HOPELESS SAVAGES

GREATEST HITS 2000–2010

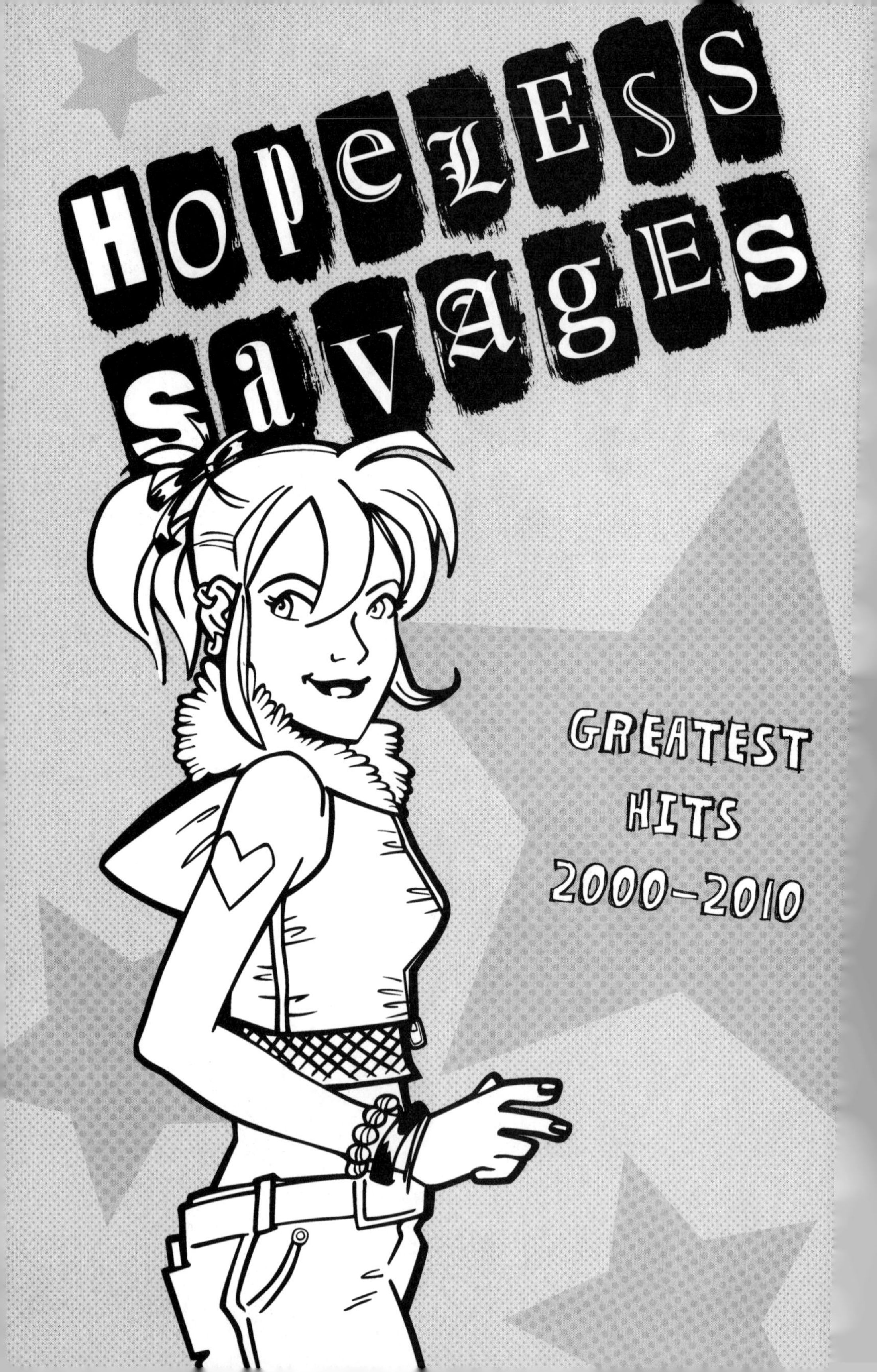
HOPELESS SAVAGES
GREATEST
HITS
2000-2010

Written by

JEN VAN METER

Illustrated by

CHRISTINE NORRIE, BRYAN LEE O'MALLEY CHYNNA CLUGSTON FLORES, and ROSS CAMPBELL

with

ANDI WATSON, VERA BROSGOL, BECKY CLOONAN, MIKE NORTON, TIM FISH, CATHERINE NORRIE, MEREDITH McCLAREN, and TERRY DODSON

introduction by

ANDY GREENWALD

book design by

KEITH WOOD

logo design by

ANDI WATSON

cover illustration by

TERRY DODSON

original series edited by

JAMIE S. RICH with JAMES LUCAS JONES

collection edited by

JAMES LUCAS JONES with JILL BEATON

HOPELESS SAVAGES

GREATEST HITS 2000–2010

Published by Oni Press, Inc.
Joe Nozemack, publisher
James Lucas Jones, editor in chief
Cory Casoni, director of marketing
Keith Wood, art director
George Rohac, operations director
Jill Beaton, associate editor
Charlie Chu, associate editor
Douglas E. Sherwood, production assistant

ONI PRESS, INC.
1305 SE Martin Luther King Jr. Blvd.
Suite A
Portland, OR 97214
USA

www.onipress.com

First edition: October 2010

ISBN: 978-1-934964-48-4

3 5 7 9 10 8 6 4 2

This collects the Oni Press miniseries *Hopeless Savages, Hopeless Savages: Ground Zero,* and *Too Much Hopeless Savages!,* as well as the one-shot *Hopeless Savages: B-Sides,* and portions of *The Oni Press Super Fun Color Special, Oni Press Color Special 2001,* and *Young Bottoms in Love.*

Hopeless Savages Book I & "Romance #1" lettered with a font provided by Larry Young.

Printed in the **United States** at **Lake Book Manufacturing, Inc.**

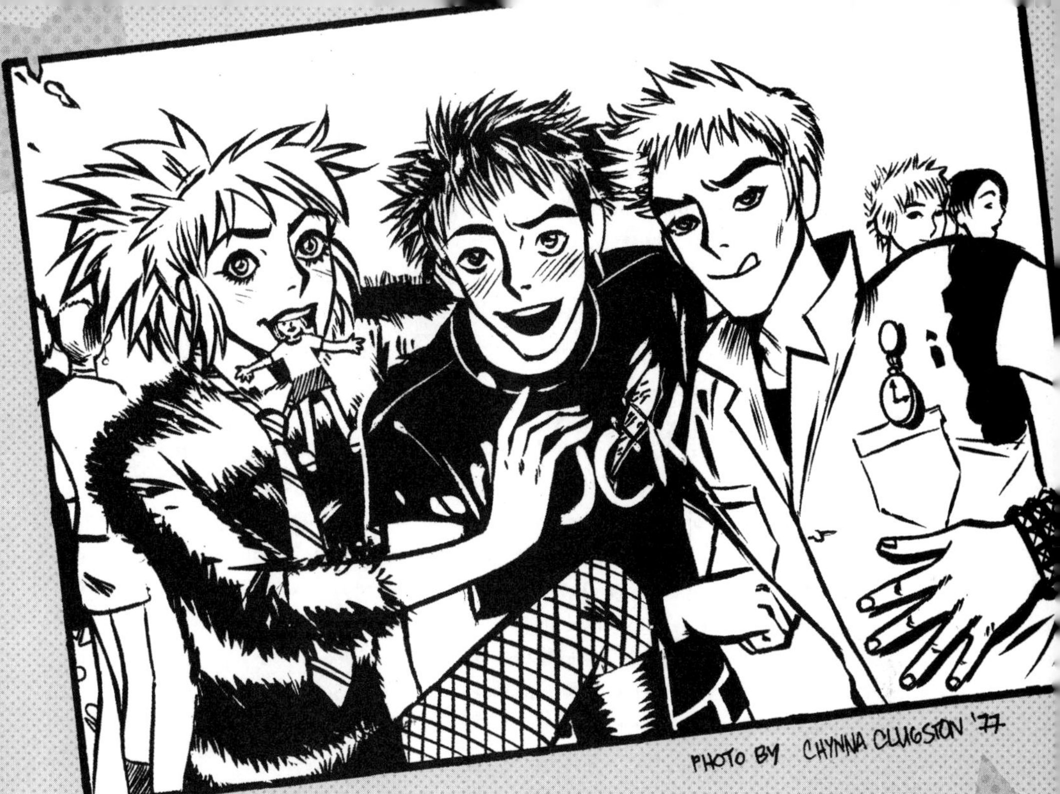
JCK

PHOTO BY CHYNNA CLUGSTON '77

ROCK & ROLL has never been about the music. OK, that's a bit harsh. How about: Rock & Roll has never just been about the music. Sure, choruses are nice, but what really hooks us at an early age doesn't come from the speakers. It's the myths. The stories. The swagger. Think: Bob Dylan's motorcycle accident and David Bowie's fashion accidents. Stevie Nicks snorting drugs and Ozzy Osbourne snorting ants. And with all the complicated backstories, burning rivalries and overreliance on face-paint it only stands to reason that many of the most music obsessed among us tend to have a long box or twelve buried in their basement: rock stars are the closest thing to real life superheroes we have. Actually, they may be better- after all, who's more indestructible: Superman or Keith Richards? And would you rather join a club called the "Justice League" (snore!) or the KISS ARMY? Kind of a no-brainer when you think about it.

Eventually, of course, we also form long and lasting connections to the songs themselves. Some of us tend to go a little overboard in our twenties and we soundtrack the minutae of our lives with all the subtlety of a John Bonham drum solo. ("The song from our first kiss! The song from our first dance! The song from our first joint tax return!") But really, even this is about myth-making: using the borrowed glamor of our favorite tunes to brighten and enhance our ordinary lives.

And then, of course, we get old. Or older, anyway. Rockstars and rock fans alike. And as lovingly curated mixtapes turn into computerized "Genius" playlists, we find ourselves coming back to the bigger-than-life stuff; the headlines, not the b-sides. The way the songs sound in our memories, not on vinyl. Our relationship with music doesn't burn out or fade away. It just... changes. Which is exactly what happened to former chart-topping sweethearts Dirk Hopeless and Nikki Savage. And why their totally imagined, utterly sincere post-punk family fairytale resonates so deeply with all of us who ever hung a bruised concert ticket on our wall, or painted our nails after reading a copy of the *NME* or tried out a cockney accent in public.

Dirk and Nikki are rock & roll superheroes, minus the capes (not that there's anything wrong with capes – James Brown had several): happily married, utterly devoted to one another and their kids, all without ever signing to a major label or learning to pronounce their "H's" properly. They're Sid & Nancy's happy ending: less heroin, more heart. And, oh, those kids. Second generation punks, it seems, revolt in their own ways: eldest Rat flirts with reverse re-bellion, working for a coffee conglomerate and (gasp) *wearing khakis* before re-discovering his inner (and outer) mohawk. Second son Twitch is his own man (he's a mod) and has one too, in the form of his fetching actor sweetheart Henry Shi (whose grandmother is a witch, of course, but you'll get to that later). First daughter Arsenal is a gothy dreamboat who drives like Jeff Gordon and fights like Jet Li.

And then there's Zero. The youngest Hopeless Savage and the least hopeless among them. If anything, Zero expects too much from the world: commitment to ideals, respect for women and parrots, and an ability to understand a colorful slang of her own invention. In these pages you'll see Zero develop from an anarchic pipsqueak with a voice that goes to eleven to... well, something only a shade more mature than that. But, really, she's the music fan still headbanging inside us all: opinionated, cheekily charming and desperate to be heard.

The three *Hopeless Savages* stories collected here are big-hearted and catchy, sharp as a perfect three-minute pop song or a crane kick from one of Arsenal's PVC boots. In these pages, Jen Van Meter, Christine Norrie, Chynna Clugston, Bryan Lee O'Malley and the rest of the talented contributors have brought rock & roll back to what we loved about it in the first place and then added fistfights with spies. I mean come on: it *is* a comic book.

TURN IT UP.

Andy Greenwald
08/10

Andy Greenwald is a journalist and screenwriter
and the author of *Nothing Feels Good: Punk Rock,
Teenagers, and Emo* (St. Martin's Press, 2003) and
Miss Misery: A Novel (Simon Spotlight Entertainment,
2006). He lives in Brooklyn.

HOPELESS SAVAGES

BOOK 1

Written by
JEN VAN METER

Art by
CHRISTINE NORRIE

Flashback art by
CHYNNA CLUGSTON FLORES

Chapter break art by
ANDI WATSON

Lettered by
ANDY LIS

Originally edited by
JAMIE S. RICH

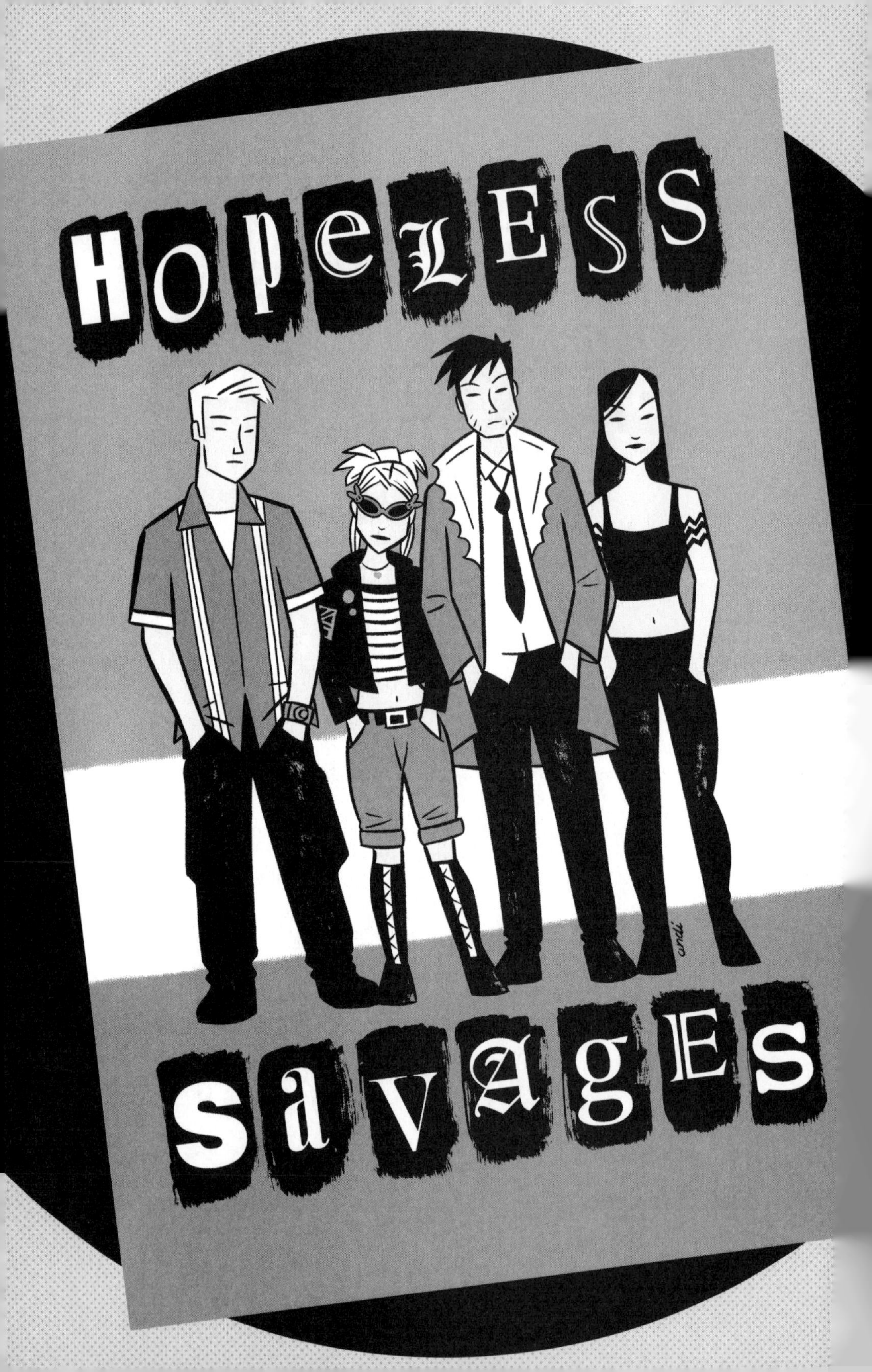
HOPELESS
SAVAGES
andi

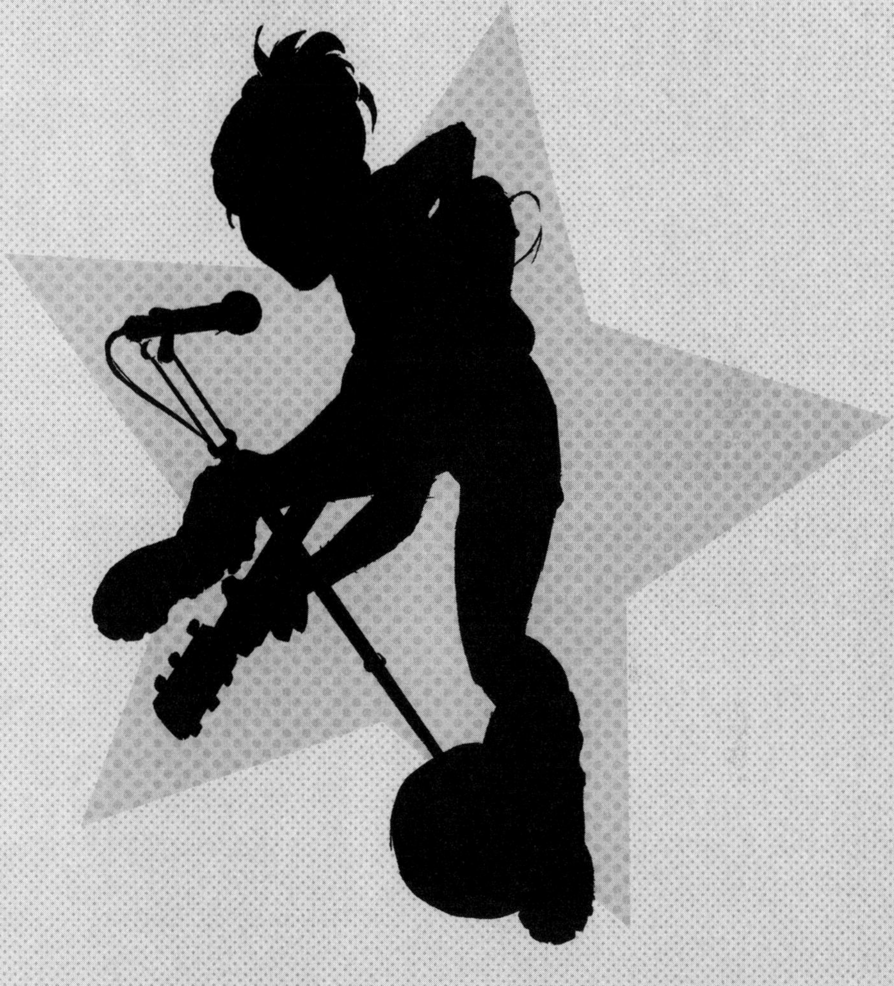

CHAPTER 1

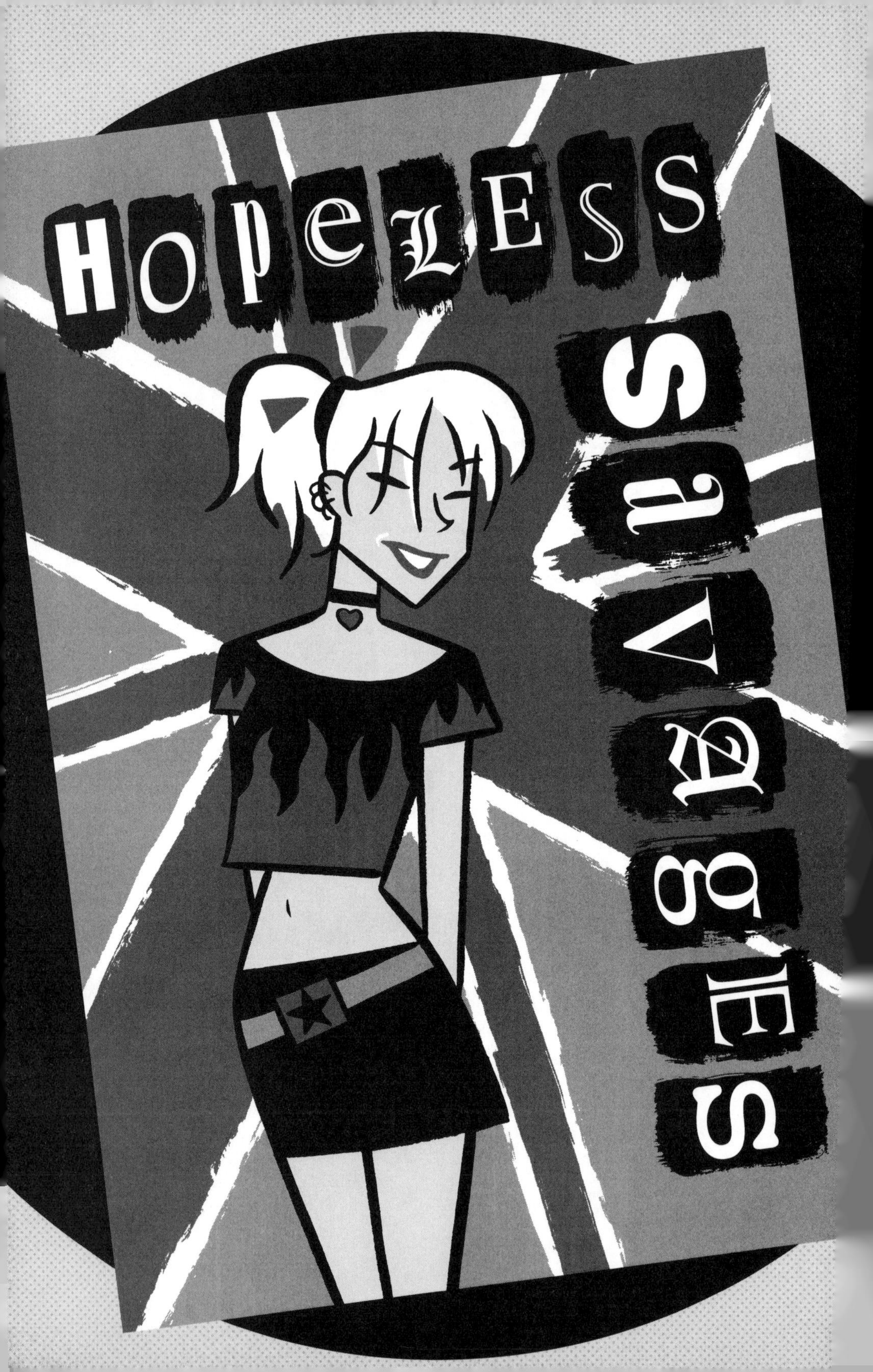
HOPELESS
SAVAGES

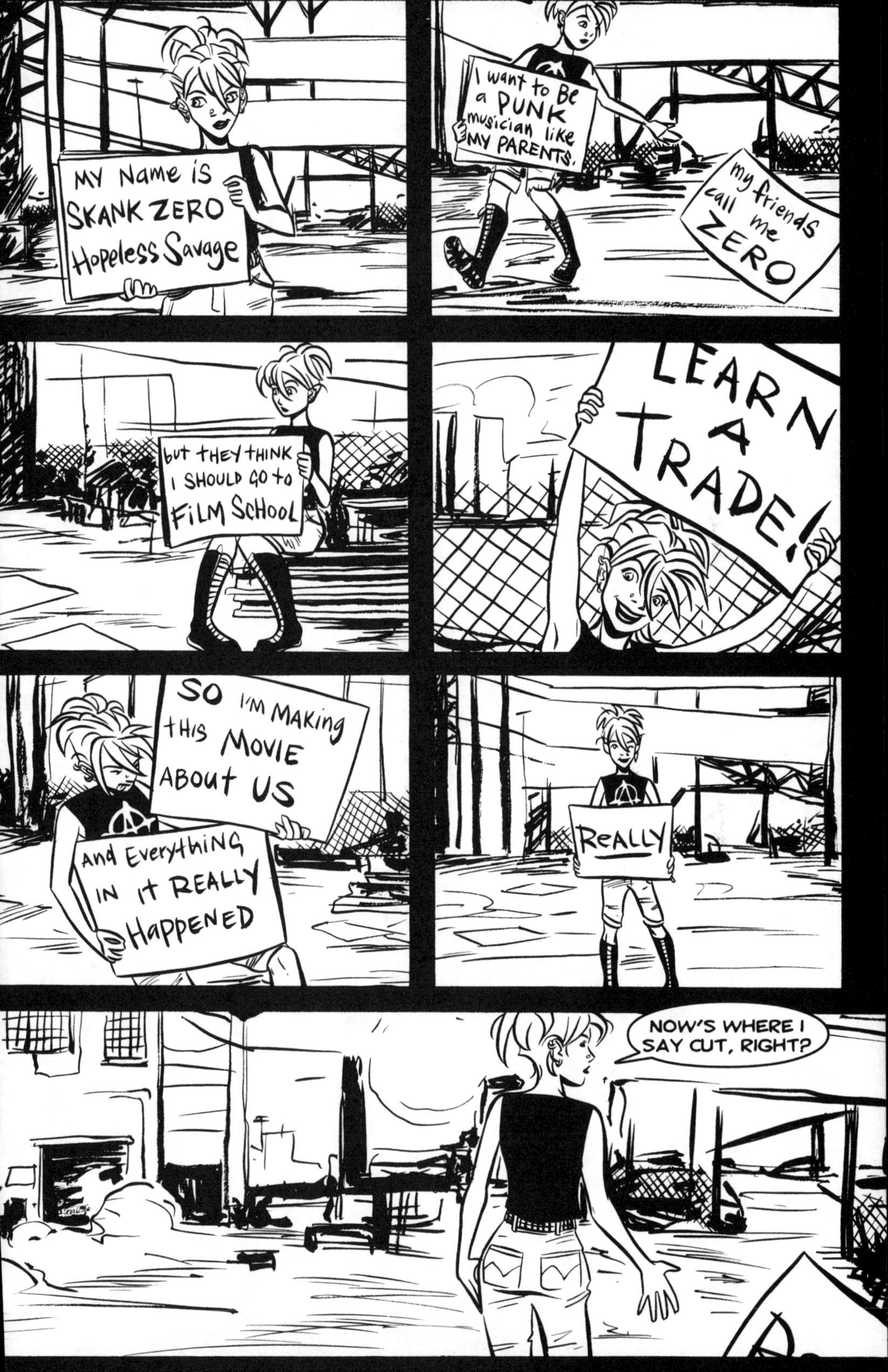
MY Name is
SKANK ZERO
Hopeless Savage
I want to Be a PUNK musician like MY PARENTS.
my friends call me ZERO
but THEY THINK I SHOULD GO to FiLM SCHOOL
LEARN A TRADE!
SO I'M MAKING tHIS MOVIE ABOUT US
And Everything IN it REALLY Happened
REALLY
NOW'S WHERE I SAY CUT, RIGHT?

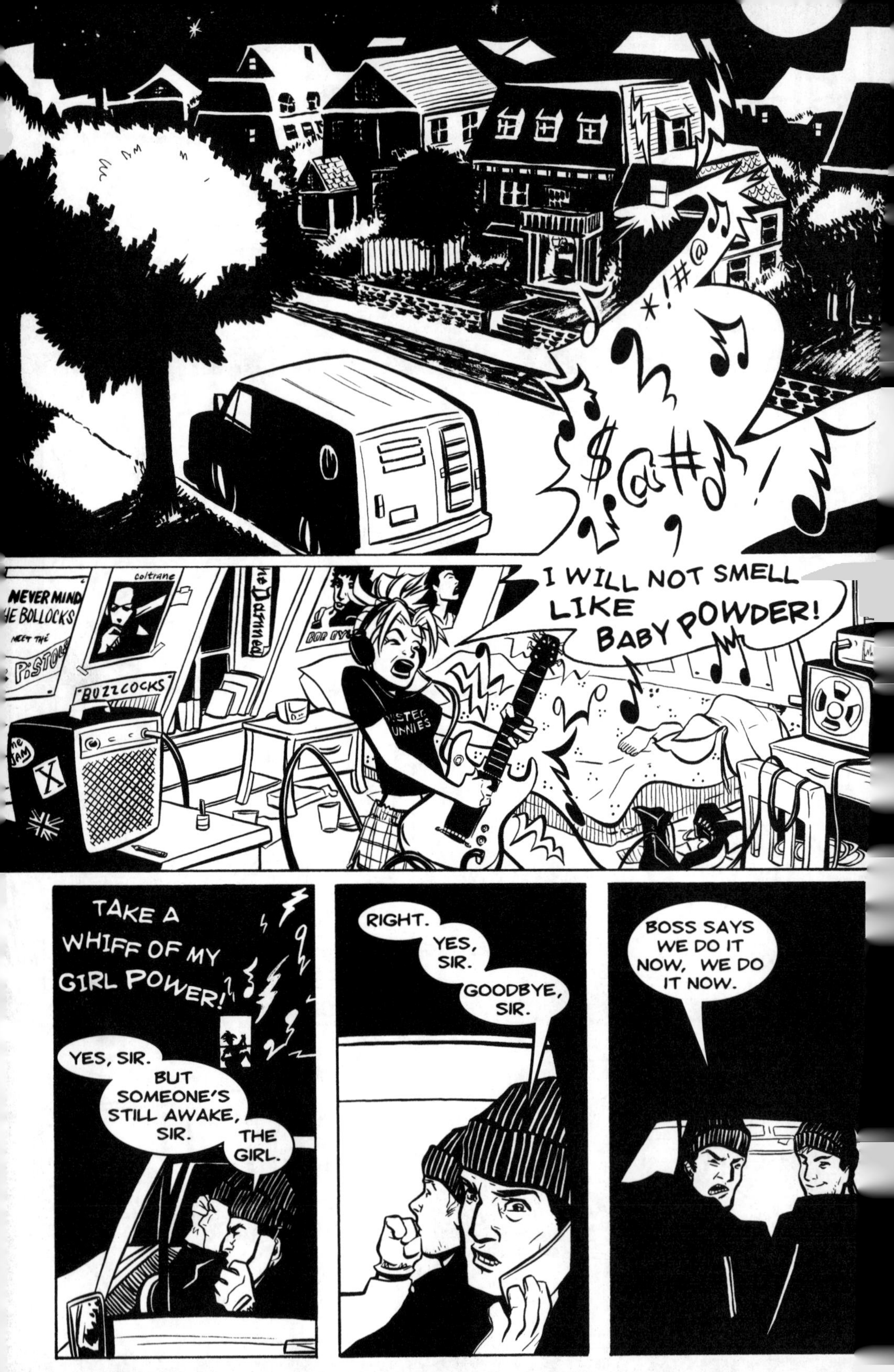
*!#@
$@#!
coltrane
NEVER MIND
BUZZCOCKS
I WILL NOT SMELL LIKE BABY POWDER!
TAKE A WHIFF OF MY GIRL POWER!
YES, SIR.
BUT SOMEONE'S STILL AWAKE, SIR.
THE GIRL.
RIGHT.
YES, SIR.
GOODBYE, SIR.
BOSS SAYS WE DO IT NOW, WE DO IT NOW.

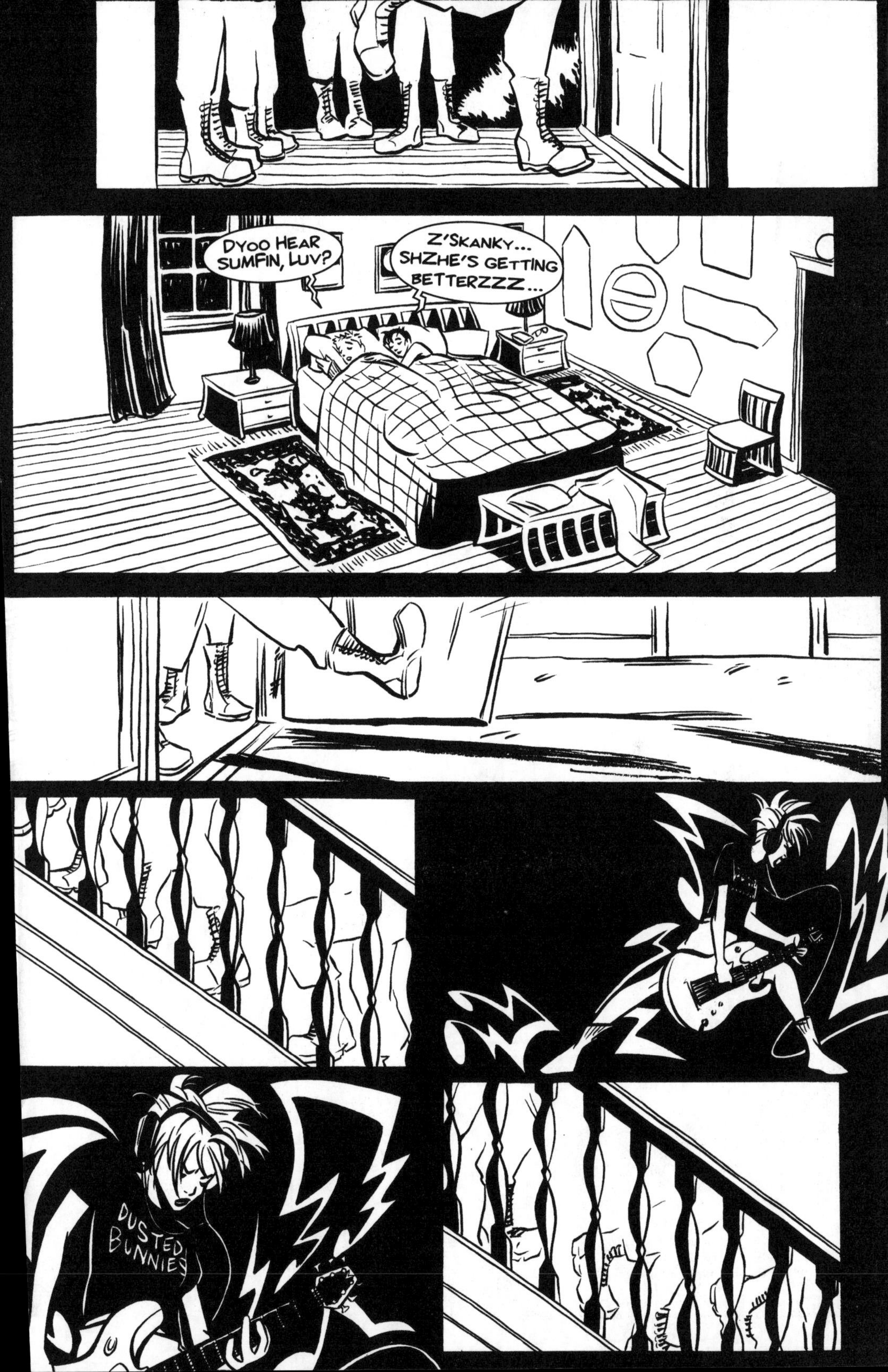
DYOO HEAR SUMFIN, LUV?
Z'SKANKY... SHZHE'S GETTING BETTERZZZ...
DUSTED BUNNIES

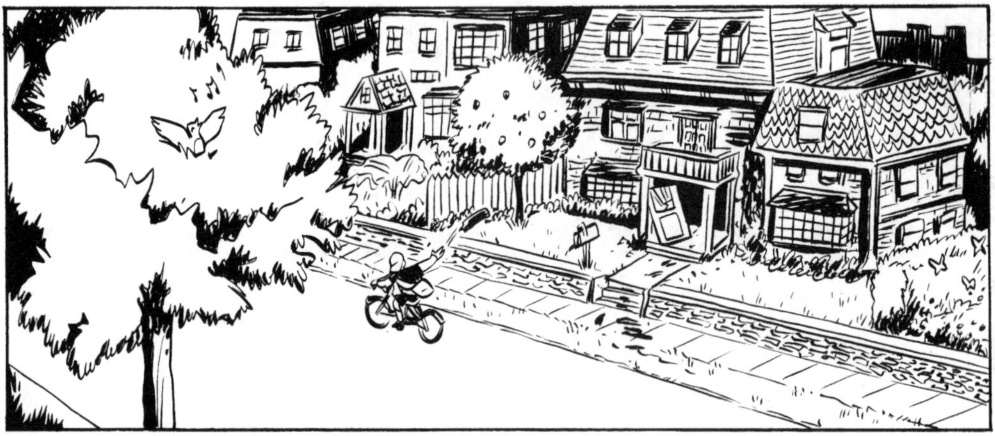

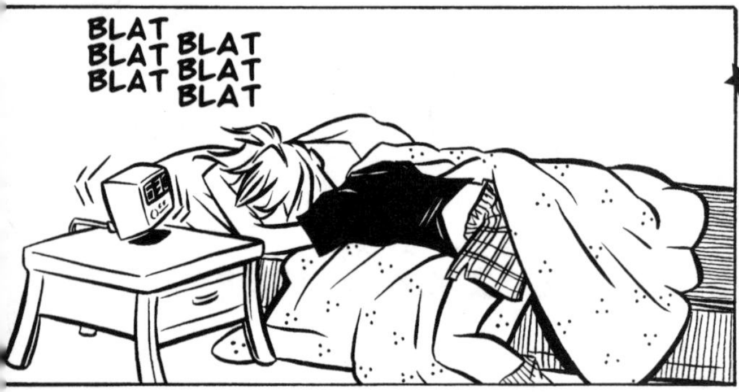
BLAT
BLAT
BLAT
BLAT
BLAT
BLAT

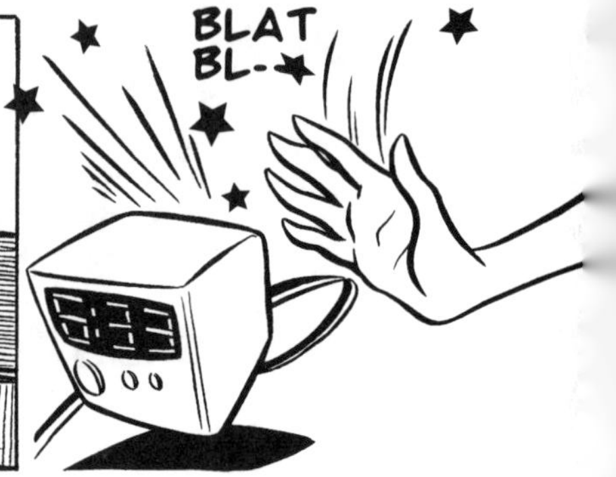
BLAT
BL--

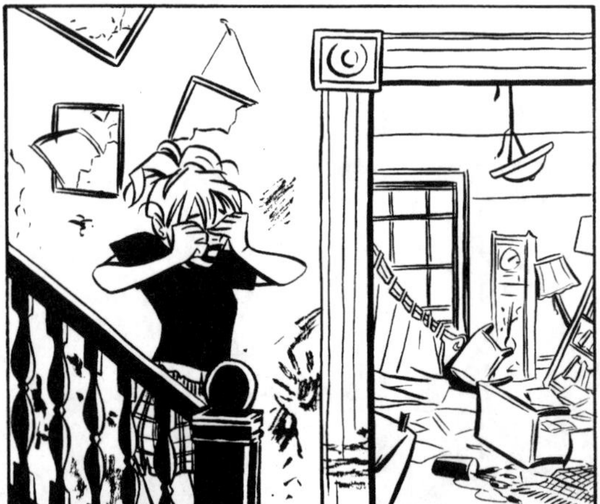

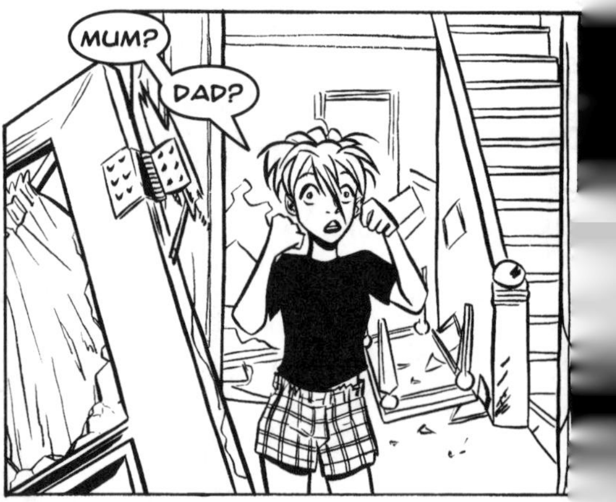
MUM?
DAD?

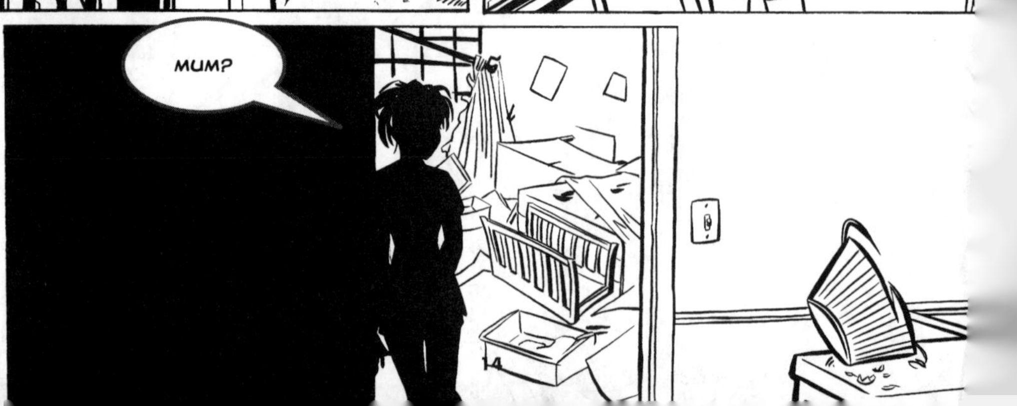
MUM?

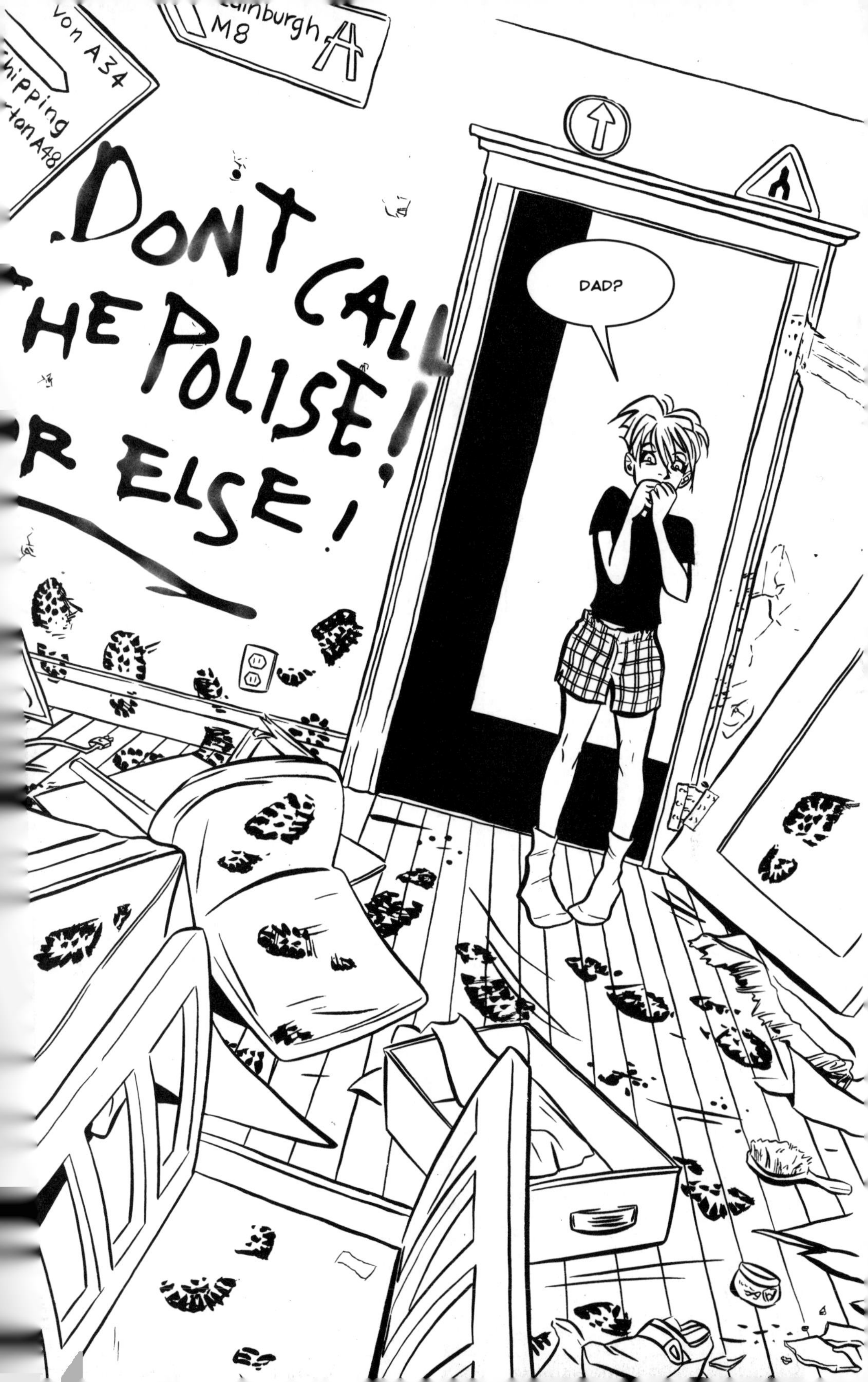

Von A34
hipping
rton A48
dinburgh
M8
DONT CALL THE POLISE OR ELSE!
DAD?

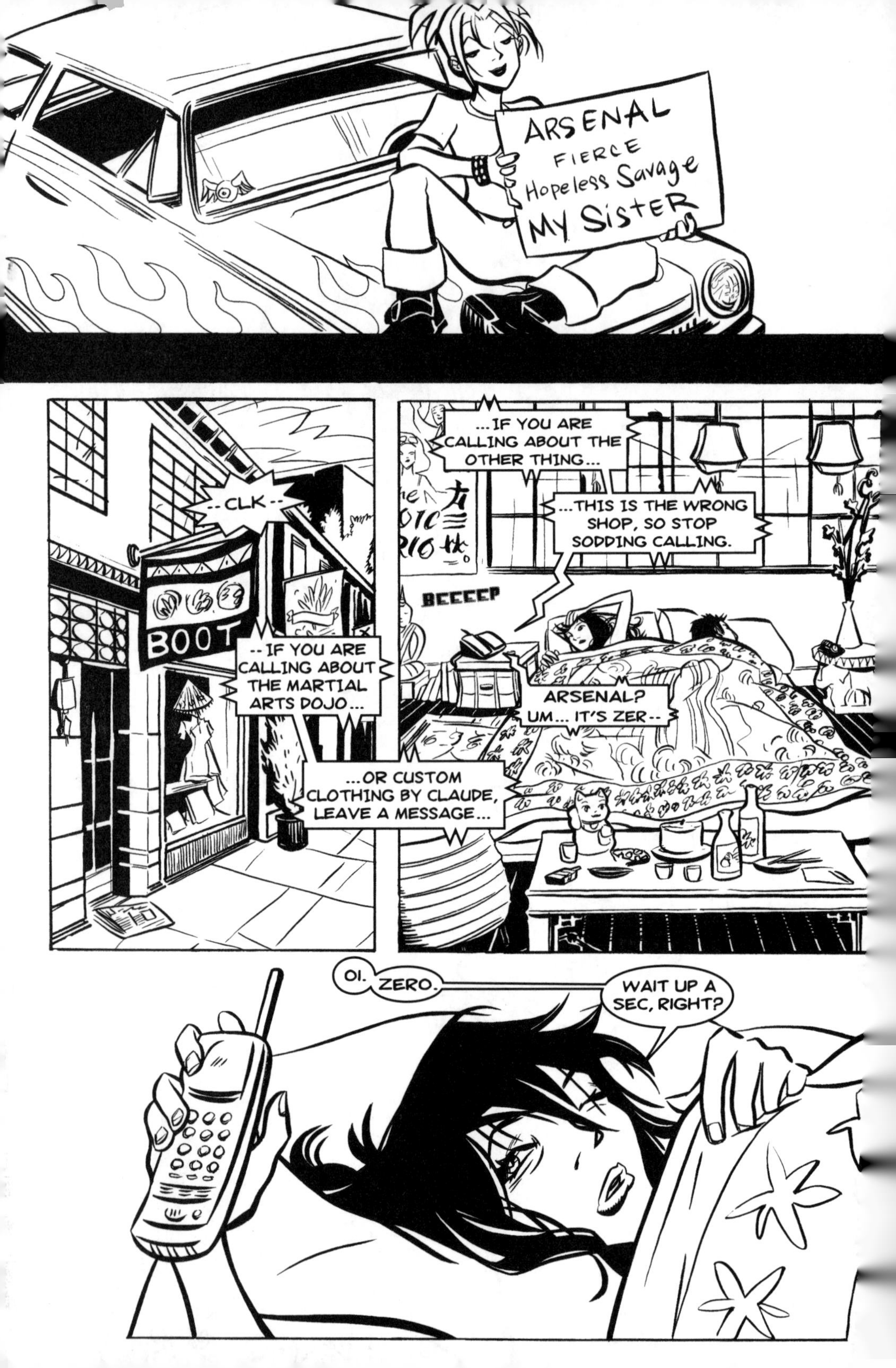
ARSENAL
FIERCE
Hopeless Savage
MY SISTER
--CLK--
--IF YOU ARE CALLING ABOUT THE MARTIAL ARTS DOJO...
...OR CUSTOM CLOTHING BY CLAUDE, LEAVE A MESSAGE...
BOOT
...IF YOU ARE CALLING ABOUT THE OTHER THING...
...THIS IS THE WRONG SHOP, SO STOP SODDING CALLING.
BEEEEP
ARSENAL? UM... IT'S ZER--
OI.
ZERO.
WAIT UP A SEC, RIGHT?

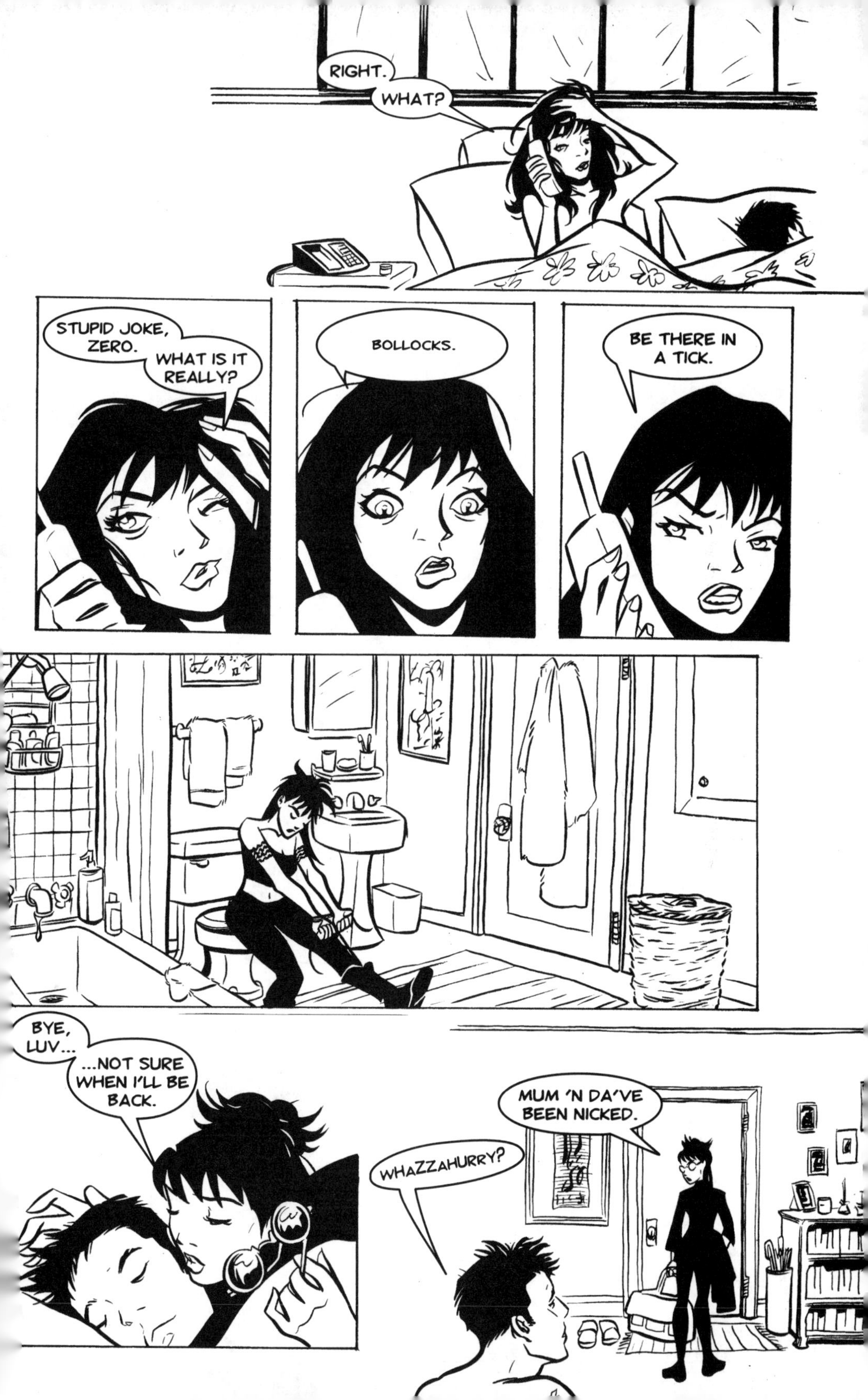
RIGHT.
WHAT?
STUPID JOKE, ZERO.
WHAT IS IT REALLY?
BOLLOCKS.
BE THERE IN A TICK.
BYE, LUV...
...NOT SURE WHEN I'LL BE BACK.
WHAZZAHURRY?
MUM 'N DA'VE BEEN NICKED.

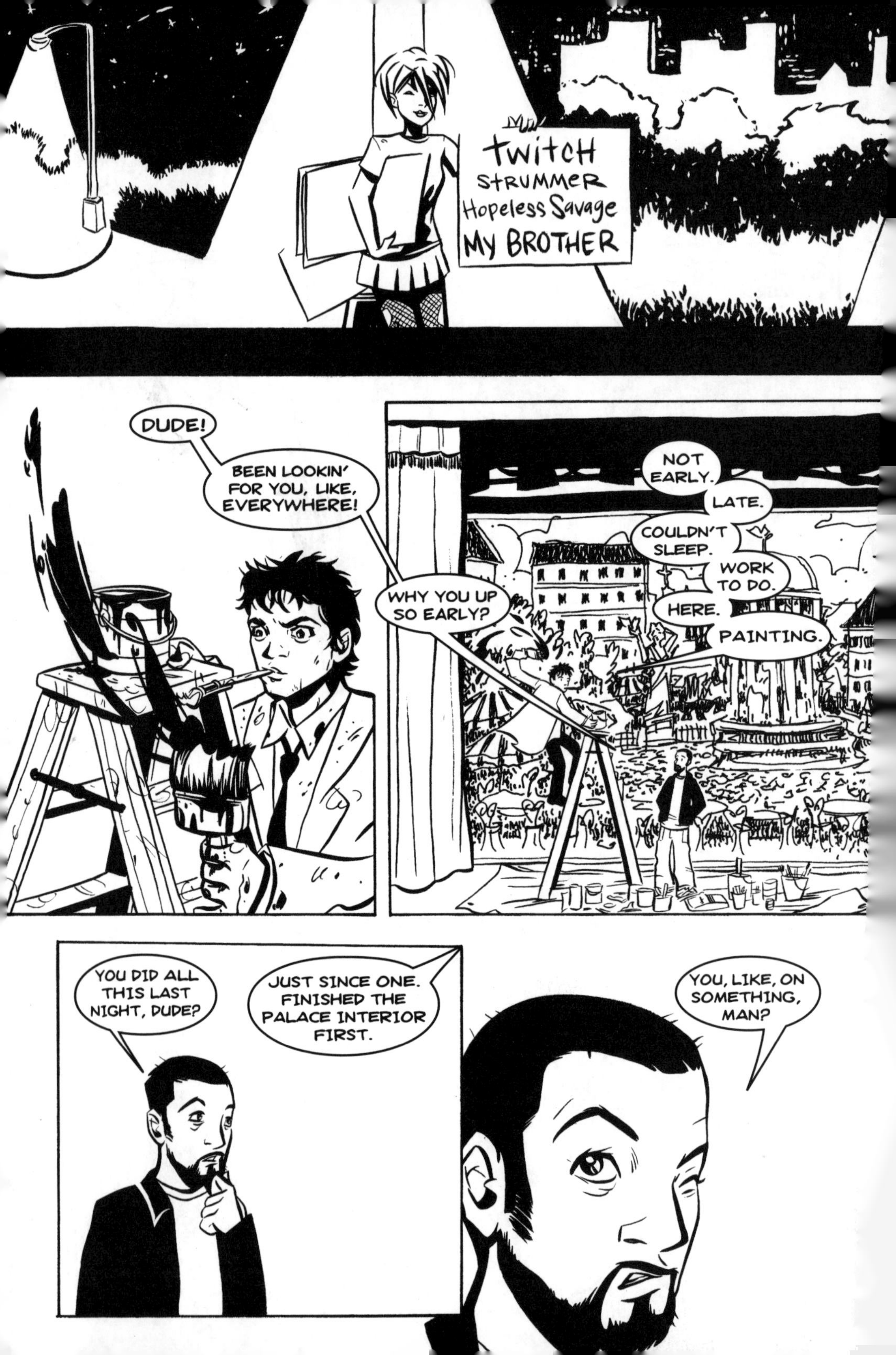
Twitch
Strummer
Hopeless Savage
My BROTHER
DUDE!
BEEN LOOKIN' FOR YOU, LIKE, EVERYWHERE!
WHY YOU UP SO EARLY?
NOT EARLY.
LATE.
COULDN'T SLEEP.
WORK TO DO.
HERE.
PAINTING.
YOU DID ALL THIS LAST NIGHT, DUDE?
JUST SINCE ONE. FINISHED THE PALACE INTERIOR FIRST.
YOU, LIKE, ON SOMETHING, MAN?

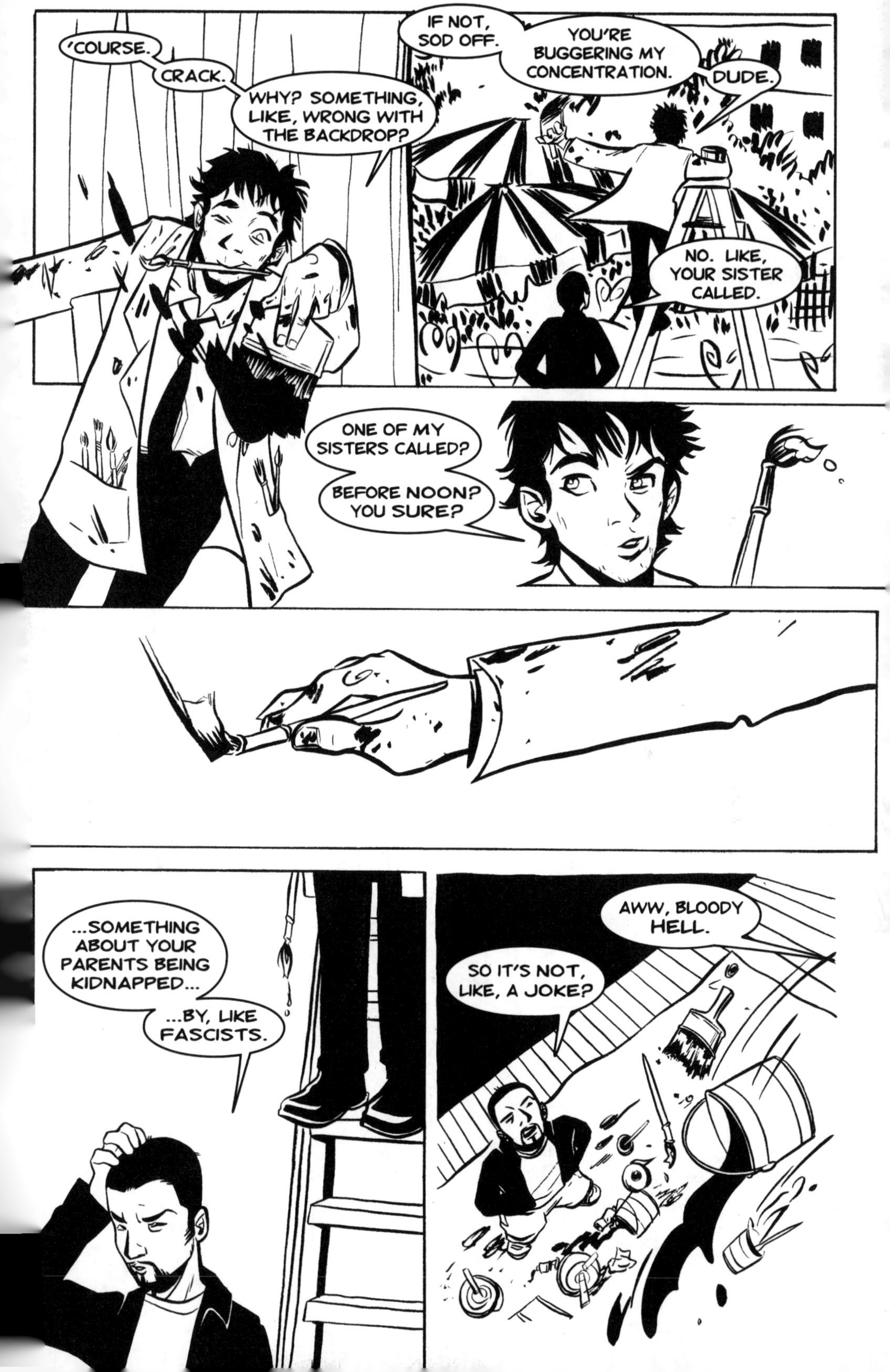
'COURSE.
CRACK.
WHY? SOMETHING, LIKE, WRONG WITH THE BACKDROP?
IF NOT, SOD OFF.
YOU'RE BUGGERING MY CONCENTRATION.
DUDE.
NO. LIKE, YOUR SISTER CALLED.
ONE OF MY SISTERS CALLED?
BEFORE NOON? YOU SURE?
...SOMETHING ABOUT YOUR PARENTS BEING KIDNAPPED...
...BY, LIKE FASCISTS.
AWW, BLOODY HELL.
SO IT'S NOT, LIKE, A JOKE?

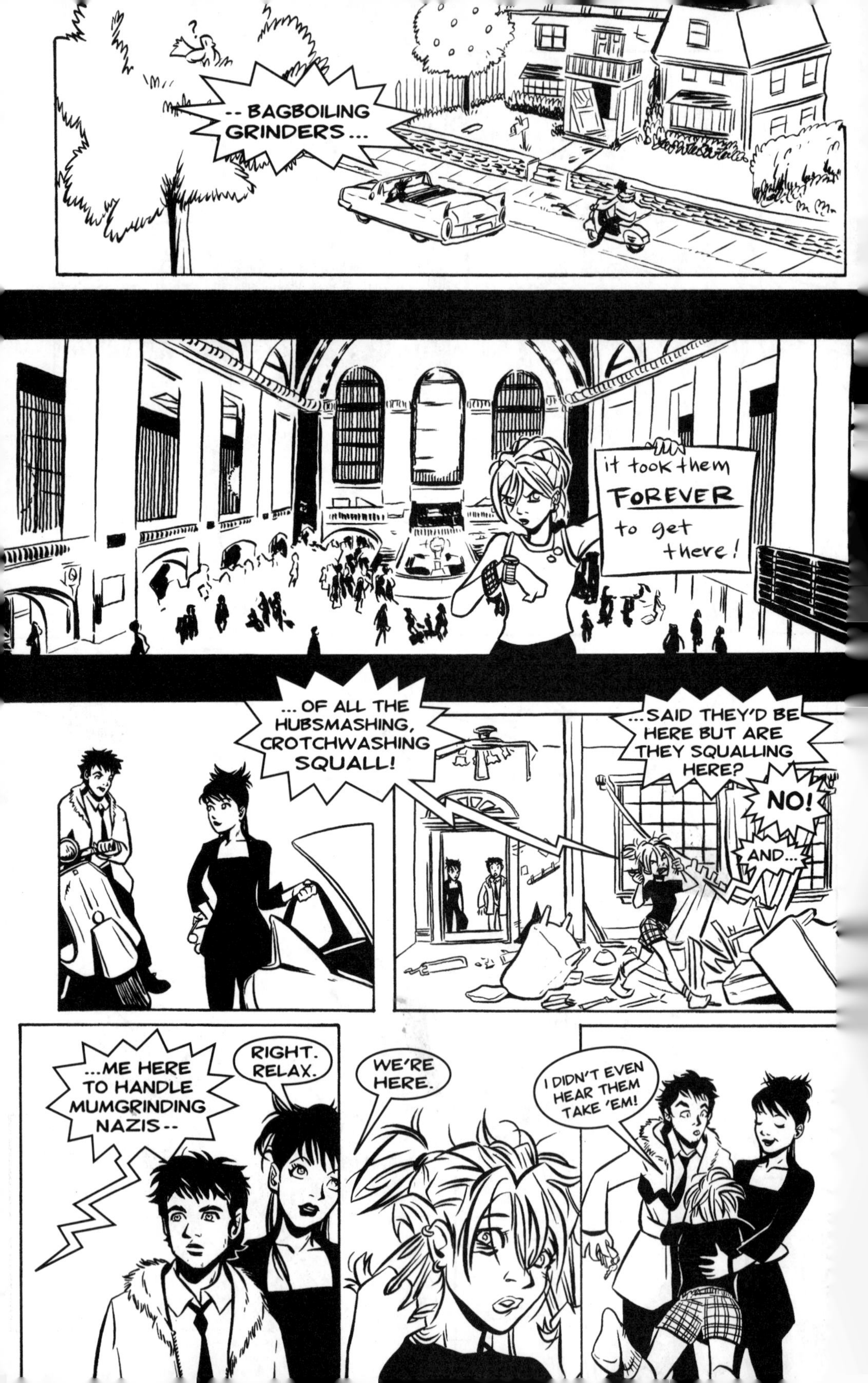
?
-- BAGBOILING GRINDERS...
it took them FOREVER to get there!
...OF ALL THE HUBSMASHING, CROTCHWASHING SQUALL!
...SAID THEY'D BE HERE BUT ARE THEY SQUALLING HERE?
NO!
AND...
...ME HERE TO HANDLE MUMGRINDING NAZIS--
RIGHT. RELAX.
WE'RE HERE.
I DIDN'T EVEN HEAR THEM TAKE 'EM!

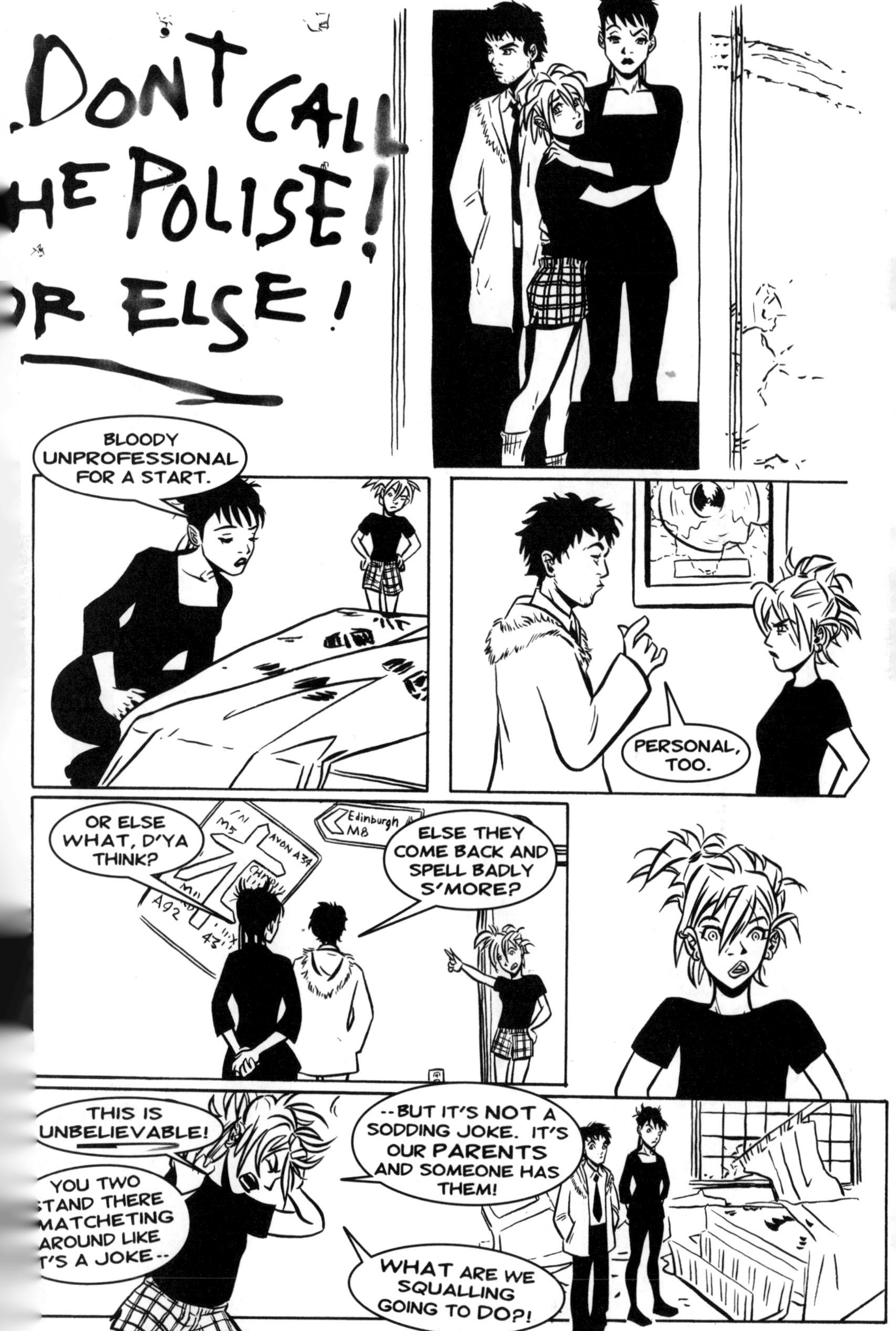
DON'T CALL
HE POLISE!
OR ELSE!
BLOODY UNPROFESSIONAL FOR A START.
PERSONAL, TOO.
OR ELSE WHAT, D'YA THINK?
Edinburgh M8
M5
AVON A34
M11
A92
ELSE THEY COME BACK AND SPELL BADLY S'MORE?
THIS IS UNBELIEVABLE!
YOU TWO STAND THERE MATCHETING AROUND LIKE IT'S A JOKE--
--BUT IT'S NOT A SODDING JOKE. IT'S OUR PARENTS AND SOMEONE HAS THEM!
WHAT ARE WE SQUALLING GOING TO DO?!

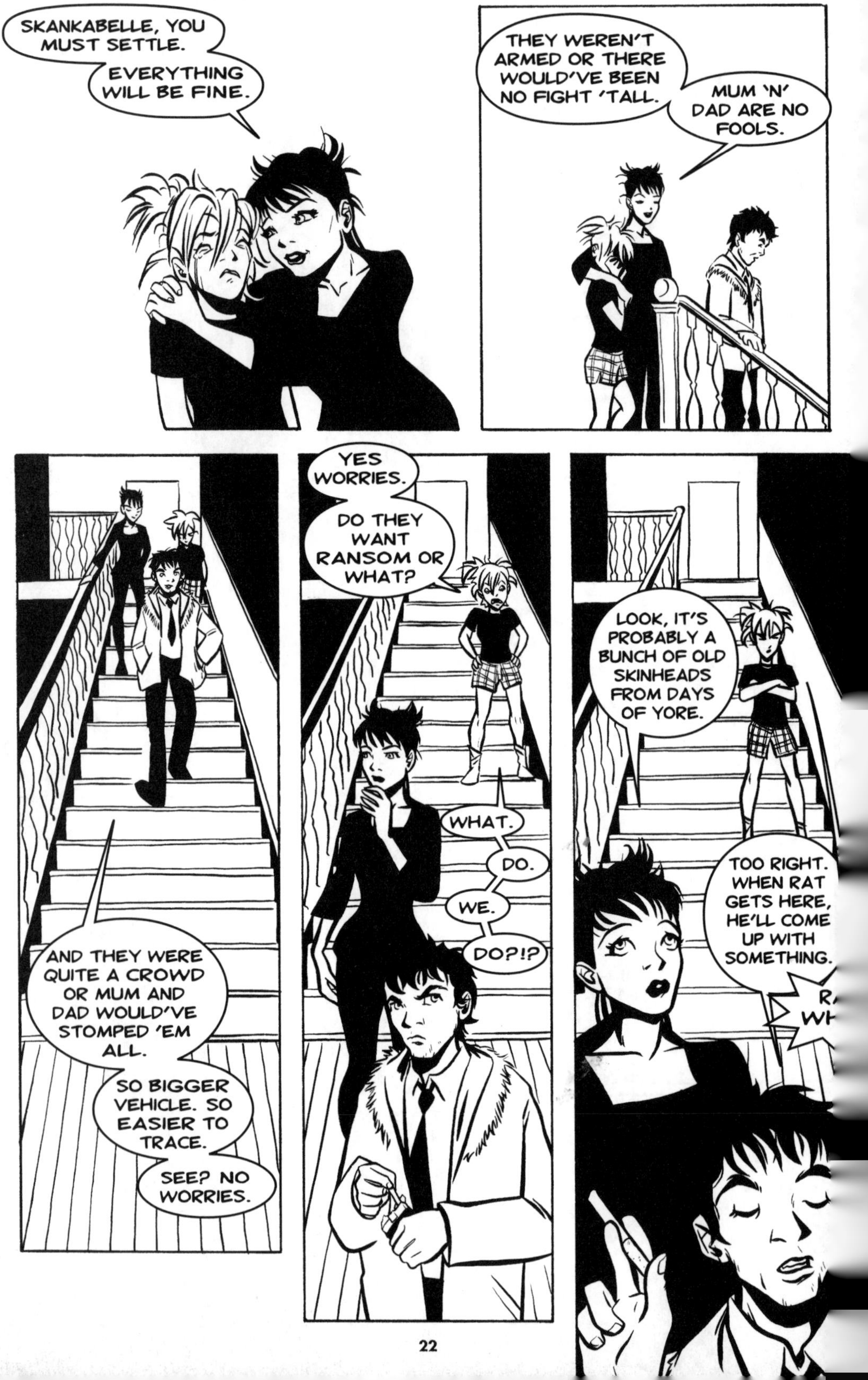
SKANKABELLE, YOU MUST SETTLE.
EVERYTHING WILL BE FINE.
THEY WEREN'T ARMED OR THERE WOULD'VE BEEN NO FIGHT 'TALL.
MUM 'N' DAD ARE NO FOOLS.
AND THEY WERE QUITE A CROWD OR MUM AND DAD WOULD'VE STOMPED 'EM ALL.
SO BIGGER VEHICLE. SO EASIER TO TRACE.
SEE? NO WORRIES.
YES WORRIES.
DO THEY WANT RANSOM OR WHAT?
WHAT.
DO.
WE.
DO?!?
LOOK, IT'S PROBABLY A BUNCH OF OLD SKINHEADS FROM DAYS OF YORE.
TOO RIGHT. WHEN RAT GETS HERE, HE'LL COME UP WITH SOMETHING.

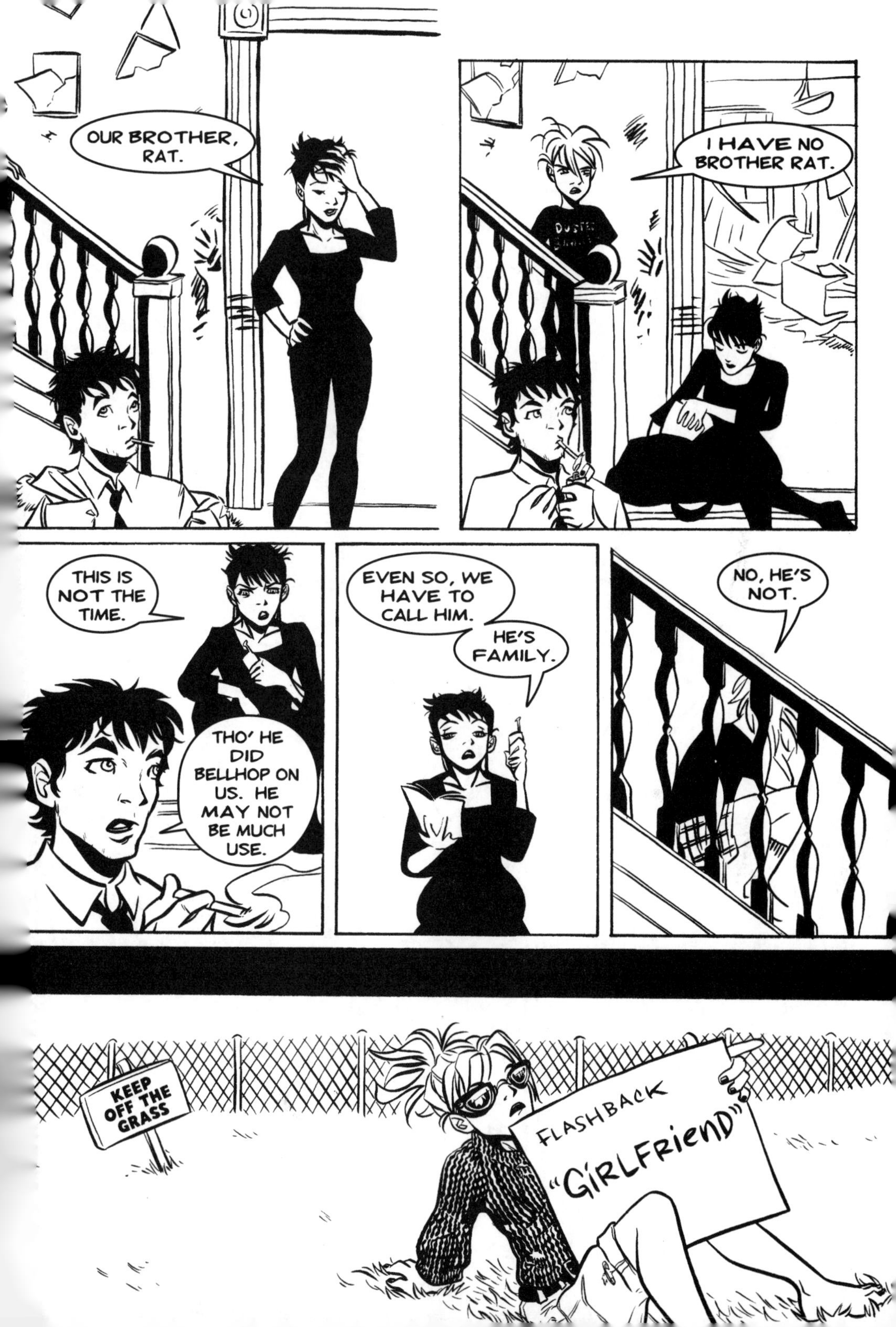
OUR BROTHER, RAT.
I HAVE NO BROTHER RAT.
THIS IS NOT THE TIME.
THO' HE DID BELLHOP ON US. HE MAY NOT BE MUCH USE.
EVEN SO, WE HAVE TO CALL HIM.
HE'S FAMILY.
NO, HE'S NOT.
KEEP OFF THE GRASS
FLASHBACK
"GIRLFRIEND"

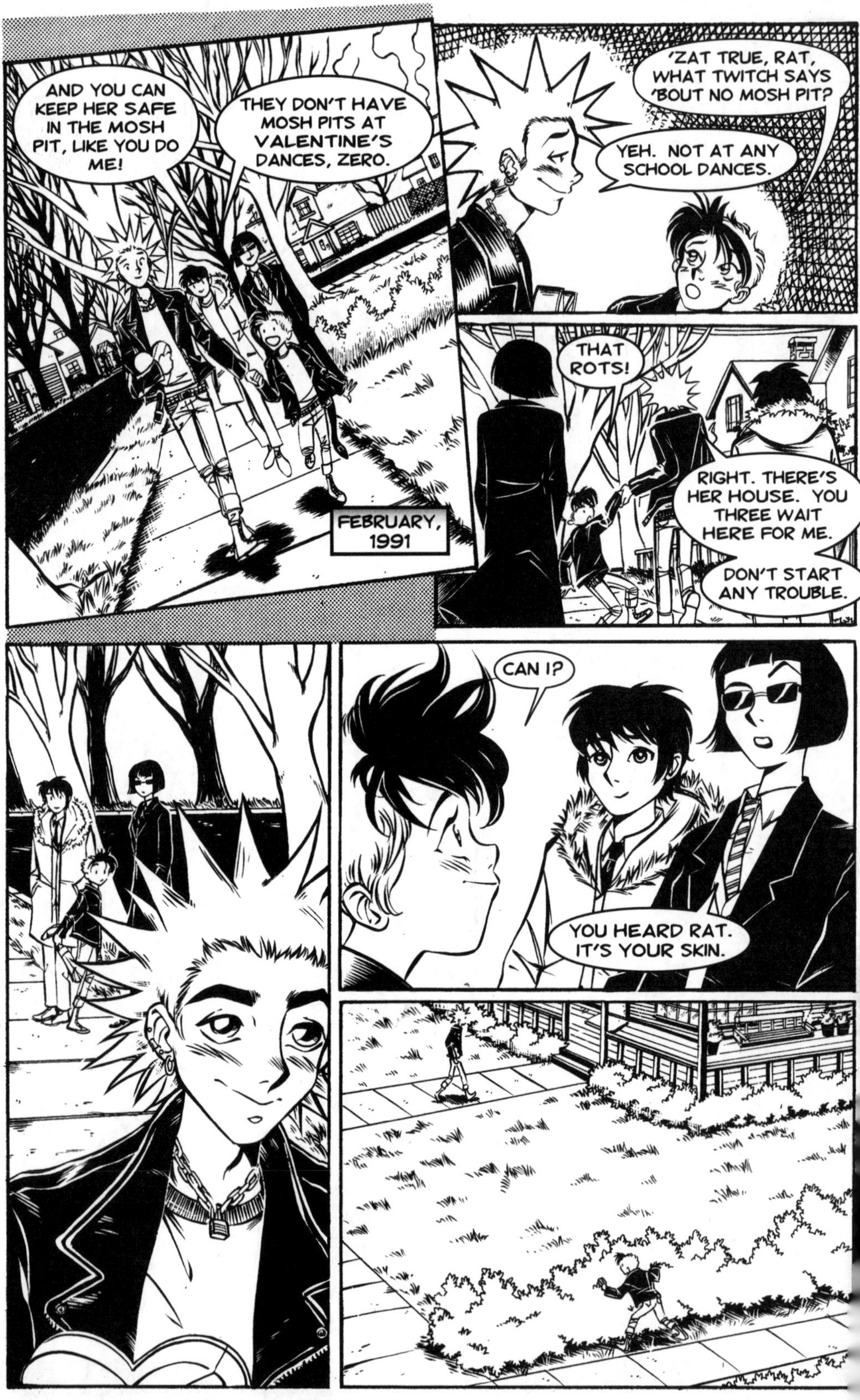
AND YOU CAN KEEP HER SAFE IN THE MOSH PIT, LIKE YOU DO ME!
THEY DON'T HAVE MOSH PITS AT VALENTINE'S DANCES, ZERO.
FEBRUARY, 1991
'ZAT TRUE, RAT, WHAT TWITCH SAYS 'BOUT NO MOSH PIT?
YEH. NOT AT ANY SCHOOL DANCES.
THAT ROTS!
RIGHT. THERE'S HER HOUSE. YOU THREE WAIT HERE FOR ME.
DON'T START ANY TROUBLE.
CAN I?
YOU HEARD RAT. IT'S YOUR SKIN.

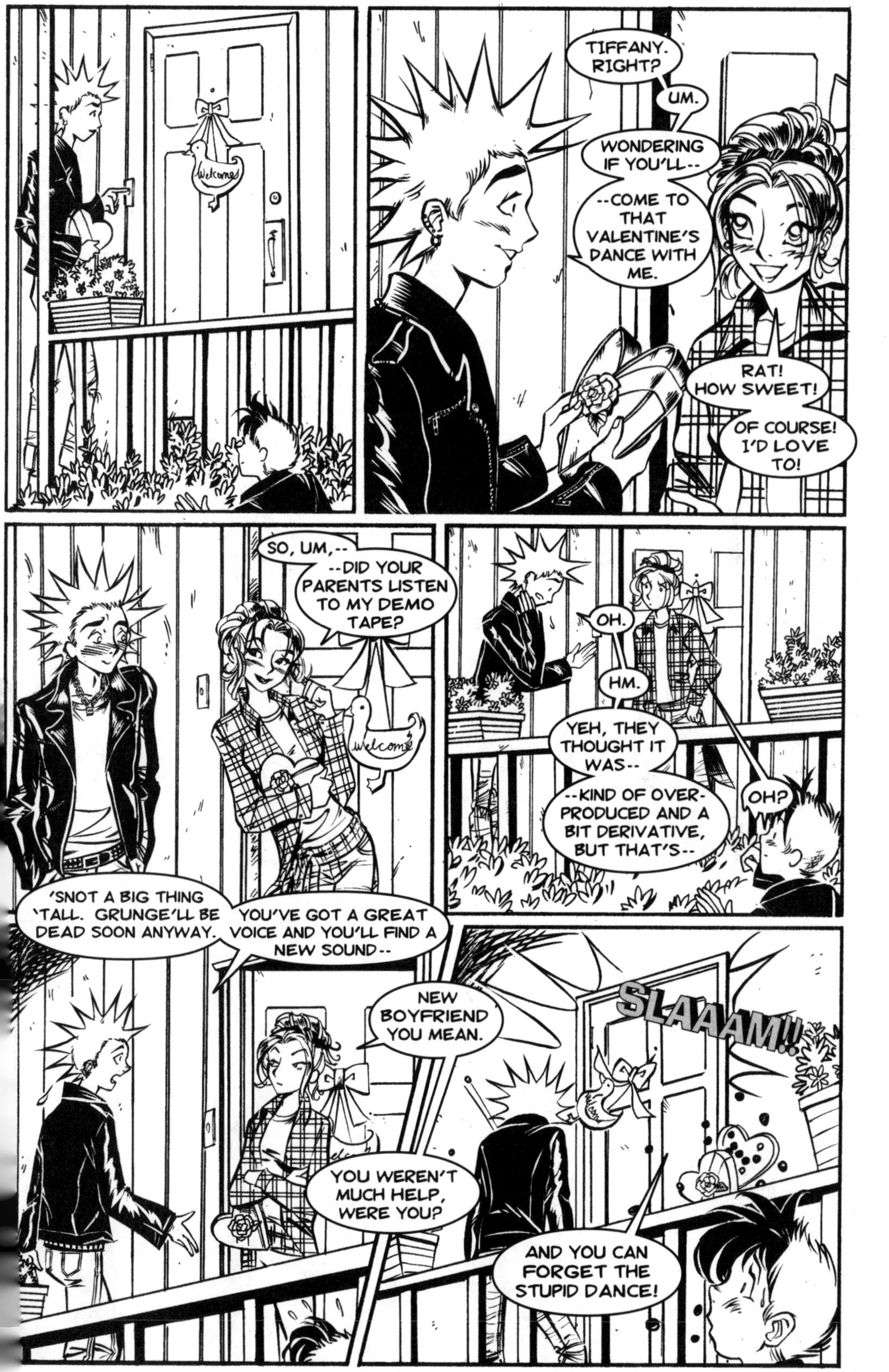
TIFFANY. RIGHT?
UM.
WONDERING IF YOU'LL--
--COME TO THAT VALENTINE'S DANCE WITH ME.
RAT! HOW SWEET!
OF COURSE! I'D LOVE TO!
SO, UM,--
--DID YOUR PARENTS LISTEN TO MY DEMO TAPE?
OH.
HM.
YEH, THEY THOUGHT IT WAS--
--KIND OF OVER-PRODUCED AND A BIT DERIVATIVE, BUT THAT'S--
OH?
'SNOT A BIG THING 'TALL. GRUNGE'LL BE DEAD SOON ANYWAY.
YOU'VE GOT A GREAT VOICE AND YOU'LL FIND A NEW SOUND--
NEW BOYFRIEND YOU MEAN.
SLAAAM!!
YOU WEREN'T MUCH HELP, WERE YOU?
AND YOU CAN FORGET THE STUPID DANCE!

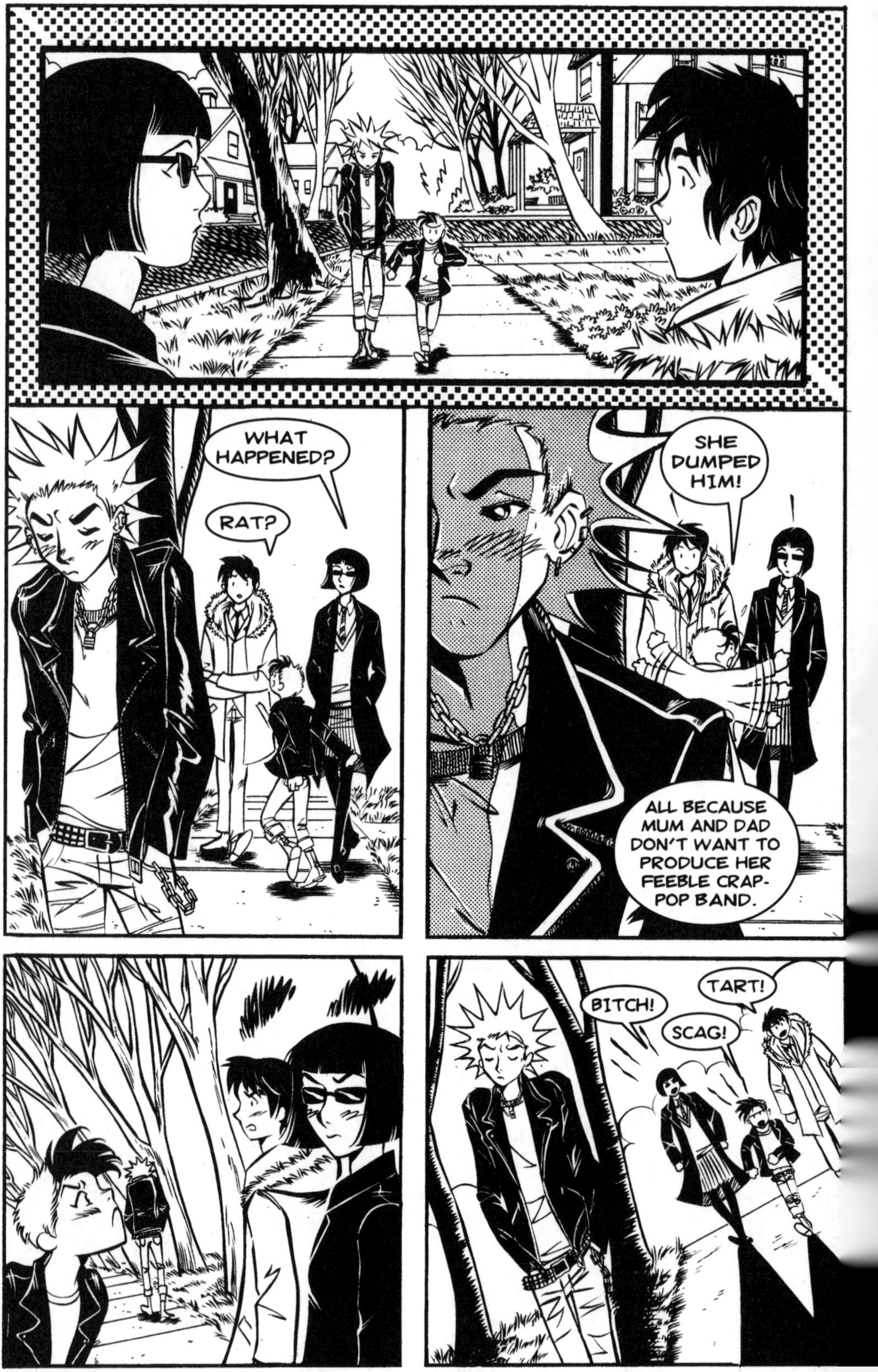
WHAT HAPPENED?
RAT?
SHE DUMPED HIM!
ALL BECAUSE MUM AND DAD DON'T WANT TO PRODUCE HER FEEBLE CRAP-POP BAND.
BITCH!
TART!
SCAG!

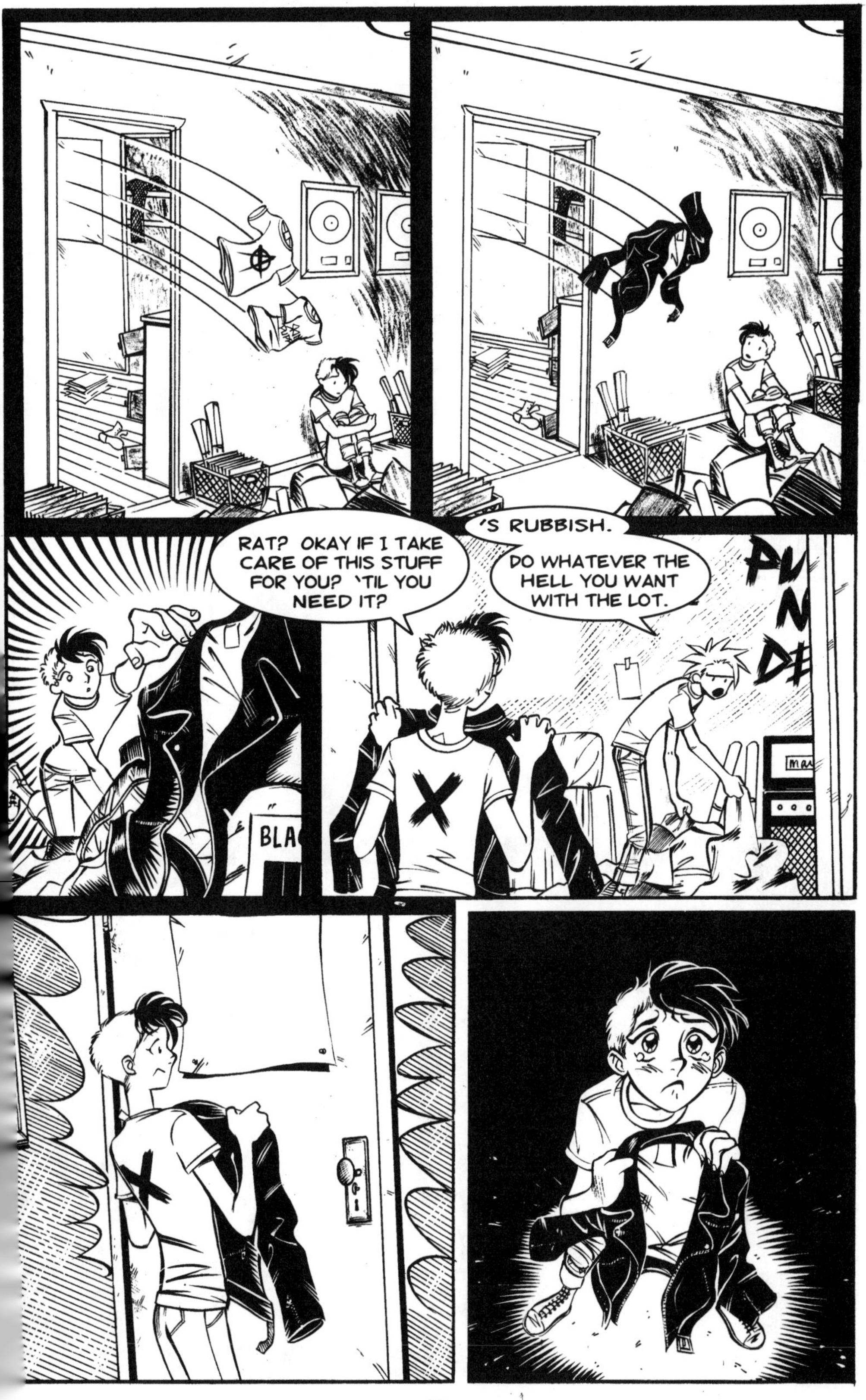
RAT? OKAY IF I TAKE CARE OF THIS STUFF FOR YOU? 'TIL YOU NEED IT?
'S RUBBISH.
DO WHATEVER THE HELL YOU WANT WITH THE LOT.
BLA

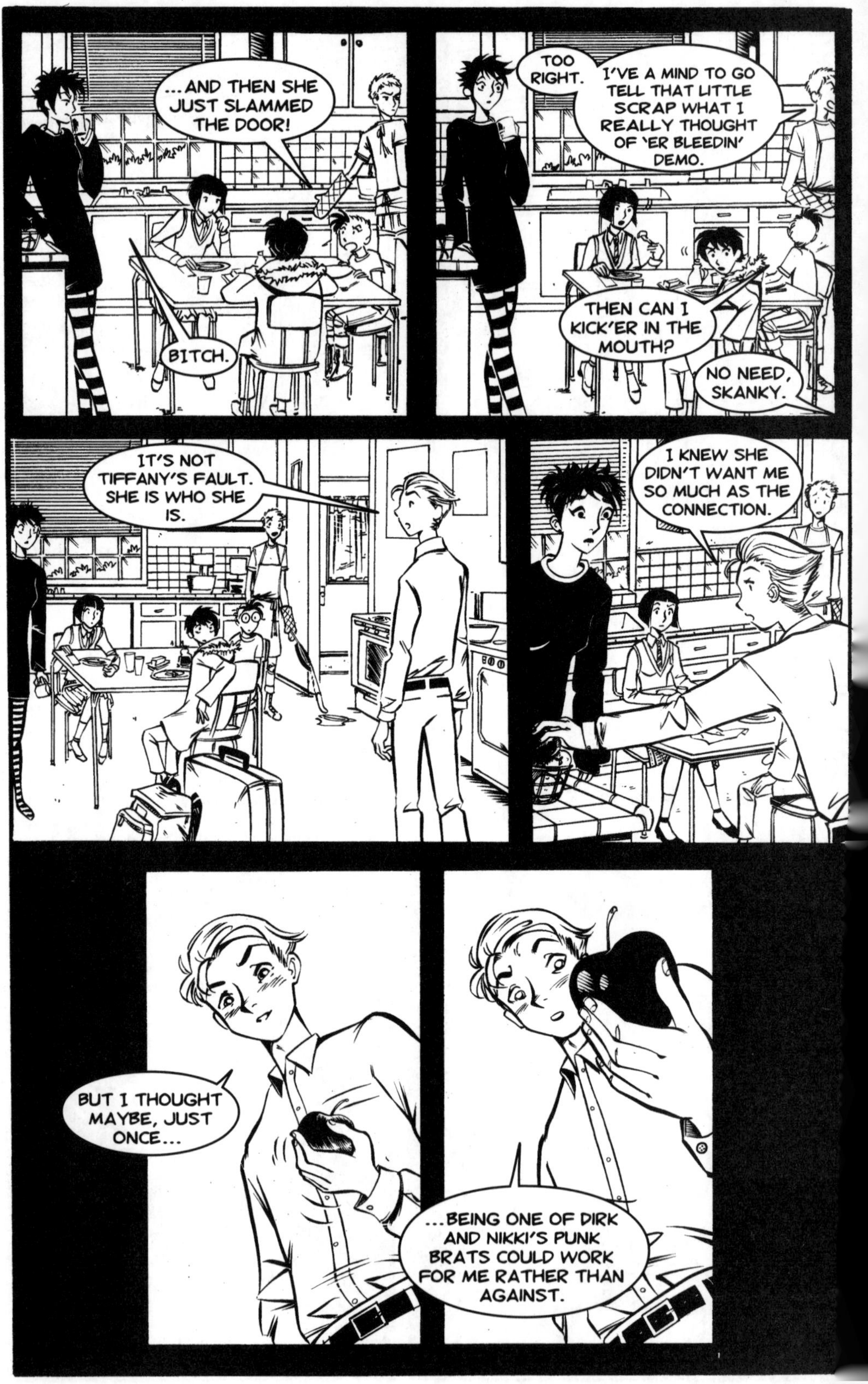
...AND THEN SHE JUST SLAMMED THE DOOR!
BITCH.
TOO RIGHT.
I'VE A MIND TO GO TELL THAT LITTLE SCRAP WHAT I REALLY THOUGHT OF 'ER BLEEDIN' DEMO.
THEN CAN I KICK'ER IN THE MOUTH?
NO NEED, SKANKY.
IT'S NOT TIFFANY'S FAULT. SHE IS WHO SHE IS.
I KNEW SHE DIDN'T WANT ME SO MUCH AS THE CONNECTION.
BUT I THOUGHT MAYBE, JUST ONCE...
...BEING ONE OF DIRK AND NIKKI'S PUNK BRATS COULD WORK FOR ME RATHER THAN AGAINST.

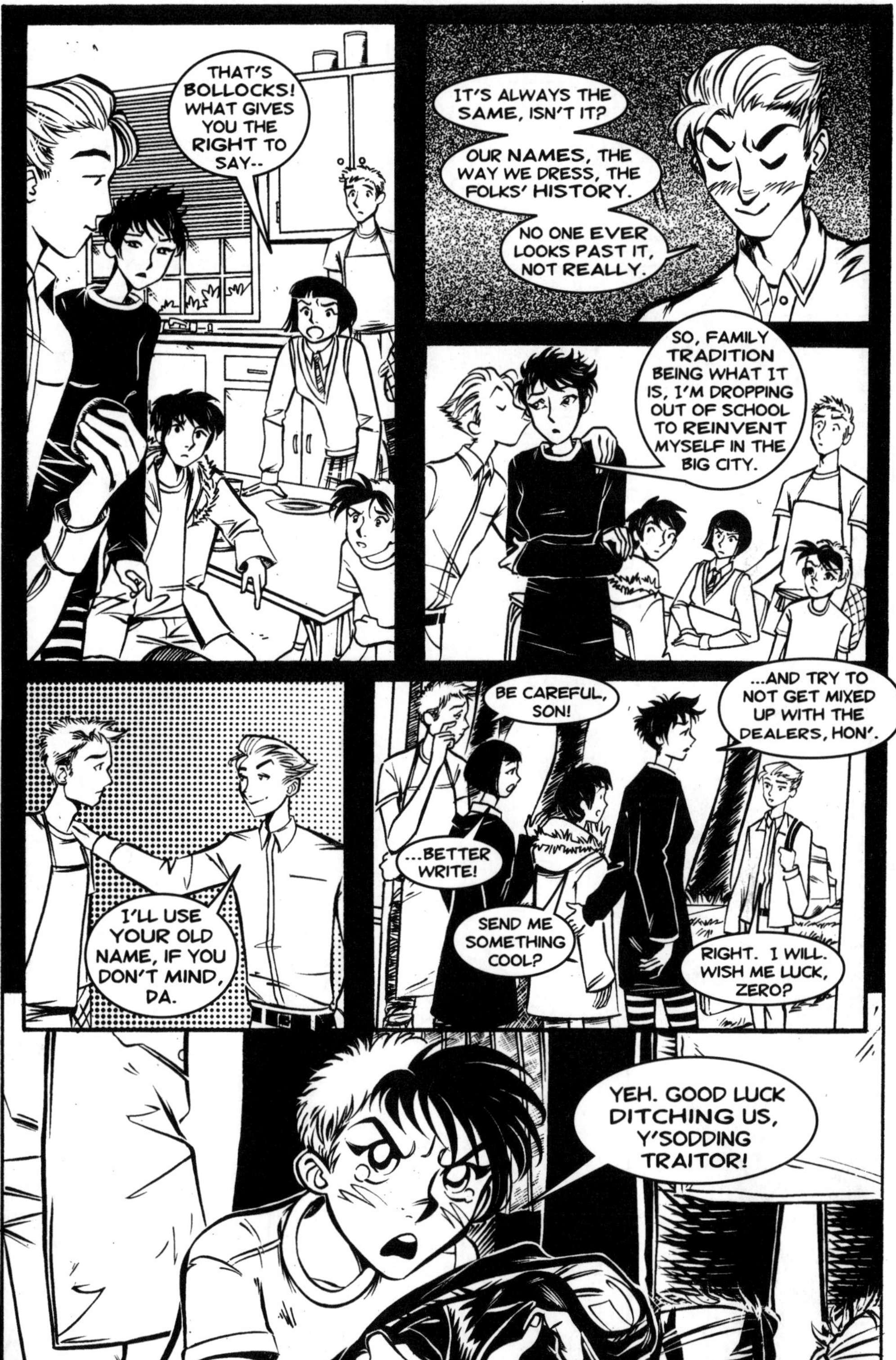
THAT'S BOLLOCKS! WHAT GIVES YOU THE RIGHT TO SAY--
IT'S ALWAYS THE SAME, ISN'T IT?
OUR NAMES, THE WAY WE DRESS, THE FOLKS' HISTORY.
NO ONE EVER LOOKS PAST IT, NOT REALLY.
SO, FAMILY TRADITION BEING WHAT IT IS, I'M DROPPING OUT OF SCHOOL TO REINVENT MYSELF IN THE BIG CITY.
I'LL USE YOUR OLD NAME, IF YOU DON'T MIND, DA.
BE CAREFUL, SON!
...AND TRY TO NOT GET MIXED UP WITH THE DEALERS, HON'.
...BETTER WRITE!
SEND ME SOMETHING COOL?
RIGHT. I WILL. WISH ME LUCK, ZERO?
YEH. GOOD LUCK DITCHING US, Y'SODDING TRAITOR!

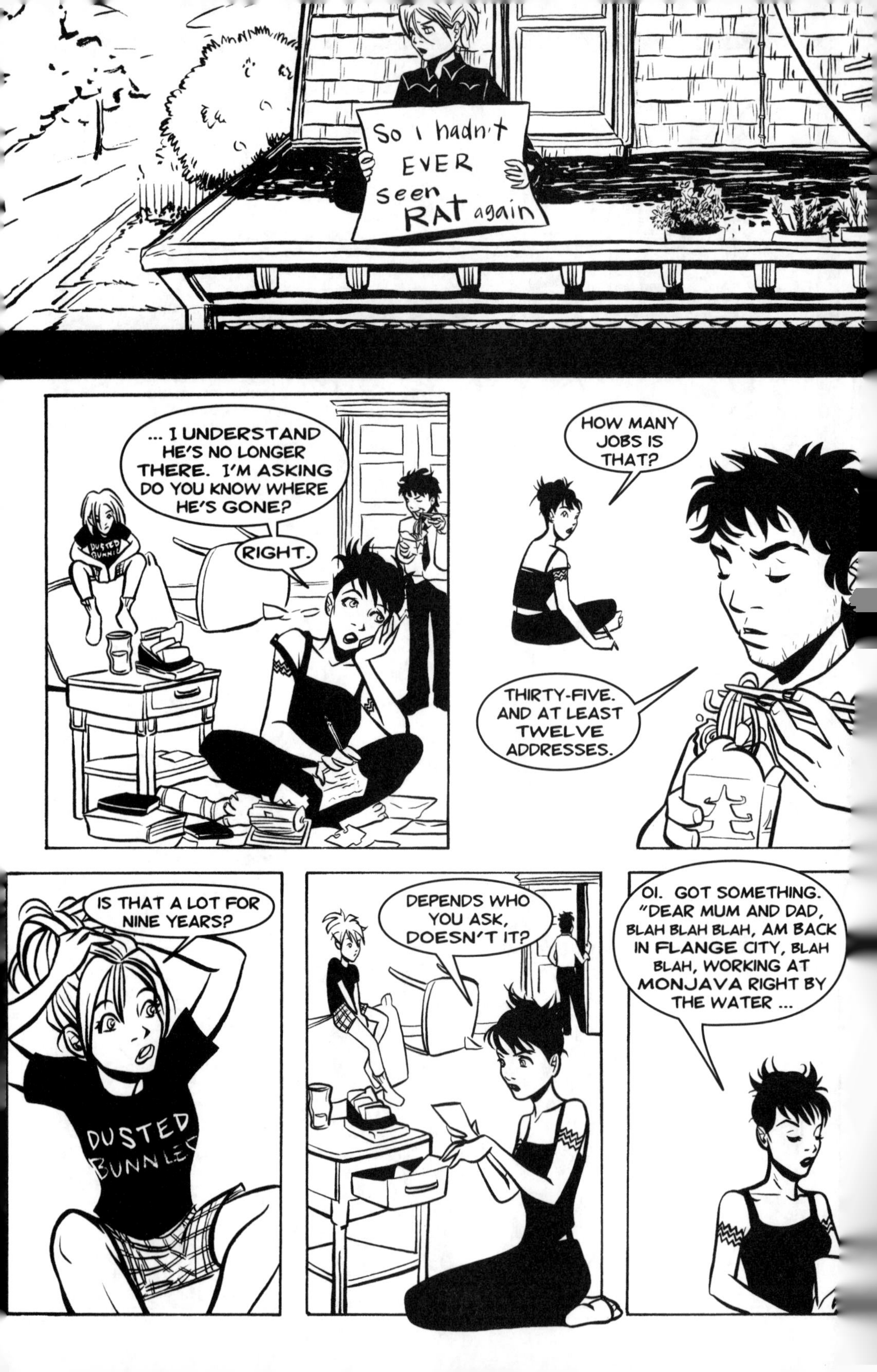
So I hadn't EVER seen RAT again
... I UNDERSTAND HE'S NO LONGER THERE. I'M ASKING DO YOU KNOW WHERE HE'S GONE?
RIGHT.
DUSTED BUNNIE
HOW MANY JOBS IS THAT?
THIRTY-FIVE. AND AT LEAST TWELVE ADDRESSES.
IS THAT A LOT FOR NINE YEARS?
DUSTED BUNNIE
DEPENDS WHO YOU ASK, DOESN'T IT?
OI. GOT SOMETHING. "DEAR MUM AND DAD, BLAH BLAH BLAH, AM BACK IN FLANGE CITY, BLAH BLAH, WORKING AT MONJAVA RIGHT BY THE WATER ...

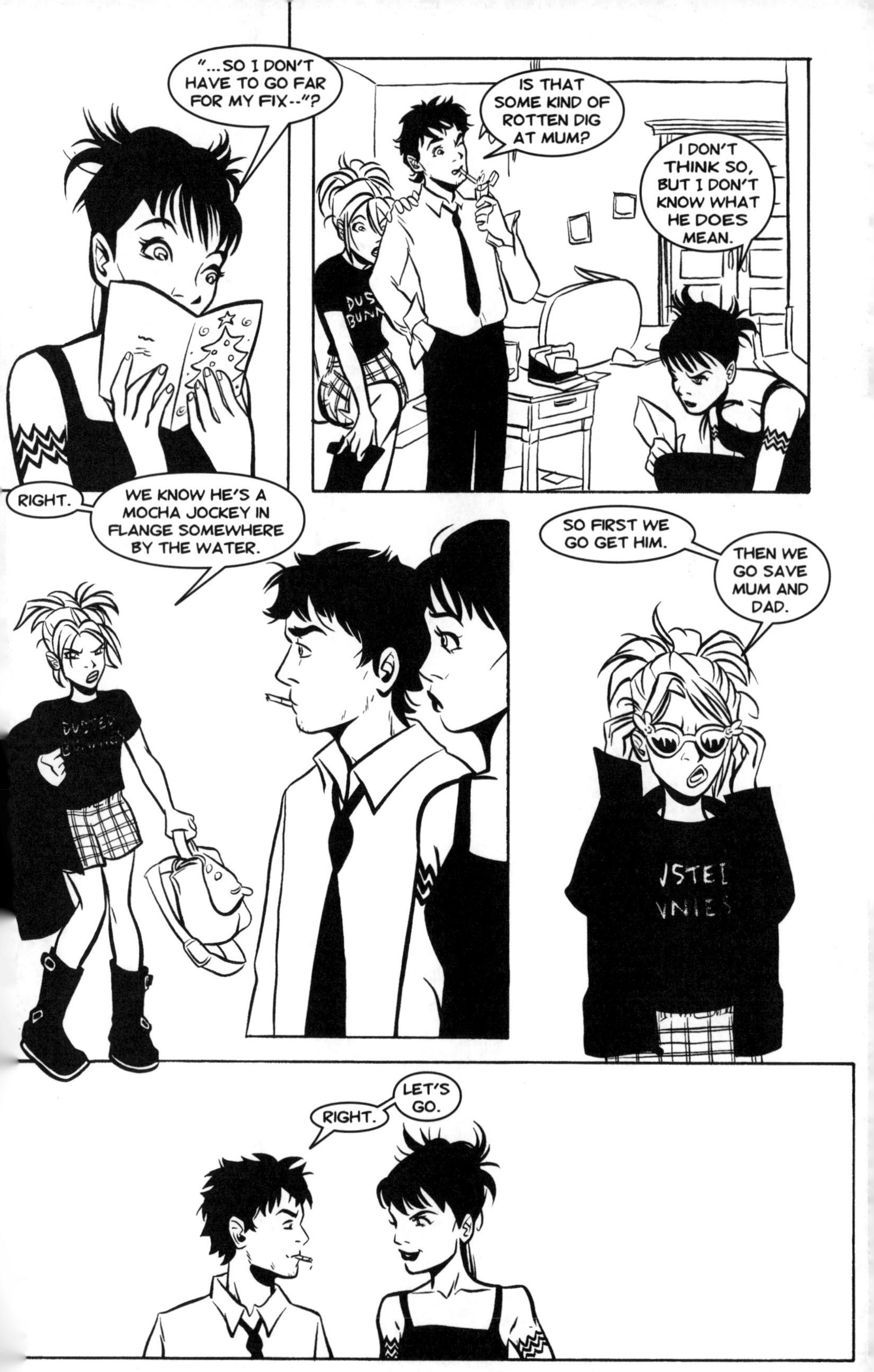
"...SO I DON'T HAVE TO GO FAR FOR MY FIX--"?
IS THAT SOME KIND OF ROTTEN DIG AT MUM?
I DON'T THINK SO, BUT I DON'T KNOW WHAT HE DOES MEAN.
RIGHT.
WE KNOW HE'S A MOCHA JOCKEY IN FLANGE SOMEWHERE BY THE WATER.
SO FIRST WE GO GET HIM.
THEN WE GO SAVE MUM AND DAD.
RIGHT.
LET'S GO.

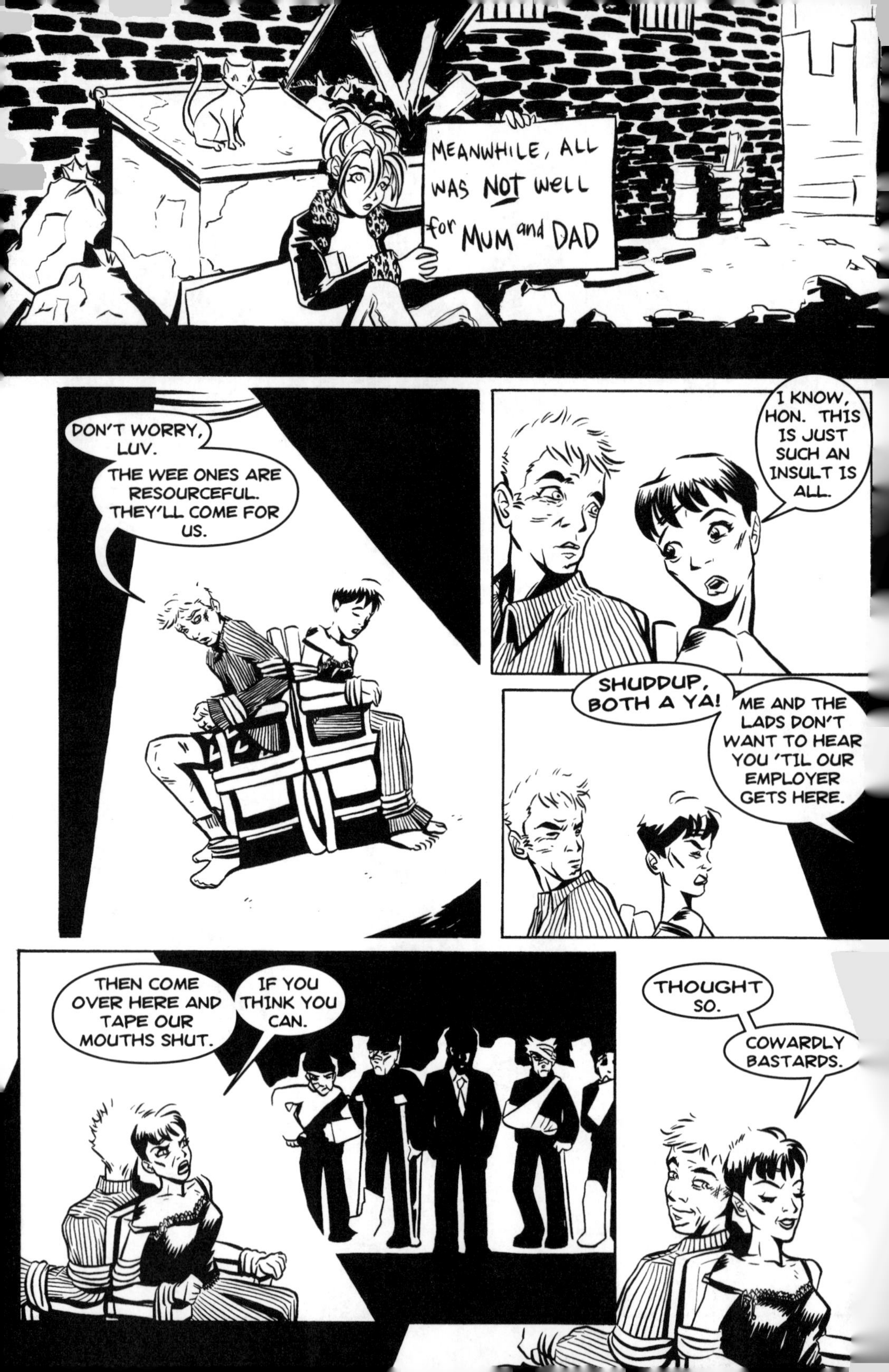

MEANWHILE, ALL WAS NOT WELL for MUM and DAD
DON'T WORRY, LUV.
THE WEE ONES ARE RESOURCEFUL. THEY'LL COME FOR US.
I KNOW, HON. THIS IS JUST SUCH AN INSULT IS ALL.
SHUDDUP, BOTH A YA!
ME AND THE LADS DON'T WANT TO HEAR YOU 'TIL OUR EMPLOYER GETS HERE.
THEN COME OVER HERE AND TAPE OUR MOUTHS SHUT.
IF YOU THINK YOU CAN.
THOUGHT SO.
COWARDLY BASTARDS.

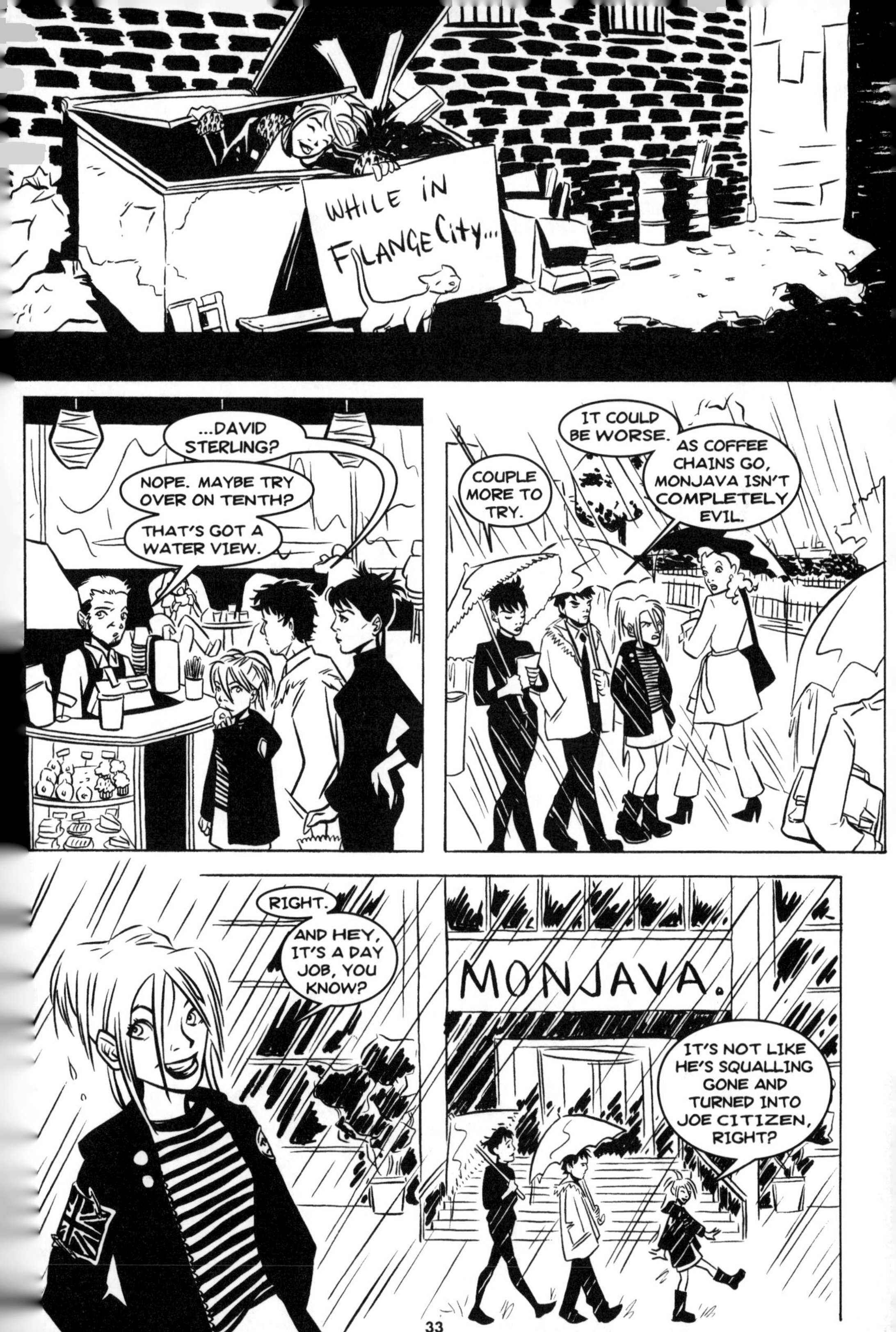
WHILE IN FLANGE City...
...DAVID STERLING?
NOPE. MAYBE TRY OVER ON TENTH?
THAT'S GOT A WATER VIEW.
COUPLE MORE TO TRY.
IT COULD BE WORSE.
AS COFFEE CHAINS GO, MONJAVA ISN'T COMPLETELY EVIL.
RIGHT.
AND HEY, IT'S A DAY JOB, YOU KNOW?
MONJAVA.
IT'S NOT LIKE HE'S SQUALLING GONE AND TURNED INTO JOE CITIZEN, RIGHT?

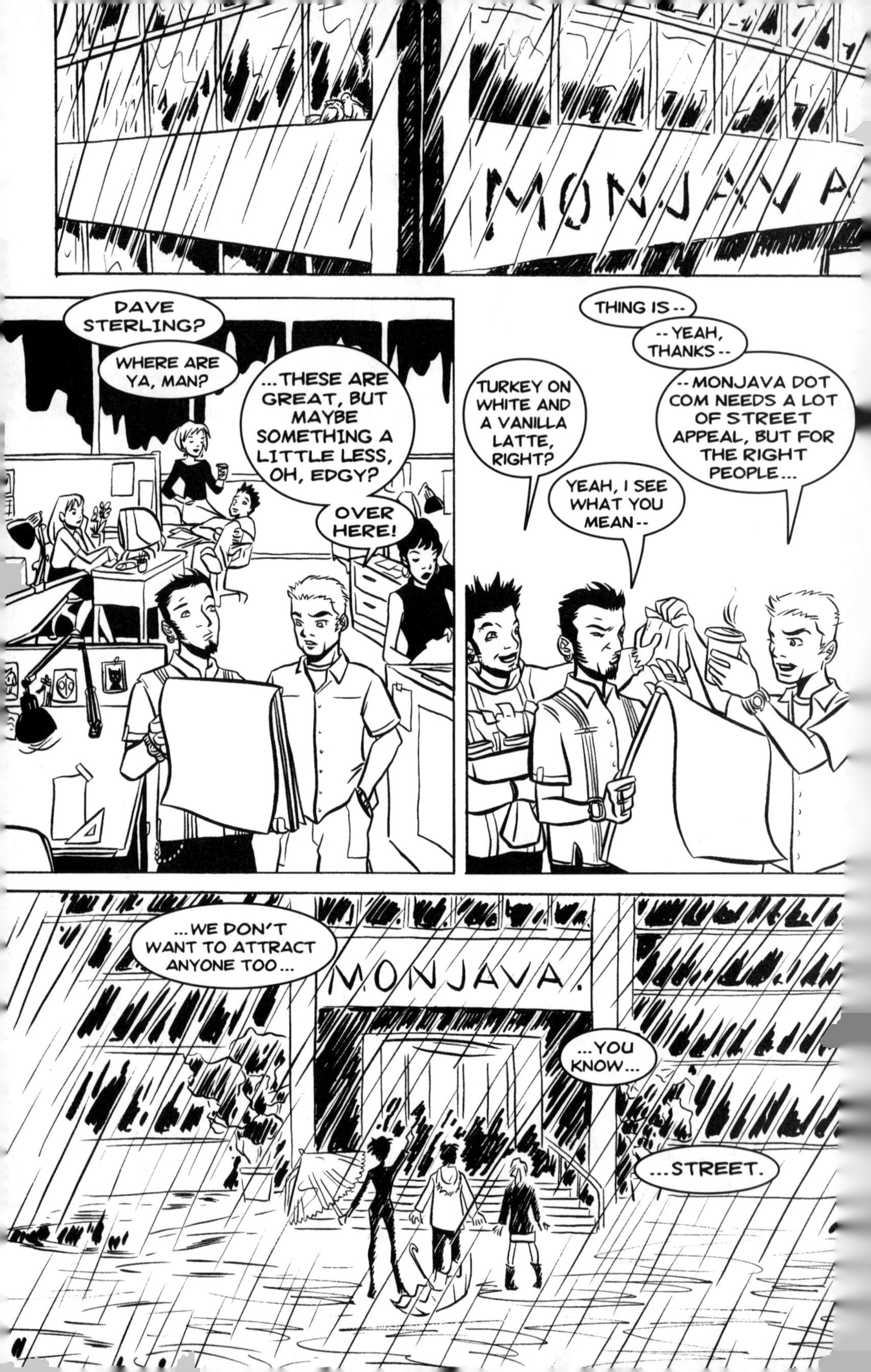
MONJAVA
DAVE STERLING?
WHERE ARE YA, MAN?
...THESE ARE GREAT, BUT MAYBE SOMETHING A LITTLE LESS, OH, EDGY?
OVER HERE!
THING IS --
-- YEAH, THANKS --
TURKEY ON WHITE AND A VANILLA LATTE, RIGHT?
-- MONJAVA DOT COM NEEDS A LOT OF STREET APPEAL, BUT FOR THE RIGHT PEOPLE...
YEAH, I SEE WHAT YOU MEAN --
...WE DON'T WANT TO ATTRACT ANYONE TOO...
MONJAVA.
...YOU KNOW...
...STREET.

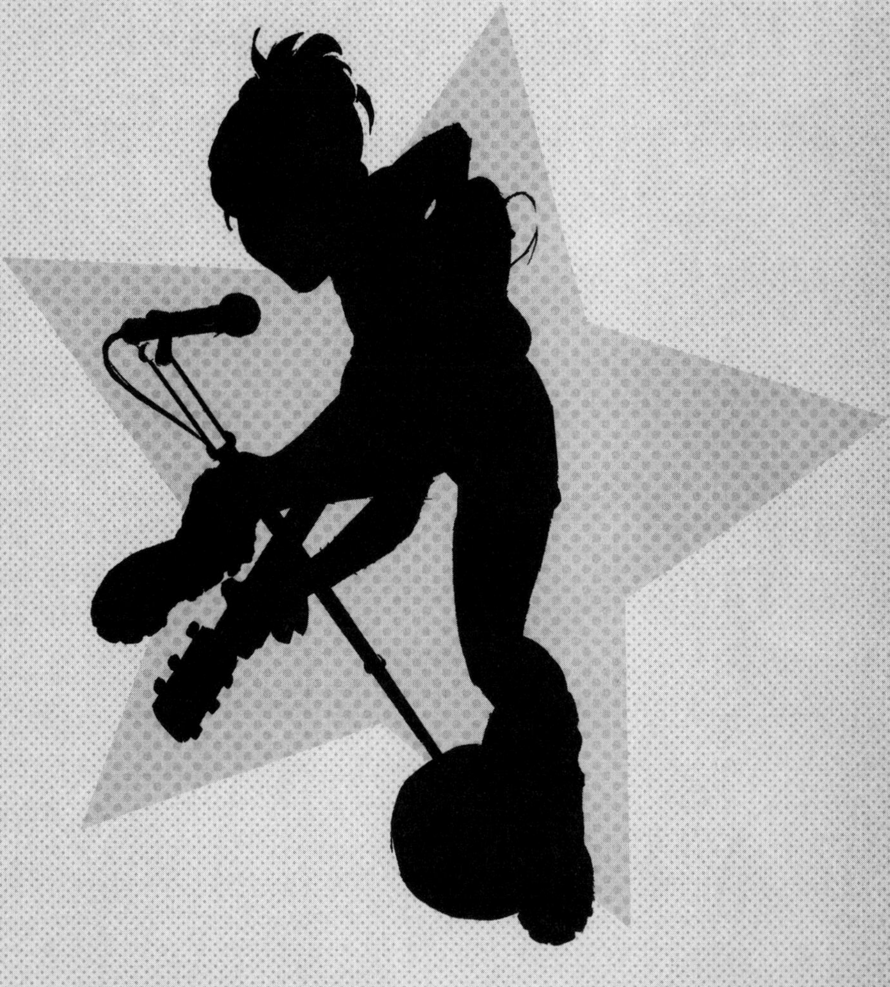

CHAPTER 2

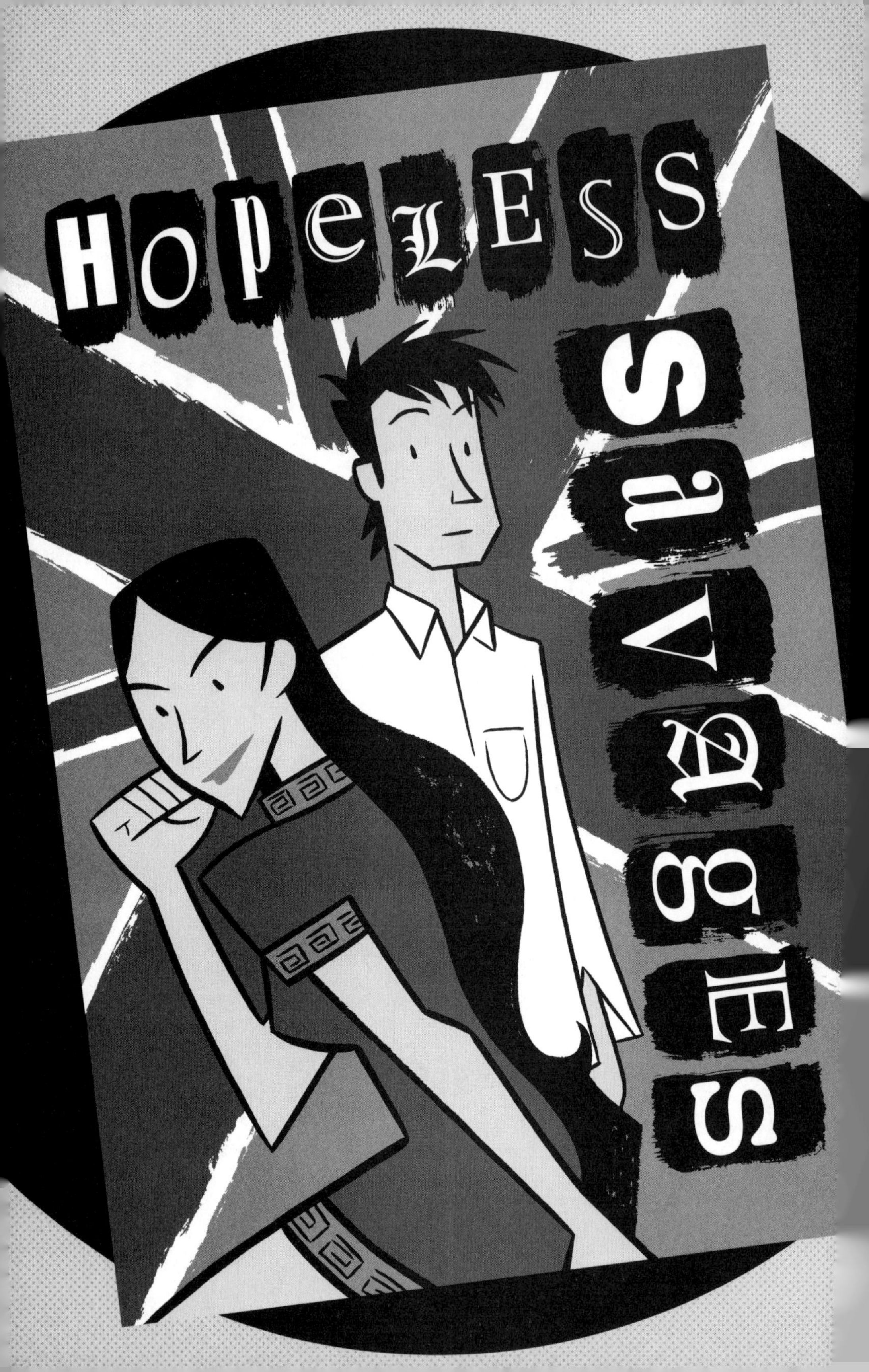
HOPELESS
SAVAGES

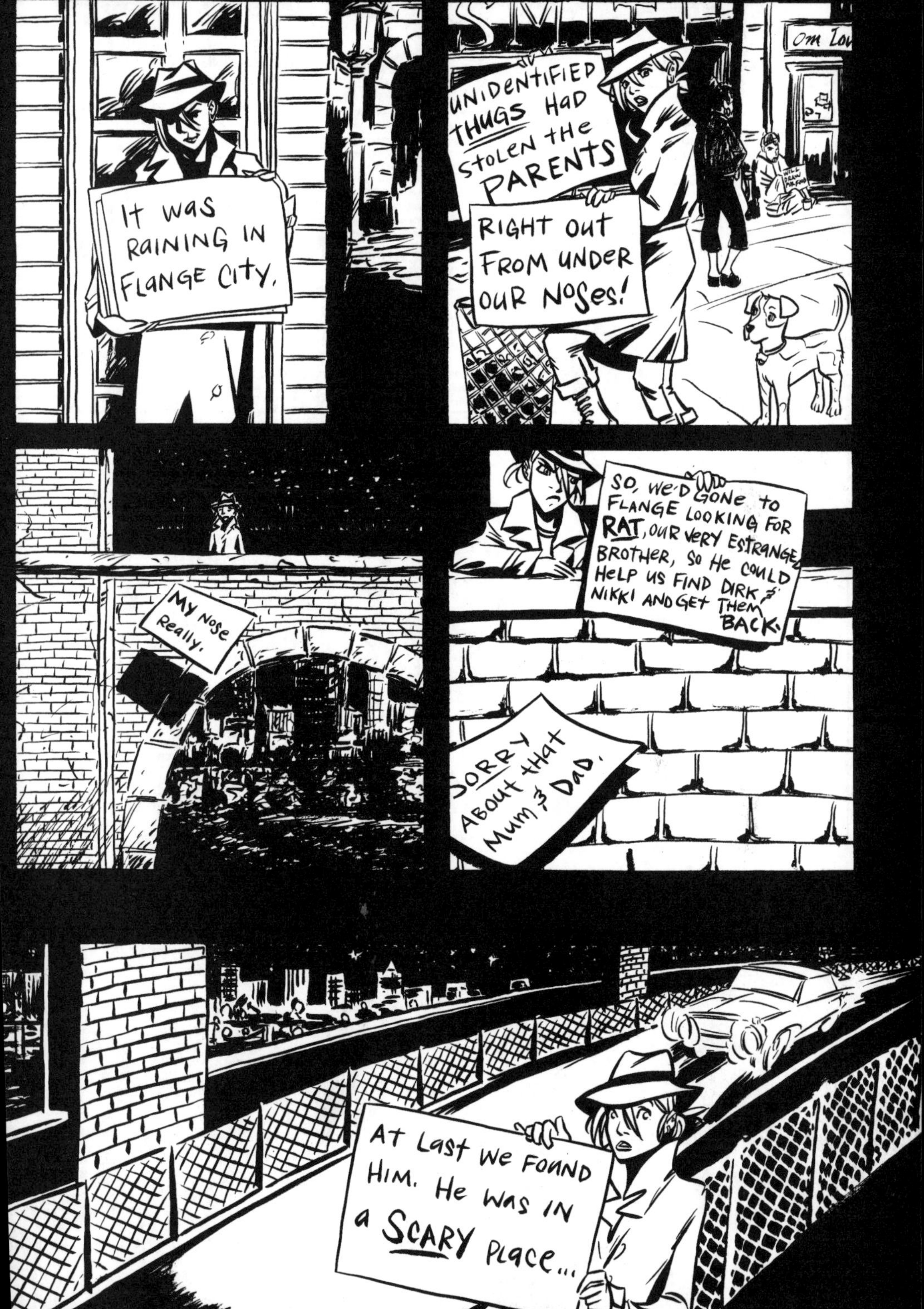
It was raining in Flange City.
Unidentified thugs had stolen the parents
right out from under our noses!
My nose really.
So, we'd gone to Flange looking for Rat, our very estranged brother, so he could help us find Dirk & Nikki and get them back.
Sorry about that Mum & Dad.
At last we found him. He was in a scary place...

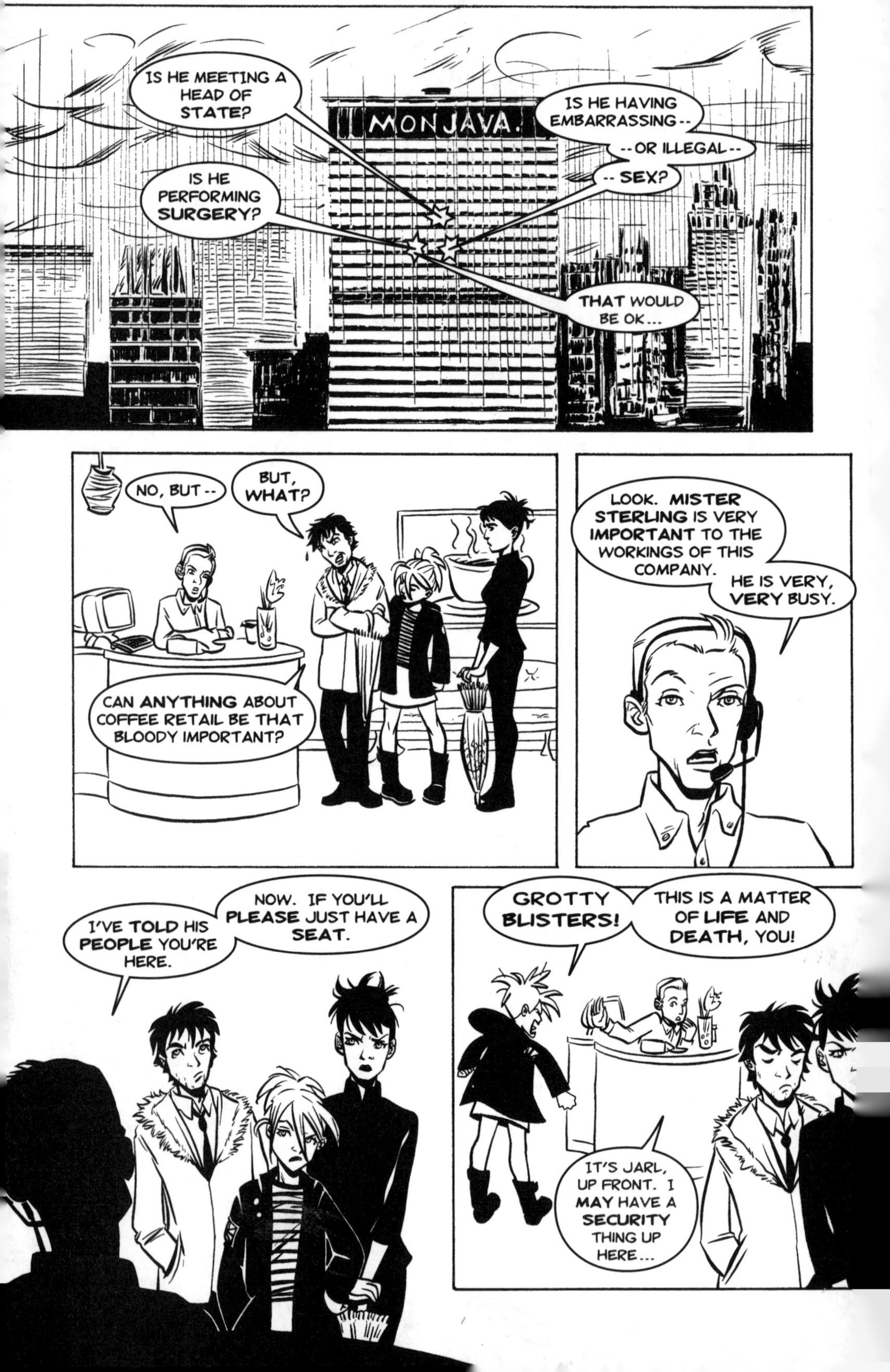

IS HE MEETING A HEAD OF STATE?
MONJAVA.
IS HE HAVING EMBARRASSING --
-- OR ILLEGAL --
-- SEX?
IS HE PERFORMING SURGERY?
THAT WOULD BE OK...
NO, BUT --
BUT, WHAT?
CAN ANYTHING ABOUT COFFEE RETAIL BE THAT BLOODY IMPORTANT?
LOOK. MISTER STERLING IS VERY IMPORTANT TO THE WORKINGS OF THIS COMPANY.
HE IS VERY, VERY BUSY.
I'VE TOLD HIS PEOPLE YOU'RE HERE.
NOW. IF YOU'LL PLEASE JUST HAVE A SEAT.
GROTTY BLISTERS!
THIS IS A MATTER OF LIFE AND DEATH, YOU!
IT'S JARL, UP FRONT. I MAY HAVE A SECURITY THING UP HERE...

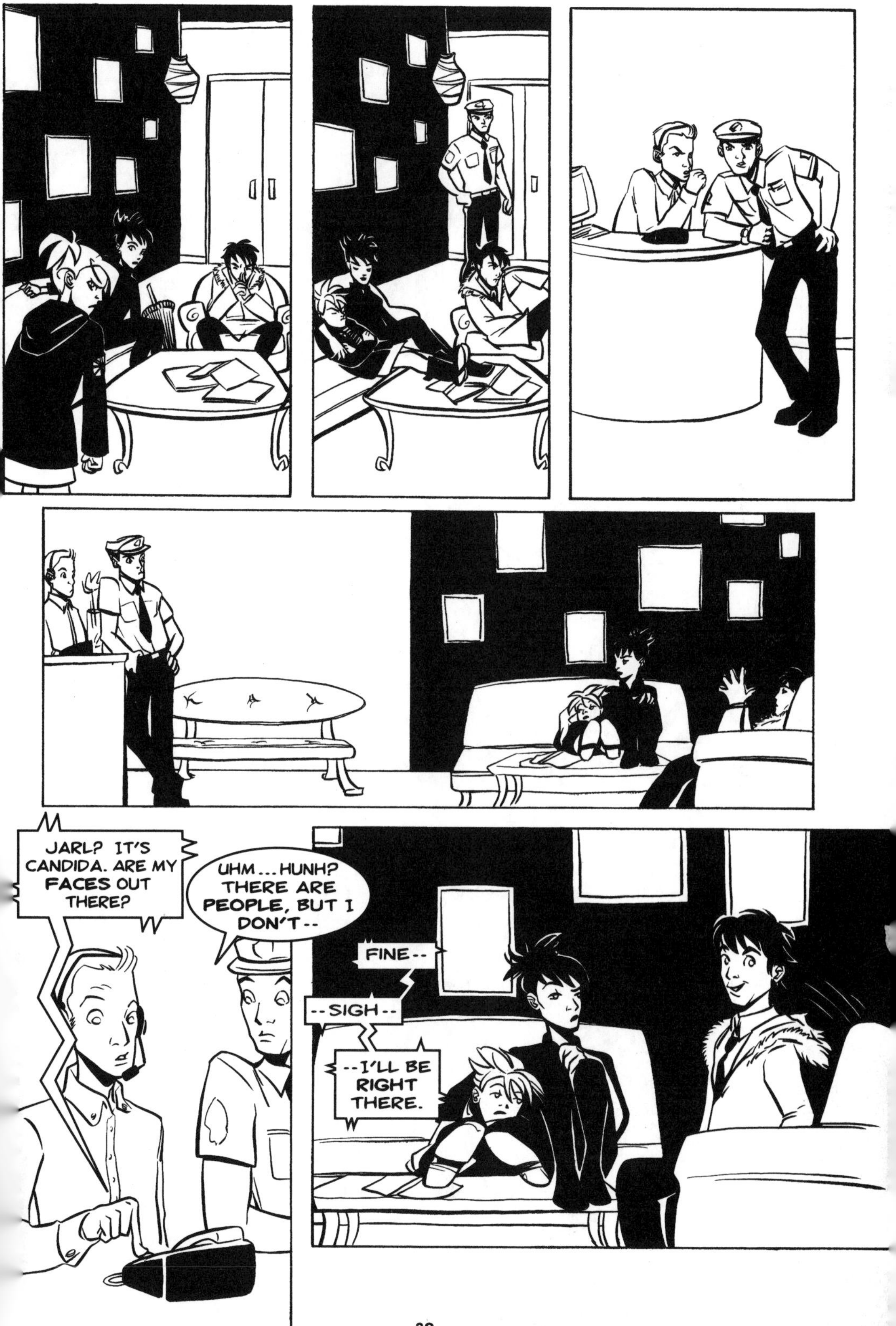
JARL? IT'S CANDIDA. ARE MY FACES OUT THERE?
UHM... HUNH? THERE ARE PEOPLE, BUT I DON'T--
FINE--
--SIGH--
--I'LL BE RIGHT THERE.

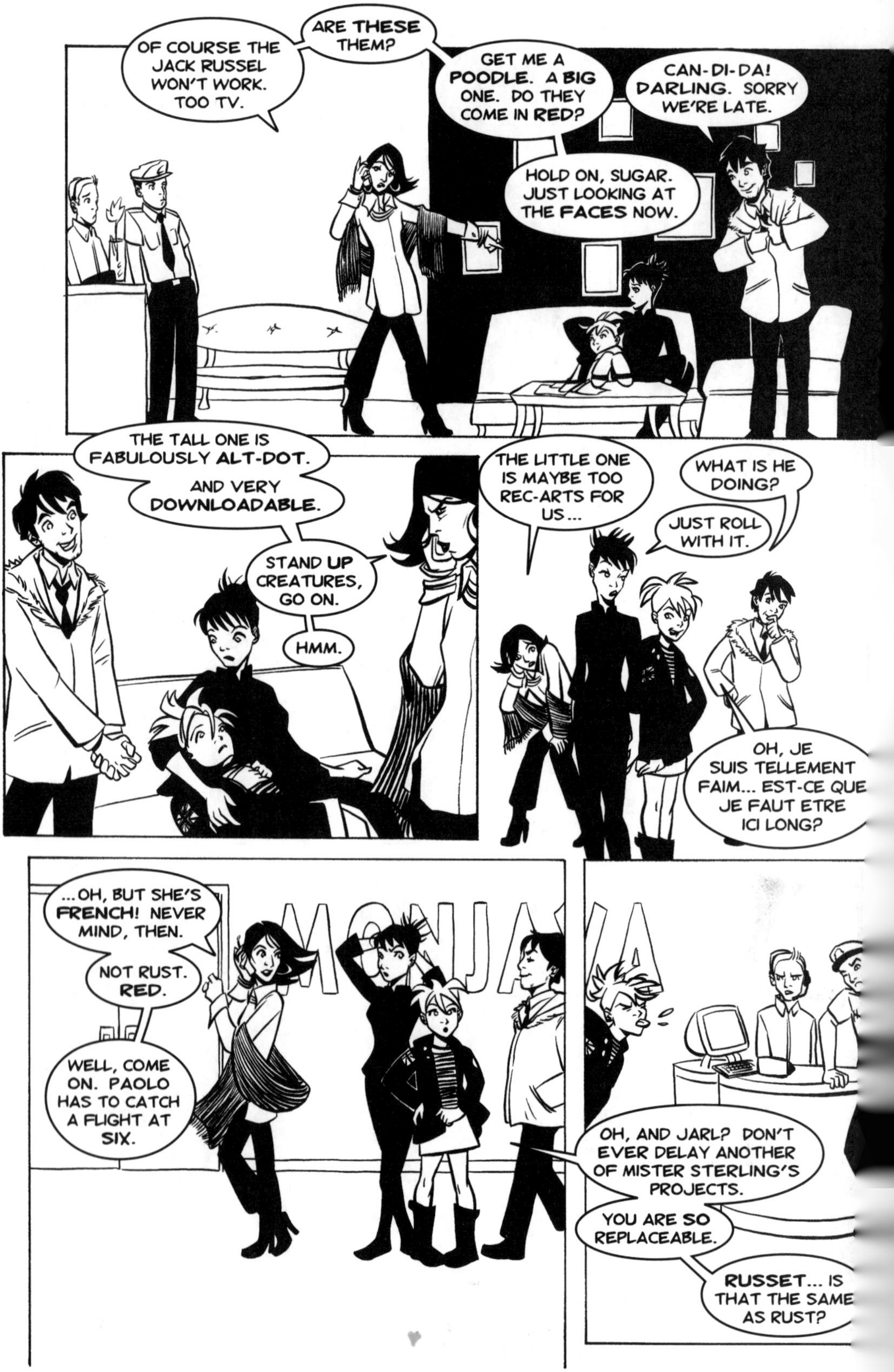
OF COURSE THE JACK RUSSEL WON'T WORK. TOO TV.
ARE THESE THEM?
GET ME A POODLE. A BIG ONE. DO THEY COME IN RED?
HOLD ON, SUGAR. JUST LOOKING AT THE FACES NOW.
CAN-DI-DA! DARLING. SORRY WE'RE LATE.
THE TALL ONE IS FABULOUSLY ALT-DOT.
AND VERY DOWNLOADABLE.
STAND UP CREATURES, GO ON.
HMM.
THE LITTLE ONE IS MAYBE TOO REC-ARTS FOR US...
WHAT IS HE DOING?
JUST ROLL WITH IT.
OH, JE SUIS TELLEMENT FAIM... EST-CE QUE JE FAUT ETRE ICI LONG?
...OH, BUT SHE'S FRENCH! NEVER MIND, THEN.
NOT RUST. RED.
WELL, COME ON. PAOLO HAS TO CATCH A FLIGHT AT SIX.
MONJAVA
OH, AND JARL? DON'T EVER DELAY ANOTHER OF MISTER STERLING'S PROJECTS.
YOU ARE SO REPLACEABLE.
RUSSET... IS THAT THE SAME AS RUST?

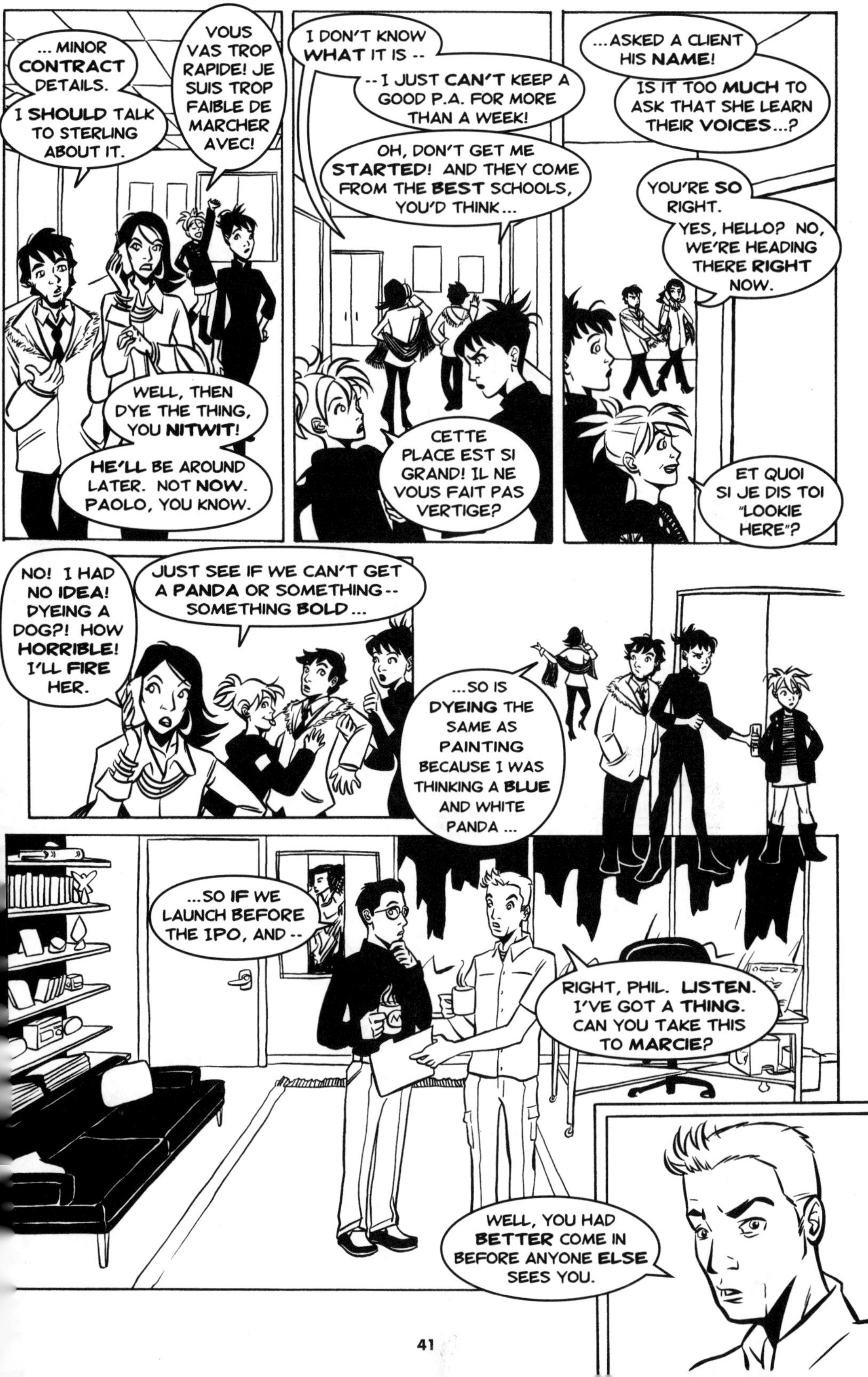
...MINOR CONTRACT DETAILS.
I SHOULD TALK TO STERLING ABOUT IT.
VOUS VAS TROP RAPIDE! JE SUIS TROP FAIBLE DE MARCHER AVEC!
WELL, THEN DYE THE THING, YOU NITWIT!
HE'LL BE AROUND LATER. NOT NOW. PAOLO, YOU KNOW.
I DON'T KNOW WHAT IT IS --
-- I JUST CAN'T KEEP A GOOD P.A. FOR MORE THAN A WEEK!
OH, DON'T GET ME STARTED! AND THEY COME FROM THE BEST SCHOOLS, YOU'D THINK...
CETTE PLACE EST SI GRAND! IL NE VOUS FAIT PAS VERTIGE?
...ASKED A CLIENT HIS NAME!
IS IT TOO MUCH TO ASK THAT SHE LEARN THEIR VOICES...?
YOU'RE SO RIGHT.
YES, HELLO? NO, WE'RE HEADING THERE RIGHT NOW.
ET QUOI SI JE DIS TOI "LOOKIE HERE"?
NO! I HAD NO IDEA! DYEING A DOG?! HOW HORRIBLE! I'LL FIRE HER.
JUST SEE IF WE CAN'T GET A PANDA OR SOMETHING -- SOMETHING BOLD...
...SO IS DYEING THE SAME AS PAINTING BECAUSE I WAS THINKING A BLUE AND WHITE PANDA ...
...SO IF WE LAUNCH BEFORE THE IPO, AND --
RIGHT, PHIL. LISTEN. I'VE GOT A THING. CAN YOU TAKE THIS TO MARCIE?
WELL, YOU HAD BETTER COME IN BEFORE ANYONE ELSE SEES YOU.

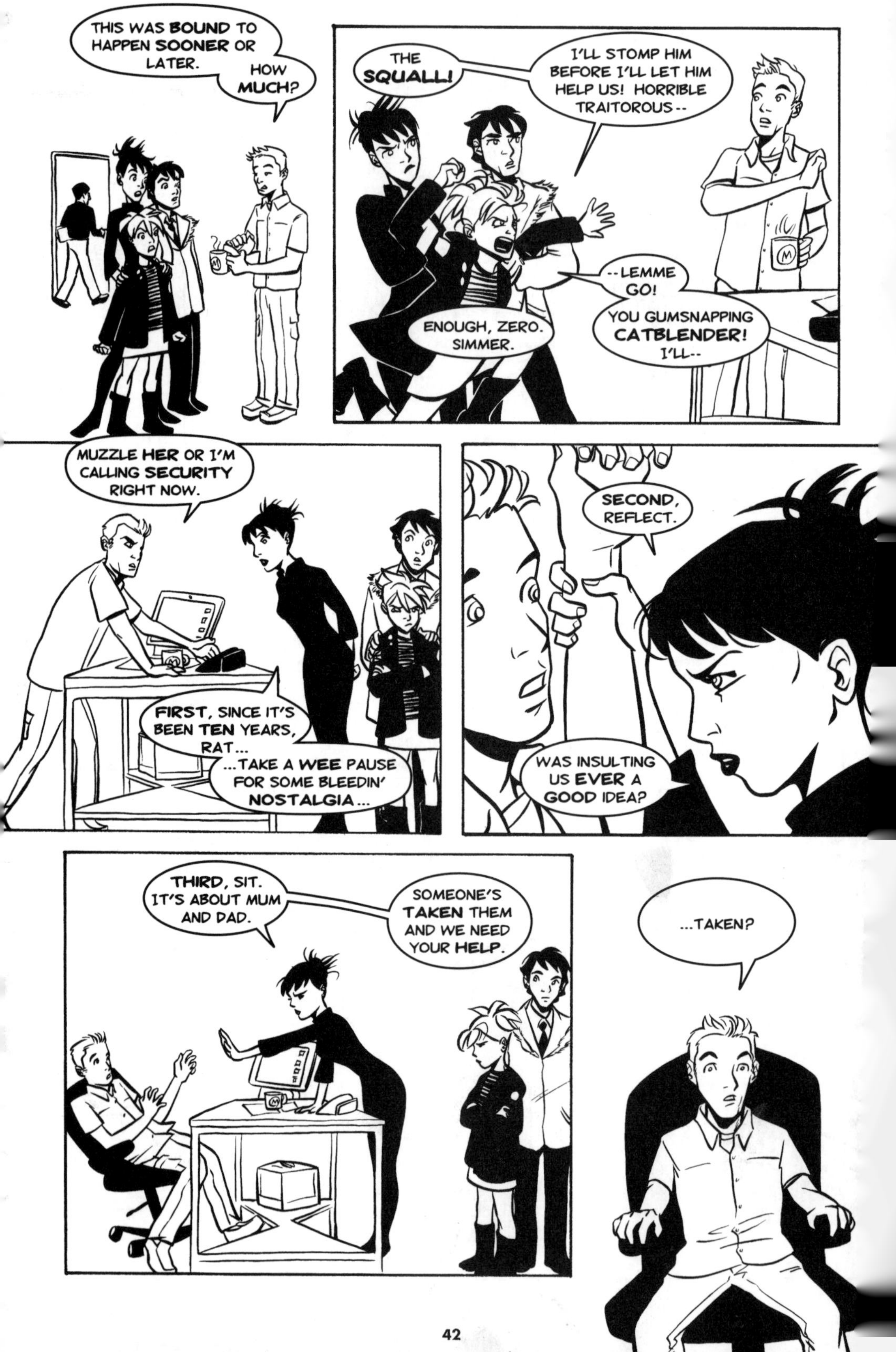
THIS WAS BOUND TO HAPPEN SOONER OR LATER.
HOW MUCH?
THE SQUALL!
I'LL STOMP HIM BEFORE I'LL LET HIM HELP US! HORRIBLE TRAITOROUS--
--LEMME GO!
YOU GUMSNAPPING CATBLENDER! I'LL--
ENOUGH, ZERO. SIMMER.
MUZZLE HER OR I'M CALLING SECURITY RIGHT NOW.
FIRST, SINCE IT'S BEEN TEN YEARS, RAT...
...TAKE A WEE PAUSE FOR SOME BLEEDIN' NOSTALGIA...
SECOND, REFLECT.
WAS INSULTING US EVER A GOOD IDEA?
THIRD, SIT. IT'S ABOUT MUM AND DAD.
SOMEONE'S TAKEN THEM AND WE NEED YOUR HELP.
...TAKEN?

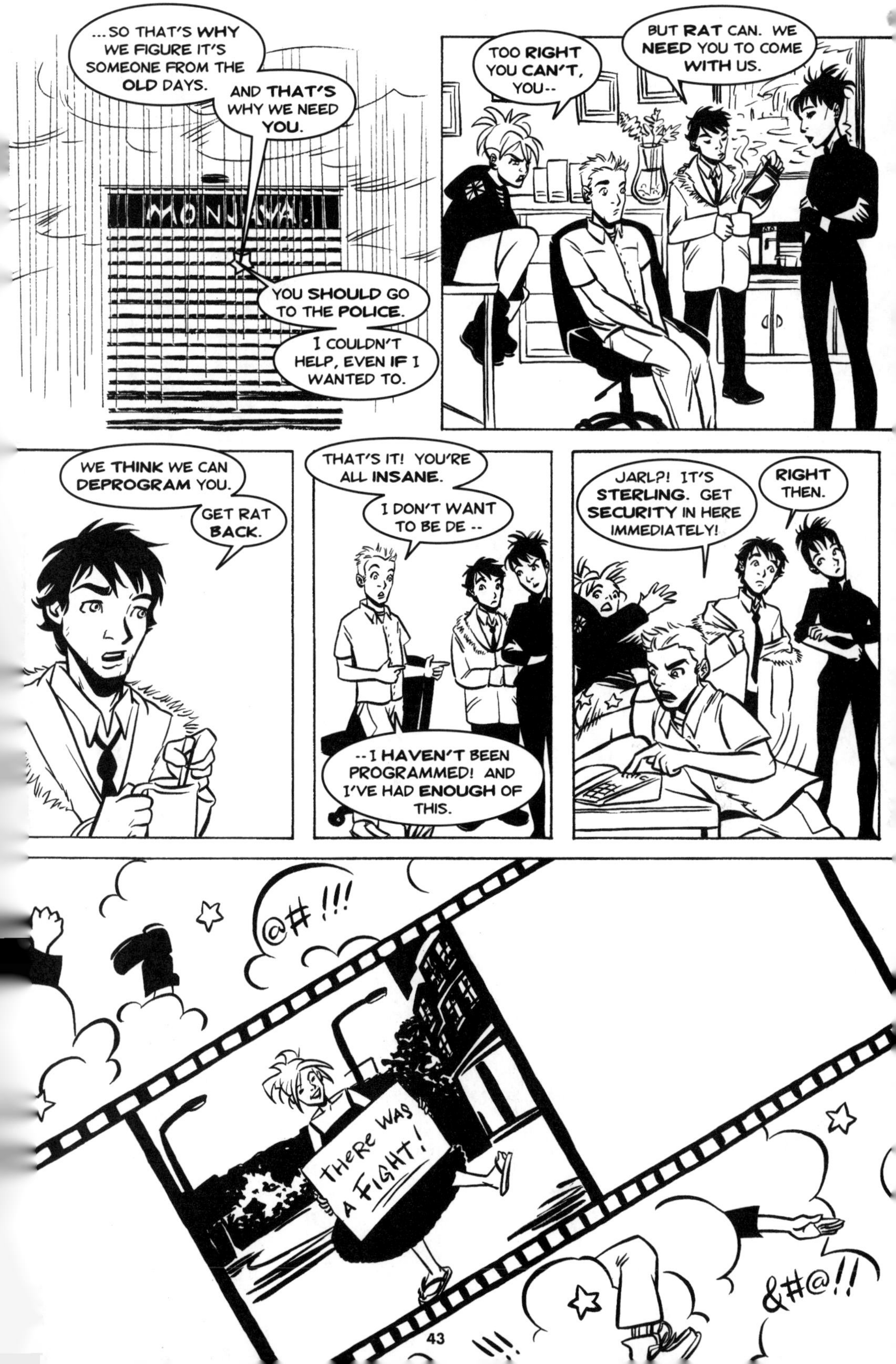
...SO THAT'S WHY WE FIGURE IT'S SOMEONE FROM THE OLD DAYS.
AND THAT'S WHY WE NEED YOU.
MONJAVA
YOU SHOULD GO TO THE POLICE.
I COULDN'T HELP, EVEN IF I WANTED TO.
TOO RIGHT YOU CAN'T, YOU--
BUT RAT CAN. WE NEED YOU TO COME WITH US.
WE THINK WE CAN DEPROGRAM YOU.
GET RAT BACK.
THAT'S IT! YOU'RE ALL INSANE.
I DON'T WANT TO BE DE --
--I HAVEN'T BEEN PROGRAMMED! AND I'VE HAD ENOUGH OF THIS.
JARL?! IT'S STERLING. GET SECURITY IN HERE IMMEDIATELY!
RIGHT THEN.
@#!!!
THERE WAS A FIGHT!
&#@!!
!!!

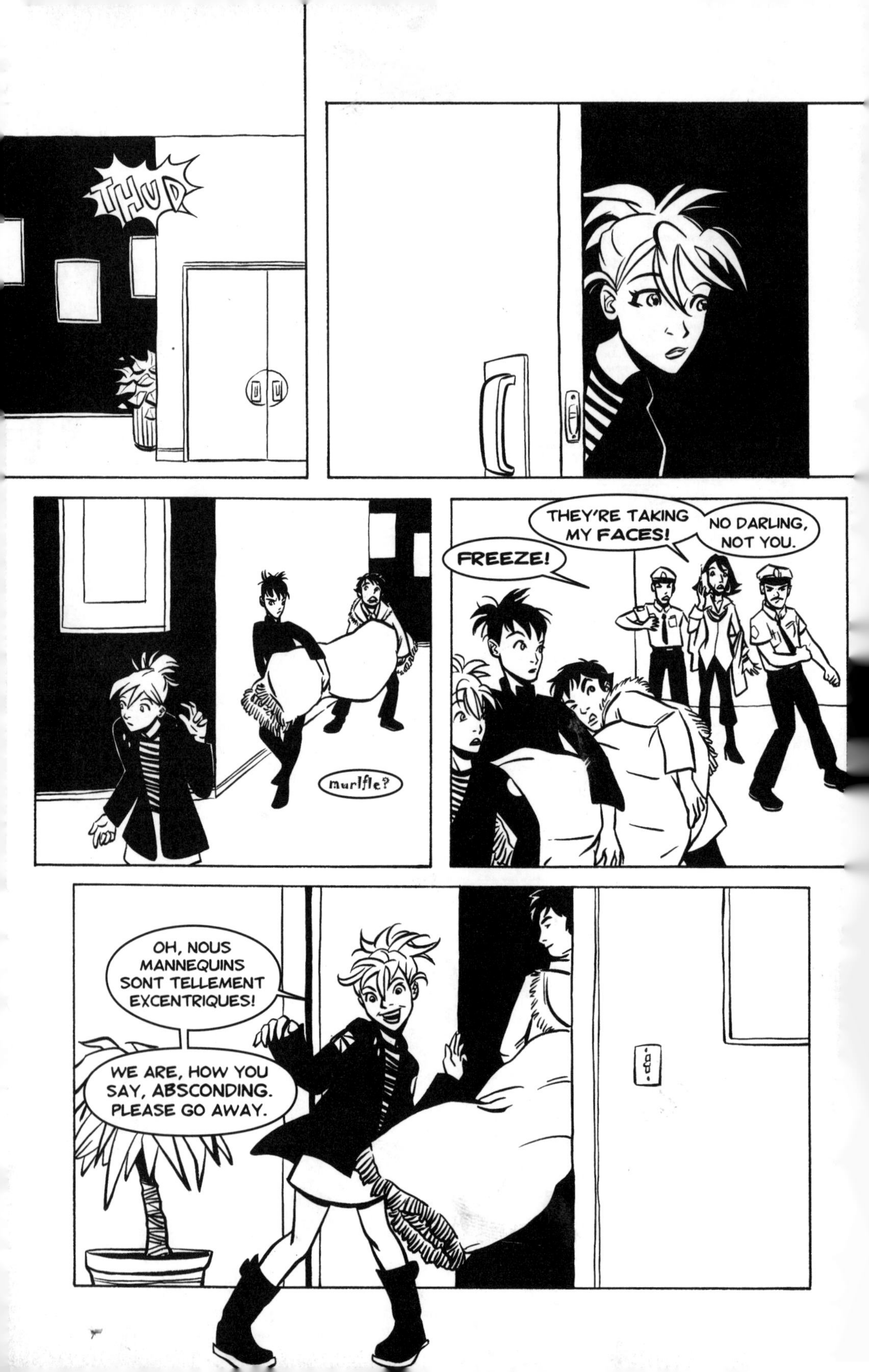
THUD
murlfle?
FREEZE!
THEY'RE TAKING MY FACES!
NO DARLING, NOT YOU.
OH, NOUS MANNEQUINS SONT TELLEMENT EXCENTRIQUES!
WE ARE, HOW YOU SAY, ABSCONDING. PLEASE GO AWAY.

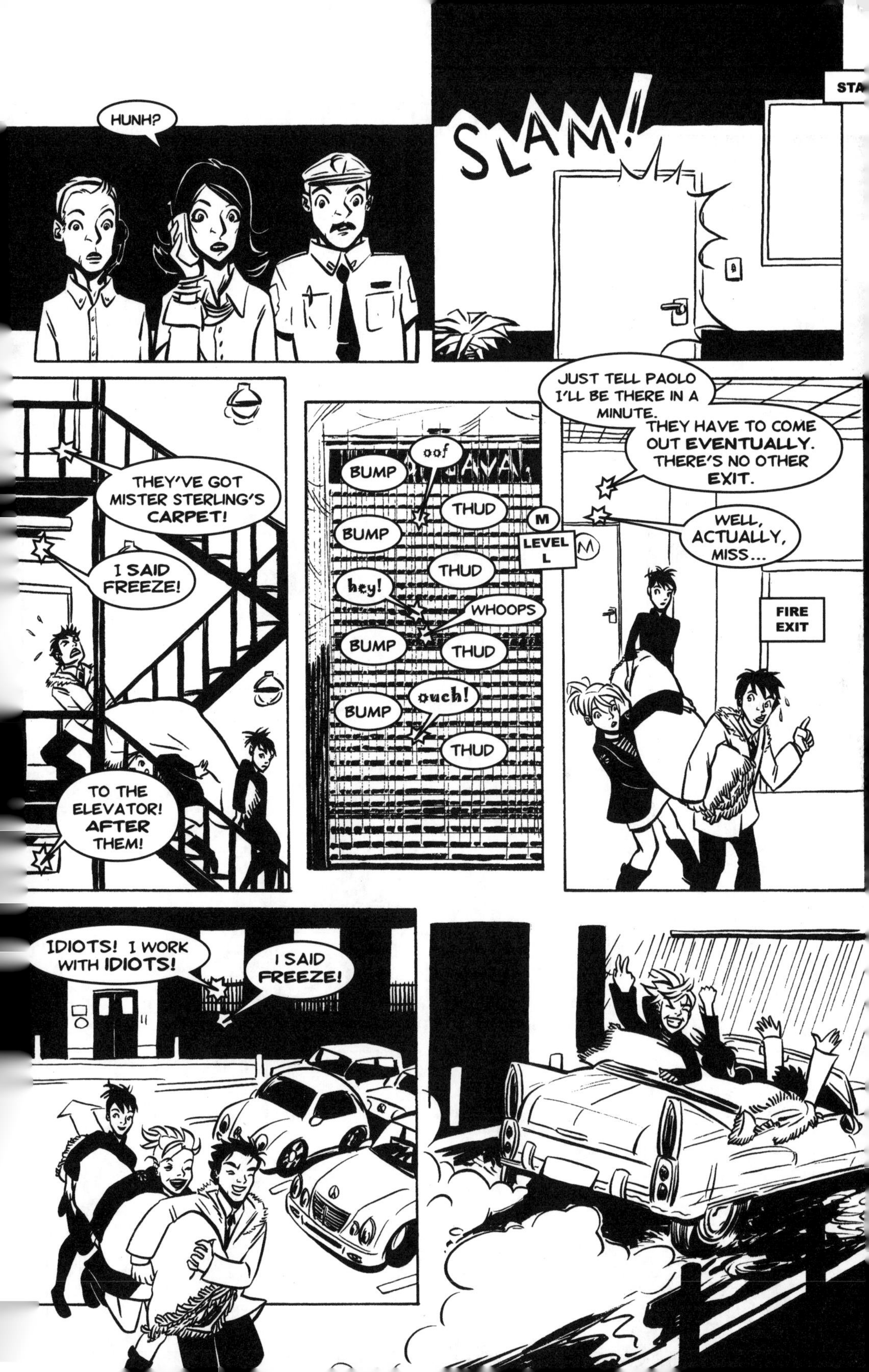
HUNH?
SLAM!
STA
THEY'VE GOT MISTER STERLING'S CARPET!
I SAID FREEZE!
TO THE ELEVATOR! AFTER THEM!
JAVA
BUMP
oof
THUD
BUMP
THUD
hey!
WHOOPS
BUMP
THUD
BUMP
ouch!
THUD
M
LEVEL L
M
JUST TELL PAOLO I'LL BE THERE IN A MINUTE.
THEY HAVE TO COME OUT EVENTUALLY. THERE'S NO OTHER EXIT.
WELL, ACTUALLY, MISS...
FIRE EXIT
IDIOTS! I WORK WITH IDIOTS!
I SAID FREEZE!

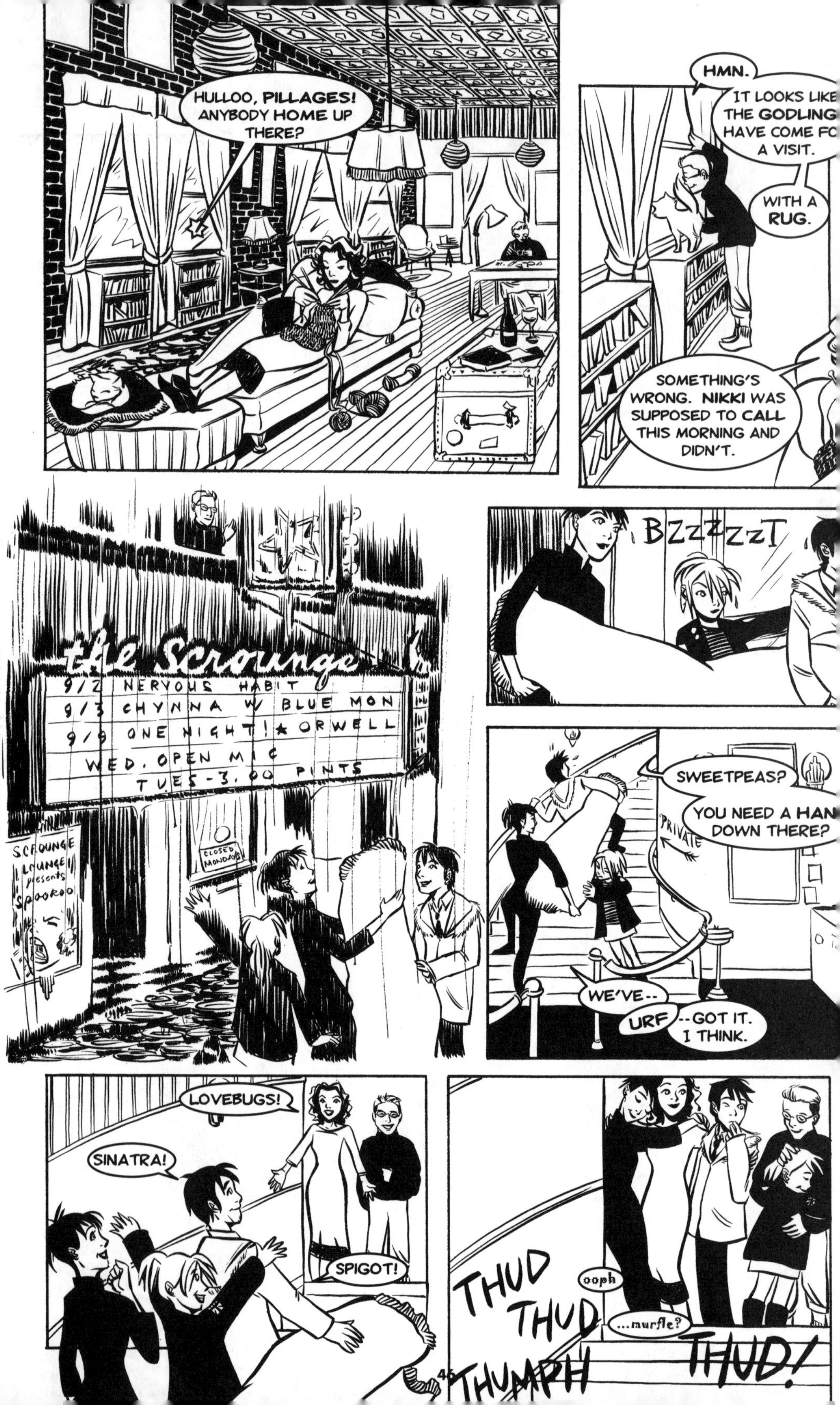
HULLOO, PILLAGES! ANYBODY HOME UP THERE?
HMN.
IT LOOKS LIKE THE GODLING HAVE COME FO A VISIT.
WITH A RUG.
SOMETHING'S WRONG. NIKKI WAS SUPPOSED TO CALL THIS MORNING AND DIDN'T.
the Scrounge
9/2 NERVOUS HABIT
9/3 CHYNNA W BLUE MON
ONE NIGHT! ★ ORWELL
WED. OPEN MIC
TUES - 3.00 PINTS
SCROUNGE LOUNGE presents Spookoo
CLOSED MONDAYS
BZZZZZT
SWEETPEAS?
YOU NEED A HAN DOWN THERE?
PRIVATE
WE'VE--
URF
--GOT IT. I THINK.
LOVEBUGS!
SINATRA!
SPIGOT!
THUD
THUD
THUMPH
ooph
...murfle?
THUD!

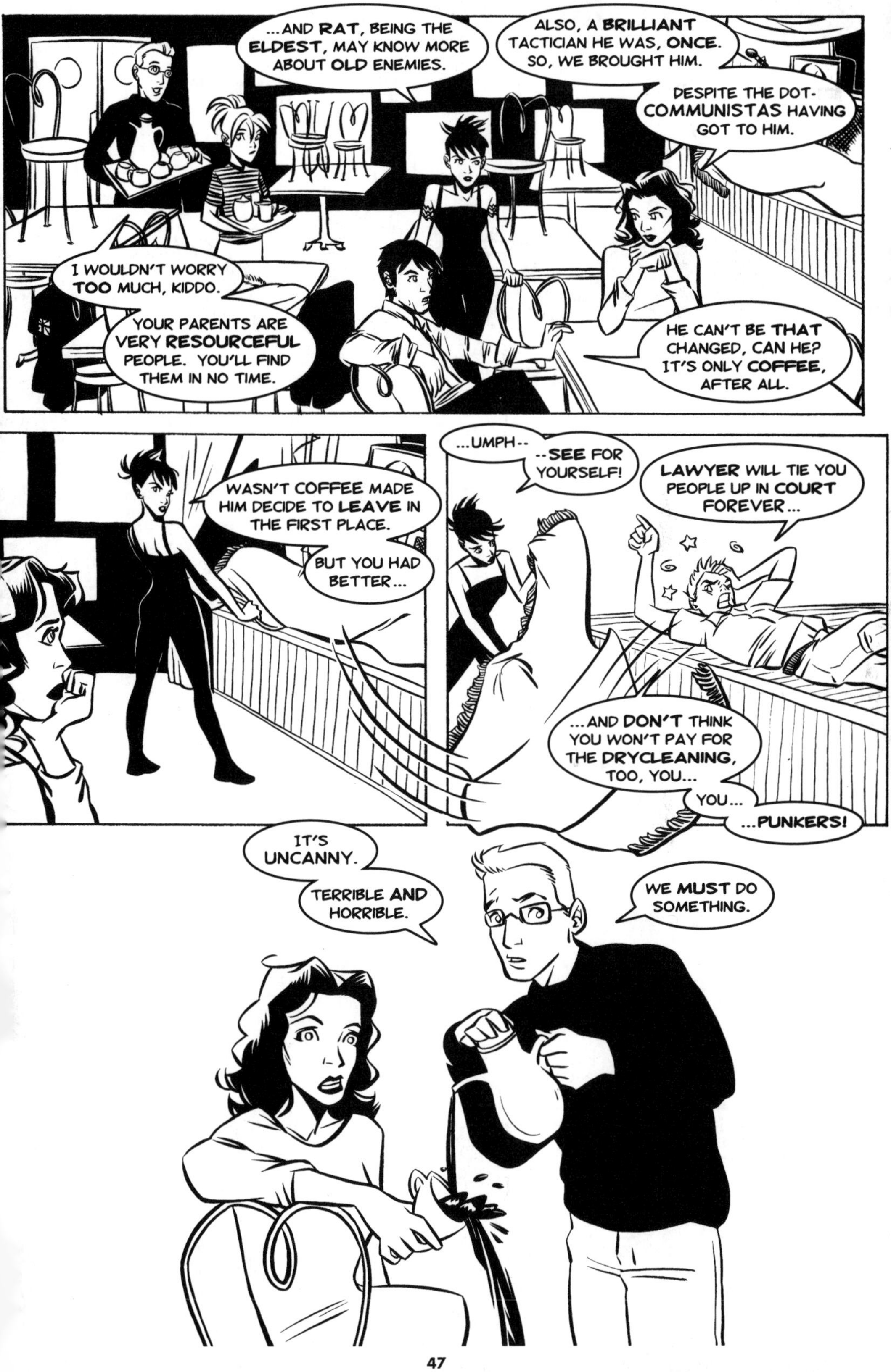
...AND RAT, BEING THE ELDEST, MAY KNOW MORE ABOUT OLD ENEMIES.
ALSO, A BRILLIANT TACTICIAN HE WAS, ONCE. SO, WE BROUGHT HIM.
DESPITE THE DOT-COMMUNISTAS HAVING GOT TO HIM.
I WOULDN'T WORRY TOO MUCH, KIDDO.
YOUR PARENTS ARE VERY RESOURCEFUL PEOPLE. YOU'LL FIND THEM IN NO TIME.
HE CAN'T BE THAT CHANGED, CAN HE? IT'S ONLY COFFEE, AFTER ALL.
WASN'T COFFEE MADE HIM DECIDE TO LEAVE IN THE FIRST PLACE.
BUT YOU HAD BETTER...
...UMPH--
--SEE FOR YOURSELF!
LAWYER WILL TIE YOU PEOPLE UP IN COURT FOREVER...
...AND DON'T THINK YOU WON'T PAY FOR THE DRYCLEANING, TOO, YOU...
YOU...
...PUNKERS!
IT'S UNCANNY.
TERRIBLE AND HORRIBLE.
WE MUST DO SOMETHING.

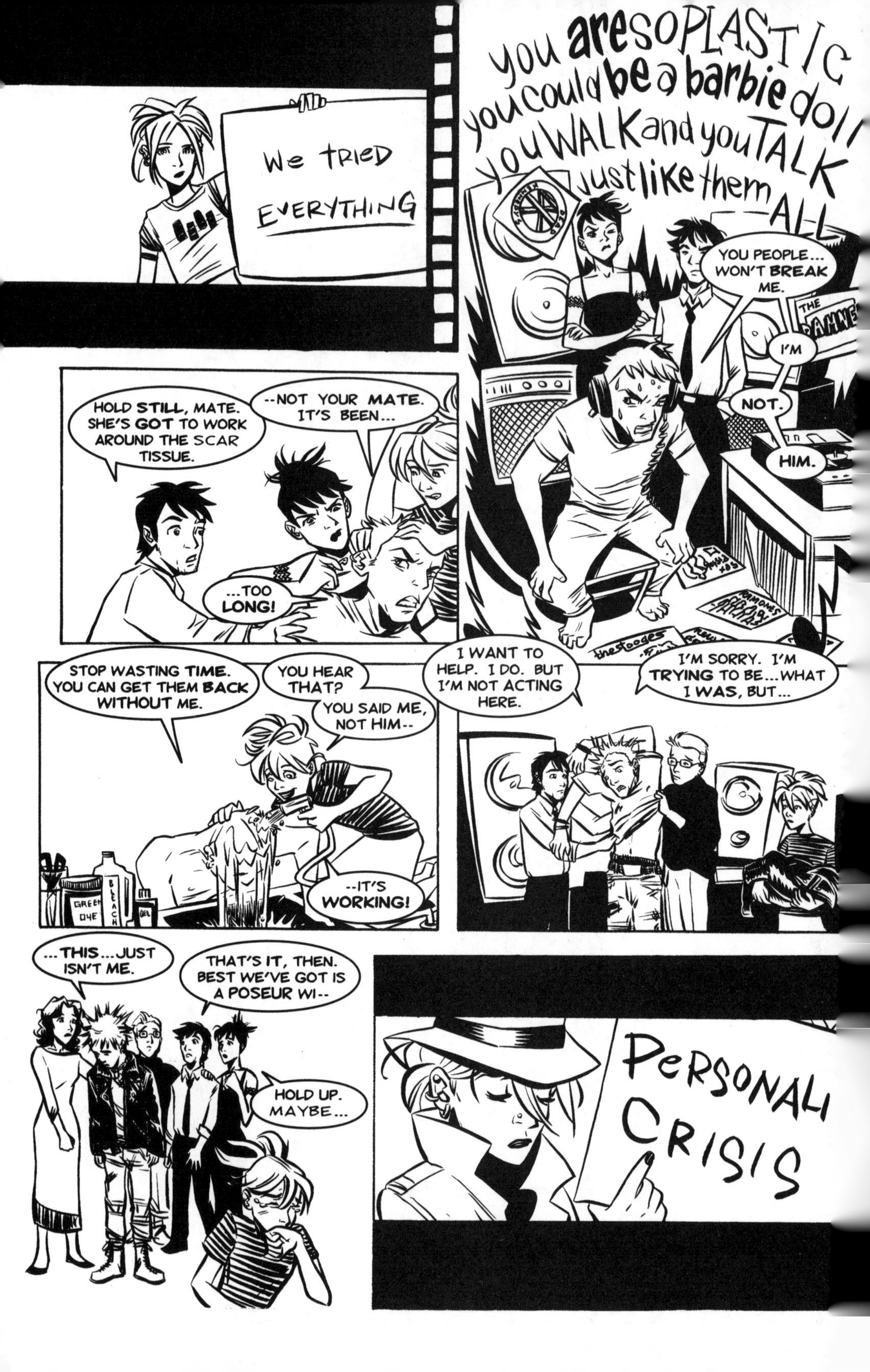

WE TRIED EVERYTHING
you are SO PLASTIC you could be a barbie doll you WALK and you TALK just like them ALL
YOU PEOPLE... WON'T BREAK ME.
I'M
NOT.
HIM.
THE RAMONES
HOLD STILL, MATE. SHE'S GOT TO WORK AROUND THE SCAR TISSUE.
--NOT YOUR MATE. IT'S BEEN...
...TOO LONG!
the stooges
STOP WASTING TIME. YOU CAN GET THEM BACK WITHOUT ME.
YOU HEAR THAT?
YOU SAID ME, NOT HIM--
--IT'S WORKING!
GREEN DYE
BLEACH
GEL
I WANT TO HELP. I DO. BUT I'M NOT ACTING HERE.
I'M SORRY. I'M TRYING TO BE...WHAT I WAS, BUT...
...THIS...JUST ISN'T ME.
THAT'S IT, THEN. BEST WE'VE GOT IS A POSEUR WI--
HOLD UP. MAYBE...
PERSONALI CRISIS

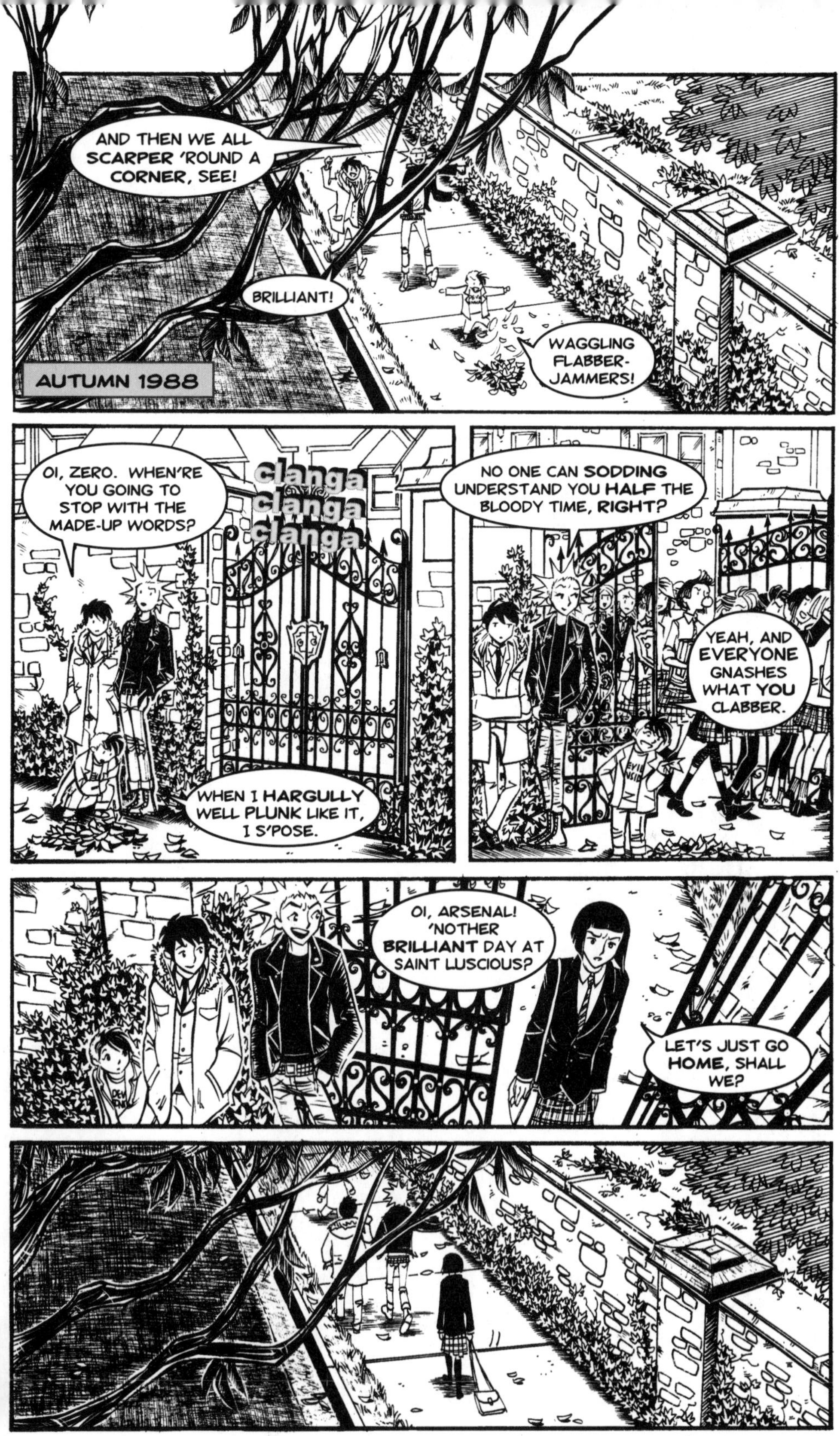
AND THEN WE ALL SCARPER 'ROUND A CORNER, SEE!
BRILLIANT!
WAGGLING FLABBER-JAMMERS!
AUTUMN 1988
OI, ZERO. WHEN'RE YOU GOING TO STOP WITH THE MADE-UP WORDS?
clanga clanga clanga
WHEN I HARGULLY WELL PLUNK LIKE IT, I S'POSE.
NO ONE CAN SODDING UNDERSTAND YOU HALF THE BLOODY TIME, RIGHT?
YEAH, AND EVERYONE GNASHES WHAT YOU CLABBER.
OI, ARSENAL! 'NOTHER BRILLIANT DAY AT SAINT LUSCIOUS?
LET'S JUST GO HOME, SHALL WE?

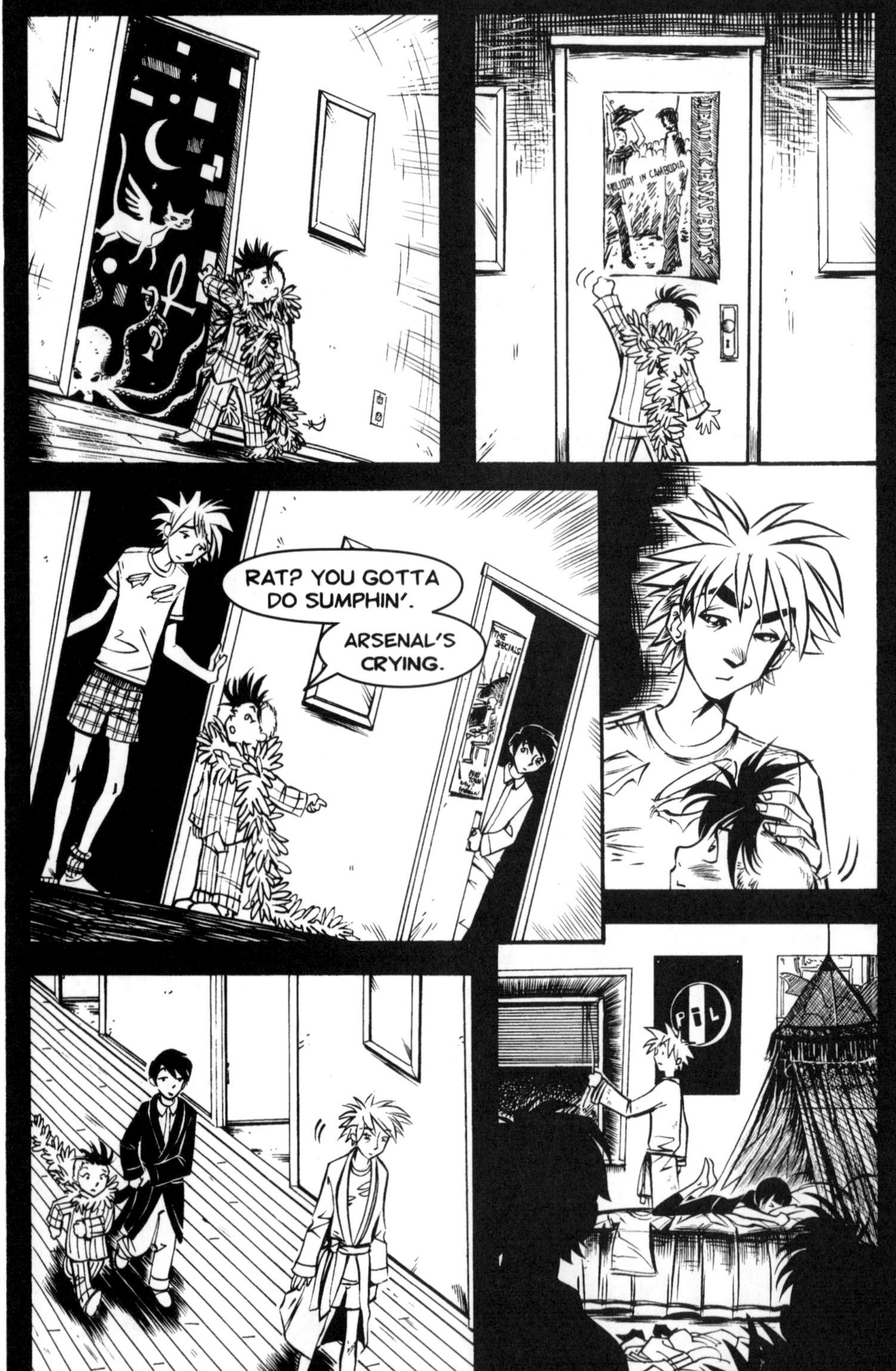
HOLIDAY IN CAMBODIA
RAT? YOU GOTTA DO SUMPHIN'.
ARSENAL'S CRYING.
THE SPECIALS
PiL

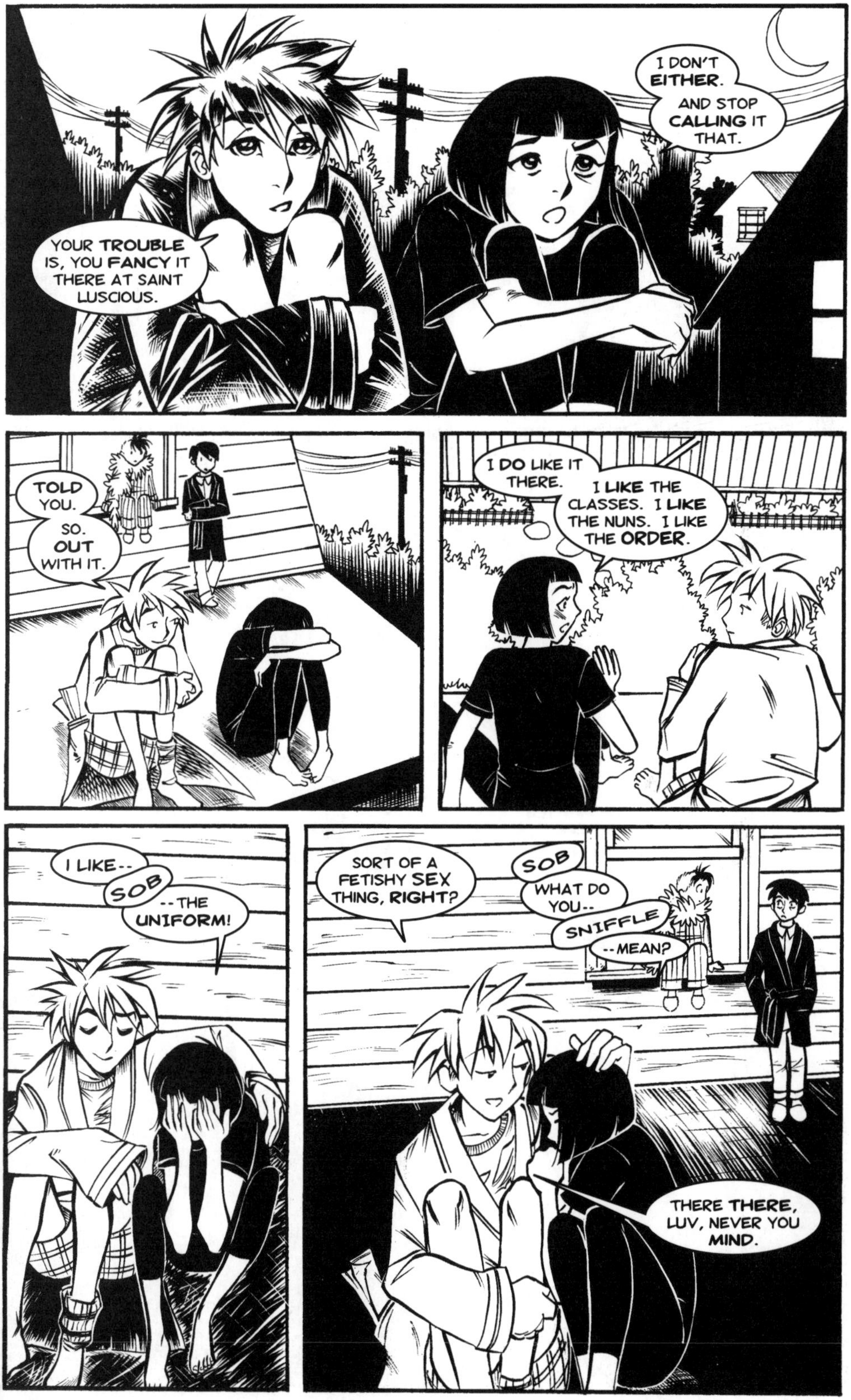
YOUR TROUBLE IS, YOU FANCY IT THERE AT SAINT LUSCIOUS.
I DON'T EITHER.
AND STOP CALLING IT THAT.
TOLD YOU.
SO. OUT WITH IT.
I DO LIKE IT THERE.
I LIKE THE CLASSES. I LIKE THE NUNS. I LIKE THE ORDER.
I LIKE--
SOB
--THE UNIFORM!
SORT OF A FETISHY SEX THING, RIGHT?
SOB
WHAT DO YOU--
SNIFFLE
--MEAN?
THERE THERE, LUV, NEVER YOU MIND.

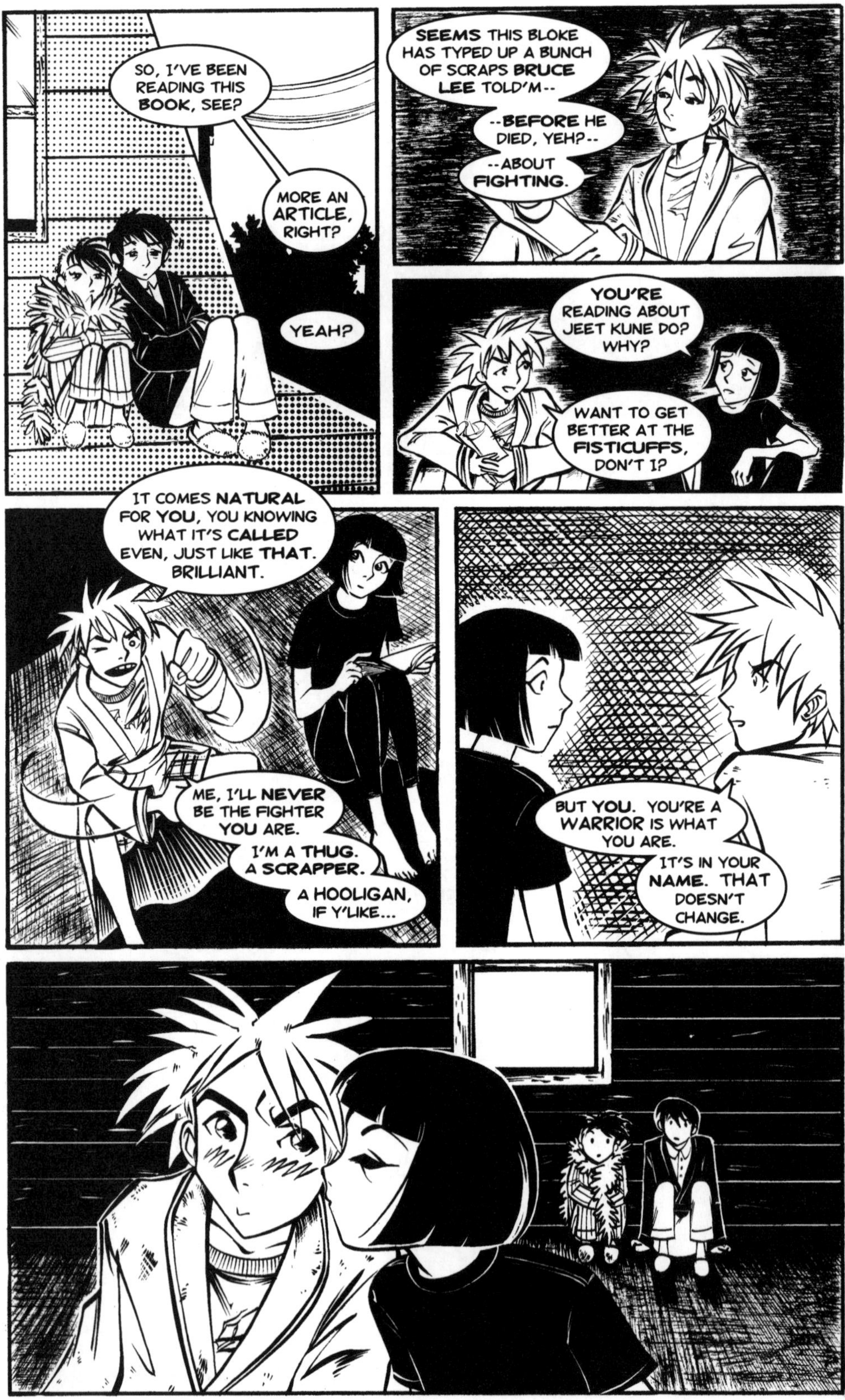
SO, I'VE BEEN READING THIS BOOK, SEE?
MORE AN ARTICLE, RIGHT?
YEAH?
SEEMS THIS BLOKE HAS TYPED UP A BUNCH OF SCRAPS BRUCE LEE TOLD'M--
--BEFORE HE DIED, YEH?--
--ABOUT FIGHTING.
YOU'RE READING ABOUT JEET KUNE DO? WHY?
WANT TO GET BETTER AT THE FISTICUFFS, DON'T I?
IT COMES NATURAL FOR YOU, YOU KNOWING WHAT IT'S CALLED EVEN, JUST LIKE THAT. BRILLIANT.
ME, I'LL NEVER BE THE FIGHTER YOU ARE.
I'M A THUG. A SCRAPPER.
A HOOLIGAN, IF Y'LIKE...
BUT YOU. YOU'RE A WARRIOR IS WHAT YOU ARE.
IT'S IN YOUR NAME. THAT DOESN'T CHANGE.

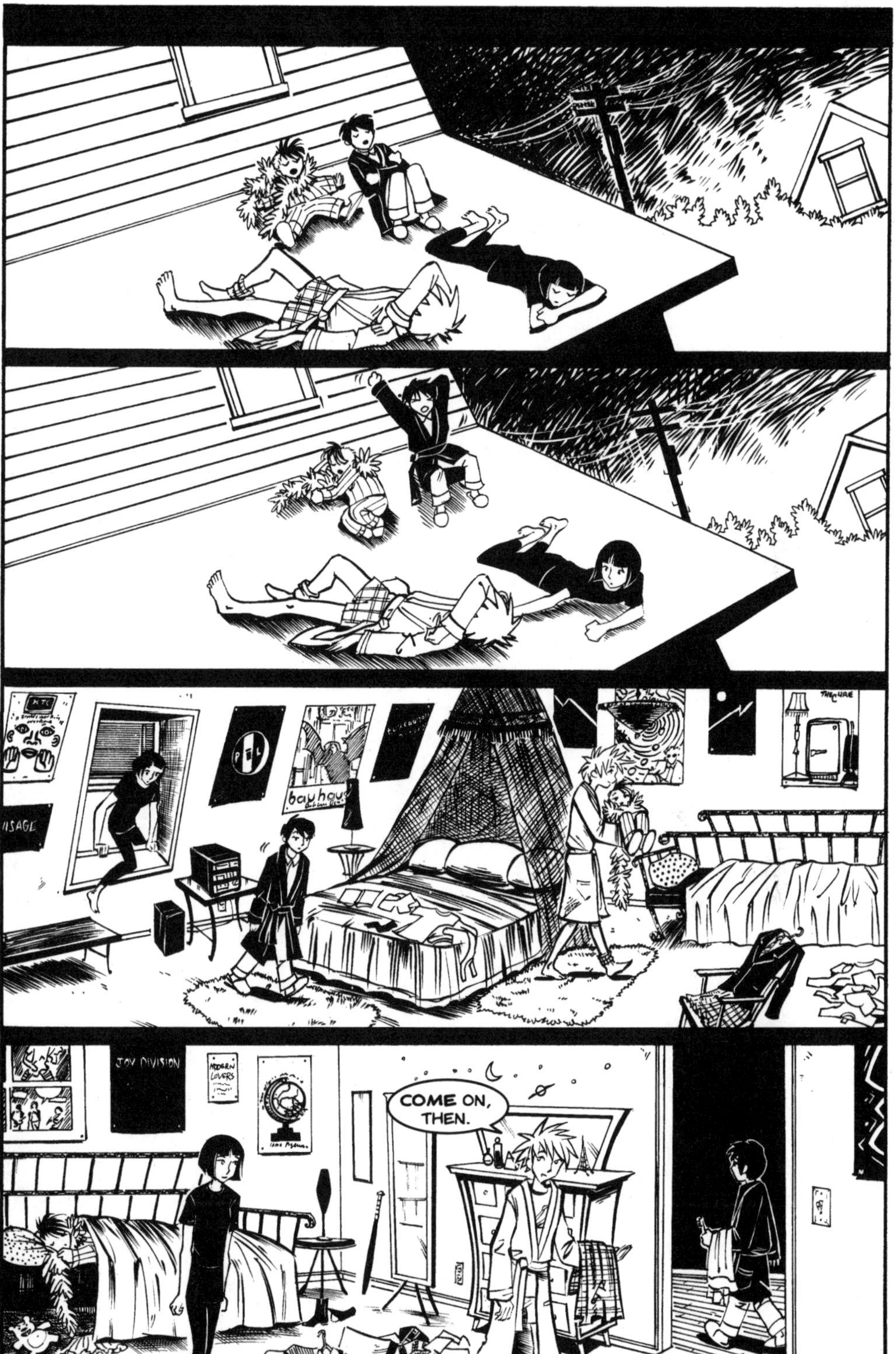
JOY DIVISION
MODERN LOVERS
COME ON, THEN.

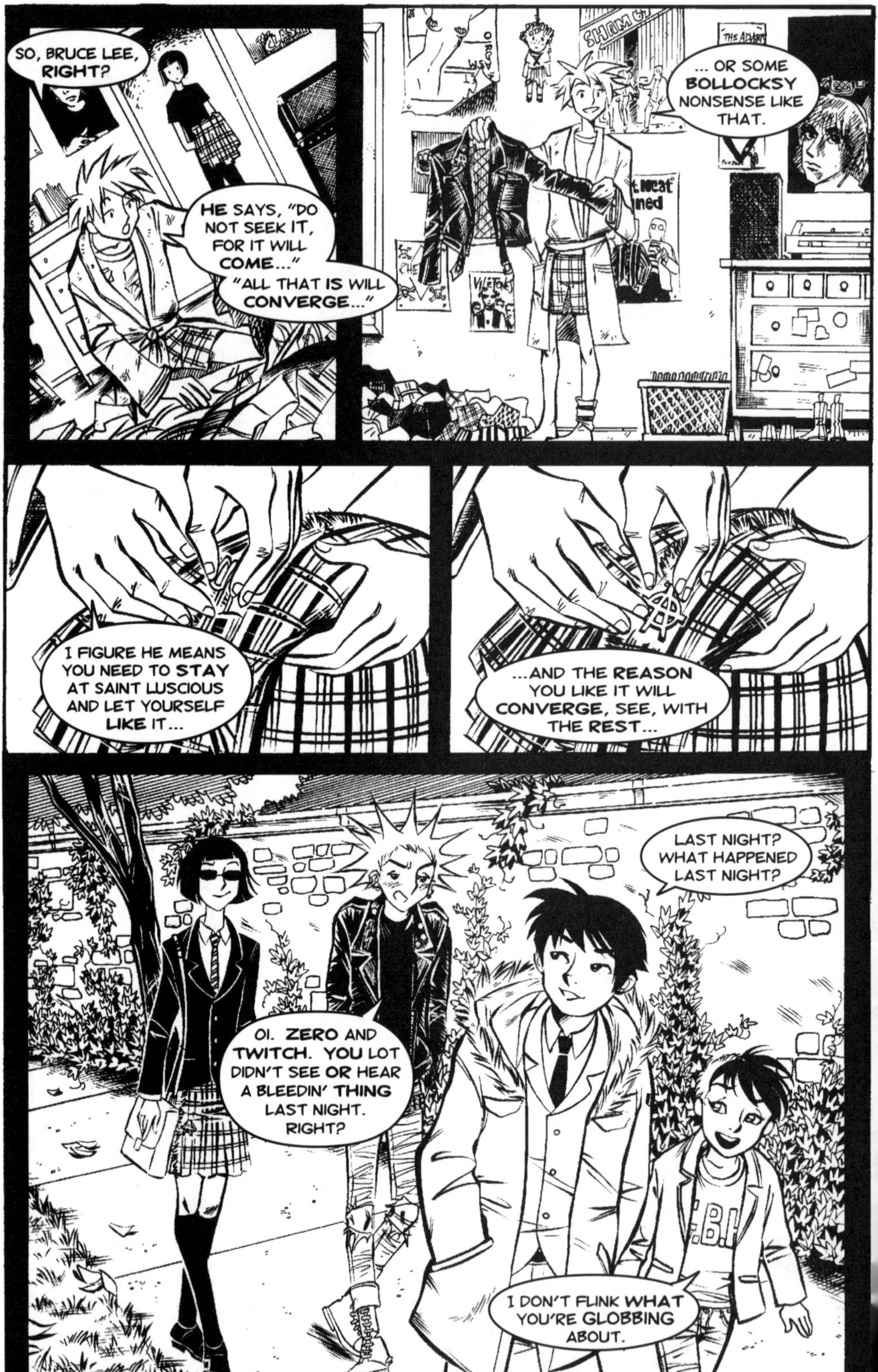

SO, BRUCE LEE, RIGHT?
HE SAYS, "DO NOT SEEK IT, FOR IT WILL COME..."
"ALL THAT IS WILL CONVERGE..."
... OR SOME BOLLOCKSY NONSENSE LIKE THAT.
I FIGURE HE MEANS YOU NEED TO STAY AT SAINT LUSCIOUS AND LET YOURSELF LIKE IT...
...AND THE REASON YOU LIKE IT WILL CONVERGE, SEE, WITH THE REST...
LAST NIGHT? WHAT HAPPENED LAST NIGHT?
OI. ZERO AND TWITCH. YOU LOT DIDN'T SEE OR HEAR A BLEEDIN' THING LAST NIGHT. RIGHT?
I DON'T FLINK WHAT YOU'RE GLOBBING ABOUT.

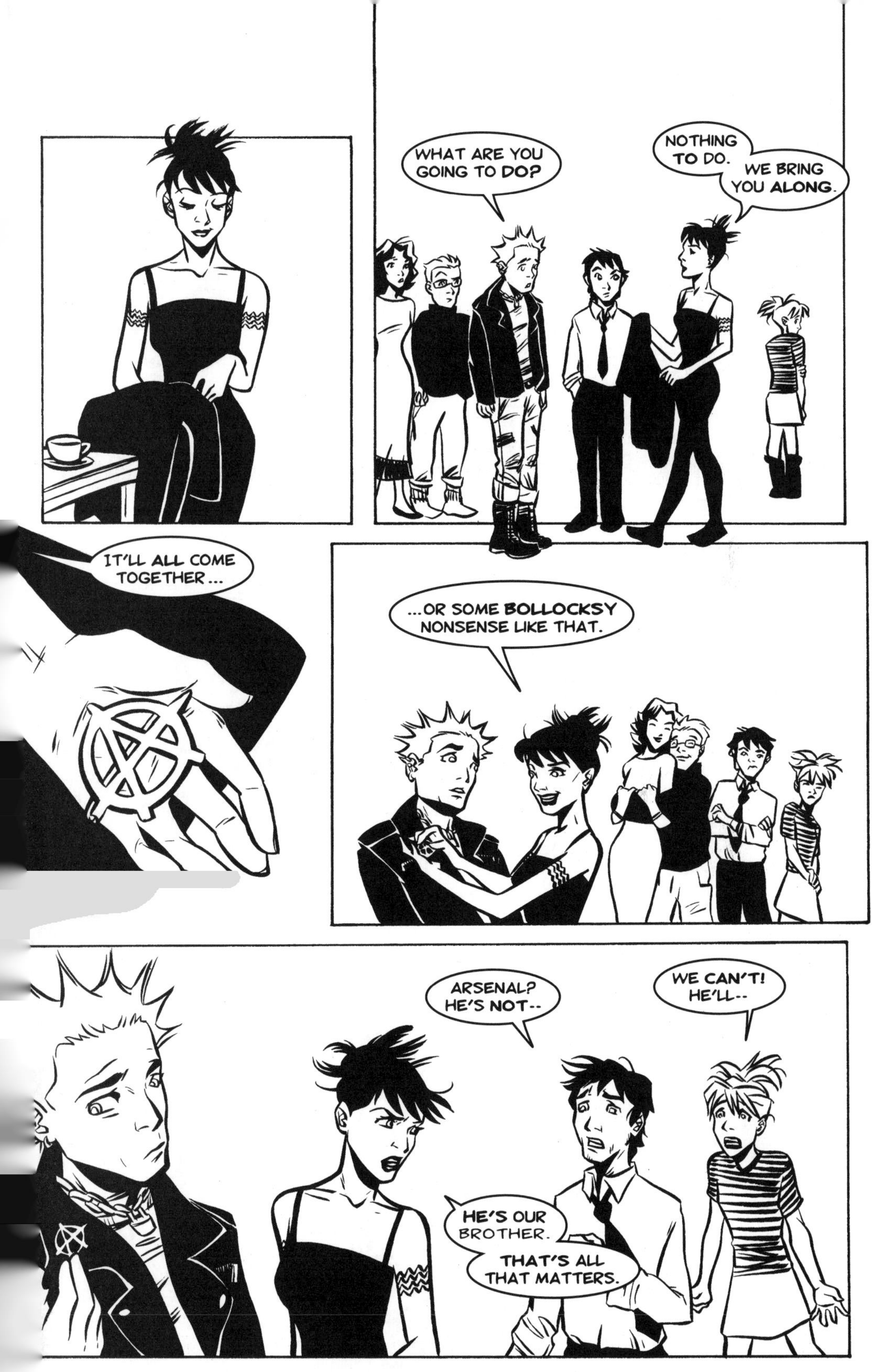
WHAT ARE YOU GOING TO DO?
NOTHING TO DO.
WE BRING YOU ALONG.
IT'LL ALL COME TOGETHER...
...OR SOME BOLLOCKSY NONSENSE LIKE THAT.
ARSENAL? HE'S NOT--
WE CAN'T! HE'LL--
HE'S OUR BROTHER.
THAT'S ALL THAT MATTERS.

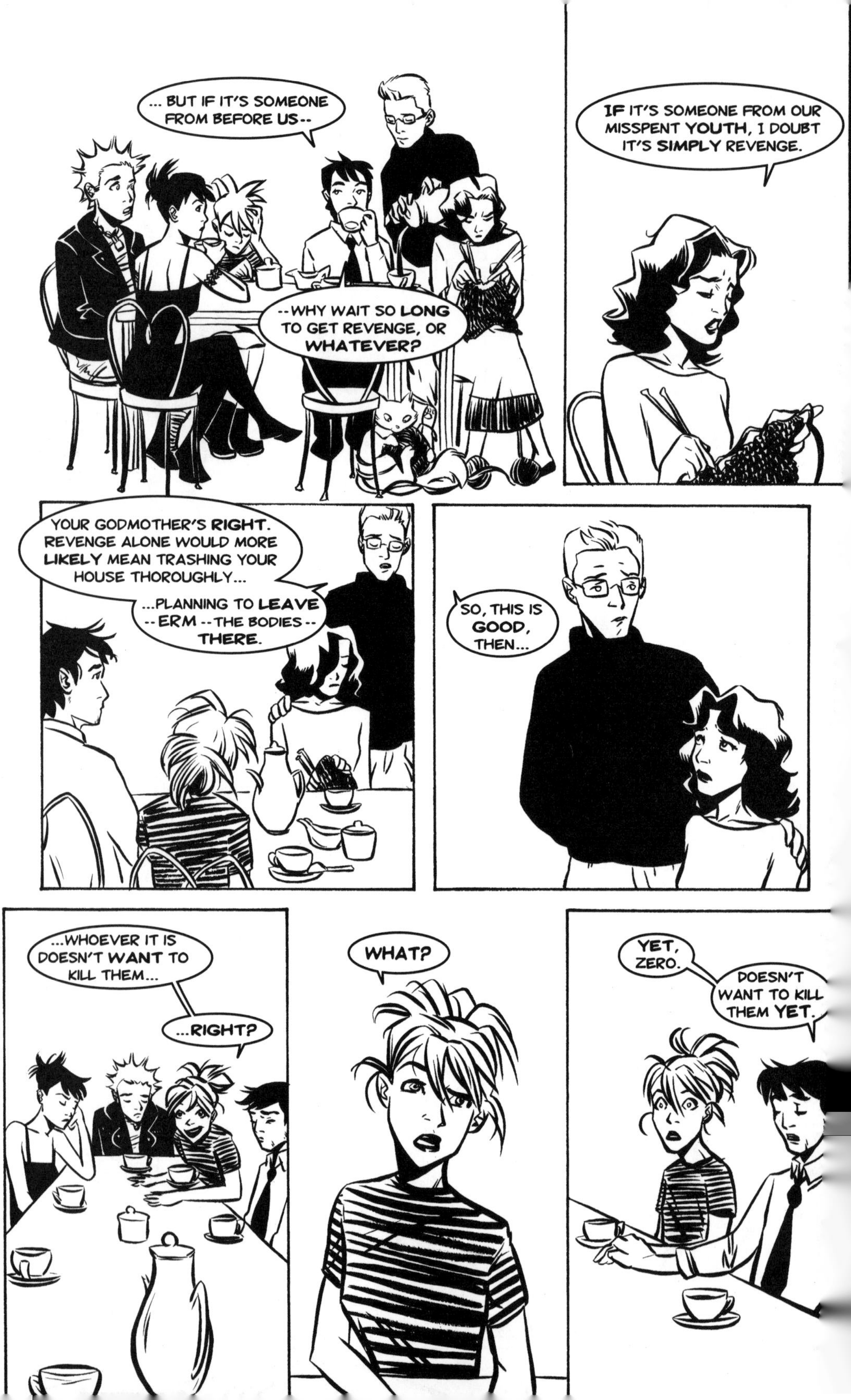
... BUT IF IT'S SOMEONE FROM BEFORE US--
--WHY WAIT SO LONG TO GET REVENGE, OR WHATEVER?
IF IT'S SOMEONE FROM OUR MISSPENT YOUTH, I DOUBT IT'S SIMPLY REVENGE.
YOUR GODMOTHER'S RIGHT. REVENGE ALONE WOULD MORE LIKELY MEAN TRASHING YOUR HOUSE THOROUGHLY...
...PLANNING TO LEAVE --ERM --THE BODIES -- THERE.
SO, THIS IS GOOD, THEN...
...WHOEVER IT IS DOESN'T WANT TO KILL THEM...
...RIGHT?
WHAT?
YET, ZERO.
DOESN'T WANT TO KILL THEM YET.

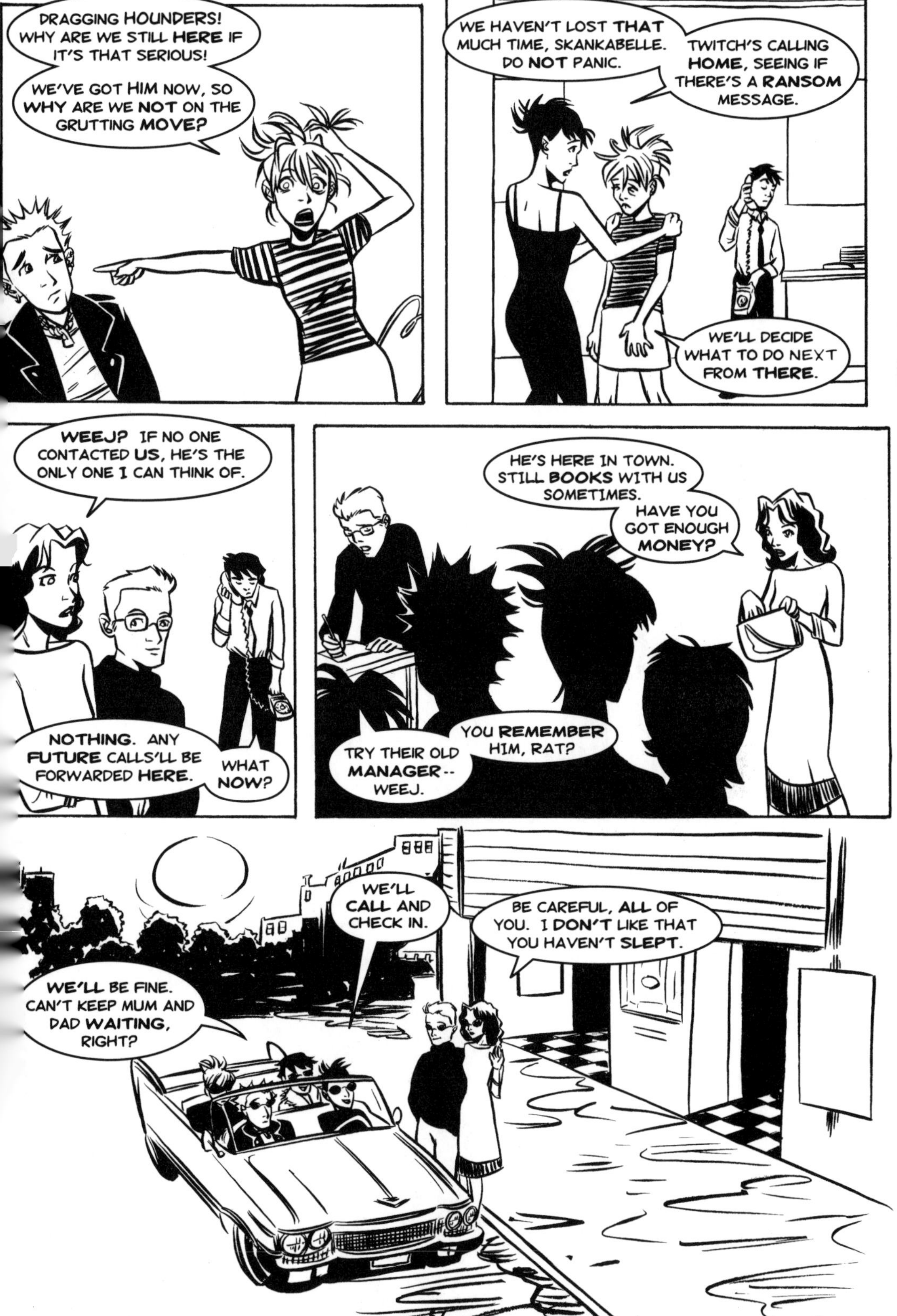
DRAGGING HOUNDERS! WHY ARE WE STILL HERE IF IT'S THAT SERIOUS!
WE'VE GOT HIM NOW, SO WHY ARE WE NOT ON THE GRUTTING MOVE?
WE HAVEN'T LOST THAT MUCH TIME, SKANKABELLE. DO NOT PANIC.
TWITCH'S CALLING HOME, SEEING IF THERE'S A RANSOM MESSAGE.
WE'LL DECIDE WHAT TO DO NEXT FROM THERE.
WEEJ? IF NO ONE CONTACTED US, HE'S THE ONLY ONE I CAN THINK OF.
NOTHING. ANY FUTURE CALLS'LL BE FORWARDED HERE.
WHAT NOW?
HE'S HERE IN TOWN. STILL BOOKS WITH US SOMETIMES.
HAVE YOU GOT ENOUGH MONEY?
YOU REMEMBER HIM, RAT?
TRY THEIR OLD MANAGER-- WEEJ.
WE'LL BE FINE. CAN'T KEEP MUM AND DAD WAITING, RIGHT?
WE'LL CALL AND CHECK IN.
BE CAREFUL, ALL OF YOU. I DON'T LIKE THAT YOU HAVEN'T SLEPT.

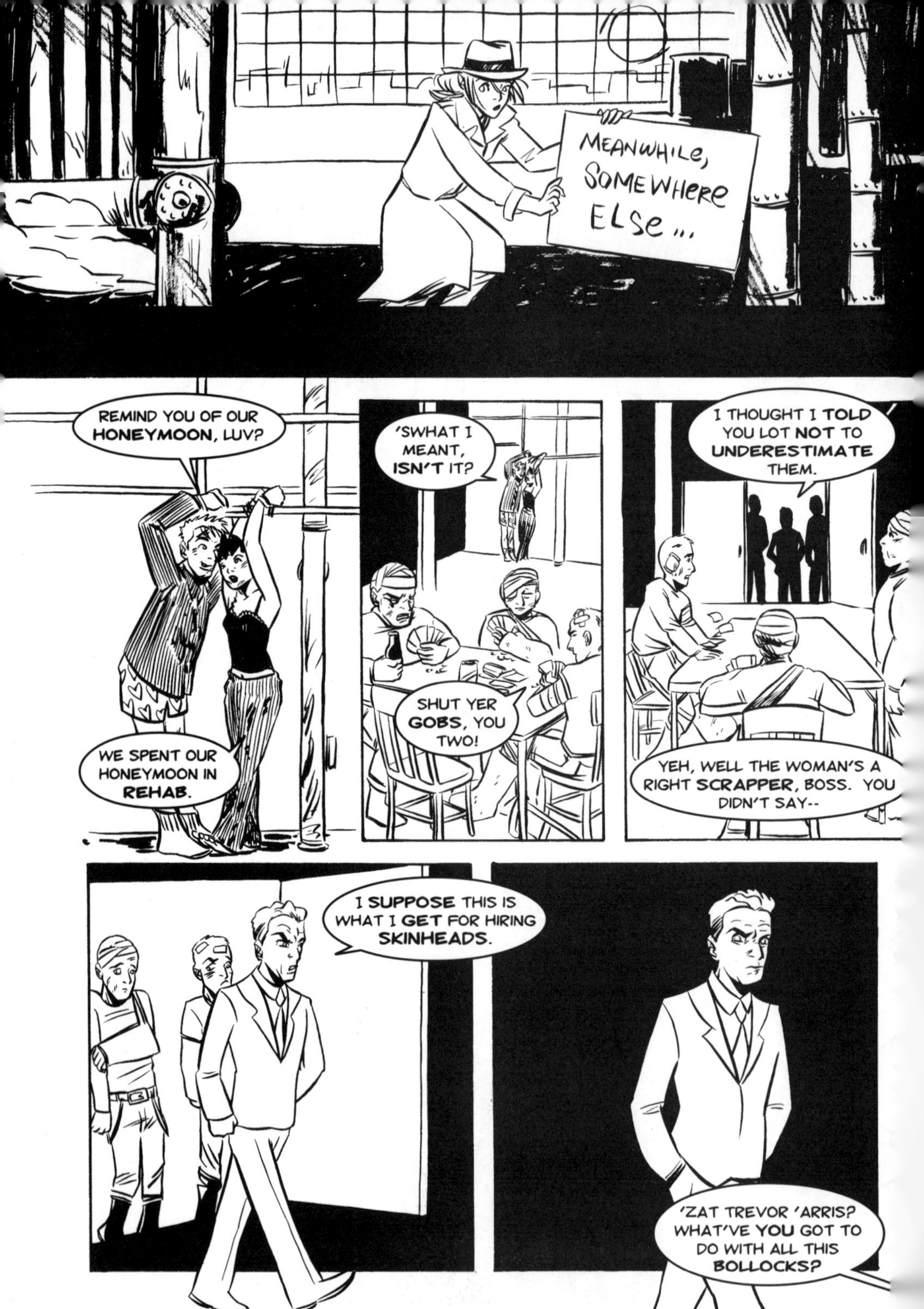
MEANWHILE, SOMEWHERE ELSE...
REMIND YOU OF OUR HONEYMOON, LUV?
WE SPENT OUR HONEYMOON IN REHAB.
'SWHAT I MEANT, ISN'T IT?
SHUT YER GOBS, YOU TWO!
I THOUGHT I TOLD YOU LOT NOT TO UNDERESTIMATE THEM.
YEH, WELL THE WOMAN'S A RIGHT SCRAPPER, BOSS. YOU DIDN'T SAY--
I SUPPOSE THIS IS WHAT I GET FOR HIRING SKINHEADS.
'ZAT TREVOR 'ARRIS? WHAT'VE YOU GOT TO DO WITH ALL THIS BOLLOCKS?

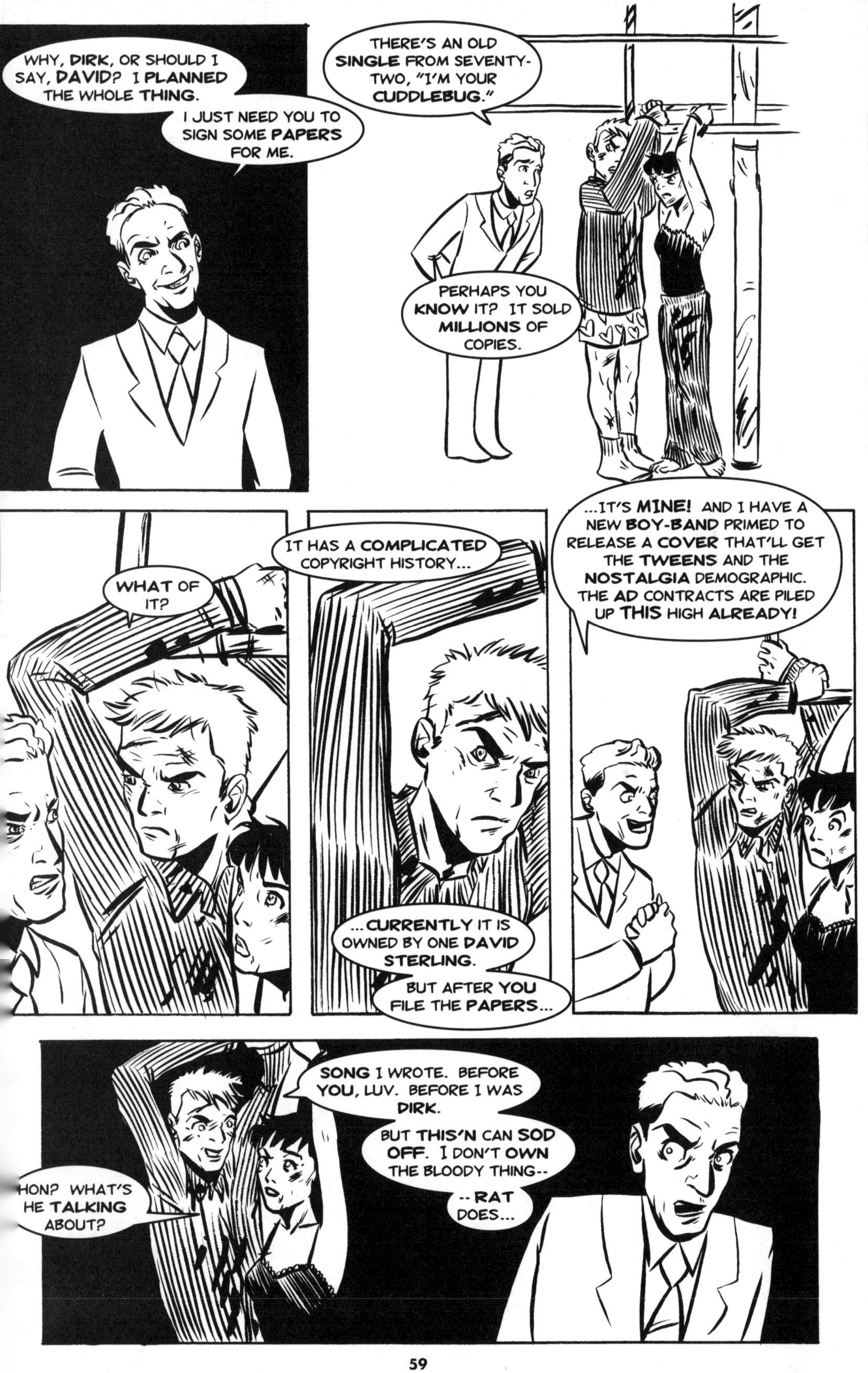
WHY, DIRK, OR SHOULD I SAY, DAVID? I PLANNED THE WHOLE THING.
I JUST NEED YOU TO SIGN SOME PAPERS FOR ME.
THERE'S AN OLD SINGLE FROM SEVENTY-TWO, "I'M YOUR CUDDLEBUG."
PERHAPS YOU KNOW IT? IT SOLD MILLIONS OF COPIES.
WHAT OF IT?
IT HAS A COMPLICATED COPYRIGHT HISTORY...
...CURRENTLY IT IS OWNED BY ONE DAVID STERLING.
BUT AFTER YOU FILE THE PAPERS...
...IT'S MINE! AND I HAVE A NEW BOY-BAND PRIMED TO RELEASE A COVER THAT'LL GET THE TWEENS AND THE NOSTALGIA DEMOGRAPHIC. THE AD CONTRACTS ARE PILED UP THIS HIGH ALREADY!
SONG I WROTE. BEFORE YOU, LUV. BEFORE I WAS DIRK.
BUT THIS'N CAN SOD OFF. I DON'T OWN THE BLOODY THING--
--RAT DOES...
HON? WHAT'S HE TALKING ABOUT?

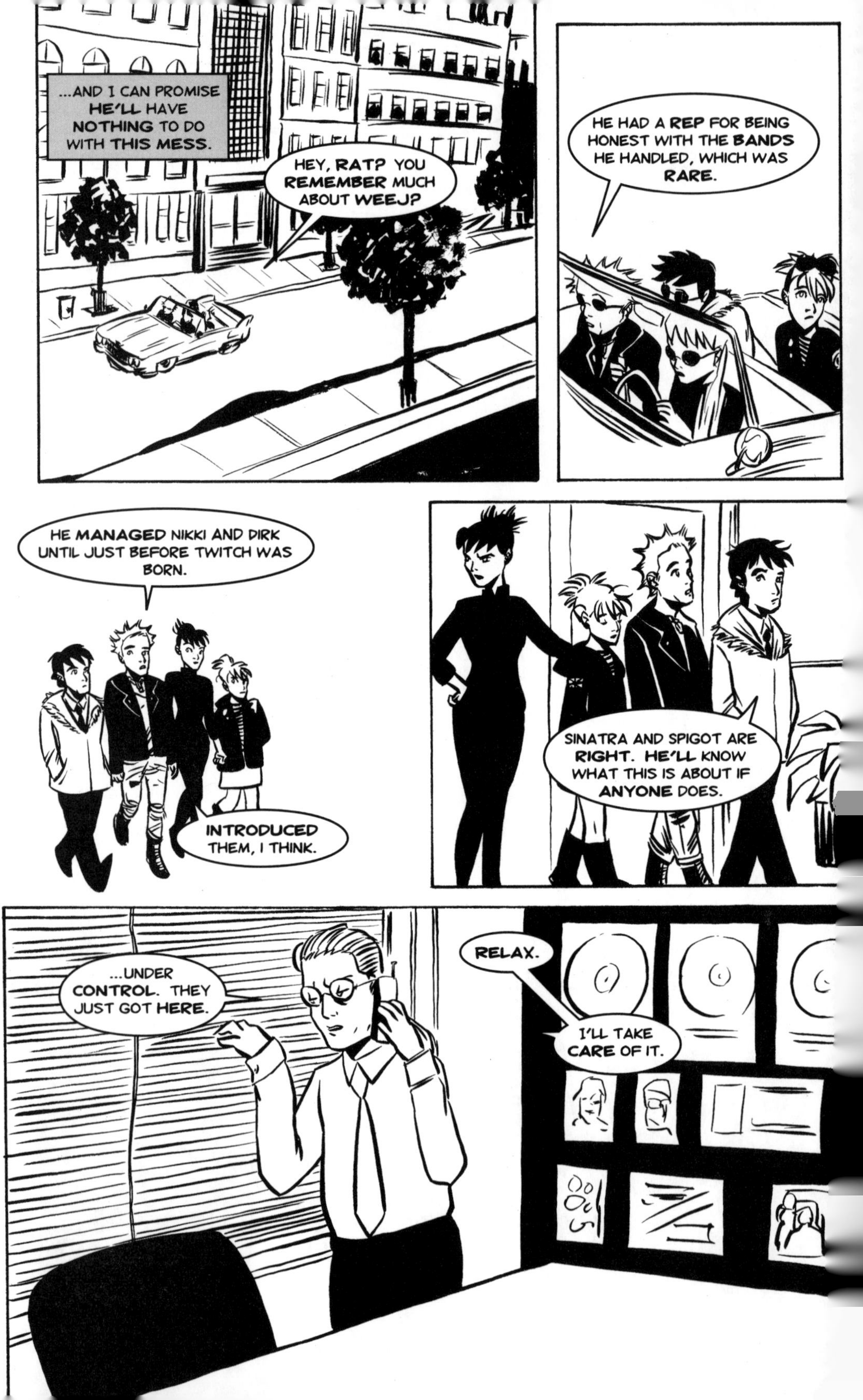
...AND I CAN PROMISE HE'LL HAVE NOTHING TO DO WITH THIS MESS.
HEY, RAT? YOU REMEMBER MUCH ABOUT WEEJ?
HE HAD A REP FOR BEING HONEST WITH THE BANDS HE HANDLED, WHICH WAS RARE.
HE MANAGED NIKKI AND DIRK UNTIL JUST BEFORE TWITCH WAS BORN.
INTRODUCED THEM, I THINK.
SINATRA AND SPIGOT ARE RIGHT. HE'LL KNOW WHAT THIS IS ABOUT IF ANYONE DOES.
...UNDER CONTROL. THEY JUST GOT HERE.
RELAX.
I'LL TAKE CARE OF IT.

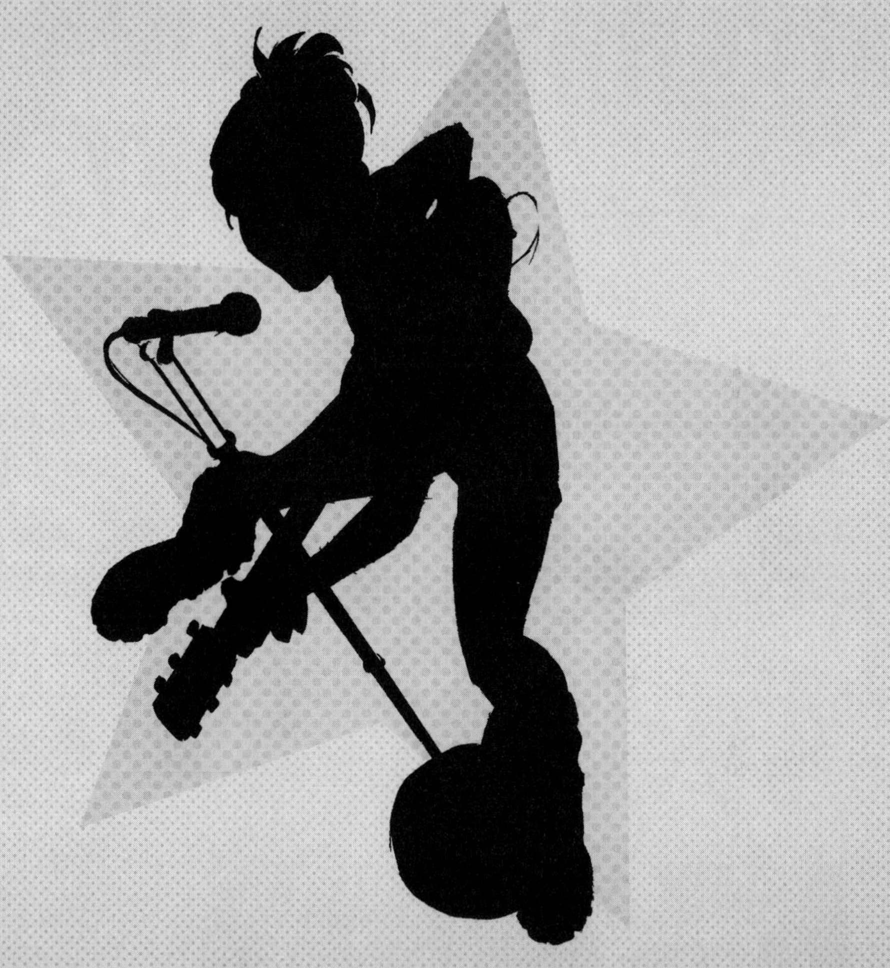

CHAPTER 3

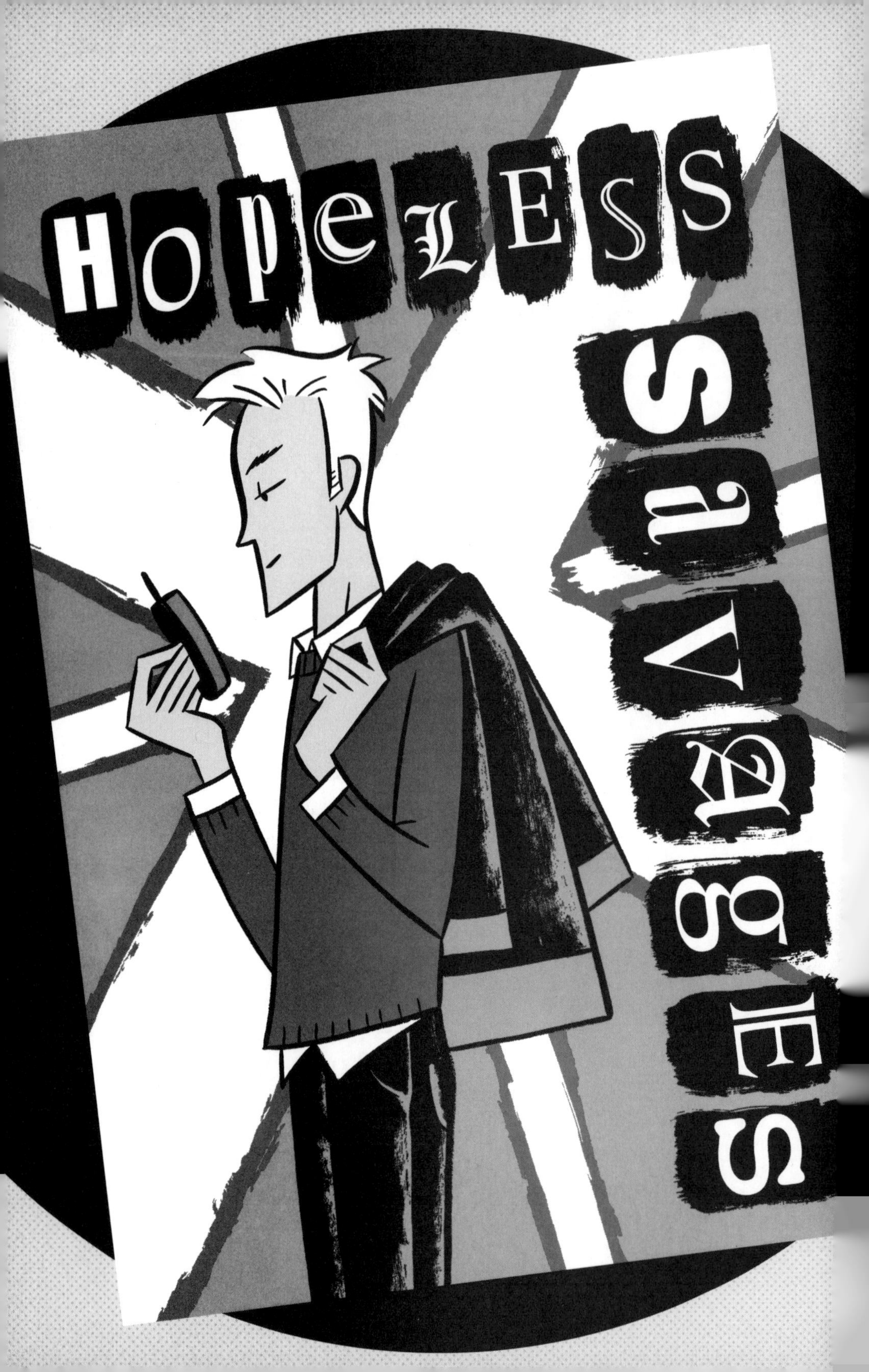
HOPELESS
SAVAGES

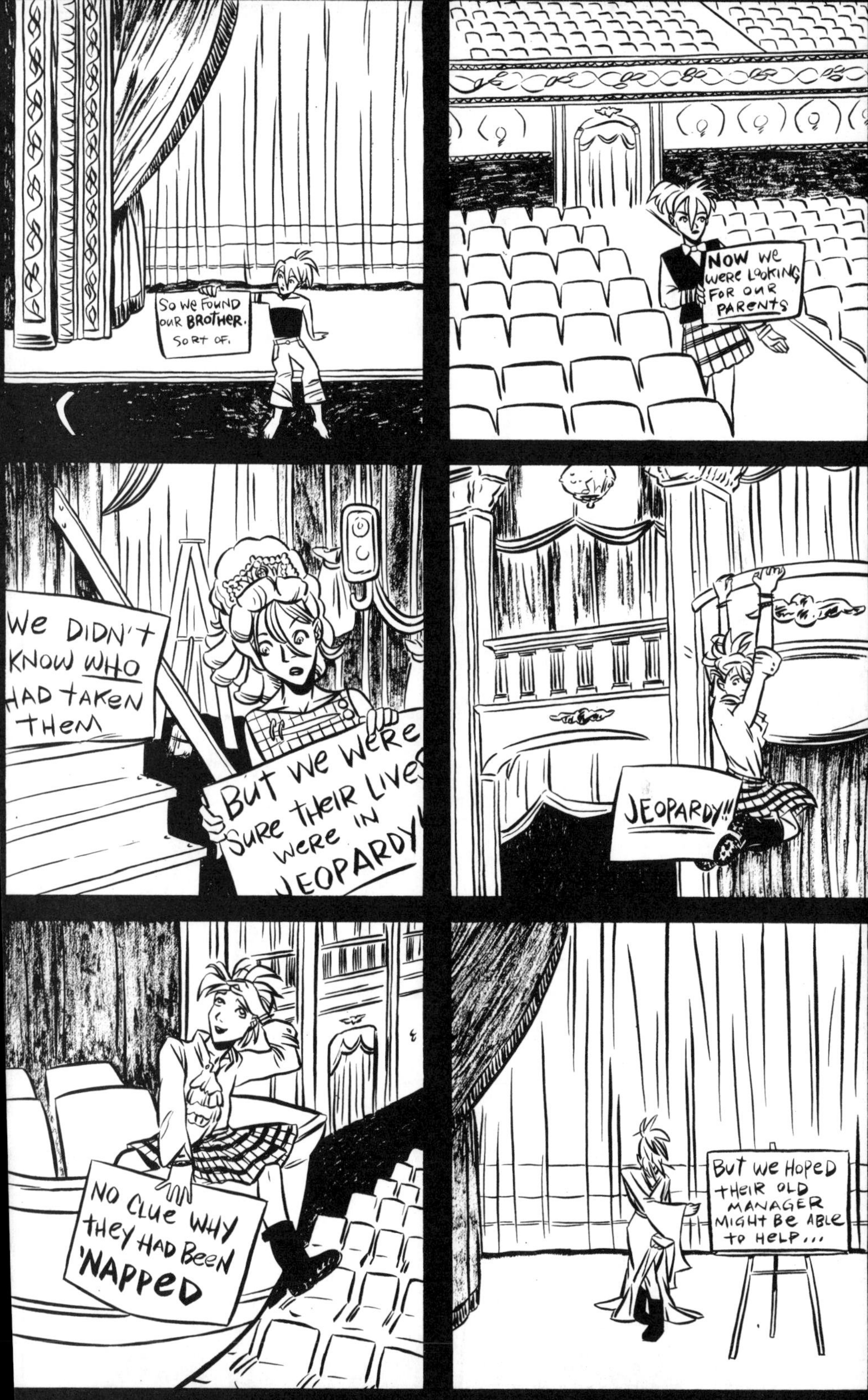
So we found our BROTHER. Sort of.
NOW we were looking for our PARENTS
We didn't know WHO had taken them
But we were sure their lives were in JEOPARDY!
JEOPARDY!!
No clue why they had been 'NAPPED
But we hoped their old manager might be able to help...

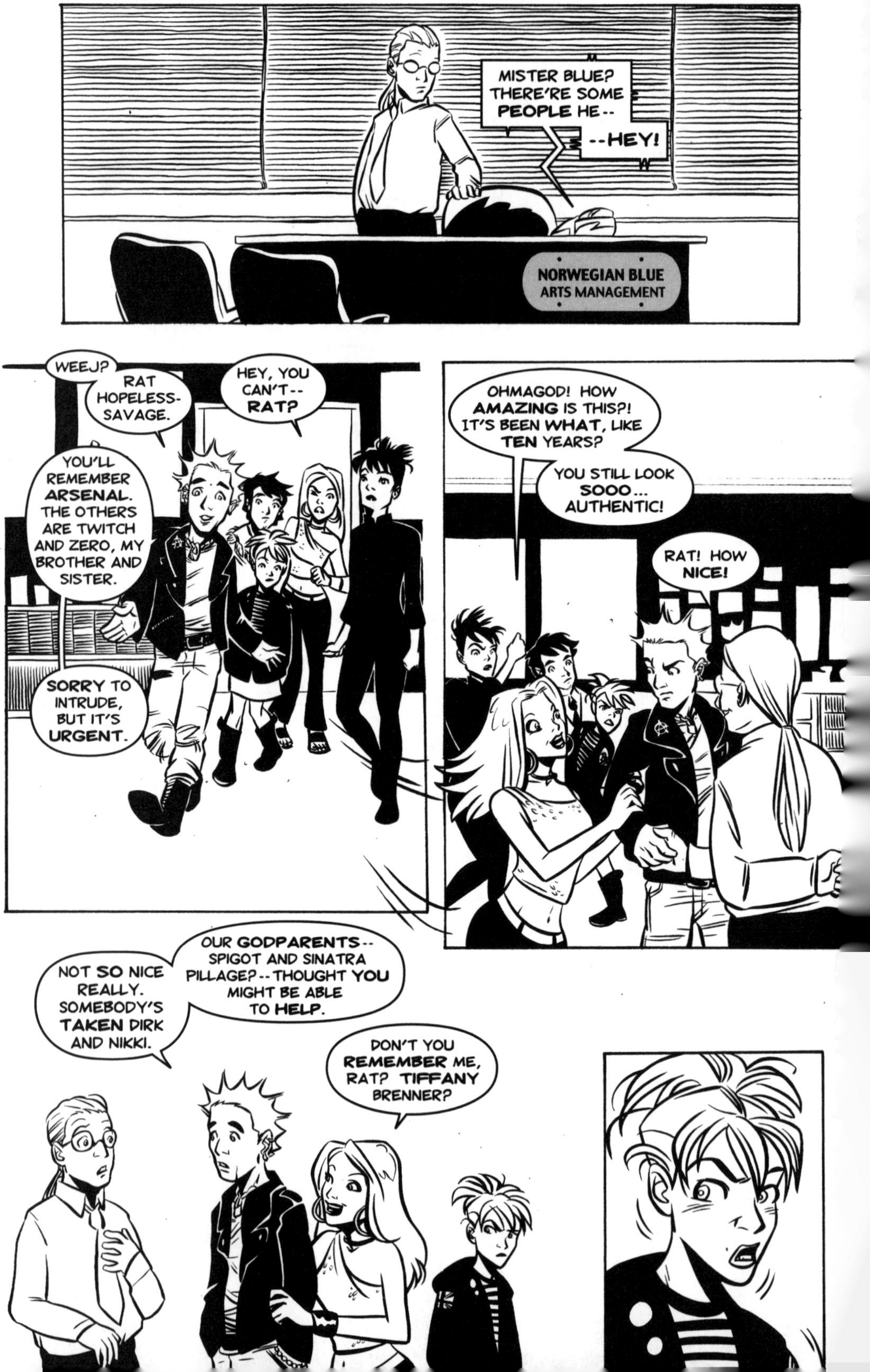
MISTER BLUE? THERE'RE SOME PEOPLE HE--
--HEY!
NORWEGIAN BLUE ARTS MANAGEMENT
WEEJ?
RAT HOPELESS-SAVAGE.
HEY, YOU CAN'T--RAT?
YOU'LL REMEMBER ARSENAL. THE OTHERS ARE TWITCH AND ZERO, MY BROTHER AND SISTER.
SORRY TO INTRUDE, BUT IT'S URGENT.
OHMAGOD! HOW AMAZING IS THIS?! IT'S BEEN WHAT, LIKE TEN YEARS?
YOU STILL LOOK SOOO... AUTHENTIC!
RAT! HOW NICE!
NOT SO NICE REALLY. SOMEBODY'S TAKEN DIRK AND NIKKI.
OUR GODPARENTS--SPIGOT AND SINATRA PILLAGE?--THOUGHT YOU MIGHT BE ABLE TO HELP.
DON'T YOU REMEMBER ME, RAT? TIFFANY BRENNER?

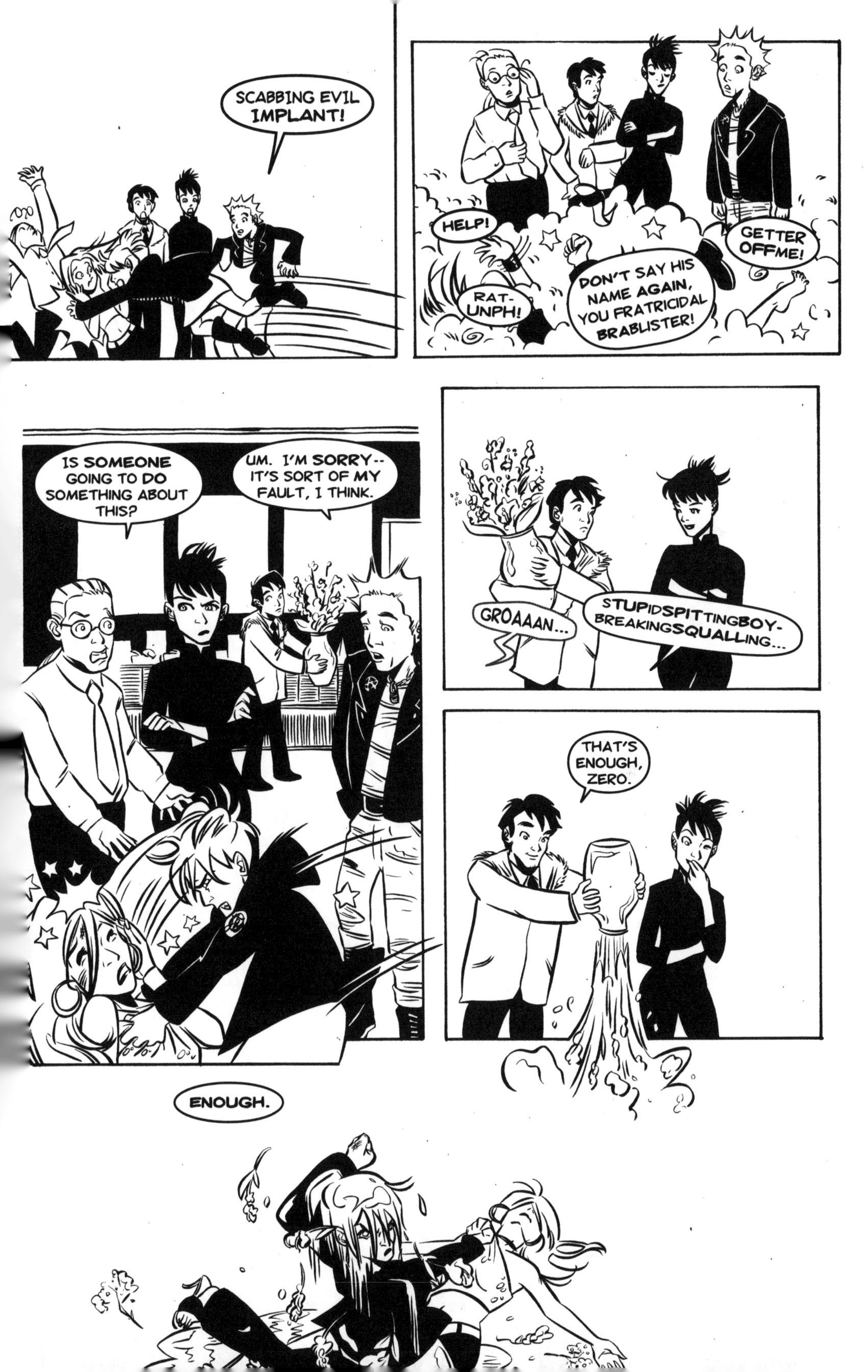
SCABBING EVIL IMPLANT!
HELP!
RAT-UNPH!
DON'T SAY HIS NAME AGAIN, YOU FRATRICIDAL BRABLISTER!
GETTER OFFME!
IS SOMEONE GOING TO DO SOMETHING ABOUT THIS?
UM. I'M SORRY-- IT'S SORT OF MY FAULT, I THINK.
GROAAAN...
STUPIDSPITTINGBOY-BREAKINGSQUALLING...
THAT'S ENOUGH, ZERO.
ENOUGH.

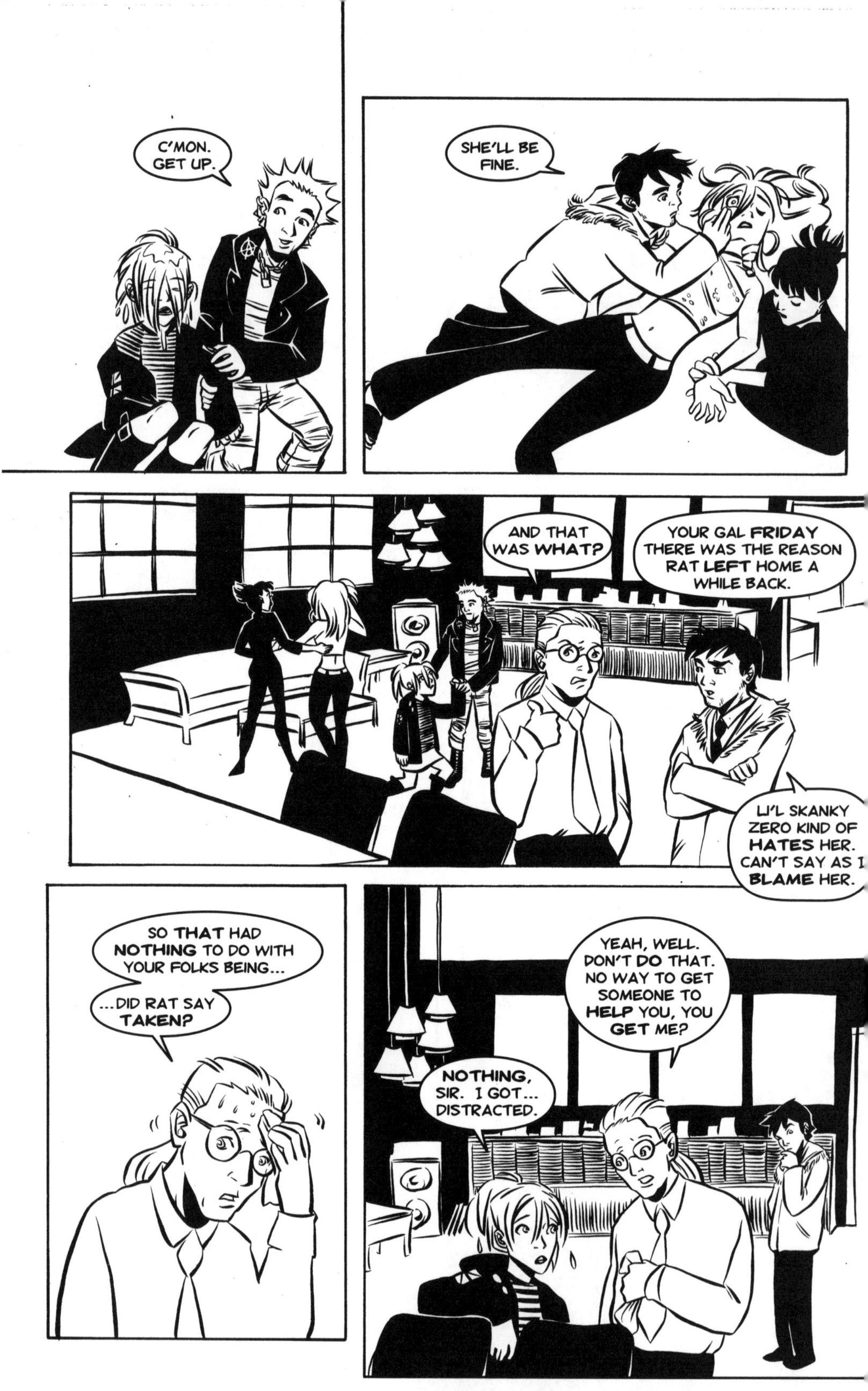
C'MON. GET UP.
SHE'LL BE FINE.
AND THAT WAS WHAT?
YOUR GAL FRIDAY THERE WAS THE REASON RAT LEFT HOME A WHILE BACK.
LI'L SKANKY ZERO KIND OF HATES HER. CAN'T SAY AS I BLAME HER.
SO THAT HAD NOTHING TO DO WITH YOUR FOLKS BEING...
...DID RAT SAY TAKEN?
YEAH, WELL. DON'T DO THAT. NO WAY TO GET SOMEONE TO HELP YOU, YOU GET ME?
NOTHING, SIR. I GOT... DISTRACTED.

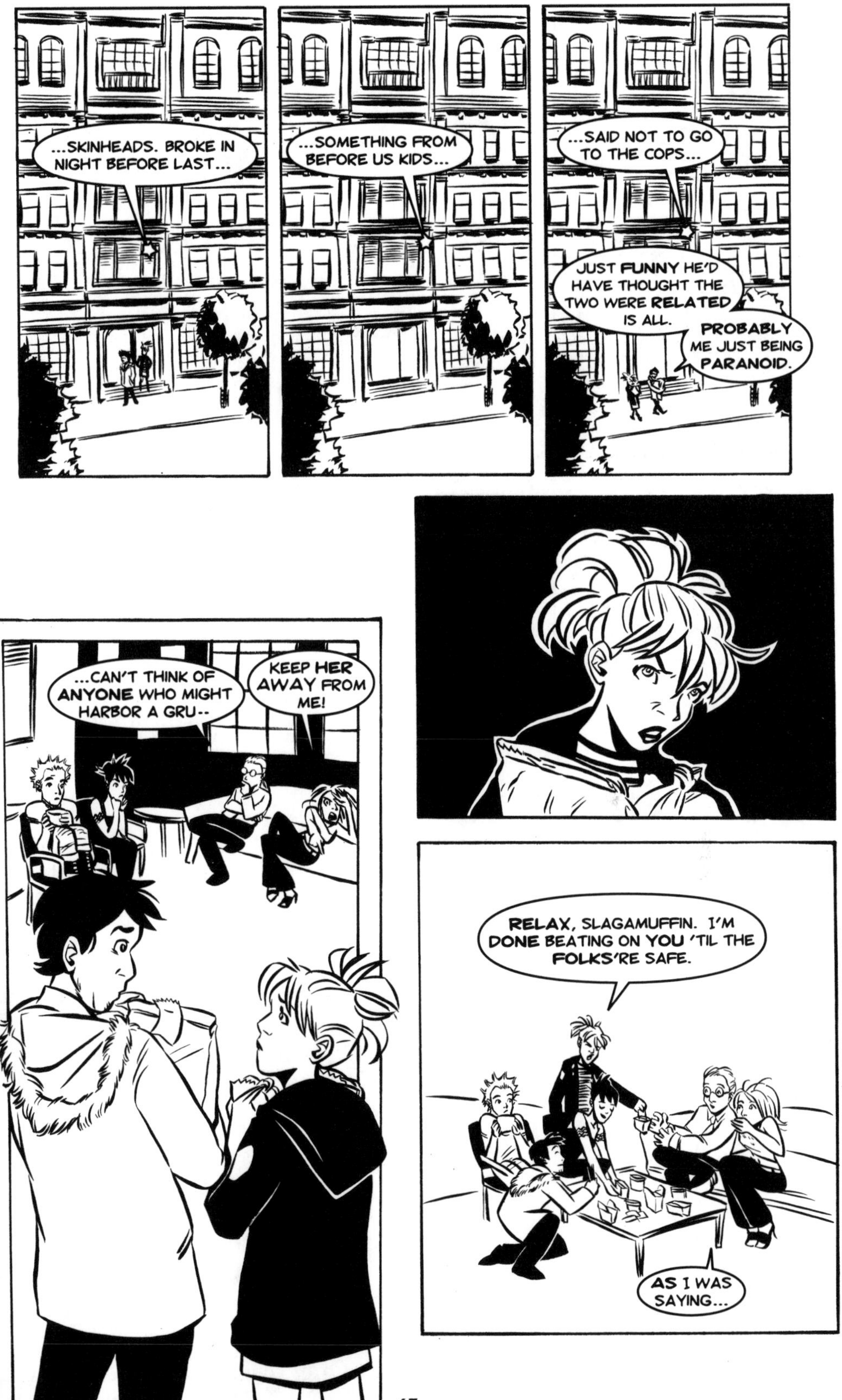

...SKINHEADS. BROKE IN NIGHT BEFORE LAST...
...SOMETHING FROM BEFORE US KIDS...
...SAID NOT TO GO TO THE COPS...
JUST FUNNY HE'D HAVE THOUGHT THE TWO WERE RELATED IS ALL.
PROBABLY ME JUST BEING PARANOID.
...CAN'T THINK OF ANYONE WHO MIGHT HARBOR A GRU--
KEEP HER AWAY FROM ME!
RELAX, SLAGAMUFFIN. I'M DONE BEATING ON YOU 'TIL THE FOLKS'RE SAFE.
AS I WAS SAYING...

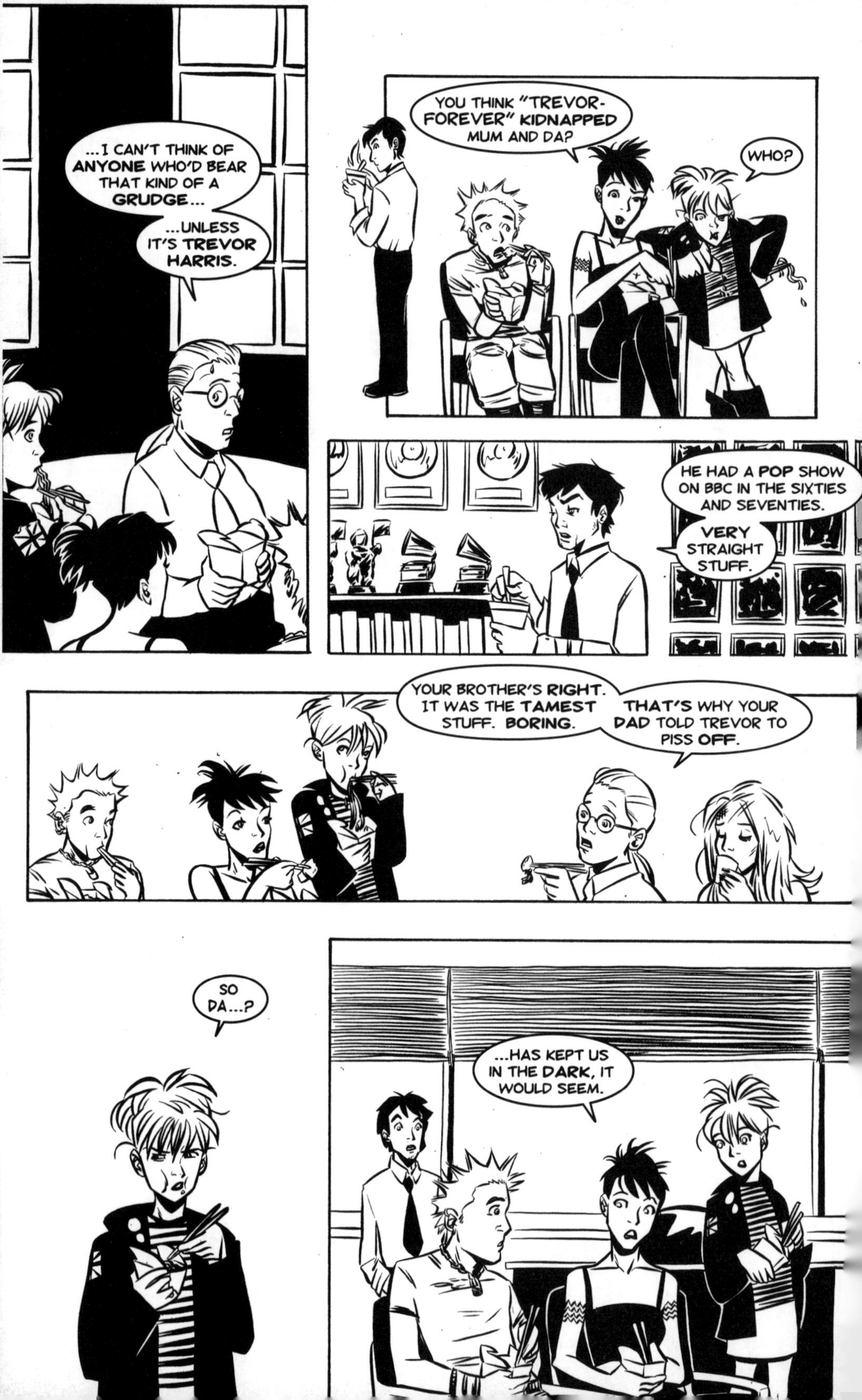
...I CAN'T THINK OF ANYONE WHO'D BEAR THAT KIND OF A GRUDGE...
...UNLESS IT'S TREVOR HARRIS.
YOU THINK "TREVOR-FOREVER" KIDNAPPED MUM AND DA?
WHO?
HE HAD A POP SHOW ON BBC IN THE SIXTIES AND SEVENTIES.
VERY STRAIGHT STUFF.
YOUR BROTHER'S RIGHT. IT WAS THE TAMEST STUFF. BORING.
THAT'S WHY YOUR DAD TOLD TREVOR TO PISS OFF.
SO DA...?
...HAS KEPT US IN THE DARK, IT WOULD SEEM.

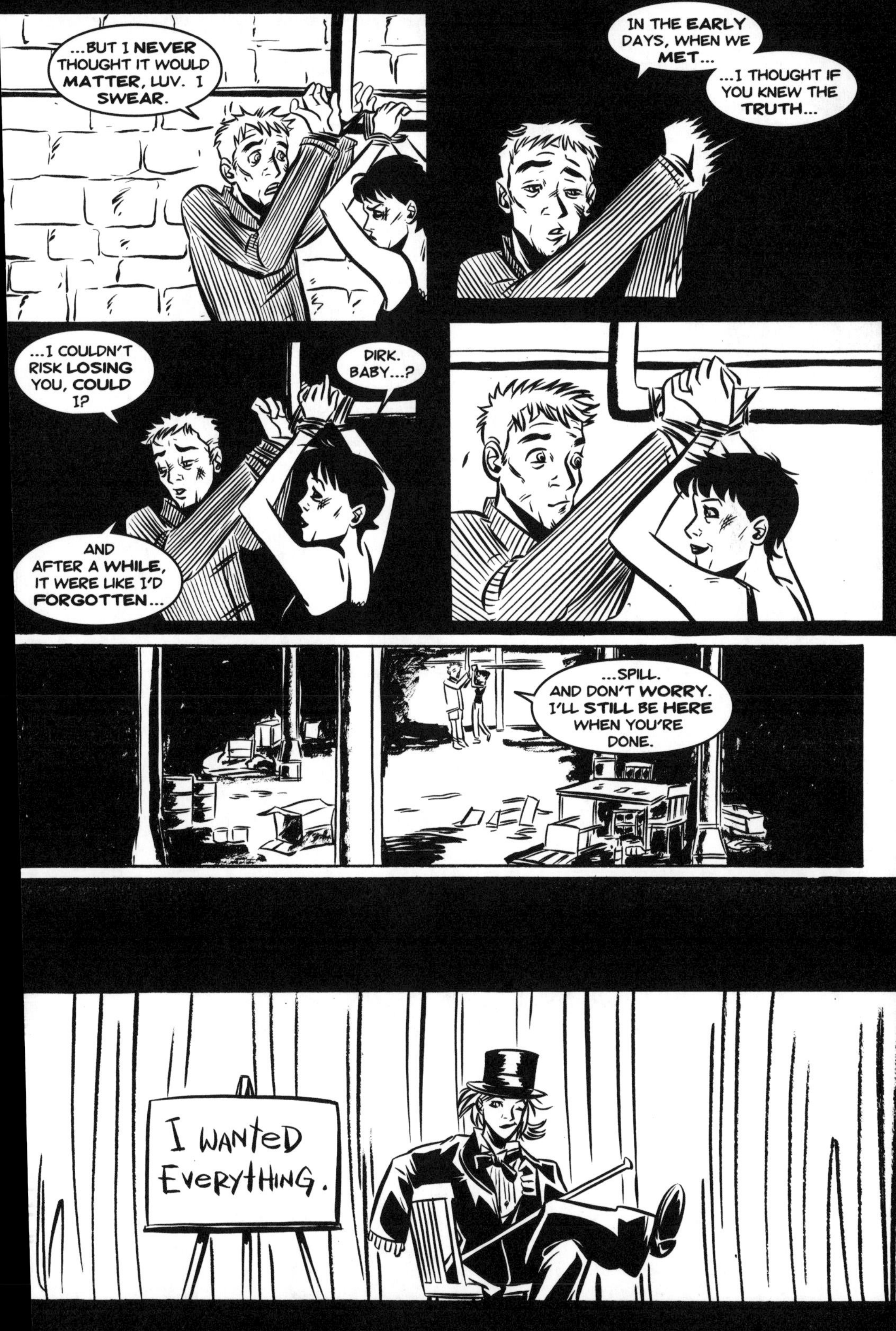
...BUT I NEVER THOUGHT IT WOULD MATTER, LUV. I SWEAR.
IN THE EARLY DAYS, WHEN WE MET...
...I THOUGHT IF YOU KNEW THE TRUTH...
...I COULDN'T RISK LOSING YOU, COULD I?
DIRK. BABY...?
AND AFTER A WHILE, IT WERE LIKE I'D FORGOTTEN...
...SPILL. AND DON'T WORRY. I'LL STILL BE HERE WHEN YOU'RE DONE.
I WANTED EVERYTHING.

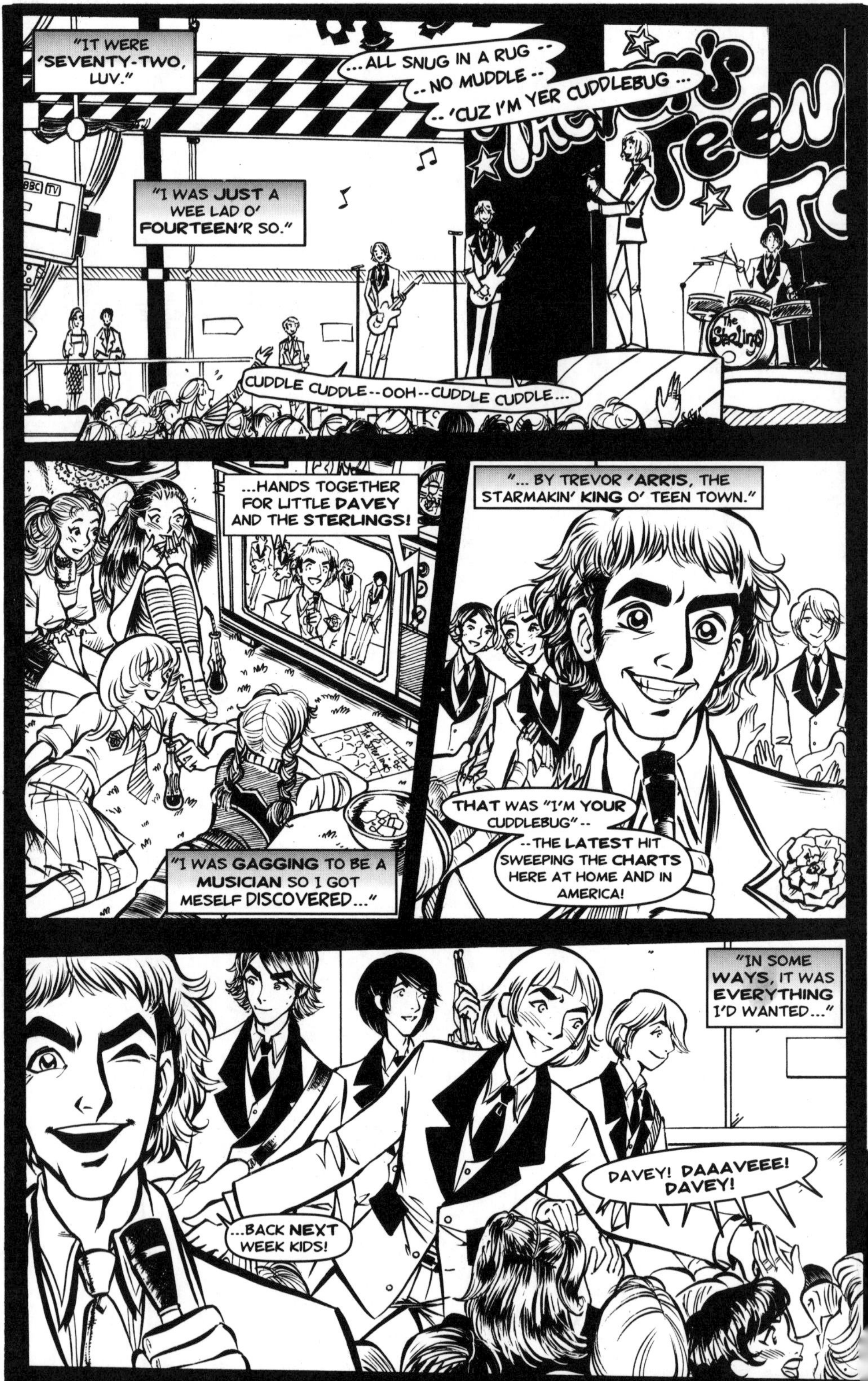
"IT WERE 'SEVENTY-TWO, LUV."
...ALL SNUG IN A RUG --
-- NO MUDDLE --
-- 'CUZ I'M YER CUDDLEBUG ...
"I WAS JUST A WEE LAD O' FOURTEEN'R SO."
CUDDLE CUDDLE--OOH--CUDDLE CUDDLE...
...HANDS TOGETHER FOR LITTLE DAVEY AND THE STERLINGS!
"I WAS GAGGING TO BE A MUSICIAN SO I GOT MESELF DISCOVERED..."
"... BY TREVOR 'ARRIS, THE STARMAKIN' KING O' TEEN TOWN."
THAT WAS "I'M YOUR CUDDLEBUG" --
--THE LATEST HIT SWEEPING THE CHARTS HERE AT HOME AND IN AMERICA!
"IN SOME WAYS, IT WAS EVERYTHING I'D WANTED..."
DAVEY! DAAAVEEE! DAVEY!
...BACK NEXT WEEK KIDS!

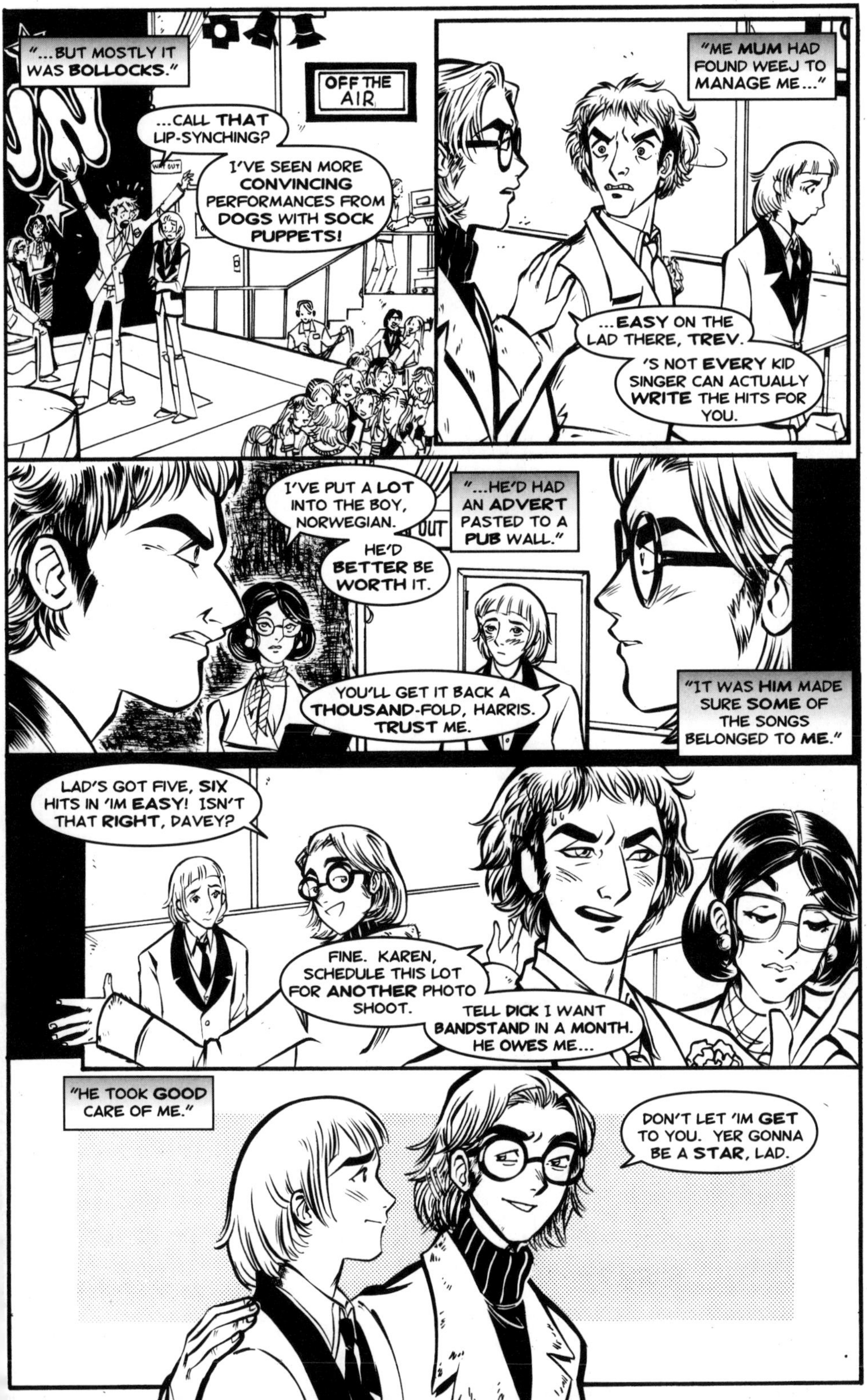
"...BUT MOSTLY IT WAS BOLLOCKS."
OFF THE AIR
...CALL THAT LIP-SYNCHING?
I'VE SEEN MORE CONVINCING PERFORMANCES FROM DOGS WITH SOCK PUPPETS!
"ME MUM HAD FOUND WEEJ TO MANAGE ME..."
...EASY ON THE LAD THERE, TREV.
'S NOT EVERY KID SINGER CAN ACTUALLY WRITE THE HITS FOR YOU.
I'VE PUT A LOT INTO THE BOY, NORWEGIAN.
HE'D BETTER BE WORTH IT.
"...HE'D HAD AN ADVERT PASTED TO A PUB WALL."
YOU'LL GET IT BACK A THOUSAND-FOLD, HARRIS. TRUST ME.
"IT WAS HIM MADE SURE SOME OF THE SONGS BELONGED TO ME."
LAD'S GOT FIVE, SIX HITS IN 'IM EASY! ISN'T THAT RIGHT, DAVEY?
FINE. KAREN, SCHEDULE THIS LOT FOR ANOTHER PHOTO SHOOT.
TELL DICK I WANT BANDSTAND IN A MONTH. HE OWES ME...
"HE TOOK GOOD CARE OF ME."
DON'T LET 'IM GET TO YOU. YER GONNA BE A STAR, LAD.

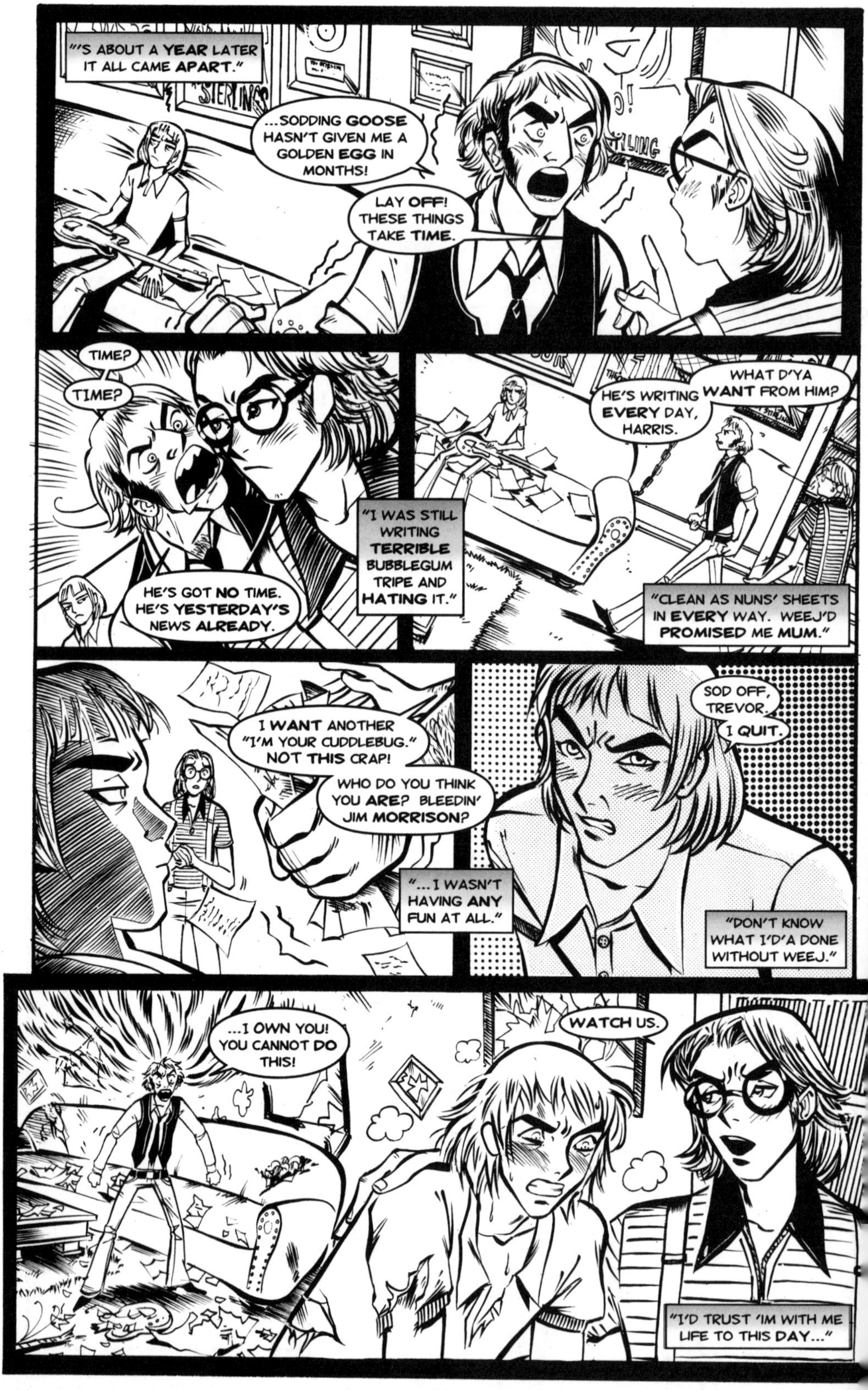
"'S ABOUT A YEAR LATER IT ALL CAME APART."
...SODDING GOOSE HASN'T GIVEN ME A GOLDEN EGG IN MONTHS!
LAY OFF! THESE THINGS TAKE TIME.
TIME?
TIME?
"I WAS STILL WRITING TERRIBLE BUBBLEGUM TRIPE AND HATING IT."
HE'S GOT NO TIME. HE'S YESTERDAY'S NEWS ALREADY.
HE'S WRITING EVERY DAY, HARRIS.
WHAT D'YA WANT FROM HIM?
"CLEAN AS NUNS' SHEETS IN EVERY WAY. WEEJ'D PROMISED ME MUM."
I WANT ANOTHER "I'M YOUR CUDDLEBUG." NOT THIS CRAP!
WHO DO YOU THINK YOU ARE? BLEEDIN' JIM MORRISON?
"...I WASN'T HAVING ANY FUN AT ALL."
SOD OFF, TREVOR.
I QUIT.
"DON'T KNOW WHAT I'D'A DONE WITHOUT WEEJ."
...I OWN YOU! YOU CANNOT DO THIS!
WATCH US.
"I'D TRUST 'IM WITH ME LIFE TO THIS DAY..."

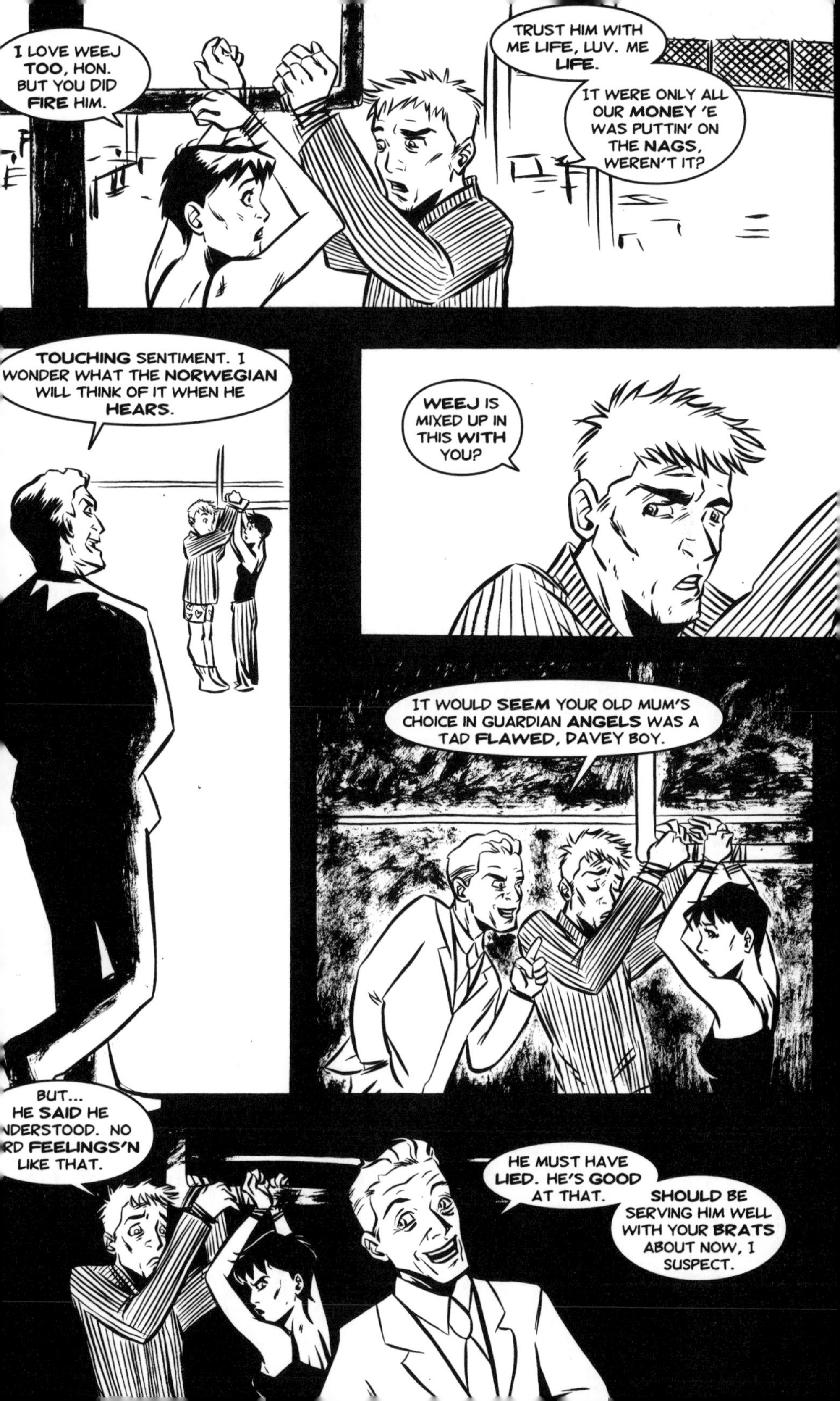
I LOVE WEEJ TOO, HON. BUT YOU DID FIRE HIM.
TRUST HIM WITH ME LIFE, LUV. ME LIFE.
IT WERE ONLY ALL OUR MONEY 'E WAS PUTTIN' ON THE NAGS, WEREN'T IT?
TOUCHING SENTIMENT. I WONDER WHAT THE NORWEGIAN WILL THINK OF IT WHEN HE HEARS.
WEEJ IS MIXED UP IN THIS WITH YOU?
IT WOULD SEEM YOUR OLD MUM'S CHOICE IN GUARDIAN ANGELS WAS A TAD FLAWED, DAVEY BOY.
BUT... HE SAID HE NDERSTOOD. NO RD FEELINGS'N LIKE THAT.
HE MUST HAVE LIED. HE'S GOOD AT THAT.
SHOULD BE SERVING HIM WELL WITH YOUR BRATS ABOUT NOW, I SUSPECT.

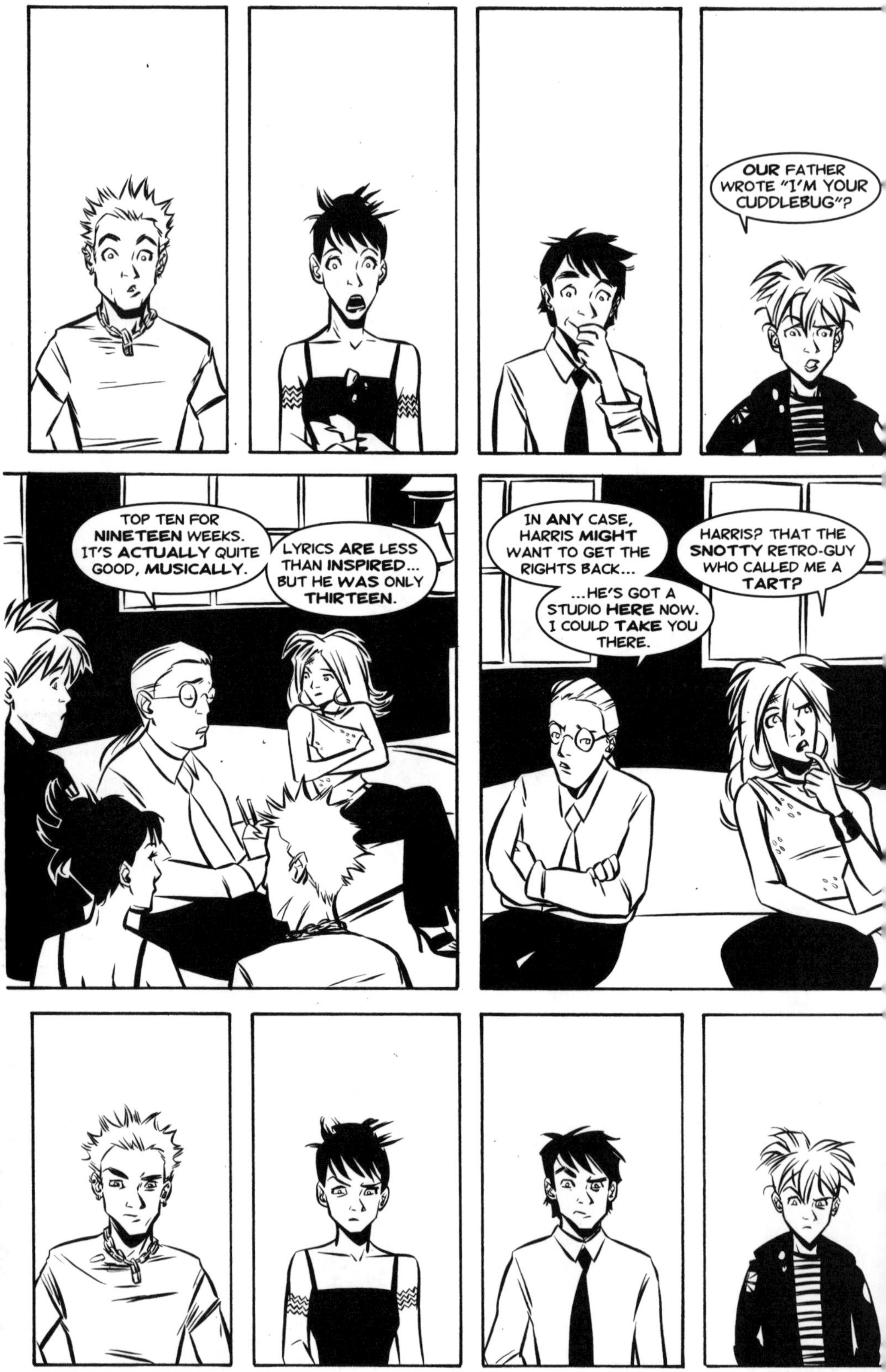
OUR FATHER WROTE "I'M YOUR CUDDLEBUG"?
TOP TEN FOR NINETEEN WEEKS. IT'S ACTUALLY QUITE GOOD, MUSICALLY.
LYRICS ARE LESS THAN INSPIRED... BUT HE WAS ONLY THIRTEEN.
IN ANY CASE, HARRIS MIGHT WANT TO GET THE RIGHTS BACK...
...HE'S GOT A STUDIO HERE NOW. I COULD TAKE YOU THERE.
HARRIS? THAT THE SNOTTY RETRO-GUY WHO CALLED ME A TART?

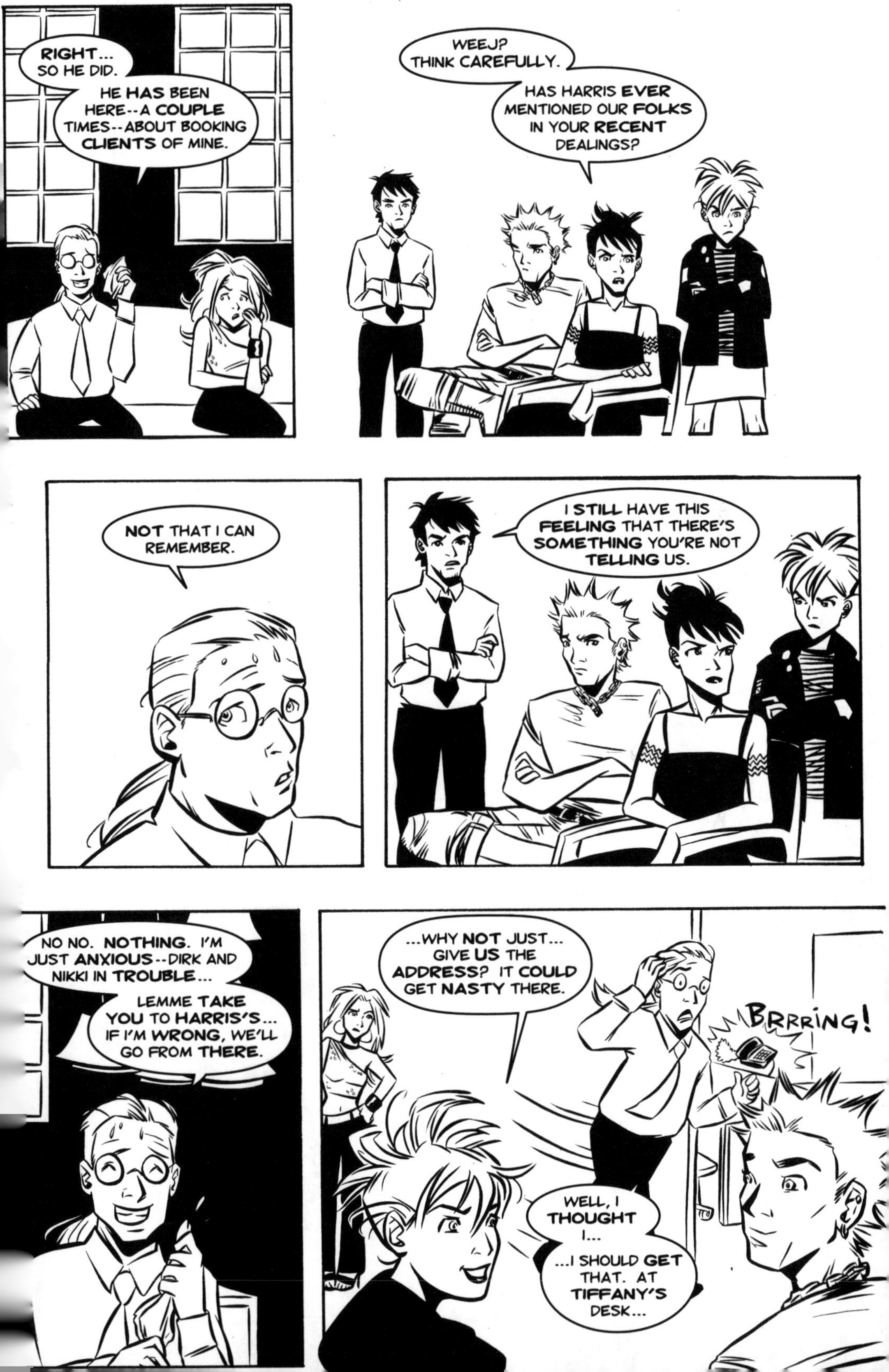
RIGHT... SO HE DID.
HE HAS BEEN HERE--A COUPLE TIMES--ABOUT BOOKING CLIENTS OF MINE.
WEEJ? THINK CAREFULLY.
HAS HARRIS EVER MENTIONED OUR FOLKS IN YOUR RECENT DEALINGS?
NOT THAT I CAN REMEMBER.
I STILL HAVE THIS FEELING THAT THERE'S SOMETHING YOU'RE NOT TELLING US.
NO NO. NOTHING. I'M JUST ANXIOUS--DIRK AND NIKKI IN TROUBLE...
LEMME TAKE YOU TO HARRIS'S... IF I'M WRONG, WE'LL GO FROM THERE.
...WHY NOT JUST... GIVE US THE ADDRESS? IT COULD GET NASTY THERE.
BRRRING!
WELL, I THOUGHT I...
...I SHOULD GET THAT. AT TIFFANY'S DESK...

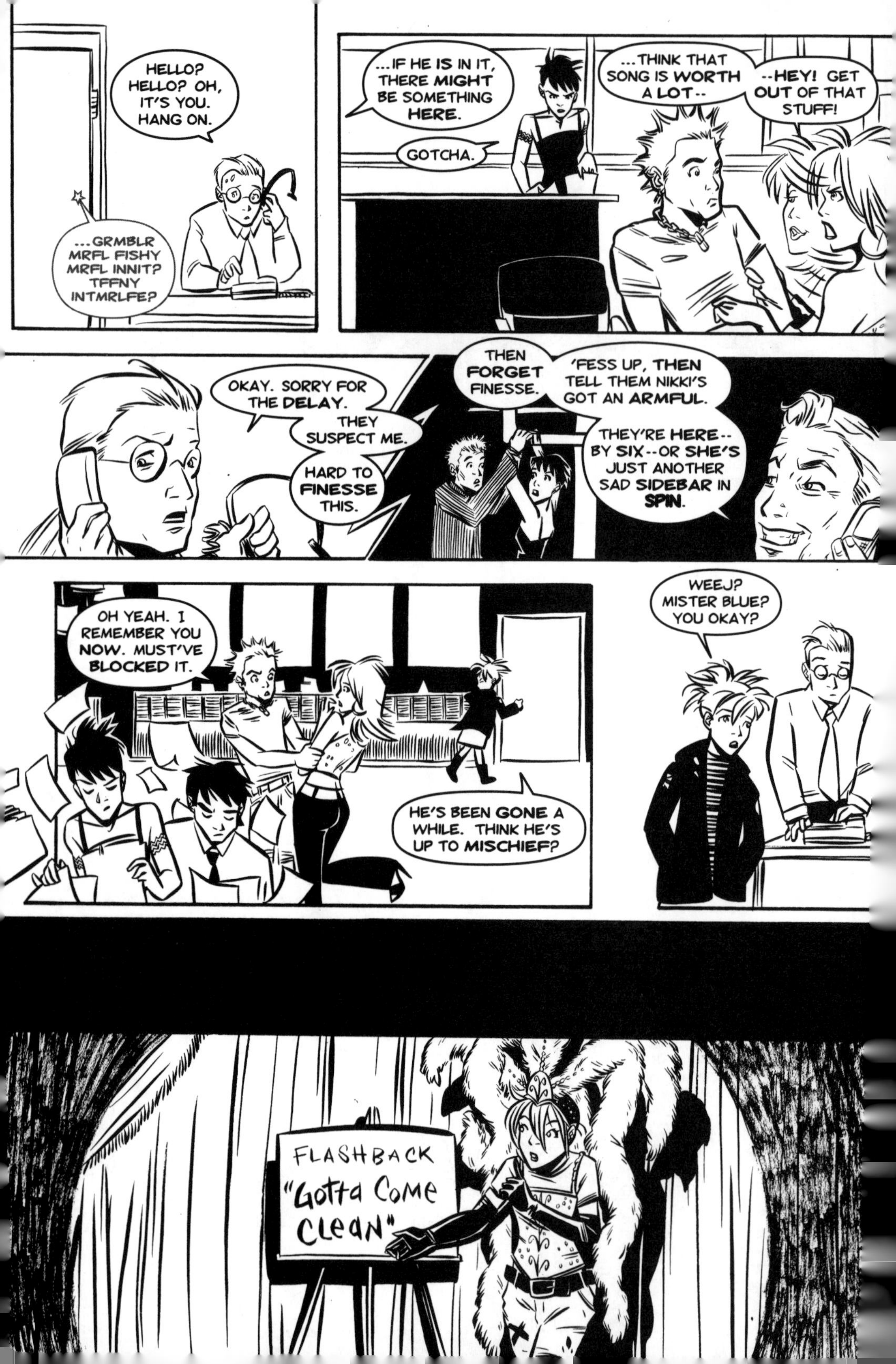
HELLO? HELLO? OH, IT'S YOU. HANG ON.
...GRMBLR MRFL FISHY MRFL INNIT? TFFNY INTMRLFE?
...IF HE IS IN IT, THERE MIGHT BE SOMETHING HERE.
GOTCHA.
...THINK THAT SONG IS WORTH A LOT--
--HEY! GET OUT OF THAT STUFF!
OKAY. SORRY FOR THE DELAY.
THEY SUSPECT ME.
HARD TO FINESSE THIS.
THEN FORGET FINESSE.
'FESS UP, THEN TELL THEM NIKKI'S GOT AN ARMFUL.
THEY'RE HERE-- BY SIX--OR SHE'S JUST ANOTHER SAD SIDEBAR IN SPIN.
OH YEAH. I REMEMBER YOU NOW. MUST'VE BLOCKED IT.
HE'S BEEN GONE A WHILE. THINK HE'S UP TO MISCHIEF?
WEEJ? MISTER BLUE? YOU OKAY?
FLASHBACK
"Gotta Come Clean"

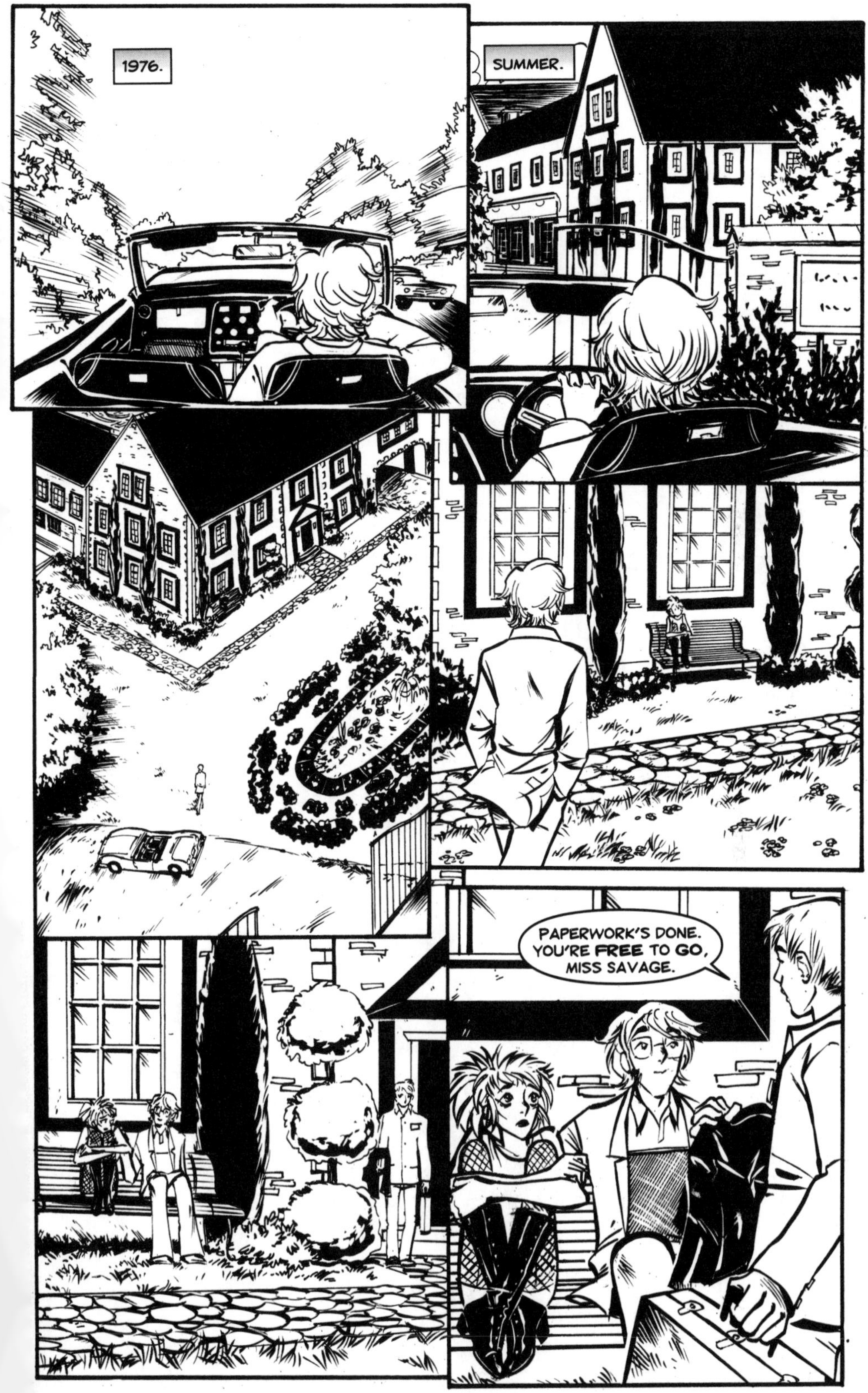
1976.
SUMMER.
PAPERWORK'S DONE. YOU'RE FREE TO GO, MISS SAVAGE.

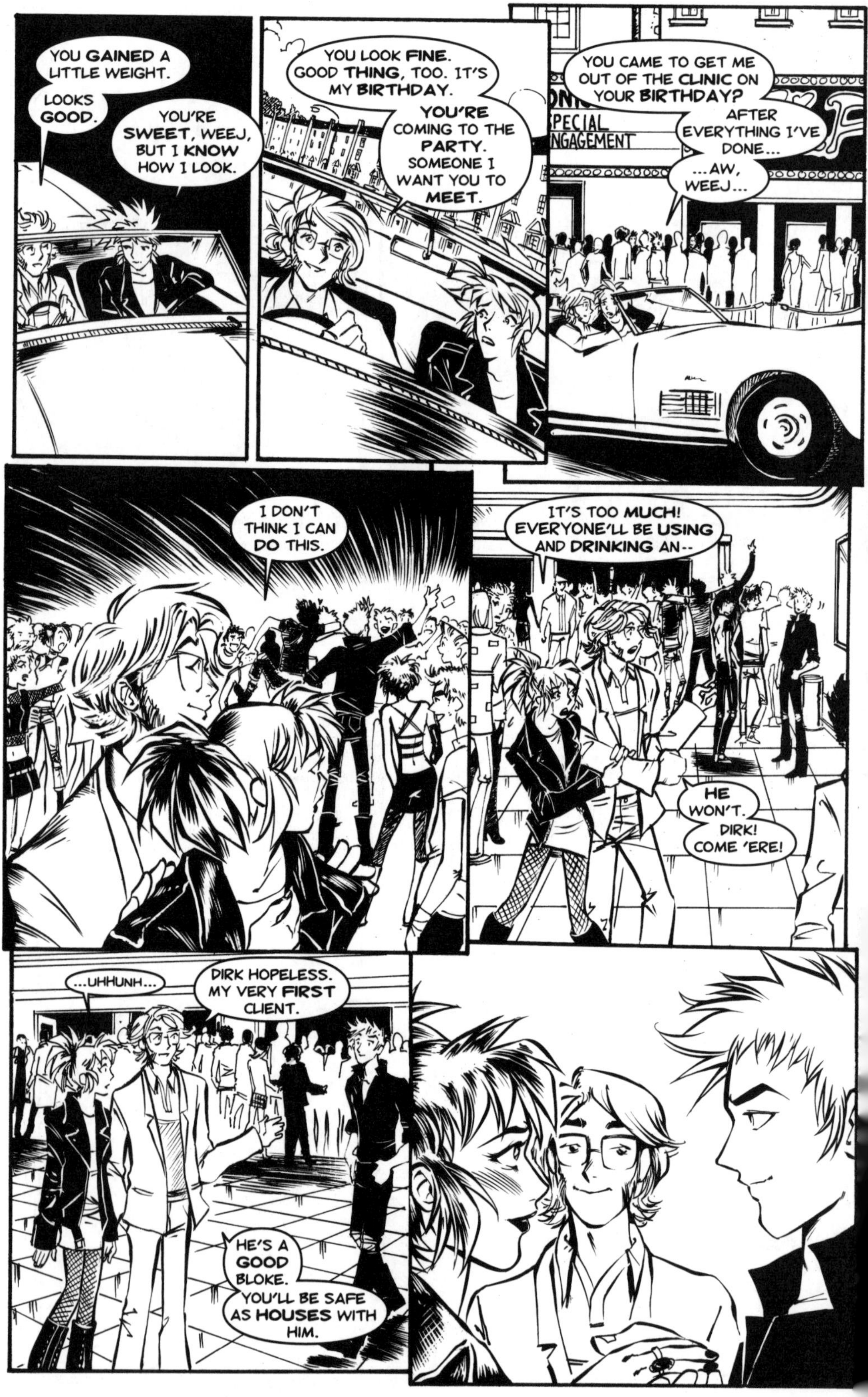
YOU GAINED A LITTLE WEIGHT.
LOOKS GOOD.
YOU'RE SWEET, WEEJ, BUT I KNOW HOW I LOOK.
YOU LOOK FINE. GOOD THING, TOO. IT'S MY BIRTHDAY.
YOU'RE COMING TO THE PARTY. SOMEONE I WANT YOU TO MEET.
SPECIAL ENGAGEMENT
YOU CAME TO GET ME OUT OF THE CLINIC ON YOUR BIRTHDAY?
AFTER EVERYTHING I'VE DONE...
...AW, WEEJ...
I DON'T THINK I CAN DO THIS.
IT'S TOO MUCH! EVERYONE'LL BE USING AND DRINKING AN--
HE WON'T. DIRK! COME 'ERE!
...UHHUNH...
DIRK HOPELESS. MY VERY FIRST CLIENT.
HE'S A GOOD BLOKE. YOU'LL BE SAFE AS HOUSES WITH HIM.

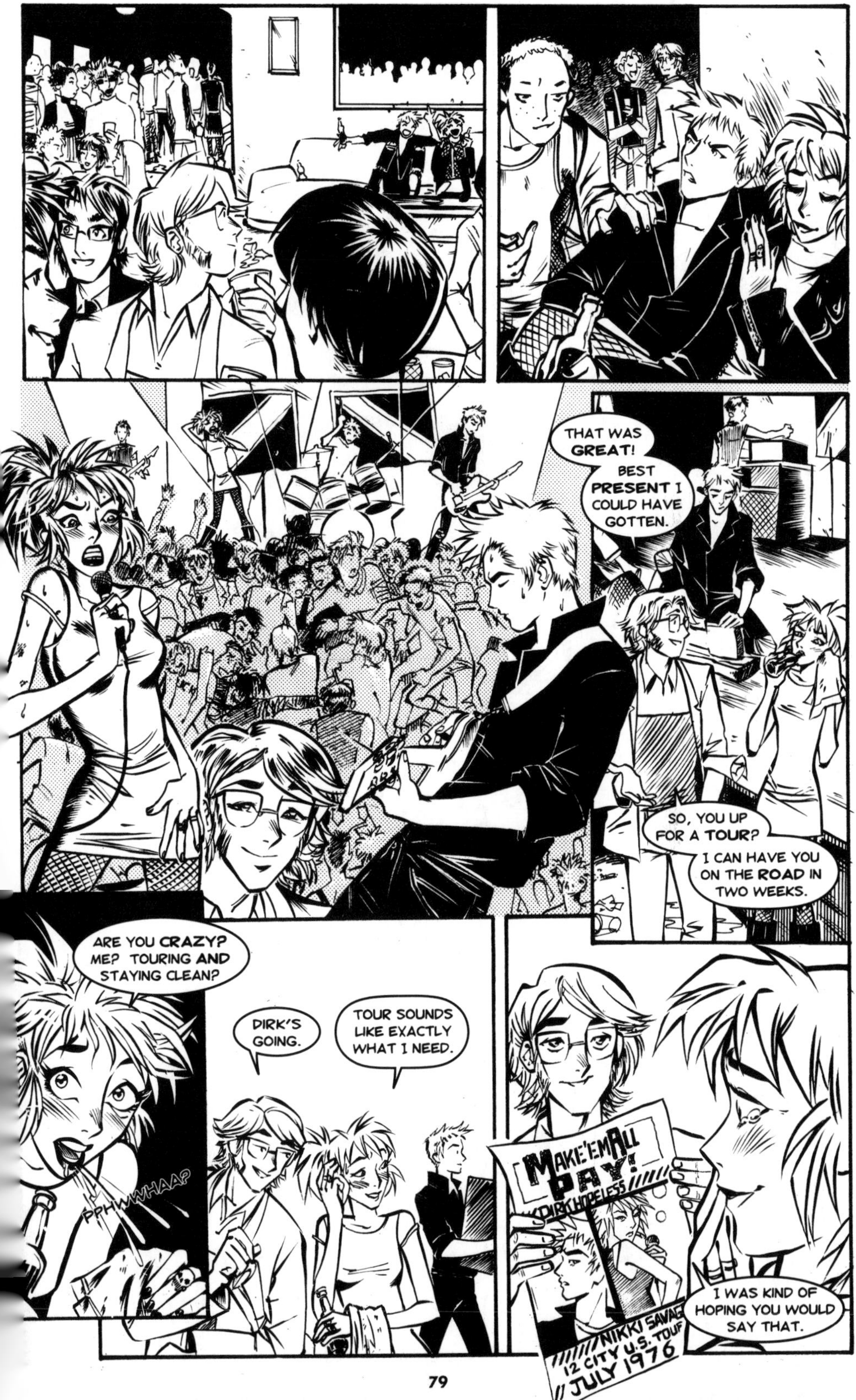

THAT WAS GREAT!
BEST PRESENT I COULD HAVE GOTTEN.
SO, YOU UP FOR A TOUR?
I CAN HAVE YOU ON THE ROAD IN TWO WEEKS.
ARE YOU CRAZY? ME? TOURING AND STAYING CLEAN?
PPHWWHAA?
DIRK'S GOING.
TOUR SOUNDS LIKE EXACTLY WHAT I NEED.
MAKE'EM ALL PAY!
DIRK HOPELESS
NIKKI SAVAGE
12 CITY U.S. TOUR
JULY 1976
I WAS KIND OF HOPING YOU WOULD SAY THAT.

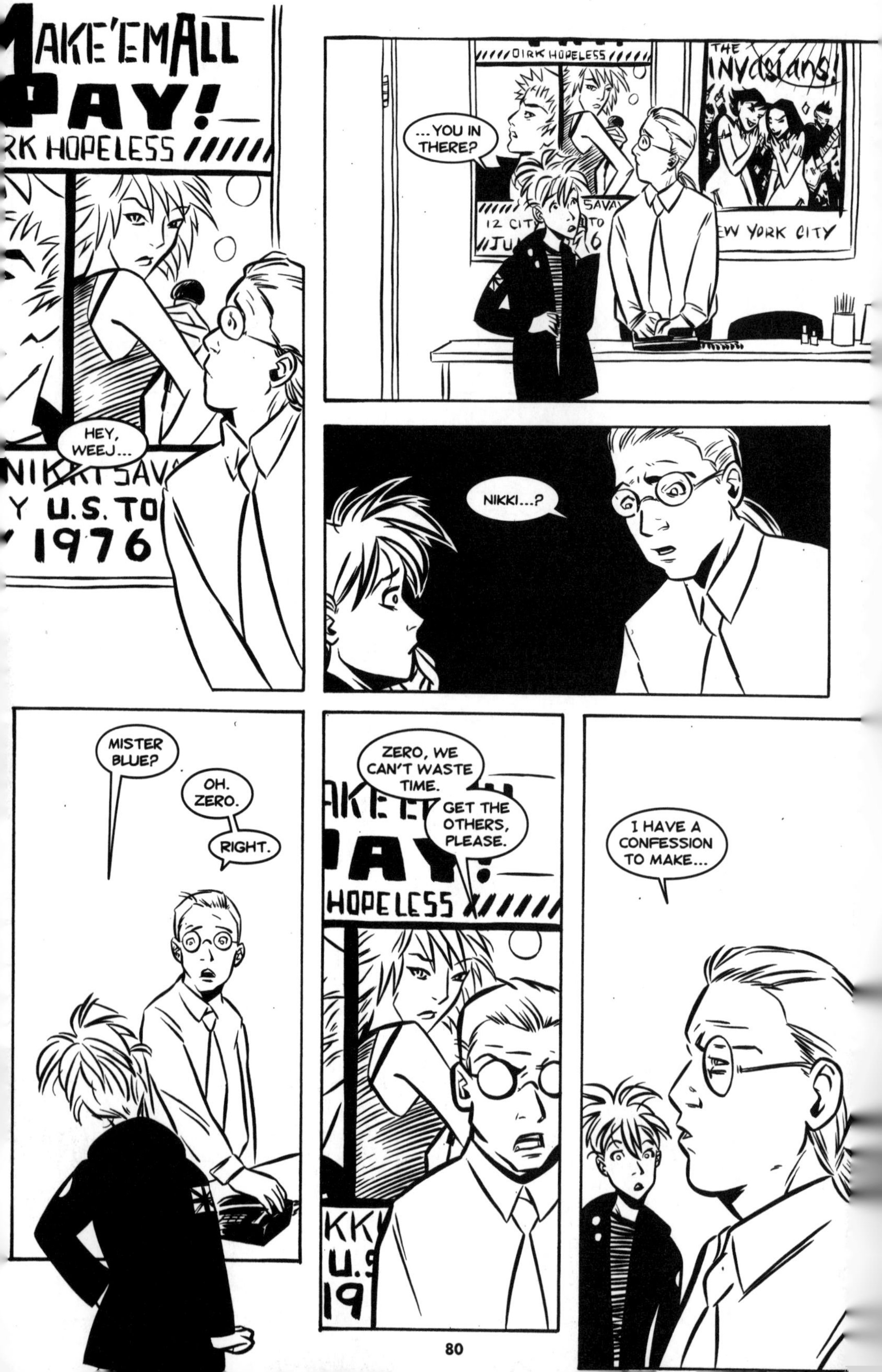

AKE'EMALL
PAY!
RK HOPELESS
HEY, WEEJ...
Y U.S. TO
1976
DIRK HOPELESS
THE INVASIANS!
EW YORK CITY
...YOU IN THERE?
NIKKI...?
MISTER BLUE?
OH. ZERO.
RIGHT.
ZERO, WE CAN'T WASTE TIME.
GET THE OTHERS, PLEASE.
HOPELESS
I HAVE A CONFESSION TO MAKE...

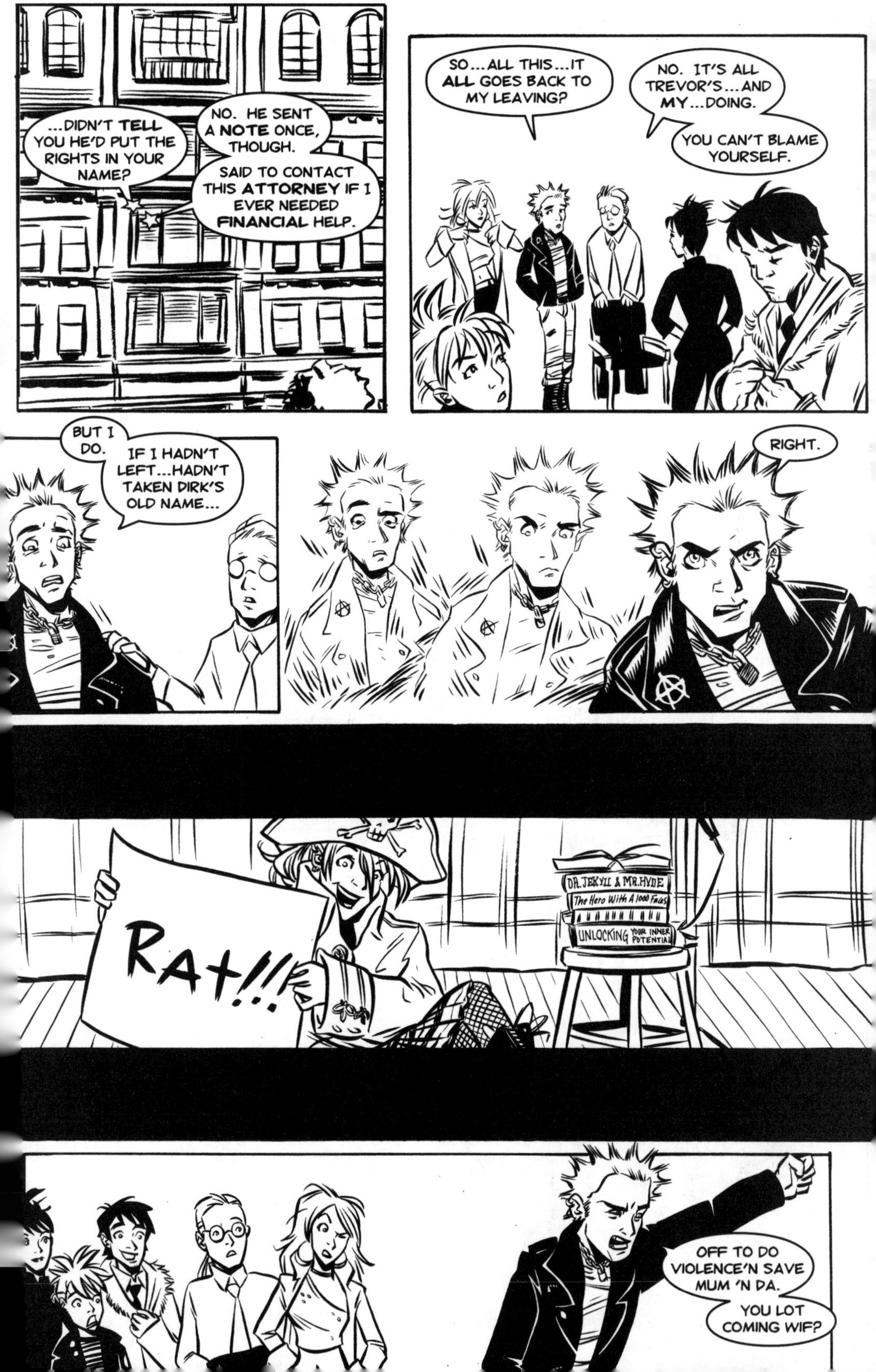

...DIDN'T TELL YOU HE'D PUT THE RIGHTS IN YOUR NAME?
NO. HE SENT A NOTE ONCE, THOUGH.
SAID TO CONTACT THIS ATTORNEY IF I EVER NEEDED FINANCIAL HELP.
SO...ALL THIS...IT ALL GOES BACK TO MY LEAVING?
NO. IT'S ALL TREVOR'S...AND MY...DOING.
YOU CAN'T BLAME YOURSELF.
BUT I DO.
IF I HADN'T LEFT...HADN'T TAKEN DIRK'S OLD NAME...
RIGHT.
RAT!!!
DR. JEKYLL & MR. HYDE
The Hero With A 1000 Faces
UNLOCKING YOUR INNER POTENTIAL
OFF TO DO VIOLENCE'N SAVE MUM 'N DA.
YOU LOT COMING WIF?

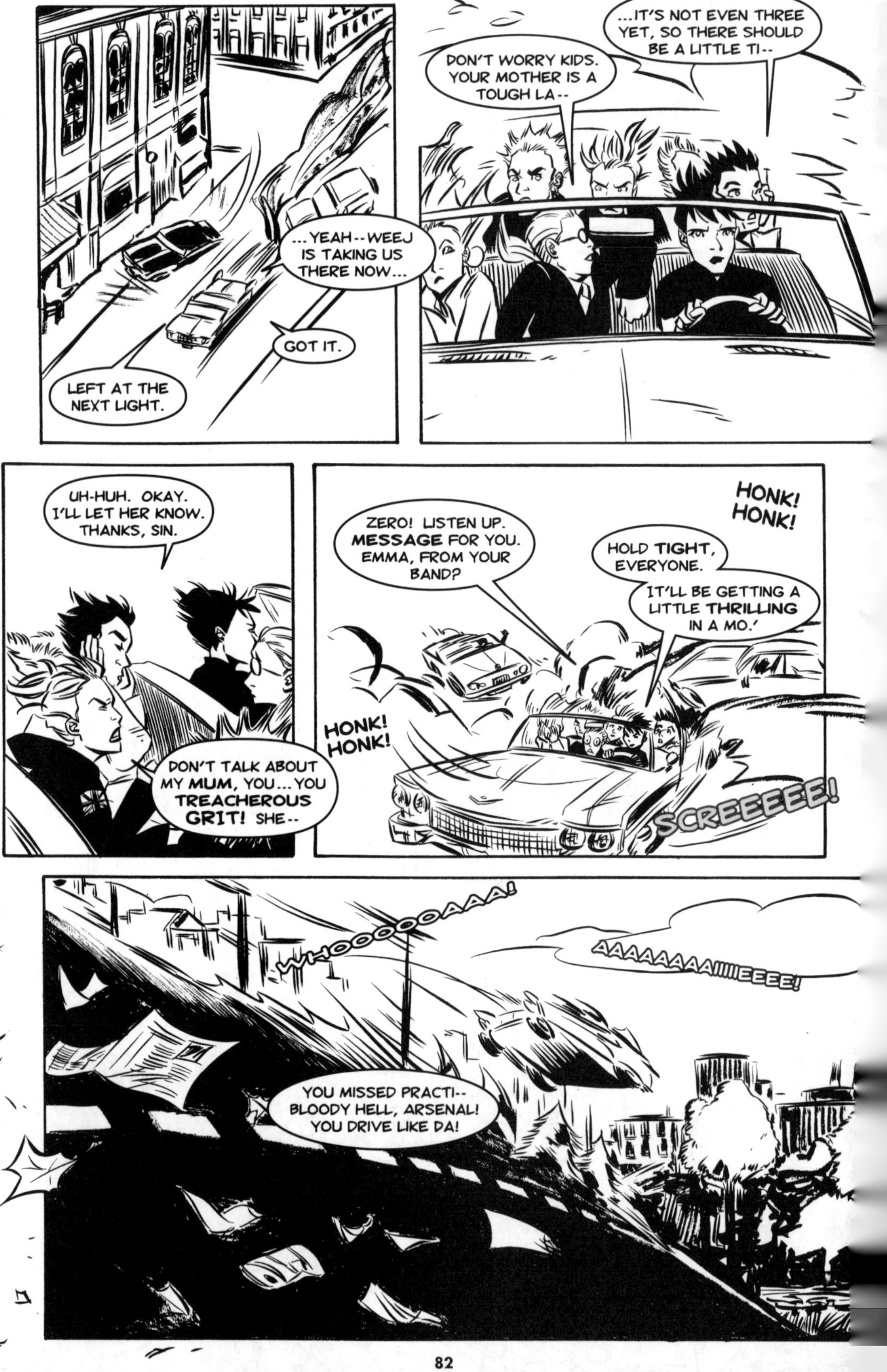
...YEAH--WEEJ IS TAKING US THERE NOW...
GOT IT.
LEFT AT THE NEXT LIGHT.
DON'T WORRY KIDS. YOUR MOTHER IS A TOUGH LA--
...IT'S NOT EVEN THREE YET, SO THERE SHOULD BE A LITTLE TI--
UH-HUH. OKAY. I'LL LET HER KNOW. THANKS, SIN.
DON'T TALK ABOUT MY MUM, YOU...YOU TREACHEROUS GRIT! SHE--
HONK! HONK!
ZERO! LISTEN UP. MESSAGE FOR YOU. EMMA, FROM YOUR BAND?
HOLD TIGHT, EVERYONE.
IT'LL BE GETTING A LITTLE THRILLING IN A MO.'
HONK! HONK!
SCREEEEEE!
WHOOOOOOOAAA!
AAAAAAAAIIIIIEEEE!
YOU MISSED PRACTI-- BLOODY HELL, ARSENAL! YOU DRIVE LIKE DA!

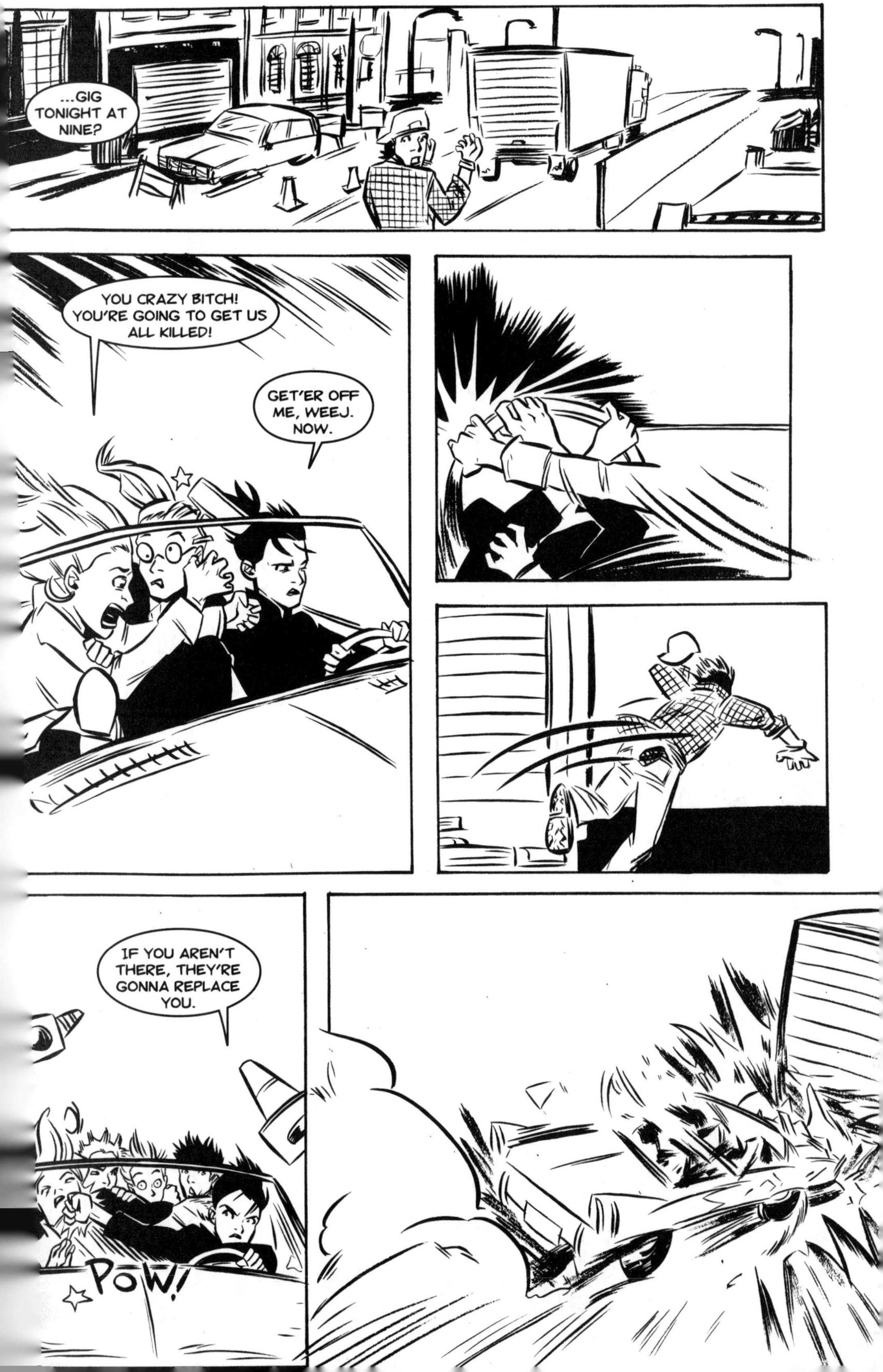
...GIG TONIGHT AT NINE?
YOU CRAZY BITCH! YOU'RE GOING TO GET US ALL KILLED!
GET'ER OFF ME, WEEJ. NOW.
IF YOU AREN'T THERE, THEY'RE GONNA REPLACE YOU.
POW!

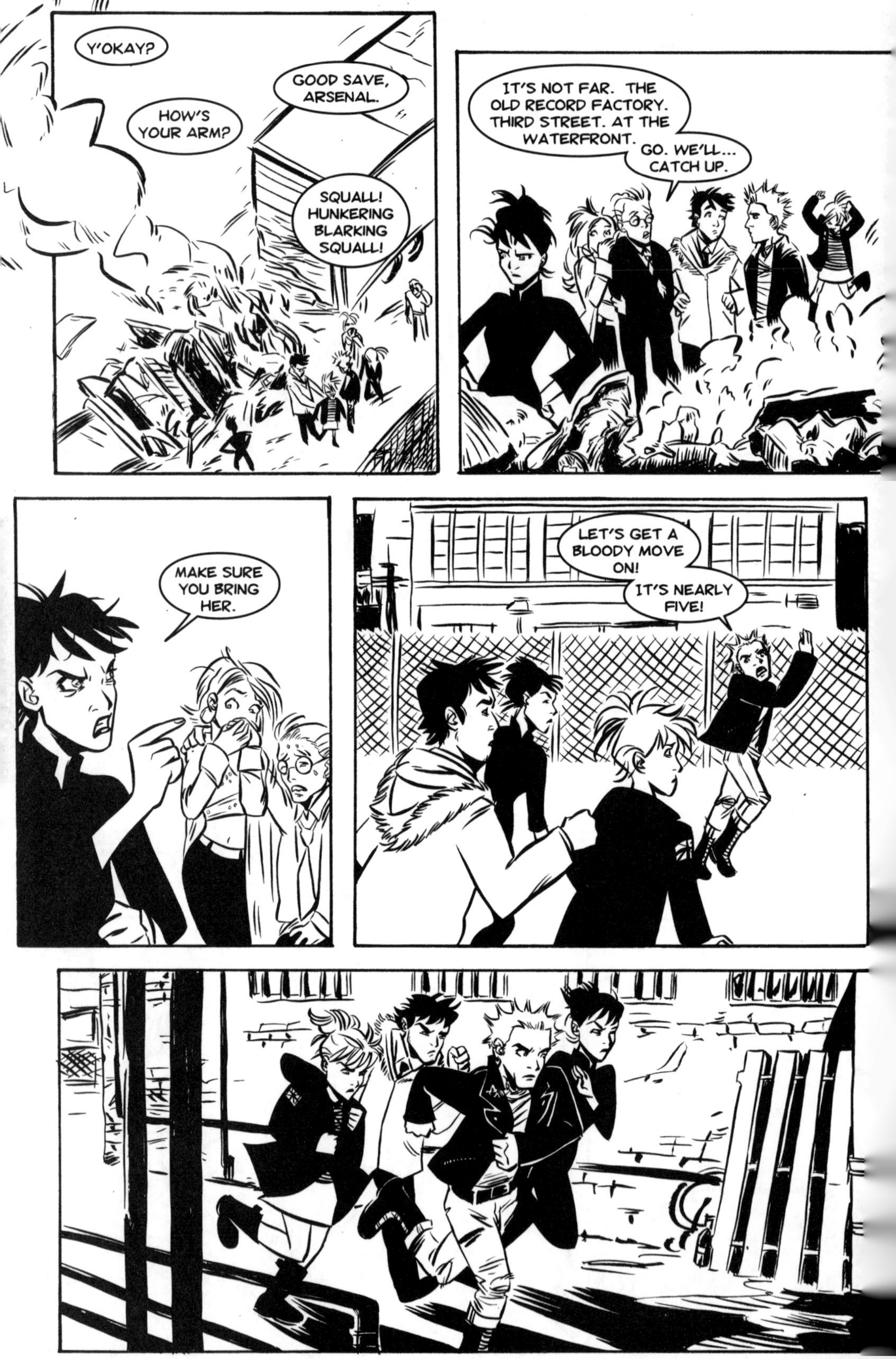
Y'OKAY?
HOW'S YOUR ARM?
GOOD SAVE, ARSENAL.
SQUALL! HUNKERING BLARKING SQUALL!
IT'S NOT FAR. THE OLD RECORD FACTORY. THIRD STREET. AT THE WATERFRONT.
GO. WE'LL... CATCH UP.
MAKE SURE YOU BRING HER.
LET'S GET A BLOODY MOVE ON!
IT'S NEARLY FIVE!

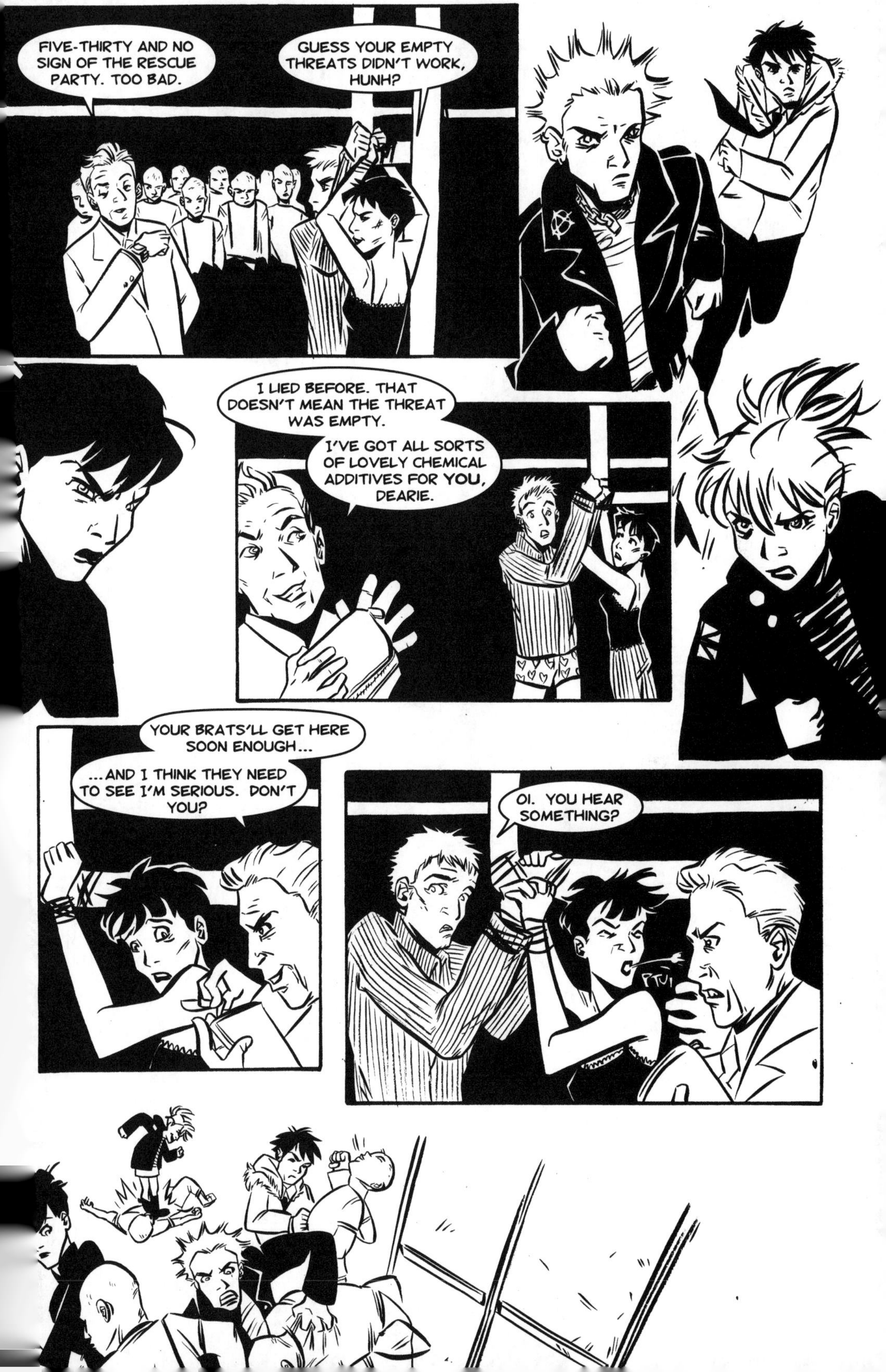
FIVE-THIRTY AND NO SIGN OF THE RESCUE PARTY. TOO BAD.
GUESS YOUR EMPTY THREATS DIDN'T WORK, HUNH?
I LIED BEFORE. THAT DOESN'T MEAN THE THREAT WAS EMPTY.
I'VE GOT ALL SORTS OF LOVELY CHEMICAL ADDITIVES FOR YOU, DEARIE.
YOUR BRATS'LL GET HERE SOON ENOUGH...
...AND I THINK THEY NEED TO SEE I'M SERIOUS. DON'T YOU?
OI. YOU HEAR SOMETHING?
PTUI

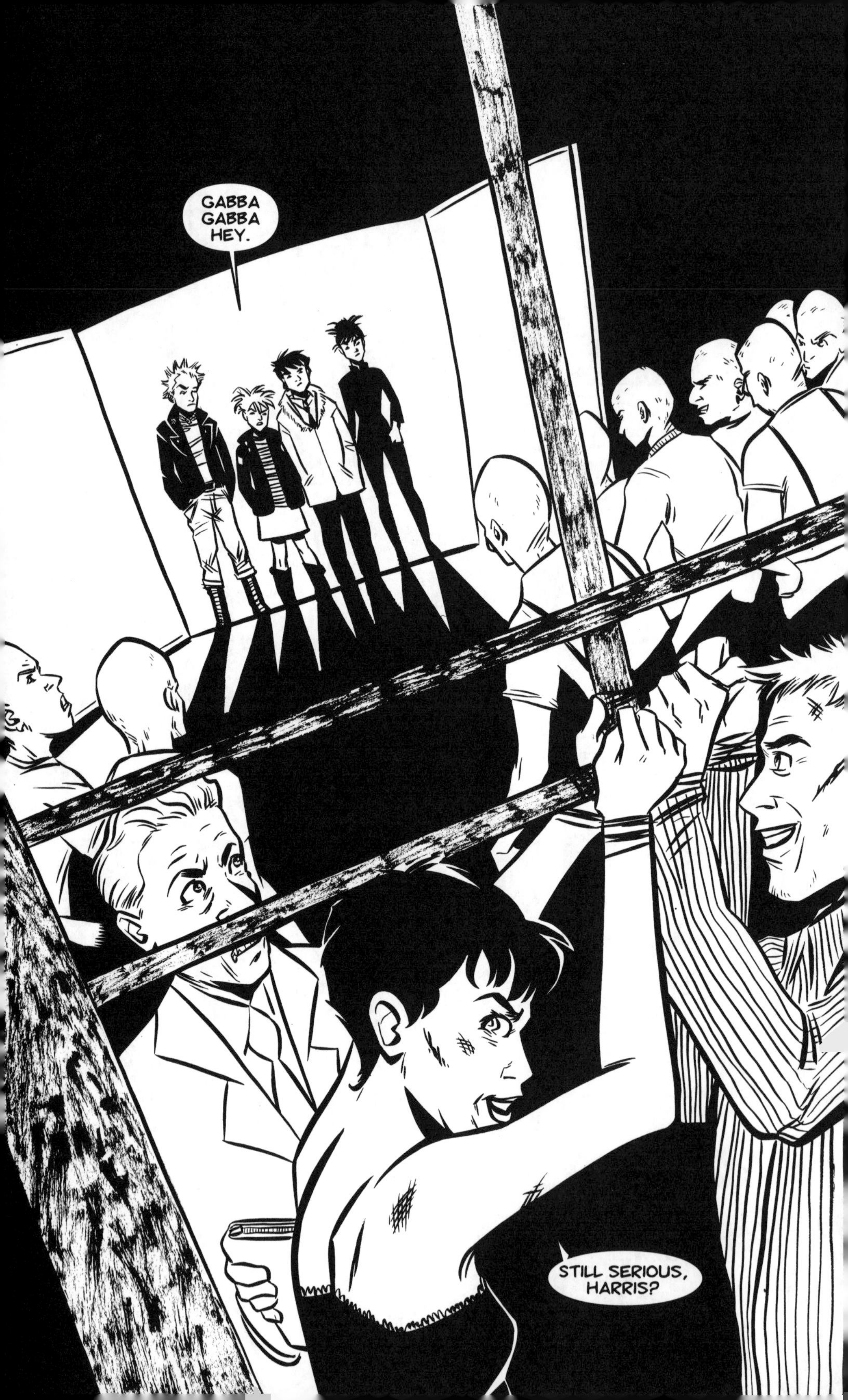
GABBA GABBA HEY.
STILL SERIOUS, HARRIS?

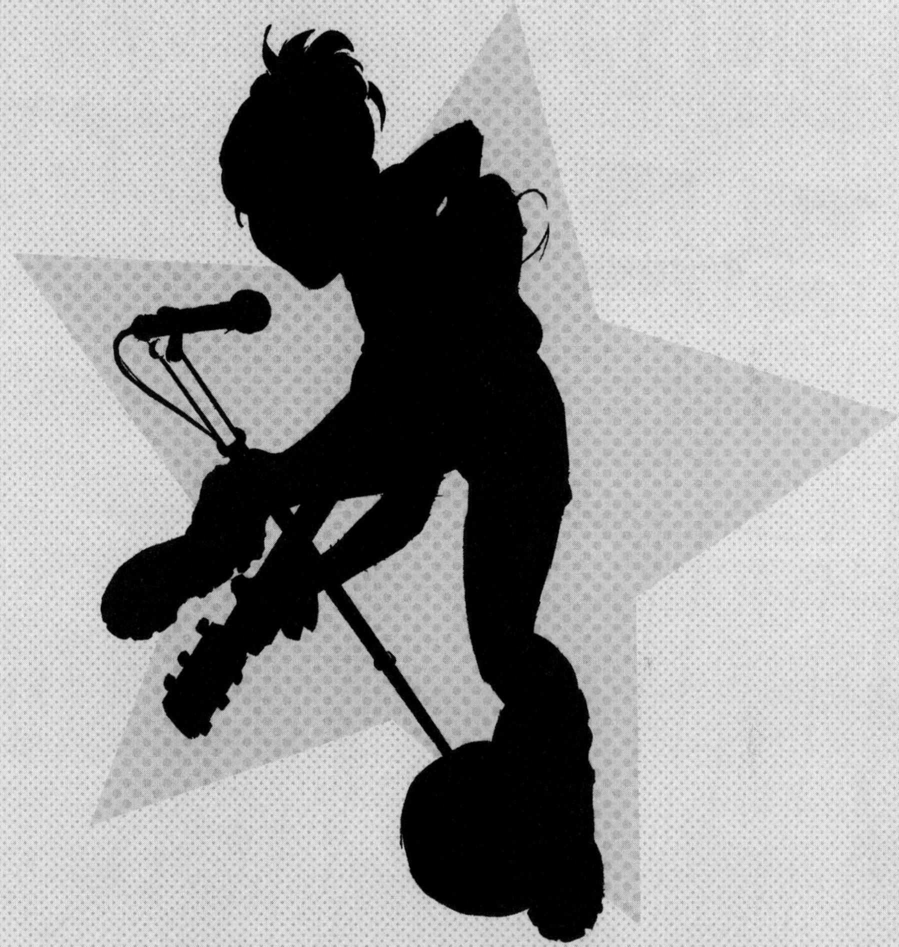

CHAPTER 4

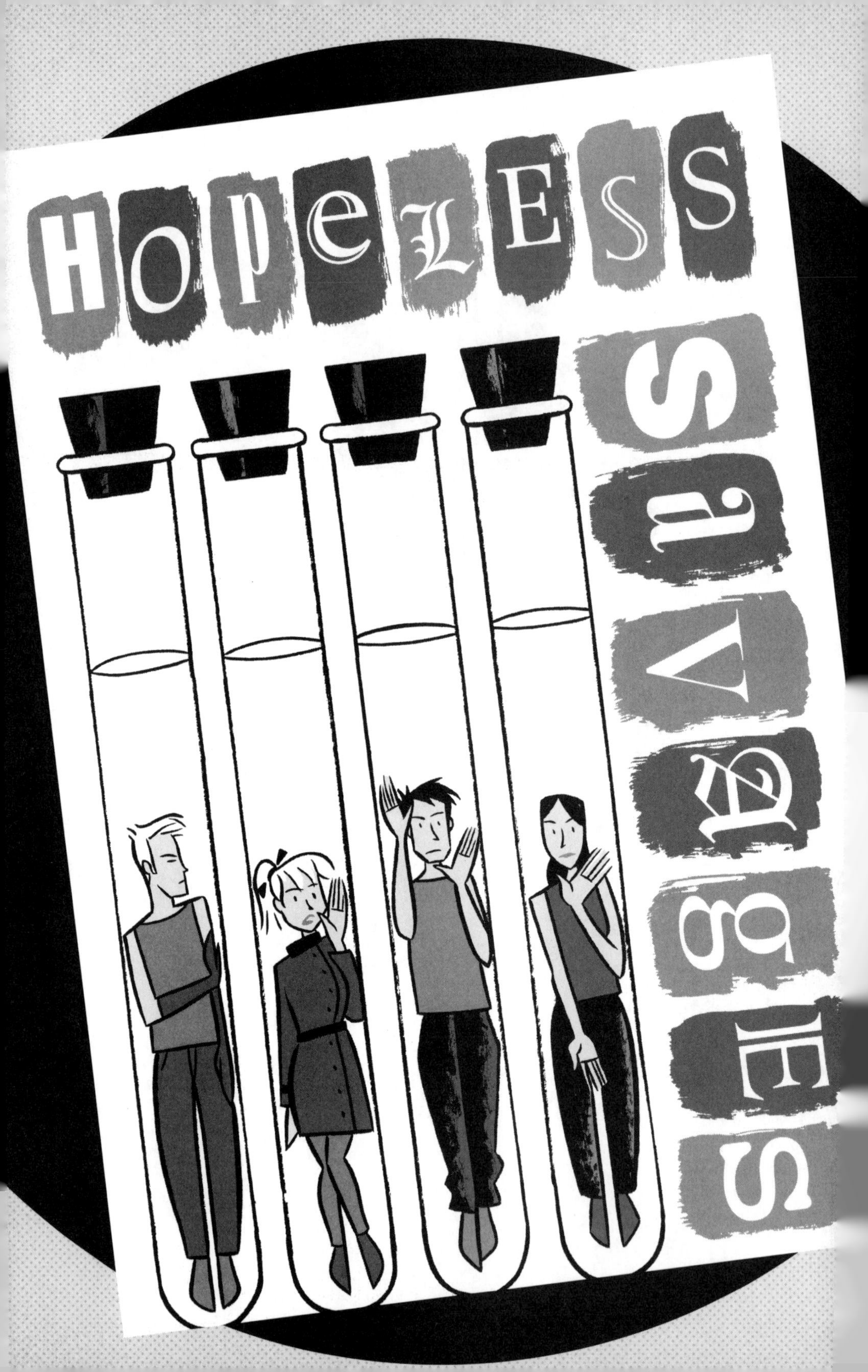
HOPELESS
SAVAGES

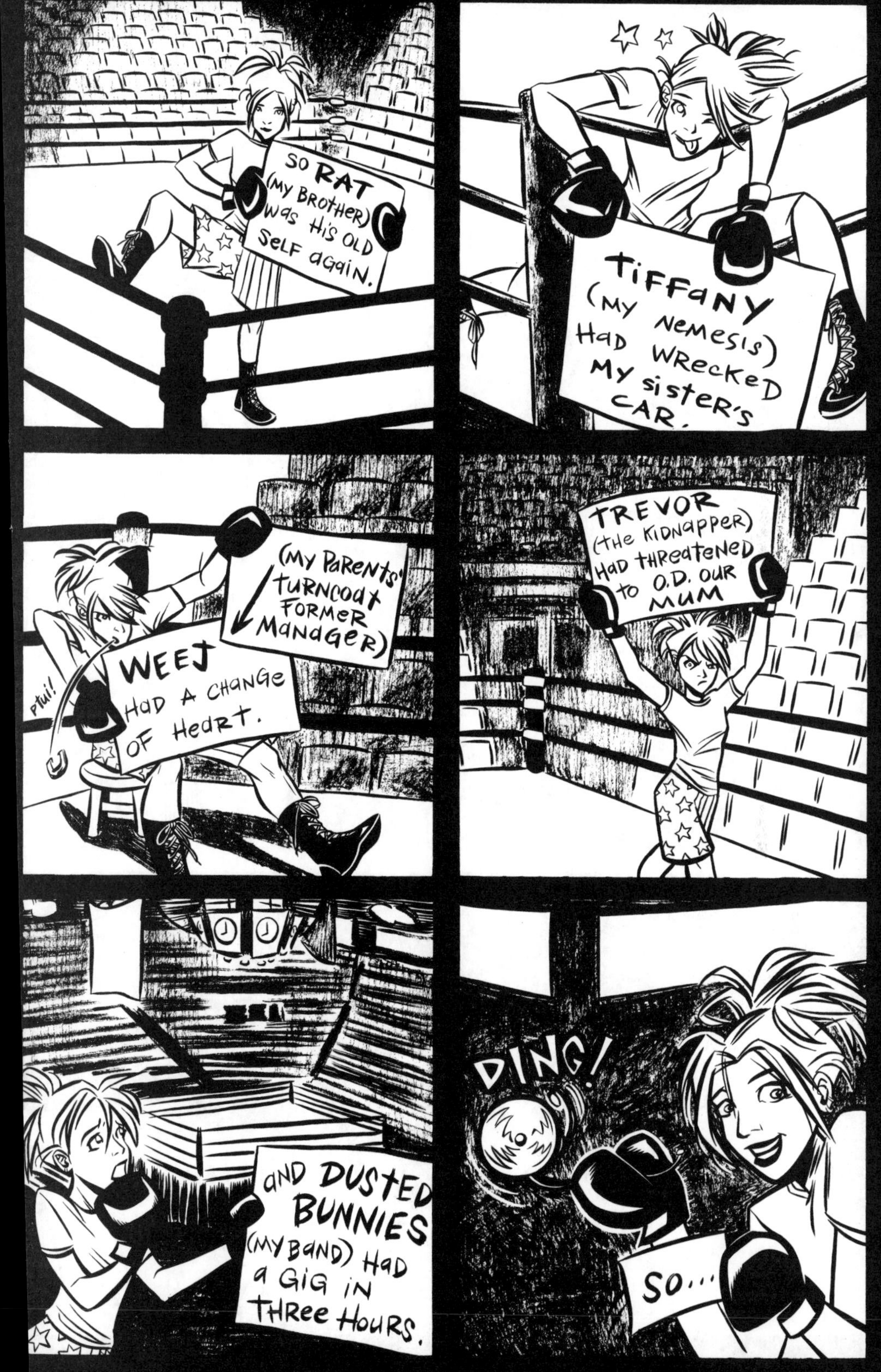
SO RAT (MY BROTHER) WAS HIS OLD SELF AGAIN.
TIFFANY (MY NEMESIS) HAD WRECKED MY SISTER'S CAR.
(MY PARENTS' TURNCOAT FORMER MANAGER)
WEEJ HAD A CHANGE OF HEART.
PTUI!
TREVOR (THE KIDNAPPER) HAD THREATENED TO O.D. OUR MUM
AND DUSTED BUNNIES (MY BAND) HAD A GIG IN THREE HOURS.
DING!
SO...

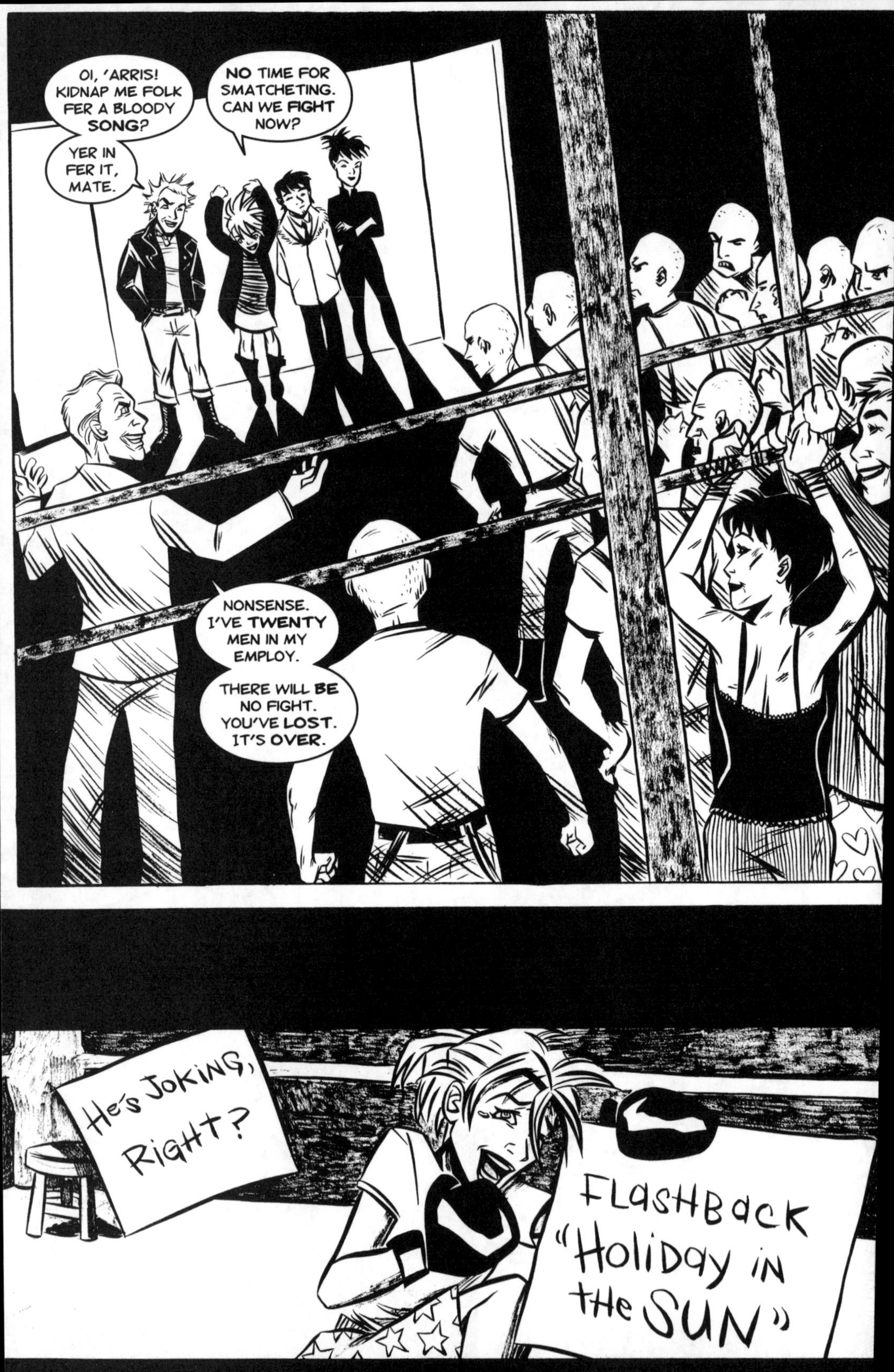
OI, 'ARRIS! KIDNAP ME FOLK FER A BLOODY SONG?
YER IN FER IT, MATE.
NO TIME FOR SMATCHETING. CAN WE FIGHT NOW?
NONSENSE. I'VE TWENTY MEN IN MY EMPLOY.
THERE WILL BE NO FIGHT. YOU'VE LOST. IT'S OVER.
He's JOKING, RIGHT?
FLASHBACK "HOLIDAY IN THE SUN"

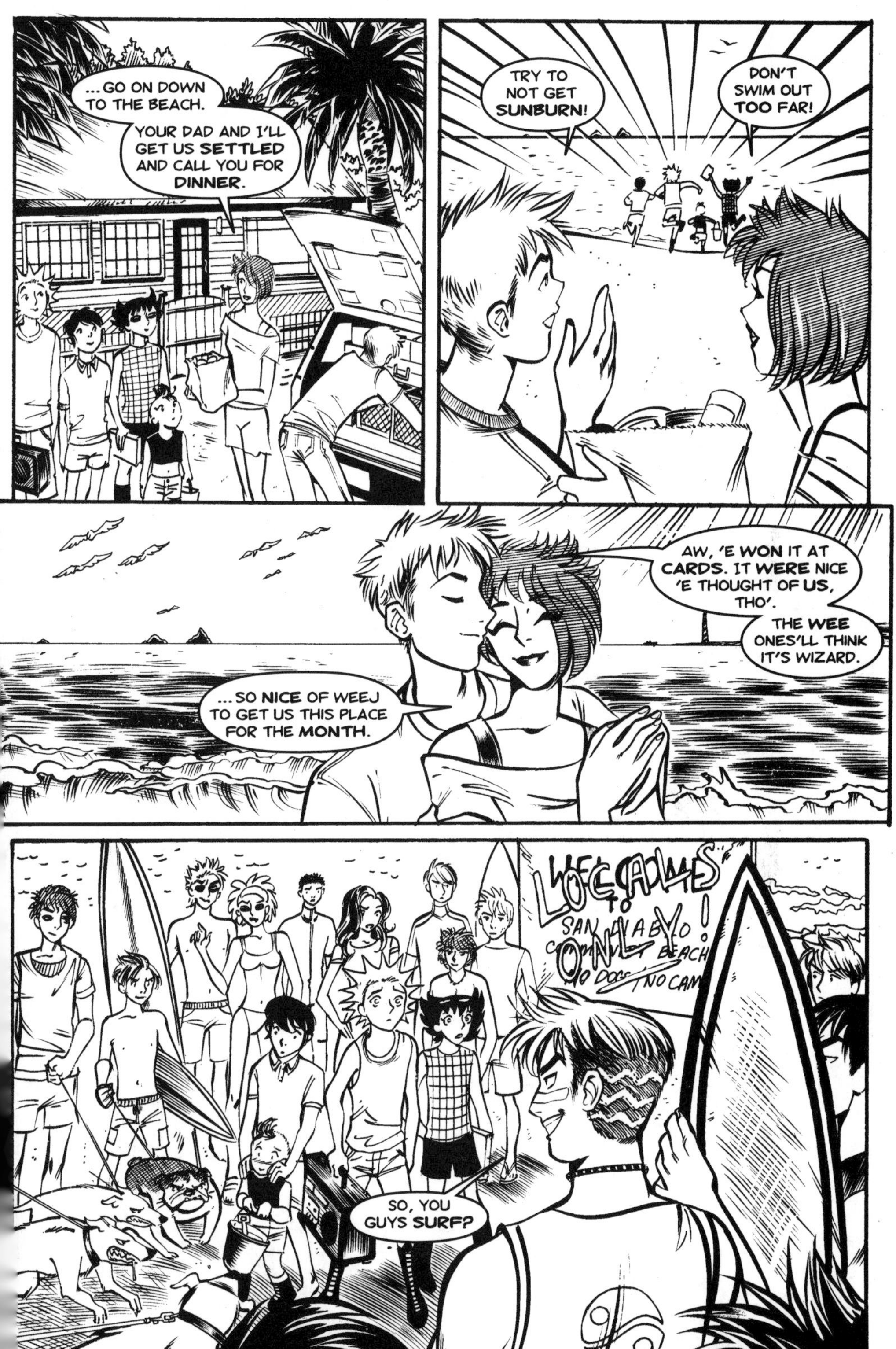
...GO ON DOWN TO THE BEACH.
YOUR DAD AND I'LL GET US SETTLED AND CALL YOU FOR DINNER.
TRY TO NOT GET SUNBURN!
DON'T SWIM OUT TOO FAR!
...SO NICE OF WEEJ TO GET US THIS PLACE FOR THE MONTH.
AW, 'E WON IT AT CARDS. IT WERE NICE 'E THOUGHT OF US, THO'.
THE WEE ONES'LL THINK IT'S WIZARD.
LOCALS ONLY!
SO, YOU GUYS SURF?

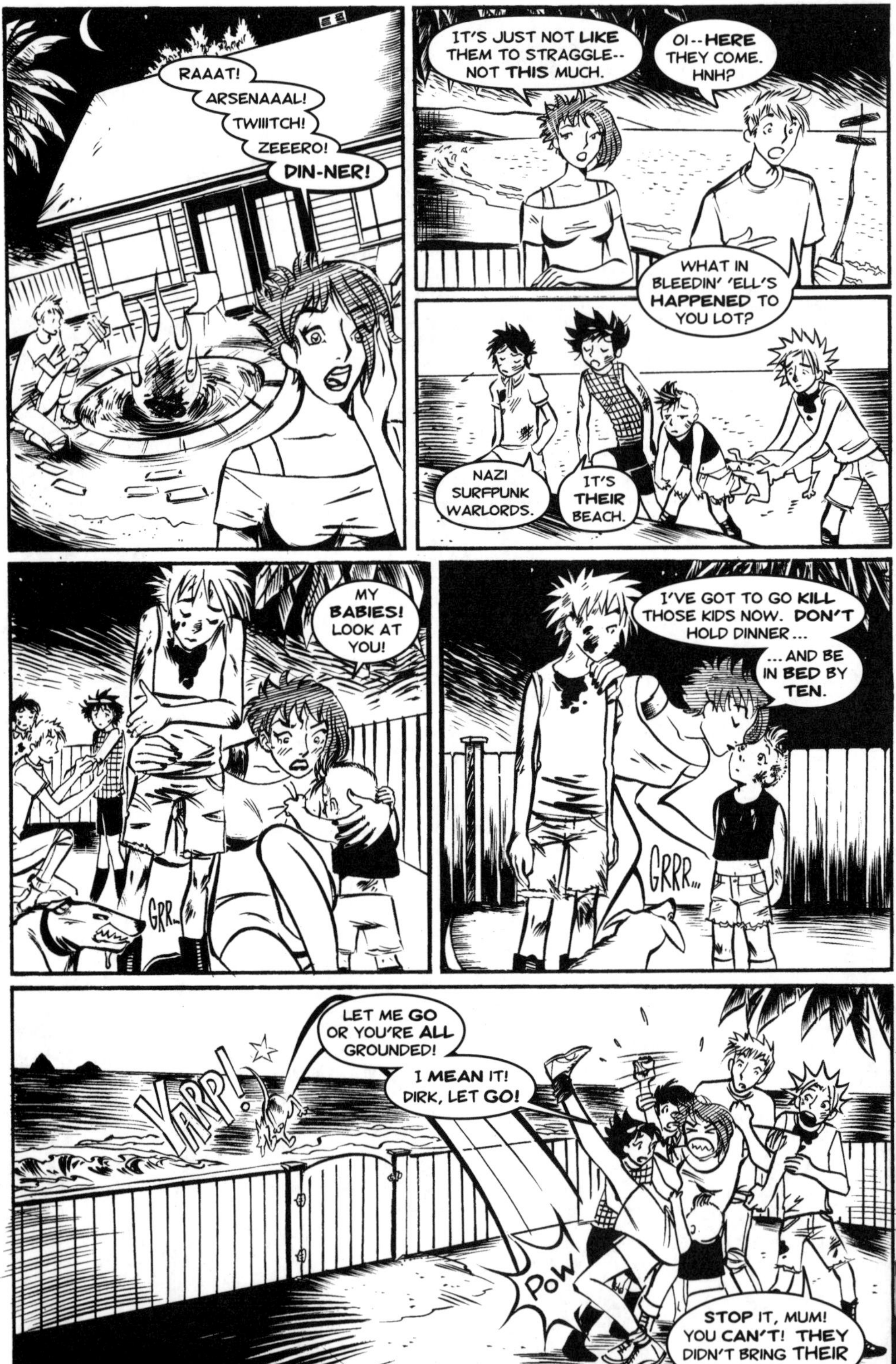
RAAAT!
ARSENAAAL!
TWIIITCH!
ZEEERO!
DIN-NER!
IT'S JUST NOT LIKE THEM TO STRAGGLE-- NOT THIS MUCH.
OI--HERE THEY COME. HNH?
WHAT IN BLEEDIN' 'ELL'S HAPPENED TO YOU LOT?
NAZI SURFPUNK WARLORDS.
IT'S THEIR BEACH.
MY BABIES! LOOK AT YOU!
GRR...
I'VE GOT TO GO KILL THOSE KIDS NOW. DON'T HOLD DINNER...
...AND BE IN BED BY TEN.
GRRR...
LET ME GO OR YOU'RE ALL GROUNDED!
I MEAN IT! DIRK, LET GO!
YARP!
POW
STOP IT, MUM! YOU CAN'T! THEY DIDN'T BRING THEIR MOTHERS!

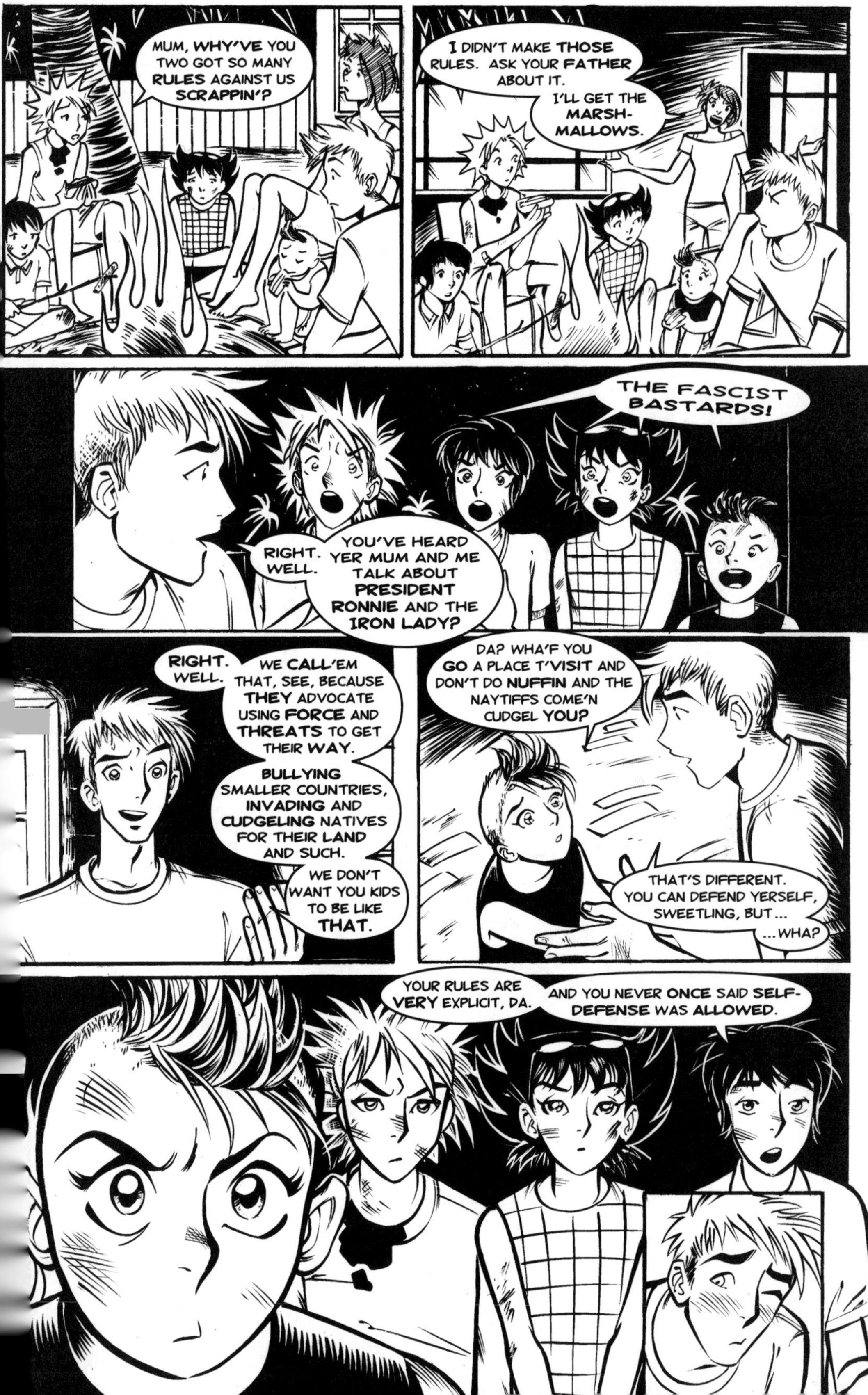
MUM, WHY'VE YOU TWO GOT SO MANY RULES AGAINST US SCRAPPIN'?
I DIDN'T MAKE THOSE RULES. ASK YOUR FATHER ABOUT IT.
I'LL GET THE MARSH-MALLOWS.
THE FASCIST BASTARDS!
RIGHT. WELL.
YOU'VE HEARD YER MUM AND ME TALK ABOUT PRESIDENT RONNIE AND THE IRON LADY?
RIGHT. WELL.
WE CALL'EM THAT, SEE, BECAUSE THEY ADVOCATE USING FORCE AND THREATS TO GET THEIR WAY.
BULLYING SMALLER COUNTRIES, INVADING AND CUDGELING NATIVES FOR THEIR LAND AND SUCH.
WE DON'T WANT YOU KIDS TO BE LIKE THAT.
DA? WHA'F YOU GO A PLACE T'VISIT AND DON'T DO NUFFIN AND THE NAYTIFFS COME'N CUDGEL YOU?
THAT'S DIFFERENT. YOU CAN DEFEND YERSELF, SWEETLING, BUT...
...WHA?
YOUR RULES ARE VERY EXPLICIT, DA.
AND YOU NEVER ONCE SAID SELF-DEFENSE WAS ALLOWED.

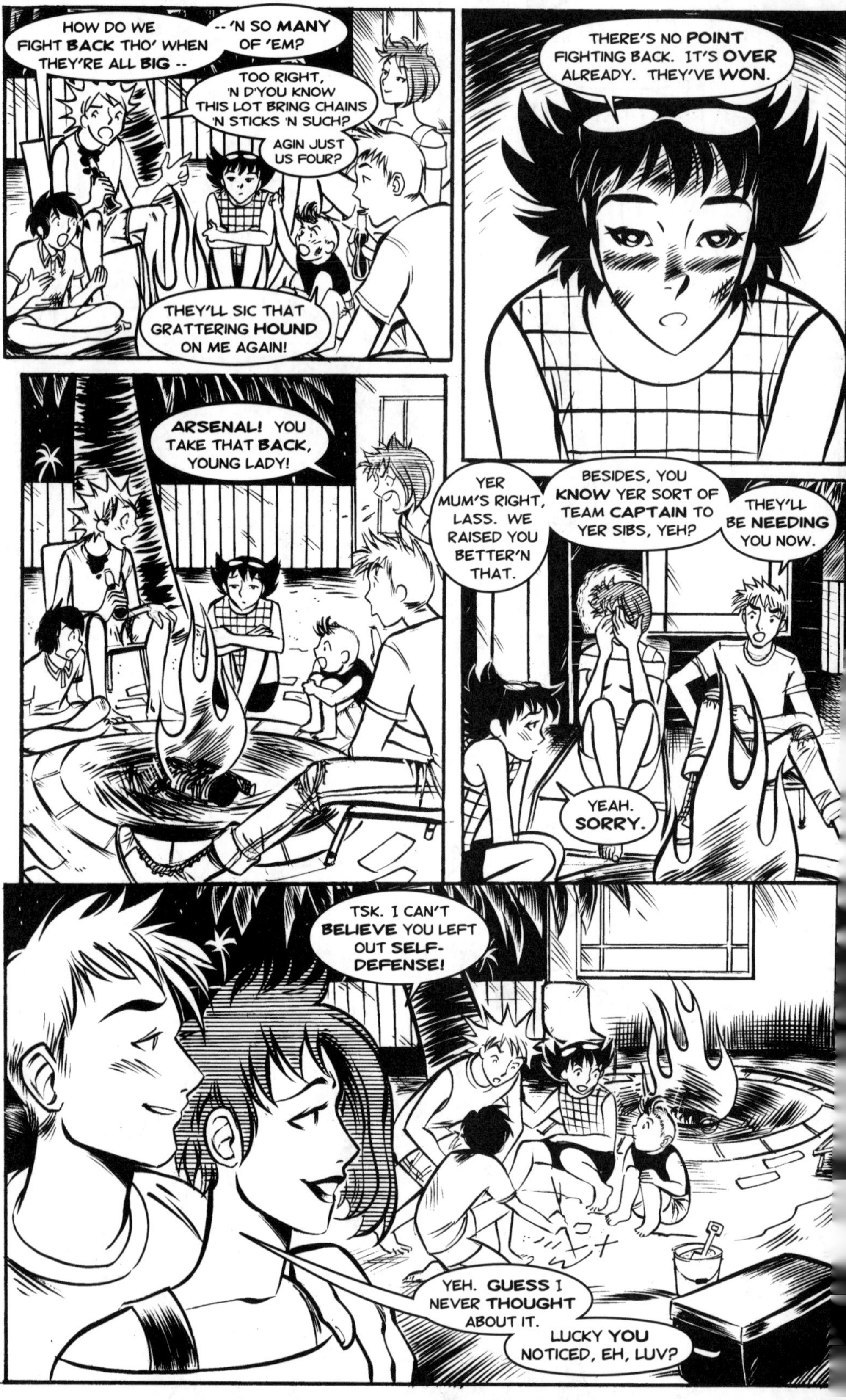
HOW DO WE FIGHT BACK THO' WHEN THEY'RE ALL BIG --
-- 'N SO MANY OF 'EM?
TOO RIGHT, 'N D'YOU KNOW THIS LOT BRING CHAINS 'N STICKS 'N SUCH?
AGIN JUST US FOUR?
THEY'LL SIC THAT GRATTERING HOUND ON ME AGAIN!
THERE'S NO POINT FIGHTING BACK. IT'S OVER ALREADY. THEY'VE WON.
ARSENAL! YOU TAKE THAT BACK, YOUNG LADY!
YER MUM'S RIGHT, LASS. WE RAISED YOU BETTER'N THAT.
BESIDES, YOU KNOW YER SORT OF TEAM CAPTAIN TO YER SIBS, YEH?
THEY'LL BE NEEDING YOU NOW.
YEAH. SORRY.
TSK. I CAN'T BELIEVE YOU LEFT OUT SELF-DEFENSE!
YEH. GUESS I NEVER THOUGHT ABOUT IT.
LUCKY YOU NOTICED, EH, LUV?

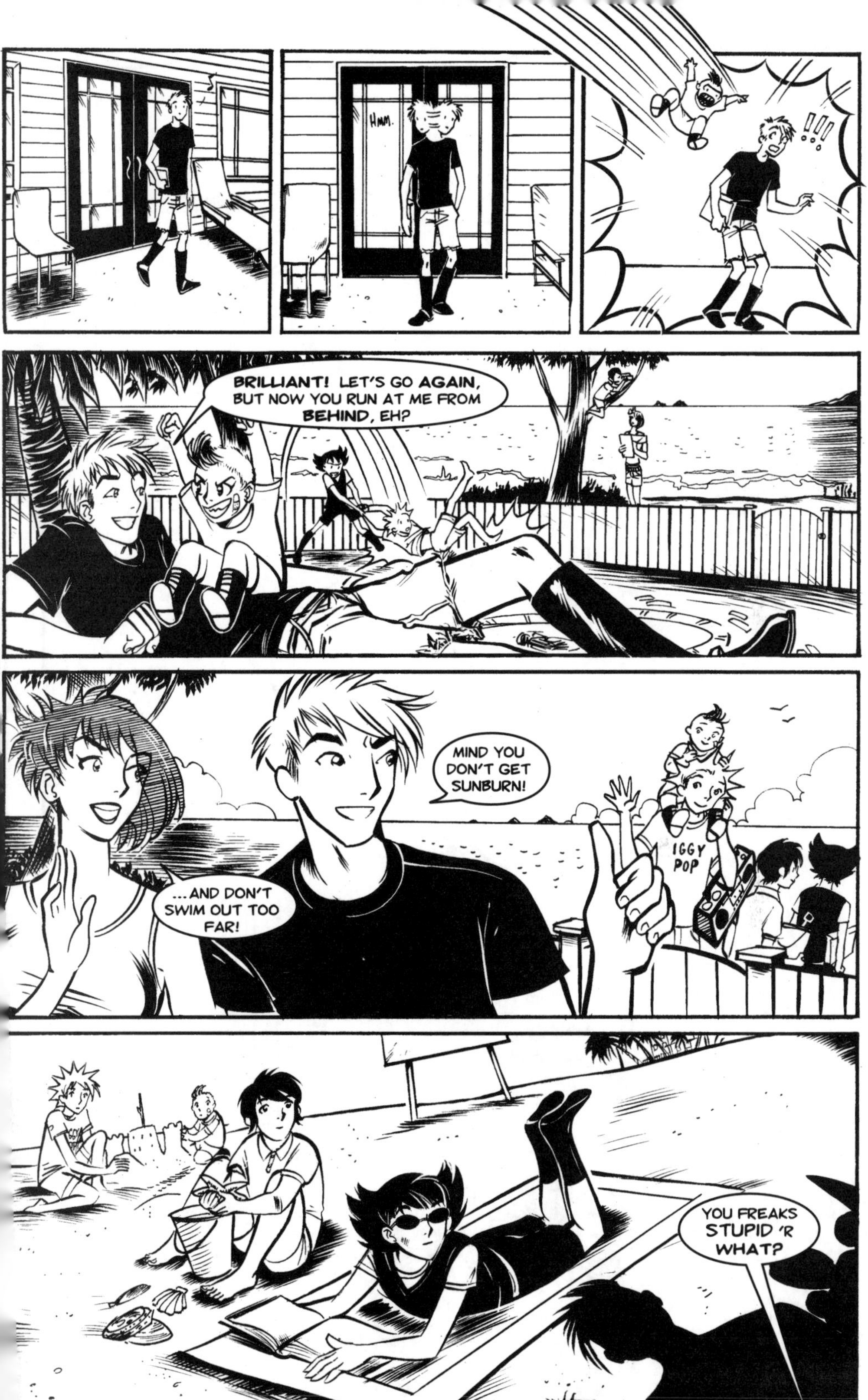
HMM.
!!!
BRILLIANT! LET'S GO AGAIN, BUT NOW YOU RUN AT ME FROM BEHIND, EH?
MIND YOU DON'T GET SUNBURN!
...AND DON'T SWIM OUT TOO FAR!
IGGY POP
YOU FREAKS STUPID 'R WHAT?

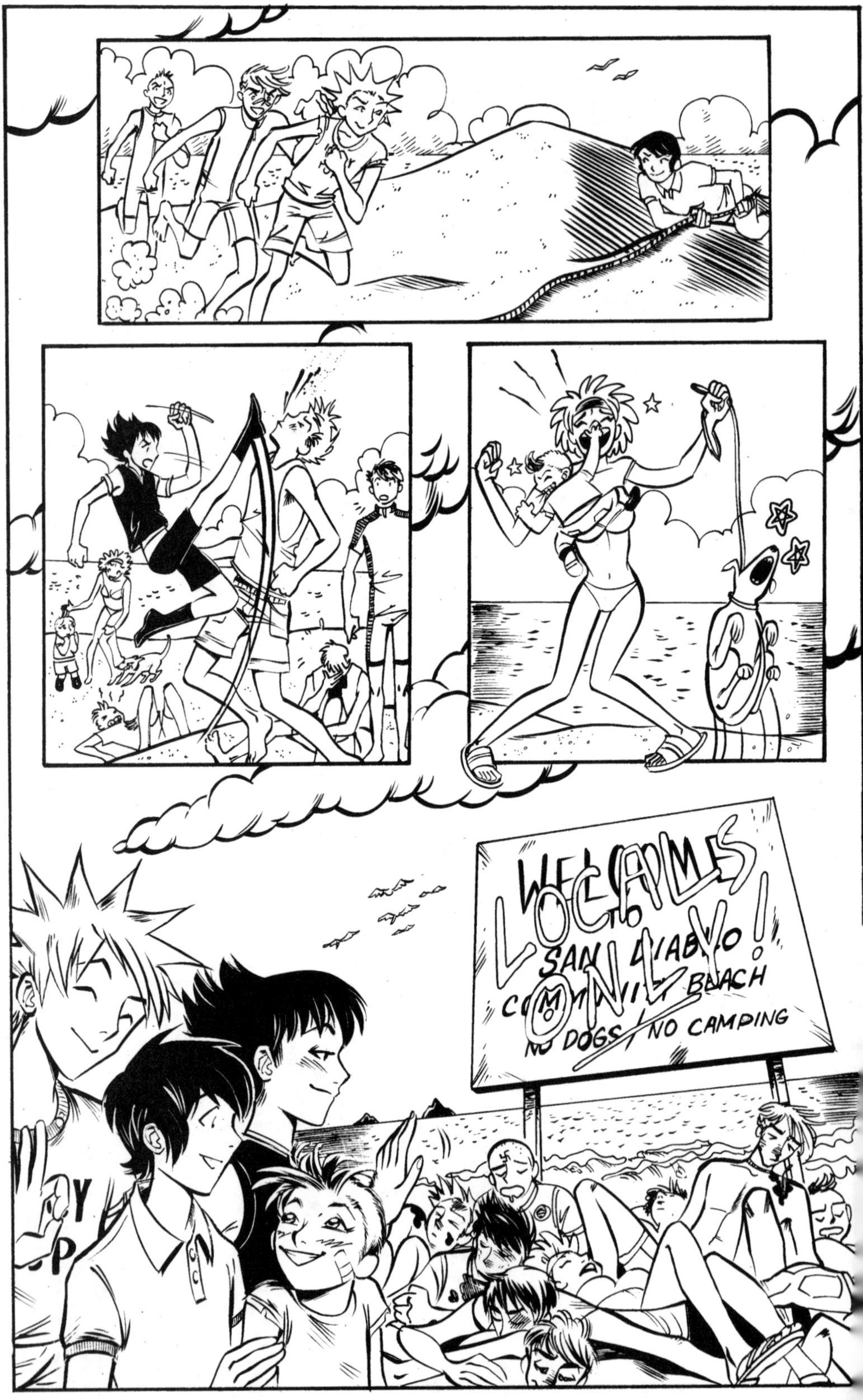
WELCOME TO SAN DIABLO COMMUNITY BEACH
NO DOGS / NO CAMPING
LOCALS ONLY!

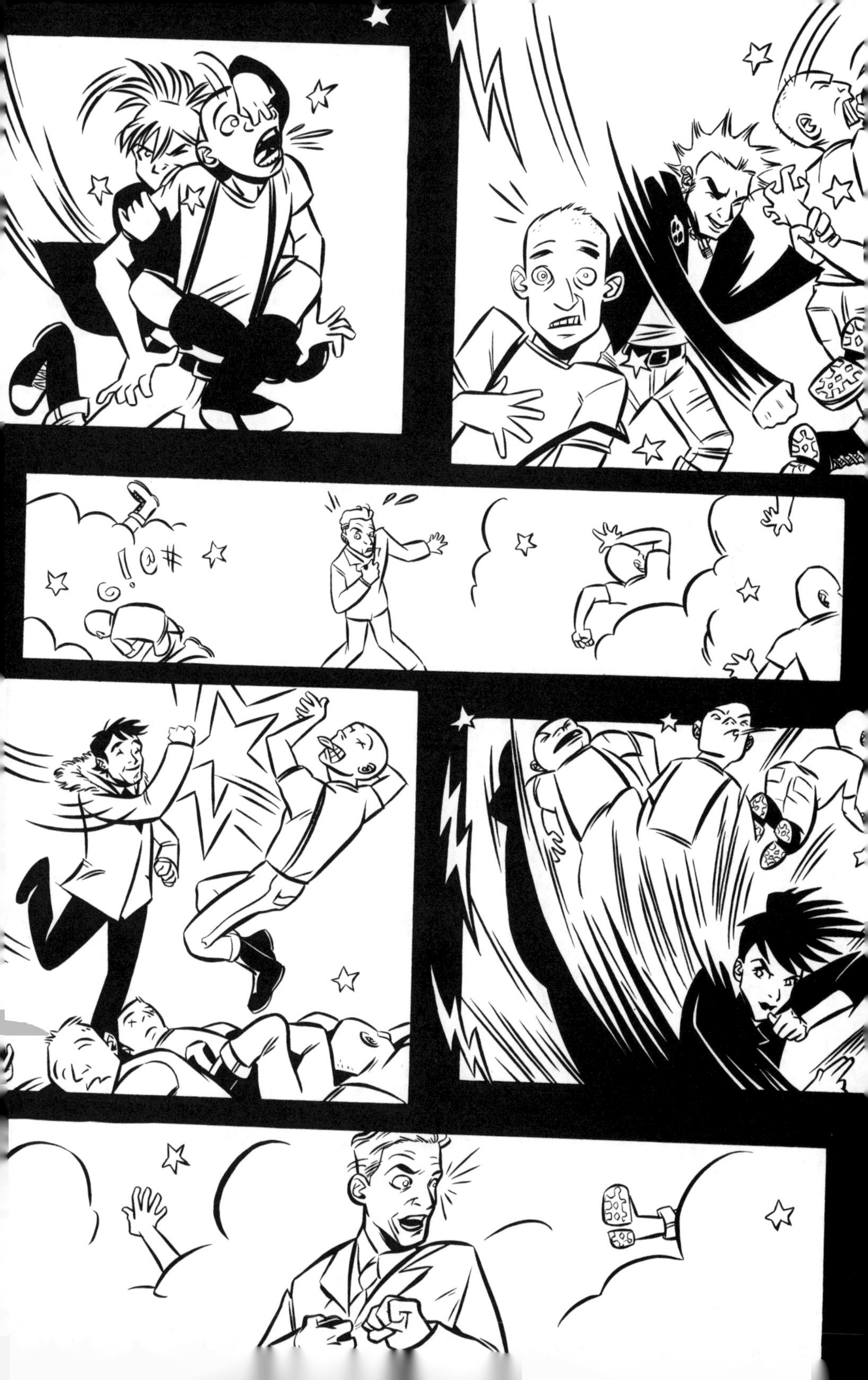

!@#

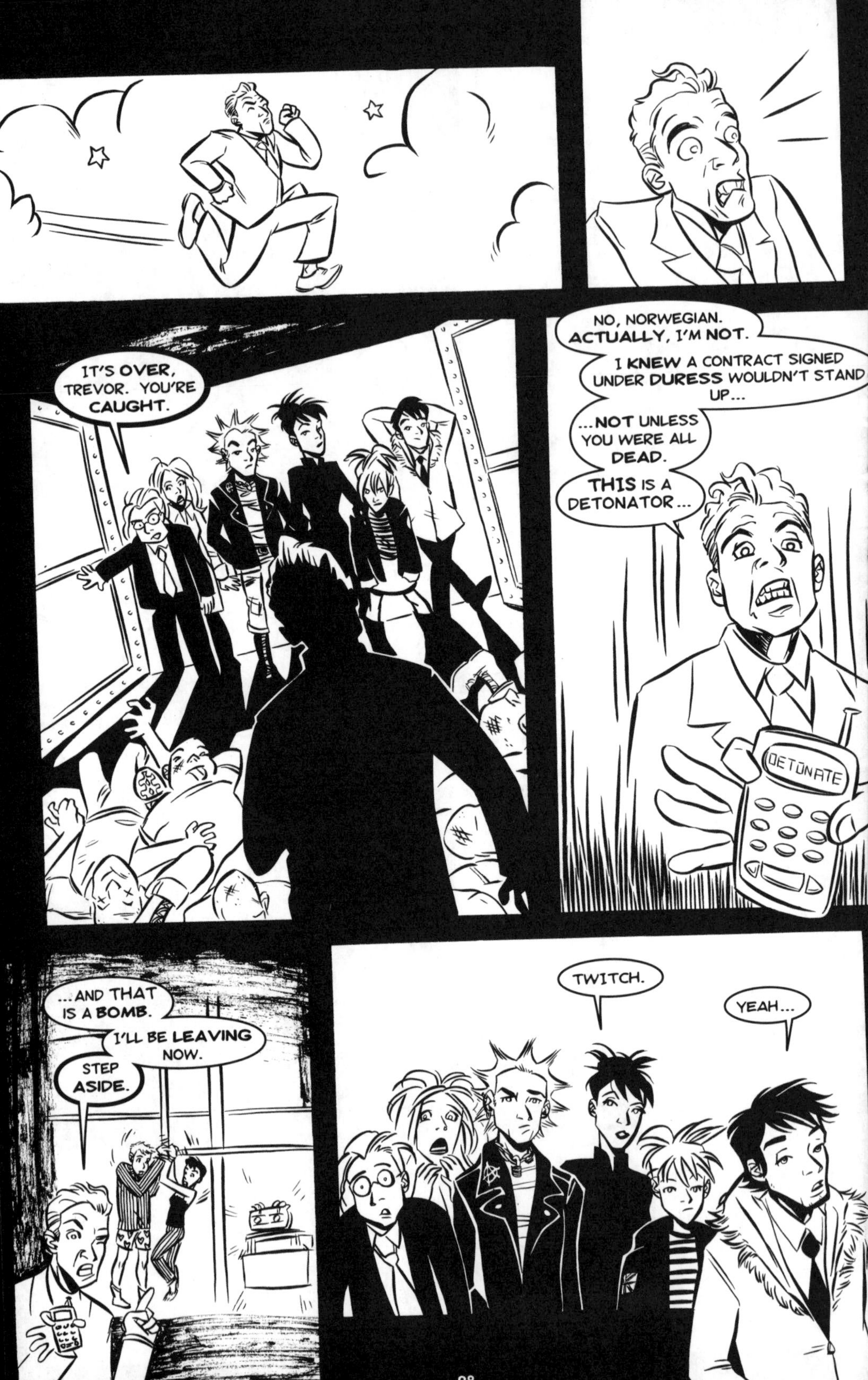
IT'S OVER, TREVOR. YOU'RE CAUGHT.
NO, NORWEGIAN. ACTUALLY, I'M NOT.
I KNEW A CONTRACT SIGNED UNDER DURESS WOULDN'T STAND UP...
...NOT UNLESS YOU WERE ALL DEAD.
THIS IS A DETONATOR...
DETONATE
...AND THAT IS A BOMB.
I'LL BE LEAVING NOW.
STEP ASIDE.
TWITCH.
YEAH...

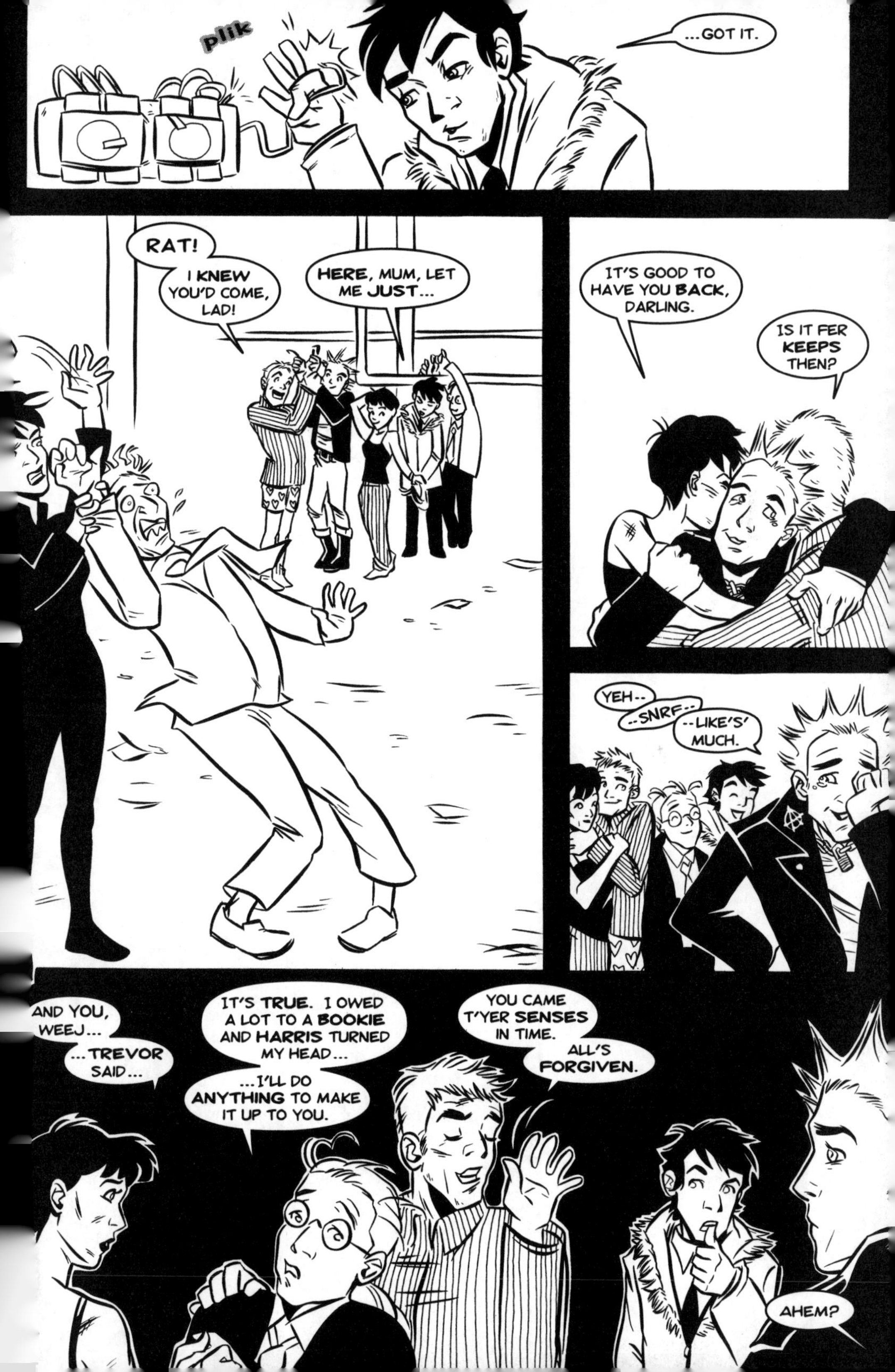
plik
...GOT IT.
RAT!
I KNEW YOU'D COME, LAD!
HERE, MUM, LET ME JUST...
IT'S GOOD TO HAVE YOU BACK, DARLING.
IS IT FER KEEPS THEN?
YEH--
--SNRF--
--LIKE'S' MUCH.
AND YOU, WEEJ...
...TREVOR SAID...
IT'S TRUE. I OWED A LOT TO A BOOKIE AND HARRIS TURNED MY HEAD...
...I'LL DO ANYTHING TO MAKE IT UP TO YOU.
YOU CAME T'YER SENSES IN TIME.
ALL'S FORGIVEN.
AHEM?

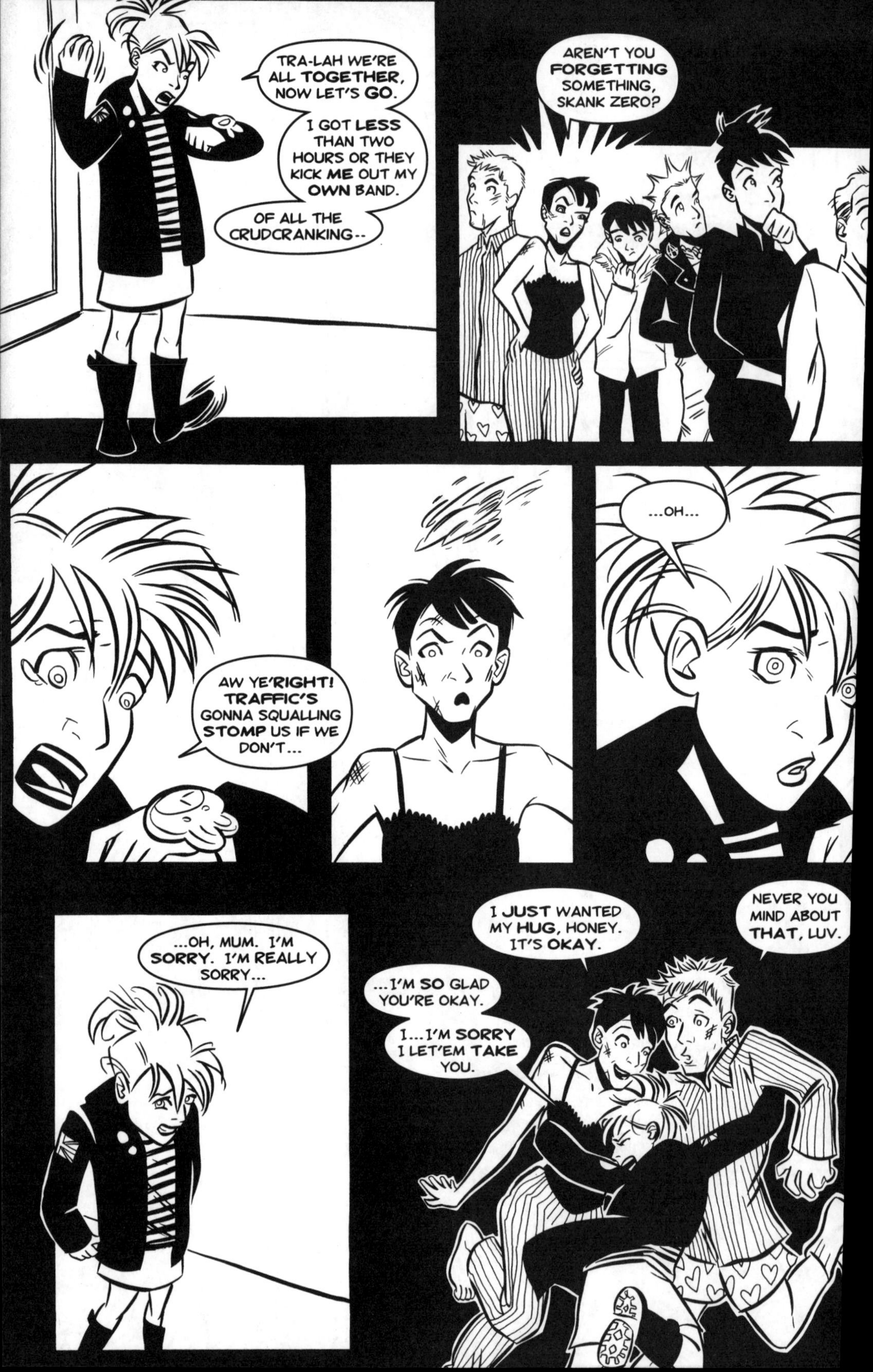
TRA-LAH WE'RE ALL TOGETHER, NOW LET'S GO.
I GOT LESS THAN TWO HOURS OR THEY KICK ME OUT MY OWN BAND.
OF ALL THE CRUDCRANKING--
AREN'T YOU FORGETTING SOMETHING, SKANK ZERO?
AW YE'RIGHT! TRAFFIC'S GONNA SQUALLING STOMP US IF WE DON'T...
...OH...
...OH, MUM. I'M SORRY. I'M REALLY SORRY...
I JUST WANTED MY HUG, HONEY. IT'S OKAY.
NEVER YOU MIND ABOUT THAT, LUV.
...I'M SO GLAD YOU'RE OKAY.
I...I'M SORRY I LET'EM TAKE YOU.

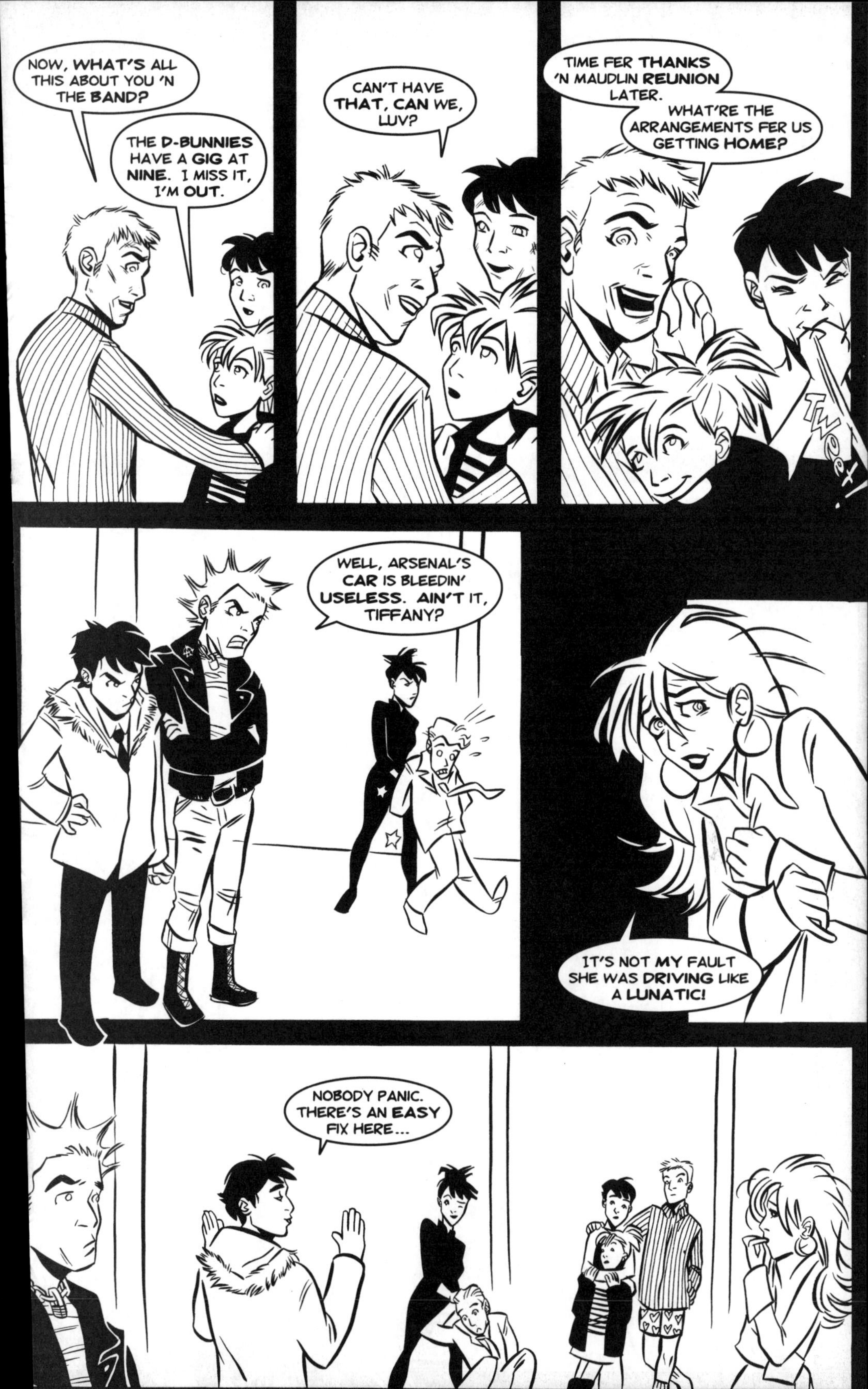
NOW, WHAT'S ALL THIS ABOUT YOU 'N THE BAND?
THE D-BUNNIES HAVE A GIG AT NINE. I MISS IT, I'M OUT.
CAN'T HAVE THAT, CAN WE, LUV?
TIME FER THANKS 'N MAUDLIN REUNION LATER.
WHAT'RE THE ARRANGEMENTS FER US GETTING HOME?
TWEET
WELL, ARSENAL'S CAR IS BLEEDIN' USELESS. AIN'T IT, TIFFANY?
IT'S NOT MY FAULT SHE WAS DRIVING LIKE A LUNATIC!
NOBODY PANIC. THERE'S AN EASY FIX HERE...

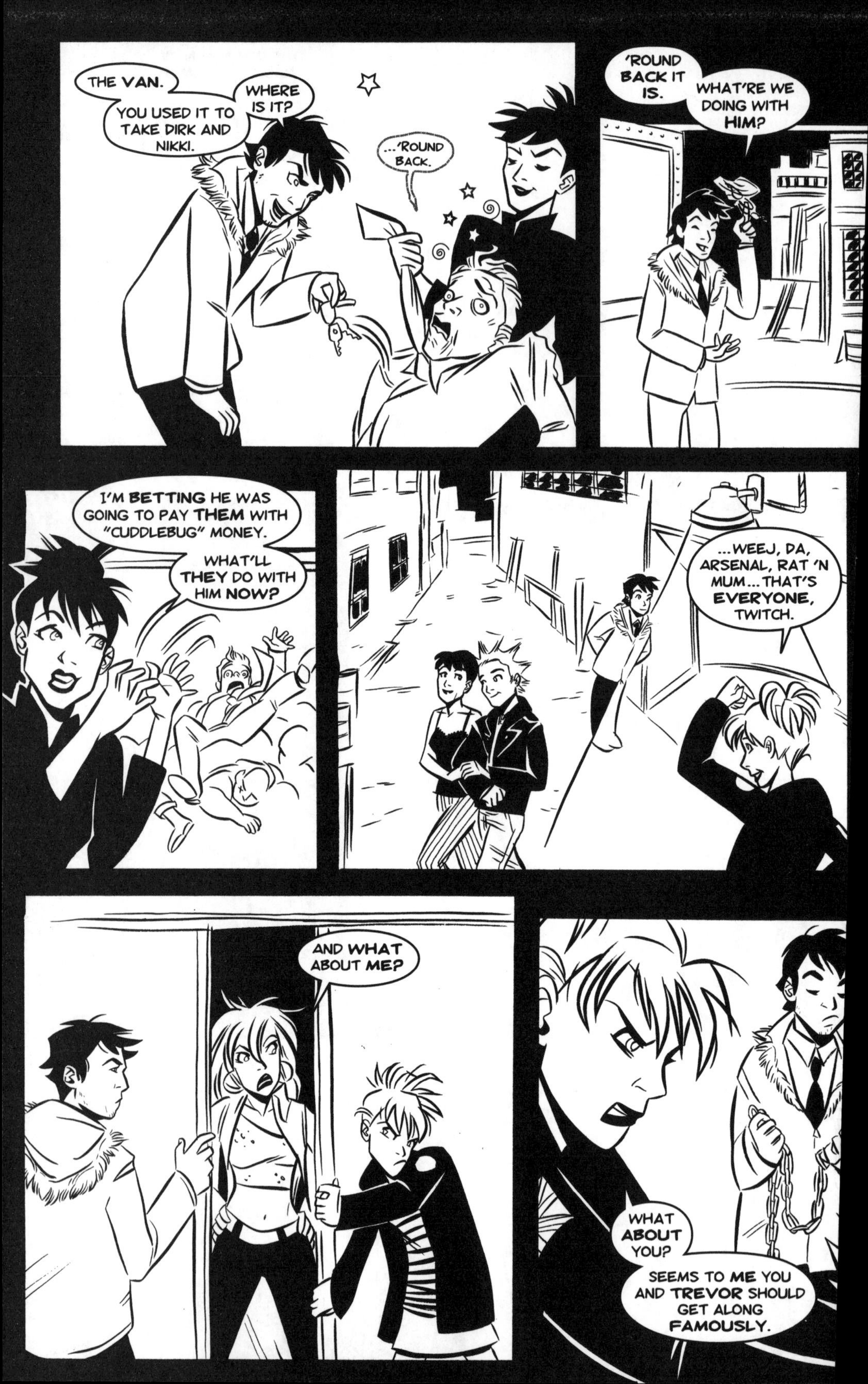
THE VAN.
YOU USED IT TO TAKE DIRK AND NIKKI.
WHERE IS IT?
...'ROUND BACK.
'ROUND BACK IT IS.
WHAT'RE WE DOING WITH HIM?
I'M BETTING HE WAS GOING TO PAY THEM WITH "CUDDLEBUG" MONEY.
WHAT'LL THEY DO WITH HIM NOW?
...WEEJ, DA, ARSENAL, RAT 'N MUM...THAT'S EVERYONE, TWITCH.
AND WHAT ABOUT ME?
WHAT ABOUT YOU?
SEEMS TO ME YOU AND TREVOR SHOULD GET ALONG FAMOUSLY.

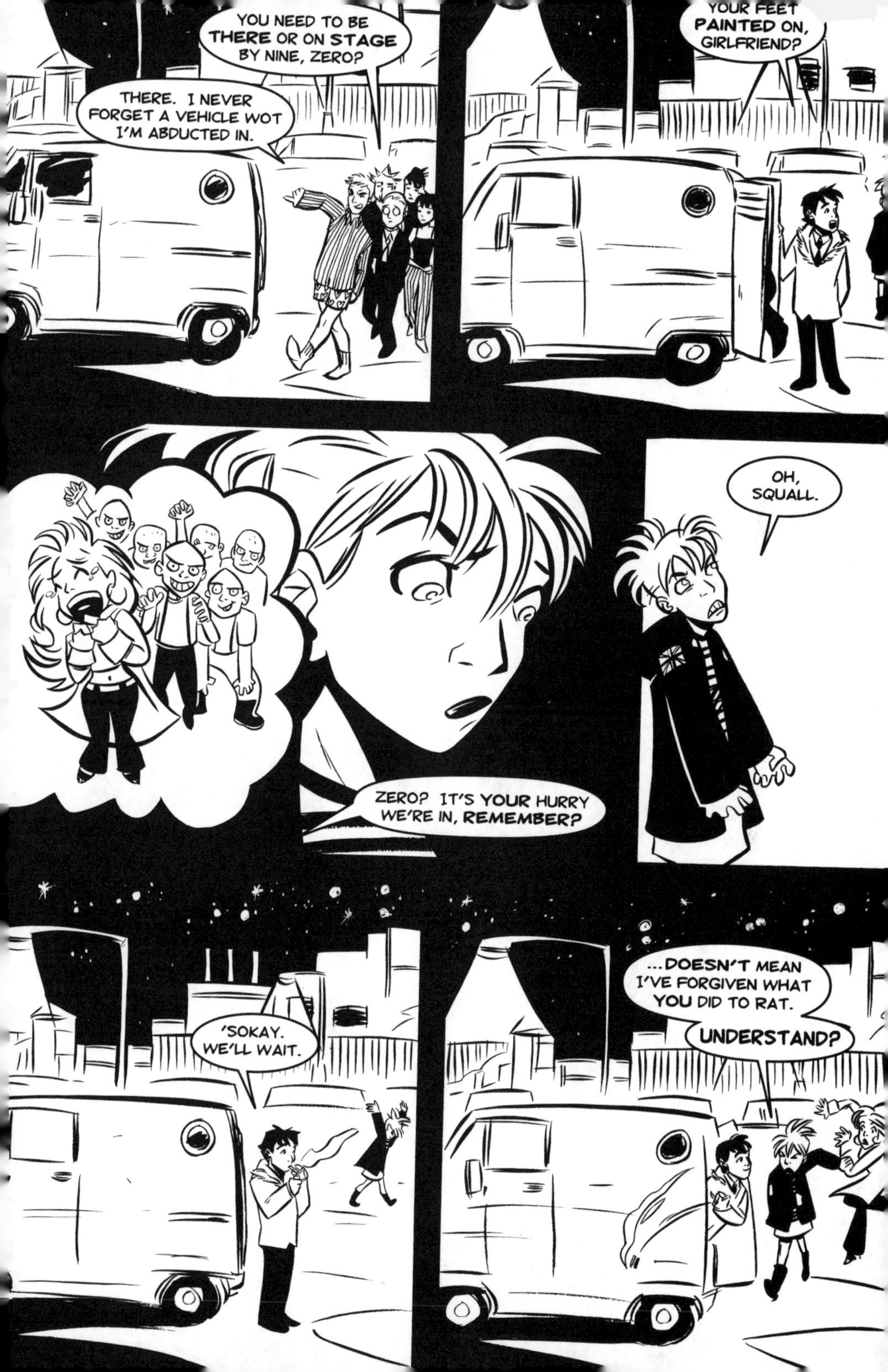
YOU NEED TO BE THERE OR ON STAGE BY NINE, ZERO?
THERE. I NEVER FORGET A VEHICLE WOT I'M ABDUCTED IN.
YOUR FEET PAINTED ON, GIRLFRIEND?
ZERO? IT'S YOUR HURRY WE'RE IN, REMEMBER?
OH, SQUALL.
'SOKAY. WE'LL WAIT.
...DOESN'T MEAN I'VE FORGIVEN WHAT YOU DID TO RAT.
UNDERSTAND?

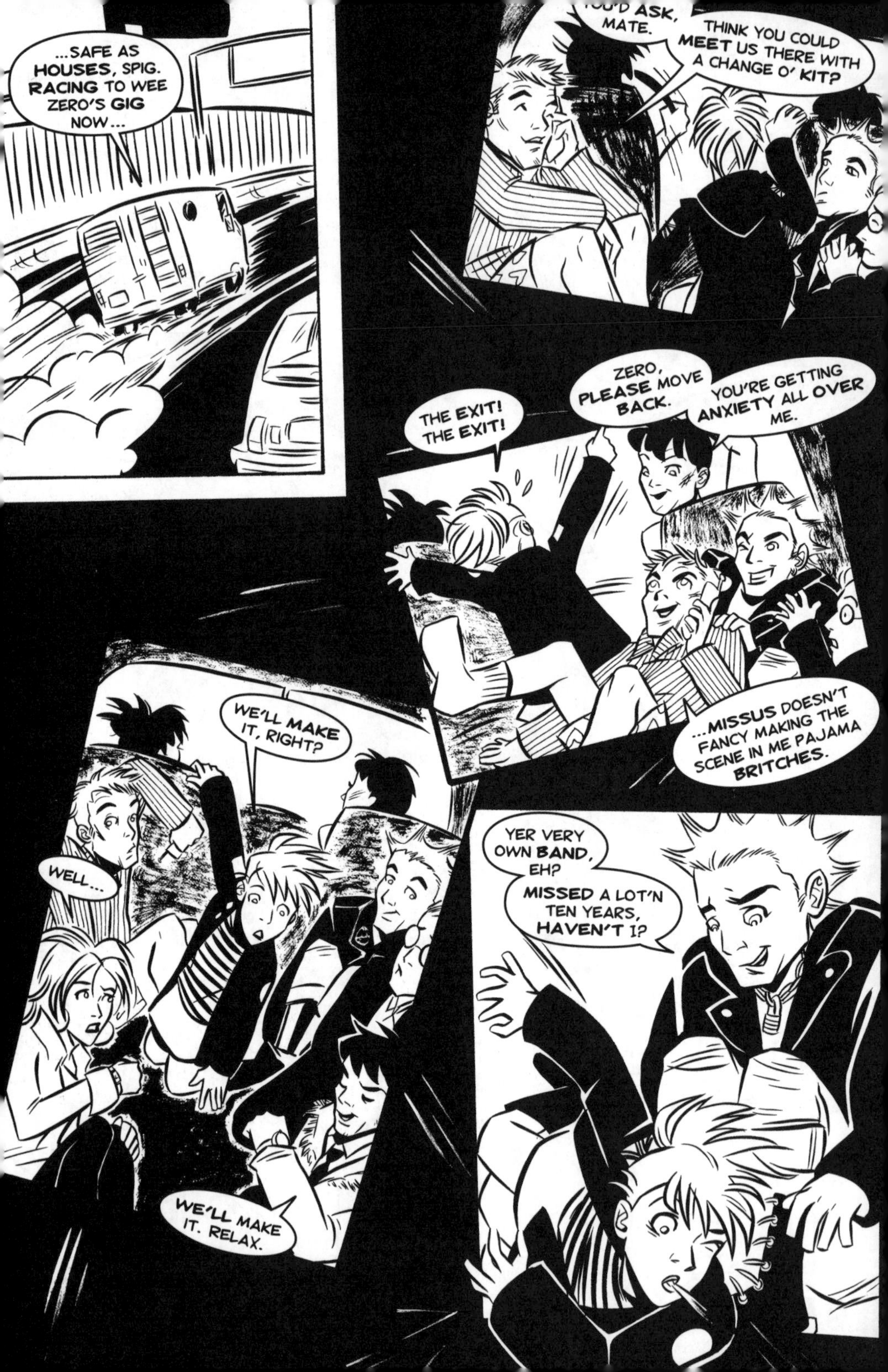
...SAFE AS HOUSES, SPIG. RACING TO WEE ZERO'S GIG NOW...
OU'D ASK, MATE.
THINK YOU COULD MEET US THERE WITH A CHANGE O' KIT?
THE EXIT! THE EXIT!
ZERO, PLEASE MOVE BACK.
YOU'RE GETTING ANXIETY ALL OVER ME.
...MISSUS DOESN'T FANCY MAKING THE SCENE IN ME PAJAMA BRITCHES.
WE'LL MAKE IT, RIGHT?
WELL...
WE'LL MAKE IT. RELAX.
YER VERY OWN BAND, EH?
MISSED A LOT'N TEN YEARS, HAVEN'T I?

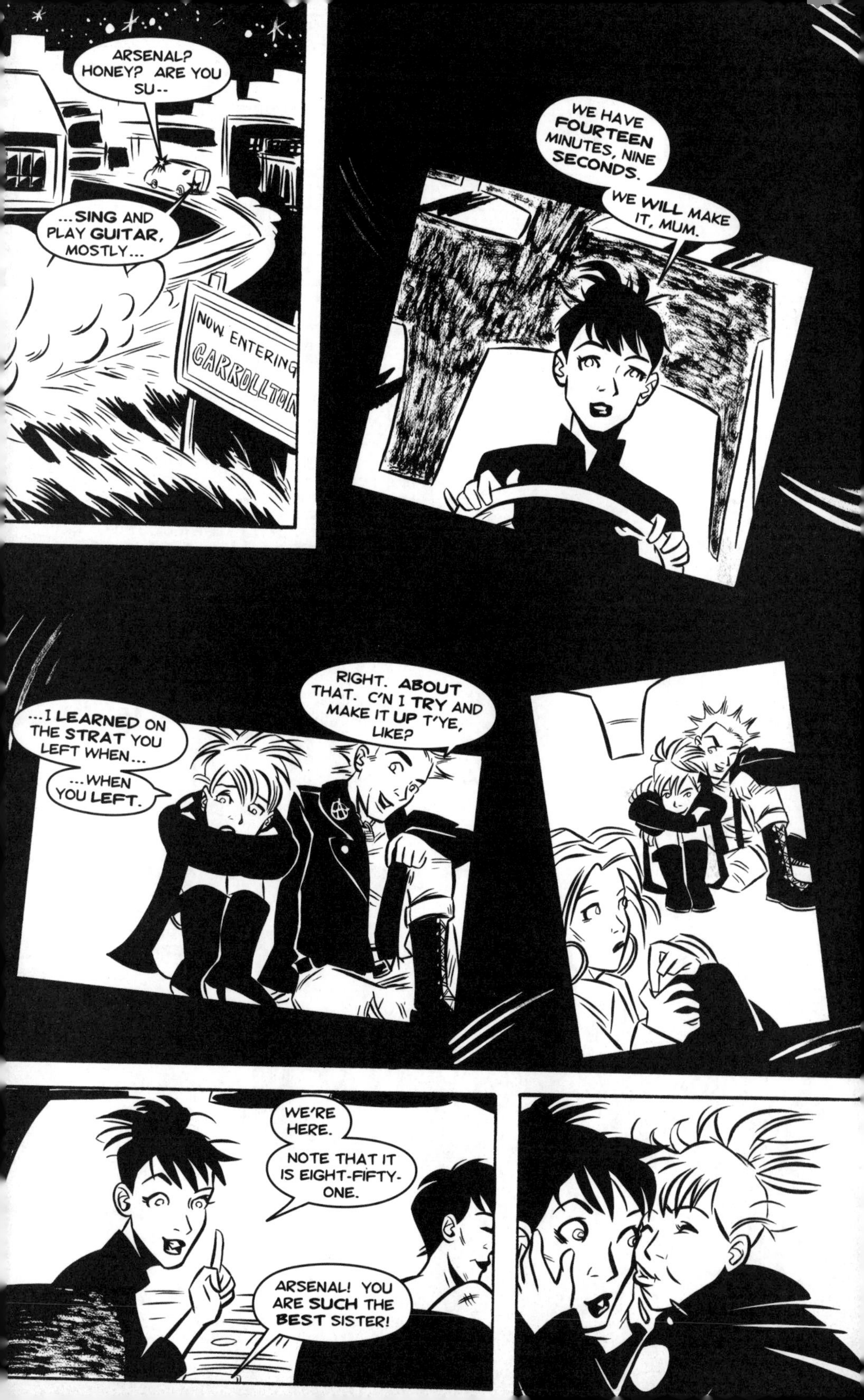
ARSENAL? HONEY? ARE YOU SU--
...SING AND PLAY GUITAR, MOSTLY...
NOW ENTERING CARROLLTON
WE HAVE FOURTEEN MINUTES, NINE SECONDS.
WE WILL MAKE IT, MUM.
...I LEARNED ON THE STRAT YOU LEFT WHEN...
...WHEN YOU LEFT.
RIGHT. ABOUT THAT. C'N I TRY AND MAKE IT UP T'YE, LIKE?
WE'RE HERE.
NOTE THAT IT IS EIGHT-FIFTY-ONE.
ARSENAL! YOU ARE SUCH THE BEST SISTER!

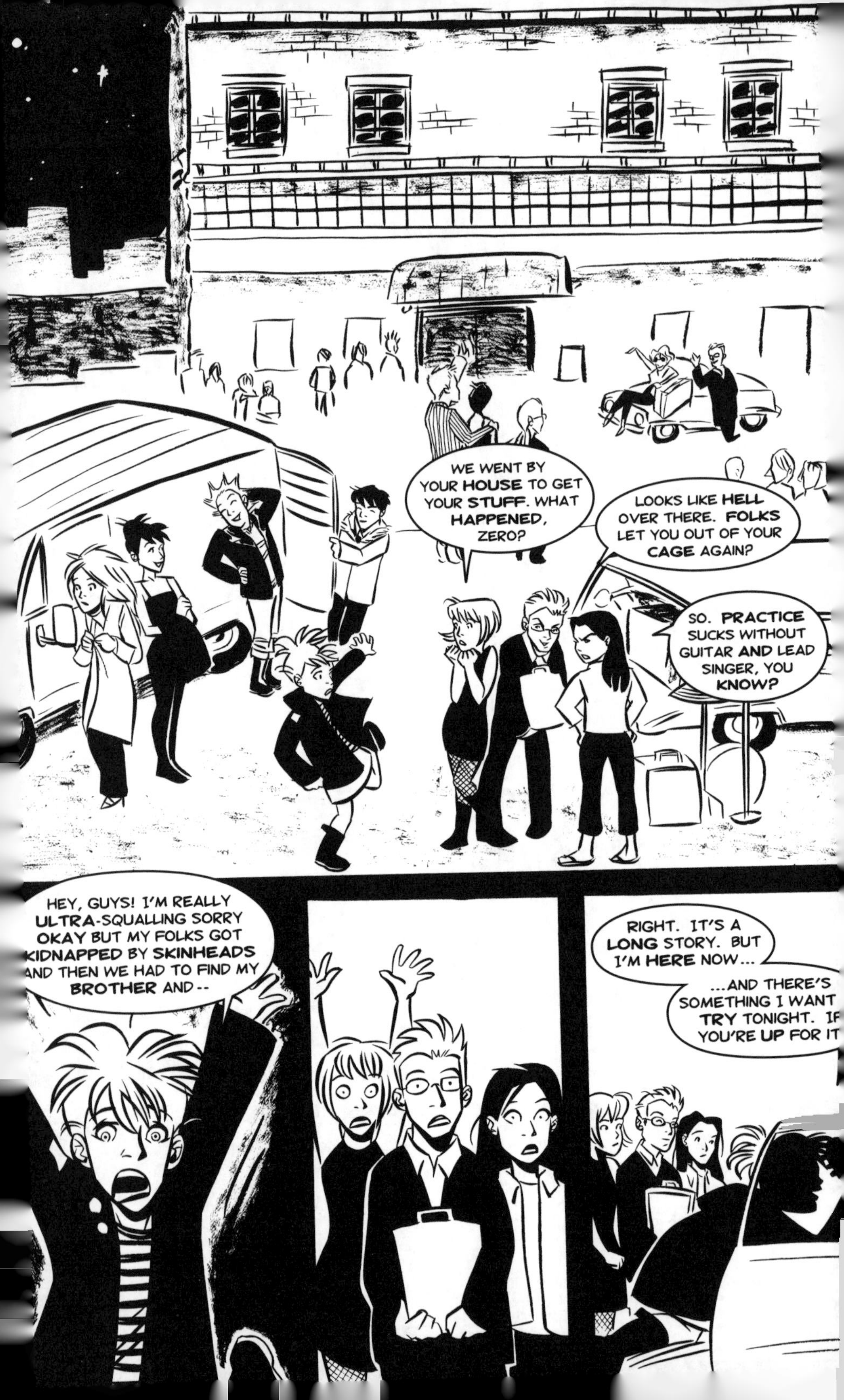

WE WENT BY YOUR HOUSE TO GET YOUR STUFF. WHAT HAPPENED, ZERO?
LOOKS LIKE HELL OVER THERE. FOLKS LET YOU OUT OF YOUR CAGE AGAIN?
SO. PRACTICE SUCKS WITHOUT GUITAR AND LEAD SINGER, YOU KNOW?
HEY, GUYS! I'M REALLY ULTRA-SQUALLING SORRY OKAY BUT MY FOLKS GOT KIDNAPPED BY SKINHEADS AND THEN WE HAD TO FIND MY BROTHER AND--
RIGHT. IT'S A LONG STORY. BUT I'M HERE NOW...
...AND THERE'S SOMETHING I WANT TRY TONIGHT. IF YOU'RE UP FOR IT

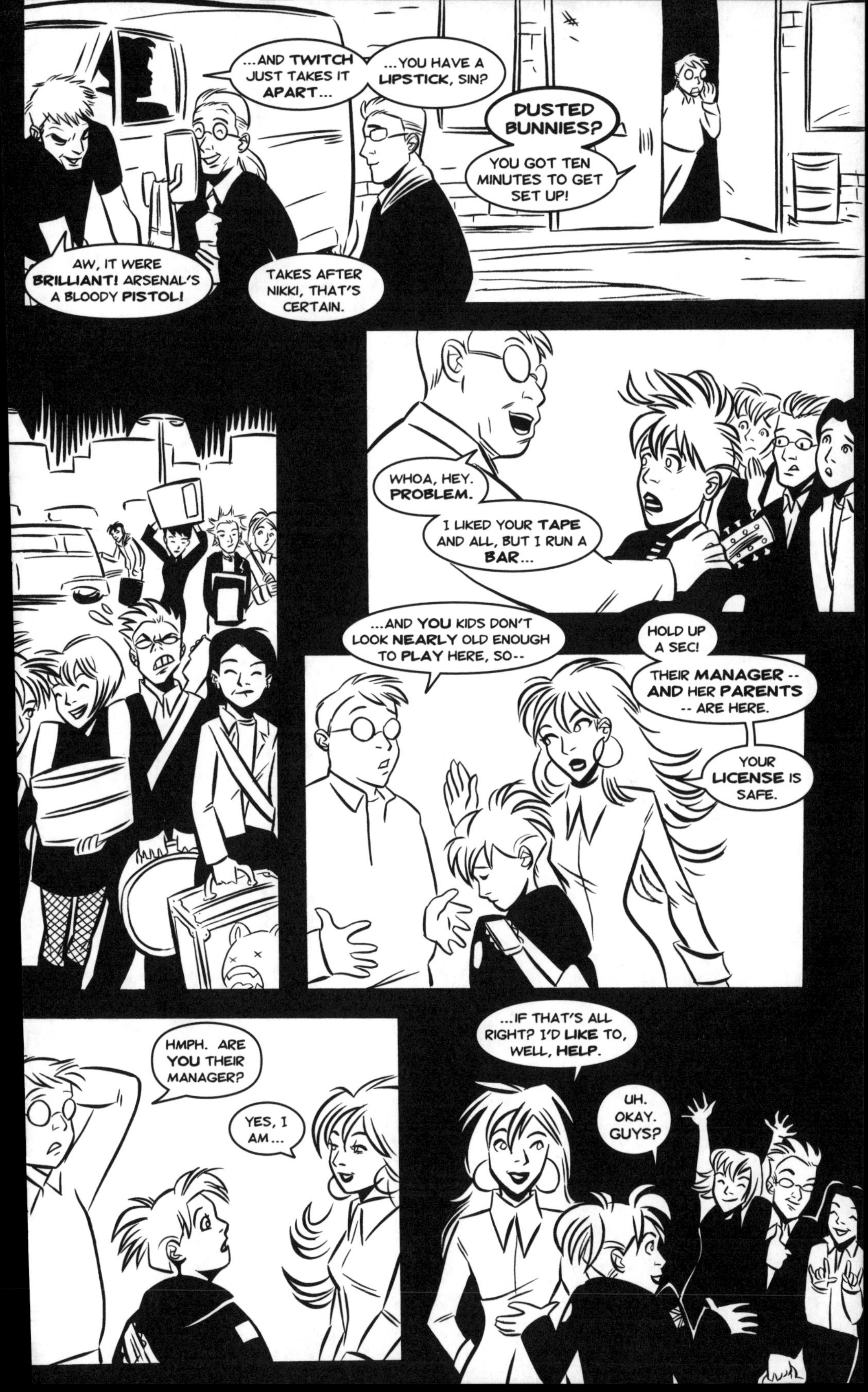
...AND TWITCH JUST TAKES IT APART...
...YOU HAVE A LIPSTICK, SIN?
DUSTED BUNNIES?
YOU GOT TEN MINUTES TO GET SET UP!
AW, IT WERE BRILLIANT! ARSENAL'S A BLOODY PISTOL!
TAKES AFTER NIKKI, THAT'S CERTAIN.
WHOA, HEY. PROBLEM.
I LIKED YOUR TAPE AND ALL, BUT I RUN A BAR...
...AND YOU KIDS DON'T LOOK NEARLY OLD ENOUGH TO PLAY HERE, SO--
HOLD UP A SEC!
THEIR MANAGER -- AND HER PARENTS -- ARE HERE.
YOUR LICENSE IS SAFE.
HMPH. ARE YOU THEIR MANAGER?
YES, I AM...
...IF THAT'S ALL RIGHT? I'D LIKE TO, WELL, HELP.
UH. OKAY. GUYS?

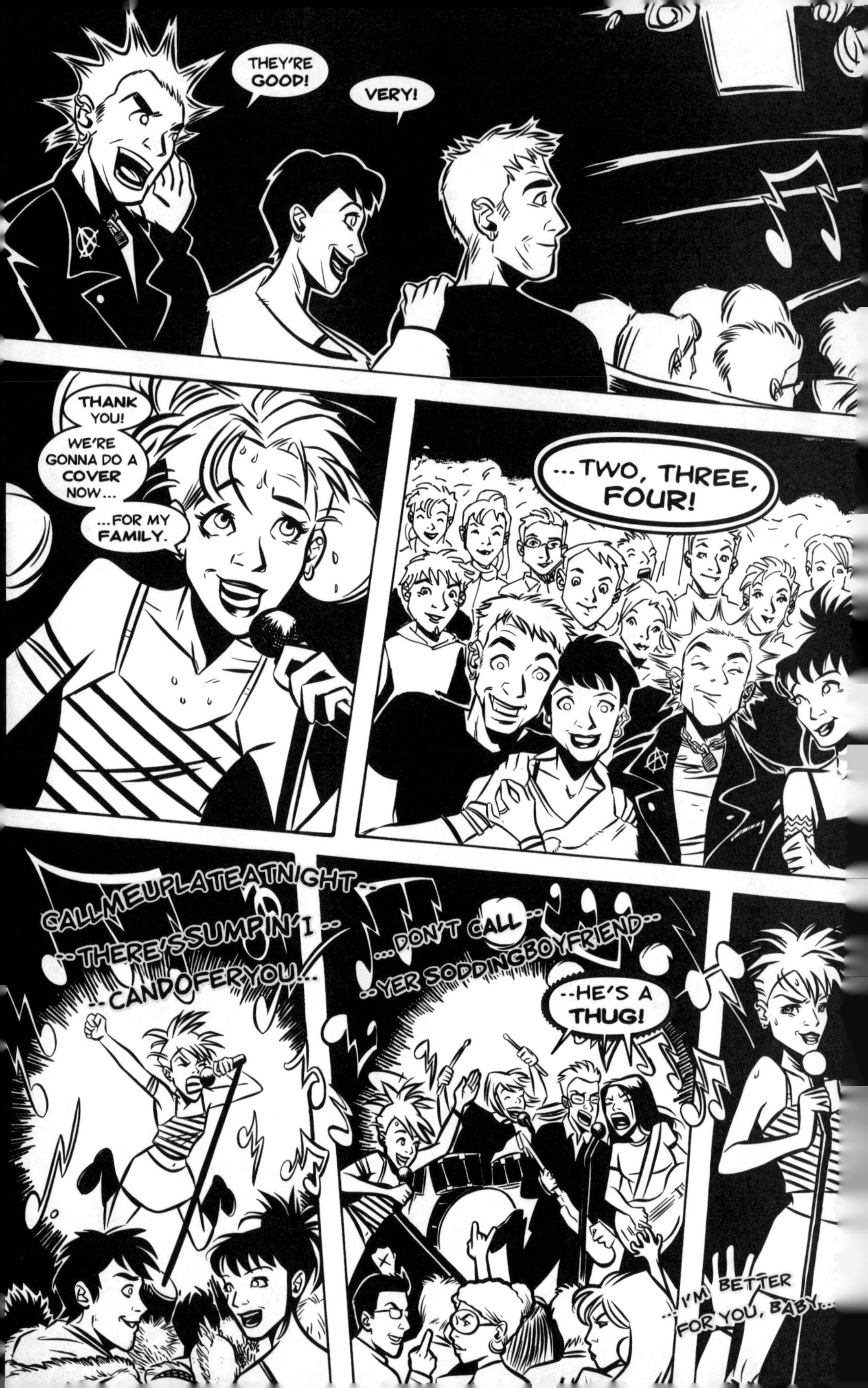
THEY'RE GOOD!
VERY!
THANK YOU!
WE'RE GONNA DO A COVER NOW...
...FOR MY FAMILY.
...TWO, THREE, FOUR!
CALLMEUPLATEATNIGHT--
--THERE'SSUMPIN'I--
--CANDOFERYOU...
...DON'T CALL--
--YER SODDINGBOYFRIEND--
--HE'S A THUG!
--I'M BETTER FOR YOU, BABY...

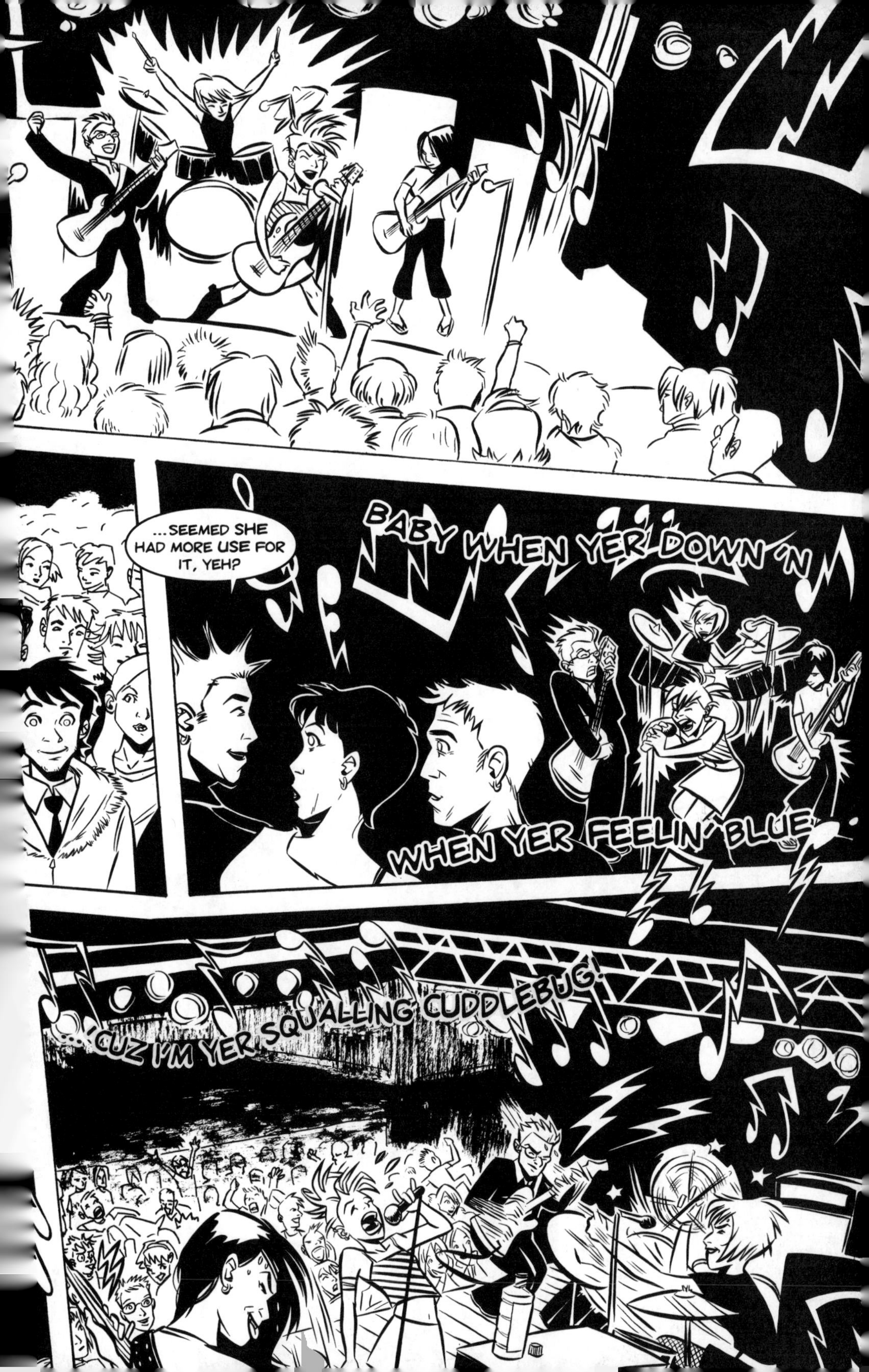
...SEEMED SHE HAD MORE USE FOR IT, YEH?
BABY WHEN YER DOWN 'N
WHEN YER FEELIN' BLUE
...CUZ I'M YER SQUALLING CUDDLEBUG!

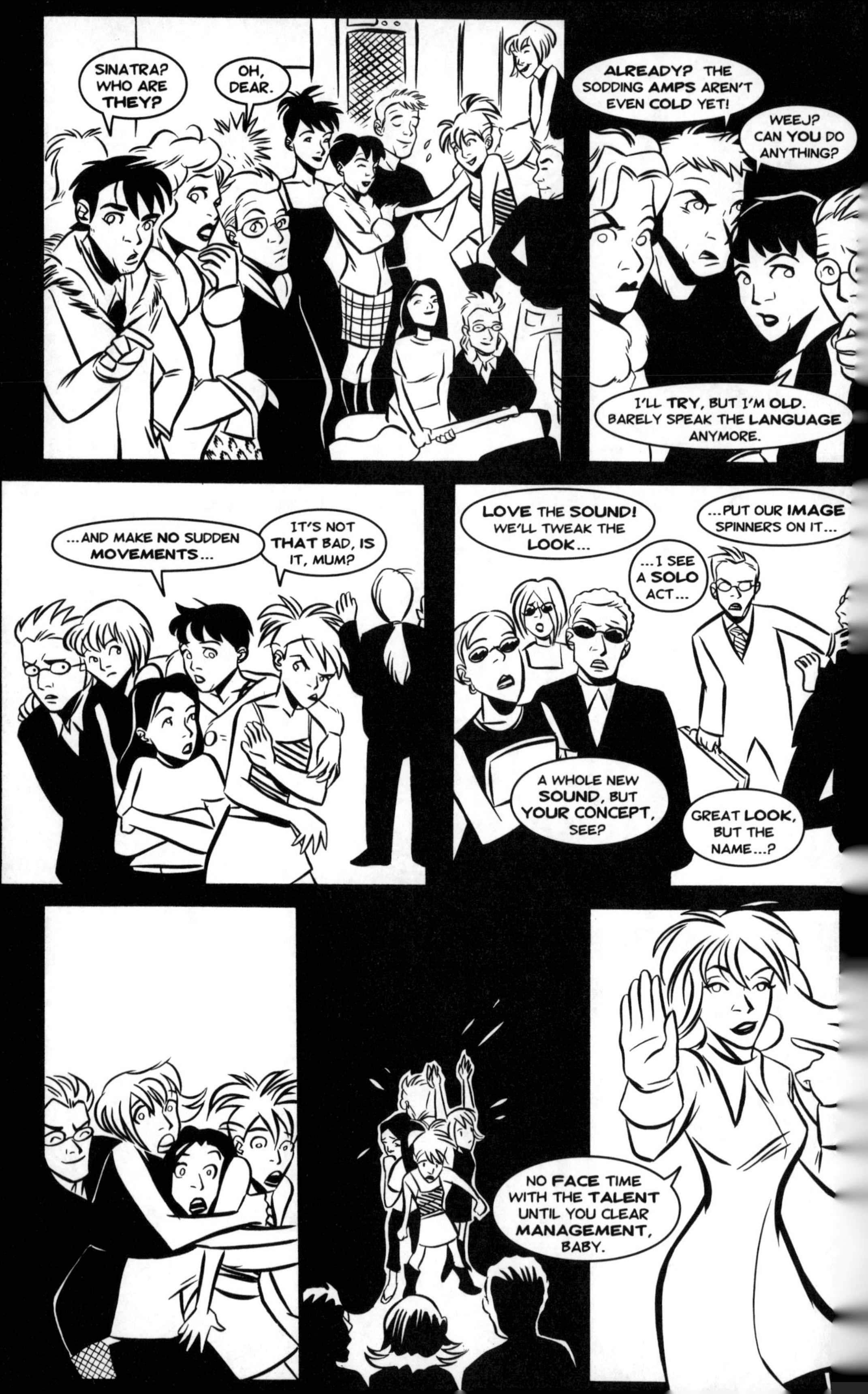
SINATRA? WHO ARE THEY?
OH, DEAR.
ALREADY? THE SODDING AMPS AREN'T EVEN COLD YET!
WEEJ? CAN YOU DO ANYTHING?
I'LL TRY, BUT I'M OLD. BARELY SPEAK THE LANGUAGE ANYMORE.
...AND MAKE NO SUDDEN MOVEMENTS...
IT'S NOT THAT BAD, IS IT, MUM?
LOVE THE SOUND! WE'LL TWEAK THE LOOK...
...I SEE A SOLO ACT...
...PUT OUR IMAGE SPINNERS ON IT...
A WHOLE NEW SOUND, BUT YOUR CONCEPT, SEE?
GREAT LOOK, BUT THE NAME...?
NO FACE TIME WITH THE TALENT UNTIL YOU CLEAR MANAGEMENT, BABY.

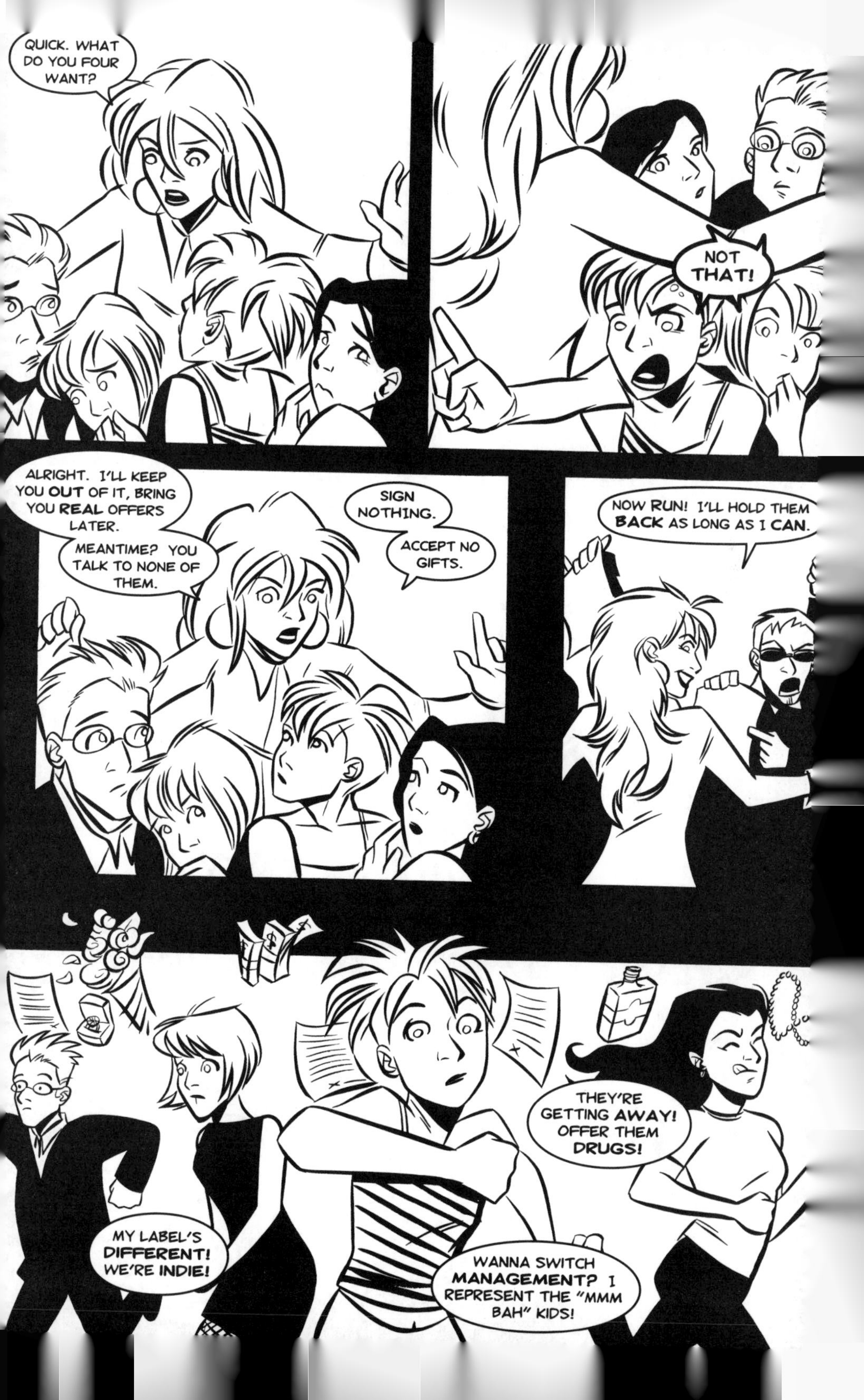
QUICK. WHAT DO YOU FOUR WANT?
NOT THAT!
ALRIGHT. I'LL KEEP YOU OUT OF IT, BRING YOU REAL OFFERS LATER.
MEANTIME? YOU TALK TO NONE OF THEM.
SIGN NOTHING.
ACCEPT NO GIFTS.
NOW RUN! I'LL HOLD THEM BACK AS LONG AS I CAN.
THEY'RE GETTING AWAY! OFFER THEM DRUGS!
MY LABEL'S DIFFERENT! WE'RE INDIE!
WANNA SWITCH MANAGEMENT? I REPRESENT THE "MMM BAH" KIDS!

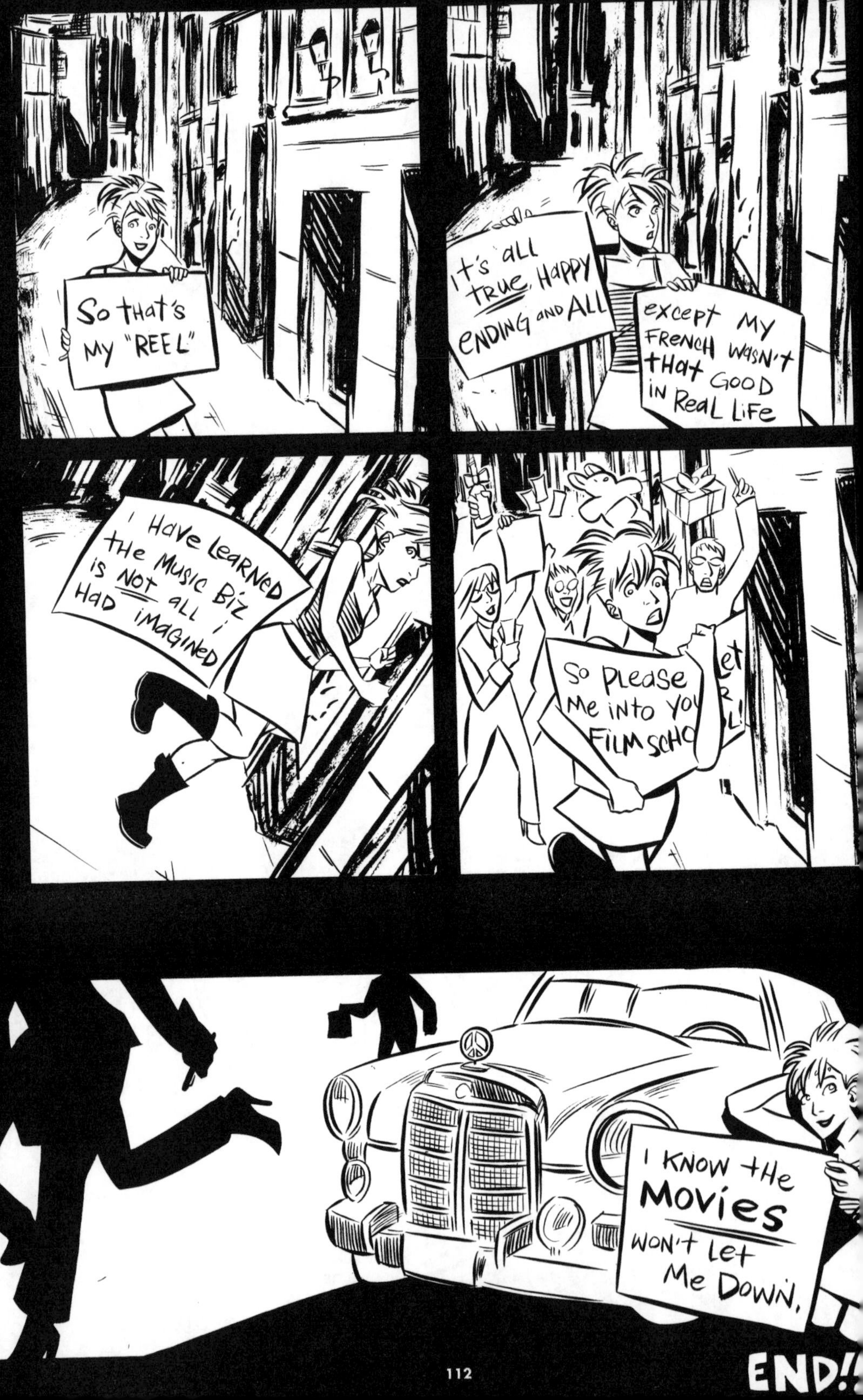
So that's my "REEL"
It's all TRUE, HAPPY ENDING AND ALL
except my FRENCH WASN'T THAT GOOD in Real Life
I Have Learned the Music Biz is NOT all I Had imagined
So Please Me into Yo FILM SCHO
let R L!
I KNOW tHe Movies won't let Me Down.
END!!

HOPELESS SAVAGES

BOOK 2: GROUND ZERO

Written by
JEN VAN METER

Art & lettering by
BRYAN LEE O'MALLEY

Chapter 3 with
CHRISTINE and KATHERINE NORRIE

Flashback art by
ANDI WATSON, CHRISTINE NORRIE, and CHYNNA CLUGSTON FLORES

Chapter break art by
TERRY DODSON

Originally edited by
JAMIE S. RICH

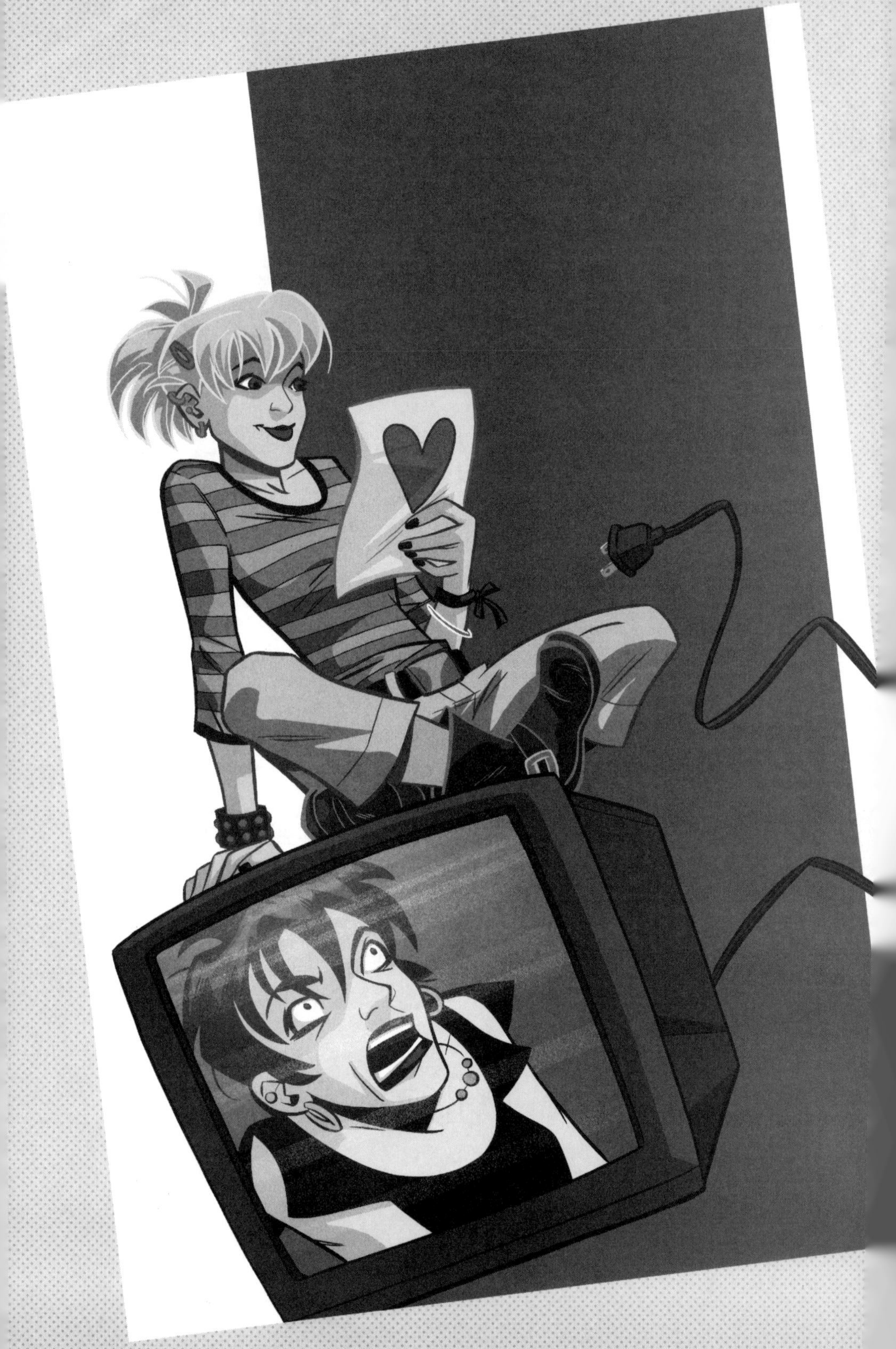

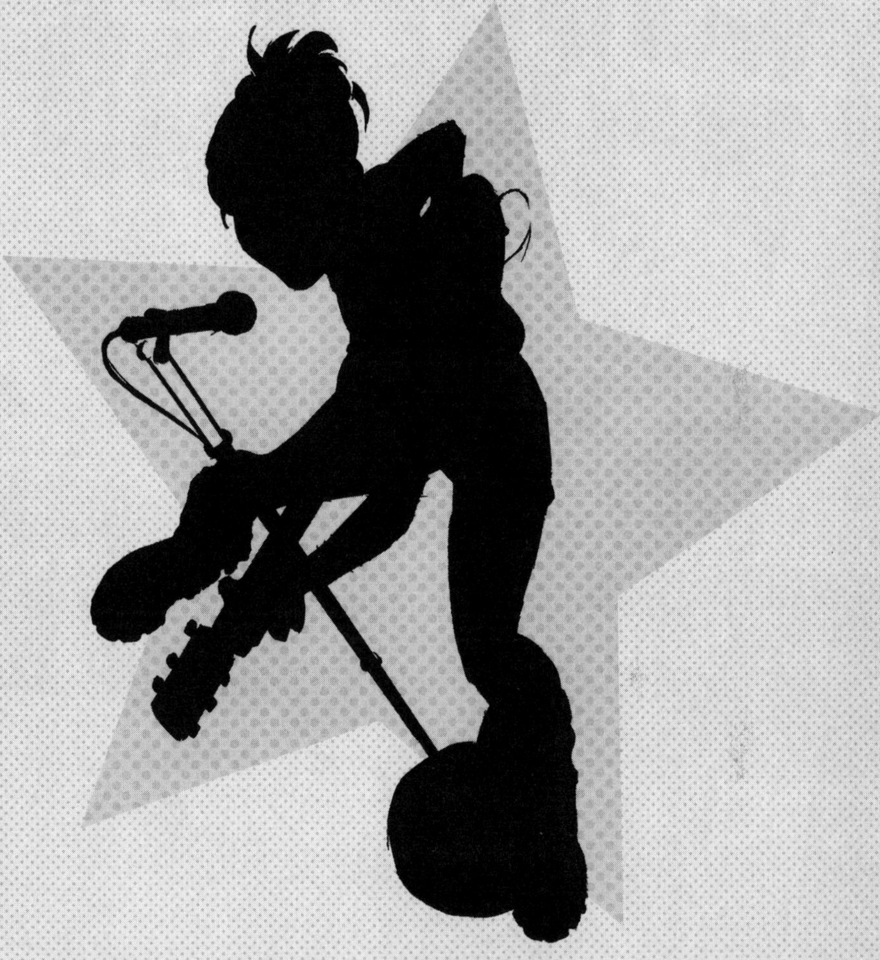

CHAPTER 1

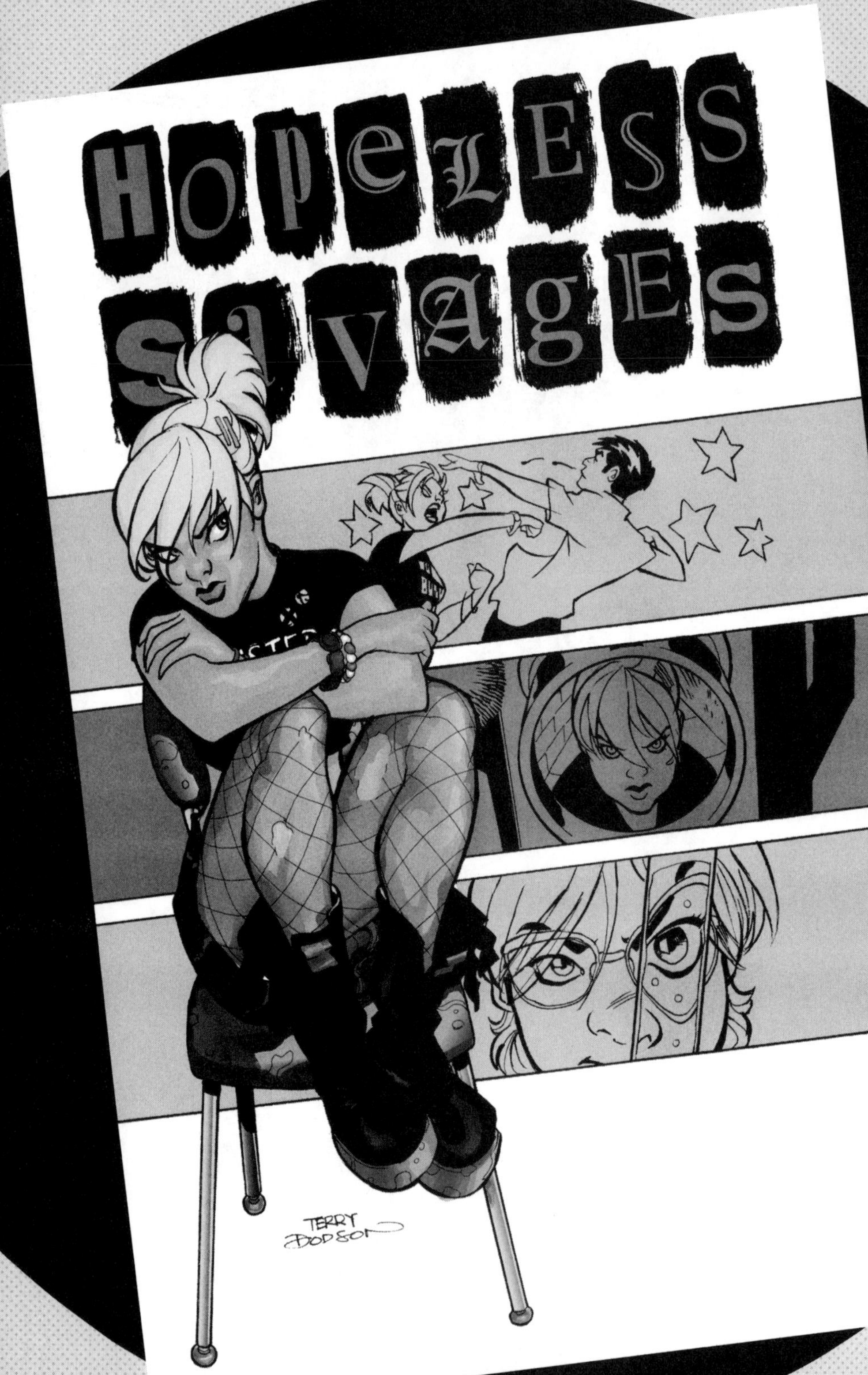
HOPELESS SAVAGES
TERRY DODSON

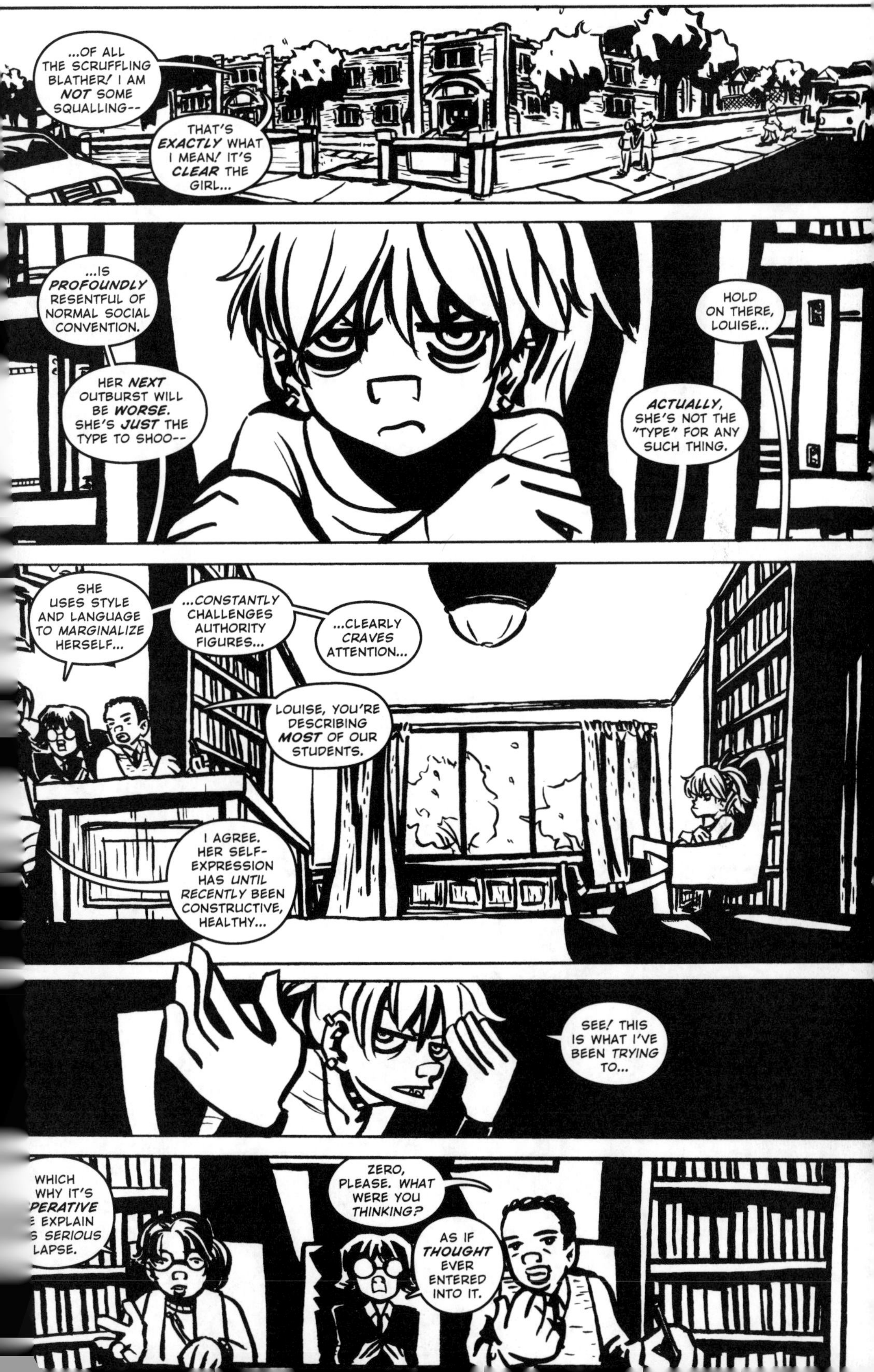
...OF ALL THE SCRUFFLING BLATHER! I AM NOT SOME SQUALLING--
THAT'S EXACTLY WHAT I MEAN! IT'S CLEAR THE GIRL...
...IS PROFOUNDLY RESENTFUL OF NORMAL SOCIAL CONVENTION.
HER NEXT OUTBURST WILL BE WORSE. SHE'S JUST THE TYPE TO SHOO--
HOLD ON THERE, LOUISE...
ACTUALLY, SHE'S NOT THE "TYPE" FOR ANY SUCH THING.
SHE USES STYLE AND LANGUAGE TO MARGINALIZE HERSELF...
...CONSTANTLY CHALLENGES AUTHORITY FIGURES...
...CLEARLY CRAVES ATTENTION...
LOUISE, YOU'RE DESCRIBING MOST OF OUR STUDENTS.
I AGREE. HER SELF-EXPRESSION HAS UNTIL RECENTLY BEEN CONSTRUCTIVE, HEALTHY...
SEE! THIS IS WHAT I'VE BEEN TRYING TO...
WHICH WHY IT'S PERATIVE E EXPLAIN S SERIOUS LAPSE.
ZERO, PLEASE. WHAT WERE YOU THINKING?
AS IF THOUGHT EVER ENTERED INTO IT.

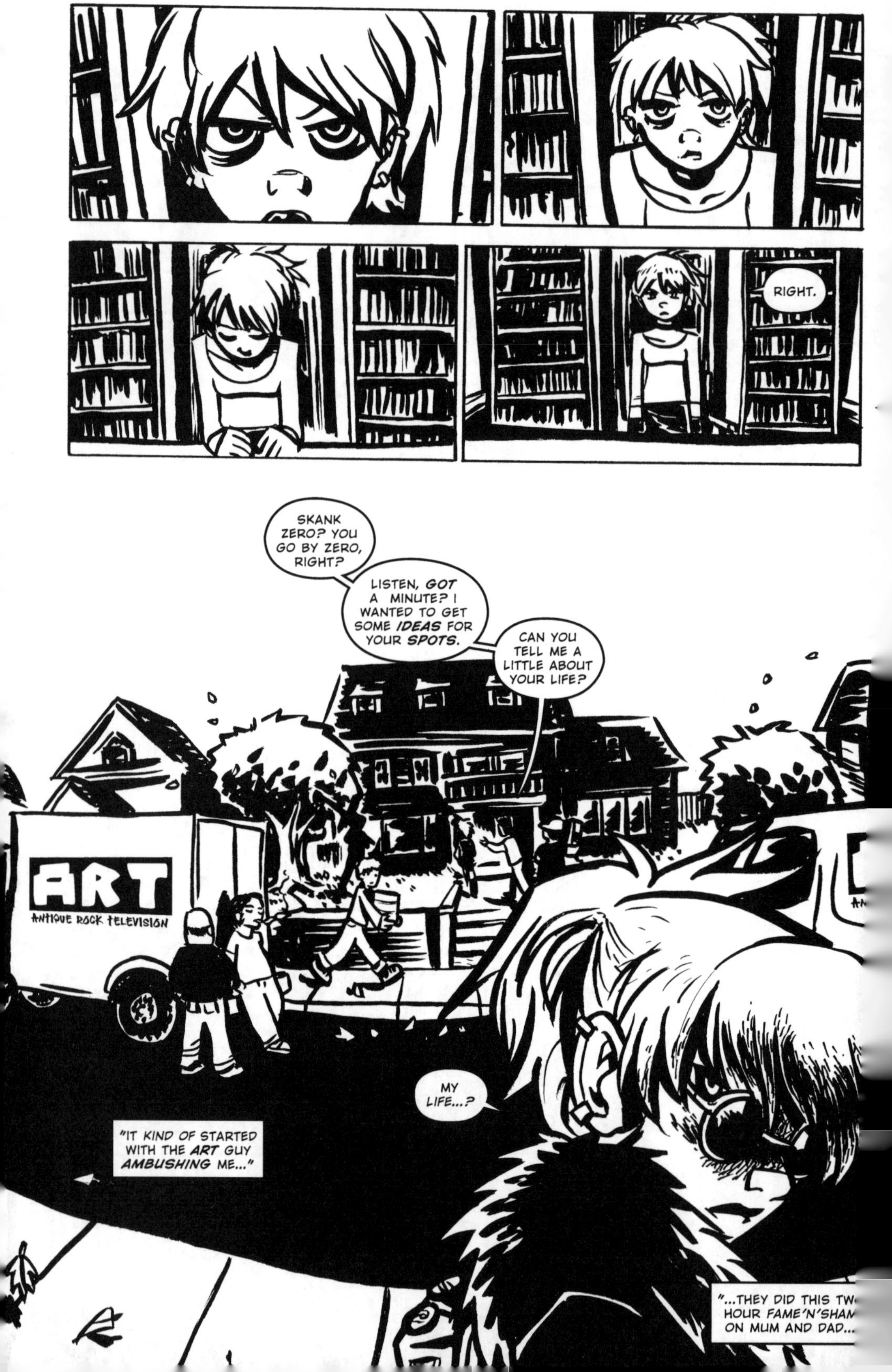
RIGHT.
SKANK ZERO? YOU GO BY ZERO, RIGHT?
LISTEN, GOT A MINUTE? I WANTED TO GET SOME IDEAS FOR YOUR SPOTS.
CAN YOU TELL ME A LITTLE ABOUT YOUR LIFE?
ART
ANTIQUE ROCK TELEVISION
MY LIFE...?
"IT KIND OF STARTED WITH THE ART GUY AMBUSHING ME..."
"...THEY DID THIS TW
HOUR FAME'N'SHAM
ON MUM AND DAD..."

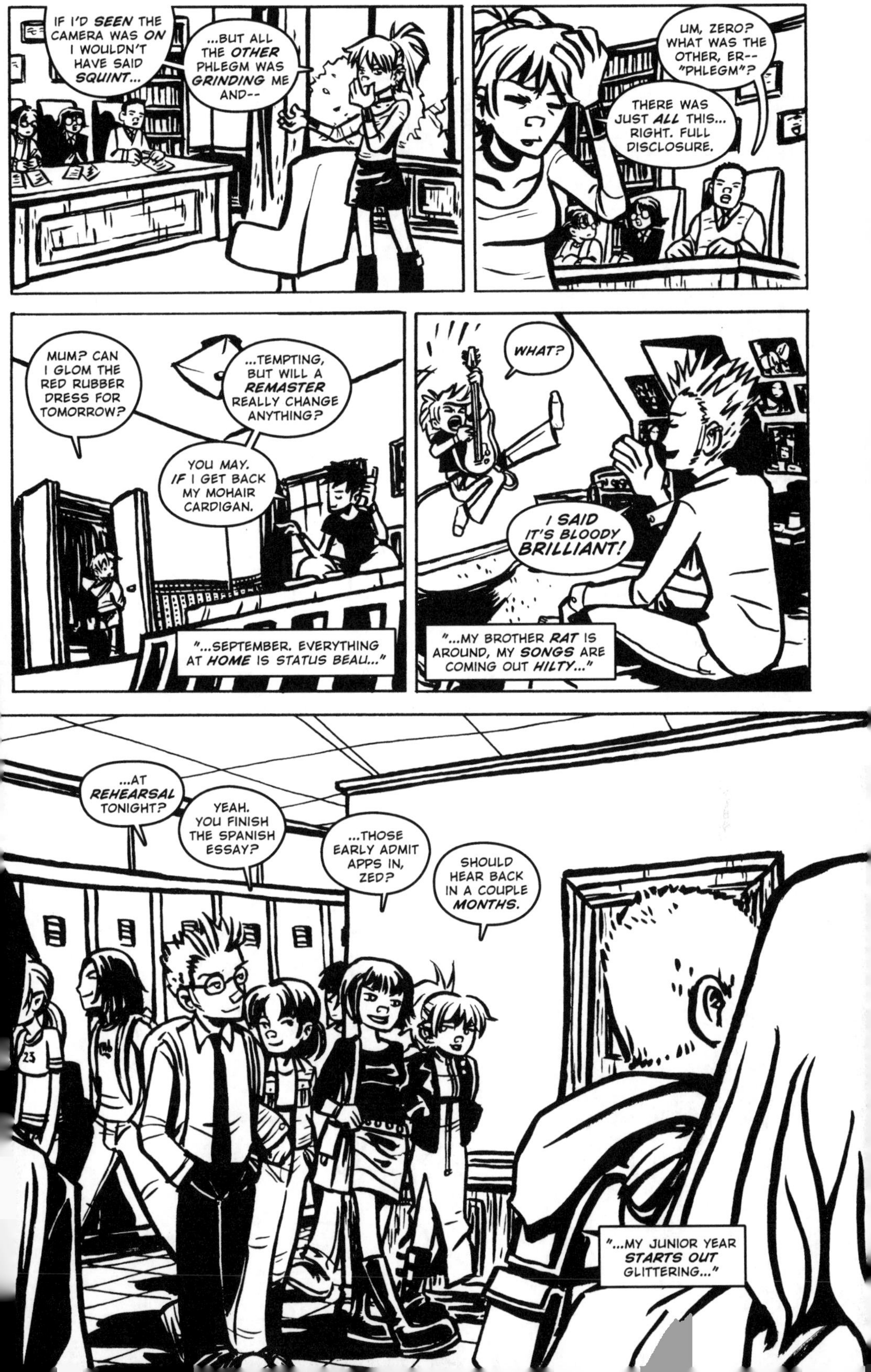
IF I'D SEEN THE CAMERA WAS ON I WOULDN'T HAVE SAID SQUINT...
...BUT ALL THE OTHER PHLEGM WAS GRINDING ME AND--
UM, ZERO? WHAT WAS THE OTHER, ER-- "PHLEGM"?
THERE WAS JUST ALL THIS... RIGHT. FULL DISCLOSURE.
MUM? CAN I GLOM THE RED RUBBER DRESS FOR TOMORROW?
...TEMPTING, BUT WILL A REMASTER REALLY CHANGE ANYTHING?
YOU MAY. IF I GET BACK MY MOHAIR CARDIGAN.
"...SEPTEMBER. EVERYTHING AT HOME IS STATUS BEAU..."
WHAT?
I SAID IT'S BLOODY BRILLIANT!
"...MY BROTHER RAT IS AROUND, MY SONGS ARE COMING OUT HILTY..."
...AT REHEARSAL TONIGHT?
YEAH. YOU FINISH THE SPANISH ESSAY?
...THOSE EARLY ADMIT APPS IN, ZED?
SHOULD HEAR BACK IN A COUPLE MONTHS.
"...MY JUNIOR YEAR STARTS OUT GLITTERING..."

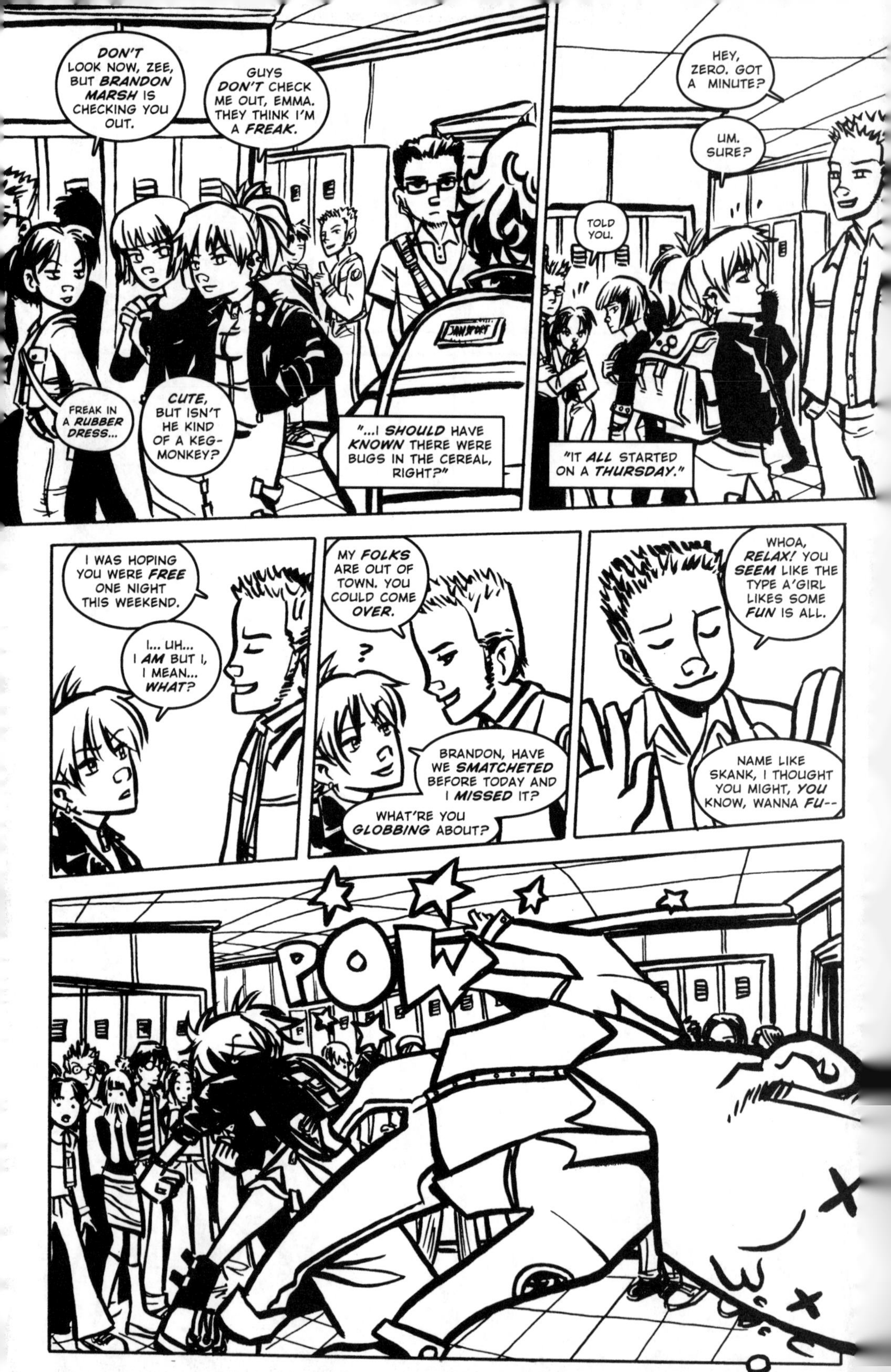
DON'T LOOK NOW, ZEE, BUT BRANDON MARSH IS CHECKING YOU OUT.
GUYS DON'T CHECK ME OUT, EMMA. THEY THINK I'M A FREAK.
FREAK IN A RUBBER DRESS...
CUTE, BUT ISN'T HE KIND OF A KEG-MONKEY?
"...I SHOULD HAVE KNOWN THERE WERE BUGS IN THE CEREAL, RIGHT?"
JANSPORT
HEY, ZERO. GOT A MINUTE?
UM. SURE?
TOLD YOU.
"IT ALL STARTED ON A THURSDAY."
I WAS HOPING YOU WERE FREE ONE NIGHT THIS WEEKEND.
I... UH... I AM BUT I, I MEAN... WHAT?
MY FOLKS ARE OUT OF TOWN. YOU COULD COME OVER.
?
BRANDON, HAVE WE SMATCHETED BEFORE TODAY AND I MISSED IT?
WHAT'RE YOU GLOBBING ABOUT?
WHOA, RELAX! YOU SEEM LIKE THE TYPE A'GIRL LIKES SOME FUN IS ALL.
NAME LIKE SKANK, I THOUGHT YOU MIGHT, YOU KNOW, WANNA FU--
POW

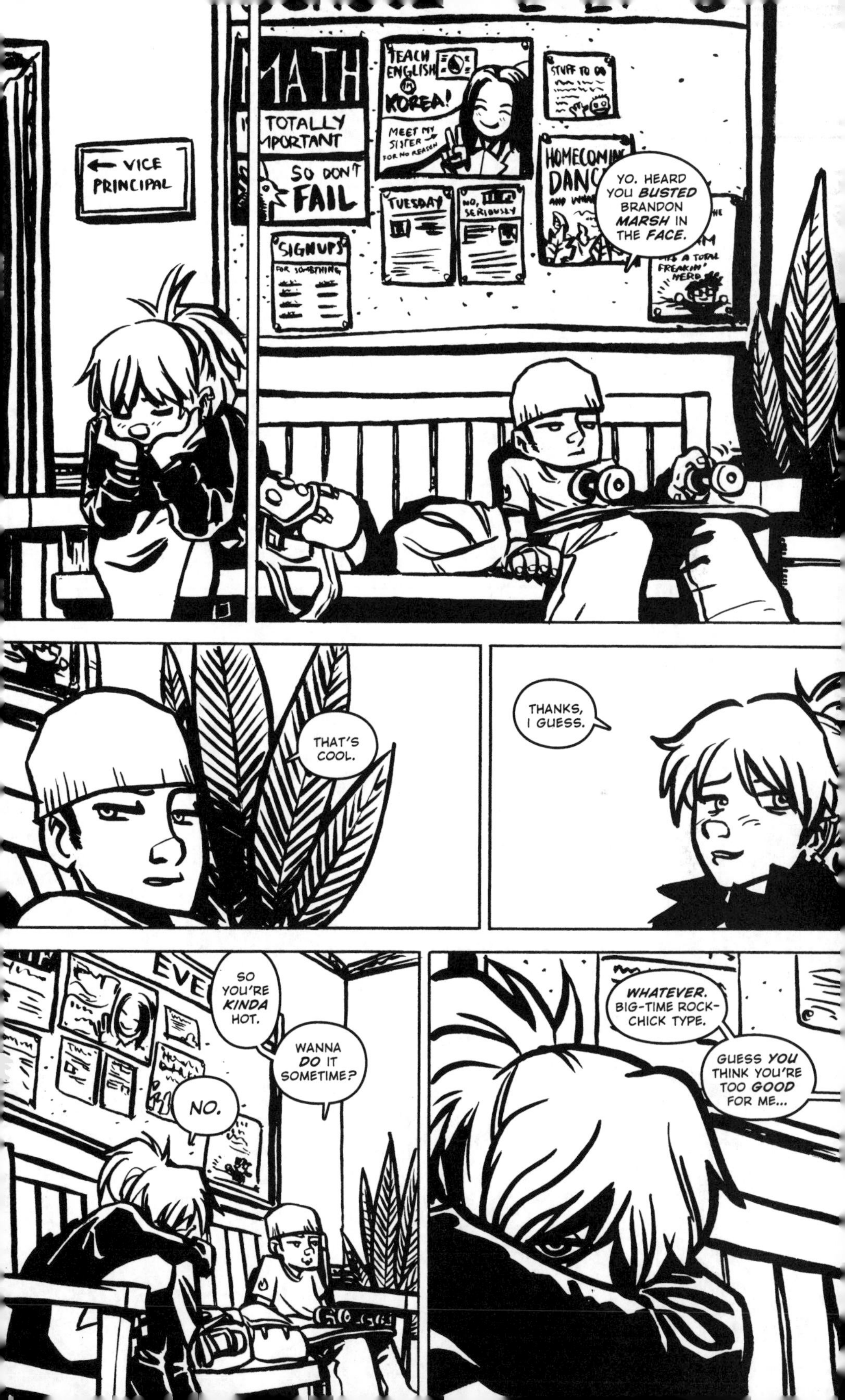
← VICE PRINCIPAL
YO. HEARD YOU BUSTED BRANDON MARSH IN THE FACE.
THAT'S COOL.
THANKS, I GUESS.
SO YOU'RE KINDA HOT.
WANNA DO IT SOMETIME?
NO.
WHATEVER. BIG-TIME ROCK-CHICK TYPE.
GUESS YOU THINK YOU'RE TOO GOOD FOR ME...

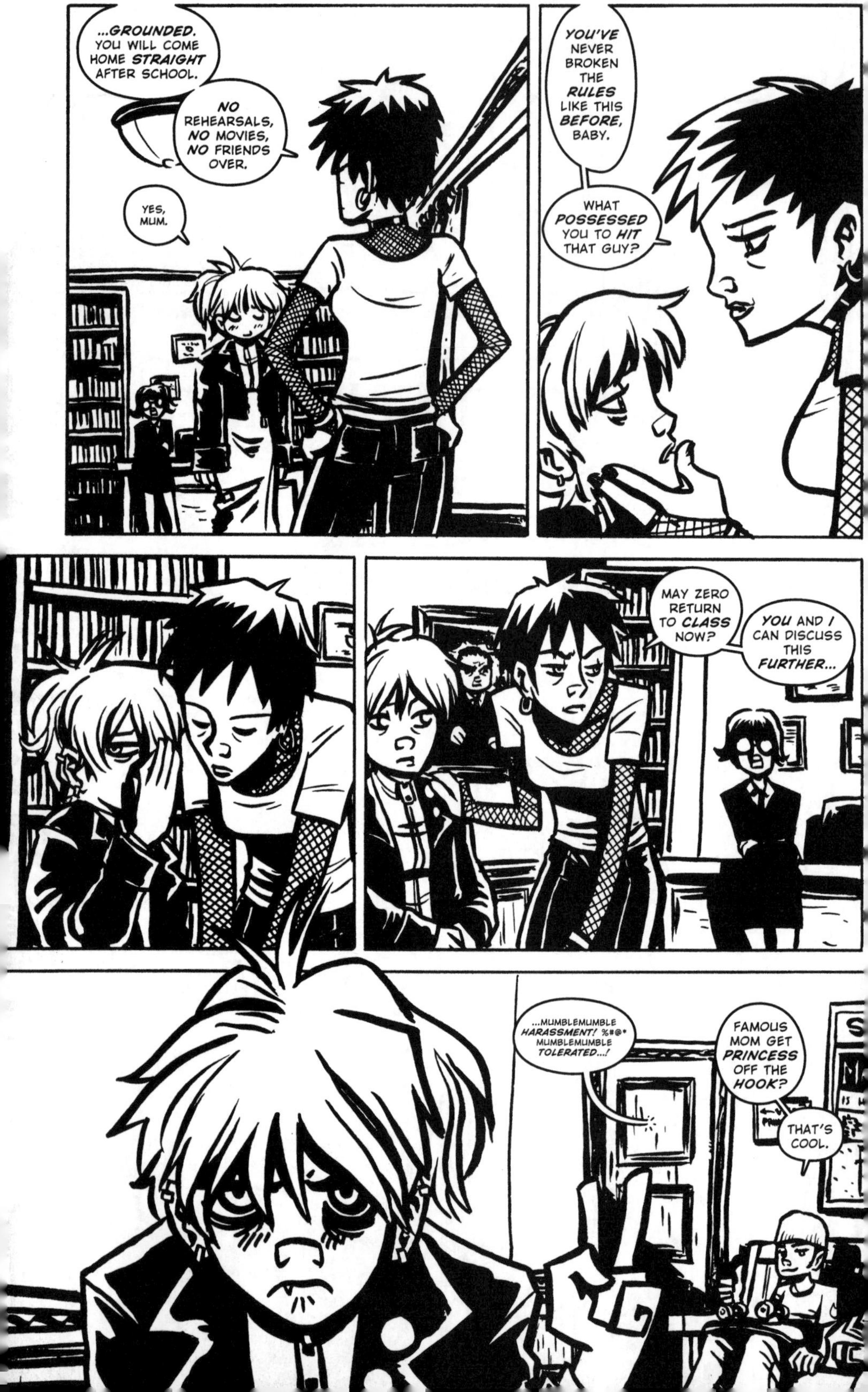
...GROUNDED. YOU WILL COME HOME STRAIGHT AFTER SCHOOL.
NO REHEARSALS, NO MOVIES, NO FRIENDS OVER.
YES, MUM.
YOU'VE NEVER BROKEN THE RULES LIKE THIS BEFORE, BABY.
WHAT POSSESSED YOU TO HIT THAT GUY?
MAY ZERO RETURN TO CLASS NOW?
YOU AND I CAN DISCUSS THIS FURTHER...
...MUMBLEMUMBLE HARASSMENT! %#@* MUMBLEMUMBLE TOLERATED...!
FAMOUS MOM GET PRINCESS OFF THE HOOK?
THAT'S COOL.

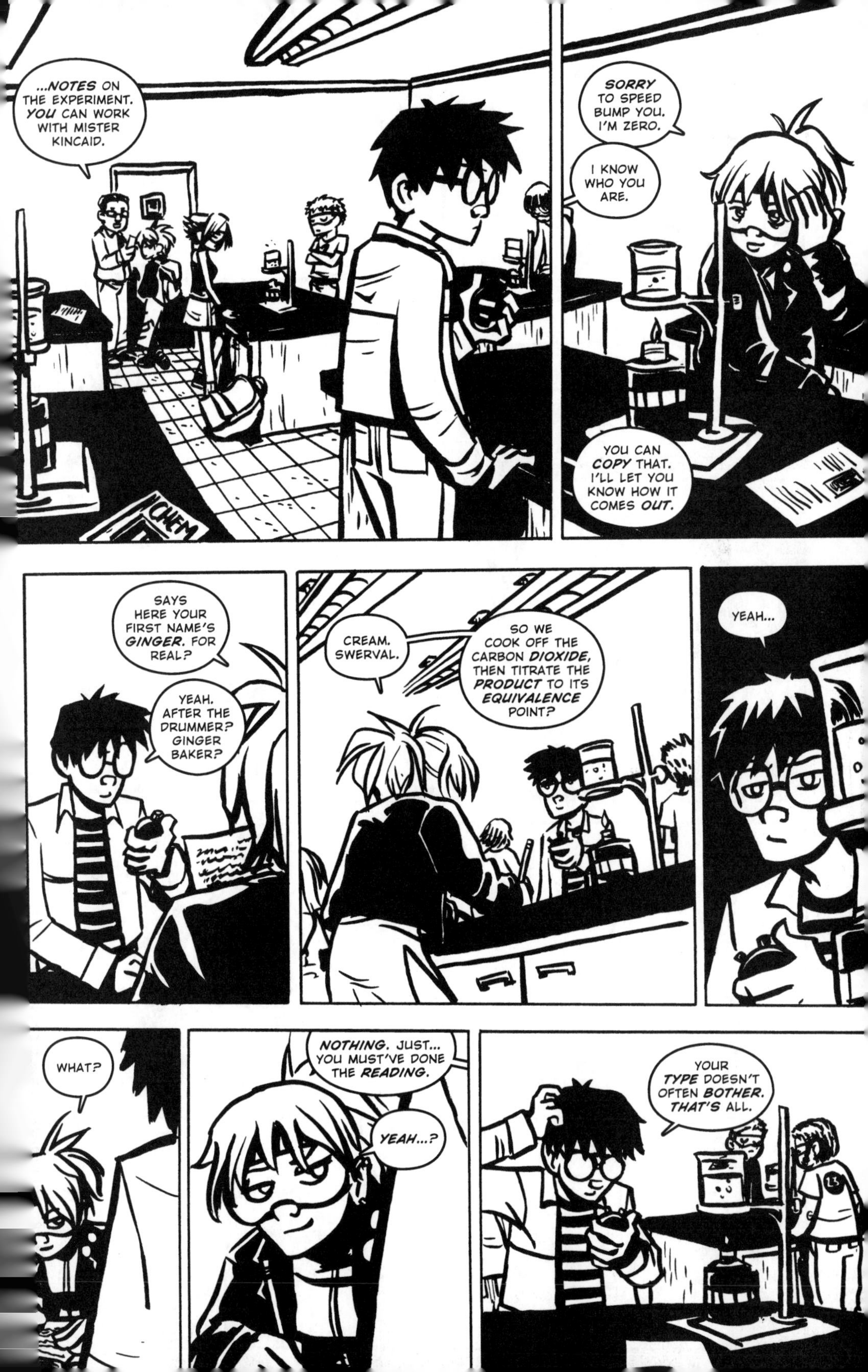
...NOTES ON THE EXPERIMENT. YOU CAN WORK WITH MISTER KINCAID.
CHEM
SORRY TO SPEED BUMP YOU. I'M ZERO.
I KNOW WHO YOU ARE.
YOU CAN COPY THAT. I'LL LET YOU KNOW HOW IT COMES OUT.
SAYS HERE YOUR FIRST NAME'S GINGER. FOR REAL?
YEAH. AFTER THE DRUMMER? GINGER BAKER?
CREAM. SWERVAL.
SO WE COOK OFF THE CARBON DIOXIDE, THEN TITRATE THE PRODUCT TO ITS EQUIVALENCE POINT?
YEAH...
WHAT?
NOTHING. JUST... YOU MUST'VE DONE THE READING.
YEAH...?
YOUR TYPE DOESN'T OFTEN BOTHER. THAT'S ALL.

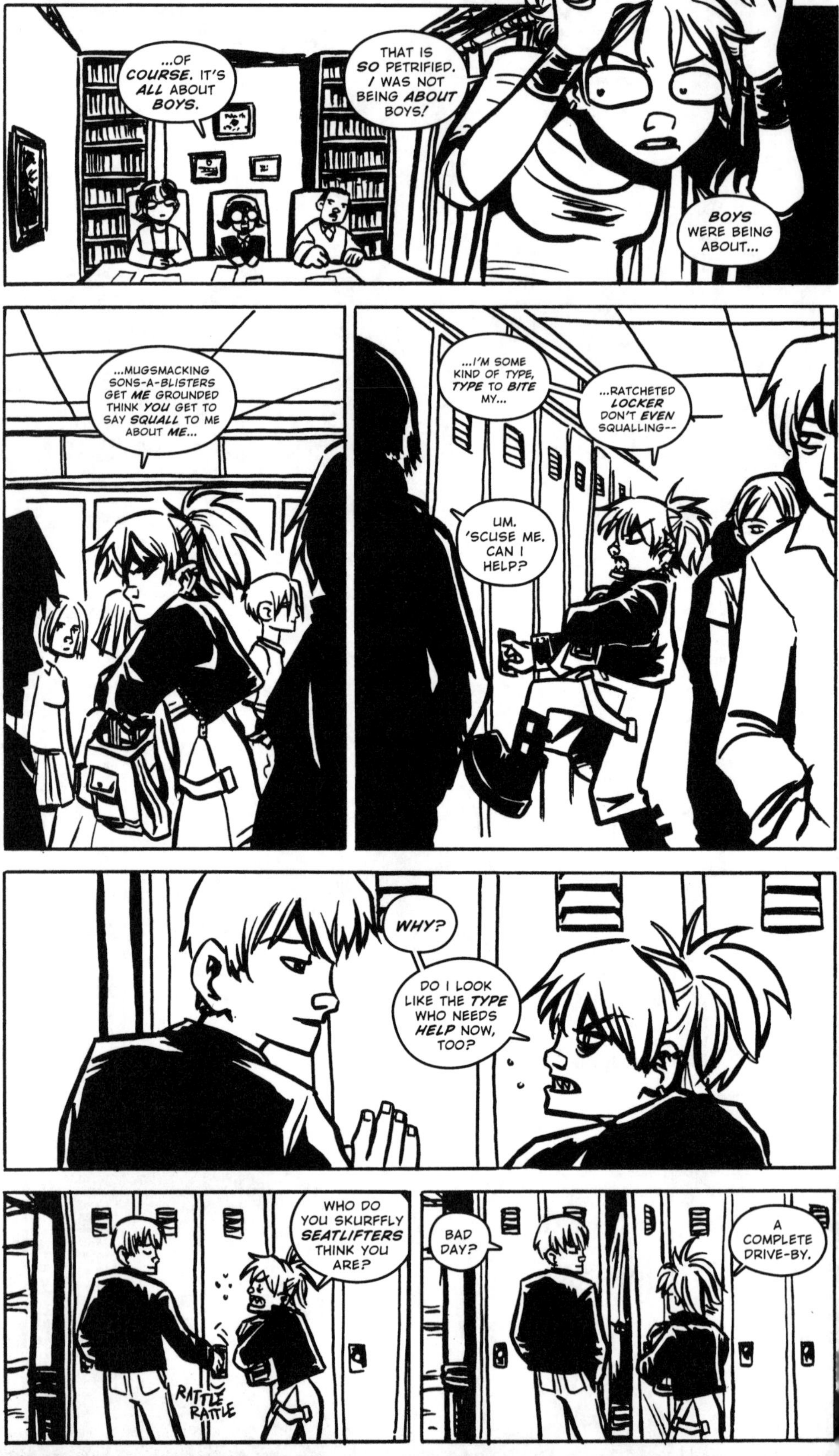
...OF COURSE. IT'S ALL ABOUT BOYS.
THAT IS SO PETRIFIED. I WAS NOT BEING ABOUT BOYS!
BOYS WERE BEING ABOUT...
...MUGSMACKING SONS-A-BLISTERS GET ME GROUNDED THINK YOU GET TO SAY SQUALL TO ME ABOUT ME...
...I'M SOME KIND OF TYPE, TYPE TO BITE MY...
...RATCHETED LOCKER DON'T EVEN SQUALLING--
UM. 'SCUSE ME. CAN I HELP?
WHY?
DO I LOOK LIKE THE TYPE WHO NEEDS HELP NOW, TOO?
WHO DO YOU SKURFFLY SEATLIFTERS THINK YOU ARE?
RATTLE RATTLE
BAD DAY?
A COMPLETE DRIVE-BY.

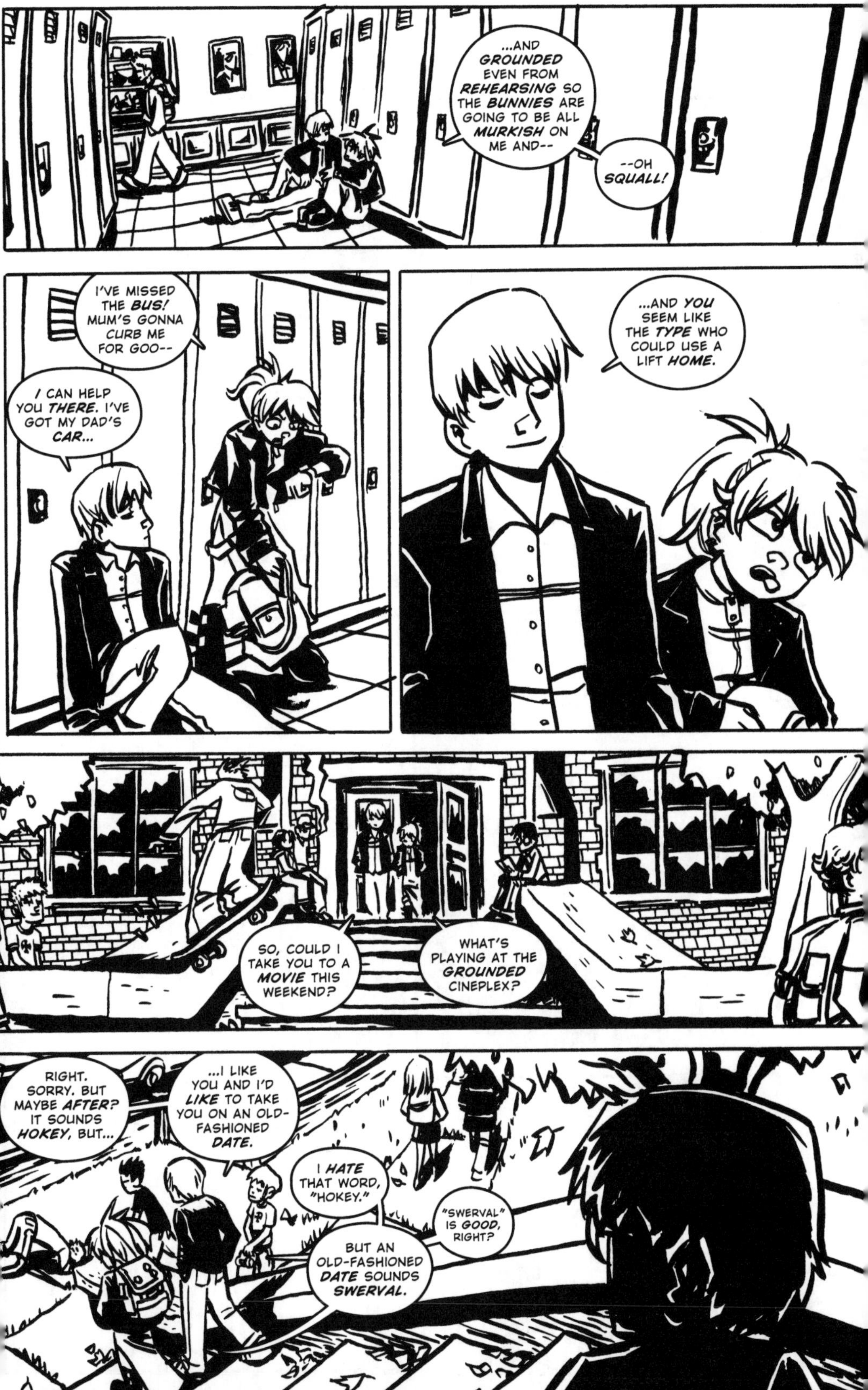
...AND GROUNDED EVEN FROM REHEARSING SO THE BUNNIES ARE GOING TO BE ALL MURKISH ON ME AND--
--OH SQUALL!
I'VE MISSED THE BUS! MUM'S GONNA CURB ME FOR GOO--
I CAN HELP YOU THERE. I'VE GOT MY DAD'S CAR...
...AND YOU SEEM LIKE THE TYPE WHO COULD USE A LIFT HOME.
SO, COULD I TAKE YOU TO A MOVIE THIS WEEKEND?
WHAT'S PLAYING AT THE GROUNDED CINEPLEX?
RIGHT. SORRY. BUT MAYBE AFTER? IT SOUNDS HOKEY, BUT...
...I LIKE YOU AND I'D LIKE TO TAKE YOU ON AN OLD-FASHIONED DATE.
I HATE THAT WORD, "HOKEY."
BUT AN OLD-FASHIONED DATE SOUNDS SWERVAL.
"SWERVAL" IS GOOD, RIGHT?

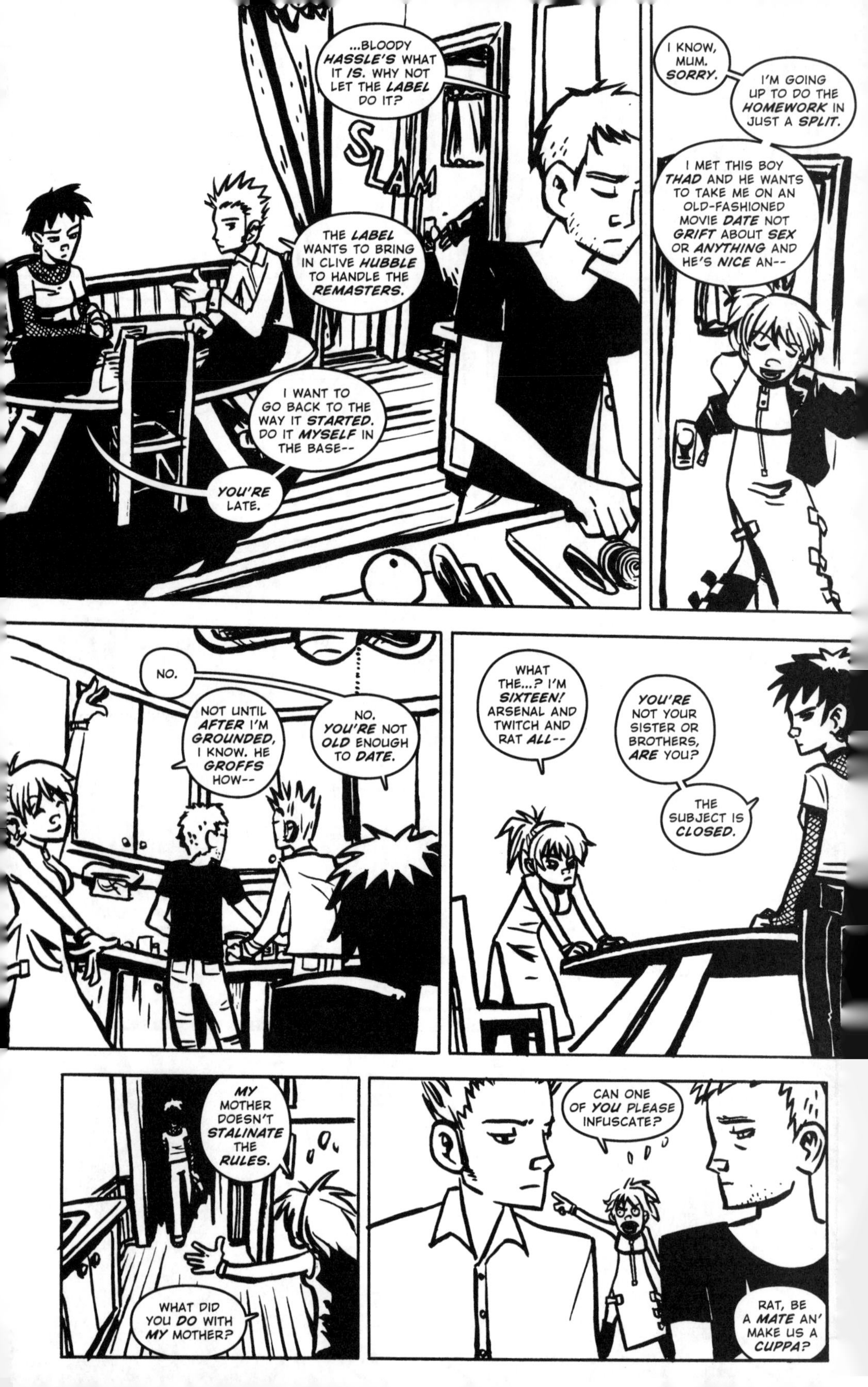
...BLOODY HASSLE'S WHAT IT IS. WHY NOT LET THE LABEL DO IT?
SLAM
THE LABEL WANTS TO BRING IN CLIVE HUBBLE TO HANDLE THE REMASTERS.
I WANT TO GO BACK TO THE WAY IT STARTED. DO IT MYSELF IN THE BASE--
YOU'RE LATE.
I KNOW, MUM. SORRY.
I'M GOING UP TO DO THE HOMEWORK IN JUST A SPLIT.
I MET THIS BOY THAD AND HE WANTS TO TAKE ME ON AN OLD-FASHIONED MOVIE DATE NOT GRIFT ABOUT SEX OR ANYTHING AND HE'S NICE AN--
NO.
NOT UNTIL AFTER I'M GROUNDED, I KNOW. HE GROFFS HOW--
NO. YOU'RE NOT OLD ENOUGH TO DATE.
WHAT THE...? I'M SIXTEEN! ARSENAL AND TWITCH AND RAT ALL--
YOU'RE NOT YOUR SISTER OR BROTHERS, ARE YOU?
THE SUBJECT IS CLOSED.
MY MOTHER DOESN'T STALINATE THE RULES.
WHAT DID YOU DO WITH MY MOTHER?
CAN ONE OF YOU PLEASE INFUSCATE?
RAT, BE A MATE AN' MAKE US A CUPPA?

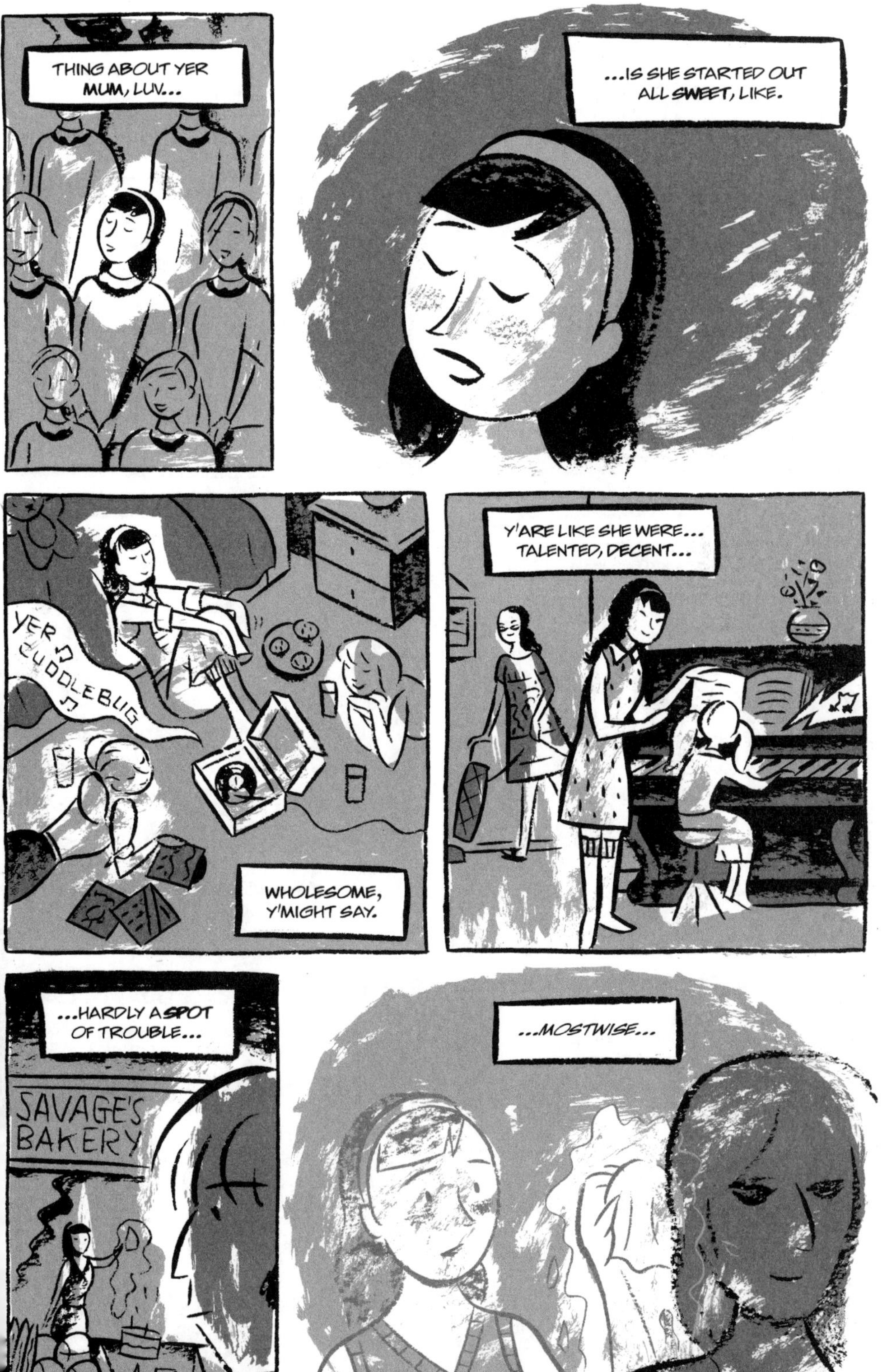
THING ABOUT YER MUM, LUV...
...IS SHE STARTED OUT ALL SWEET, LIKE.
YER CUDDLEBUG
WHOLESOME, Y'MIGHT SAY.
Y'ARE LIKE SHE WERE... TALENTED, DECENT...
...HARDLY A SPOT OF TROUBLE...
SAVAGE'S BAKERY
...MOSTWISE...

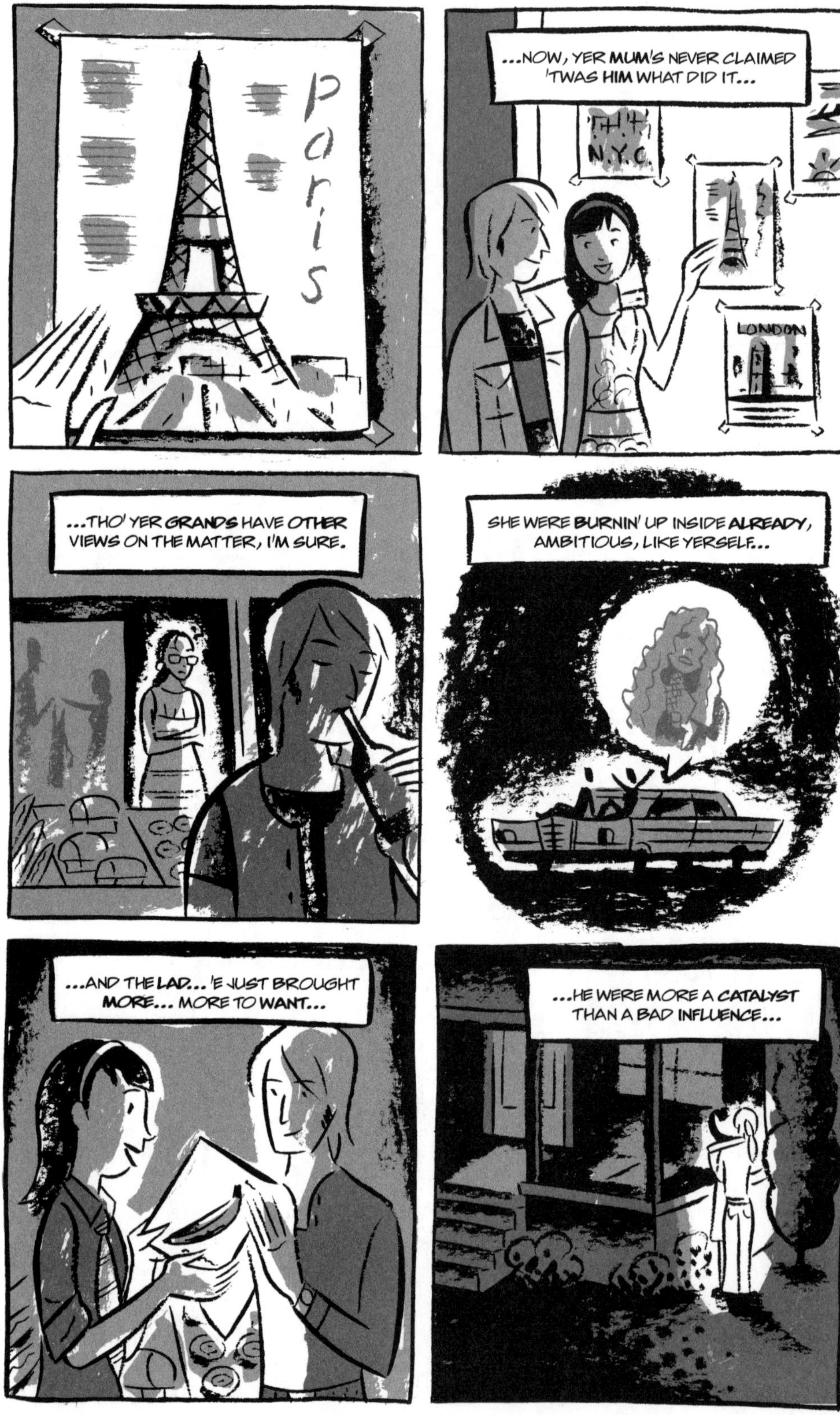
Paris
...NOW, YER MUM'S NEVER CLAIMED 'TWAS HIM WHAT DID IT...
N.Y.C.
LONDON
...THO' YER GRANDS HAVE OTHER VIEWS ON THE MATTER, I'M SURE.
SHE WERE BURNIN' UP INSIDE ALREADY, AMBITIOUS, LIKE YERSELF...
...AND THE LAD... 'E JUST BROUGHT MORE... MORE TO WANT...
...HE WERE MORE A CATALYST THAN A BAD INFLUENCE...

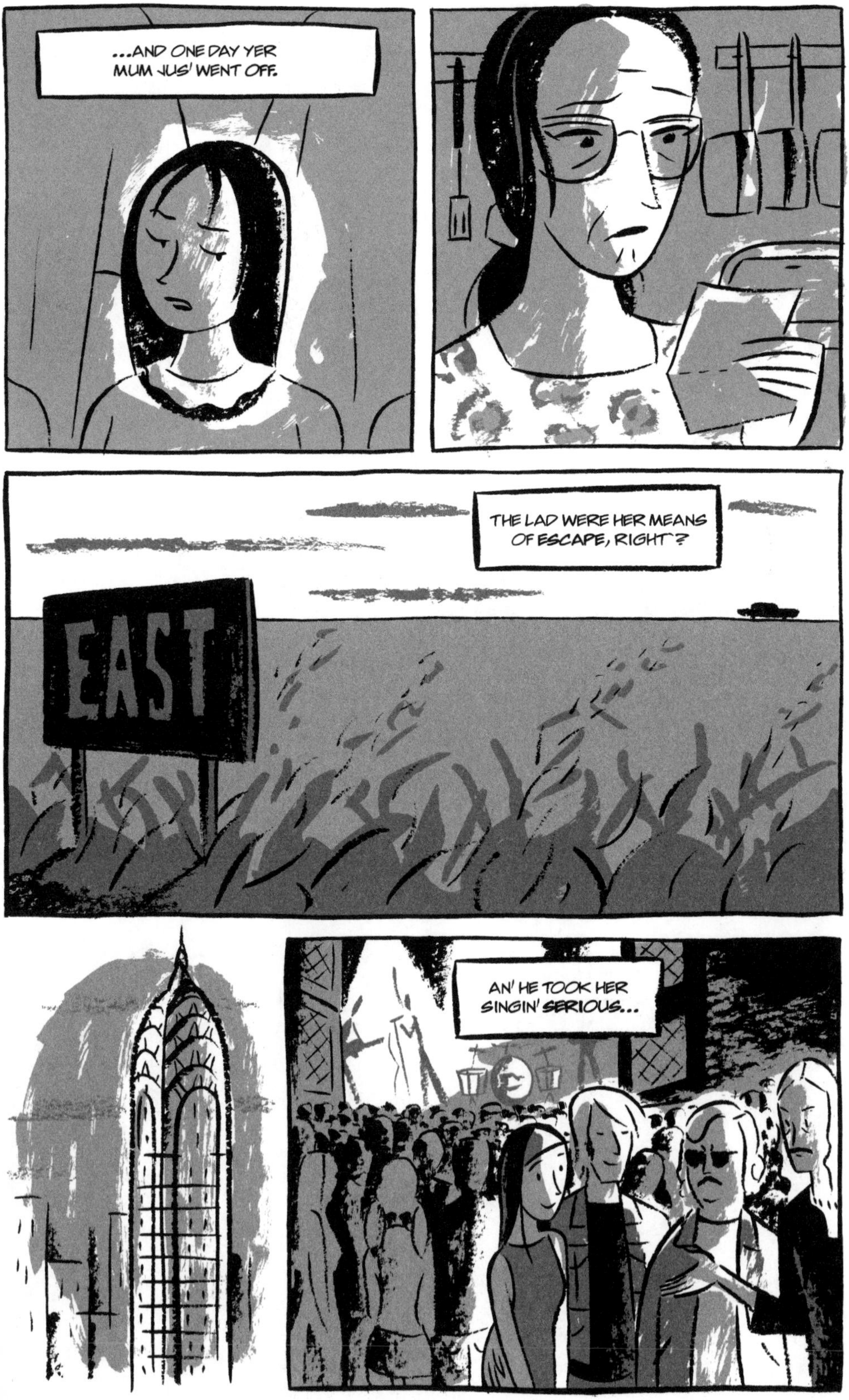
...AND ONE DAY YER MUM JUS' WENT OFF.
THE LAD WERE HER MEANS OF ESCAPE, RIGHT?
EAST
AN' HE TOOK HER SINGIN' SERIOUS...

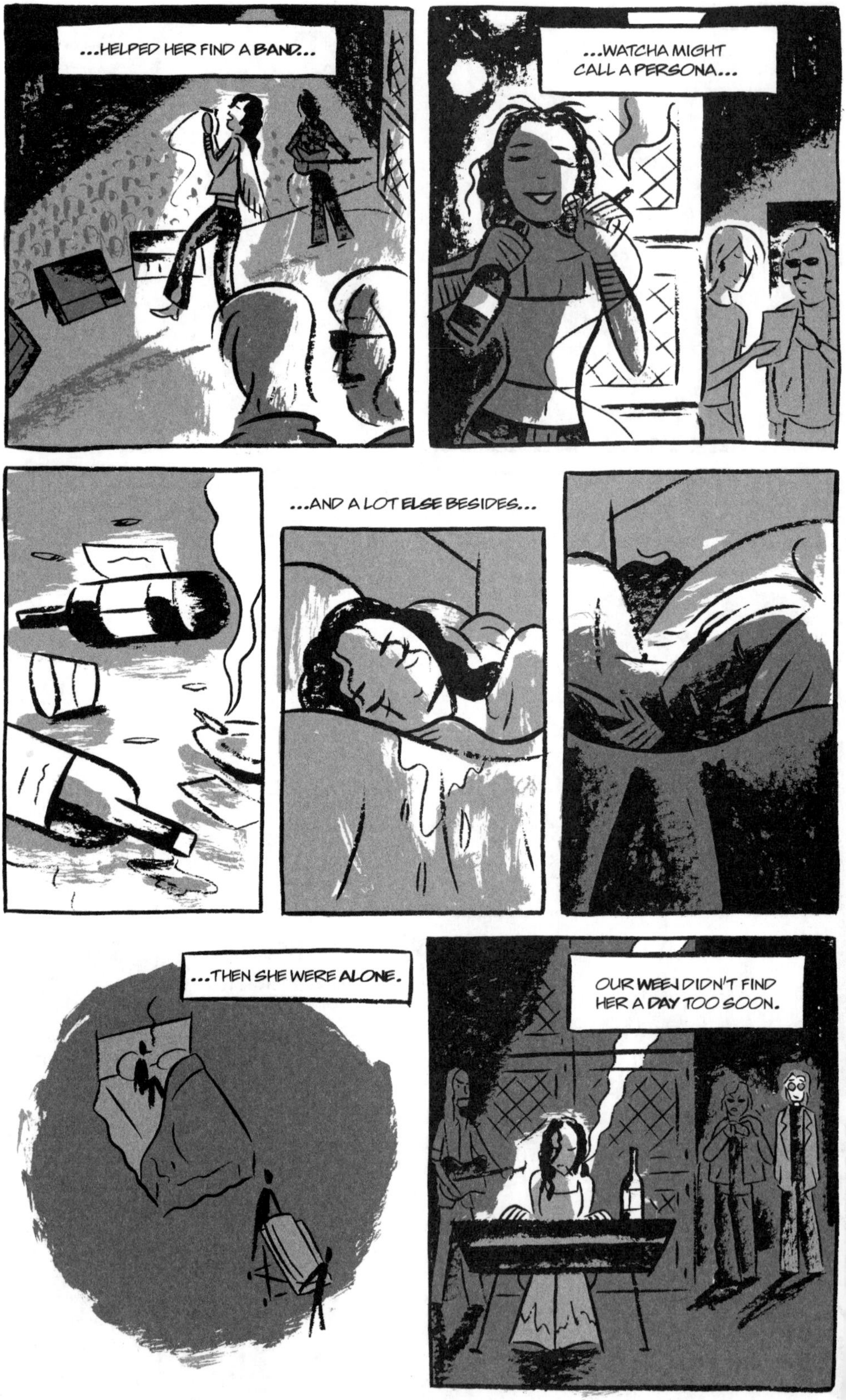
...HELPED HER FIND A BAND...
...WATCHA MIGHT CALL A PERSONA...
...AND A LOT ELSE BESIDES...
...THEN SHE WERE ALONE.
OUR WEEJ DIDN'T FIND HER A DAY TOO SOON.

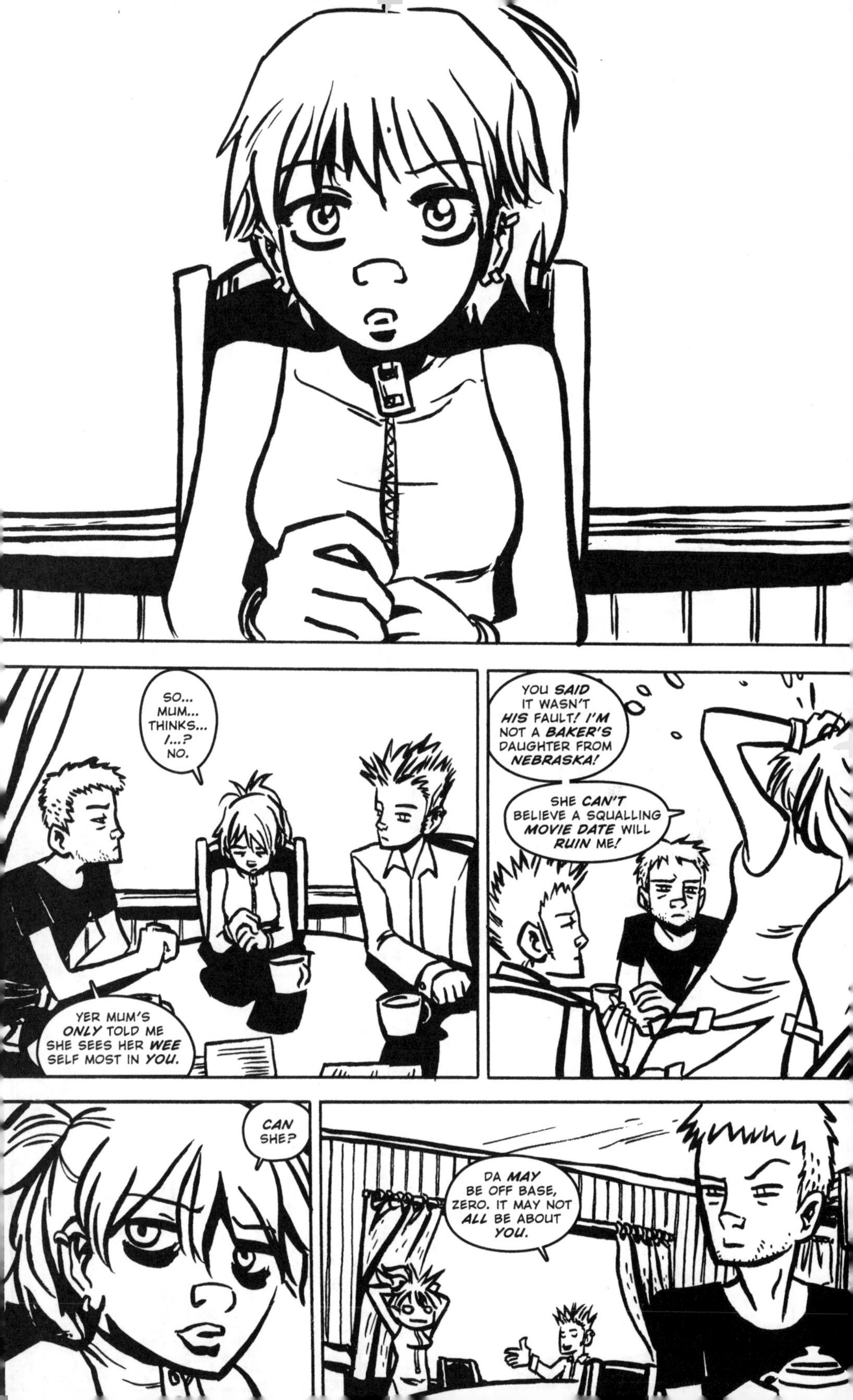

SO... MUM... THINKS... I...? NO.
YER MUM'S ONLY TOLD ME SHE SEES HER WEE SELF MOST IN YOU.
YOU SAID IT WASN'T HIS FAULT! I'M NOT A BAKER'S DAUGHTER FROM NEBRASKA!
SHE CAN'T BELIEVE A SQUALLING MOVIE DATE WILL RUIN ME!
CAN SHE?
DA MAY BE OFF BASE, ZERO. IT MAY NOT ALL BE ABOUT YOU.

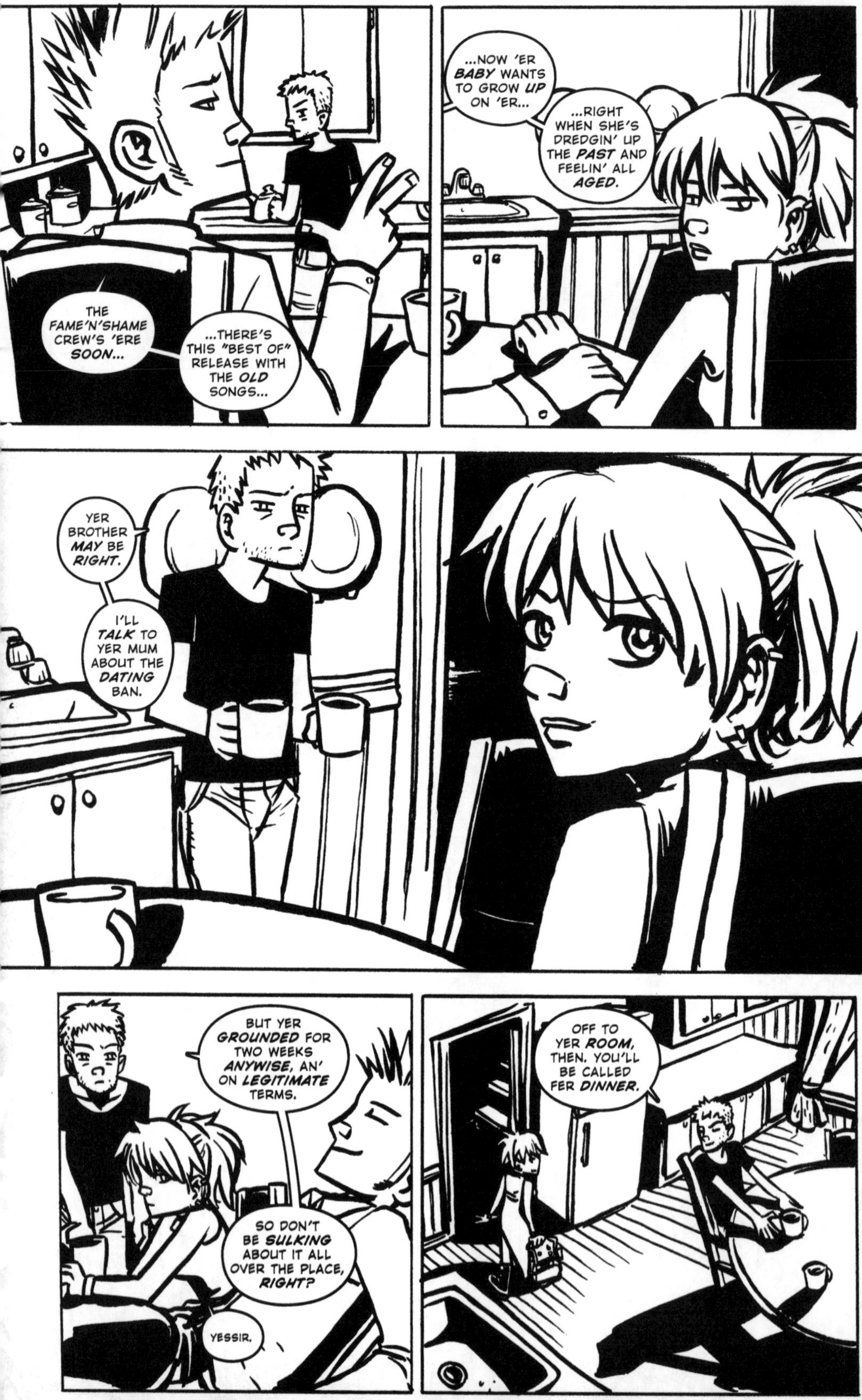
THE FAME'N'SHAME CREW'S 'ERE SOON...
...THERE'S THIS "BEST OF" RELEASE WITH THE OLD SONGS...
...NOW 'ER BABY WANTS TO GROW UP ON 'ER...
...RIGHT WHEN SHE'S DREDGIN' UP THE PAST AND FEELIN' ALL AGED.
YER BROTHER MAY BE RIGHT.
I'LL TALK TO YER MUM ABOUT THE DATING BAN.
BUT YER GROUNDED FOR TWO WEEKS ANYWISE, AN' ON LEGITIMATE TERMS.
SO DON'T BE SULKING ABOUT IT ALL OVER THE PLACE, RIGHT?
YESSIR.
OFF TO YER ROOM, THEN. YOU'LL BE CALLED FER DINNER.

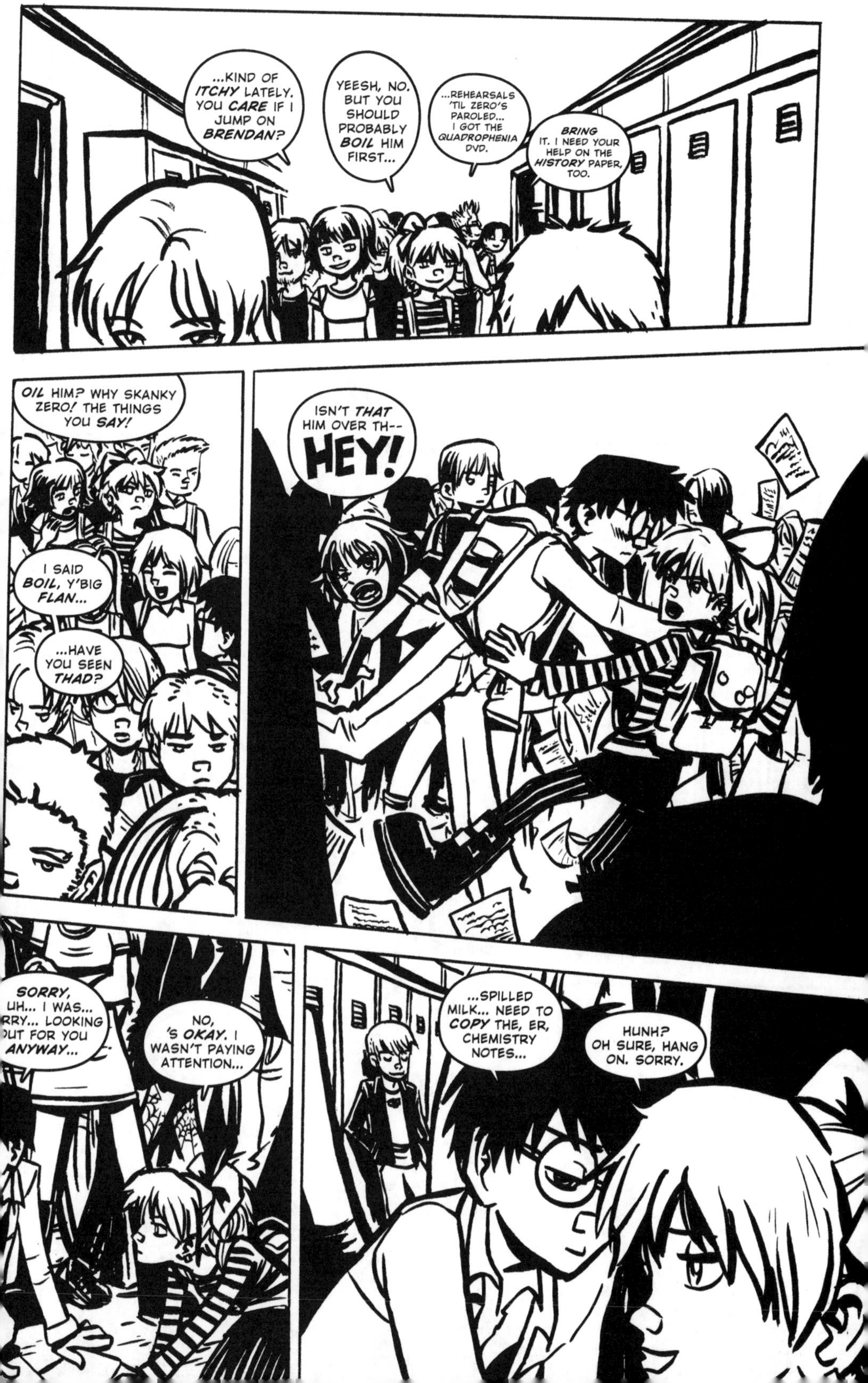

...KIND OF ITCHY LATELY. YOU CARE IF I JUMP ON BRENDAN?
YEESH, NO. BUT YOU SHOULD PROBABLY BOIL HIM FIRST...
...REHEARSALS 'TIL ZERO'S PAROLED... I GOT THE QUADROPHENIA DVD.
BRING IT. I NEED YOUR HELP ON THE HISTORY PAPER, TOO.
OIL HIM? WHY SKANKY ZERO! THE THINGS YOU SAY!
I SAID BOIL, Y'BIG FLAN...
...HAVE YOU SEEN THAD?
ISN'T THAT HIM OVER TH--
HEY!
SORRY, UH... I WAS... RRY... LOOKING OUT FOR YOU ANYWAY...
NO, 'S OKAY. I WASN'T PAYING ATTENTION...
...SPILLED MILK... NEED TO COPY THE, ER, CHEMISTRY NOTES...
HUNH? OH SURE, HANG ON. SORRY.

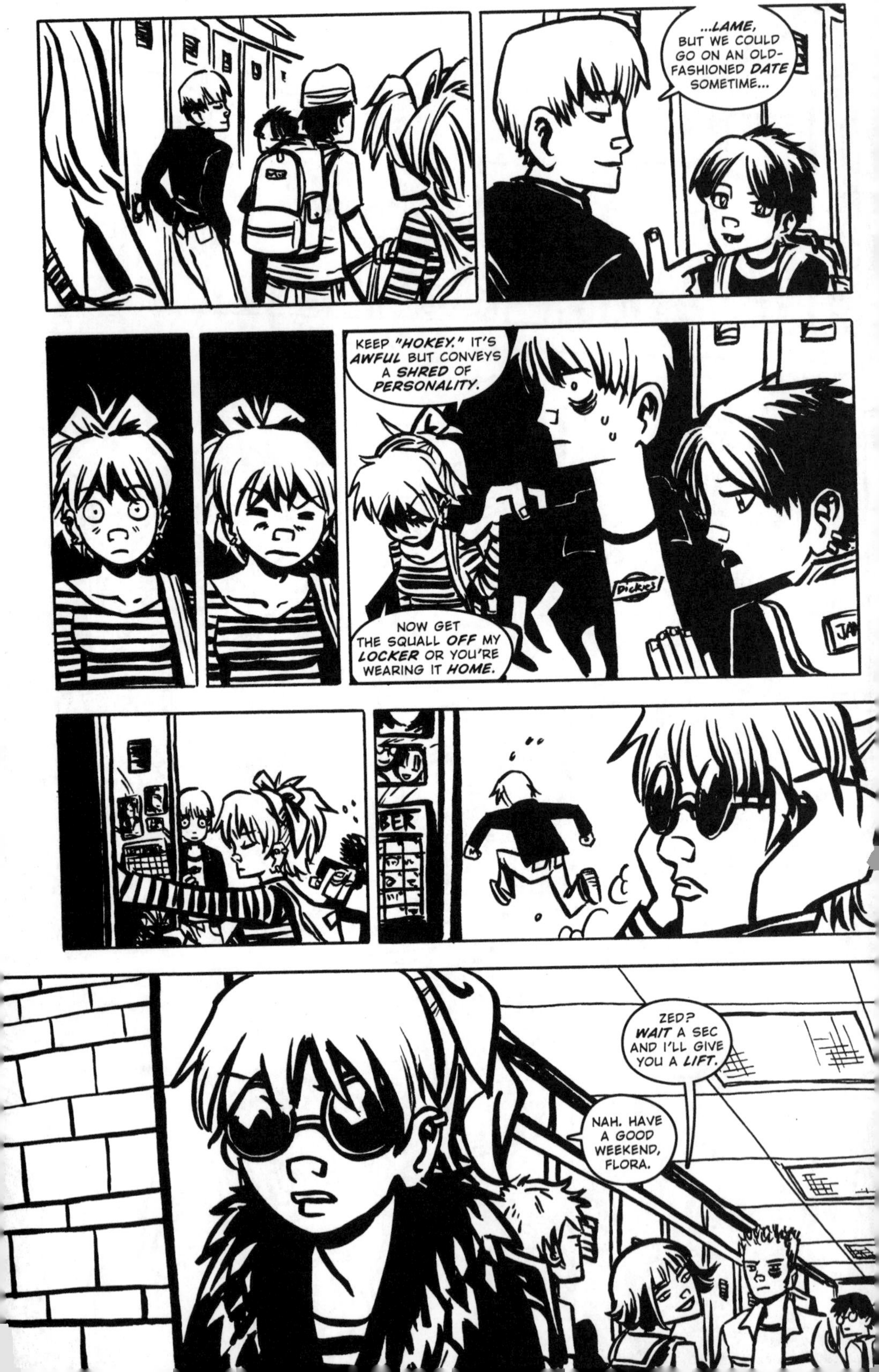
...LAME, BUT WE COULD GO ON AN OLD-FASHIONED DATE SOMETIME...
KEEP "HOKEY." IT'S AWFUL BUT CONVEYS A SHRED OF PERSONALITY.
NOW GET THE SQUALL OFF MY LOCKER OR YOU'RE WEARING IT HOME.
ZED? WAIT A SEC AND I'LL GIVE YOU A LIFT.
NAH. HAVE A GOOD WEEKEND, FLORA.

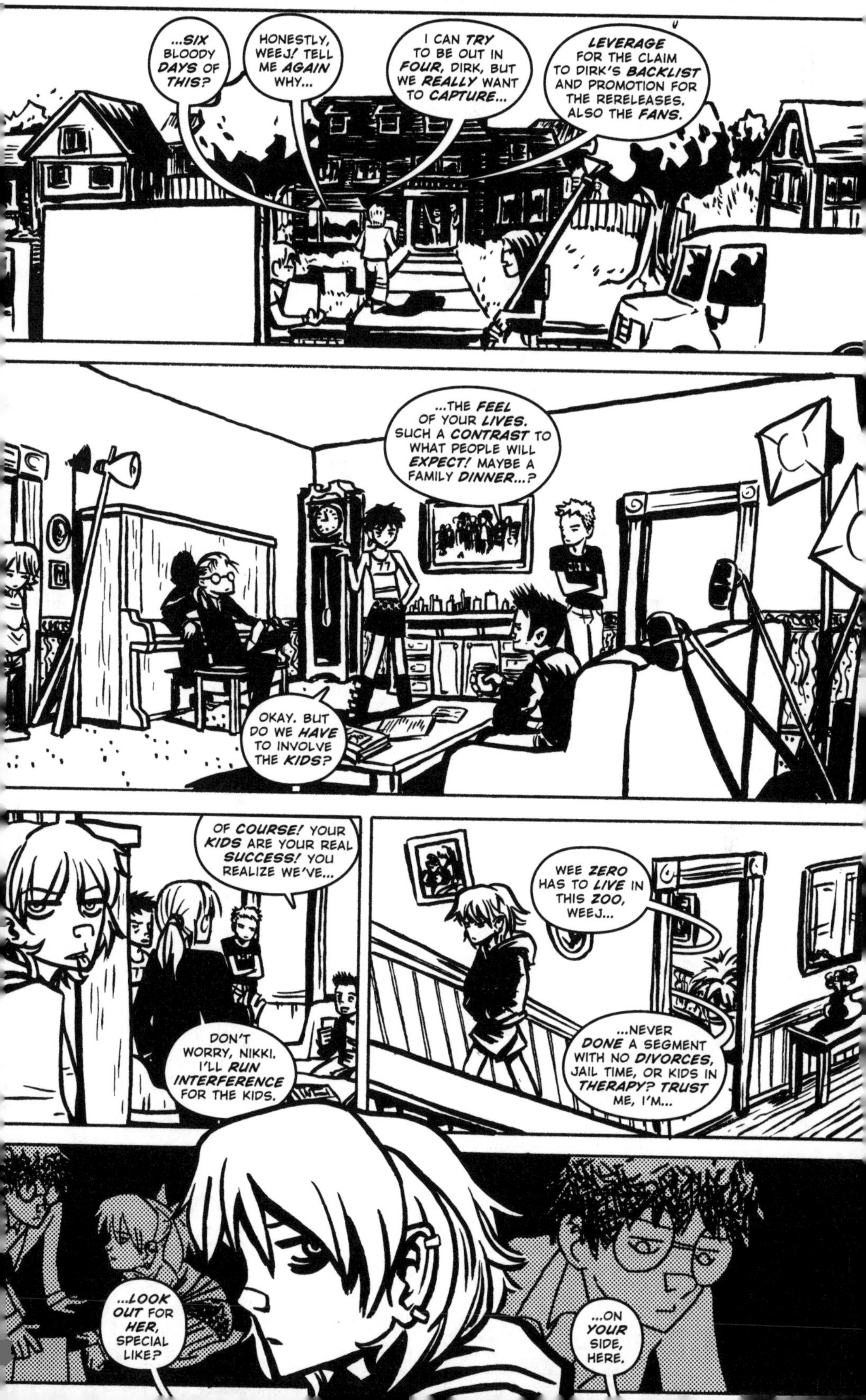
...SIX BLOODY DAYS OF THIS?
HONESTLY, WEEJ! TELL ME AGAIN WHY...
I CAN TRY TO BE OUT IN FOUR, DIRK, BUT WE REALLY WANT TO CAPTURE...
LEVERAGE FOR THE CLAIM TO DIRK'S BACKLIST AND PROMOTION FOR THE RERELEASES. ALSO THE FANS.
...THE FEEL OF YOUR LIVES. SUCH A CONTRAST TO WHAT PEOPLE WILL EXPECT! MAYBE A FAMILY DINNER...?
OKAY. BUT DO WE HAVE TO INVOLVE THE KIDS?
OF COURSE! YOUR KIDS ARE YOUR REAL SUCCESS! YOU REALIZE WE'VE...
DON'T WORRY, NIKKI. I'LL RUN INTERFERENCE FOR THE KIDS.
WEE ZERO HAS TO LIVE IN THIS ZOO, WEEJ...
...NEVER DONE A SEGMENT WITH NO DIVORCES, JAIL TIME, OR KIDS IN THERAPY? TRUST ME, I'M...
...LOOK OUT FOR HER, SPECIAL LIKE?
...ON YOUR SIDE, HERE.

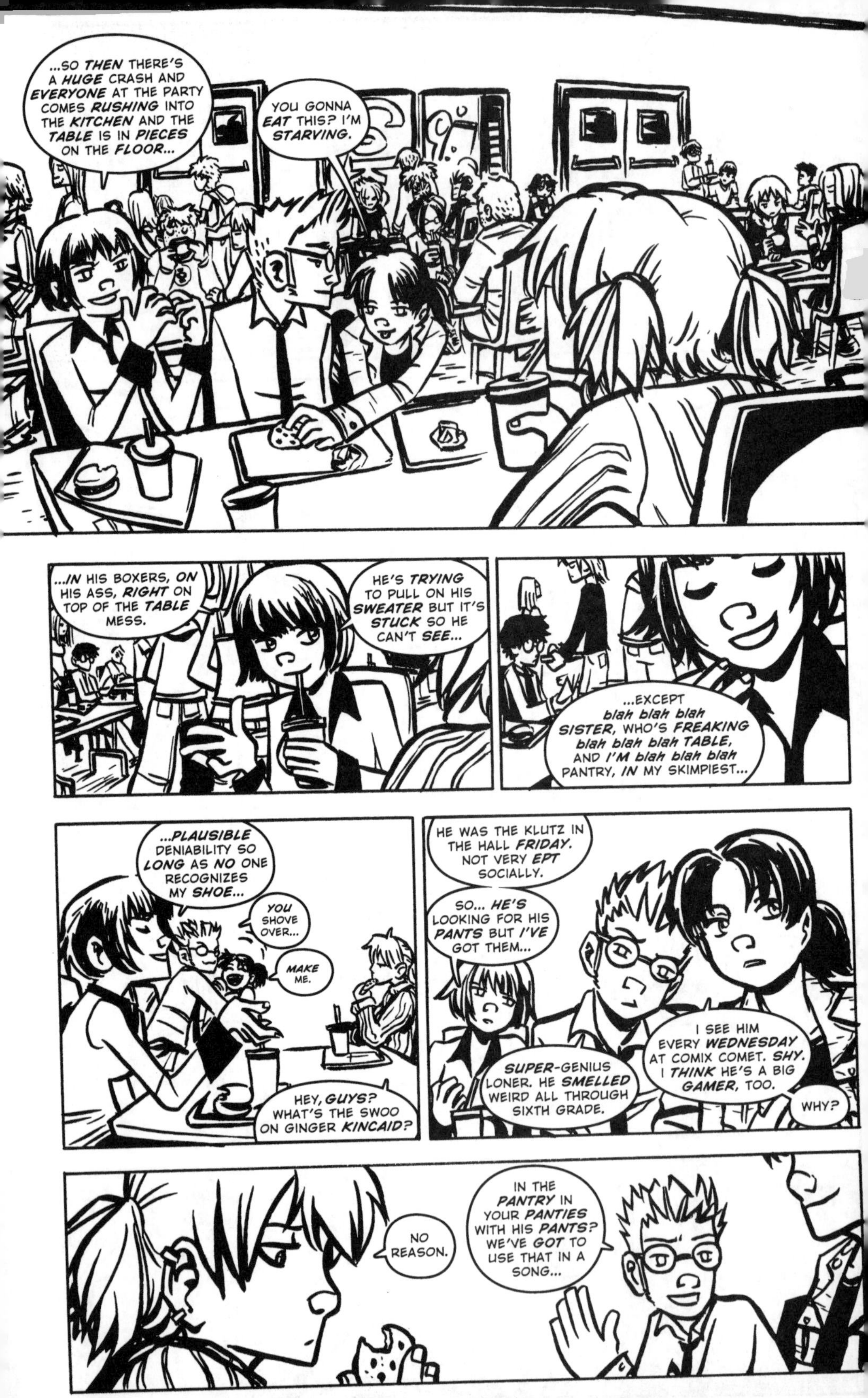
...SO THEN THERE'S A HUGE CRASH AND EVERYONE AT THE PARTY COMES RUSHING INTO THE KITCHEN AND THE TABLE IS IN PIECES ON THE FLOOR...
YOU GONNA EAT THIS? I'M STARVING.
...IN HIS BOXERS, ON HIS ASS, RIGHT ON TOP OF THE TABLE MESS.
HE'S TRYING TO PULL ON HIS SWEATER BUT IT'S STUCK SO HE CAN'T SEE...
...EXCEPT blah blah blah SISTER, WHO'S FREAKING blah blah blah TABLE, AND I'M blah blah blah PANTRY, IN MY SKIMPIEST...
...PLAUSIBLE DENIABILITY SO LONG AS NO ONE RECOGNIZES MY SHOE...
YOU SHOVE OVER...
MAKE ME.
HEY, GUYS? WHAT'S THE SWOO ON GINGER KINCAID?
HE WAS THE KLUTZ IN THE HALL FRIDAY. NOT VERY EPT SOCIALLY.
SO... HE'S LOOKING FOR HIS PANTS BUT I'VE GOT THEM...
SUPER-GENIUS LONER. HE SMELLED WEIRD ALL THROUGH SIXTH GRADE.
I SEE HIM EVERY WEDNESDAY AT COMIX COMET. SHY. I THINK HE'S A BIG GAMER, TOO.
WHY?
NO REASON.
IN THE PANTRY IN YOUR PANTIES WITH HIS PANTS? WE'VE GOT TO USE THAT IN A SONG...

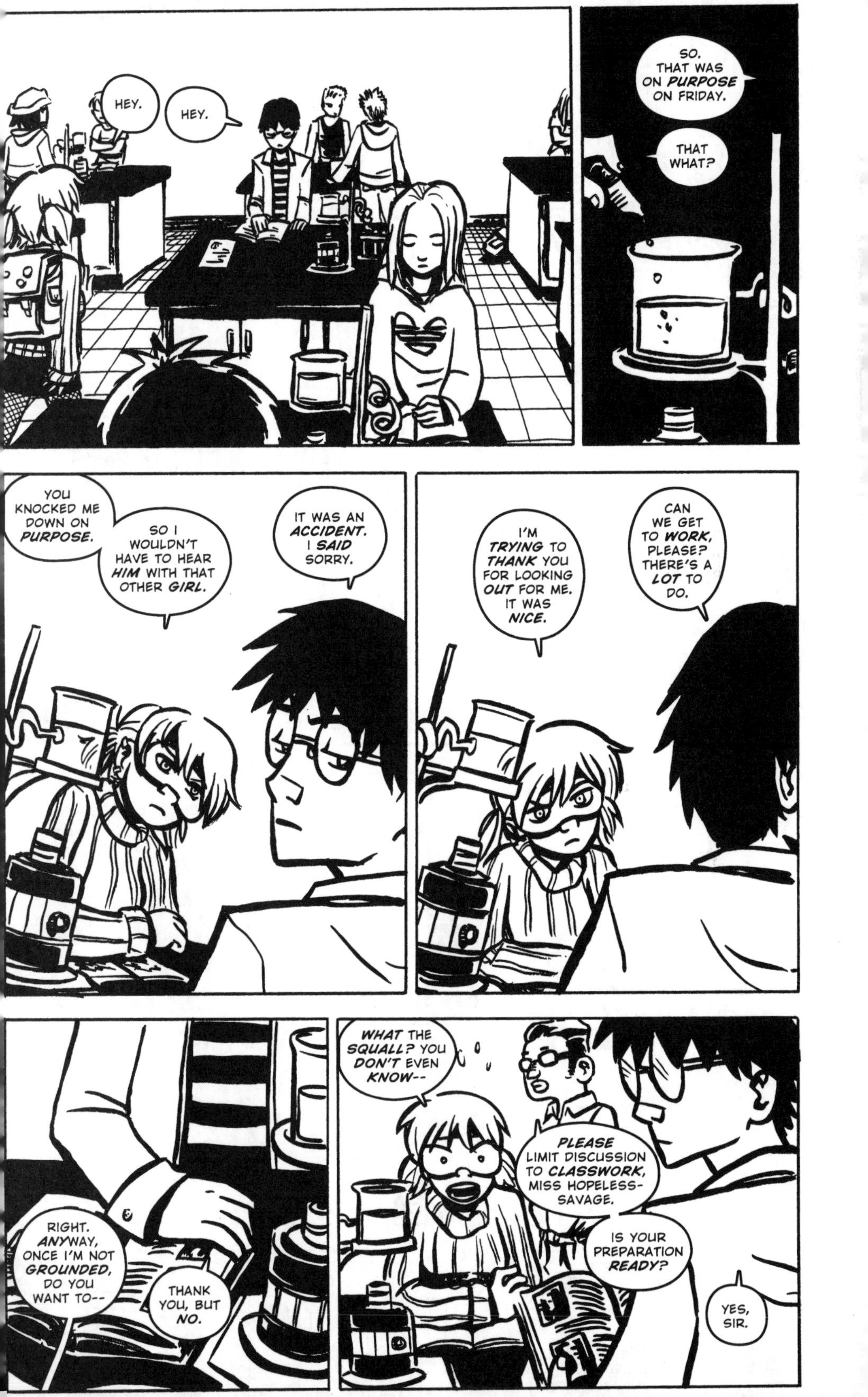
HEY.
HEY.
SO. THAT WAS ON PURPOSE ON FRIDAY.
THAT WHAT?
YOU KNOCKED ME DOWN ON PURPOSE.
SO I WOULDN'T HAVE TO HEAR HIM WITH THAT OTHER GIRL.
IT WAS AN ACCIDENT. I SAID SORRY.
I'M TRYING TO THANK YOU FOR LOOKING OUT FOR ME. IT WAS NICE.
CAN WE GET TO WORK, PLEASE? THERE'S A LOT TO DO.
RIGHT. ANYWAY, ONCE I'M NOT GROUNDED, DO YOU WANT TO--
THANK YOU, BUT NO.
WHAT THE SQUALL? YOU DON'T EVEN KNOW--
PLEASE LIMIT DISCUSSION TO CLASSWORK, MISS HOPELESS-SAVAGE.
IS YOUR PREPARATION READY?
YES, SIR.

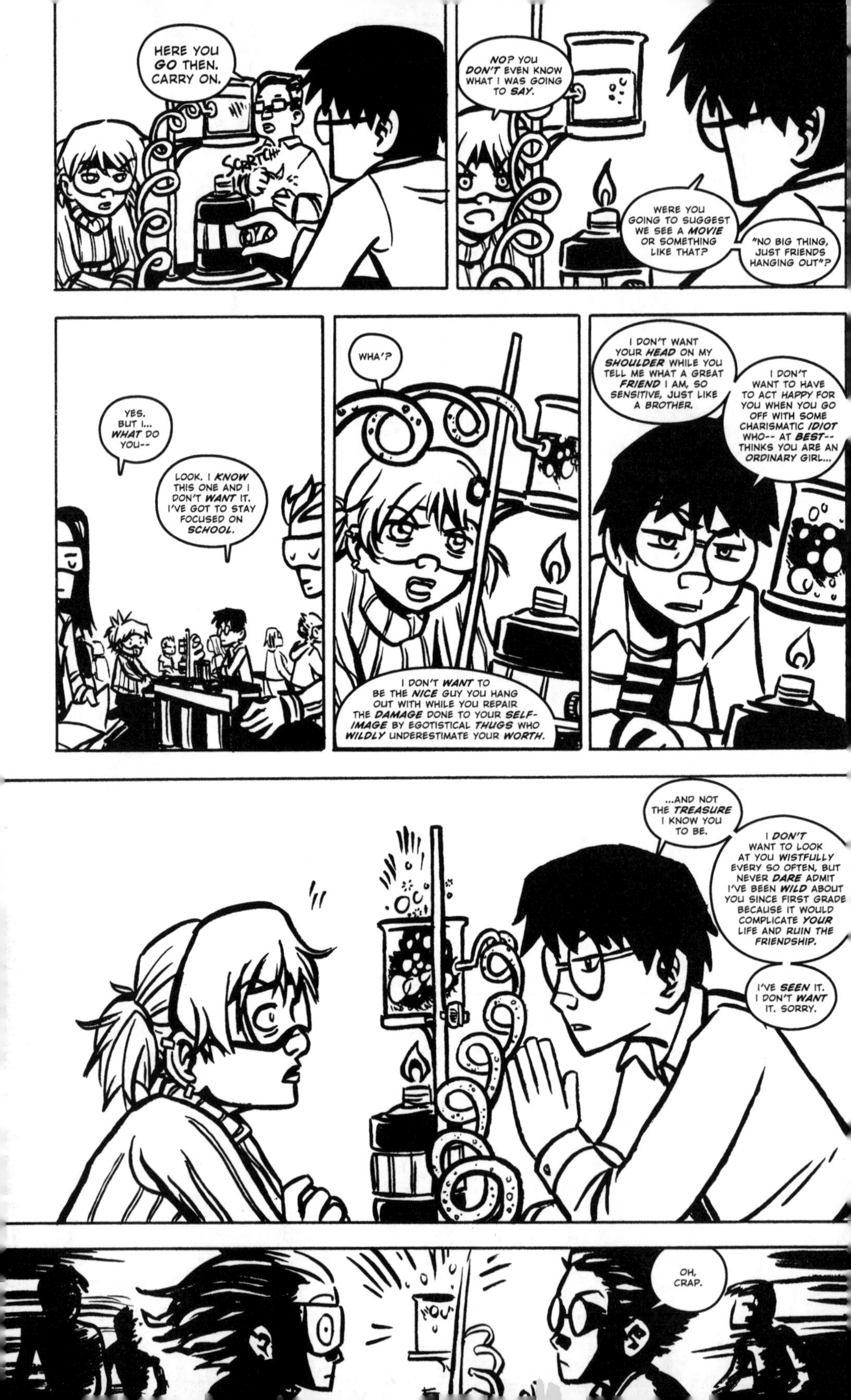
HERE YOU GO THEN. CARRY ON.
SCRTCH
NO? YOU DON'T EVEN KNOW WHAT I WAS GOING TO SAY.
WERE YOU GOING TO SUGGEST WE SEE A MOVIE OR SOMETHING LIKE THAT?
"NO BIG THING, JUST FRIENDS HANGING OUT"?
YES. BUT I... WHAT DO YOU--
LOOK. I KNOW THIS ONE AND I DON'T WANT IT. I'VE GOT TO STAY FOCUSED ON SCHOOL.
WHA'?
I DON'T WANT TO BE THE NICE GUY YOU HANG OUT WITH WHILE YOU REPAIR THE DAMAGE DONE TO YOUR SELF-IMAGE BY EGOTISTICAL THUGS WHO WILDLY UNDERESTIMATE YOUR WORTH.
I DON'T WANT YOUR HEAD ON MY SHOULDER WHILE YOU TELL ME WHAT A GREAT FRIEND I AM, SO SENSITIVE, JUST LIKE A BROTHER.
I DON'T WANT TO HAVE TO ACT HAPPY FOR YOU WHEN YOU GO OFF WITH SOME CHARISMATIC IDIOT WHO-- AT BEST-- THINKS YOU ARE AN ORDINARY GIRL...
...AND NOT THE TREASURE I KNOW YOU TO BE.
I DON'T WANT TO LOOK AT YOU WISTFULLY EVERY SO OFTEN, BUT NEVER DARE ADMIT I'VE BEEN WILD ABOUT YOU SINCE FIRST GRADE BECAUSE IT WOULD COMPLICATE YOUR LIFE AND RUIN THE FRIENDSHIP.
I'VE SEEN IT. I DON'T WANT IT. SORRY.
OH, CRAP.

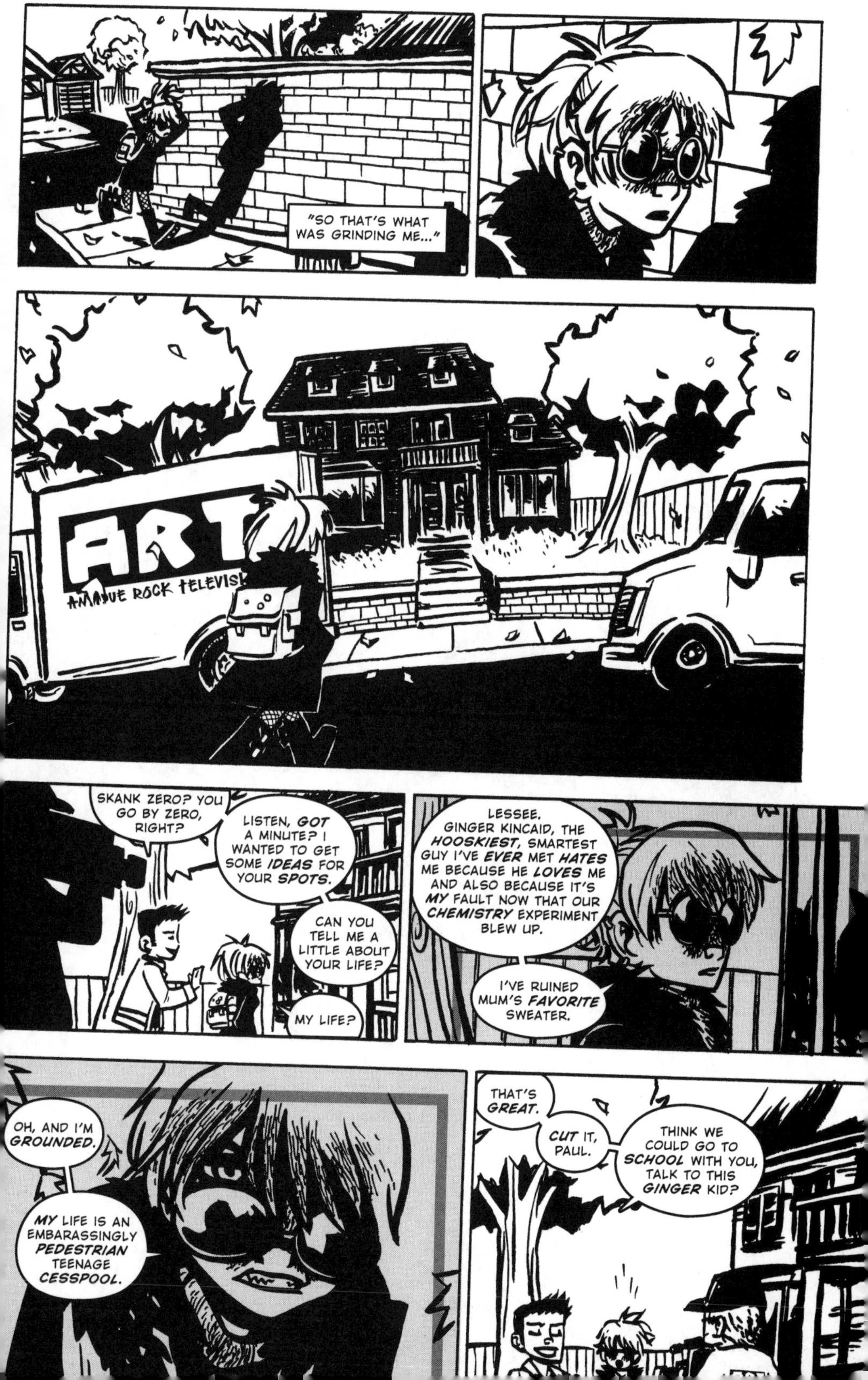

"SO THAT'S WHAT WAS GRINDING ME..."
ART
SKANK ZERO? YOU GO BY ZERO, RIGHT?
LISTEN, GOT A MINUTE? I WANTED TO GET SOME IDEAS FOR YOUR SPOTS.
CAN YOU TELL ME A LITTLE ABOUT YOUR LIFE?
MY LIFE?
LESSEE. GINGER KINCAID, THE HOOSKIEST, SMARTEST GUY I'VE EVER MET HATES ME BECAUSE HE LOVES ME AND ALSO BECAUSE IT'S MY FAULT NOW THAT OUR CHEMISTRY EXPERIMENT BLEW UP.
I'VE RUINED MUM'S FAVORITE SWEATER.
OH, AND I'M GROUNDED.
MY LIFE IS AN EMBARASSINGLY PEDESTRIAN TEENAGE CESSPOOL.
THAT'S GREAT.
CUT IT, PAUL.
THINK WE COULD GO TO SCHOOL WITH YOU, TALK TO THIS GINGER KID?

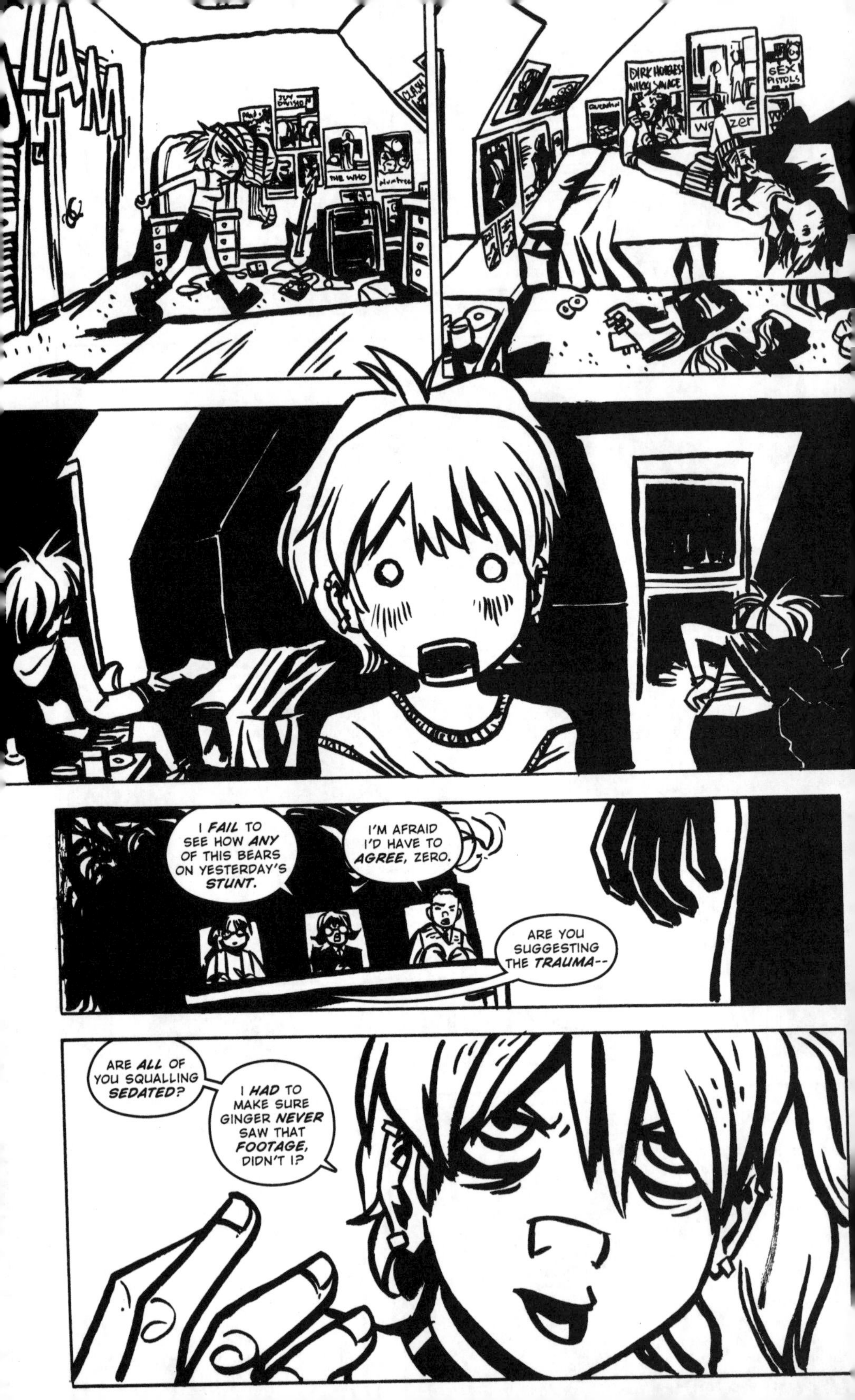
SLAM
CLASH
THE WHO
DIRK HODGES NIKKI SAVAGE
SEX PISTOLS
weezer
I FAIL TO SEE HOW ANY OF THIS BEARS ON YESTERDAY'S STUNT.
I'M AFRAID I'D HAVE TO AGREE, ZERO.
ARE YOU SUGGESTING THE TRAUMA--
ARE ALL OF YOU SQUALLING SEDATED?
I HAD TO MAKE SURE GINGER NEVER SAW THAT FOOTAGE, DIDN'T I?

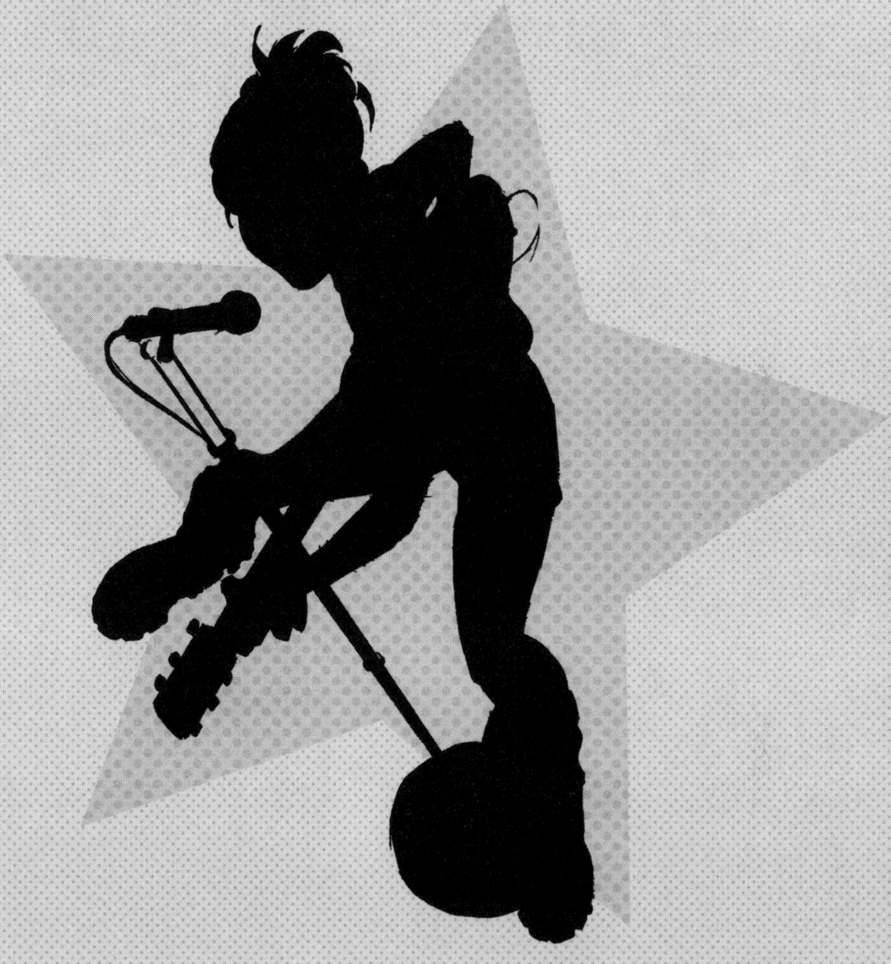

CHAPTER 2

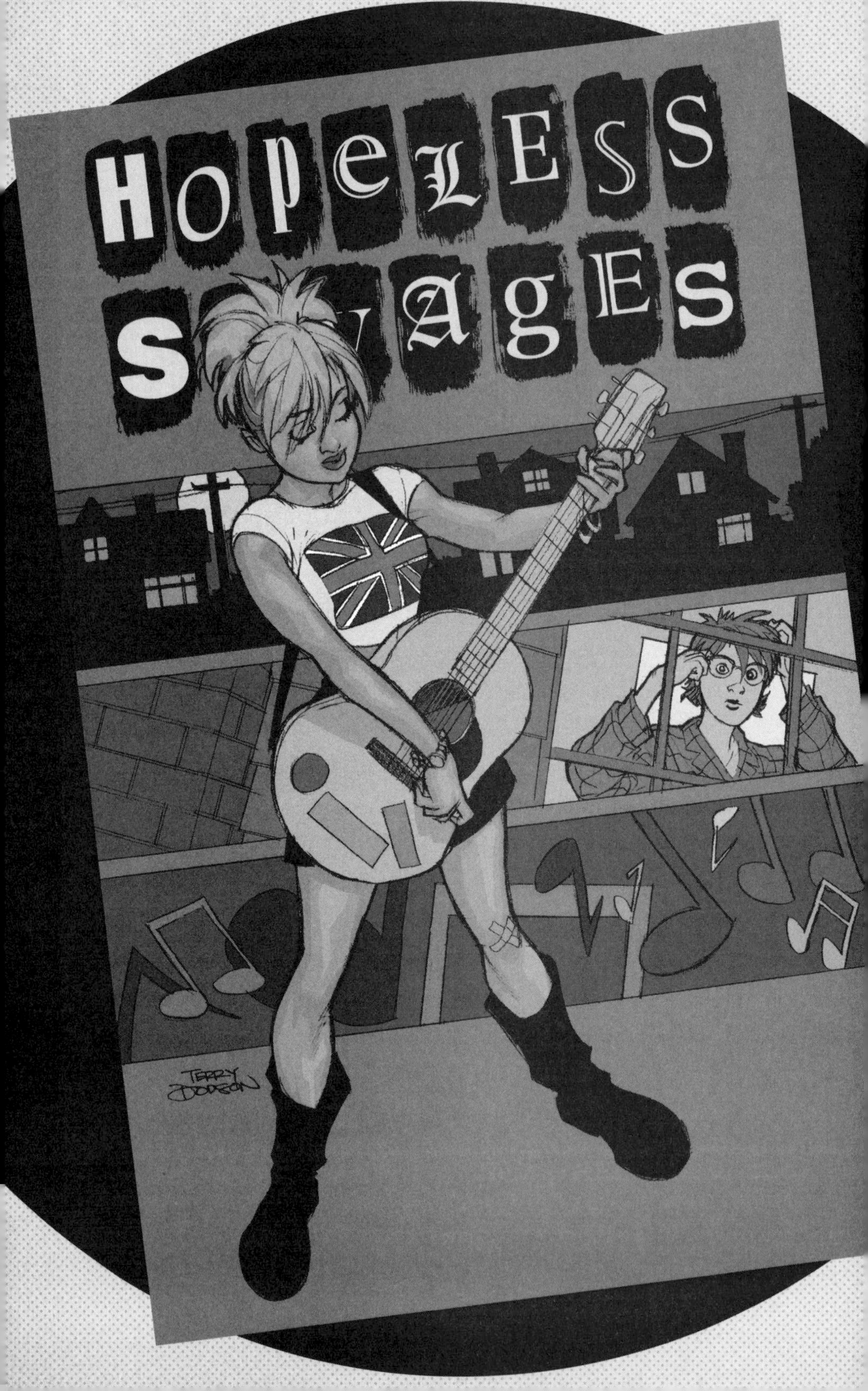
HOPELESS
S VAGES
TERRY DODSON

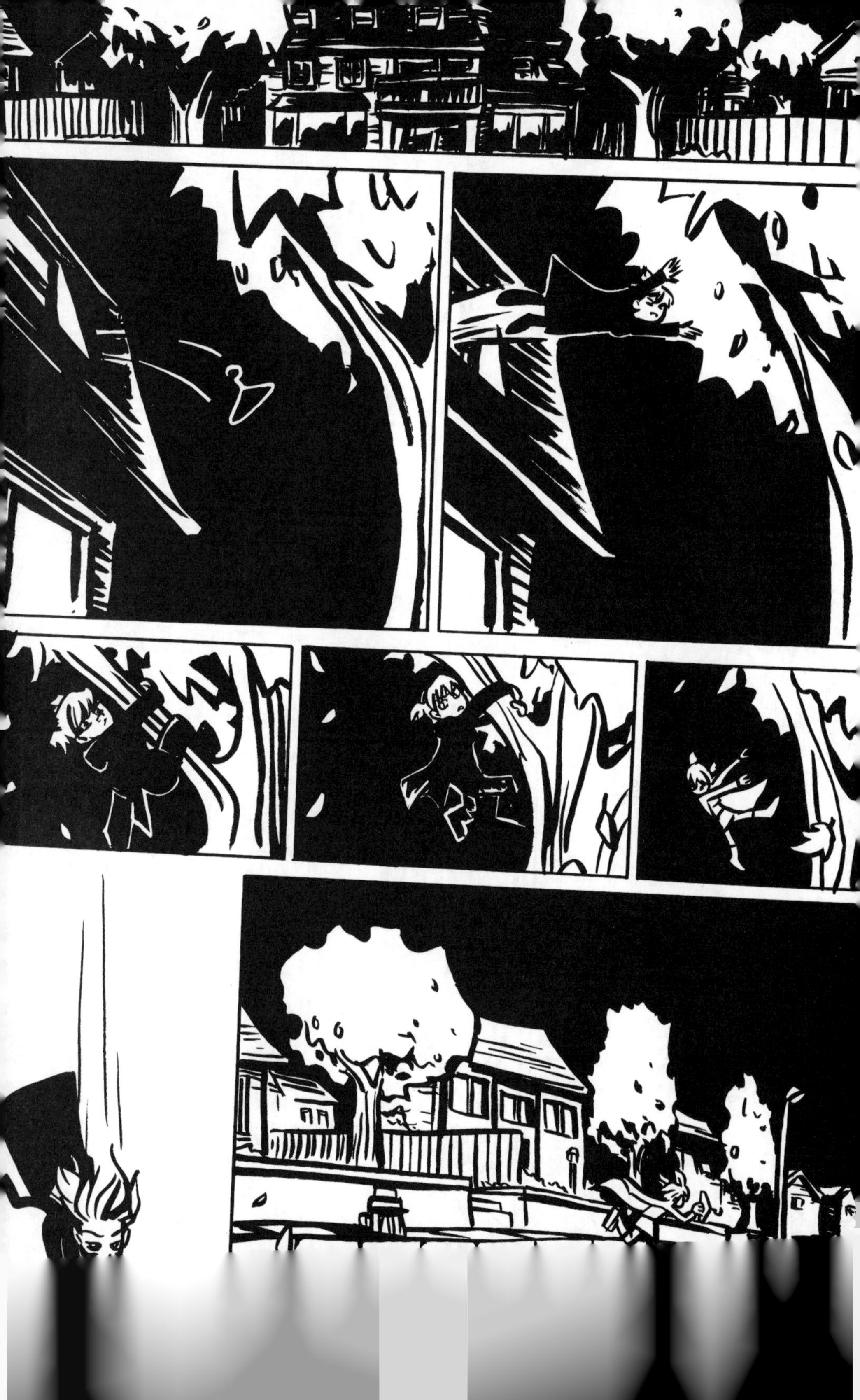

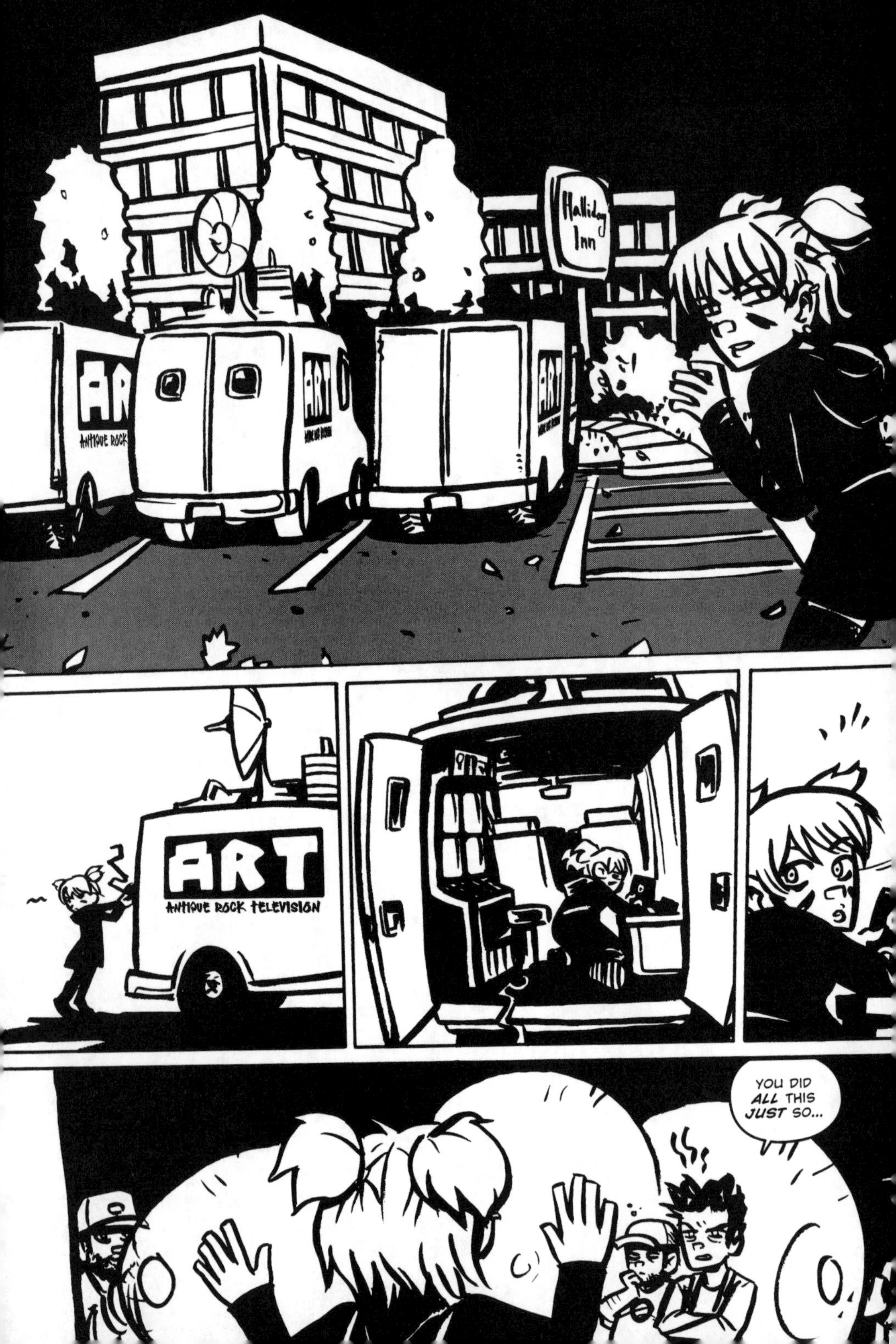
Halliday Inn
ART
ANTIQUE ROCK
ART
ART
ART
ANTIQUE ROCK TELEVISION
YOU DID ALL THIS JUST SO...

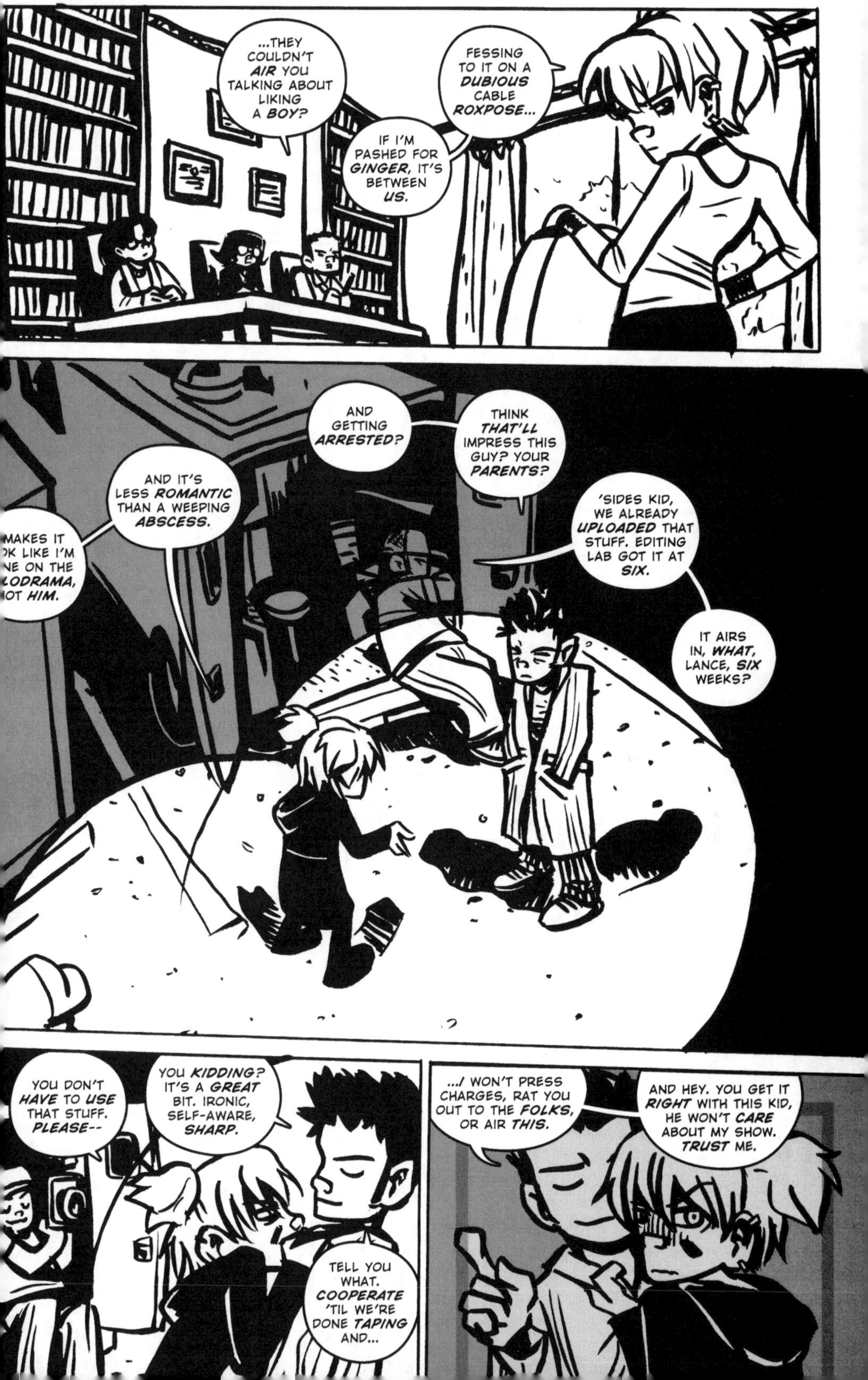
...THEY COULDN'T AIR YOU TALKING ABOUT LIKING A BOY?
FESSING TO IT ON A DUBIOUS CABLE ROXPOSE...
IF I'M PASHED FOR GINGER, IT'S BETWEEN US.
AND GETTING ARRESTED?
THINK THAT'LL IMPRESS THIS GUY? YOUR PARENTS?
AND IT'S LESS ROMANTIC THAN A WEEPING ABSCESS.
'SIDES KID, WE ALREADY UPLOADED THAT STUFF. EDITING LAB GOT IT AT SIX.
IT AIRS IN, WHAT, LANCE, SIX WEEKS?
YOU DON'T HAVE TO USE THAT STUFF. PLEASE--
YOU KIDDING? IT'S A GREAT BIT. IRONIC, SELF-AWARE, SHARP.
TELL YOU WHAT. COOPERATE 'TIL WE'RE DONE TAPING AND...
...I WON'T PRESS CHARGES, RAT YOU OUT TO THE FOLKS, OR AIR THIS.
AND HEY. YOU GET IT RIGHT WITH THIS KID, HE WON'T CARE ABOUT MY SHOW. TRUST ME.

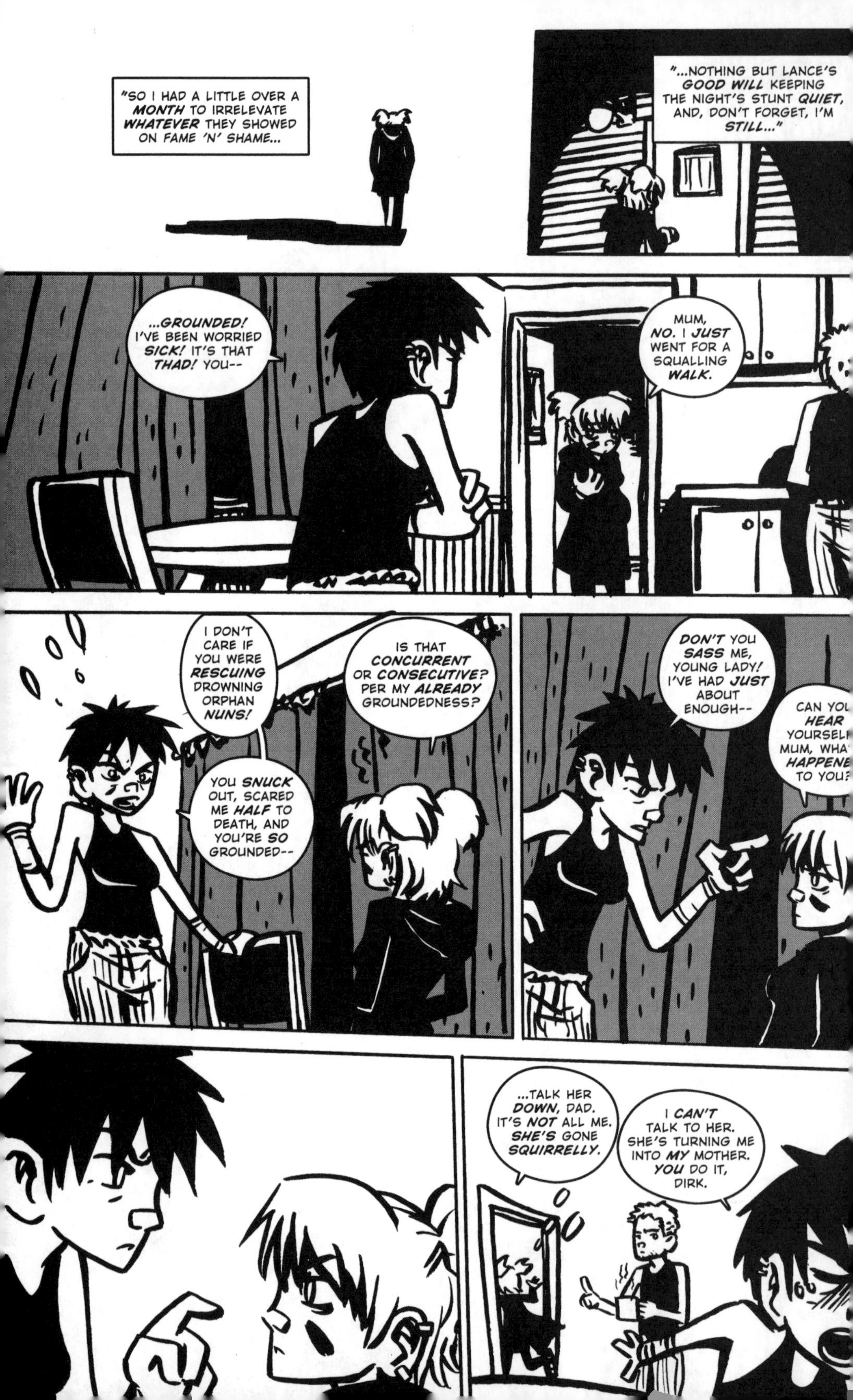
"SO I HAD A LITTLE OVER A MONTH TO IRRELEVATE WHATEVER THEY SHOWED ON FAME 'N' SHAME...
"...NOTHING BUT LANCE'S GOOD WILL KEEPING THE NIGHT'S STUNT QUIET, AND, DON'T FORGET, I'M STILL..."
...GROUNDED! I'VE BEEN WORRIED SICK! IT'S THAT THAD! YOU--
MUM, NO. I JUST WENT FOR A SQUALLING WALK.
I DON'T CARE IF YOU WERE RESCUING DROWNING ORPHAN NUNS!
YOU SNUCK OUT, SCARED ME HALF TO DEATH, AND YOU'RE SO GROUNDED--
IS THAT CONCURRENT OR CONSECUTIVE? PER MY ALREADY GROUNDEDNESS?
DON'T YOU SASS ME, YOUNG LADY! I'VE HAD JUST ABOUT ENOUGH--
...TALK HER DOWN, DAD. IT'S NOT ALL ME. SHE'S GONE SQUIRRELLY.
I CAN'T TALK TO HER. SHE'S TURNING ME INTO MY MOTHER. YOU DO IT, DIRK.

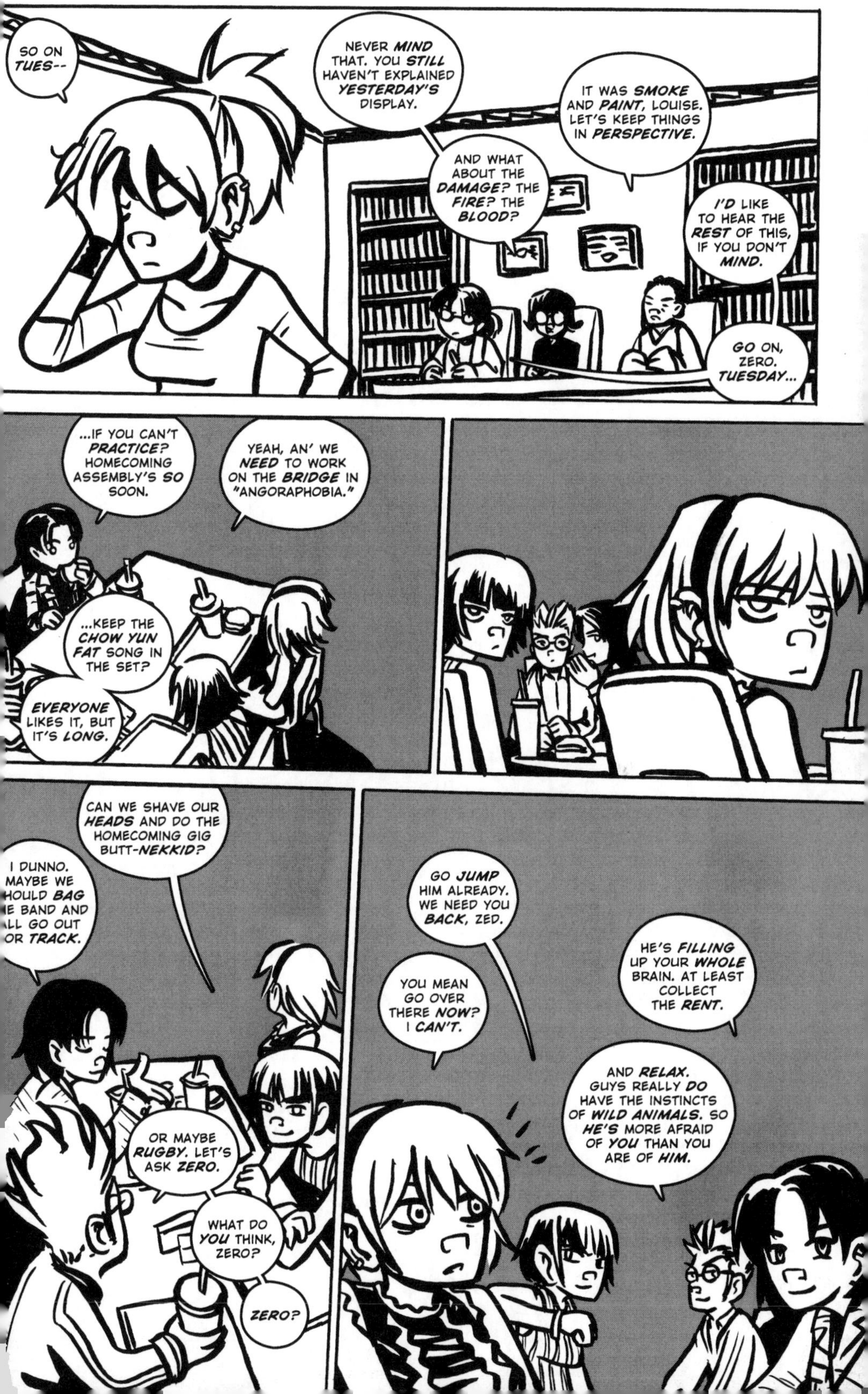
SO ON TUES--
NEVER MIND THAT. YOU STILL HAVEN'T EXPLAINED YESTERDAY'S DISPLAY.
AND WHAT ABOUT THE DAMAGE? THE FIRE? THE BLOOD?
IT WAS SMOKE AND PAINT, LOUISE. LET'S KEEP THINGS IN PERSPECTIVE.
I'D LIKE TO HEAR THE REST OF THIS, IF YOU DON'T MIND.
GO ON, ZERO. TUESDAY...
...IF YOU CAN'T PRACTICE? HOMECOMING ASSEMBLY'S SO SOON.
YEAH, AN' WE NEED TO WORK ON THE BRIDGE IN "ANGORAPHOBIA."
...KEEP THE CHOW YUN FAT SONG IN THE SET?
EVERYONE LIKES IT, BUT IT'S LONG.
CAN WE SHAVE OUR HEADS AND DO THE HOMECOMING GIG BUTT-NEKKID?
I DUNNO. MAYBE WE HOULD BAG E BAND AND LL GO OUT OR TRACK.
OR MAYBE RUGBY. LET'S ASK ZERO.
WHAT DO YOU THINK, ZERO?
ZERO?
GO JUMP HIM ALREADY. WE NEED YOU BACK, ZED.
YOU MEAN GO OVER THERE NOW? I CAN'T.
HE'S FILLING UP YOUR WHOLE BRAIN. AT LEAST COLLECT THE RENT.
AND RELAX. GUYS REALLY DO HAVE THE INSTINCTS OF WILD ANIMALS. SO HE'S MORE AFRAID OF YOU THAN YOU ARE OF HIM.

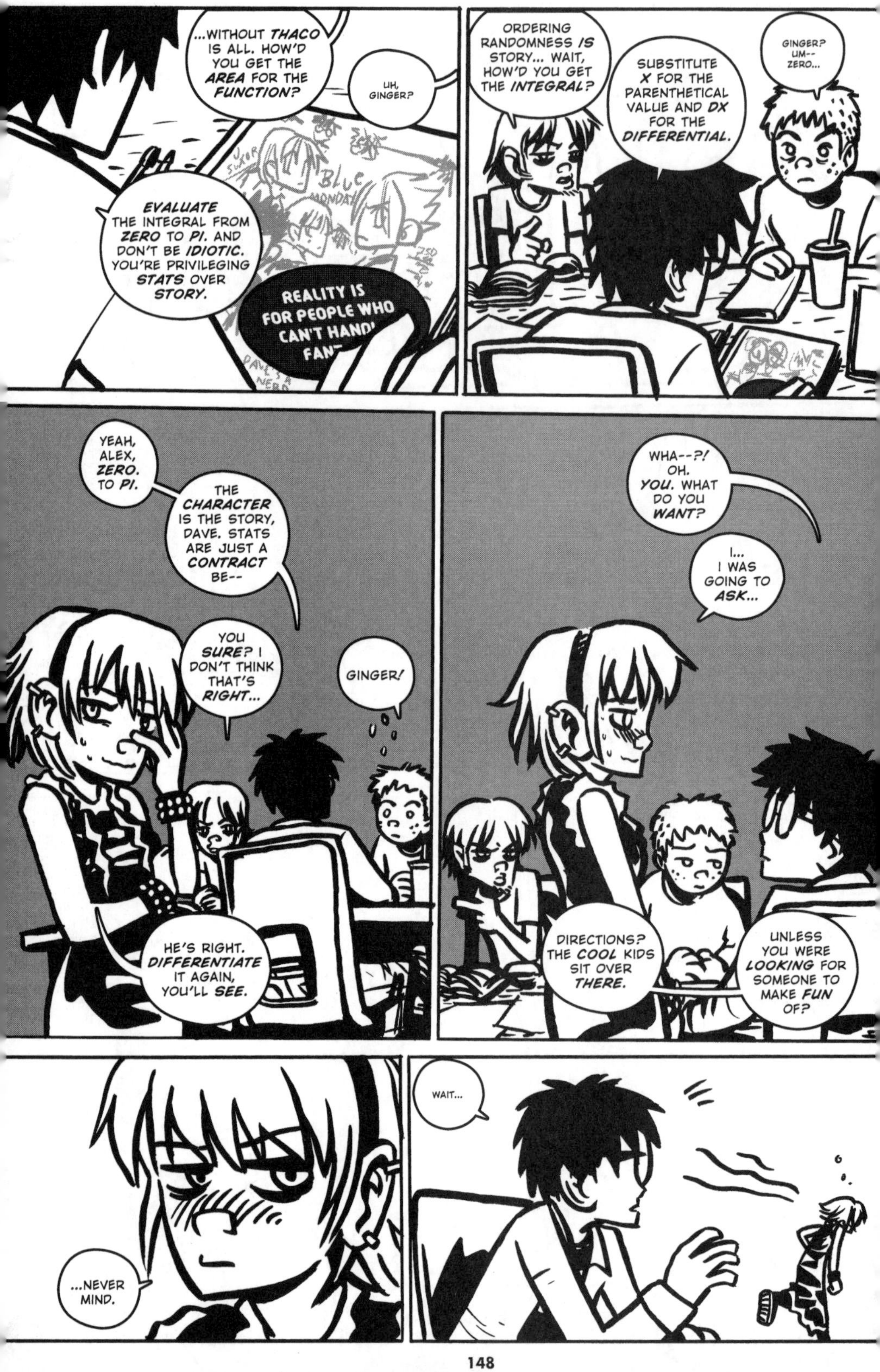
...WITHOUT THACO IS ALL. HOW'D YOU GET THE AREA FOR THE FUNCTION?
UH, GINGER?
EVALUATE THE INTEGRAL FROM ZERO TO PI. AND DON'T BE IDIOTIC. YOU'RE PRIVILEGING STATS OVER STORY.
REALITY IS FOR PEOPLE WHO
ORDERING RANDOMNESS IS STORY... WAIT, HOW'D YOU GET THE INTEGRAL?
SUBSTITUTE X FOR THE PARENTHETICAL VALUE AND DX FOR THE DIFFERENTIAL.
GINGER? UM-- ZERO...
YEAH, ALEX, ZERO. TO PI.
THE CHARACTER IS THE STORY, DAVE. STATS ARE JUST A CONTRACT BE--
YOU SURE? I DON'T THINK THAT'S RIGHT...
GINGER!
HE'S RIGHT. DIFFERENTIATE IT AGAIN, YOU'LL SEE.
WHA--?! OH. YOU. WHAT DO YOU WANT?
I... I WAS GOING TO ASK...
DIRECTIONS? THE COOL KIDS SIT OVER THERE.
UNLESS YOU WERE LOOKING FOR SOMEONE TO MAKE FUN OF?
...NEVER MIND.
WAIT...

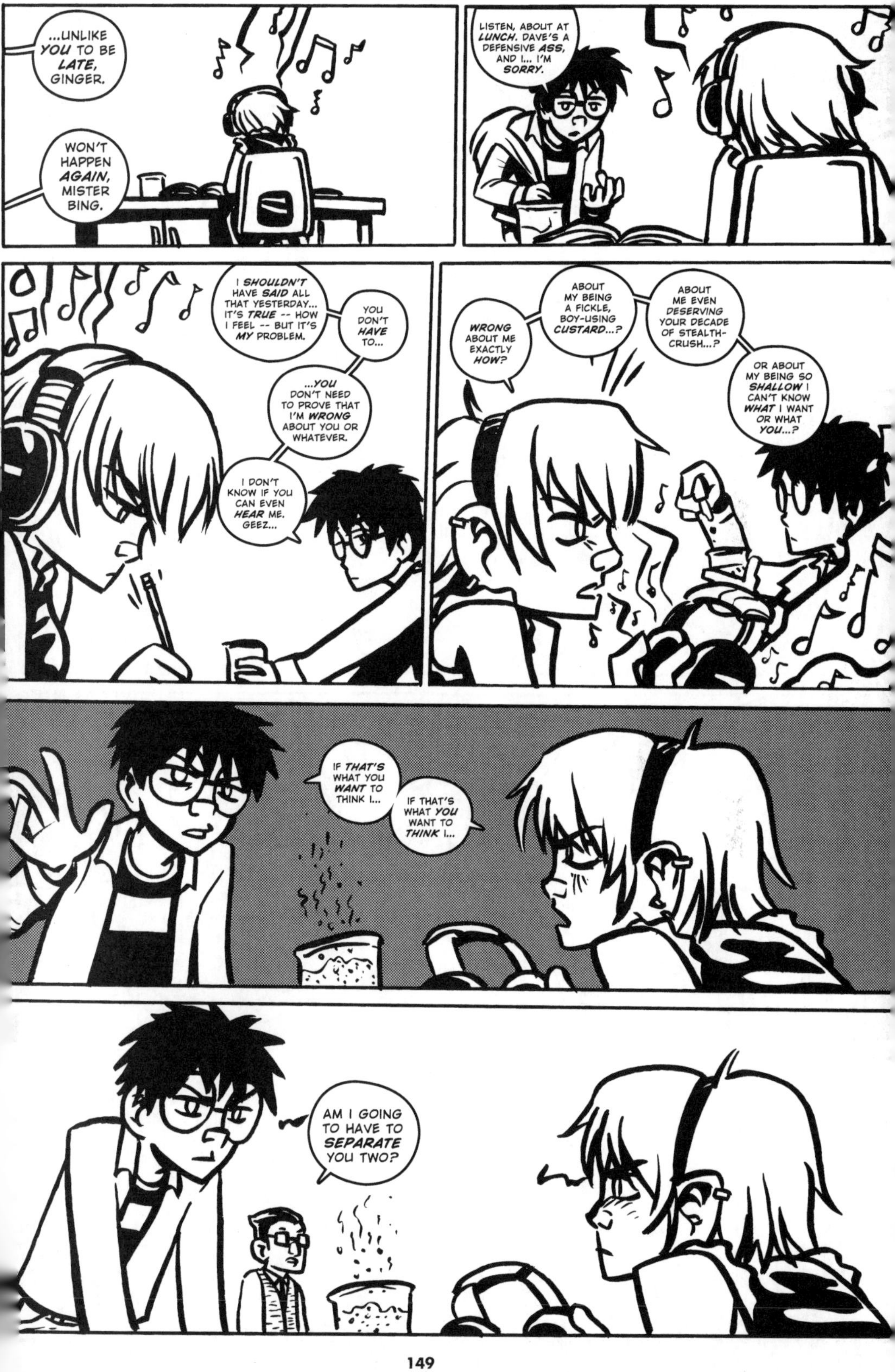
...UNLIKE YOU TO BE LATE, GINGER.
WON'T HAPPEN AGAIN, MISTER BING.
LISTEN, ABOUT AT LUNCH. DAVE'S A DEFENSIVE ASS, AND I... I'M SORRY.
I SHOULDN'T HAVE SAID ALL THAT YESTERDAY... IT'S TRUE -- HOW I FEEL -- BUT IT'S MY PROBLEM.
YOU DON'T HAVE TO...
...YOU DON'T NEED TO PROVE THAT I'M WRONG ABOUT YOU OR WHATEVER.
I DON'T KNOW IF YOU CAN EVEN HEAR ME. GEEZ...
WRONG ABOUT ME EXACTLY HOW?
ABOUT MY BEING A FICKLE, BOY-USING CUSTARD...?
ABOUT ME EVEN DESERVING YOUR DECADE OF STEALTH-CRUSH...?
OR ABOUT MY BEING SO SHALLOW I CAN'T KNOW WHAT I WANT OR WHAT YOU...?
IF THAT'S WHAT YOU WANT TO THINK I...
IF THAT'S WHAT YOU WANT TO THINK I...
AM I GOING TO HAVE TO SEPARATE YOU TWO?

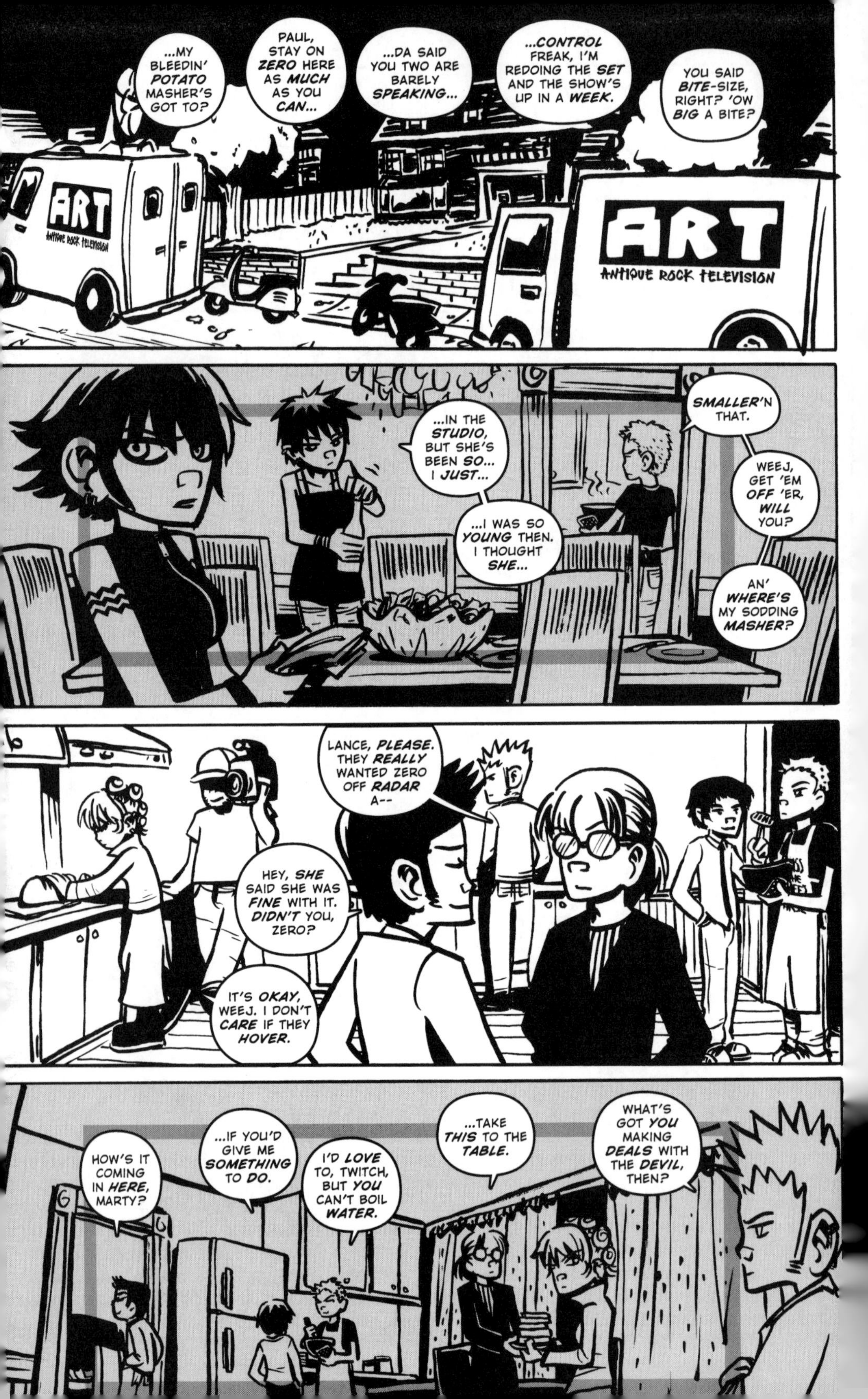
...MY BLEEDIN' POTATO MASHER'S GOT TO?
PAUL, STAY ON ZERO HERE AS MUCH AS YOU CAN...
...DA SAID YOU TWO ARE BARELY SPEAKING...
...CONTROL FREAK, I'M REDOING THE SET AND THE SHOW'S UP IN A WEEK.
YOU SAID BITE-SIZE, RIGHT? 'OW BIG A BITE?
ART
ANTIQUE ROCK TELEVISION
ART
ANTIQUE ROCK TELEVISION
...IN THE STUDIO, BUT SHE'S BEEN SO... I JUST...
...I WAS SO YOUNG THEN. I THOUGHT SHE...
SMALLER'N THAT.
WEEJ, GET 'EM OFF 'ER, WILL YOU?
AN' WHERE'S MY SODDING MASHER?
LANCE, PLEASE. THEY REALLY WANTED ZERO OFF RADAR A--
HEY, SHE SAID SHE WAS FINE WITH IT. DIDN'T YOU, ZERO?
IT'S OKAY, WEEJ. I DON'T CARE IF THEY HOVER.
HOW'S IT COMING IN HERE, MARTY?
...IF YOU'D GIVE ME SOMETHING TO DO.
I'D LOVE TO, TWITCH, BUT YOU CAN'T BOIL WATER.
...TAKE THIS TO THE TABLE.
WHAT'S GOT YOU MAKING DEALS WITH THE DEVIL, THEN?

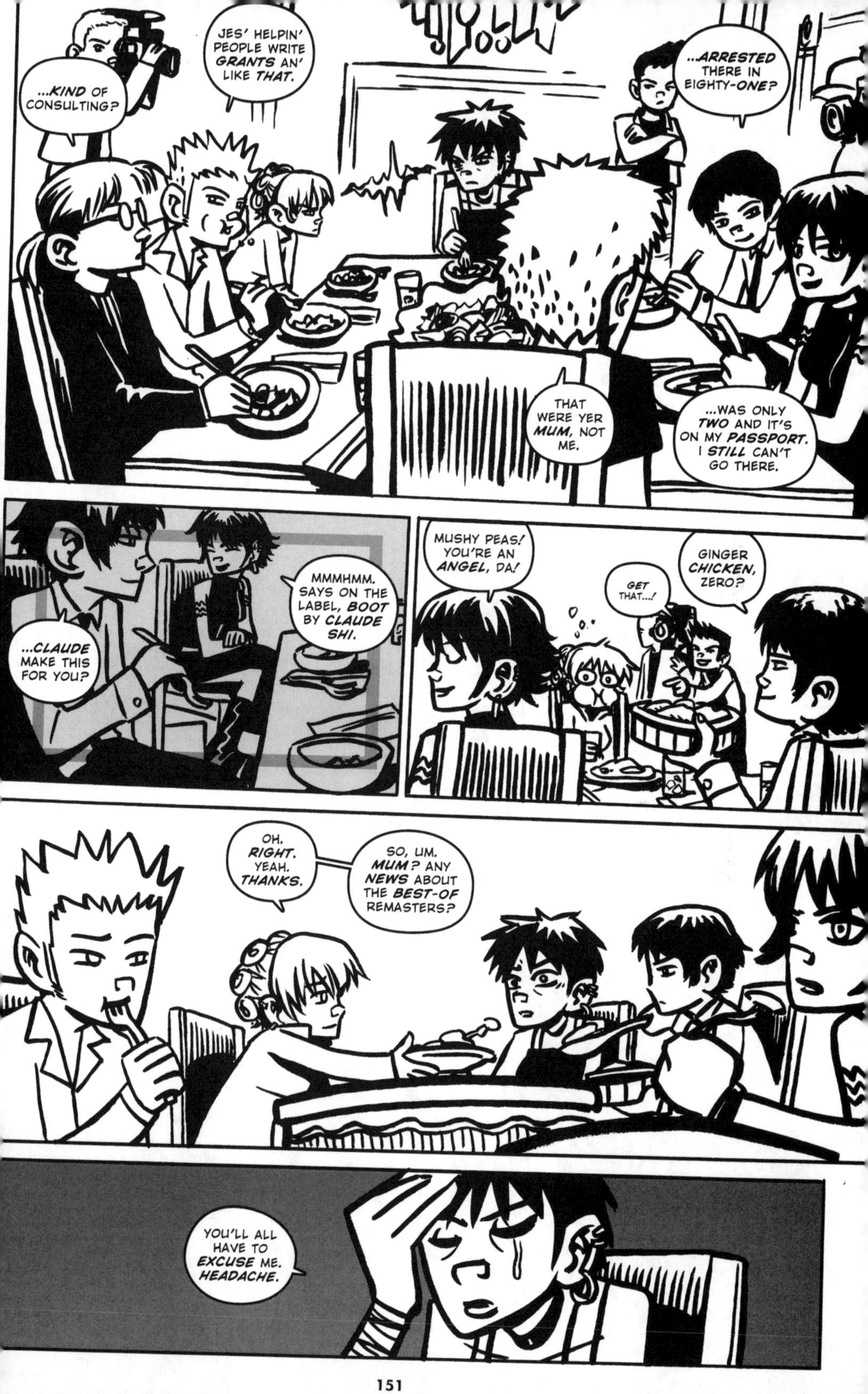
...KIND OF CONSULTING?
JES' HELPIN' PEOPLE WRITE GRANTS AN' LIKE THAT.
...ARRESTED THERE IN EIGHTY-ONE?
THAT WERE YER MUM, NOT ME.
...WAS ONLY TWO AND IT'S ON MY PASSPORT. I STILL CAN'T GO THERE.
...CLAUDE MAKE THIS FOR YOU?
MMMHMM. SAYS ON THE LABEL, BOOT BY CLAUDE SHI.
MUSHY PEAS! YOU'RE AN ANGEL, DA!
GET THAT...!
GINGER CHICKEN, ZERO?
OH. RIGHT. YEAH. THANKS.
SO, UM. MUM? ANY NEWS ABOUT THE BEST-OF REMASTERS?
YOU'LL ALL HAVE TO EXCUSE ME. HEADACHE.

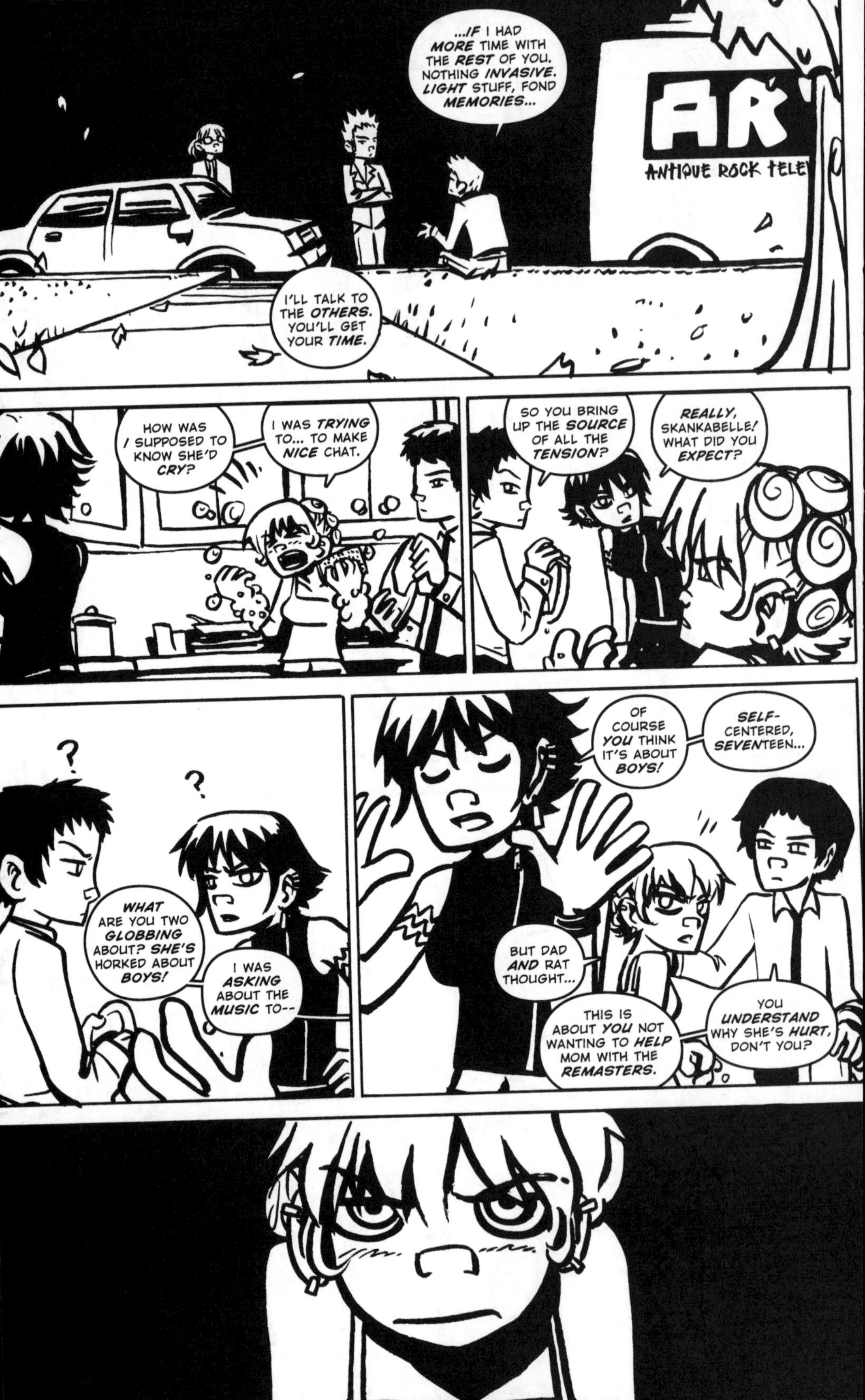
...IF I HAD MORE TIME WITH THE REST OF YOU. NOTHING INVASIVE. LIGHT STUFF, FOND MEMORIES...
AR
ANTIQUE ROCK TELE
I'LL TALK TO THE OTHERS. YOU'LL GET YOUR TIME.
HOW WAS I SUPPOSED TO KNOW SHE'D CRY?
I WAS TRYING TO... TO MAKE NICE CHAT.
SO YOU BRING UP THE SOURCE OF ALL THE TENSION?
REALLY, SKANKABELLE! WHAT DID YOU EXPECT?
?
?
WHAT ARE YOU TWO GLOBBING ABOUT? SHE'S HORKED ABOUT BOYS!
I WAS ASKING ABOUT THE MUSIC TO--
OF COURSE YOU THINK IT'S ABOUT BOYS!
SELF-CENTERED, SEVENTEEN...
BUT DAD AND RAT THOUGHT...
THIS IS ABOUT YOU NOT WANTING TO HELP MOM WITH THE REMASTERS.
YOU UNDERSTAND WHY SHE'S HURT, DON'T YOU?

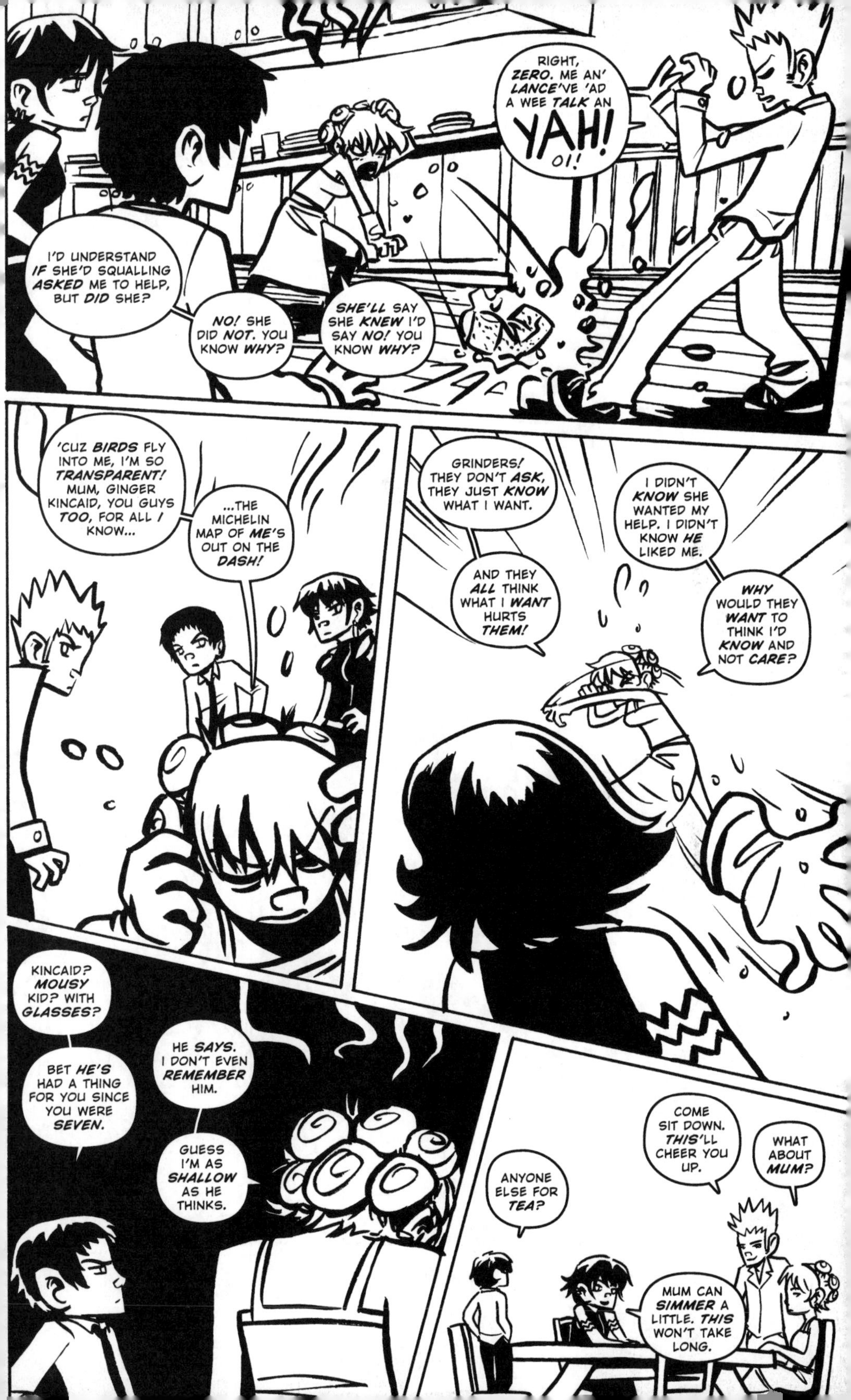

RIGHT, ZERO. ME AN' LANCE'VE 'AD A WEE TALK AN YAH! OI!
I'D UNDERSTAND IF SHE'D SQUALLING ASKED ME TO HELP, BUT DID SHE?
NO! SHE DID NOT. YOU KNOW WHY?
SHE'LL SAY SHE KNEW I'D SAY NO! YOU KNOW WHY?
'CUZ BIRDS FLY INTO ME, I'M SO TRANSPARENT! MUM, GINGER KINCAID, YOU GUYS TOO, FOR ALL I KNOW...
...THE MICHELIN MAP OF ME'S OUT ON THE DASH!
GRINDERS! THEY DON'T ASK, THEY JUST KNOW WHAT I WANT.
AND THEY ALL THINK WHAT I WANT HURTS THEM!
I DIDN'T KNOW SHE WANTED MY HELP. I DIDN'T KNOW HE LIKED ME.
WHY WOULD THEY WANT TO THINK I'D KNOW AND NOT CARE?
KINCAID? MOUSY KID? WITH GLASSES?
BET HE'S HAD A THING FOR YOU SINCE YOU WERE SEVEN.
HE SAYS. I DON'T EVEN REMEMBER HIM.
GUESS I'M AS SHALLOW AS HE THINKS.
ANYONE ELSE FOR TEA?
COME SIT DOWN. THIS'LL CHEER YOU UP.
WHAT ABOUT MUM?
MUM CAN SIMMER A LITTLE. THIS WON'T TAKE LONG.

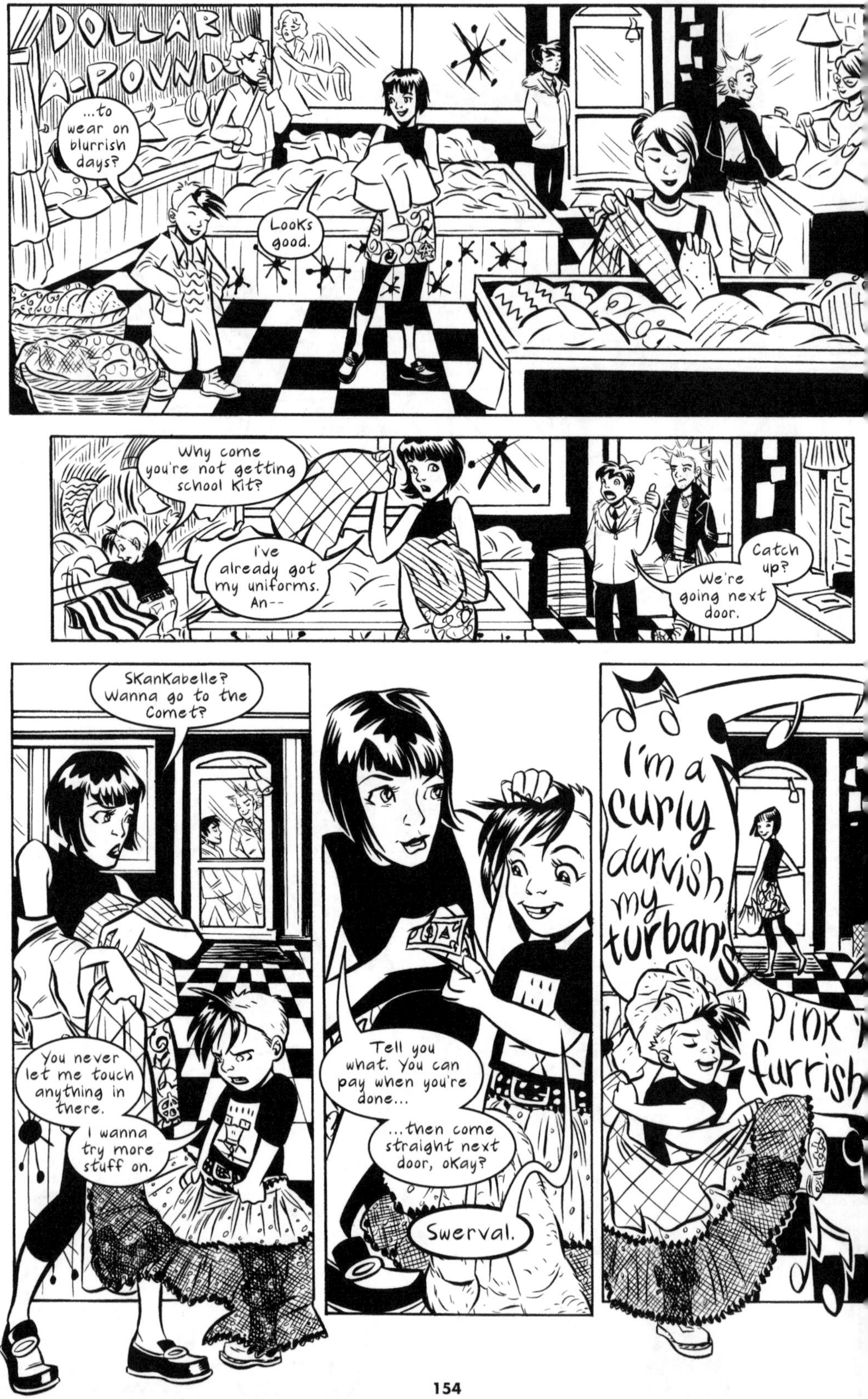
DOLLAR A-POUND
...to wear on blurrish days?
Looks good.
Why come you're not getting school Kit?
I've already got my uniforms. An--
Catch up?
We're going next door.
SKanKabelle? Wanna go to the Comet?
You never let me touch anything in there.
I wanna try more stuff on.
Tell you what. You can pay when you're done...
...then come straight next door, oKay?
Swerval.
I'm a curly durvish my turban's pink 'n furrish

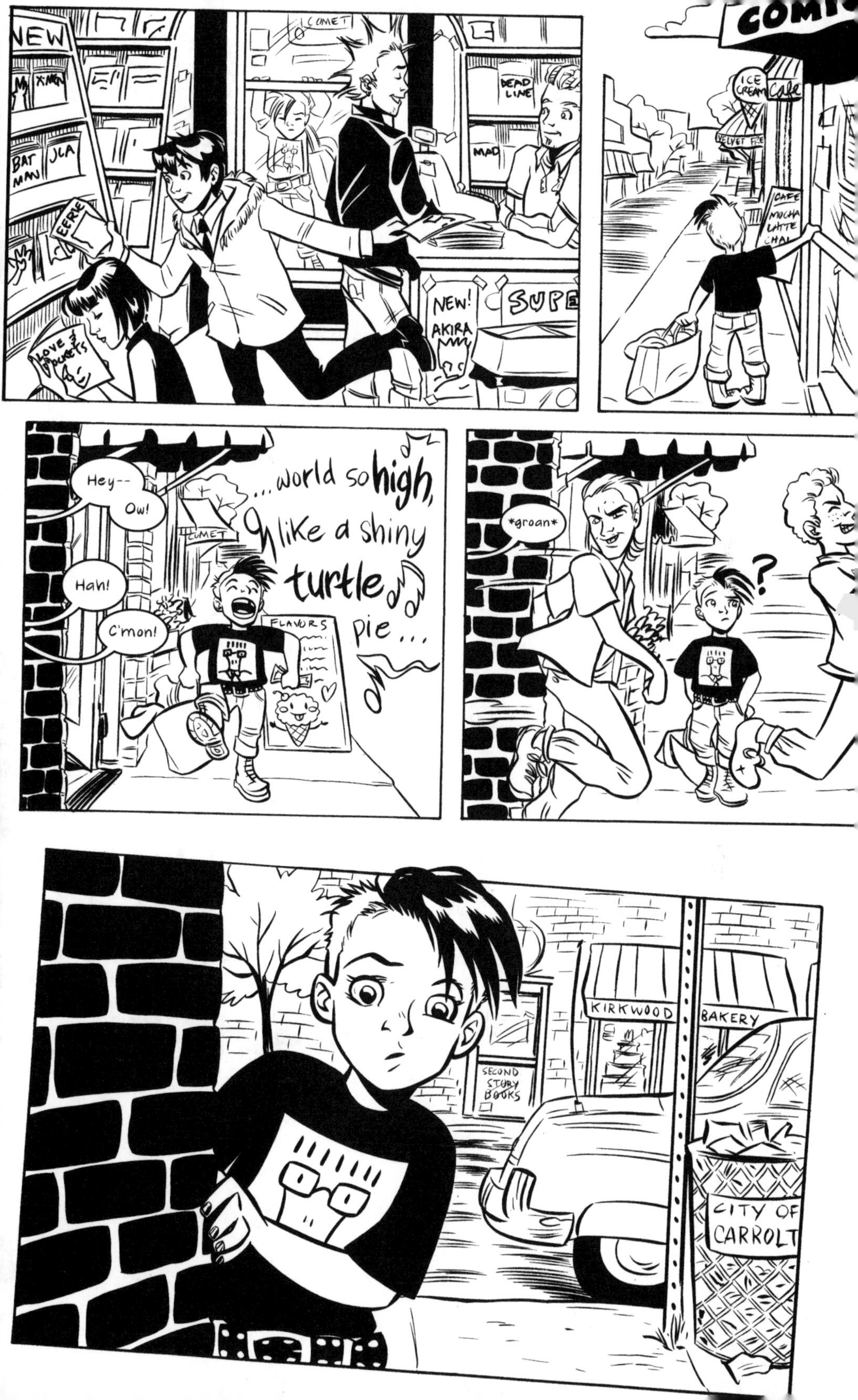
NEW
X-MEN
BATMAN
JLA
EERIE
COMET
DEAD LINE
MAD
LOVE & ROCKETS
NEW! AKIRA
SUPE
COMI
ICE CREAM
CAFE
VELVET FREE
CAFE MOCHA LATTE CHAI
Hey--
Ow!
Hah!
C'mon!
...world so high, like a shiny turtle pie...
COMET
FLAVORS
groan
?
KIRKWOOD BAKERY
SECOND STORY BOOKS
CITY OF CARROLT

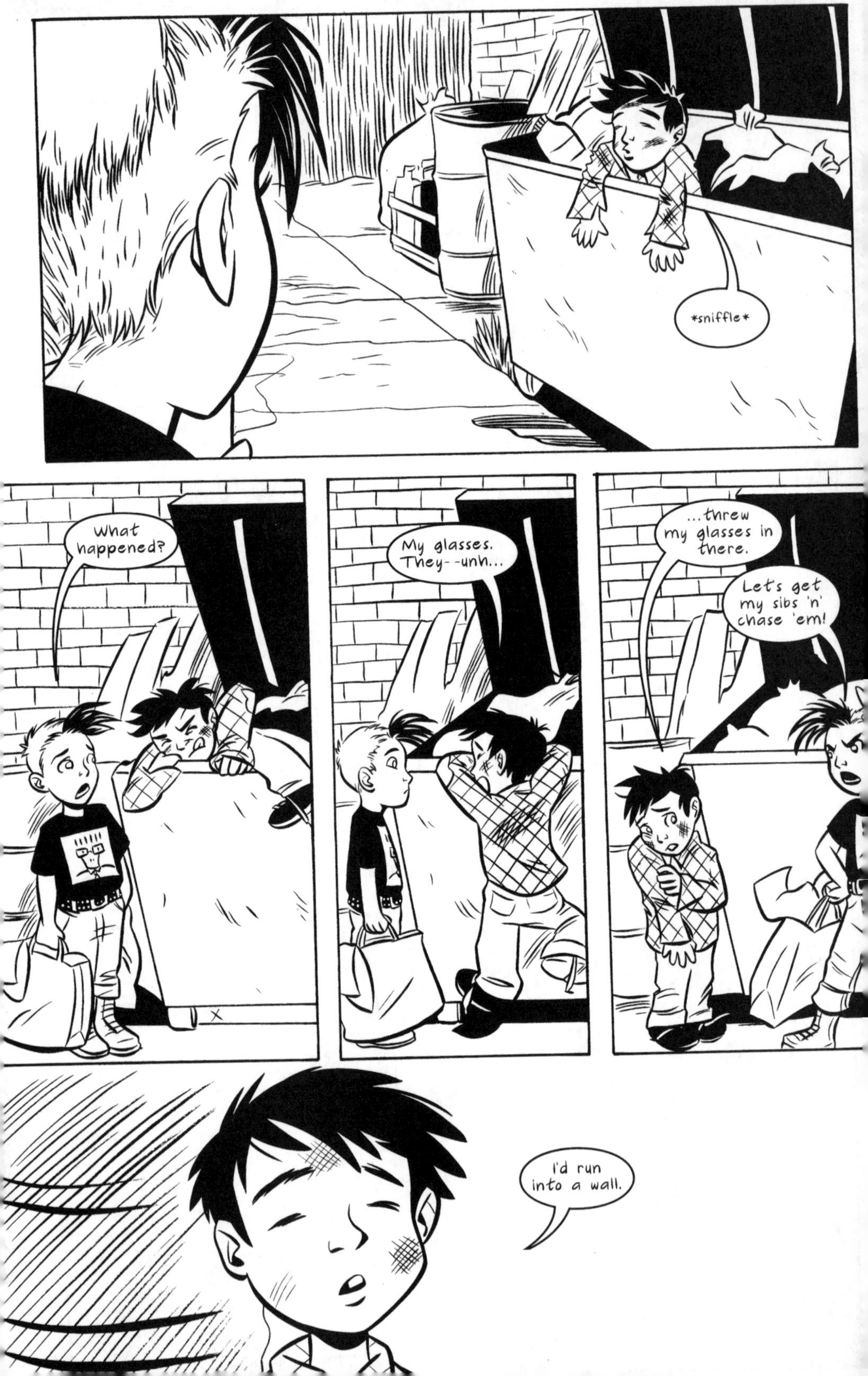
sniffle
What happened?
My glasses. They--unh...
...threw my glasses in there.
Let's get my sibs 'n' chase 'em!
I'd run into a wall.

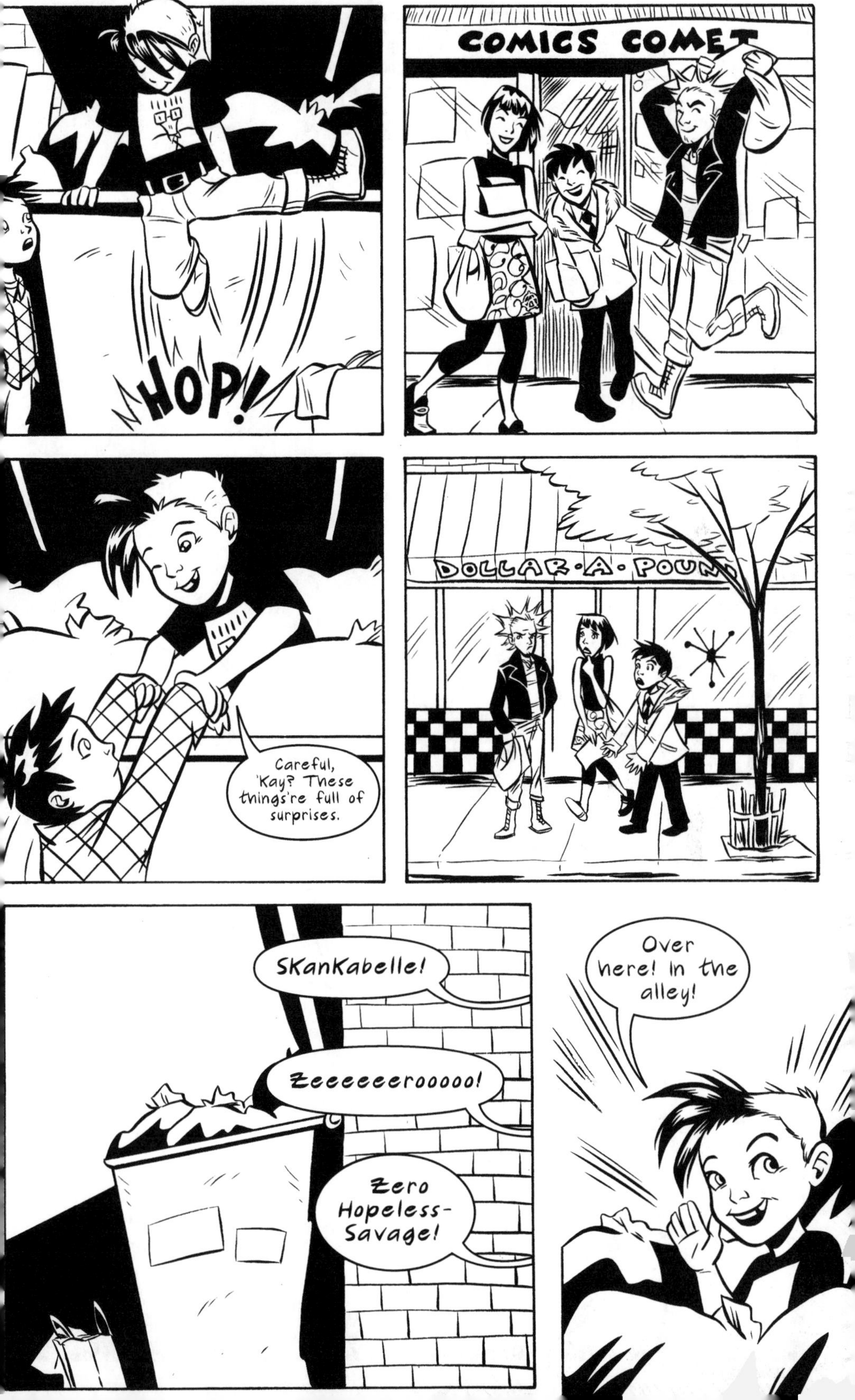
HOP!
COMICS COMET
Careful, 'Kay? These things're full of surprises.
DOLLAR-A-POUN
SKanKabelle!
Zeeeeeerooooo!
Zero Hopeless-Savage!
Over here! In the alley!

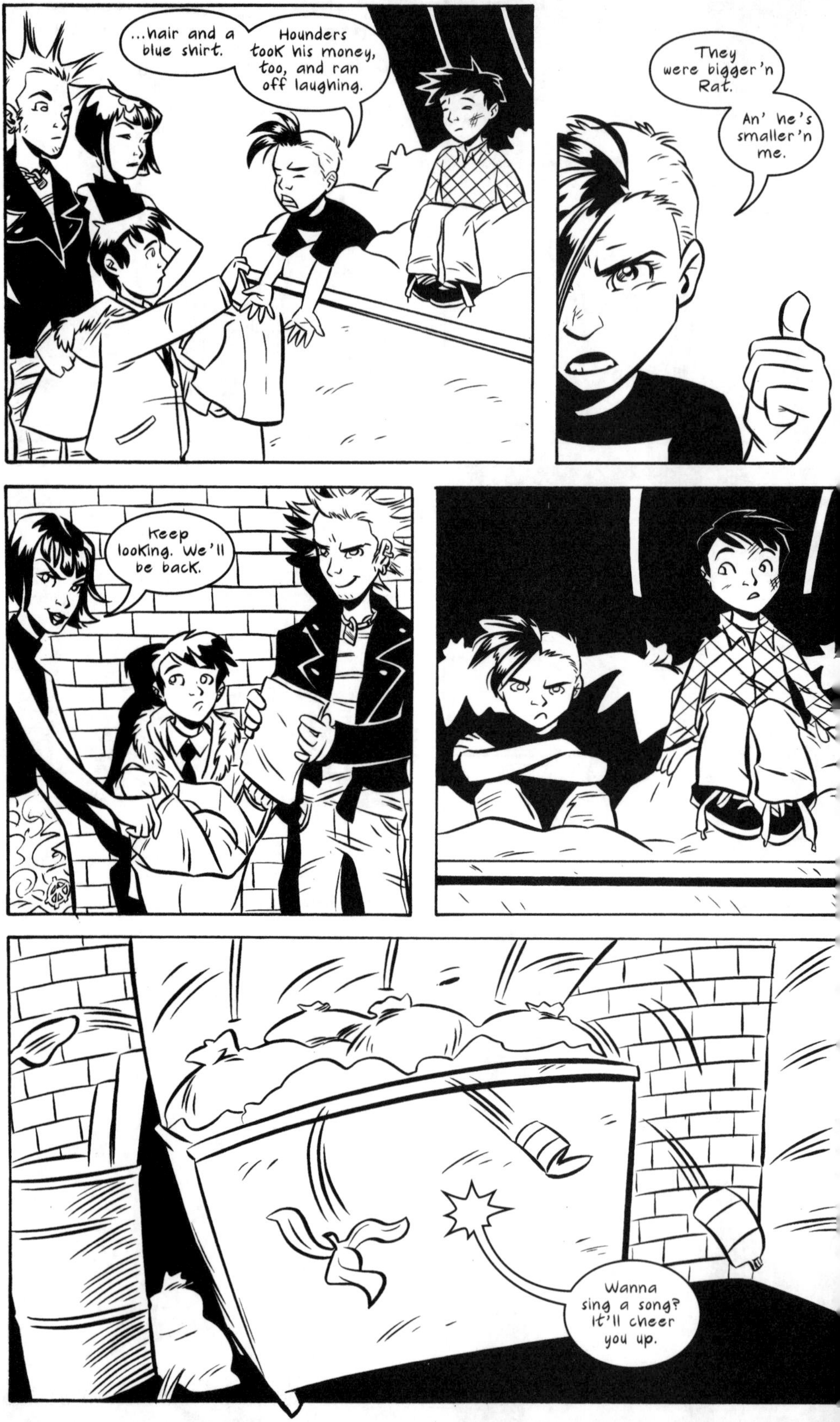
...hair and a blue shirt.
Hounders took his money, too, and ran off laughing.
They were bigger'n Rat.
An' he's smaller'n me.
Keep looking. We'll be back.
Wanna sing a song? It'll cheer you up.

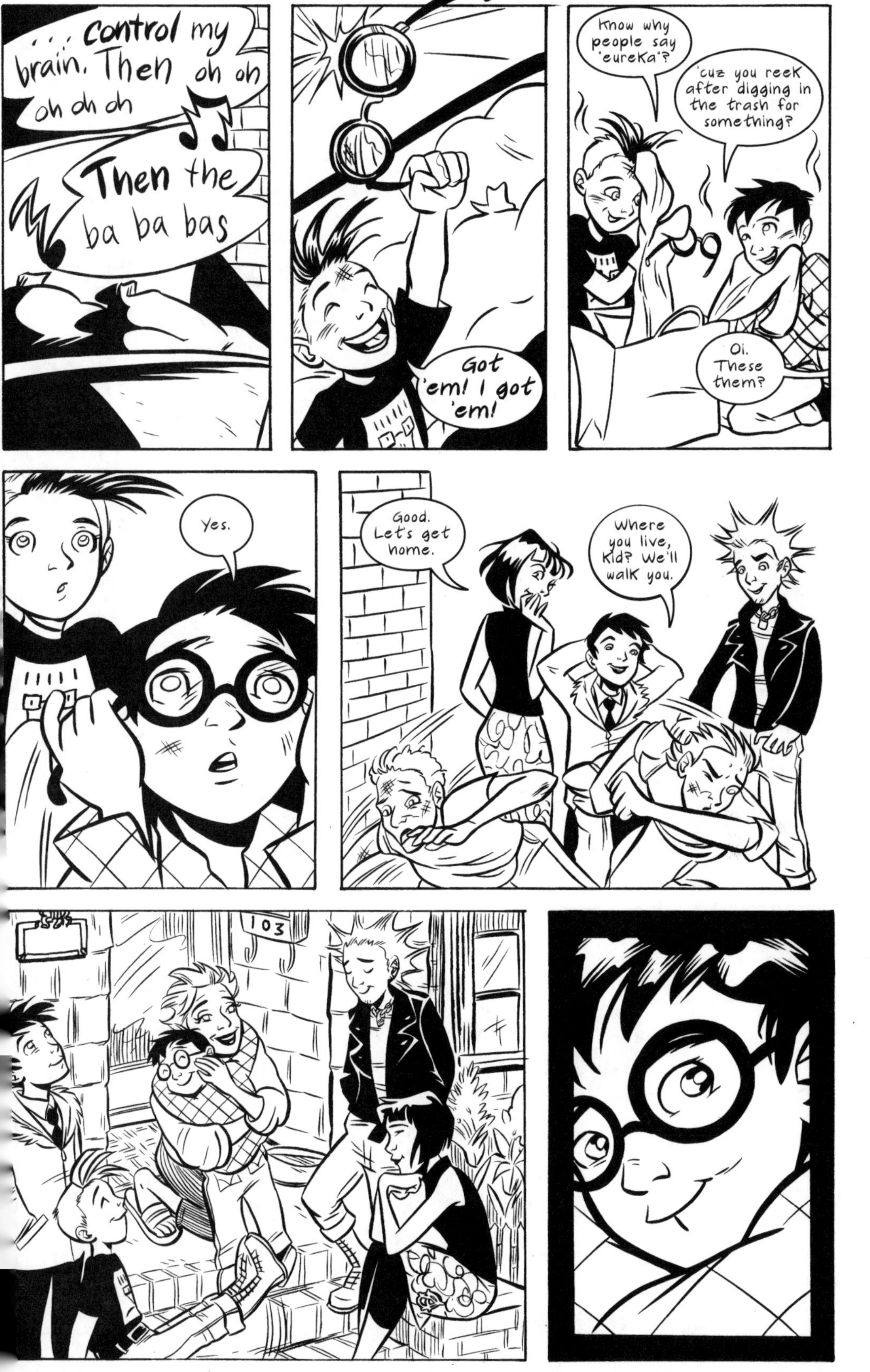
. . . Control my brain. Then oh oh oh oh oh
Then the ba ba bas
Got 'em! I got 'em!
Know why people say "eureka"?
'cuz you reek after digging in the trash for something?
Oi. These them?
Yes.
Good. Let's get home.
Where you live, kid? We'll walk you.
103

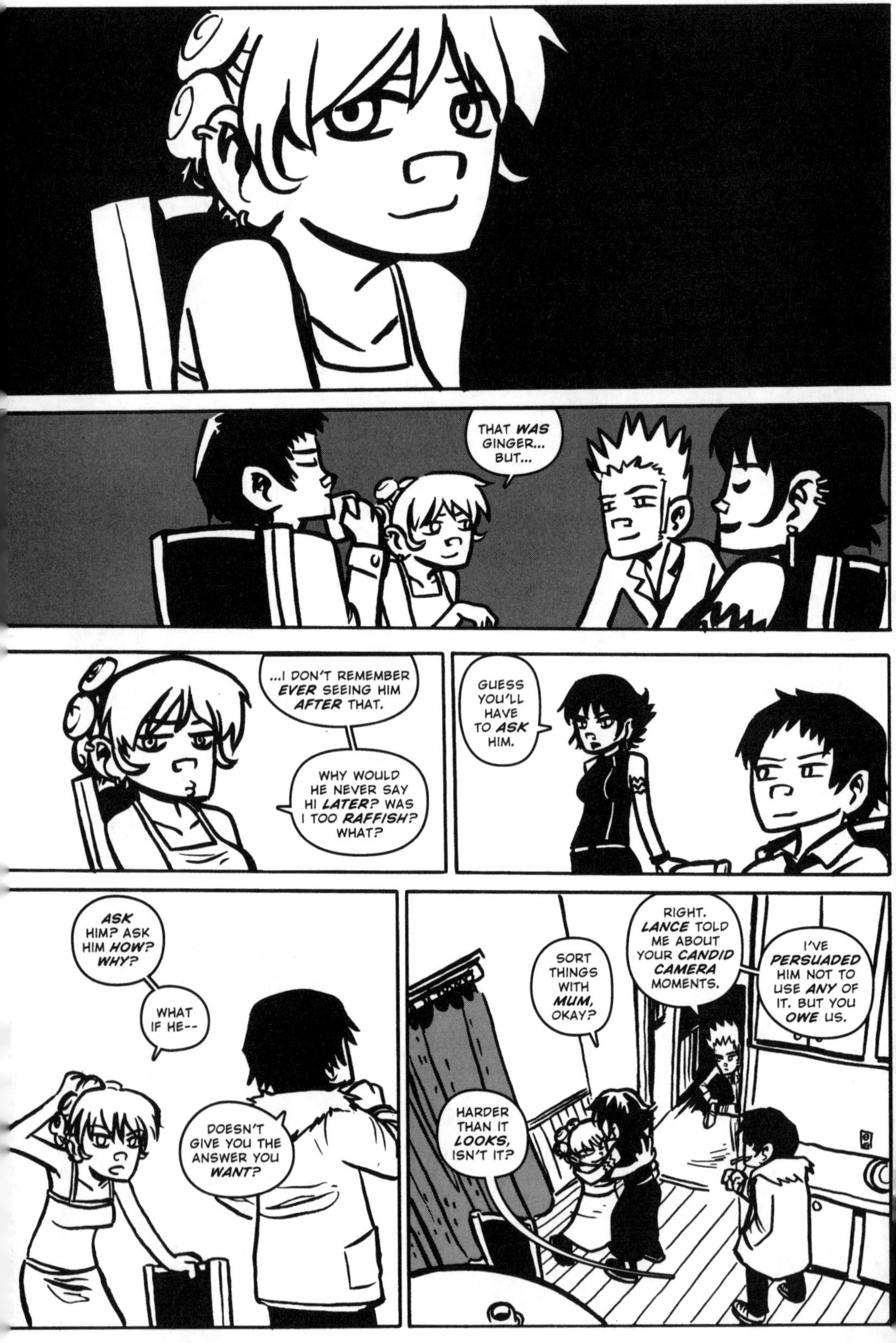
THAT *WAS* GINGER... BUT...
...I DON'T REMEMBER *EVER* SEEING HIM *AFTER* THAT.
WHY WOULD HE NEVER SAY HI *LATER*? WAS I TOO *RAFFISH*? WHAT?
GUESS YOU'LL HAVE TO *ASK* HIM.
ASK HIM? ASK HIM *HOW*? *WHY*?
WHAT IF HE--
DOESN'T GIVE YOU THE ANSWER YOU *WANT*?
SORT THINGS WITH *MUM*, OKAY?
HARDER THAN IT *LOOKS*, ISN'T IT?
RIGHT. *LANCE* TOLD ME ABOUT YOUR *CANDID CAMERA* MOMENTS.
I'VE *PERSUADED* HIM NOT TO USE *ANY* OF IT. BUT YOU *OWE* US.

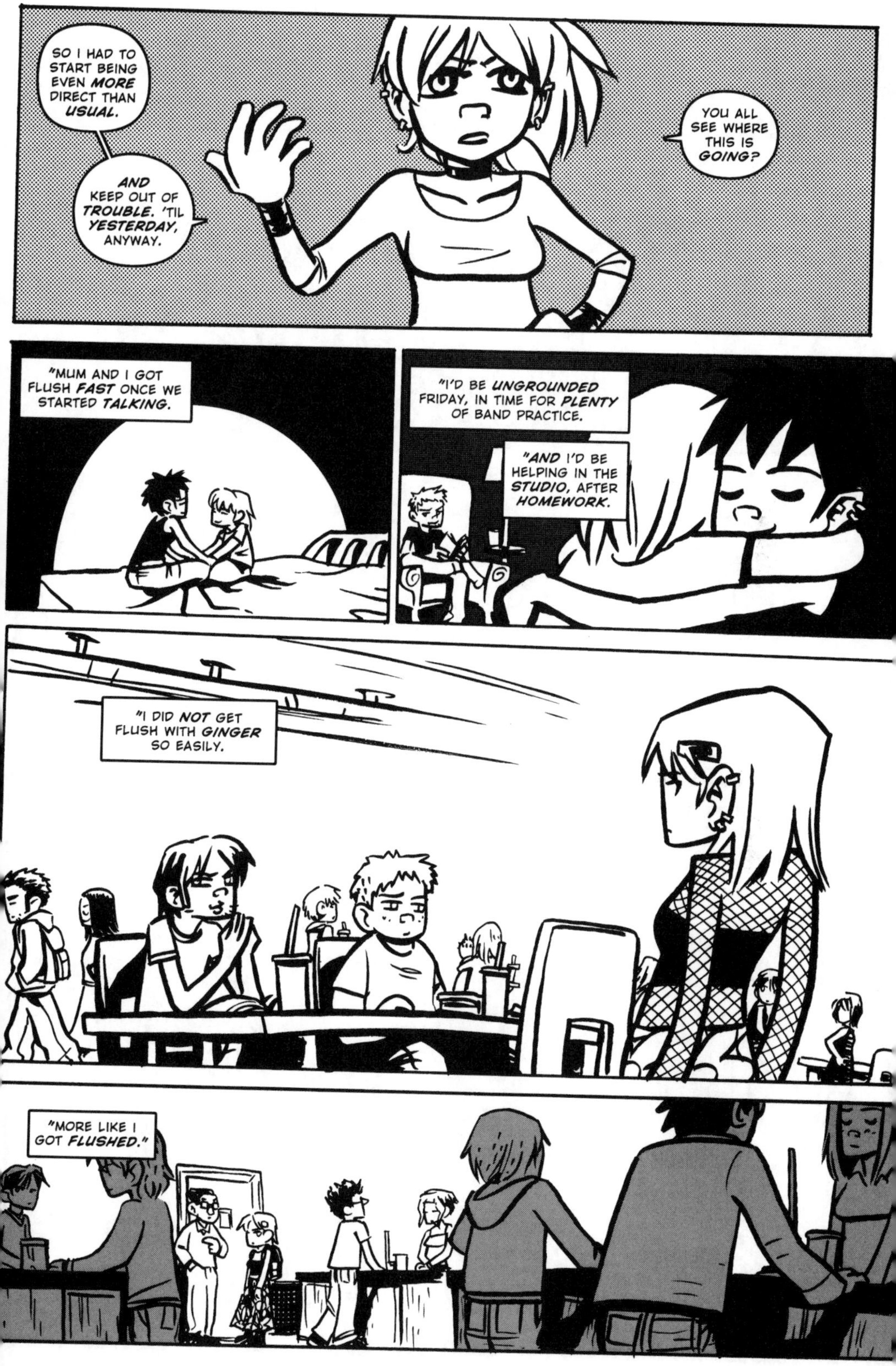
SO I HAD TO START BEING EVEN MORE DIRECT THAN USUAL.
AND KEEP OUT OF TROUBLE. 'TIL YESTERDAY, ANYWAY.
YOU ALL SEE WHERE THIS IS GOING?
"MUM AND I GOT FLUSH FAST ONCE WE STARTED TALKING.
"I'D BE UNGROUNDED FRIDAY, IN TIME FOR PLENTY OF BAND PRACTICE.
"AND I'D BE HELPING IN THE STUDIO, AFTER HOMEWORK.
"I DID NOT GET FLUSH WITH GINGER SO EASILY.
"MORE LIKE I GOT FLUSHED."

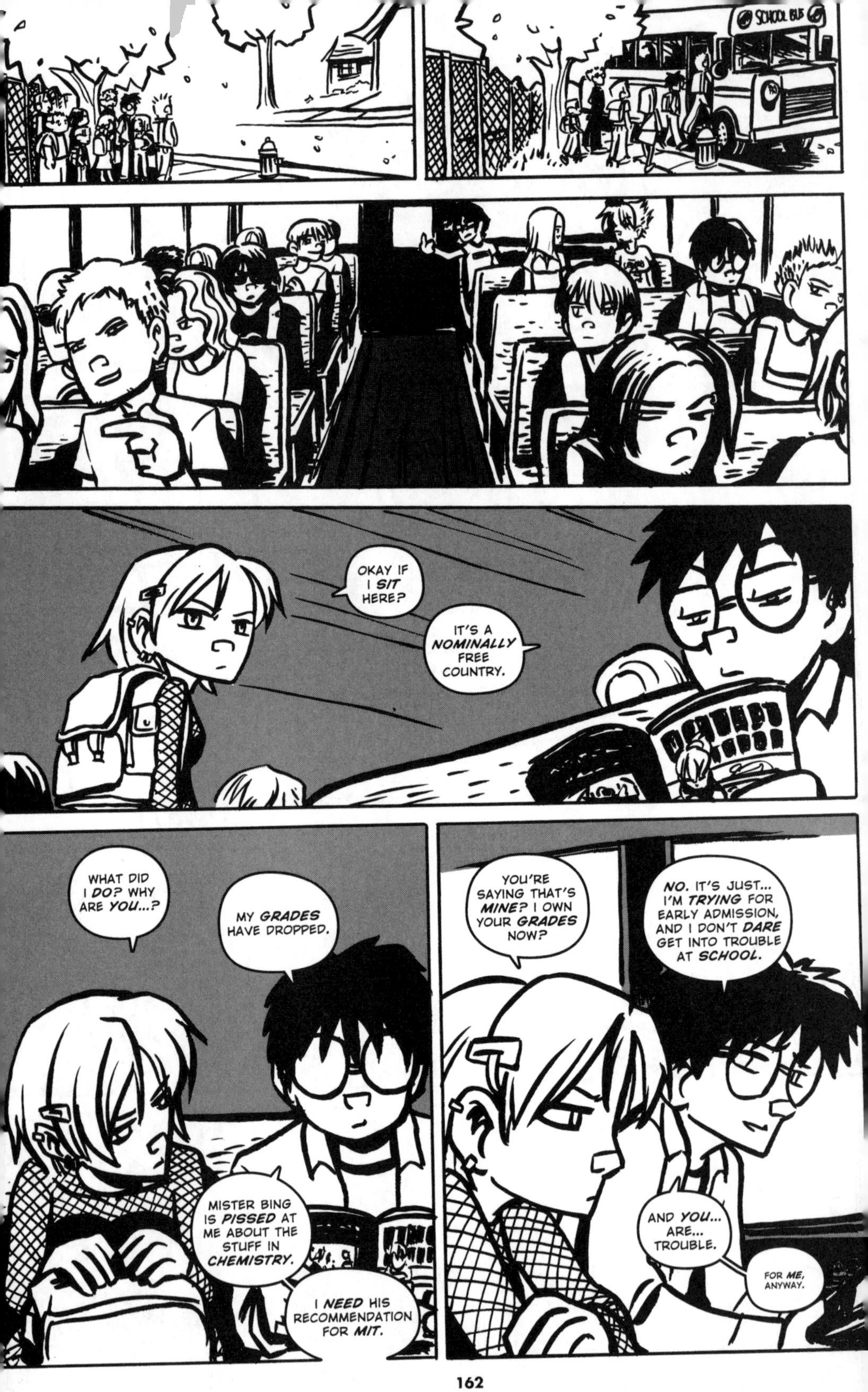
SCHOOL BUS
OKAY IF I *SIT* HERE?
IT'S A *NOMINALLY* FREE COUNTRY.
WHAT DID I *DO?* WHY ARE *YOU...?*
MY *GRADES* HAVE DROPPED.
MISTER BING IS *PISSED* AT ME ABOUT THE STUFF IN *CHEMISTRY.*
I *NEED* HIS RECOMMENDATION FOR *MIT.*
YOU'RE SAYING THAT'S *MINE?* I OWN YOUR *GRADES* NOW?
NO. IT'S JUST... I'M *TRYING* FOR EARLY ADMISSION, AND I DON'T *DARE* GET INTO TROUBLE AT *SCHOOL.*
AND *YOU...* ARE... TROUBLE.
FOR *ME,* ANYWAY.

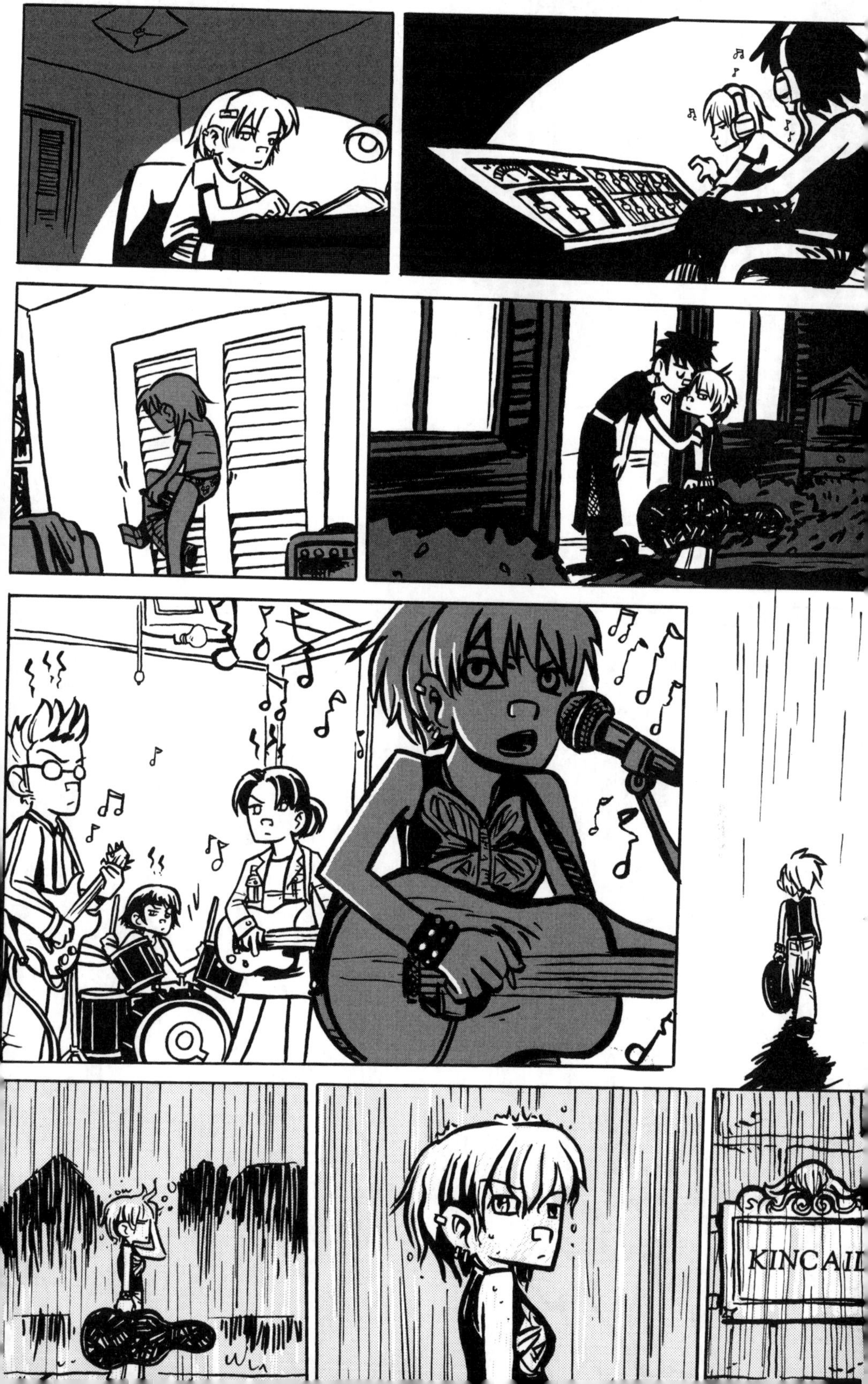

OW
KINCAII

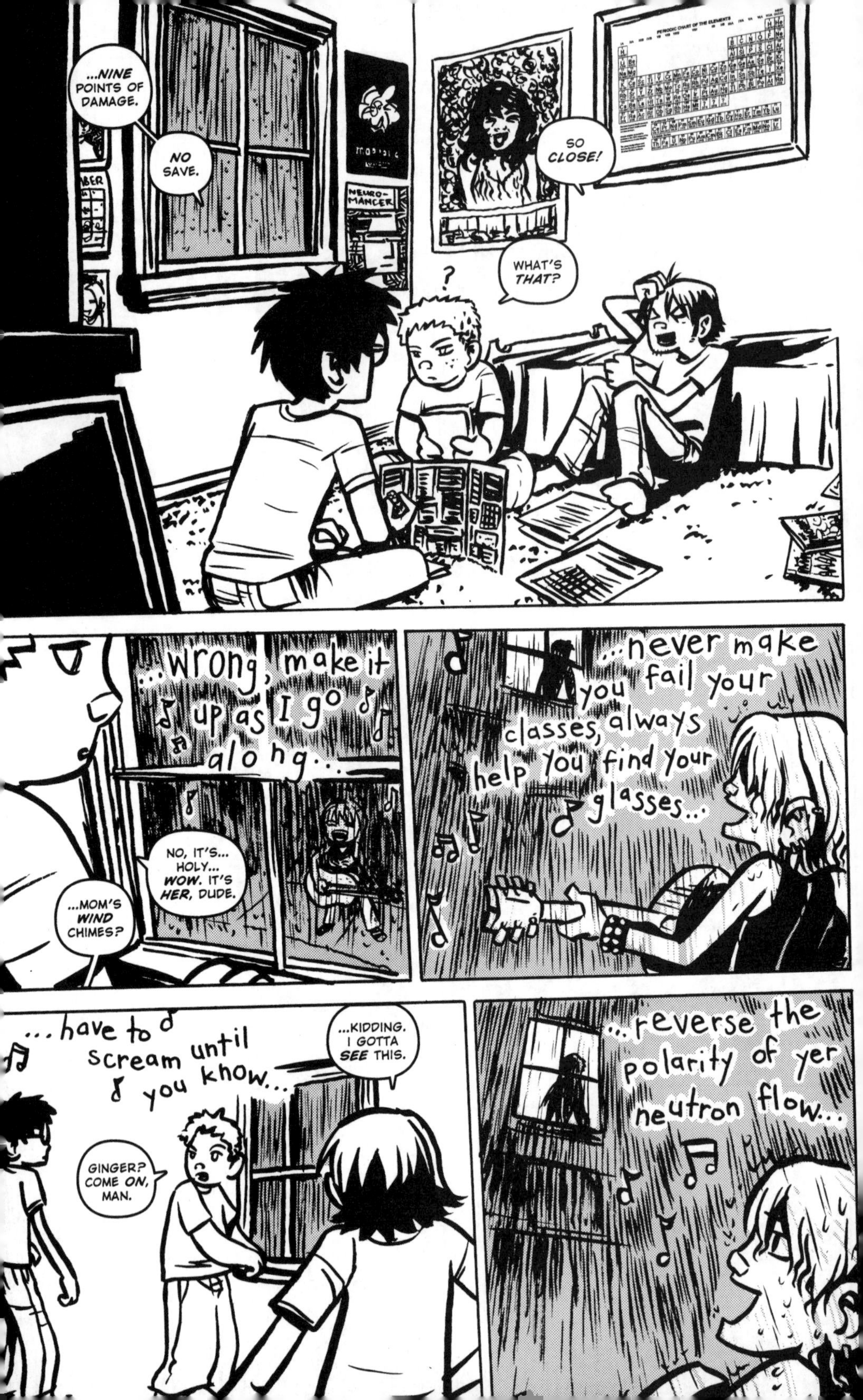
...NINE POINTS OF DAMAGE.
NO SAVE.
SO CLOSE!
NEURO-MANCER
WHAT'S THAT?
...wrong, make it up as I go along...
...MOM'S WIND CHIMES?
NO, IT'S... HOLY... WOW. IT'S HER, DUDE.
...never make you fail your classes, always help you find your glasses...
...have to scream until you know...
GINGER? COME ON, MAN.
...KIDDING. I GOTTA SEE THIS.
...reverse the polarity of yer neutron flow...

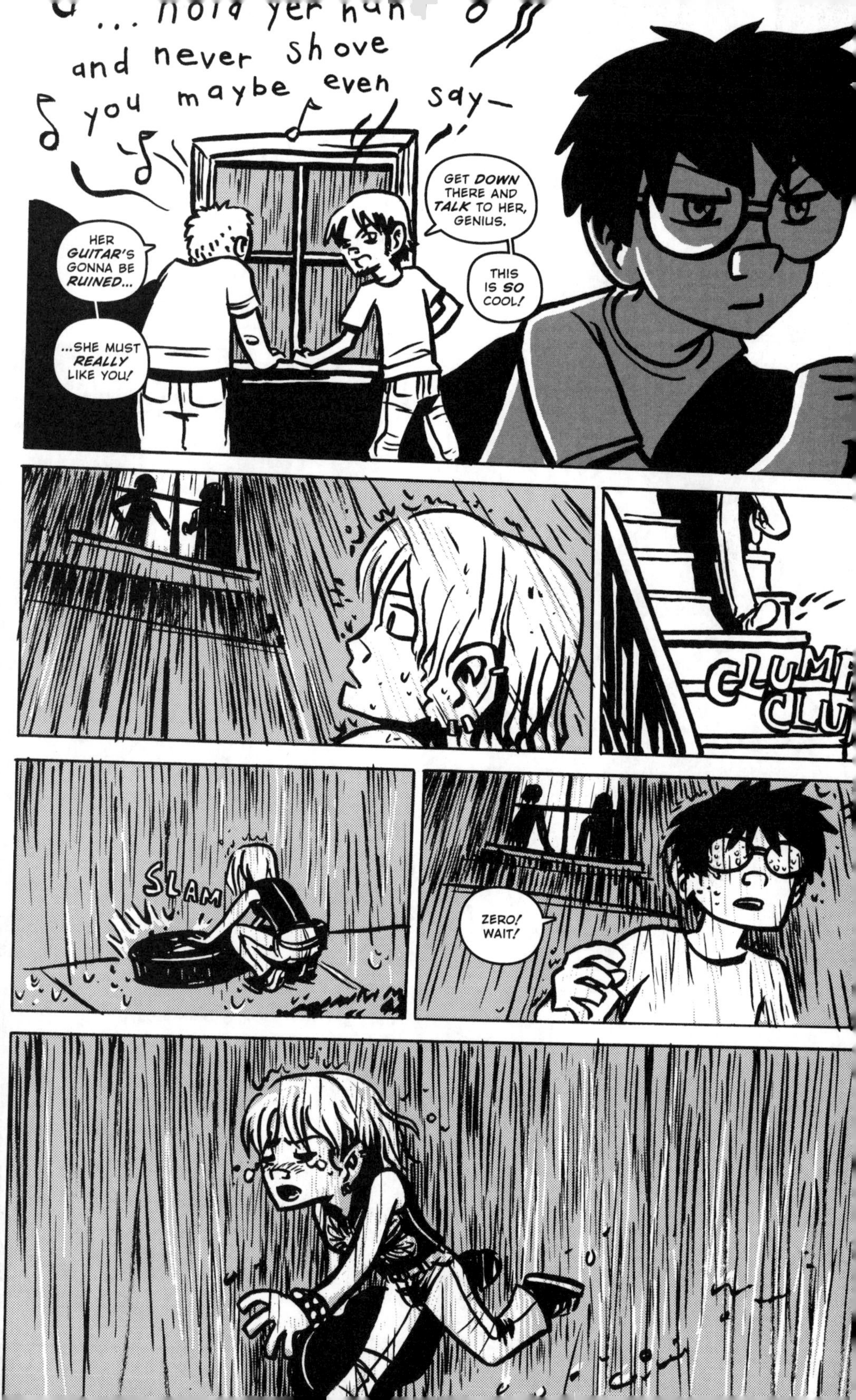
...hold yer han
and never shove
you maybe even say—
HER GUITAR'S GONNA BE RUINED...
...SHE MUST REALLY LIKE YOU!
GET DOWN THERE AND TALK TO HER, GENIUS.
THIS IS SO COOL!
CLUMP
CLU
SLAM
ZERO! WAIT!

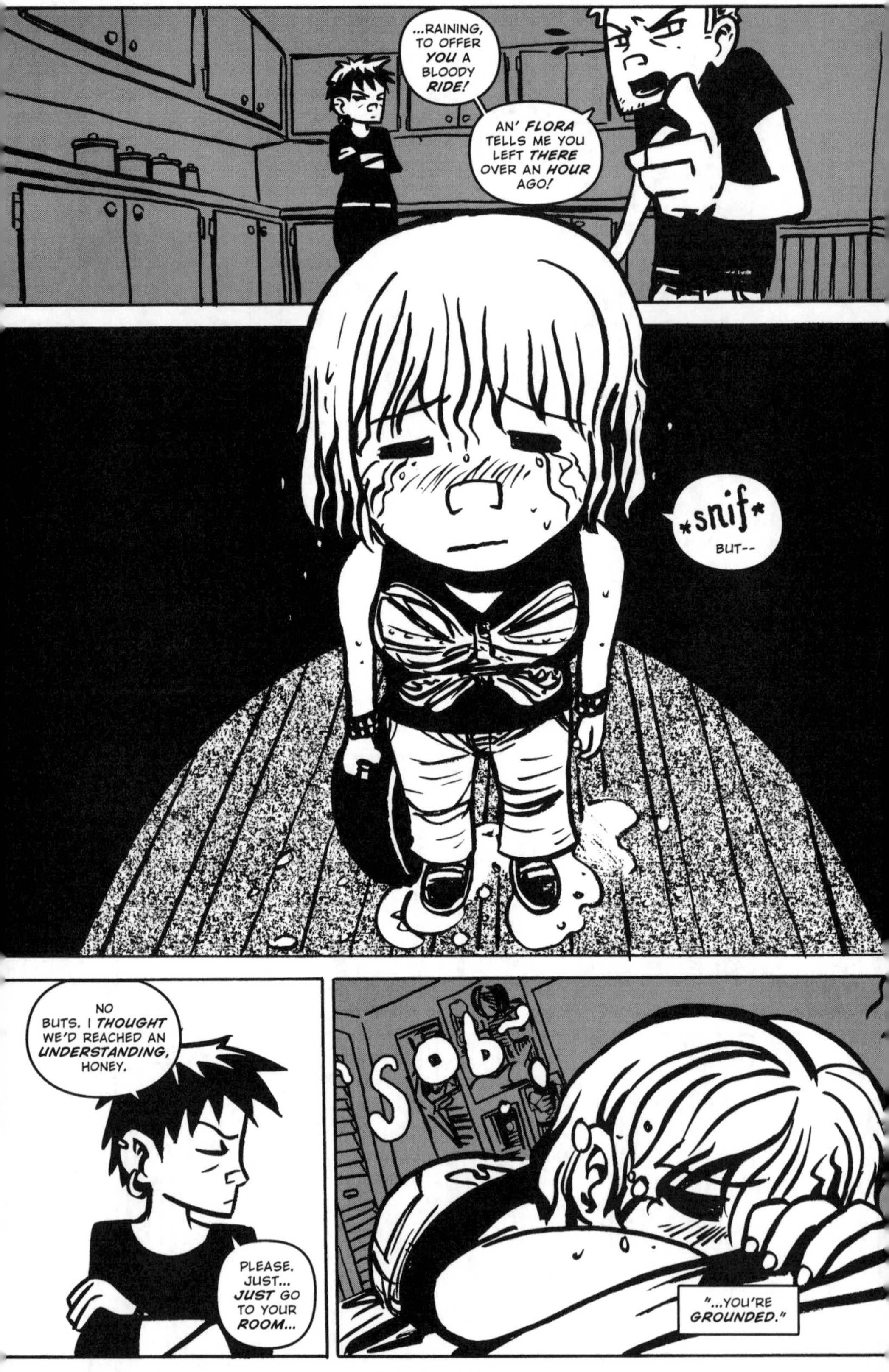
...RAINING, TO OFFER *YOU* A BLOODY *RIDE!*
AN' *FLORA* TELLS ME YOU LEFT *THERE* OVER AN *HOUR* AGO!
snif BUT--
NO BUTS. I *THOUGHT* WE'D REACHED AN *UNDERSTANDING,* HONEY.
PLEASE. JUST... *JUST* GO TO YOUR *ROOM...*
SOB
"...YOU'RE *GROUNDED.*"

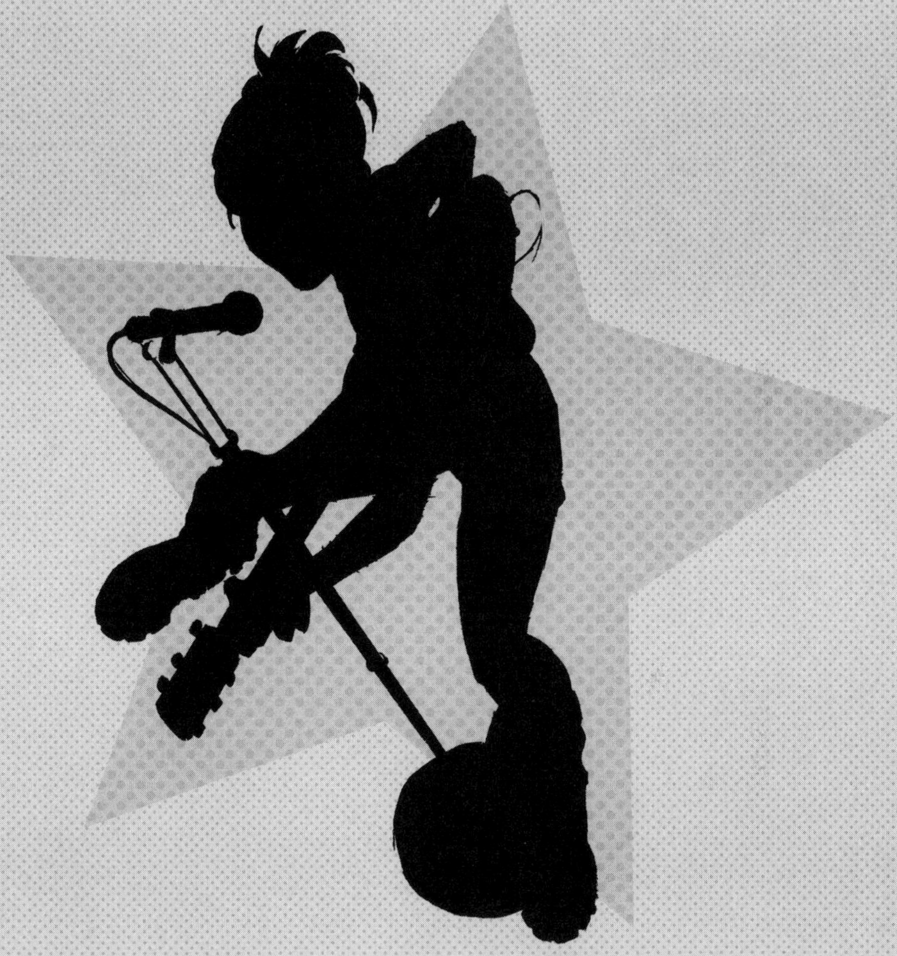

CHAPTER 3

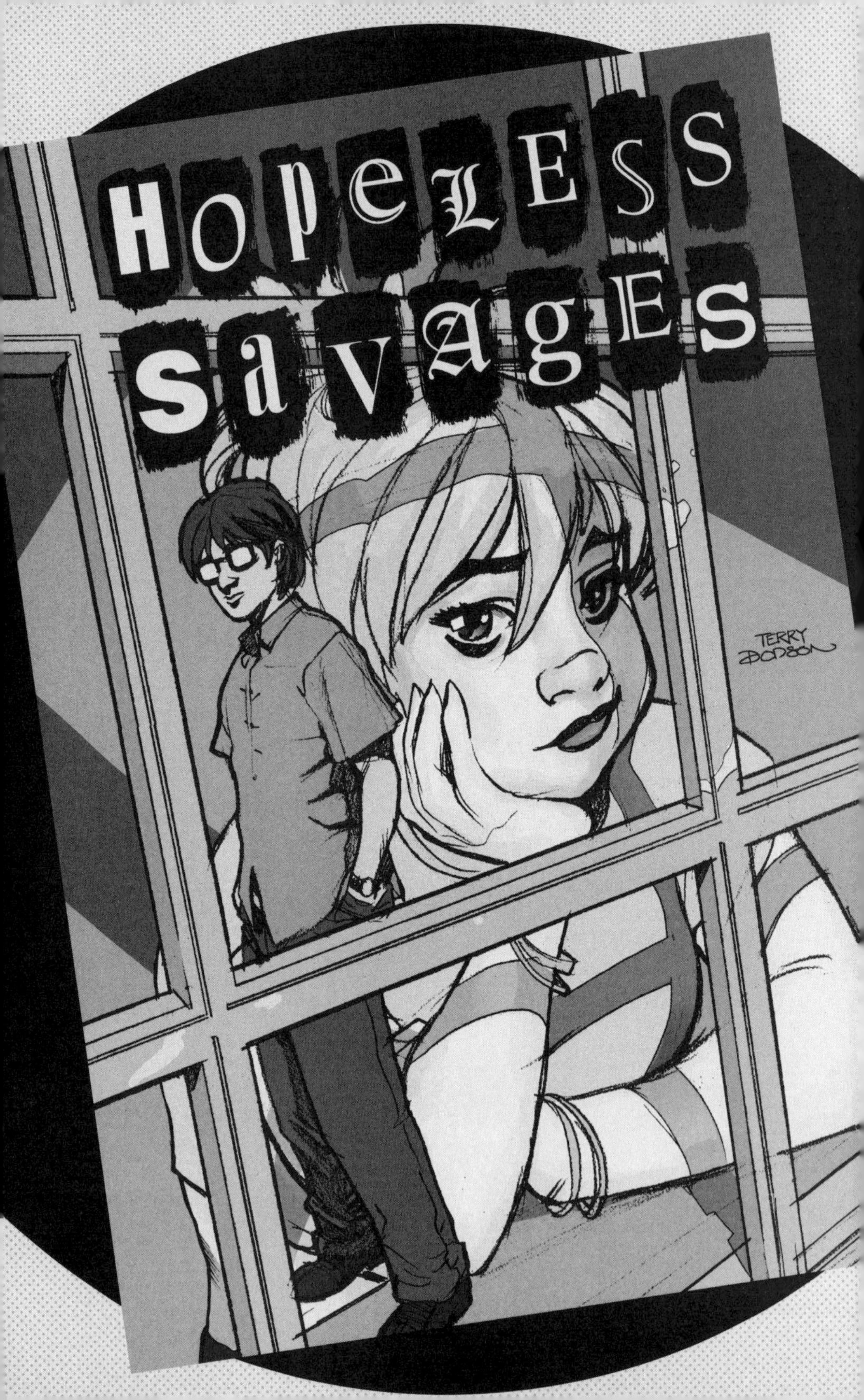
HOPELESS
SAVAGES
TERRY
DODSON

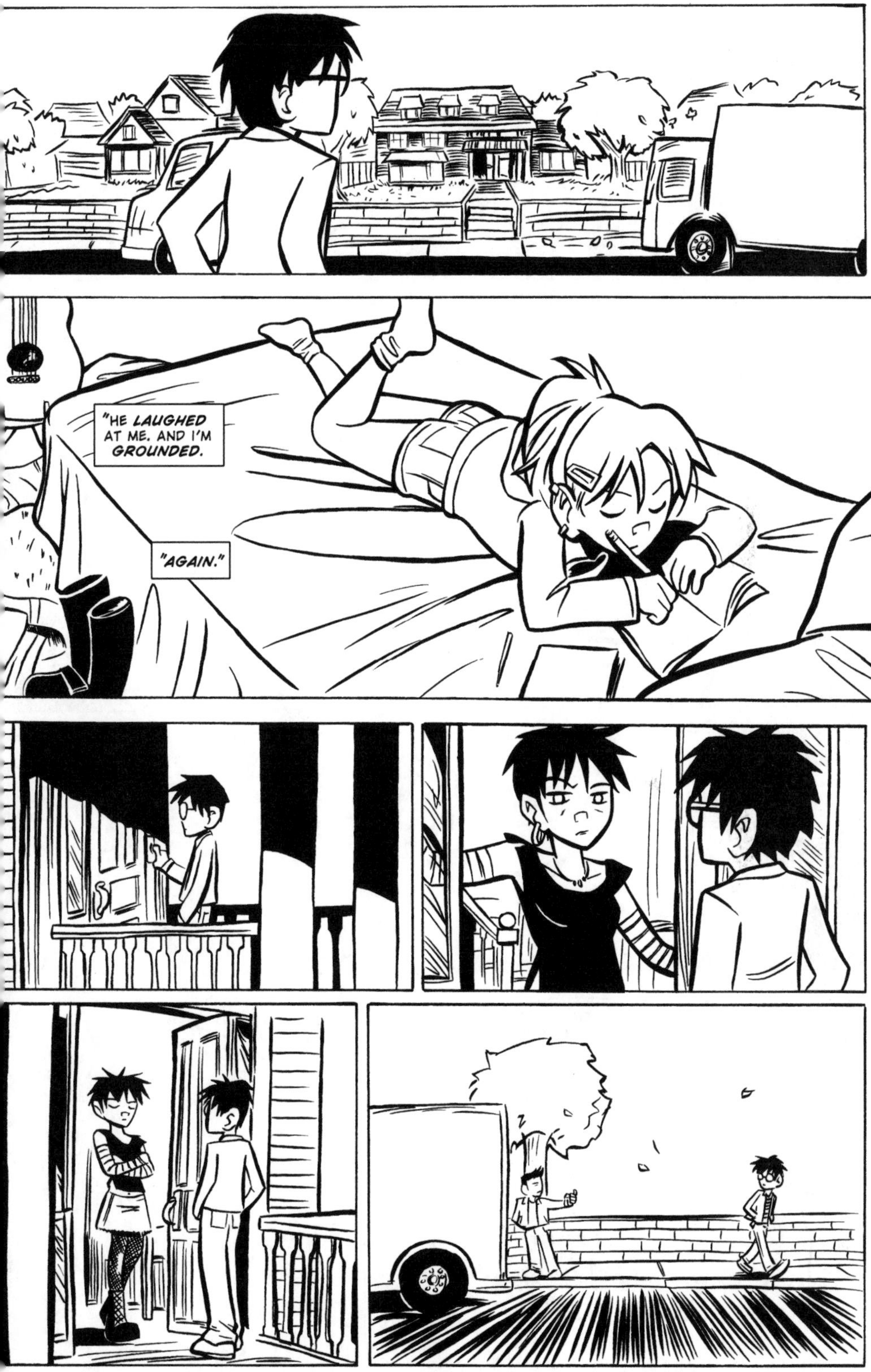
"HE LAUGHED AT ME. AND I'M GROUNDED.
"AGAIN."

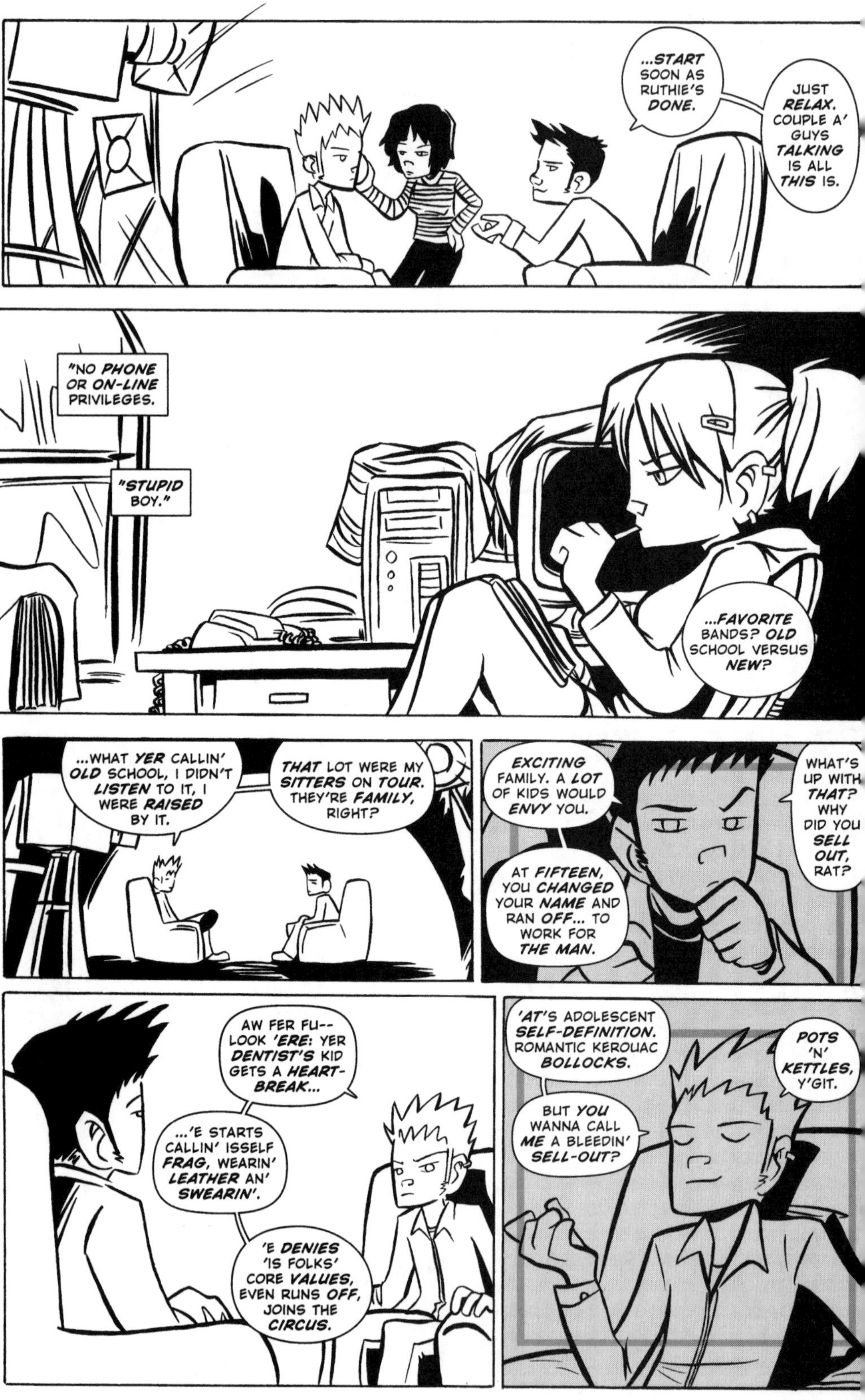

JUST RELAX. COUPLE A' GUYS TALKING IS ALL THIS IS.
...START SOON AS RUTHIE'S DONE.
"NO PHONE OR ON-LINE PRIVILEGES.
"STUPID BOY."
...FAVORITE BANDS? OLD SCHOOL VERSUS NEW?
...WHAT YER CALLIN' OLD SCHOOL, I DIDN'T LISTEN TO IT, I WERE RAISED BY IT.
THAT LOT WERE MY SITTERS ON TOUR. THEY'RE FAMILY, RIGHT?
EXCITING FAMILY. A LOT OF KIDS WOULD ENVY YOU.
AT FIFTEEN, YOU CHANGED YOUR NAME AND RAN OFF... TO WORK FOR THE MAN.
WHAT'S UP WITH THAT? WHY DID YOU SELL OUT, RAT?
AW FER FU-- LOOK 'ERE: YER DENTIST'S KID GETS A HEART-BREAK...
...'E STARTS CALLIN' ISSELF FRAG, WEARIN' LEATHER AN' SWEARIN'.
'E DENIES 'IS FOLKS' CORE VALUES, EVEN RUNS OFF, JOINS THE CIRCUS.
'AT'S ADOLESCENT SELF-DEFINITION. ROMANTIC KEROUAC BOLLOCKS.
BUT YOU WANNA CALL ME A BLEEDIN' SELL-OUT?
POTS 'N' KETTLES, Y'GIT.

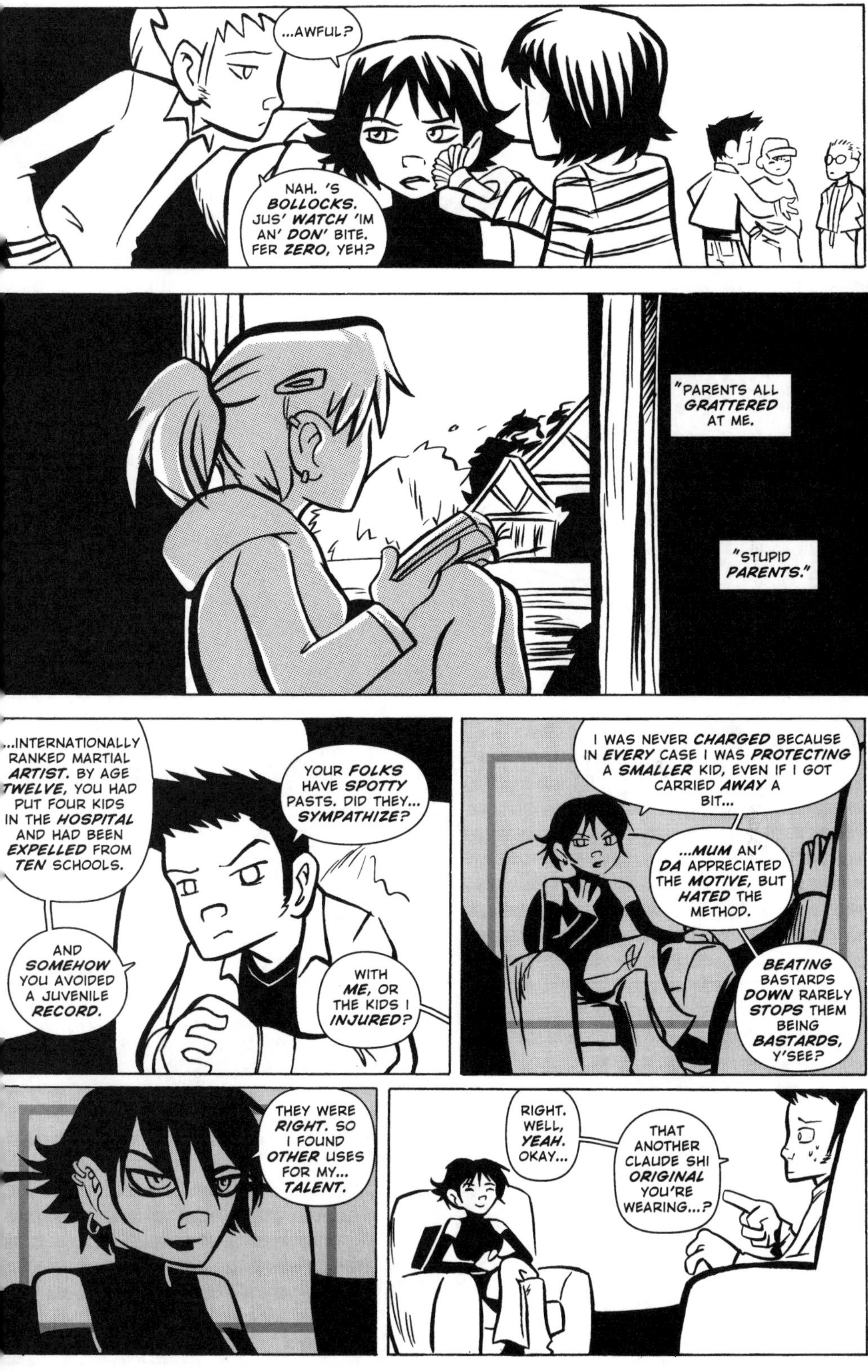
...AWFUL?
NAH. 'S BOLLOCKS. JUS' WATCH 'IM AN' DON' BITE. FER ZERO, YEH?
"PARENTS ALL GRATTERED AT ME.
"STUPID PARENTS."
...INTERNATIONALLY RANKED MARTIAL ARTIST. BY AGE TWELVE, YOU HAD PUT FOUR KIDS IN THE HOSPITAL AND HAD BEEN EXPELLED FROM TEN SCHOOLS.
AND SOMEHOW YOU AVOIDED A JUVENILE RECORD.
YOUR FOLKS HAVE SPOTTY PASTS. DID THEY... SYMPATHIZE?
WITH ME, OR THE KIDS I INJURED?
I WAS NEVER CHARGED BECAUSE IN EVERY CASE I WAS PROTECTING A SMALLER KID, EVEN IF I GOT CARRIED AWAY A BIT...
...MUM AN' DA APPRECIATED THE MOTIVE, BUT HATED THE METHOD.
BEATING BASTARDS DOWN RARELY STOPS THEM BEING BASTARDS, Y'SEE?
THEY WERE RIGHT. SO I FOUND OTHER USES FOR MY... TALENT.
RIGHT. WELL, YEAH. OKAY...
THAT ANOTHER CLAUDE SHI ORIGINAL YOU'RE WEARING...?

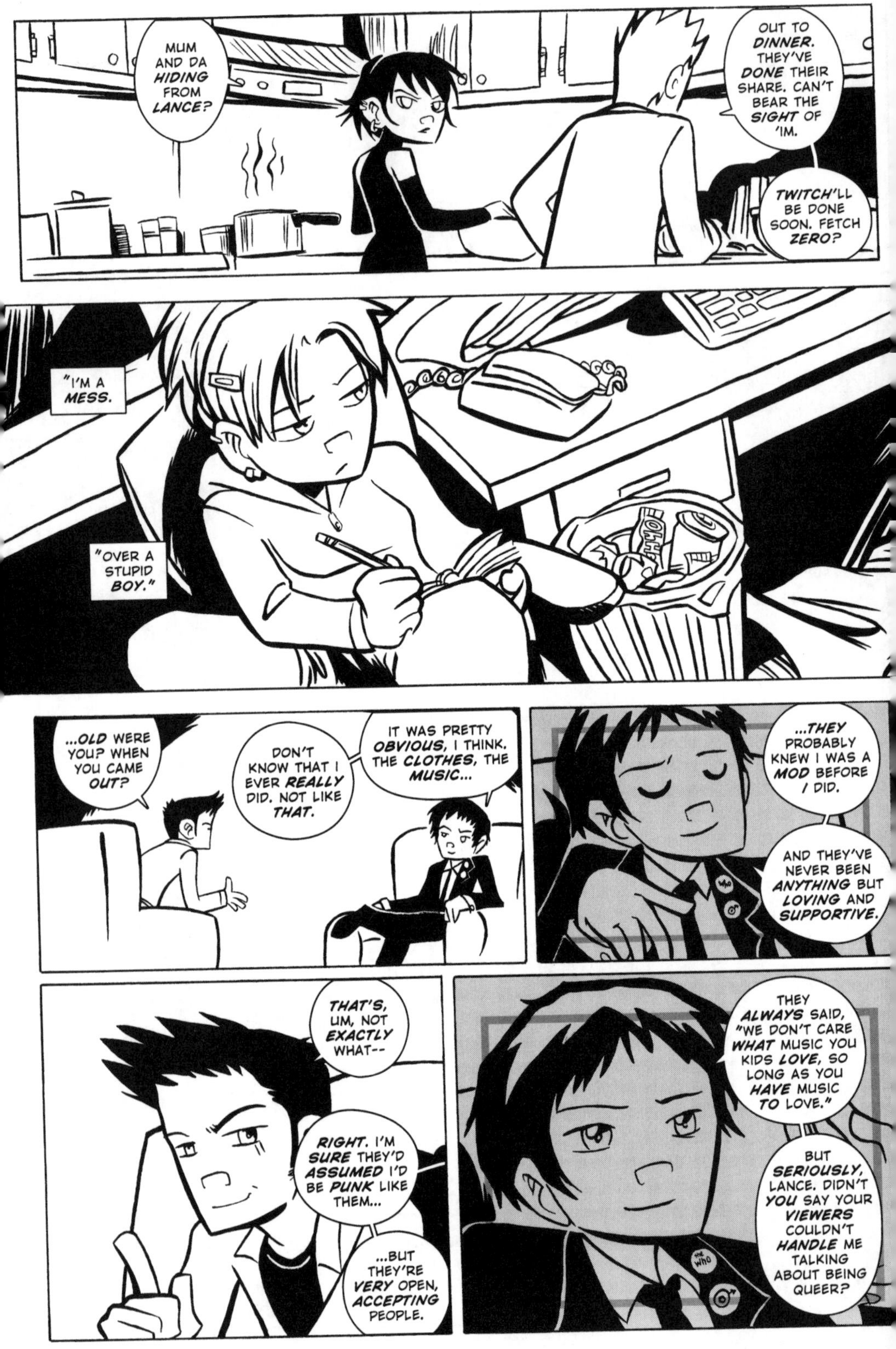
MUM AND DA HIDING FROM LANCE?
OUT TO DINNER. THEY'VE DONE THEIR SHARE. CAN'T BEAR THE SIGHT OF 'IM.
TWITCH'LL BE DONE SOON. FETCH ZERO?
"I'M A MESS.
"OVER A STUPID BOY."
...OLD WERE YOU? WHEN YOU CAME OUT?
DON'T KNOW THAT I EVER REALLY DID. NOT LIKE THAT.
IT WAS PRETTY OBVIOUS, I THINK. THE CLOTHES, THE MUSIC...
...THEY PROBABLY KNEW I WAS A MOD BEFORE I DID.
AND THEY'VE NEVER BEEN ANYTHING BUT LOVING AND SUPPORTIVE.
THAT'S, UM, NOT EXACTLY WHAT--
RIGHT. I'M SURE THEY'D ASSUMED I'D BE PUNK LIKE THEM...
...BUT THEY'RE VERY OPEN, ACCEPTING PEOPLE.
THEY ALWAYS SAID, "WE DON'T CARE WHAT MUSIC YOU KIDS LOVE, SO LONG AS YOU HAVE MUSIC TO LOVE."
BUT SERIOUSLY, LANCE. DIDN'T YOU SAY YOUR VIEWERS COULDN'T HANDLE ME TALKING ABOUT BEING QUEER?

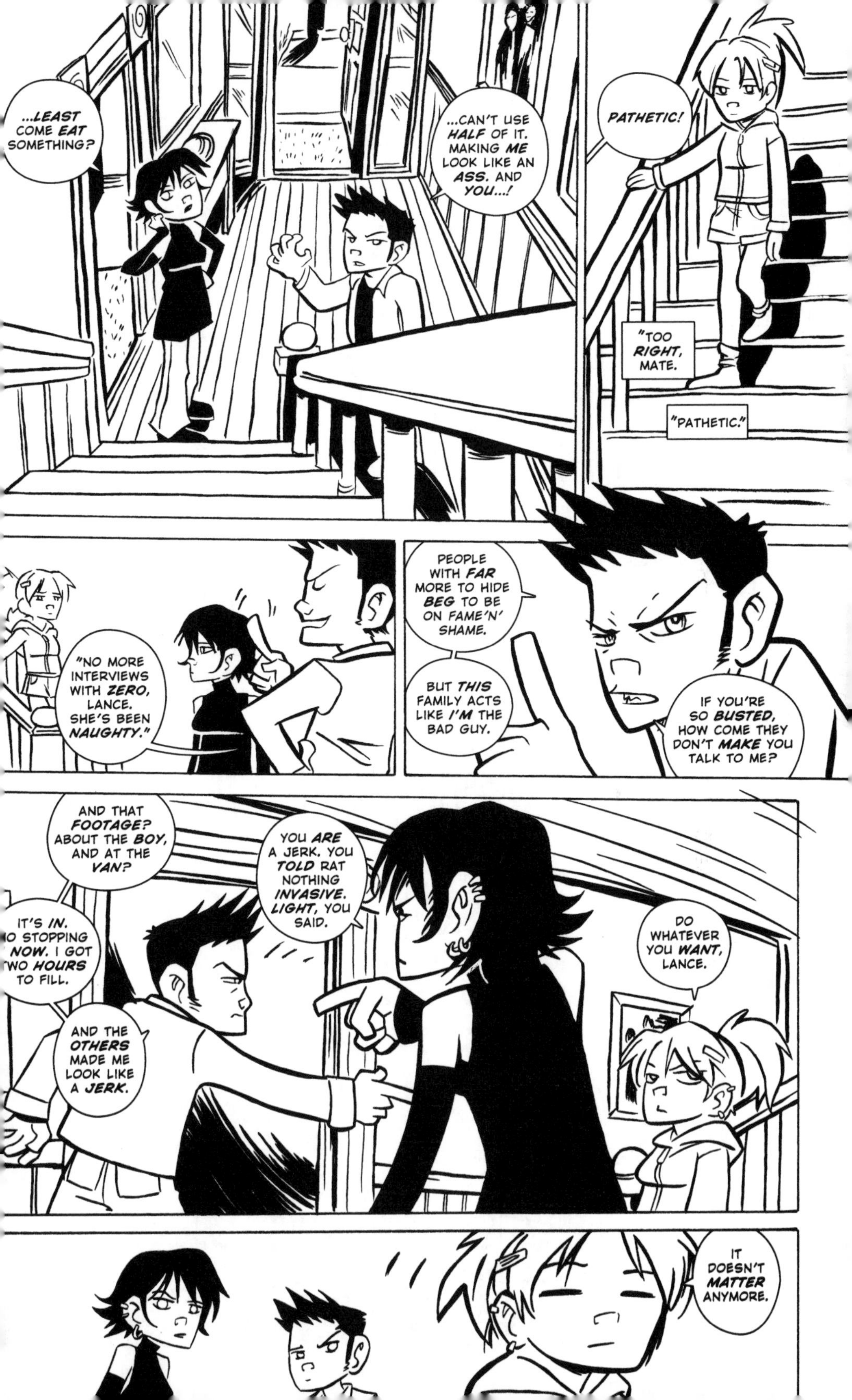
...LEAST COME EAT SOMETHING?
...CAN'T USE HALF OF IT. MAKING ME LOOK LIKE AN ASS. AND YOU...!
PATHETIC!
"TOO RIGHT, MATE.
"PATHETIC."
"NO MORE INTERVIEWS WITH ZERO, LANCE. SHE'S BEEN NAUGHTY."
PEOPLE WITH FAR MORE TO HIDE BEG TO BE ON FAME'N' SHAME.
BUT THIS FAMILY ACTS LIKE I'M THE BAD GUY.
IF YOU'RE SO BUSTED, HOW COME THEY DON'T MAKE YOU TALK TO ME?
AND THAT FOOTAGE? ABOUT THE BOY, AND AT THE VAN?
IT'S IN. O STOPPING NOW. I GOT TWO HOURS TO FILL.
AND THE OTHERS MADE ME LOOK LIKE A JERK.
YOU ARE A JERK. YOU TOLD RAT NOTHING INVASIVE. LIGHT, YOU SAID.
DO WHATEVER YOU WANT, LANCE.
IT DOESN'T MATTER ANYMORE.

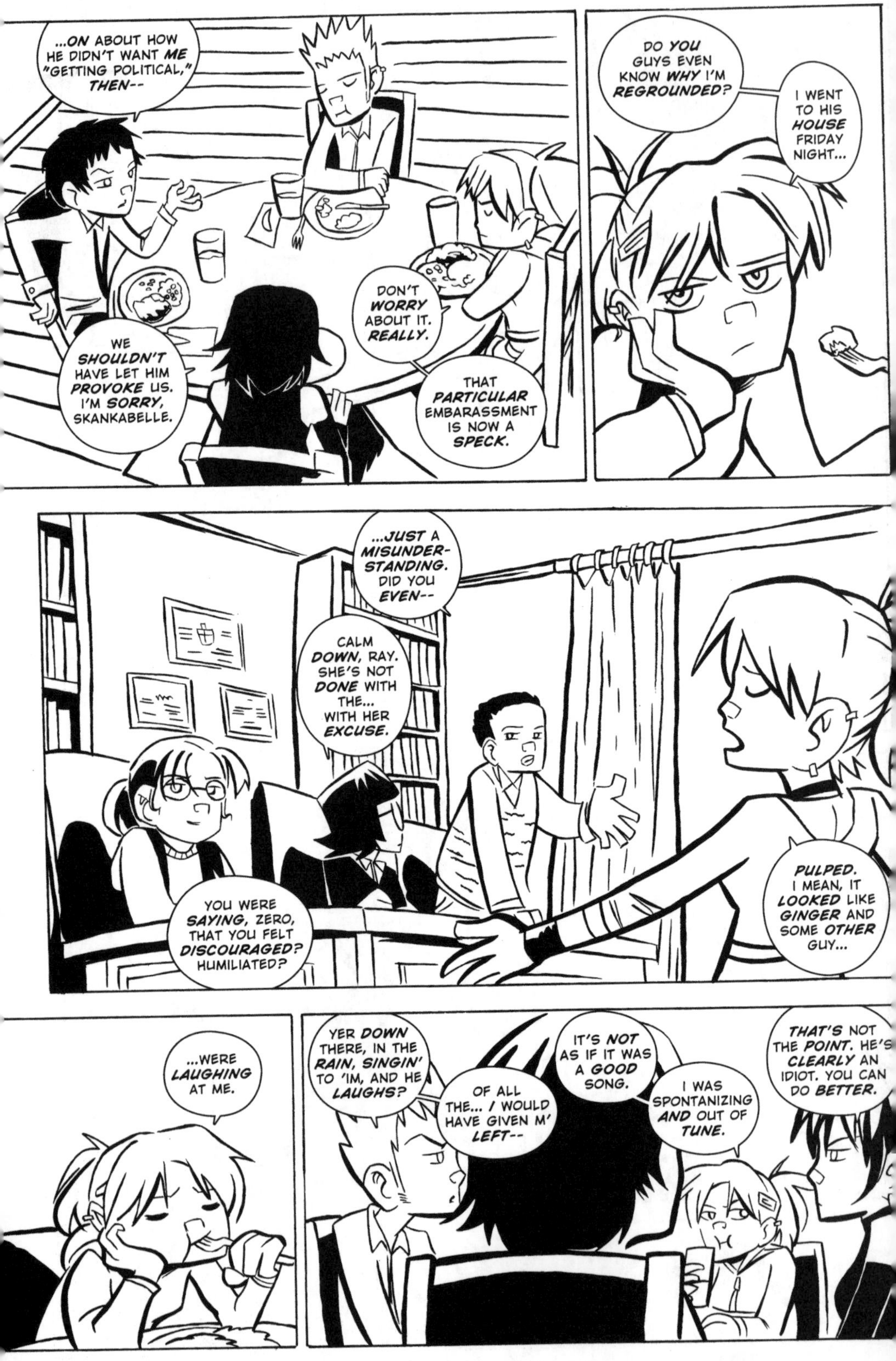
...ON ABOUT HOW HE DIDN'T WANT ME "GETTING POLITICAL," THEN--
WE SHOULDN'T HAVE LET HIM PROVOKE US. I'M SORRY, SKANKABELLE.
DON'T WORRY ABOUT IT. REALLY.
THAT PARTICULAR EMBARASSMENT IS NOW A SPECK.
DO YOU GUYS EVEN KNOW WHY I'M REGROUNDED?
I WENT TO HIS HOUSE FRIDAY NIGHT...
...JUST A MISUNDER-STANDING. DID YOU EVEN--
CALM DOWN, RAY. SHE'S NOT DONE WITH THE... WITH HER EXCUSE.
YOU WERE SAYING, ZERO, THAT YOU FELT DISCOURAGED? HUMILIATED?
PULPED. I MEAN, IT LOOKED LIKE GINGER AND SOME OTHER GUY...
...WERE LAUGHING AT ME.
YER DOWN THERE, IN THE RAIN, SINGIN' TO 'IM, AND HE LAUGHS?
OF ALL THE... I WOULD HAVE GIVEN M' LEFT--
IT'S NOT AS IF IT WAS A GOOD SONG.
I WAS SPONTANIZING AND OUT OF TUNE.
THAT'S NOT THE POINT. HE'S CLEARLY AN IDIOT. YOU CAN DO BETTER.

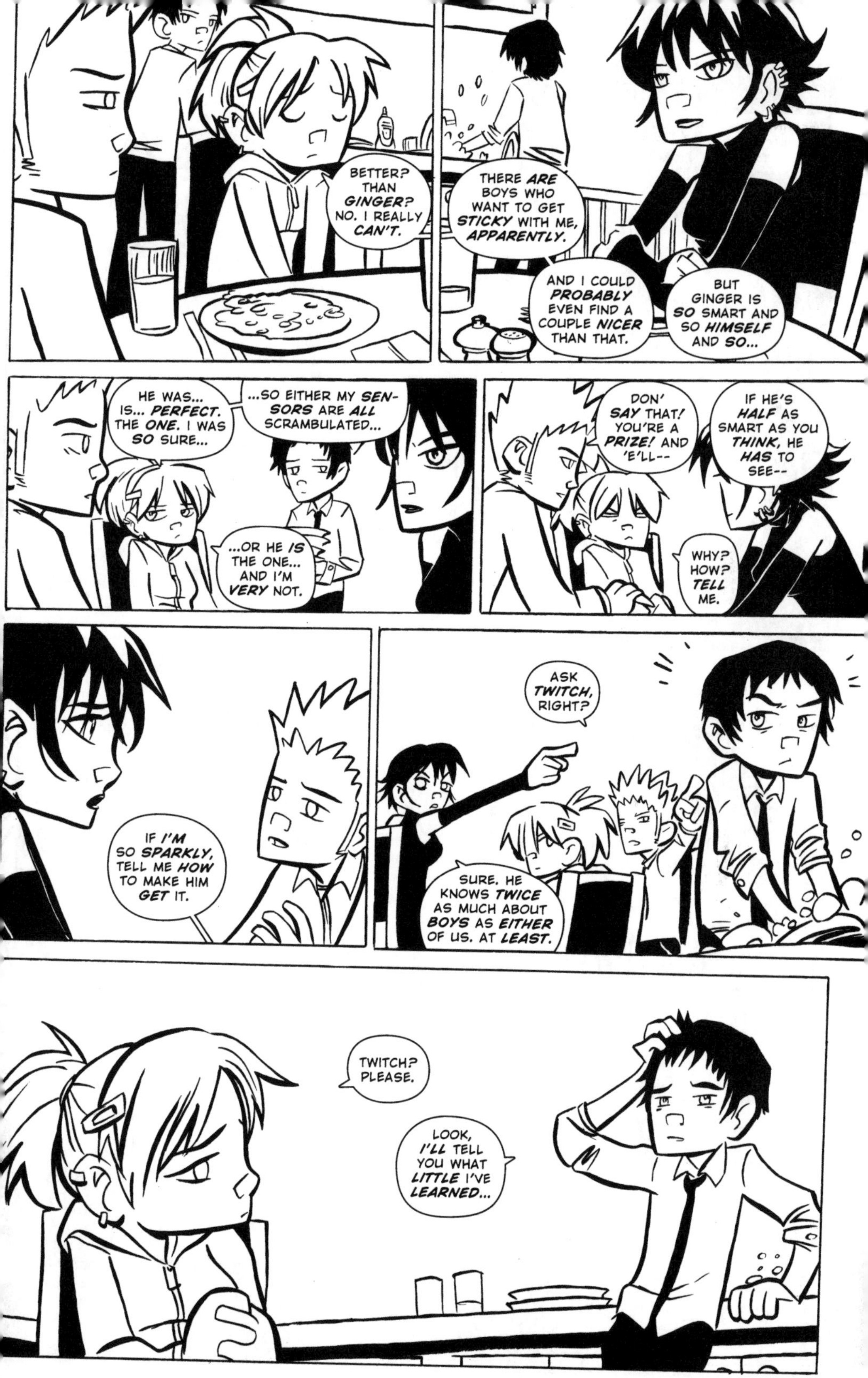
BETTER? THAN GINGER? NO. I REALLY CAN'T.
THERE ARE BOYS WHO WANT TO GET STICKY WITH ME, APPARENTLY.
AND I COULD PROBABLY EVEN FIND A COUPLE NICER THAN THAT.
BUT GINGER IS SO SMART AND SO HIMSELF AND SO...
HE WAS... IS... PERFECT. THE ONE. I WAS SO SURE...
...SO EITHER MY SENSORS ARE ALL SCRAMBULATED...
...OR HE IS THE ONE... AND I'M VERY NOT.
DON' SAY THAT! YOU'RE A PRIZE! AND 'E'LL--
IF HE'S HALF AS SMART AS YOU THINK, HE HAS TO SEE--
WHY? HOW? TELL ME.
IF I'M SO SPARKLY, TELL ME HOW TO MAKE HIM GET IT.
ASK TWITCH, RIGHT?
SURE. HE KNOWS TWICE AS MUCH ABOUT BOYS AS EITHER OF US. AT LEAST.
TWITCH? PLEASE.
LOOK, I'LL TELL YOU WHAT LITTLE I'VE LEARNED...

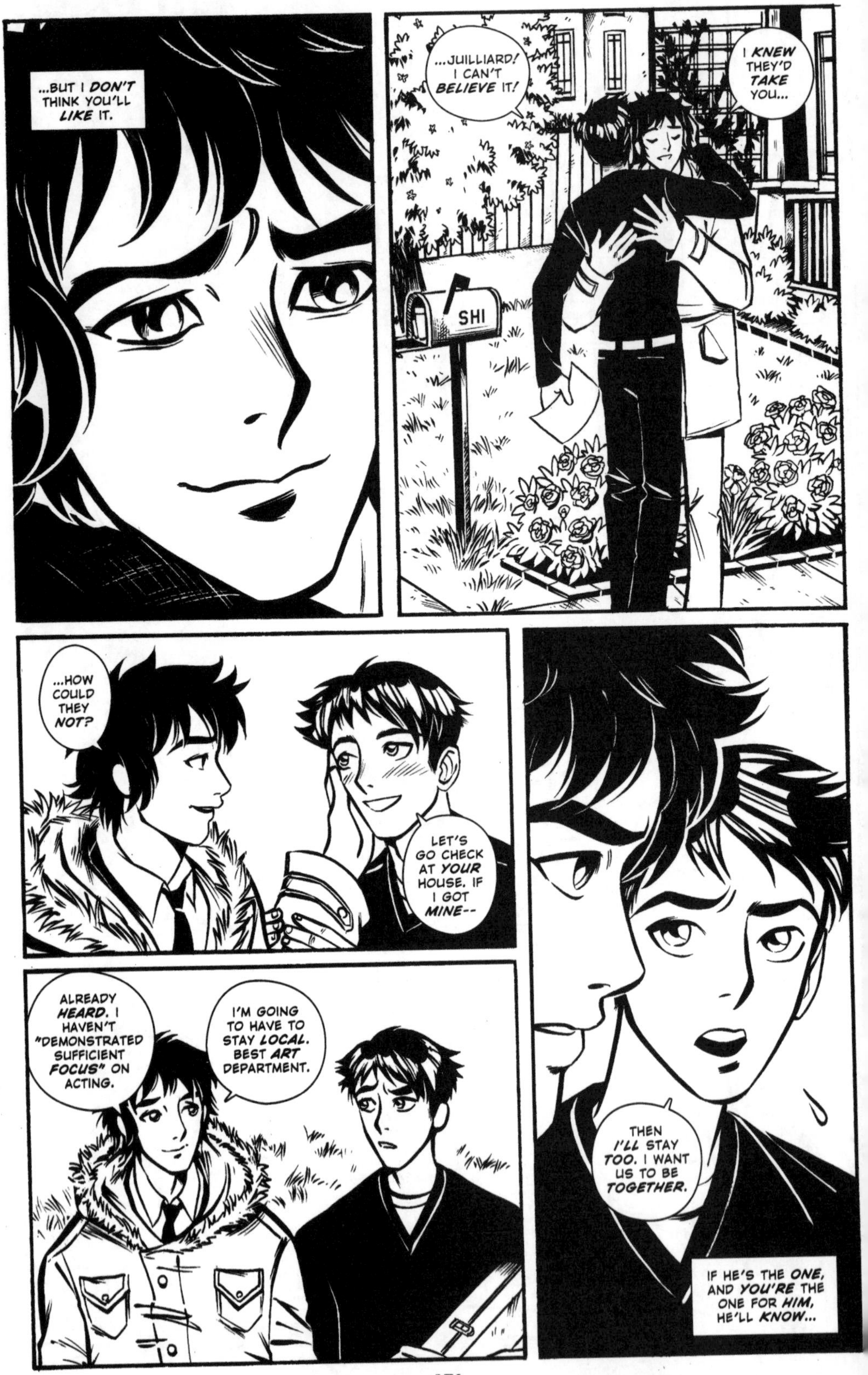
...BUT I DON'T THINK YOU'LL LIKE IT.
...JUILLIARD! I CAN'T BELIEVE IT!
I KNEW THEY'D TAKE YOU...
SHI
...HOW COULD THEY NOT?
LET'S GO CHECK AT YOUR HOUSE. IF I GOT MINE--
THEN I'LL STAY TOO. I WANT US TO BE TOGETHER.
ALREADY HEARD. I HAVEN'T "DEMONSTRATED SUFFICIENT FOCUS" ON ACTING.
I'M GOING TO HAVE TO STAY LOCAL. BEST ART DEPARTMENT.
IF HE'S THE ONE, AND YOU'RE THE ONE FOR HIM, HE'LL KNOW...

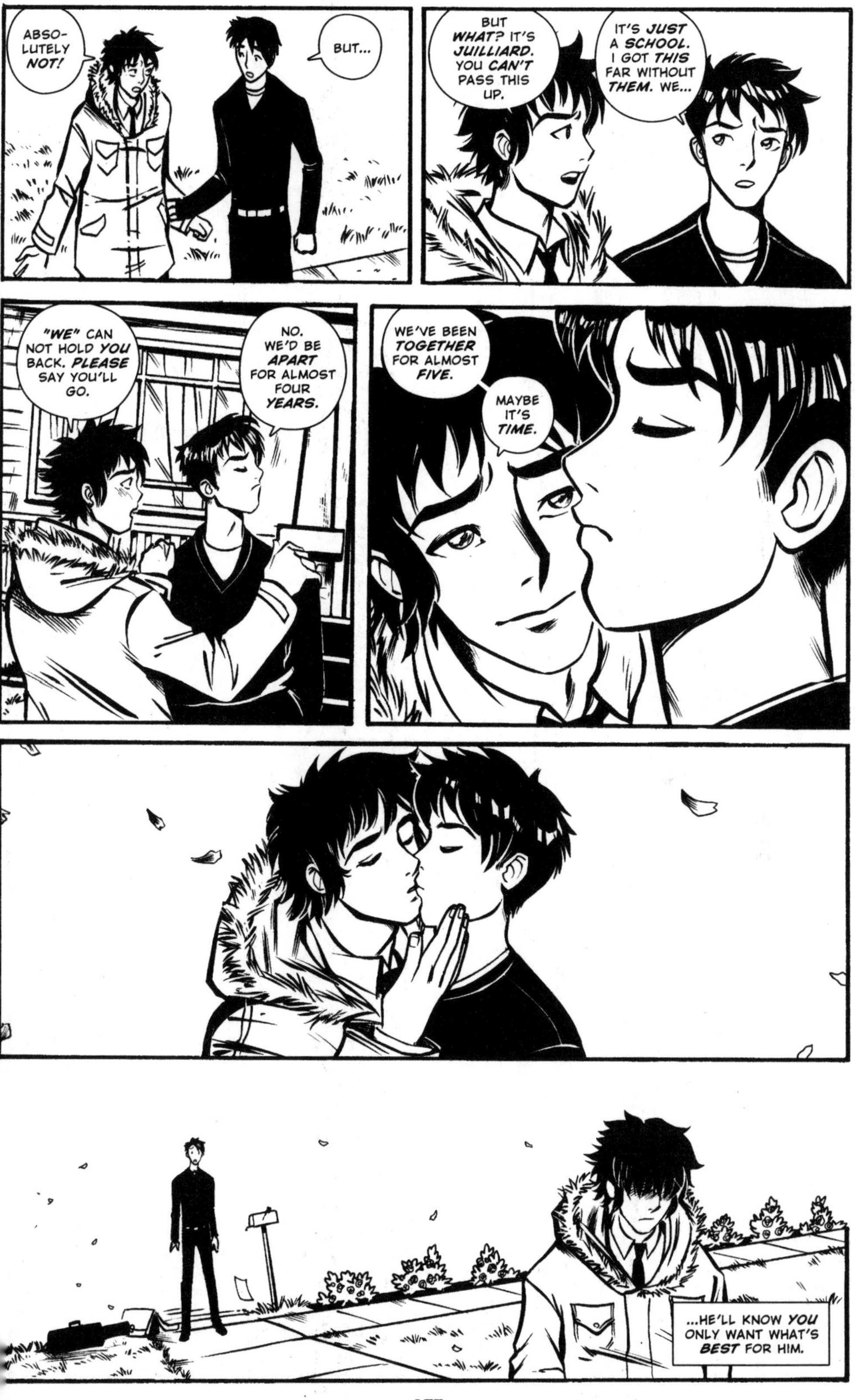
ABSO-LUTELY NOT!
BUT...
BUT WHAT? IT'S JUILLIARD. YOU CAN'T PASS THIS UP.
IT'S JUST A SCHOOL. I GOT THIS FAR WITHOUT THEM. WE...
"WE" CAN NOT HOLD YOU BACK. PLEASE SAY YOU'LL GO.
NO. WE'D BE APART FOR ALMOST FOUR YEARS.
WE'VE BEEN TOGETHER FOR ALMOST FIVE.
MAYBE IT'S TIME.
...HE'LL KNOW YOU ONLY WANT WHAT'S BEST FOR HIM.

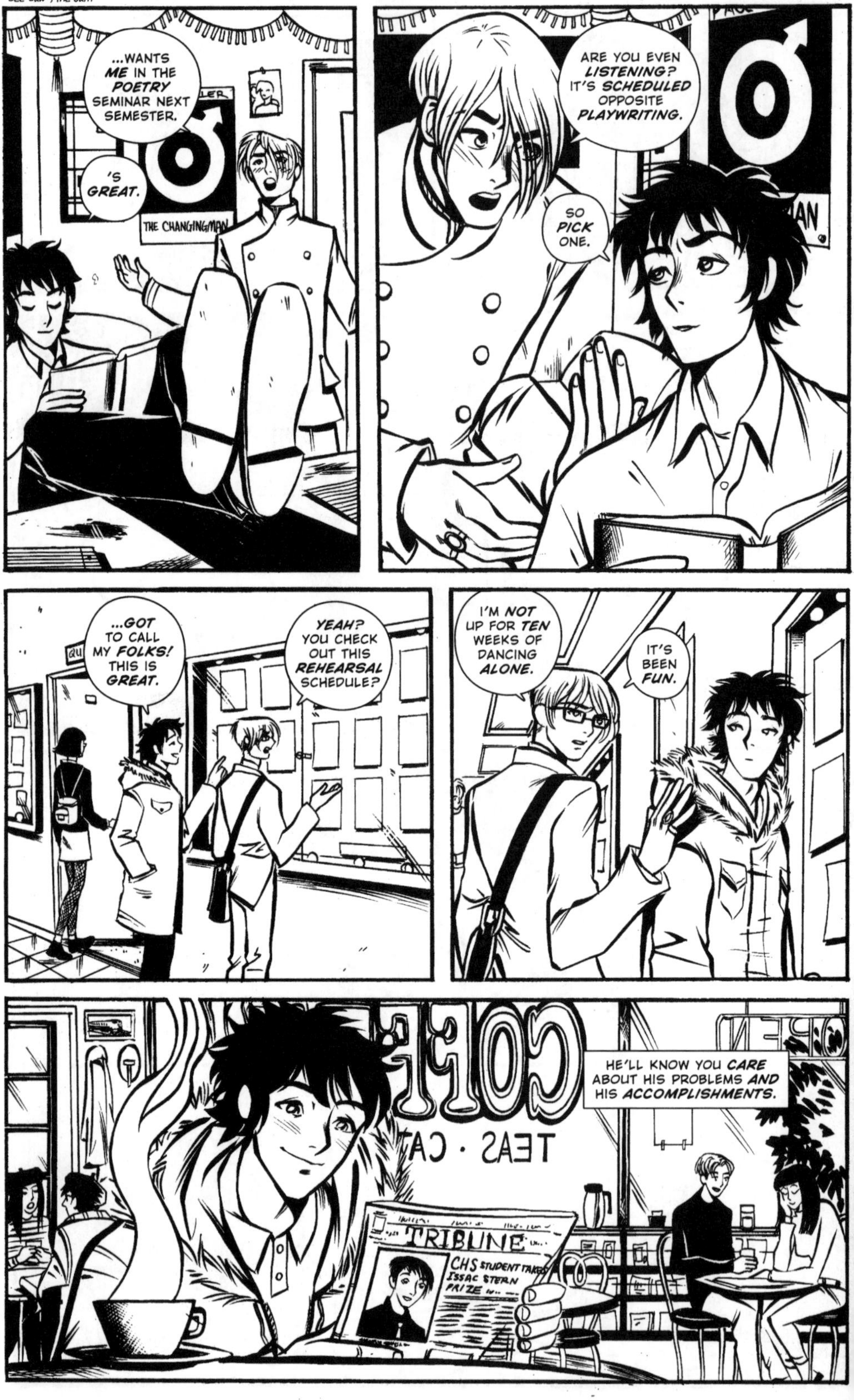
...WANTS ME IN THE POETRY SEMINAR NEXT SEMESTER.
'S GREAT.
THE CHANGINGMAN
ARE YOU EVEN LISTENING? IT'S SCHEDULED OPPOSITE PLAYWRITING.
SO PICK ONE.
...GOT TO CALL MY FOLKS! THIS IS GREAT.
YEAH? YOU CHECK OUT THIS REHEARSAL SCHEDULE?
I'M NOT UP FOR TEN WEEKS OF DANCING ALONE.
IT'S BEEN FUN.
HE'LL KNOW YOU CARE ABOUT HIS PROBLEMS AND HIS ACCOMPLISHMENTS.
TEAS · CA
TRIBUNE
CHS STUDENT TAKES ISSAC STERN PRIZE ...

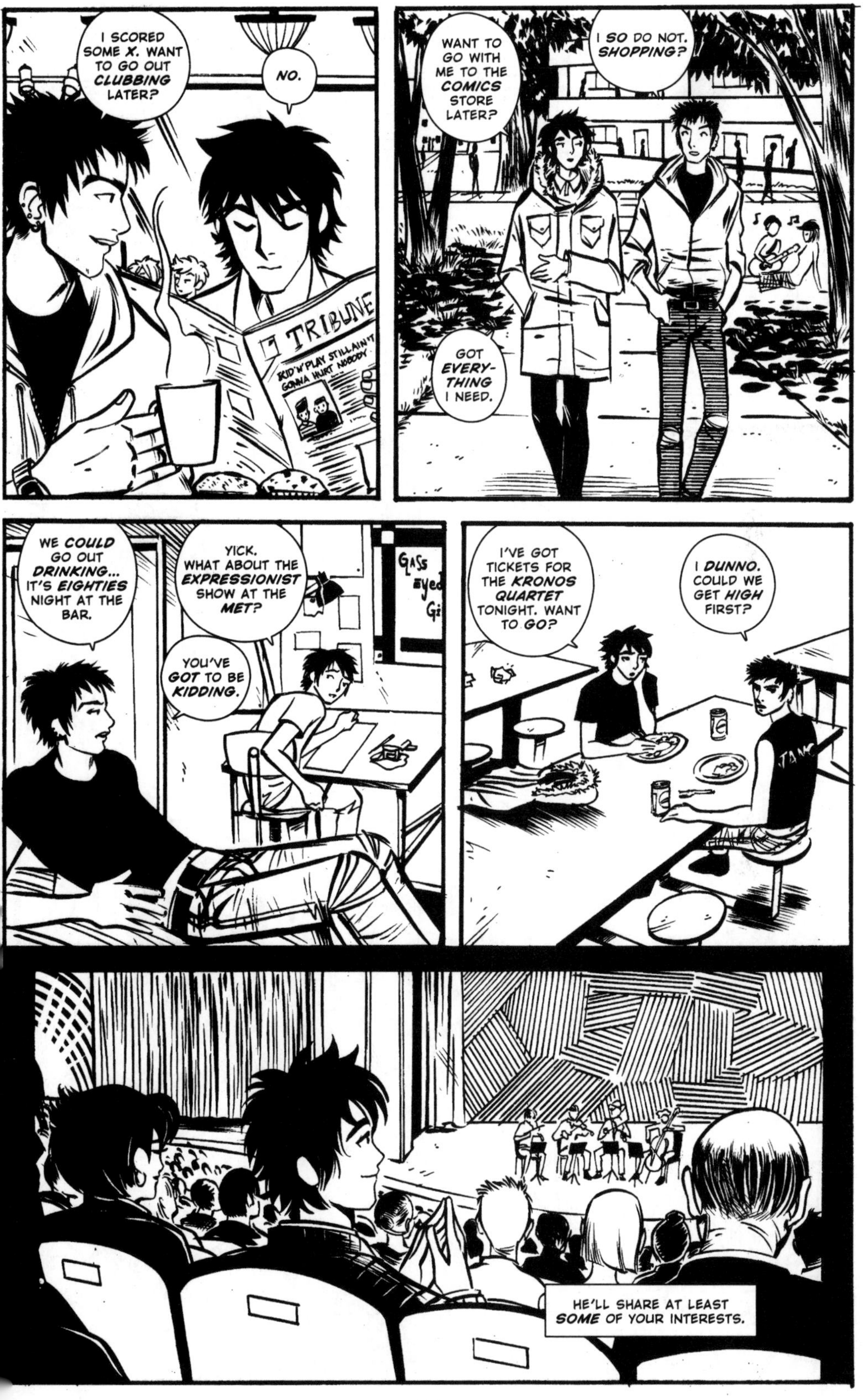
I SCORED SOME X. WANT TO GO OUT CLUBBING LATER?
NO.
TRIBUNE
KID 'N' PLAY STILL AIN'T GONNA HURT NOBODY
WANT TO GO WITH ME TO THE COMICS STORE LATER?
I SO DO NOT. SHOPPING?
GOT EVERYTHING I NEED.
WE COULD GO OUT DRINKING... IT'S EIGHTIES NIGHT AT THE BAR.
YICK. WHAT ABOUT THE EXPRESSIONIST SHOW AT THE MET?
YOU'VE GOT TO BE KIDDING.
I'VE GOT TICKETS FOR THE KRONOS QUARTET TONIGHT. WANT TO GO?
I DUNNO. COULD WE GET HIGH FIRST?
HE'LL SHARE AT LEAST SOME OF YOUR INTERESTS.

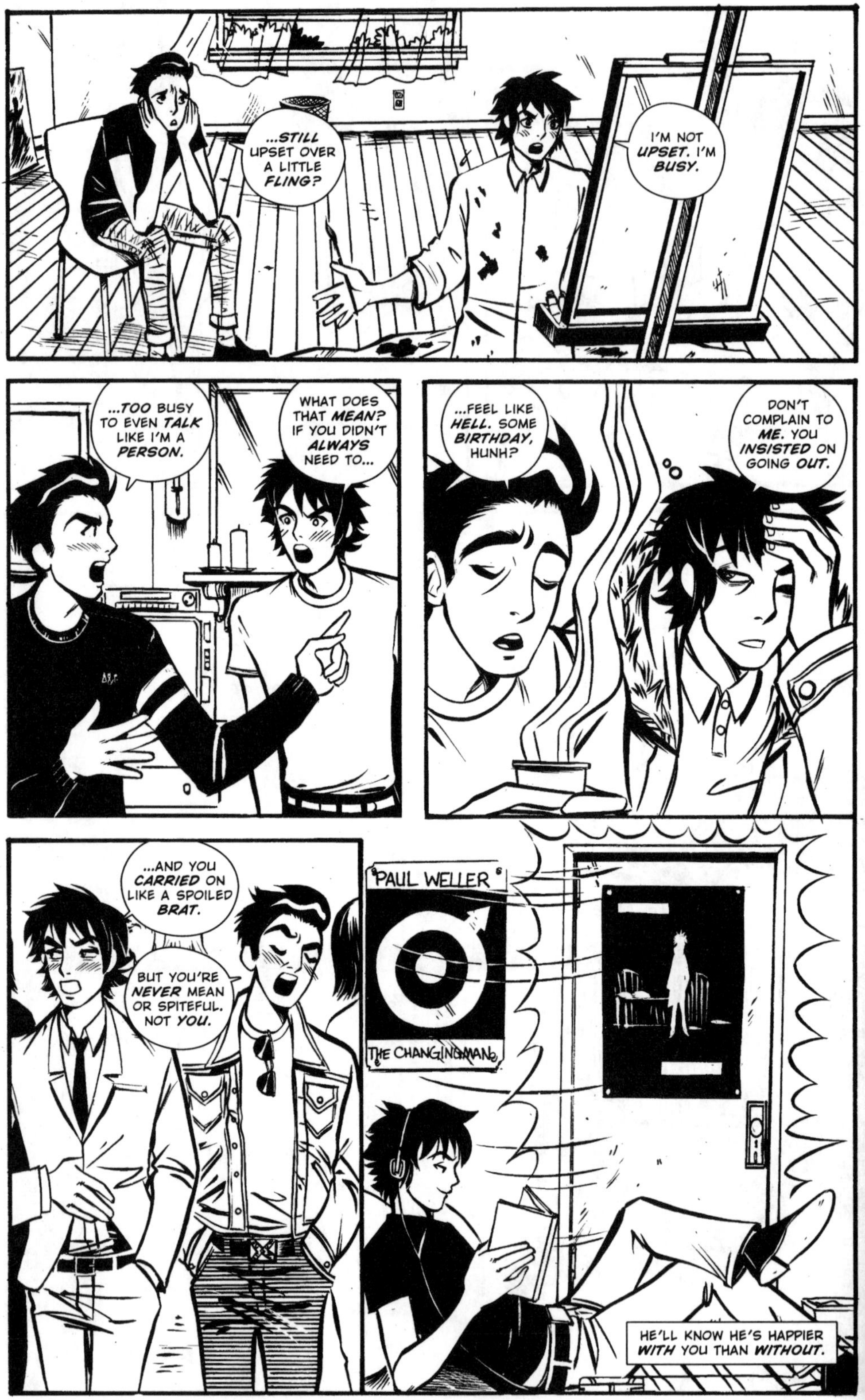
...STILL UPSET OVER A LITTLE FLING?
I'M NOT UPSET. I'M BUSY.
...TOO BUSY TO EVEN TALK LIKE I'M A PERSON.
WHAT DOES THAT MEAN? IF YOU DIDN'T ALWAYS NEED TO...
...FEEL LIKE HELL. SOME BIRTHDAY, HUNH?
DON'T COMPLAIN TO ME. YOU INSISTED ON GOING OUT.
...AND YOU CARRIED ON LIKE A SPOILED BRAT.
BUT YOU'RE NEVER MEAN OR SPITEFUL. NOT YOU.
PAUL WELLER
THE CHANGINGMAN
HE'LL KNOW HE'S HAPPIER WITH YOU THAN WITHOUT.

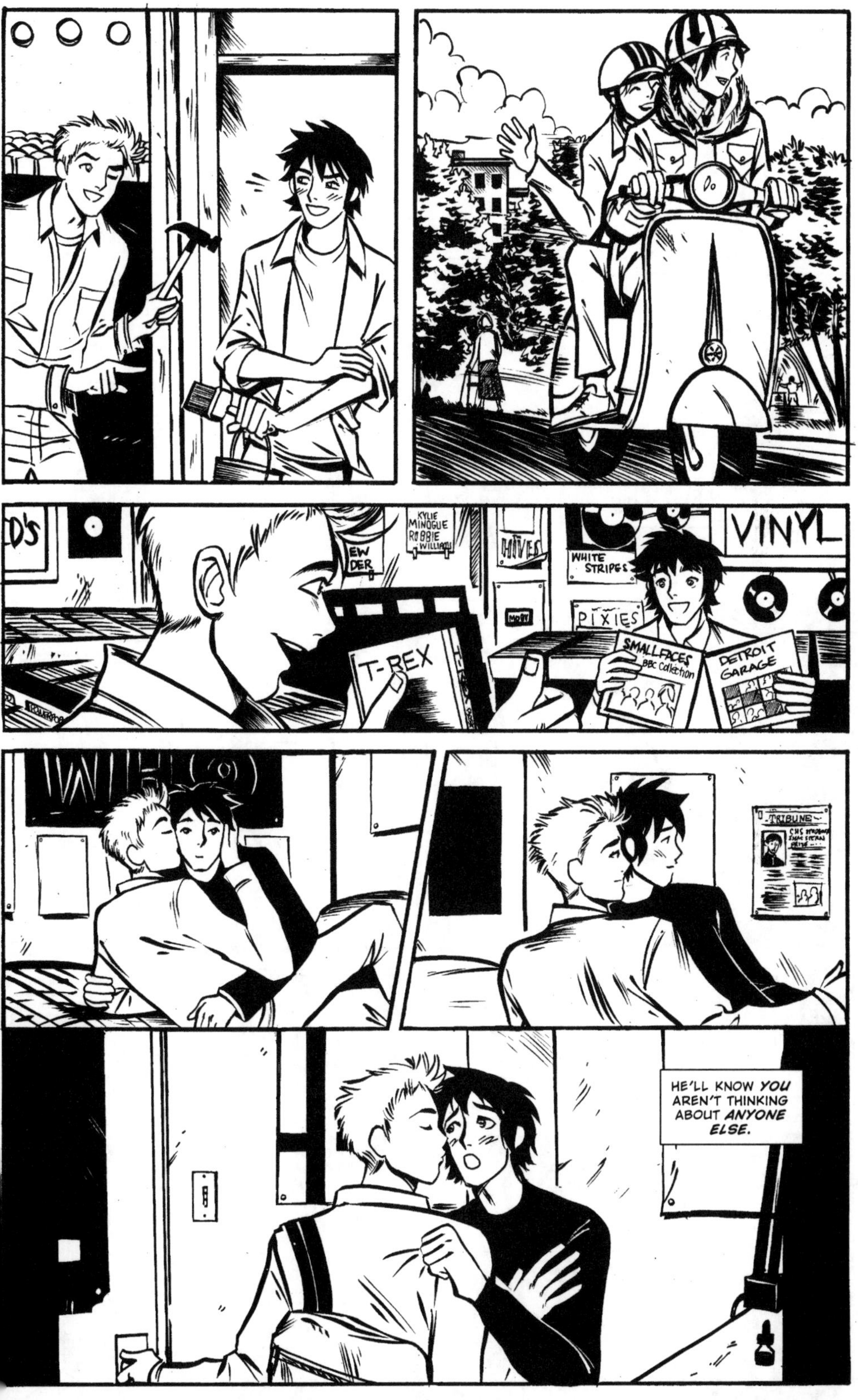
KYLIE MINOGUE
ROBBIE WILLIAMS
VINYL
WHITE STRIPES
PIXIES
T-REX
SMALLFACES
BBC Collection
DETROIT GARAGE
TRIBUNE
HE'LL KNOW *YOU* AREN'T THINKING ABOUT *ANYONE ELSE.*

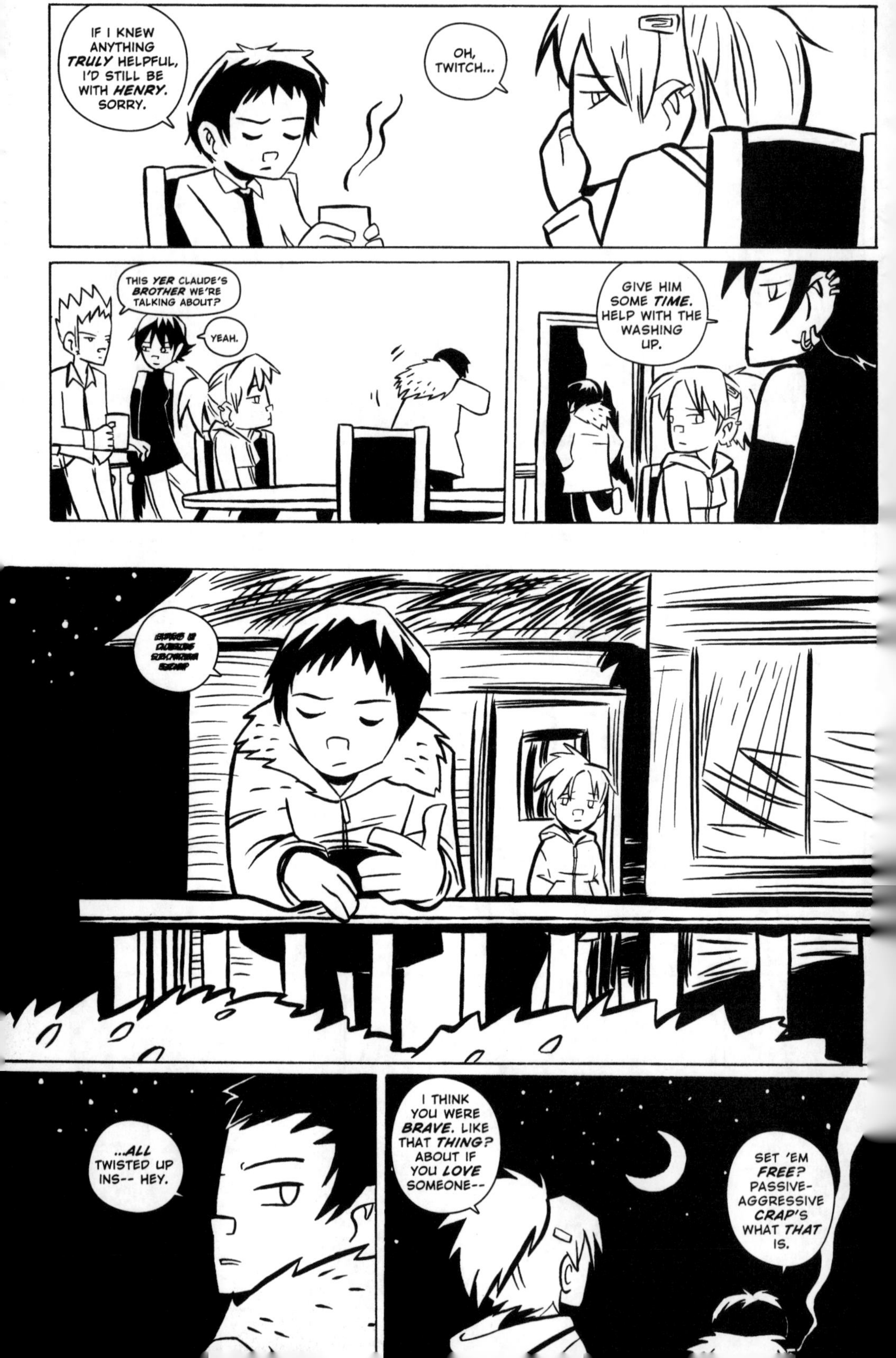
IF I KNEW ANYTHING TRULY HELPFUL, I'D STILL BE WITH HENRY. SORRY.
OH, TWITCH...
THIS YER CLAUDE'S BROTHER WE'RE TALKING ABOUT?
YEAH.
GIVE HIM SOME TIME. HELP WITH THE WASHING UP.
...ALL TWISTED UP INS-- HEY.
I THINK YOU WERE BRAVE. LIKE THAT THING? ABOUT IF YOU LOVE SOMEONE--
SET 'EM FREE? PASSIVE-AGGRESSIVE CRAP'S WHAT THAT IS.

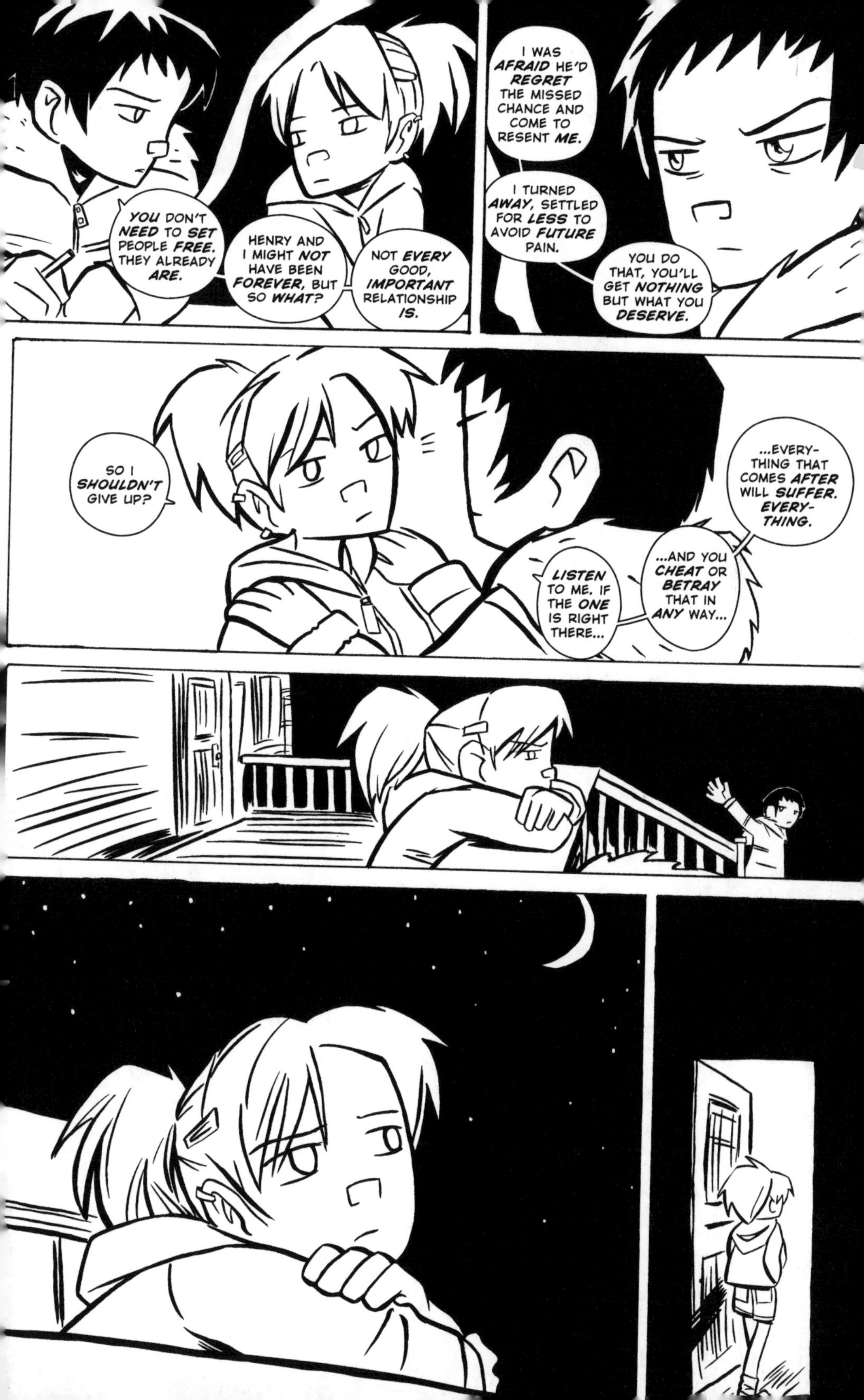
YOU DON'T NEED TO SET PEOPLE FREE. THEY ALREADY ARE.
HENRY AND I MIGHT NOT HAVE BEEN FOREVER, BUT SO WHAT?
NOT EVERY GOOD, IMPORTANT RELATIONSHIP IS.
I WAS AFRAID HE'D REGRET THE MISSED CHANCE AND COME TO RESENT ME.
I TURNED AWAY, SETTLED FOR LESS TO AVOID FUTURE PAIN.
YOU DO THAT, YOU'LL GET NOTHING BUT WHAT YOU DESERVE.
SO I SHOULDN'T GIVE UP?
LISTEN TO ME. IF THE ONE IS RIGHT THERE...
...AND YOU CHEAT OR BETRAY THAT IN ANY WAY...
...EVERYTHING THAT COMES AFTER WILL SUFFER. EVERYTHING.

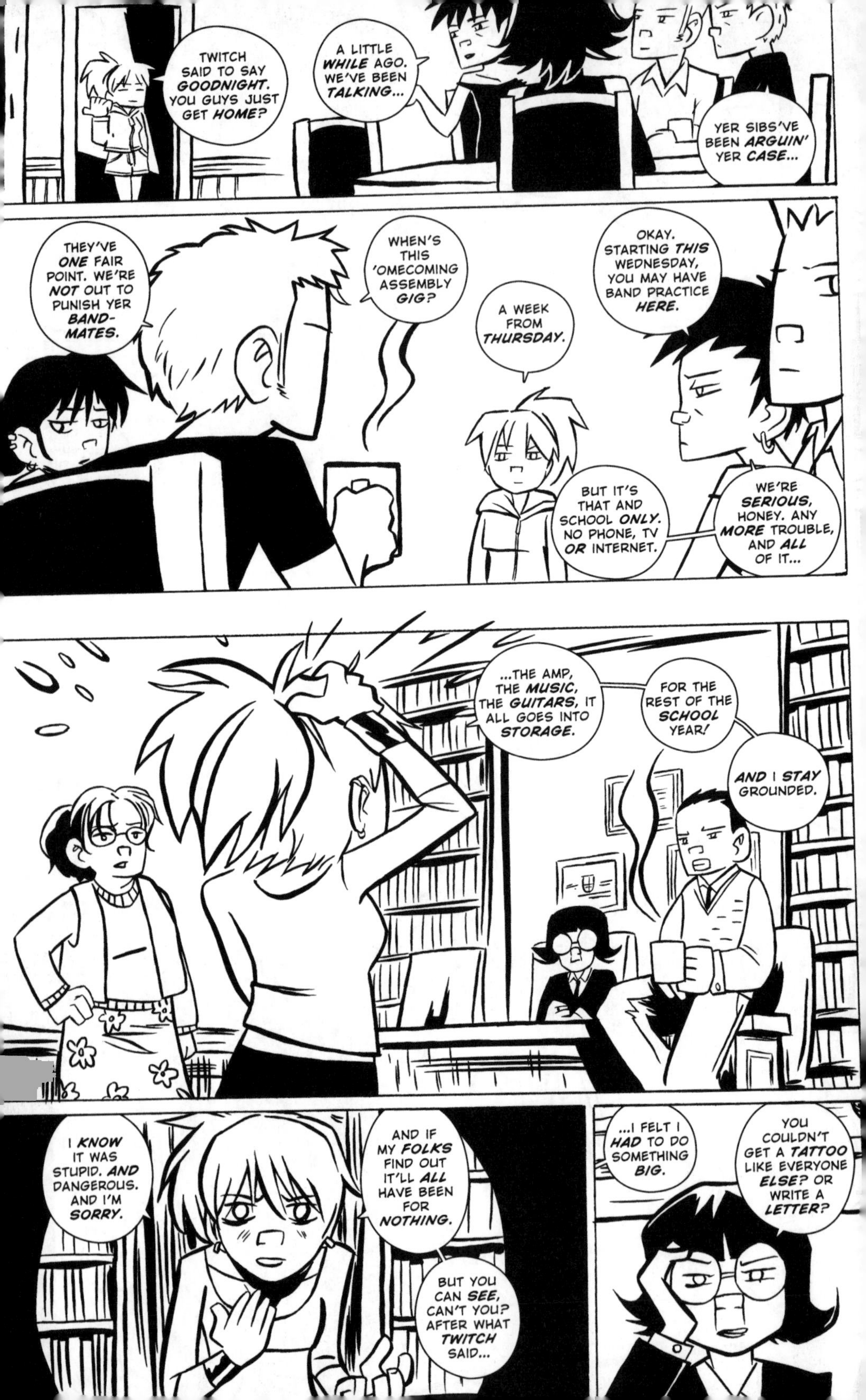
TWITCH SAID TO SAY GOODNIGHT. YOU GUYS JUST GET HOME?
A LITTLE WHILE AGO. WE'VE BEEN TALKING...
YER SIBS'VE BEEN ARGUIN' YER CASE...
THEY'VE ONE FAIR POINT. WE'RE NOT OUT TO PUNISH YER BAND-MATES.
WHEN'S THIS 'OMECOMING ASSEMBLY GIG?
A WEEK FROM THURSDAY.
OKAY. STARTING THIS WEDNESDAY, YOU MAY HAVE BAND PRACTICE HERE.
BUT IT'S THAT AND SCHOOL ONLY. NO PHONE, TV OR INTERNET.
WE'RE SERIOUS, HONEY. ANY MORE TROUBLE, AND ALL OF IT...
...THE AMP, THE MUSIC, THE GUITARS, IT ALL GOES INTO STORAGE.
FOR THE REST OF THE SCHOOL YEAR!
AND I STAY GROUNDED.
I KNOW IT WAS STUPID. AND DANGEROUS. AND I'M SORRY.
AND IF MY FOLKS FIND OUT IT'LL ALL HAVE BEEN FOR NOTHING.
BUT YOU CAN SEE, CAN'T YOU? AFTER WHAT TWITCH SAID...
...I FELT I HAD TO DO SOMETHING BIG.
YOU COULDN'T GET A TATTOO LIKE EVERYONE ELSE? OR WRITE A LETTER?

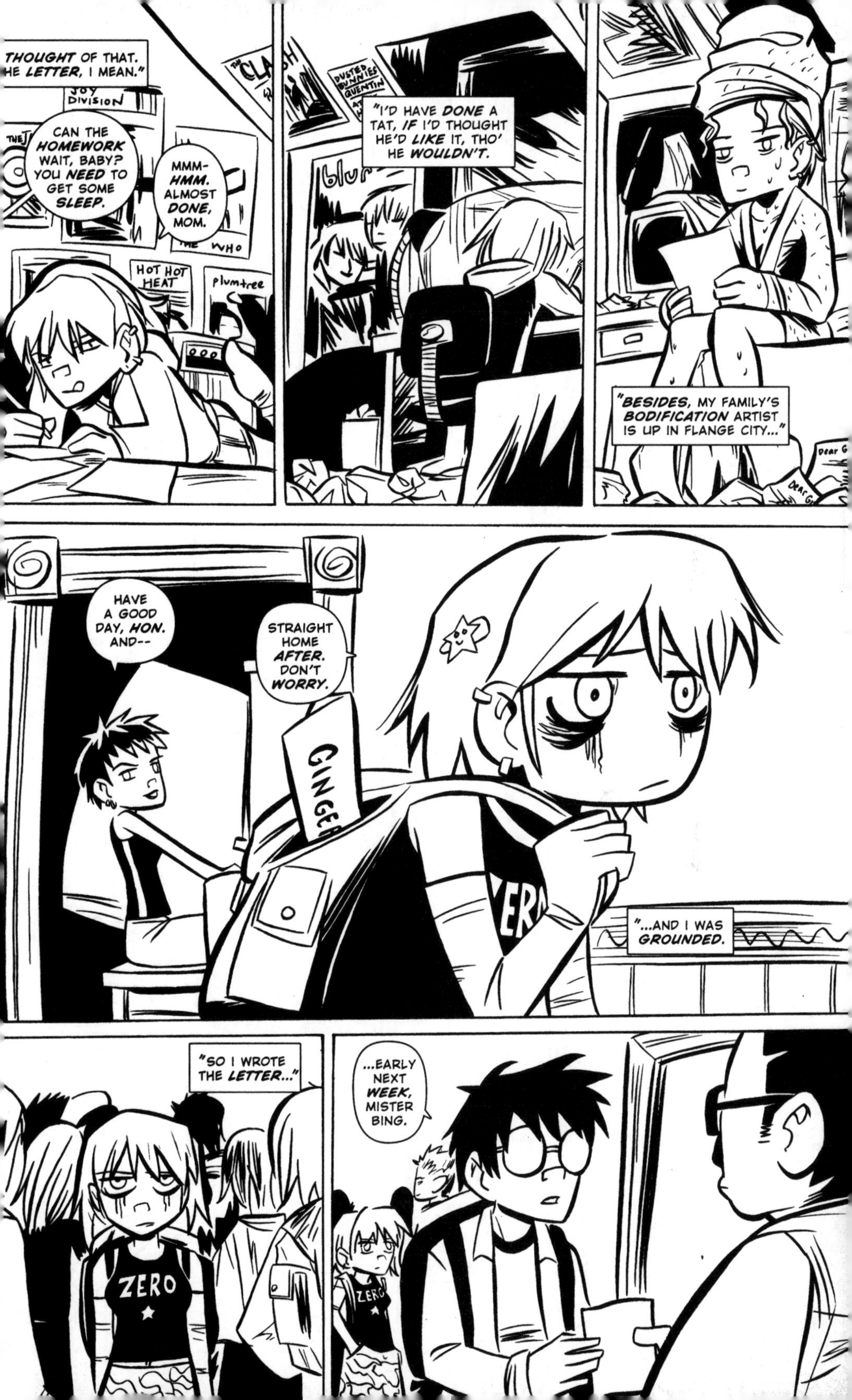
"THOUGHT OF THAT. HE LETTER, I MEAN."
JOY DIVISION
CAN THE HOMEWORK WAIT, BABY? YOU NEED TO GET SOME SLEEP.
MMM-HMM. ALMOST DONE, MOM.
THE WHO
HOT HOT HEAT
plumtree
THE CLASH
DUSTED BUNNIES QUENTIN
"I'D HAVE DONE A TAT, IF I'D THOUGHT HE'D LIKE IT, THO' HE WOULDN'T.
blur
"BESIDES, MY FAMILY'S BODIFICATION ARTIST IS UP IN FLANGE CITY..."
Dear G
HAVE A GOOD DAY, HON. AND--
STRAIGHT HOME AFTER. DON'T WORRY.
GINGER
"...AND I WAS GROUNDED.
"SO I WROTE THE LETTER..."
ZERO
...EARLY NEXT WEEK, MISTER BING.
ZERO

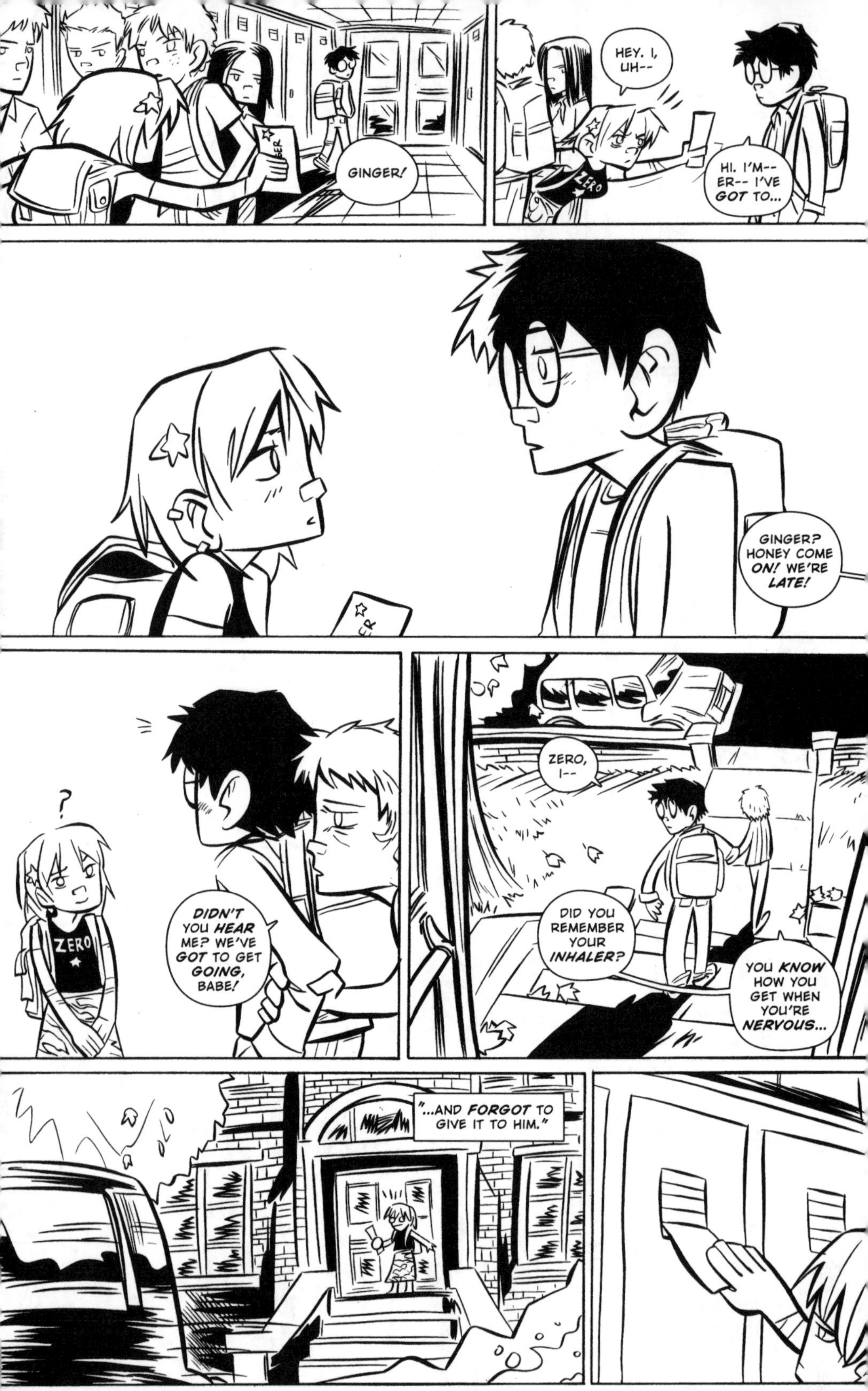
GINGER!
HEY. I, UH--
HI. I'M-- ER-- I'VE GOT TO...
GINGER? HONEY COME ON! WE'RE LATE!
DIDN'T YOU HEAR ME? WE'VE GOT TO GET GOING, BABE!
ZERO, I--
DID YOU REMEMBER YOUR INHALER?
YOU KNOW HOW YOU GET WHEN YOU'RE NERVOUS...
"...AND FORGOT TO GIVE IT TO HIM."

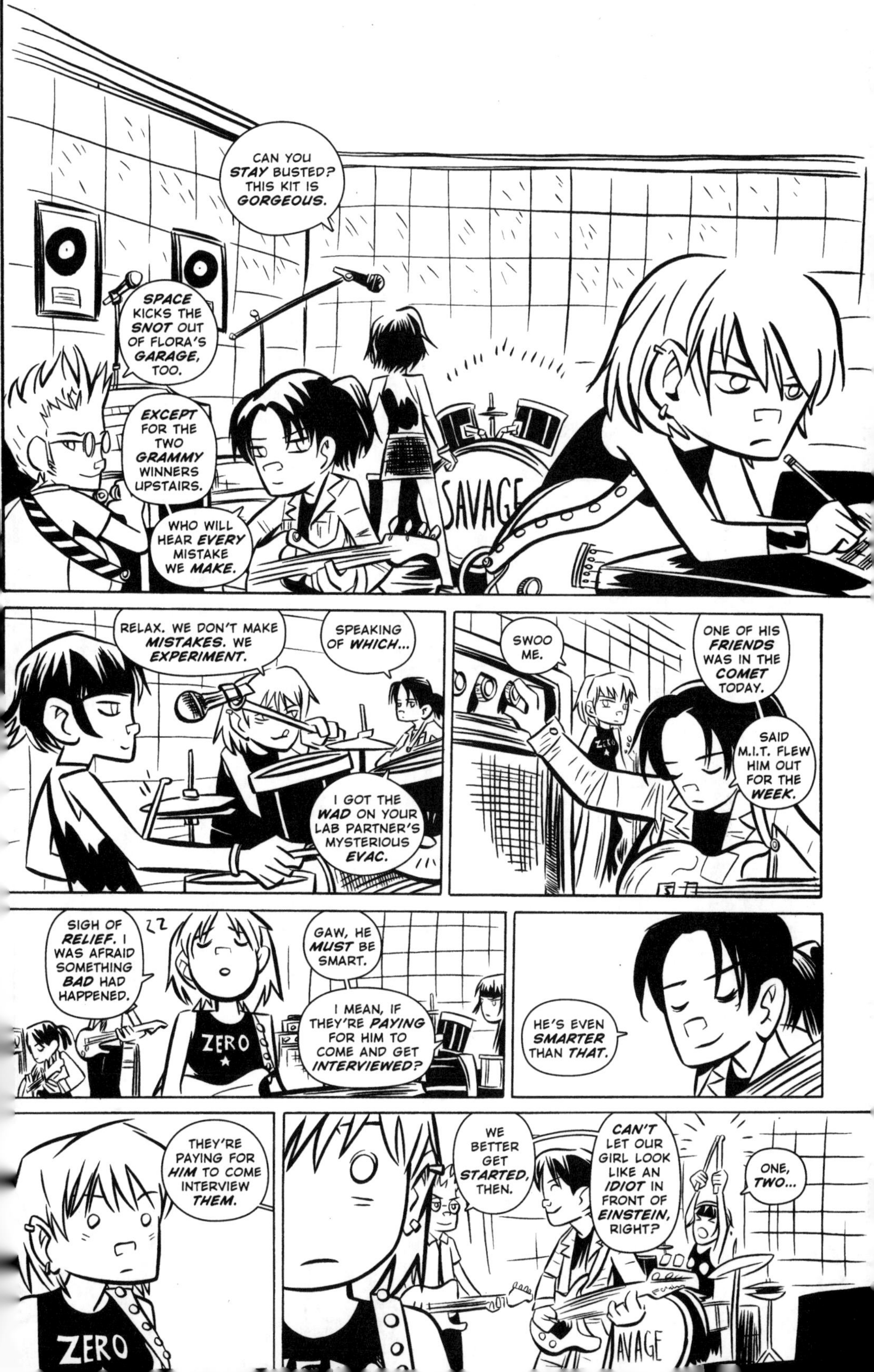
CAN YOU STAY BUSTED? THIS KIT IS GORGEOUS.
SPACE KICKS THE SNOT OUT OF FLORA'S GARAGE, TOO.
EXCEPT FOR THE TWO GRAMMY WINNERS UPSTAIRS.
WHO WILL HEAR EVERY MISTAKE WE MAKE.
SAVAGE
RELAX. WE DON'T MAKE MISTAKES. WE EXPERIMENT.
SPEAKING OF WHICH...
I GOT THE WAD ON YOUR LAB PARTNER'S MYSTERIOUS EVAC.
SWOO ME.
ONE OF HIS FRIENDS WAS IN THE COMET TODAY.
SAID M.I.T. FLEW HIM OUT FOR THE WEEK.
SIGH OF RELIEF. I WAS AFRAID SOMETHING BAD HAD HAPPENED.
GAW, HE MUST BE SMART.
I MEAN, IF THEY'RE PAYING FOR HIM TO COME AND GET INTERVIEWED?
ZERO
HE'S EVEN SMARTER THAN THAT.
THEY'RE PAYING FOR HIM TO COME INTERVIEW THEM.
ZERO
WE BETTER GET STARTED, THEN.
CAN'T LET OUR GIRL LOOK LIKE AN IDIOT IN FRONT OF EINSTEIN, RIGHT?
ONE, TWO...
AVAGE

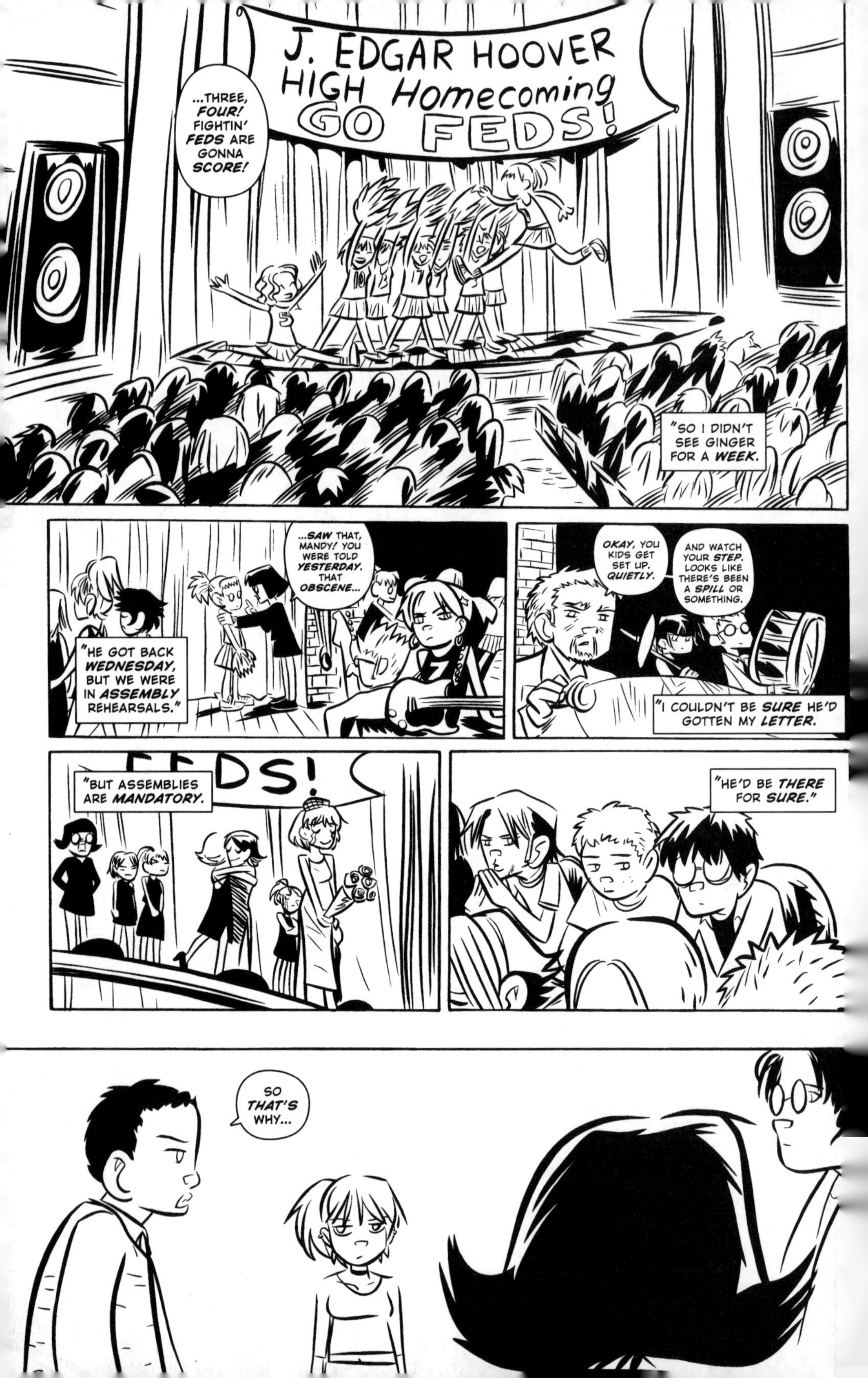
J. EDGAR HOOVER HIGH Homecoming GO FEDS!
...THREE, FOUR! FIGHTIN' FEDS ARE GONNA SCORE!
"SO I DIDN'T SEE GINGER FOR A WEEK.
"HE GOT BACK WEDNESDAY, BUT WE WERE IN ASSEMBLY REHEARSALS."
...SAW THAT, MANDY! YOU WERE TOLD YESTERDAY. THAT OBSCENE...
OKAY, YOU KIDS GET SET UP. QUIETLY.
AND WATCH YOUR STEP. LOOKS LIKE THERE'S BEEN A SPILL OR SOMETHING.
"I COULDN'T BE SURE HE'D GOTTEN MY LETTER.
"BUT ASSEMBLIES ARE MANDATORY.
DS!
"HE'D BE THERE FOR SURE."
SO THAT'S WHY...

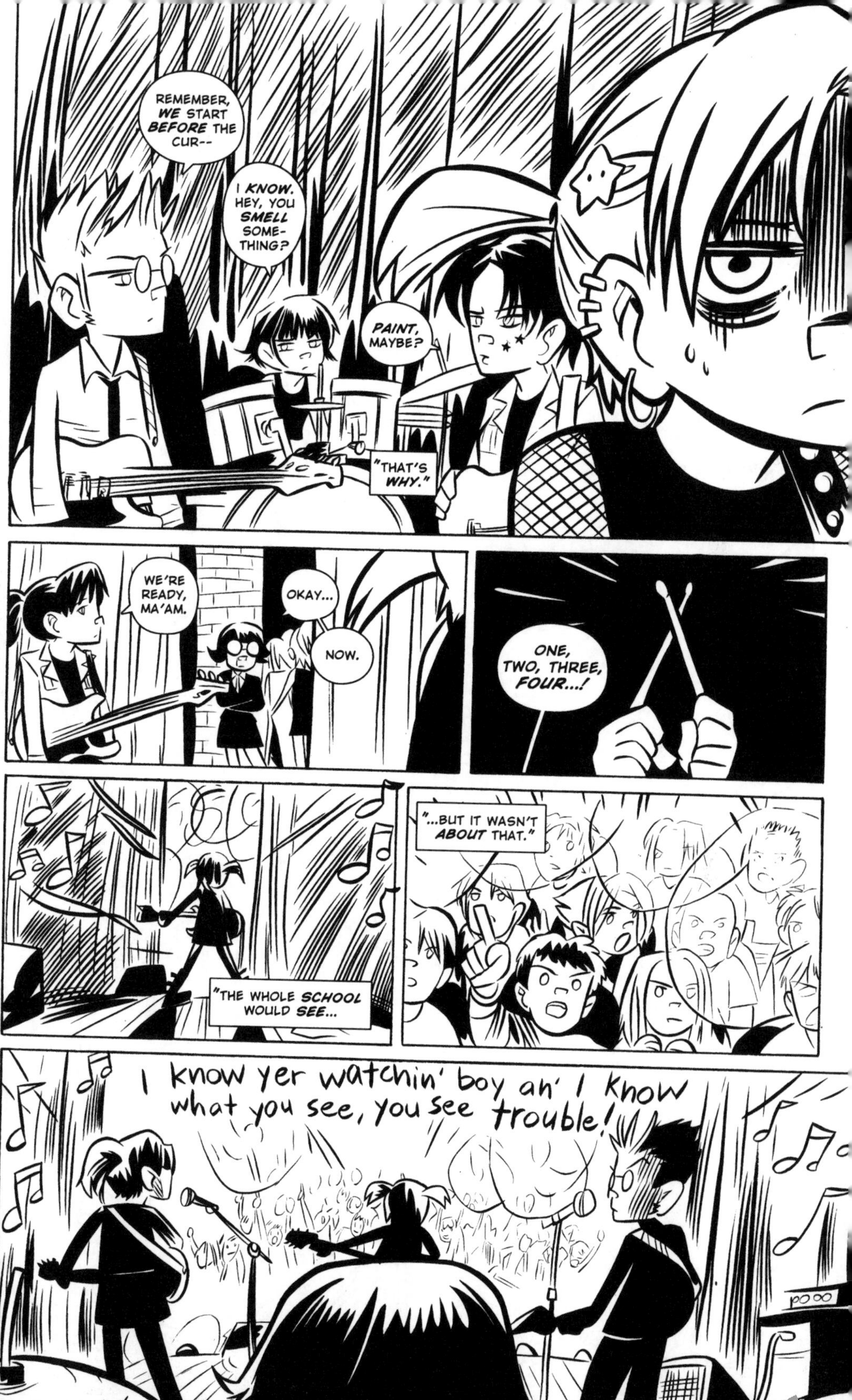

REMEMBER, WE START BEFORE THE CUR--
I KNOW. HEY, YOU SMELL SOME-THING?
PAINT, MAYBE?
"THAT'S WHY."
WE'RE READY, MA'AM.
OKAY...
NOW.
ONE, TWO, THREE, FOUR...!
"THE WHOLE SCHOOL WOULD SEE...
"...BUT IT WASN'T ABOUT THAT."
I know yer watchin' boy an' I know what you see, you see trouble!

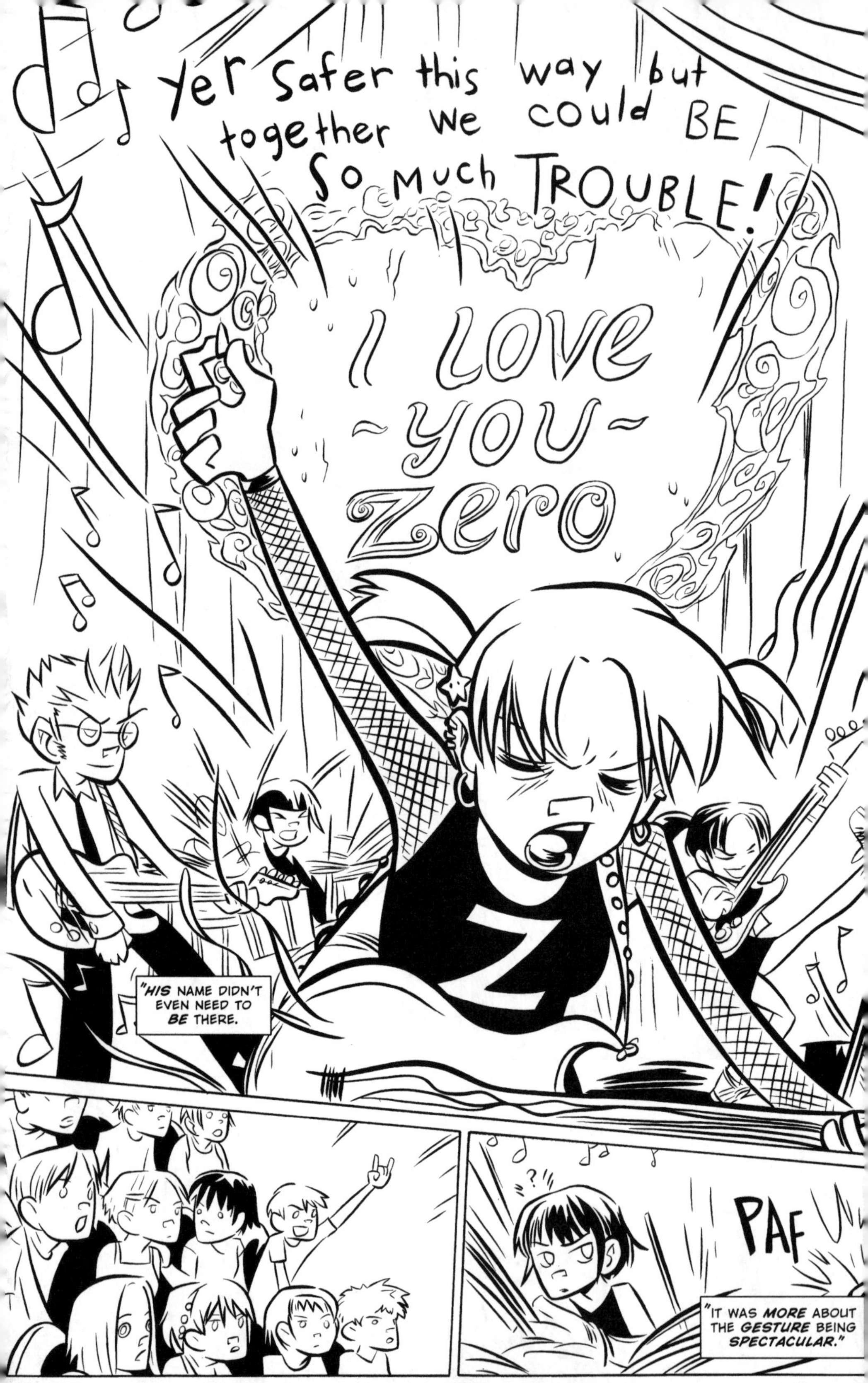

Yer safer this way but together we could BE So much TROUBLE!
I LOVE ~YOU~ ZERO
"HIS NAME DIDN'T EVEN NEED TO BE THERE.
PAF
"IT WAS MORE ABOUT THE GESTURE BEING SPECTACULAR."

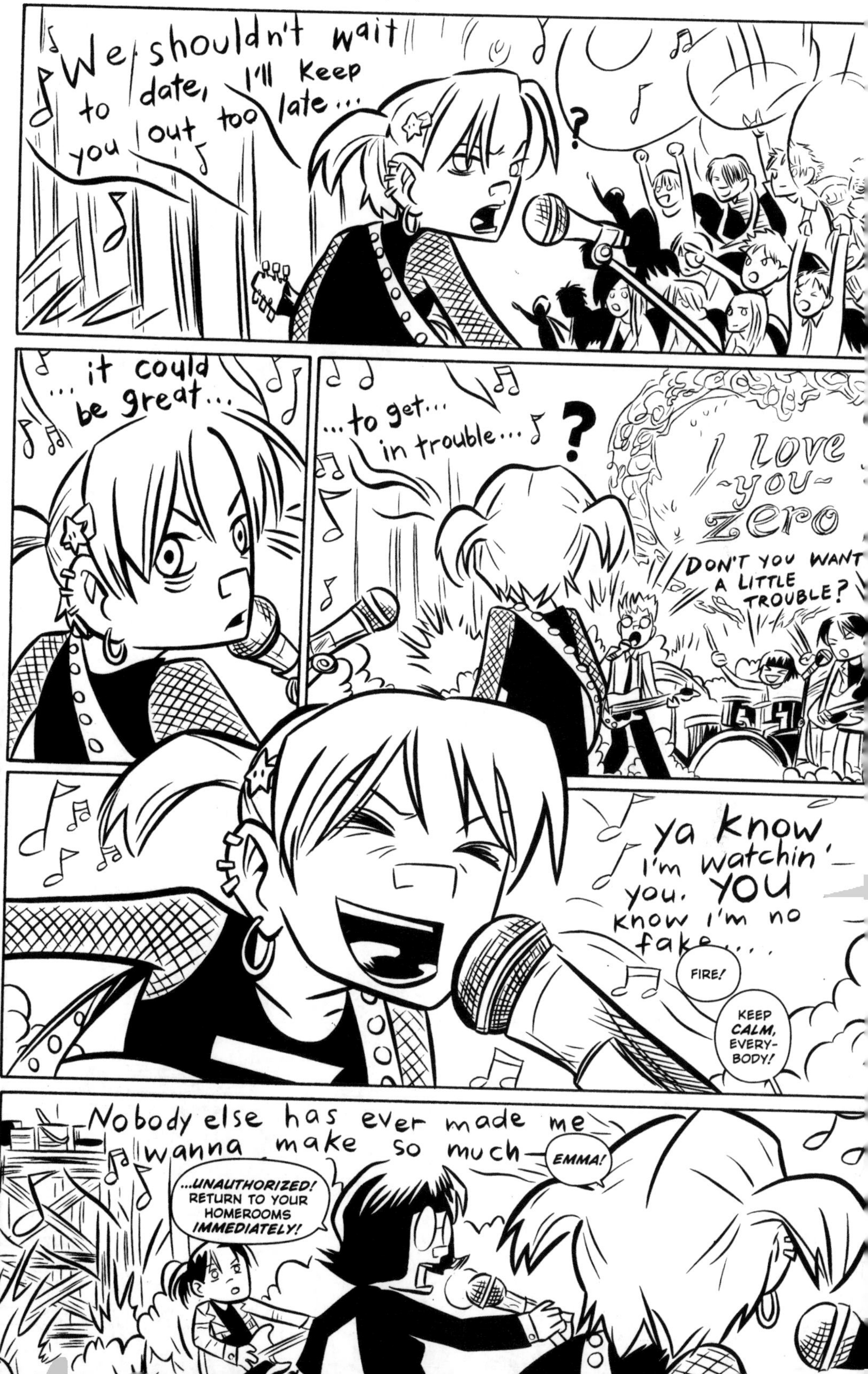
We shouldn't wait to date, I'll keep you out too late...
?
...it could be great...
...to get... in trouble...
?
I love you zero
DON'T YOU WANT A LITTLE TROUBLE?
ya know, I'm watchin' you. YOU know I'm no fake...
FIRE!
KEEP CALM, EVERYBODY!
Nobody else has ever made me wanna make so much—
EMMA!
...UNAUTHORIZED! RETURN TO YOUR HOMEROOMS IMMEDIATELY!

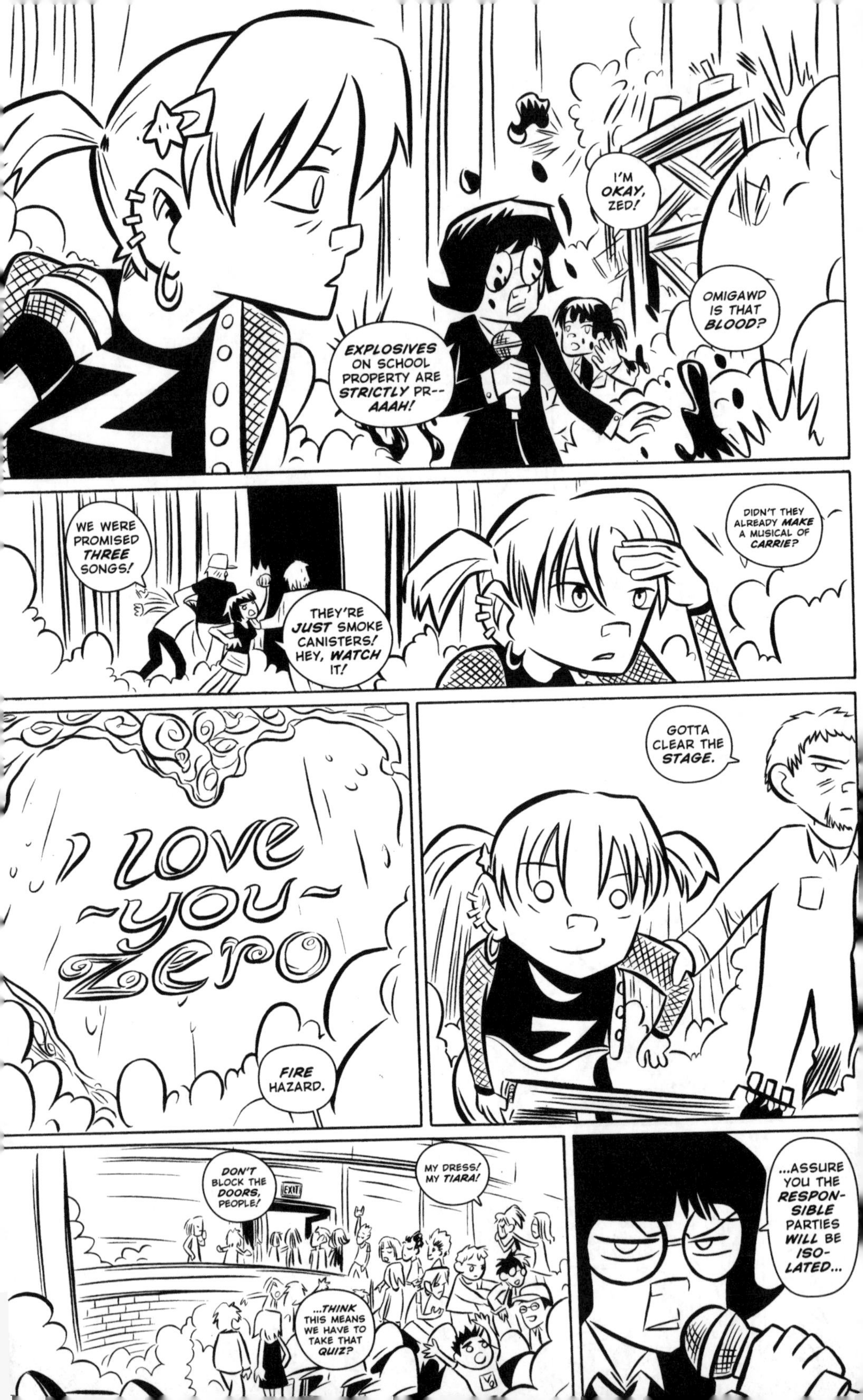
I'M OKAY, ZED!
OMIGAWD IS THAT BLOOD?
EXPLOSIVES ON SCHOOL PROPERTY ARE STRICTLY PR-- AAAH!
WE WERE PROMISED THREE SONGS!
THEY'RE JUST SMOKE CANISTERS! HEY, WATCH IT!
DIDN'T THEY ALREADY MAKE A MUSICAL OF CARRIE?
I LOVE YOU ZERO
FIRE HAZARD.
GOTTA CLEAR THE STAGE.
DON'T BLOCK THE DOORS, PEOPLE!
EXIT
MY DRESS! MY TIARA!
...THINK THIS MEANS WE HAVE TO TAKE THAT QUIZ?
...ASSURE YOU THE RESPONSIBLE PARTIES WILL BE ISOLATED...

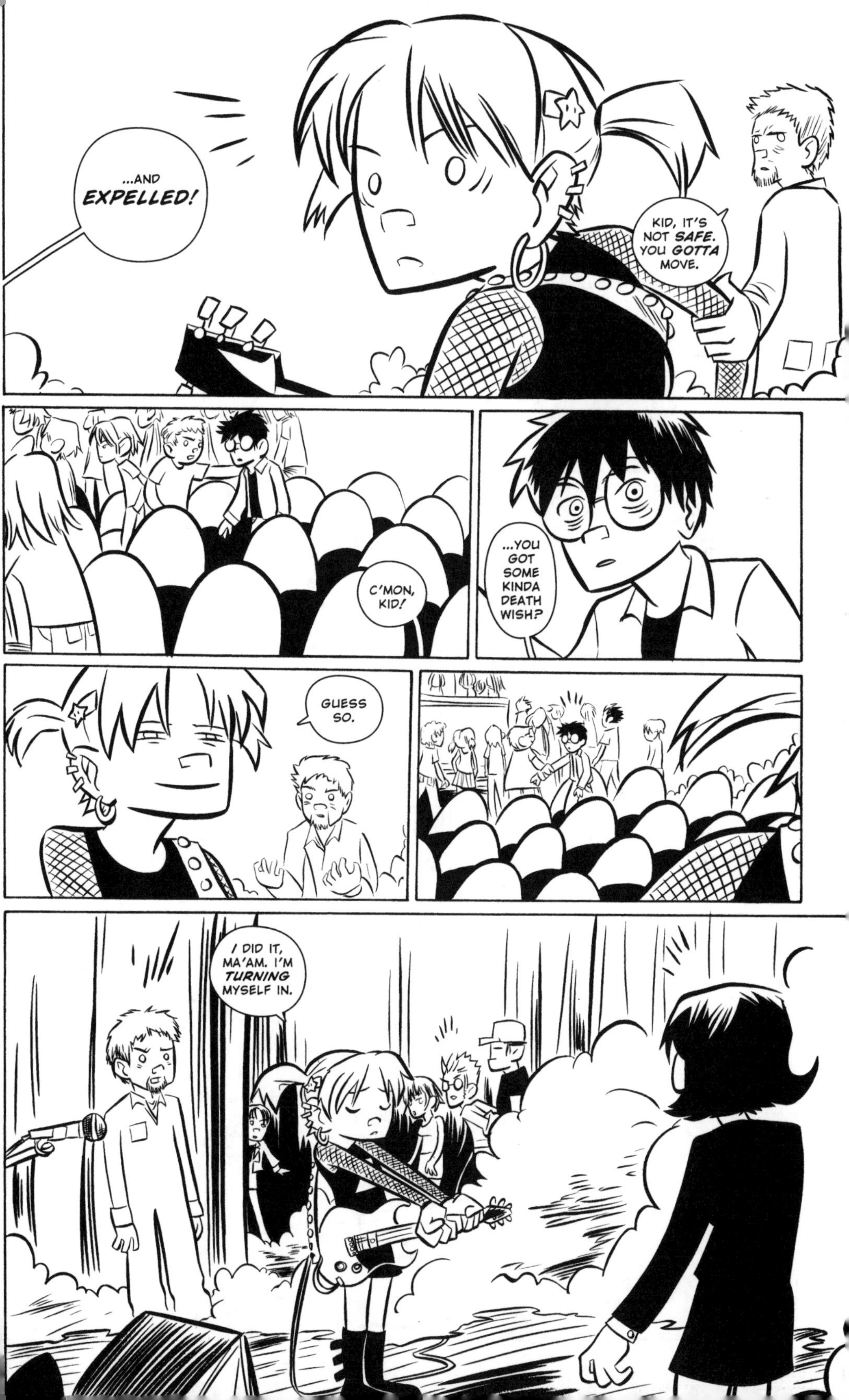
...AND EXPELLED!
KID, IT'S NOT SAFE. YOU GOTTA MOVE.
C'MON, KID!
...YOU GOT SOME KINDA DEATH WISH?
GUESS SO.
I DID IT, MA'AM. I'M TURNING MYSELF IN.

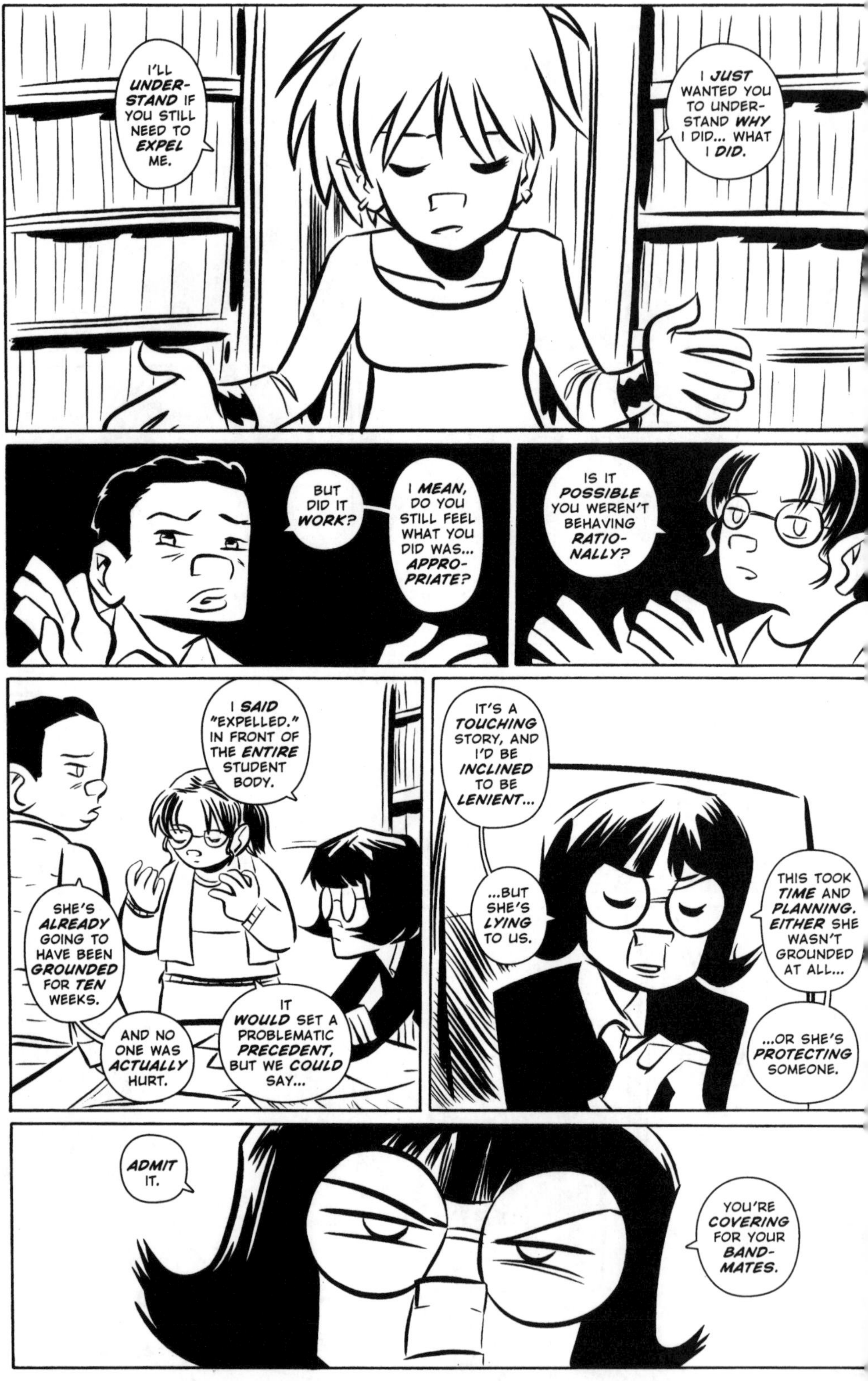

I'LL UNDERSTAND IF YOU STILL NEED TO EXPEL ME.
I JUST WANTED YOU TO UNDERSTAND WHY I DID... WHAT I DID.
BUT DID IT WORK?
I MEAN, DO YOU STILL FEEL WHAT YOU DID WAS... APPROPRIATE?
IS IT POSSIBLE YOU WEREN'T BEHAVING RATIONALLY?
I SAID "EXPELLED." IN FRONT OF THE ENTIRE STUDENT BODY.
SHE'S ALREADY GOING TO HAVE BEEN GROUNDED FOR TEN WEEKS.
AND NO ONE WAS ACTUALLY HURT.
IT WOULD SET A PROBLEMATIC PRECEDENT, BUT WE COULD SAY...
IT'S A TOUCHING STORY, AND I'D BE INCLINED TO BE LENIENT...
...BUT SHE'S LYING TO US.
THIS TOOK TIME AND PLANNING. EITHER SHE WASN'T GROUNDED AT ALL...
...OR SHE'S PROTECTING SOMEONE.
ADMIT IT.
YOU'RE COVERING FOR YOUR BAND-MATES.

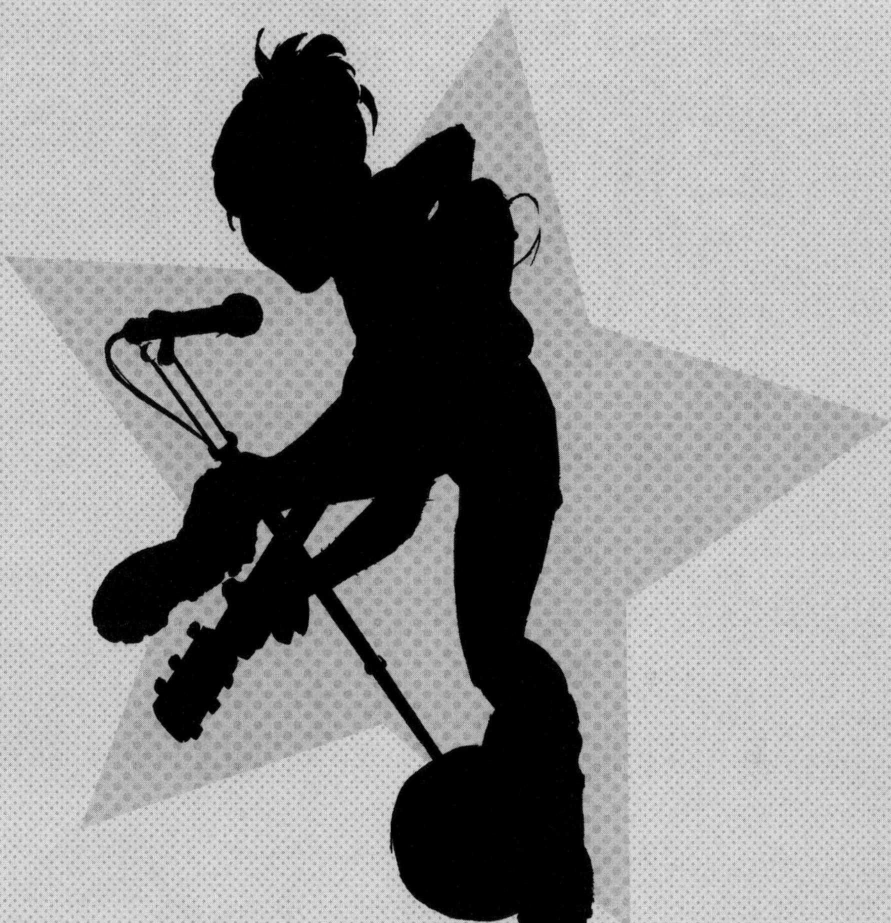

CHAPTER 4

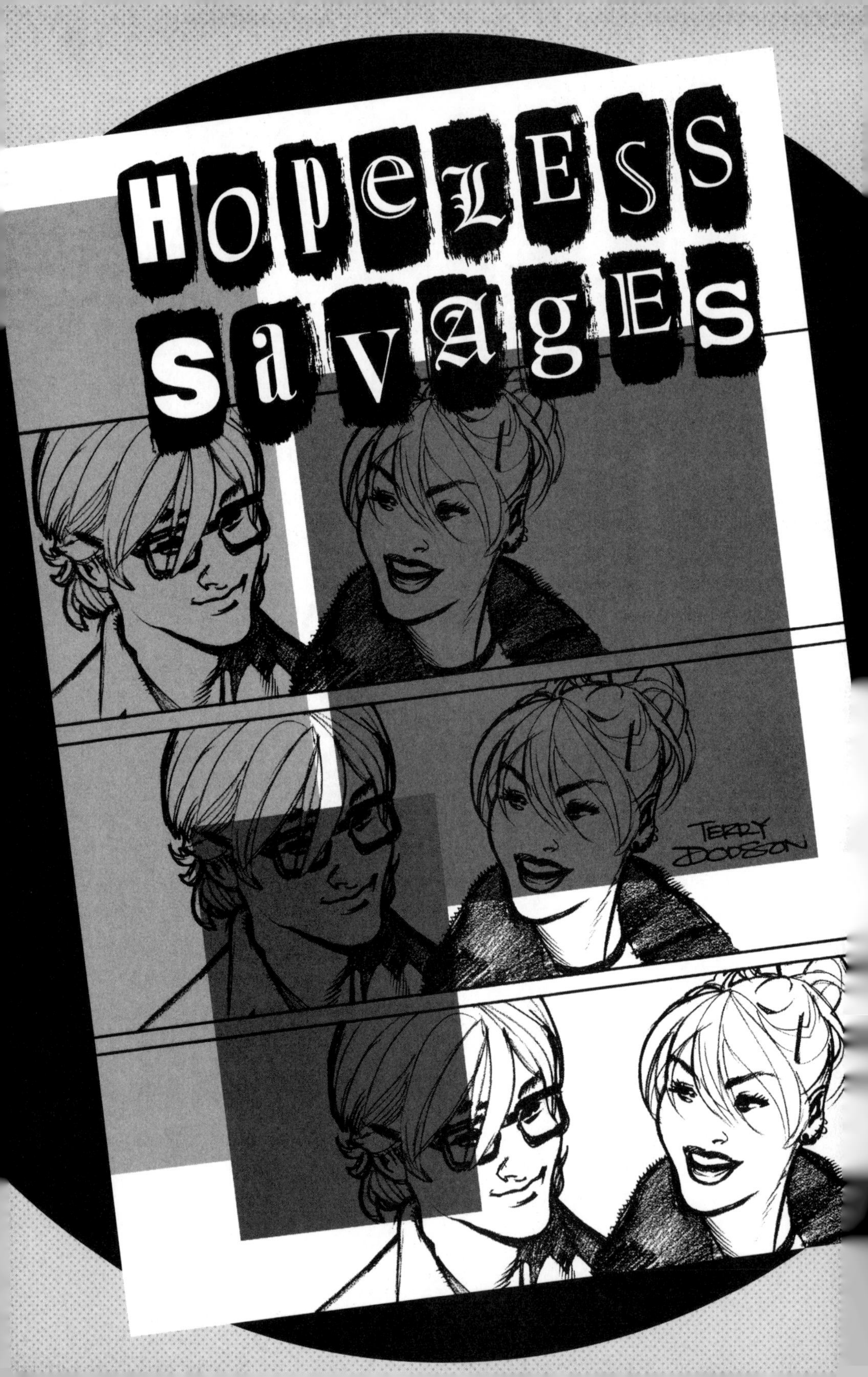
HOPELESS SAVAGES
TERRY DODSON

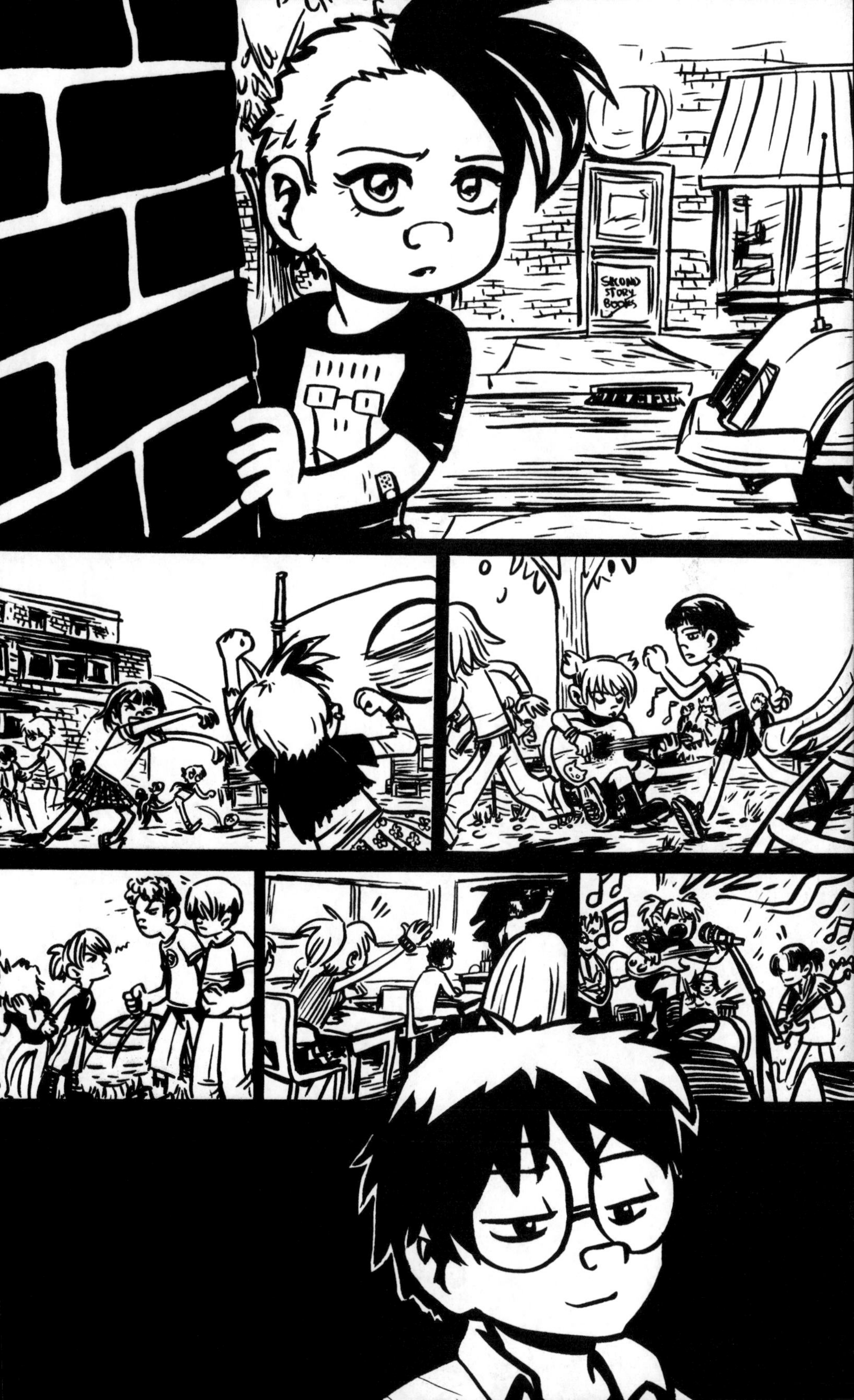
SECOND STORY BOOKS

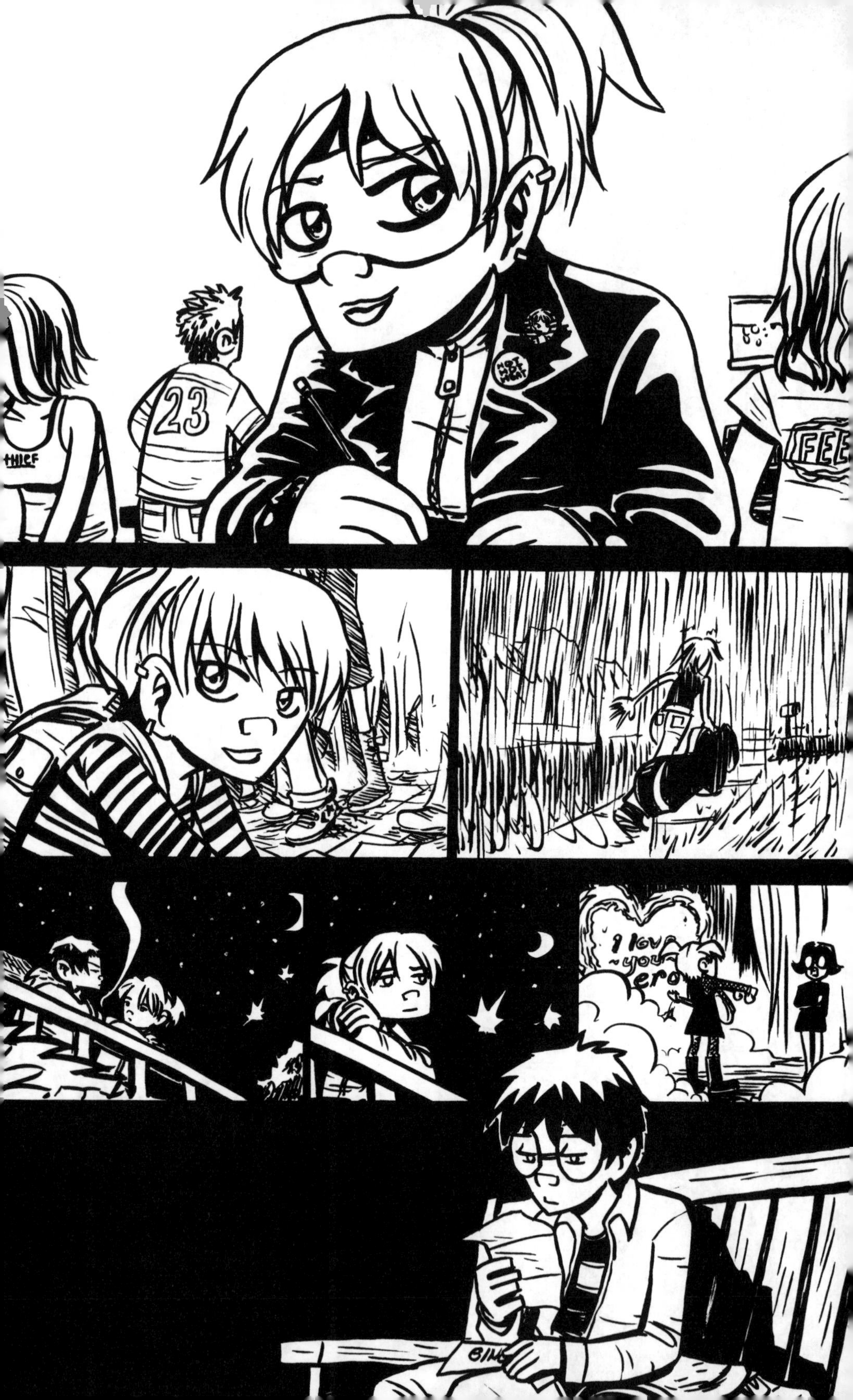
THIEF
23
FEE
I love you ero

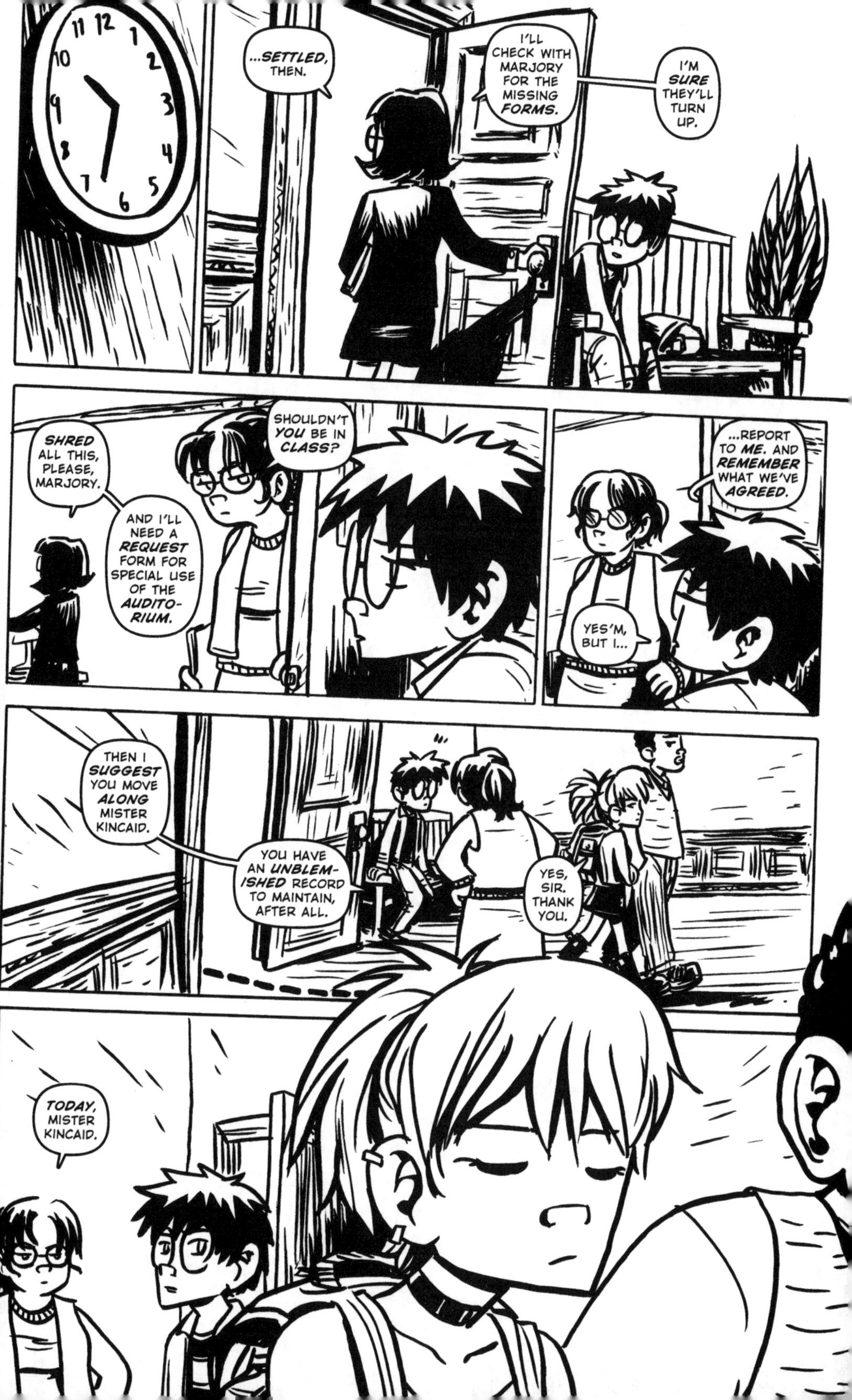

...SETTLED, THEN.
I'LL CHECK WITH MARJORY FOR THE MISSING FORMS.
I'M SURE THEY'LL TURN UP.
SHRED ALL THIS, PLEASE, MARJORY.
AND I'LL NEED A REQUEST FORM FOR SPECIAL USE OF THE AUDITORIUM.
SHOULDN'T YOU BE IN CLASS?
...REPORT TO ME. AND REMEMBER WHAT WE'VE AGREED.
YES'M, BUT I...
THEN I SUGGEST YOU MOVE ALONG MISTER KINCAID.
YOU HAVE AN UNBLEMISHED RECORD TO MAINTAIN, AFTER ALL.
YES, SIR. THANK YOU.
TODAY, MISTER KINCAID.

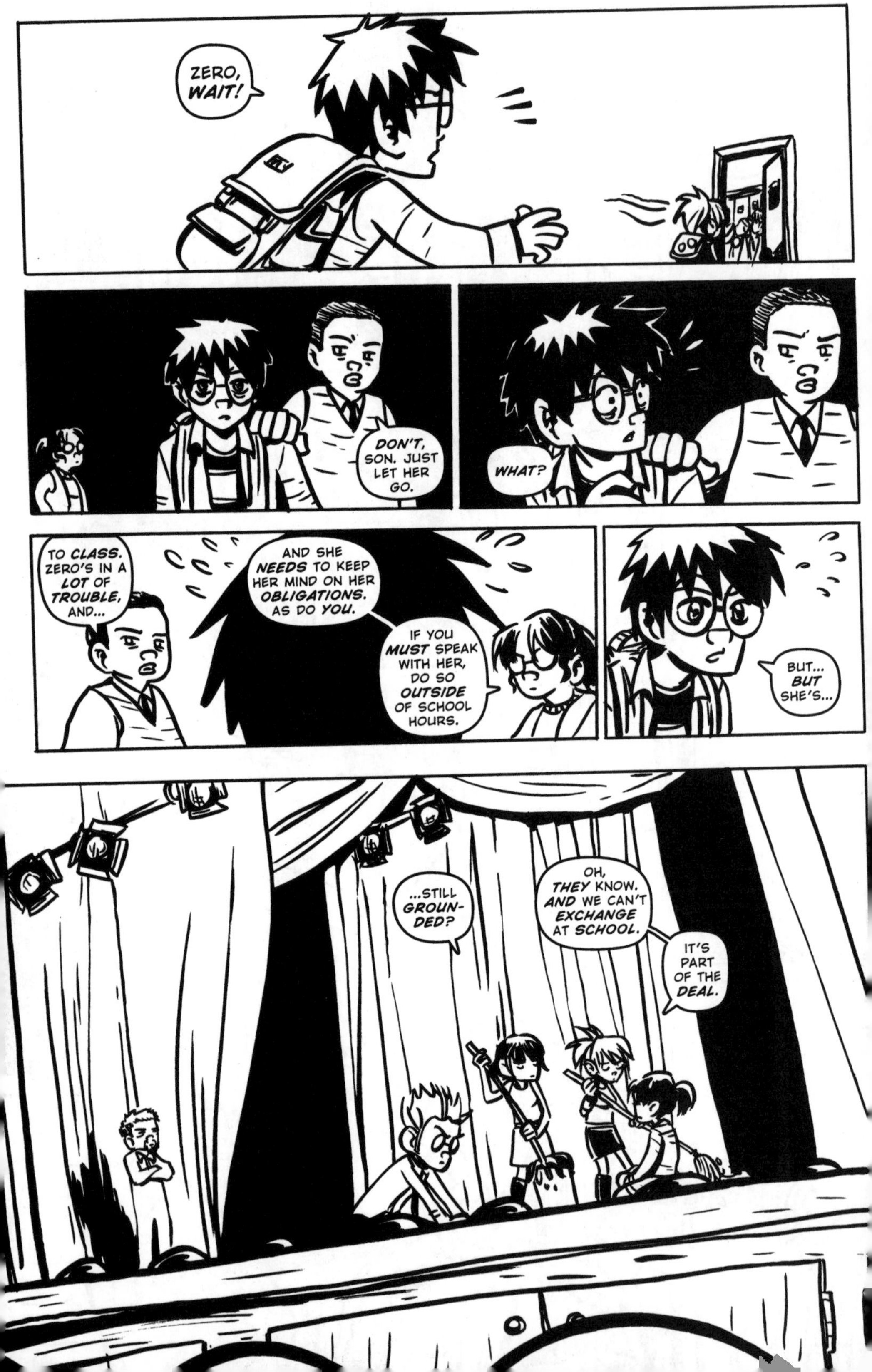

ZERO, WAIT!
DON'T, SON. JUST LET HER GO.
WHAT?
TO CLASS. ZERO'S IN A LOT OF TROUBLE, AND...
AND SHE NEEDS TO KEEP HER MIND ON HER OBLIGATIONS. AS DO YOU.
IF YOU MUST SPEAK WITH HER, DO SO OUTSIDE OF SCHOOL HOURS.
BUT... BUT SHE'S...
...STILL GROUNDED?
OH, THEY KNOW. AND WE CAN'T EXCHANGE AT SCHOOL.
IT'S PART OF THE DEAL.

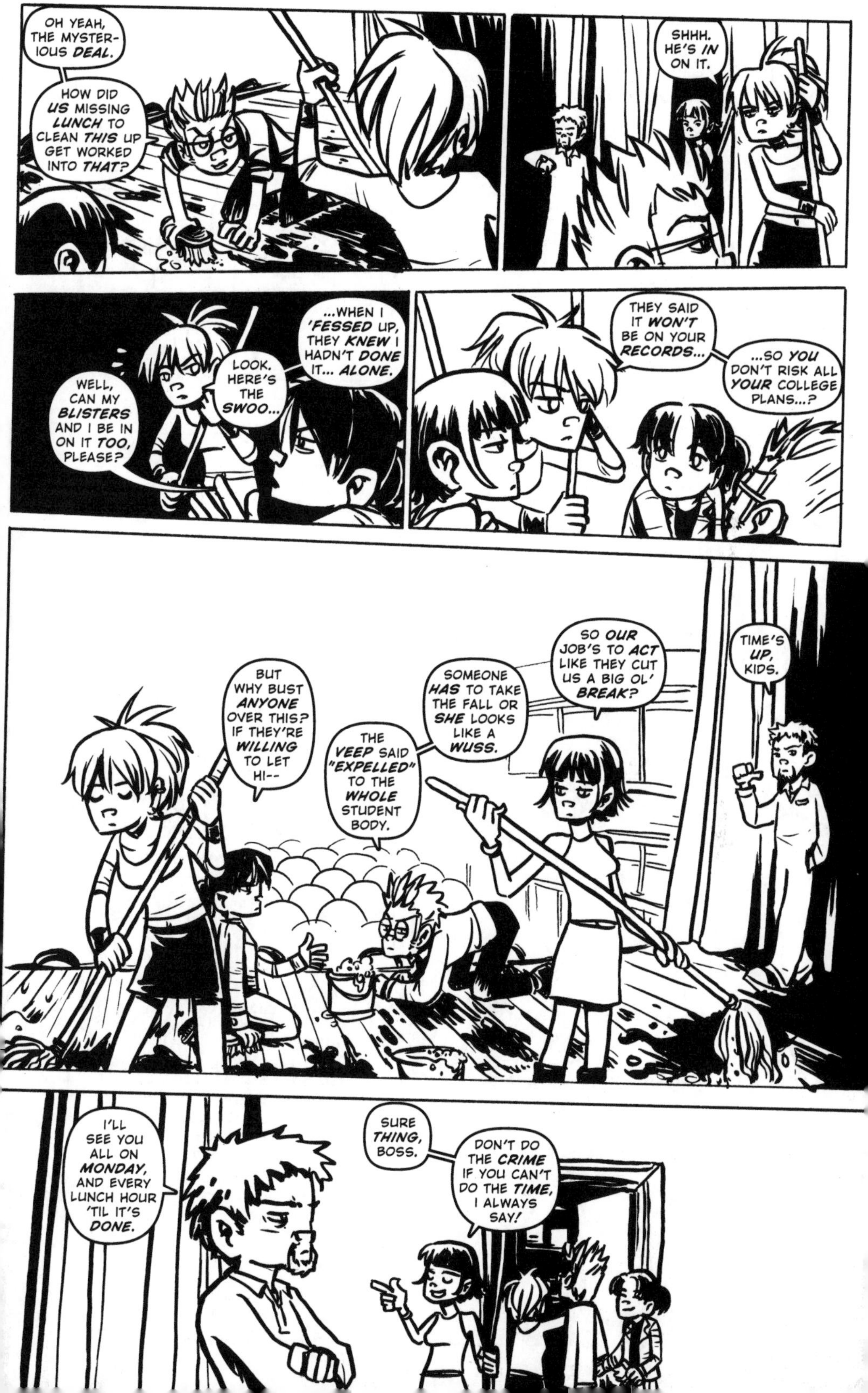
OH YEAH, THE MYSTERIOUS DEAL.
HOW DID US MISSING LUNCH TO CLEAN THIS UP GET WORKED INTO THAT?
SHHH. HE'S IN ON IT.
WELL, CAN MY BLISTERS AND I BE IN ON IT TOO, PLEASE?
LOOK. HERE'S THE SWOO...
...WHEN I 'FESSED UP, THEY KNEW I HADN'T DONE IT... ALONE.
THEY SAID IT WON'T BE ON YOUR RECORDS...
...SO YOU DON'T RISK ALL YOUR COLLEGE PLANS...?
BUT WHY BUST ANYONE OVER THIS? IF THEY'RE WILLING TO LET HI--
THE VEEP SAID "EXPELLED" TO THE WHOLE STUDENT BODY.
SOMEONE HAS TO TAKE THE FALL OR SHE LOOKS LIKE A WUSS.
SO OUR JOB'S TO ACT LIKE THEY CUT US A BIG OL' BREAK?
TIME'S UP, KIDS.
I'LL SEE YOU ALL ON MONDAY, AND EVERY LUNCH HOUR 'TIL IT'S DONE.
SURE THING, BOSS.
DON'T DO THE CRIME IF YOU CAN'T DO THE TIME, I ALWAYS SAY!

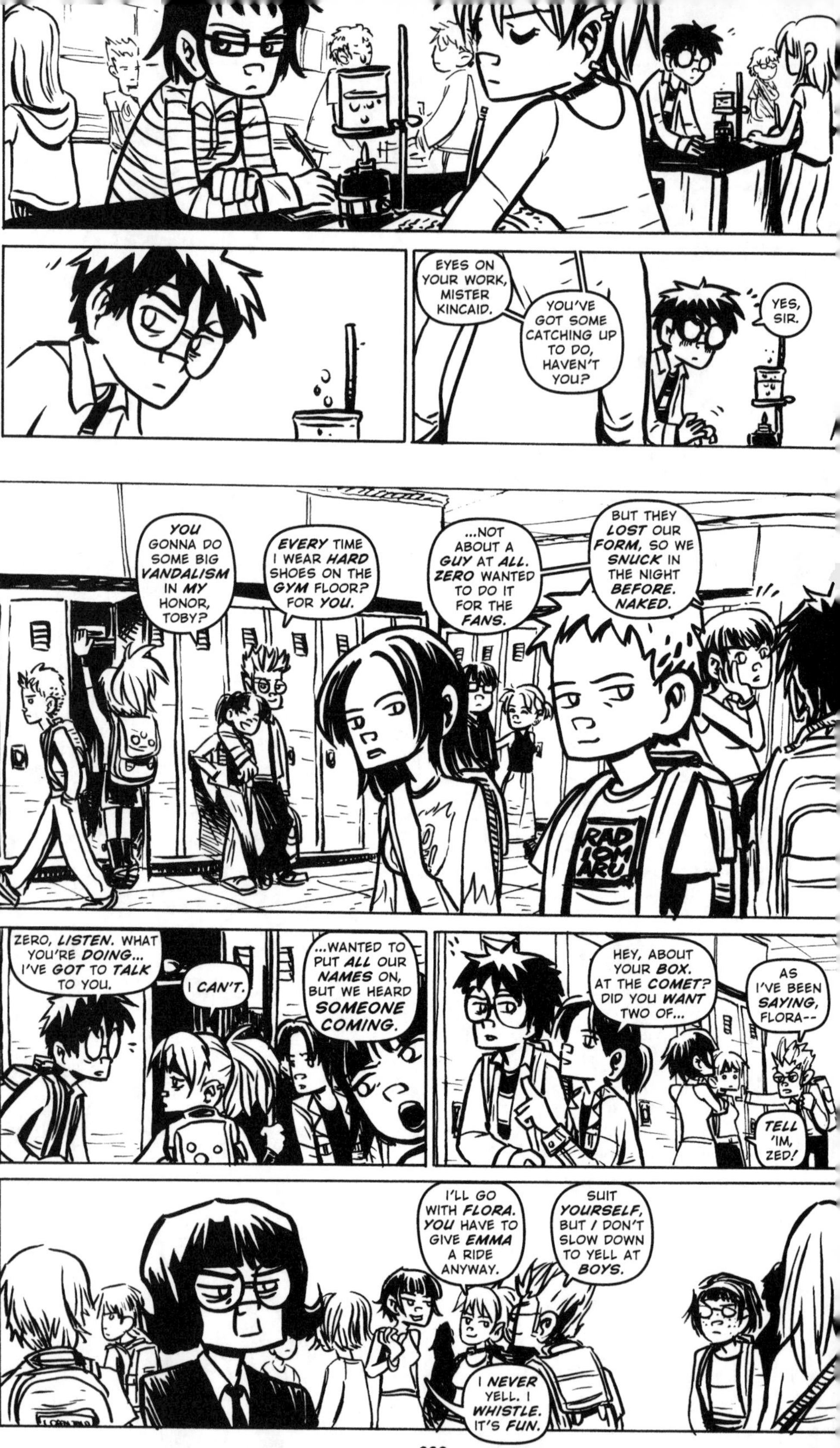
EYES ON YOUR WORK, MISTER KINCAID.
YOU'VE GOT SOME CATCHING UP TO DO, HAVEN'T YOU?
YES, SIR.
YOU GONNA DO SOME BIG VANDALISM IN MY HONOR, TOBY?
EVERY TIME I WEAR HARD SHOES ON THE GYM FLOOR? FOR YOU.
...NOT ABOUT A GUY AT ALL. ZERO WANTED TO DO IT FOR THE FANS.
BUT THEY LOST OUR FORM, SO WE SNUCK IN THE NIGHT BEFORE. NAKED.
RAD IOM ARU
ZERO, LISTEN. WHAT YOU'RE DOING... I'VE GOT TO TALK TO YOU.
I CAN'T.
...WANTED TO PUT ALL OUR NAMES ON, BUT WE HEARD SOMEONE COMING.
HEY, ABOUT YOUR BOX. AT THE COMET? DID YOU WANT TWO OF...
AS I'VE BEEN SAYING, FLORA--
TELL 'IM, ZED!
I'LL GO WITH FLORA. YOU HAVE TO GIVE EMMA A RIDE ANYWAY.
SUIT YOURSELF, BUT I DON'T SLOW DOWN TO YELL AT BOYS.
I NEVER YELL. I WHISTLE. IT'S FUN.

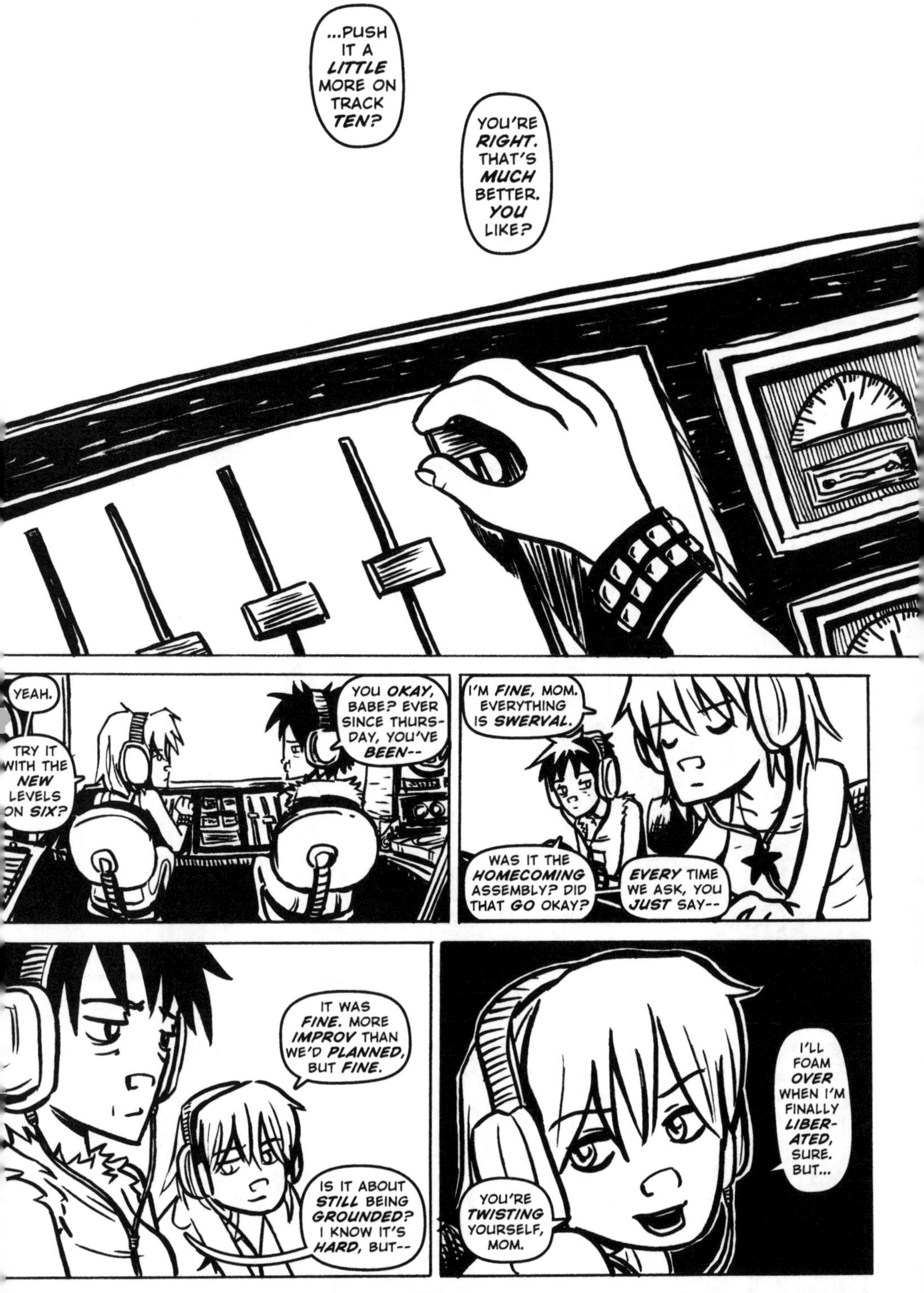
...PUSH IT A LITTLE MORE ON TRACK TEN?
YOU'RE RIGHT. THAT'S MUCH BETTER. YOU LIKE?
YEAH.
TRY IT WITH THE NEW LEVELS ON SIX?
YOU OKAY, BABE? EVER SINCE THURS-DAY, YOU'VE BEEN--
I'M FINE, MOM. EVERYTHING IS SWERVAL.
WAS IT THE HOMECOMING ASSEMBLY? DID THAT GO OKAY?
EVERY TIME WE ASK, YOU JUST SAY--
IT WAS FINE. MORE IMPROV THAN WE'D PLANNED, BUT FINE.
IS IT ABOUT STILL BEING GROUNDED? I KNOW IT'S HARD, BUT--
I'LL FOAM OVER WHEN I'M FINALLY LIBER-ATED, SURE. BUT...
YOU'RE TWISTING YOURSELF, MOM.

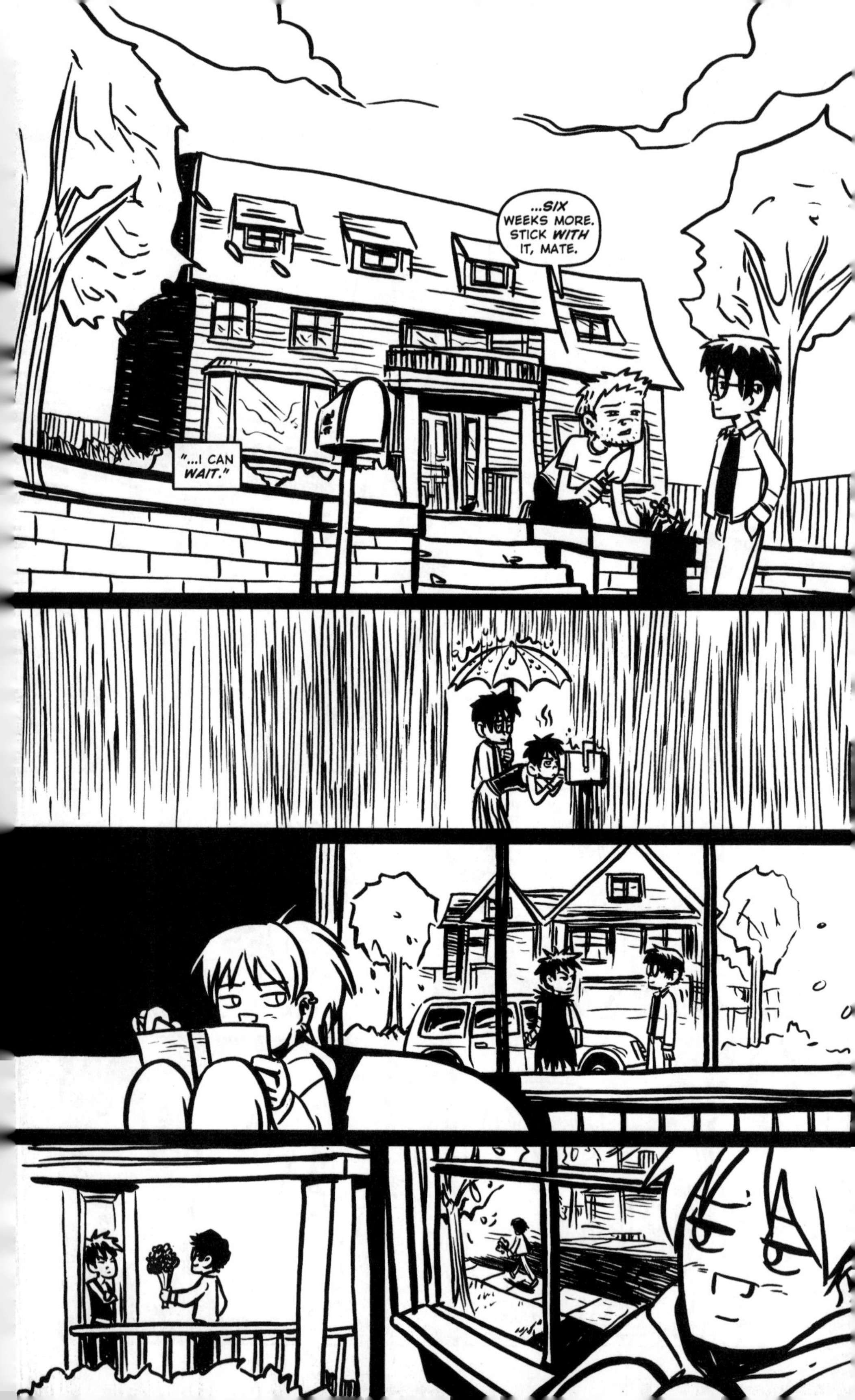
...SIX WEEKS MORE. STICK WITH IT, MATE.
"...I CAN WAIT."

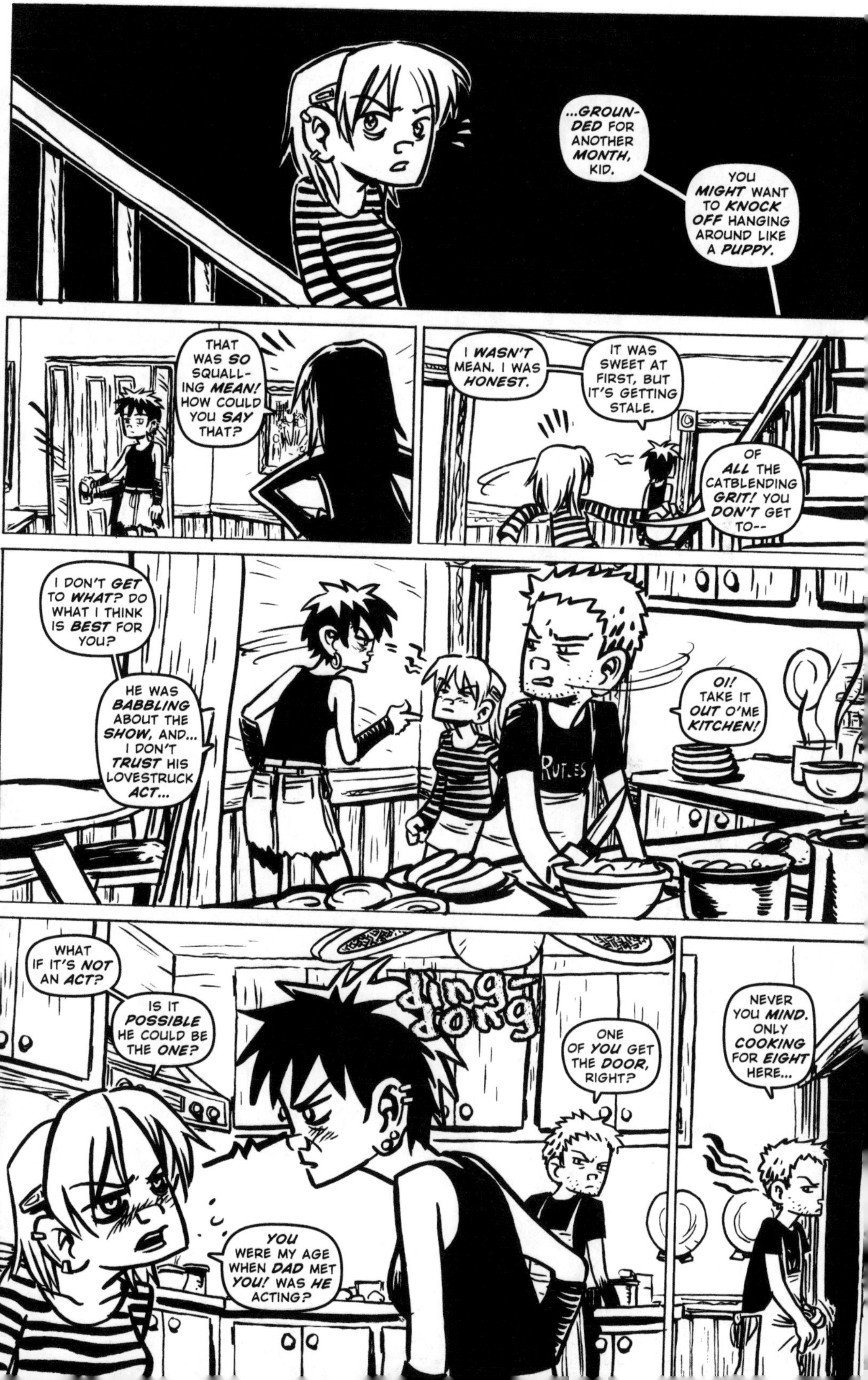
...GROUNDED FOR ANOTHER MONTH, KID.
YOU MIGHT WANT TO KNOCK OFF HANGING AROUND LIKE A PUPPY.
THAT WAS SO SQUALLING MEAN! HOW COULD YOU SAY THAT?
I WASN'T MEAN. I WAS HONEST.
IT WAS SWEET AT FIRST, BUT IT'S GETTING STALE.
OF ALL THE CATBLENDING GRIT! YOU DON'T GET TO--
I DON'T GET TO WHAT? DO WHAT I THINK IS BEST FOR YOU?
HE WAS BABBLING ABOUT THE SHOW, AND... I DON'T TRUST HIS LOVESTRUCK ACT...
OI! TAKE IT OUT O'ME KITCHEN!
RUTLES
WHAT IF IT'S NOT AN ACT?
IS IT POSSIBLE HE COULD BE THE ONE?
ding-dong
ONE OF YOU GET THE DOOR, RIGHT?
NEVER YOU MIND. ONLY COOKING FOR EIGHT HERE...
YOU WERE MY AGE WHEN DAD MET YOU! WAS HE ACTING?

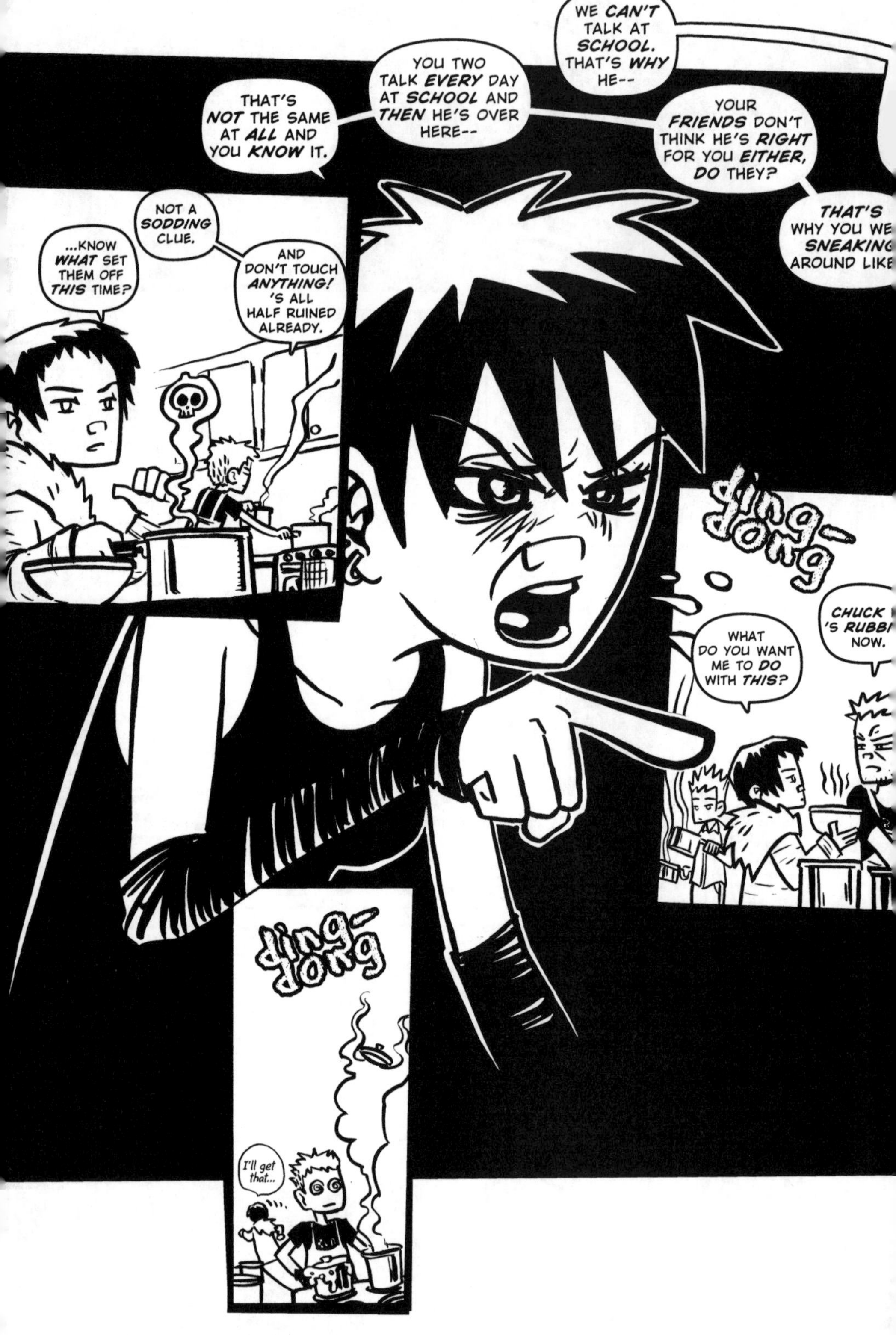
THAT'S NOT THE SAME AT ALL AND YOU KNOW IT.
YOU TWO TALK EVERY DAY AT SCHOOL AND THEN HE'S OVER HERE--
WE CAN'T TALK AT SCHOOL. THAT'S WHY HE--
YOUR FRIENDS DON'T THINK HE'S RIGHT FOR YOU EITHER, DO THEY?
THAT'S WHY YOU WE
SNEAKING AROUND LIKE
...KNOW WHAT SET THEM OFF THIS TIME?
NOT A SODDING CLUE.
AND DON'T TOUCH ANYTHING! 'S ALL HALF RUINED ALREADY.
ding-dong
WHAT DO YOU WANT ME TO DO WITH THIS?
CHUCK
'S RUBBI
NOW.
ding-dong
I'll get that...

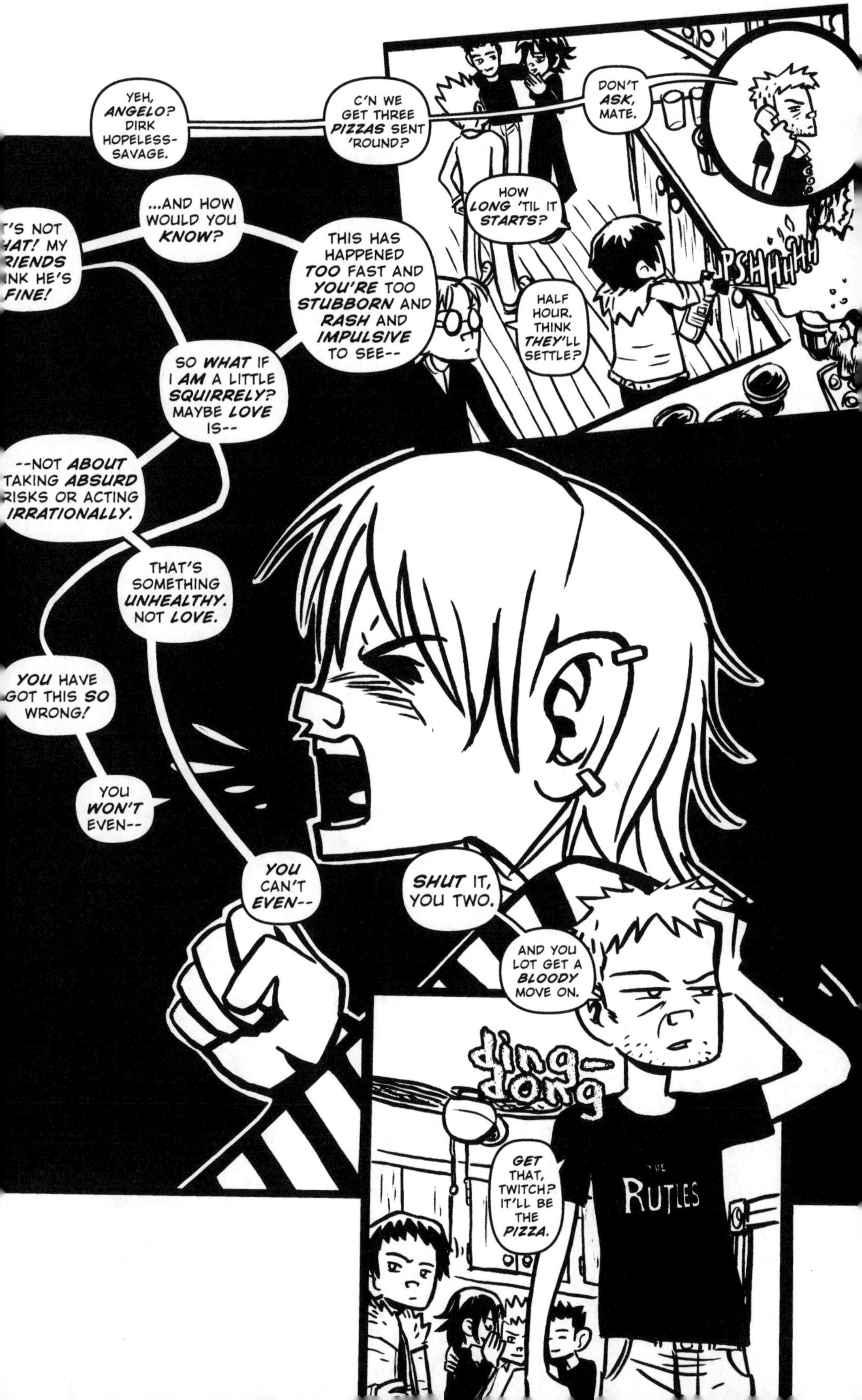
YEH, ANGELO? DIRK HOPELESS-SAVAGE.
C'N WE GET THREE PIZZAS SENT 'ROUND?
DON'T ASK, MATE.
HOW LONG 'TIL IT STARTS?
HALF HOUR. THINK THEY'LL SETTLE?
T'S NOT HAT! MY RIENDS INK HE'S FINE!
...AND HOW WOULD YOU KNOW?
THIS HAS HAPPENED TOO FAST AND YOU'RE TOO STUBBORN AND RASH AND IMPULSIVE TO SEE--
SO WHAT IF I AM A LITTLE SQUIRRELY? MAYBE LOVE IS--
--NOT ABOUT TAKING ABSURD RISKS OR ACTING IRRATIONALLY.
THAT'S SOMETHING UNHEALTHY. NOT LOVE.
YOU HAVE GOT THIS SO WRONG!
YOU WON'T EVEN--
YOU CAN'T EVEN--
SHUT IT, YOU TWO.
AND YOU LOT GET A BLOODY MOVE ON.
ding-dong
GET THAT, TWITCH? IT'LL BE THE PIZZA.
THE RUTLES

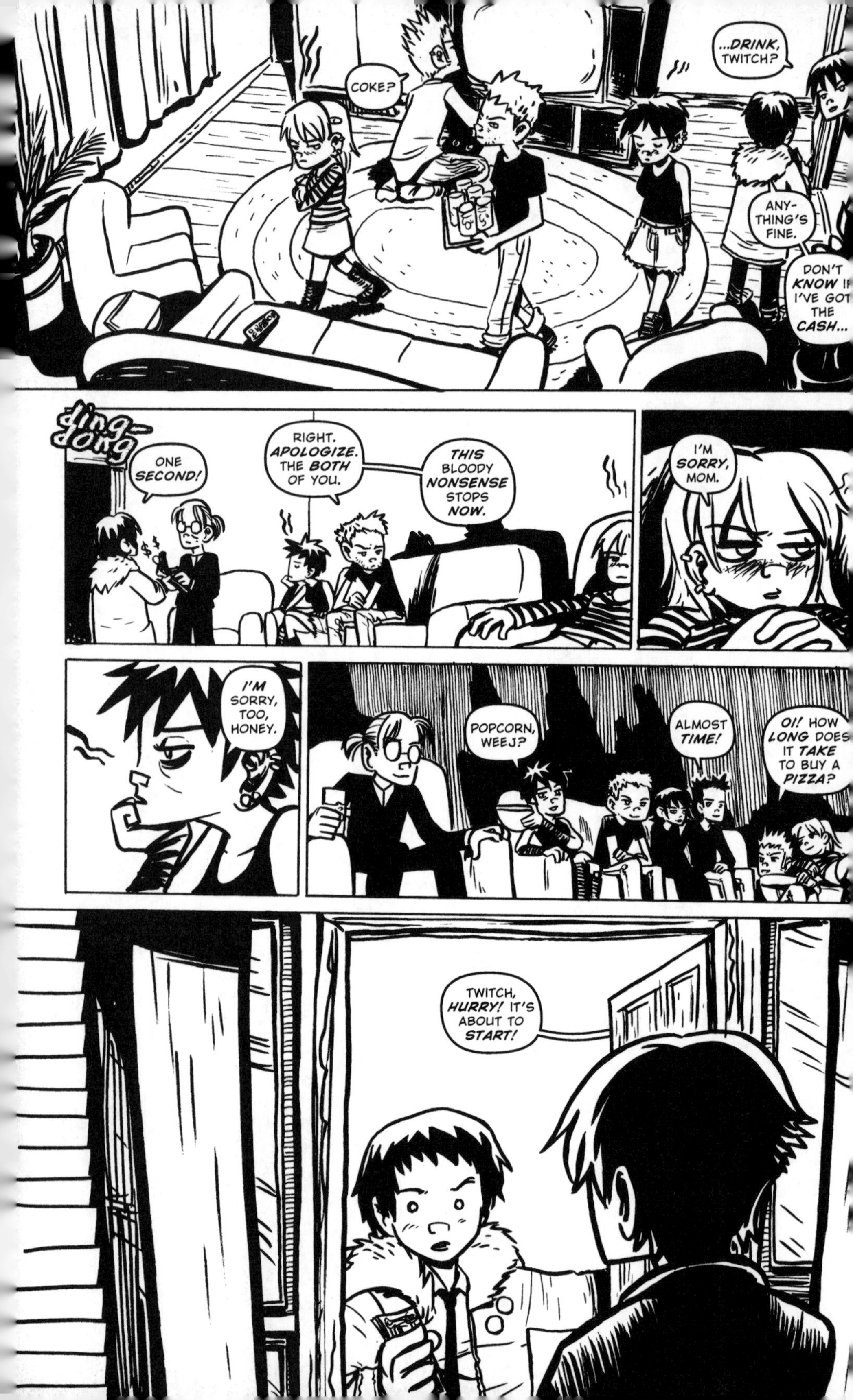
COKE?
...DRINK, TWITCH?
ANY-THING'S FINE.
DON'T KNOW IF I'VE GOT THE CASH...
ding-dong
ONE SECOND!
RIGHT. APOLOGIZE. THE BOTH OF YOU.
THIS BLOODY NONSENSE STOPS NOW.
I'M SORRY, MOM.
I'M SORRY, TOO, HONEY.
POPCORN, WEEJ?
ALMOST TIME!
OI! HOW LONG DOES IT TAKE TO BUY A PIZZA?
TWITCH, HURRY! IT'S ABOUT TO START!

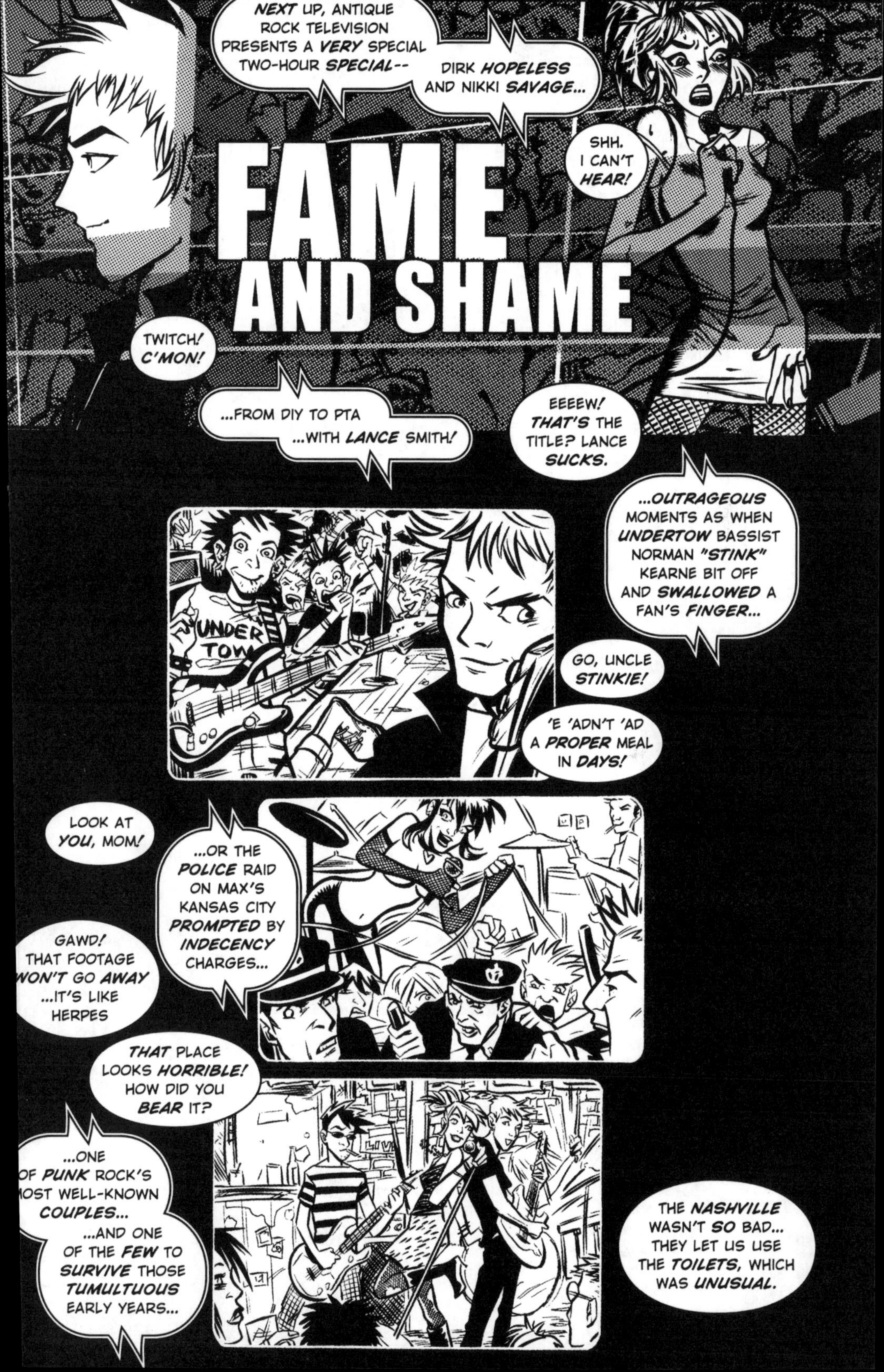
NEXT UP, ANTIQUE ROCK TELEVISION PRESENTS A VERY SPECIAL TWO-HOUR SPECIAL--
DIRK HOPELESS AND NIKKI SAVAGE...
SHH. I CAN'T HEAR!
FAME AND SHAME
TWITCH! C'MON!
...FROM DIY TO PTA ...WITH LANCE SMITH!
EEEEW! THAT'S THE TITLE? LANCE SUCKS.
...OUTRAGEOUS MOMENTS AS WHEN UNDERTOW BASSIST NORMAN "STINK" KEARNE BIT OFF AND SWALLOWED A FAN'S FINGER...
UNDERTOW
GO, UNCLE STINKIE!
'E 'ADN'T 'AD A PROPER MEAL IN DAYS!
LOOK AT YOU, MOM!
...OR THE POLICE RAID ON MAX'S KANSAS CITY PROMPTED BY INDECENCY CHARGES...
GAWD! THAT FOOTAGE WON'T GO AWAY ...IT'S LIKE HERPES
THAT PLACE LOOKS HORRIBLE! HOW DID YOU BEAR IT?
...ONE OF PUNK ROCK'S MOST WELL-KNOWN COUPLES... ...AND ONE OF THE FEW TO SURVIVE THOSE TUMULTUOUS EARLY YEARS...
THE NASHVILLE WASN'T SO BAD... THEY LET US USE THE TOILETS, WHICH WAS UNUSUAL.

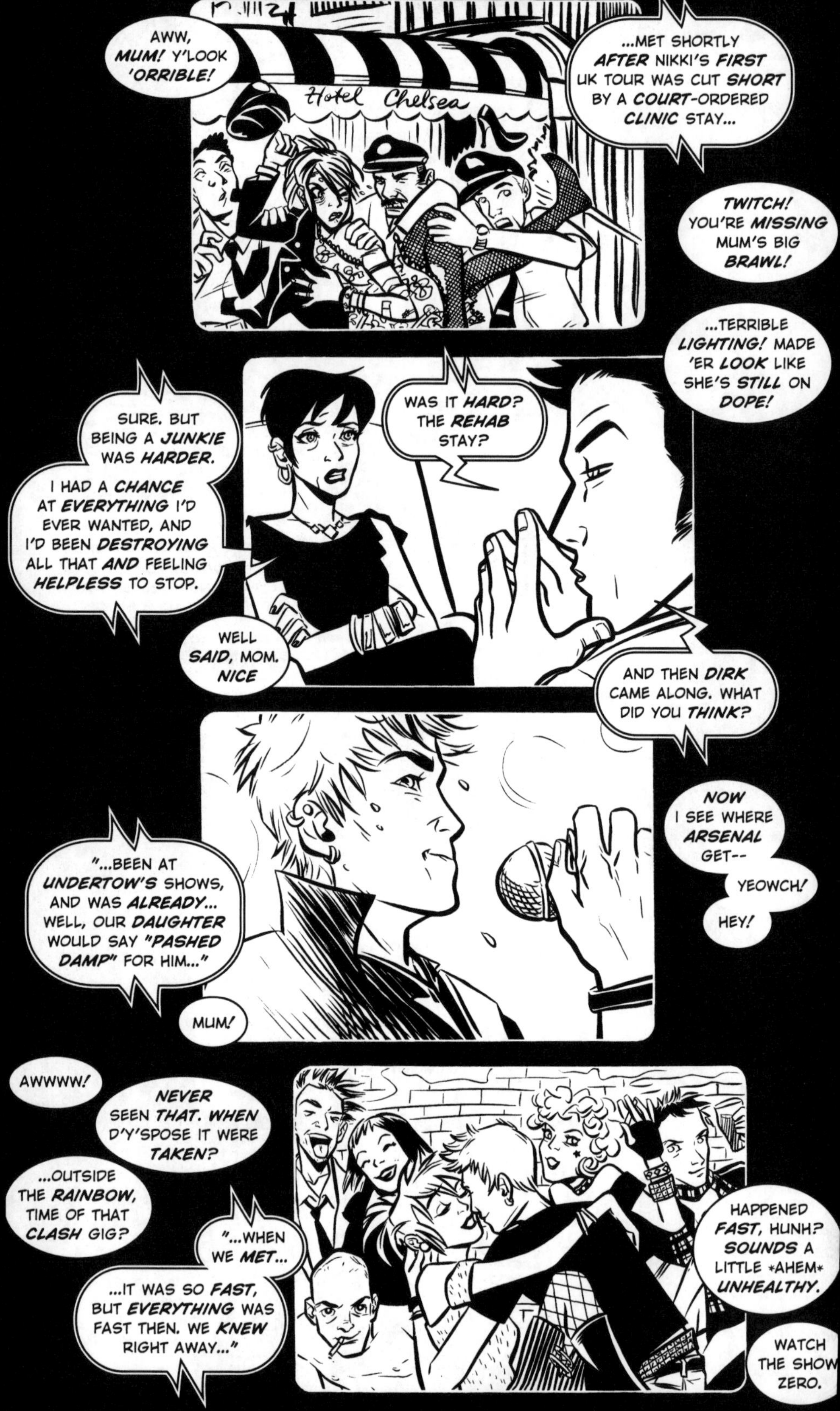

AWW, MUM! Y'LOOK 'ORRIBLE!
...MET SHORTLY AFTER NIKKI'S FIRST UK TOUR WAS CUT SHORT BY A COURT-ORDERED CLINIC STAY...
Hotel Chelsea
TWITCH! YOU'RE MISSING MUM'S BIG BRAWL!
...TERRIBLE LIGHTING! MADE 'ER LOOK LIKE SHE'S STILL ON DOPE!
WAS IT HARD? THE REHAB STAY?
SURE. BUT BEING A JUNKIE WAS HARDER.
I HAD A CHANCE AT EVERYTHING I'D EVER WANTED, AND I'D BEEN DESTROYING ALL THAT AND FEELING HELPLESS TO STOP.
WELL SAID, MOM. NICE
AND THEN DIRK CAME ALONG. WHAT DID YOU THINK?
"...BEEN AT UNDERTOW'S SHOWS, AND WAS ALREADY... WELL, OUR DAUGHTER WOULD SAY "PASHED DAMP" FOR HIM..."
NOW I SEE WHERE ARSENAL GET--
YEOWCH!
HEY!
MUM!
AWWWW!
NEVER SEEN THAT. WHEN D'Y'SPOSE IT WERE TAKEN?
...OUTSIDE THE RAINBOW, TIME OF THAT CLASH GIG?
"...WHEN WE MET...
...IT WAS SO FAST, BUT EVERYTHING WAS FAST THEN. WE KNEW RIGHT AWAY..."
HAPPENED FAST, HUNH? SOUNDS A LITTLE *AHEM* UNHEALTHY.
WATCH THE SHOW ZERO.

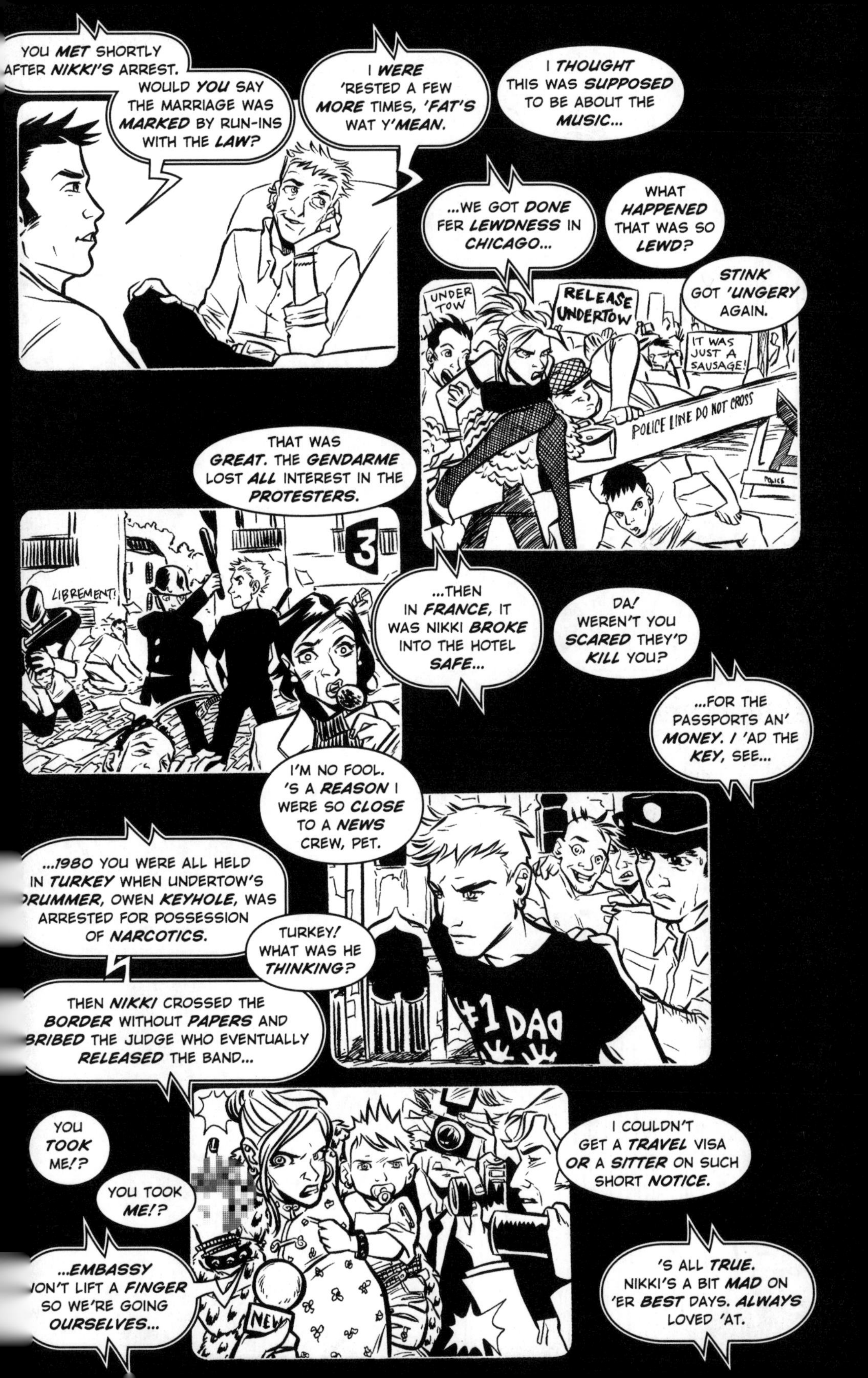
YOU MET SHORTLY AFTER NIKKI'S ARREST.
WOULD YOU SAY THE MARRIAGE WAS MARKED BY RUN-INS WITH THE LAW?
I WERE 'RESTED A FEW MORE TIMES, 'FAT'S WAT Y'MEAN.
I THOUGHT THIS WAS SUPPOSED TO BE ABOUT THE MUSIC...
...WE GOT DONE FER LEWDNESS IN CHICAGO...
WHAT HAPPENED THAT WAS SO LEWD?
STINK GOT 'UNGERY AGAIN.
UNDER TOW
RELEASE UNDERTOW
IT WAS JUST A SAUSAGE!
POLICE LINE DO NOT CROSS
THAT WAS GREAT. THE GENDARME LOST ALL INTEREST IN THE PROTESTERS.
LIBREMENT!
3
...THEN IN FRANCE, IT WAS NIKKI BROKE INTO THE HOTEL SAFE...
DA! WEREN'T YOU SCARED THEY'D KILL YOU?
...FOR THE PASSPORTS AN' MONEY. I 'AD THE KEY, SEE...
I'M NO FOOL. 'S A REASON I WERE SO CLOSE TO A NEWS CREW, PET.
...1980 YOU WERE ALL HELD IN TURKEY WHEN UNDERTOW'S DRUMMER, OWEN KEYHOLE, WAS ARRESTED FOR POSSESSION OF NARCOTICS.
TURKEY! WHAT WAS HE THINKING?
THEN NIKKI CROSSED THE BORDER WITHOUT PAPERS AND BRIBED THE JUDGE WHO EVENTUALLY RELEASED THE BAND...
#1 DAD
YOU TOOK ME!?
YOU TOOK ME!?
I COULDN'T GET A TRAVEL VISA OR A SITTER ON SUCH SHORT NOTICE.
...EMBASSY WON'T LIFT A FINGER SO WE'RE GOING OURSELVES...
NEWS
'S ALL TRUE. NIKKI'S A BIT MAD ON 'ER BEST DAYS. ALWAYS LOVED 'AT.

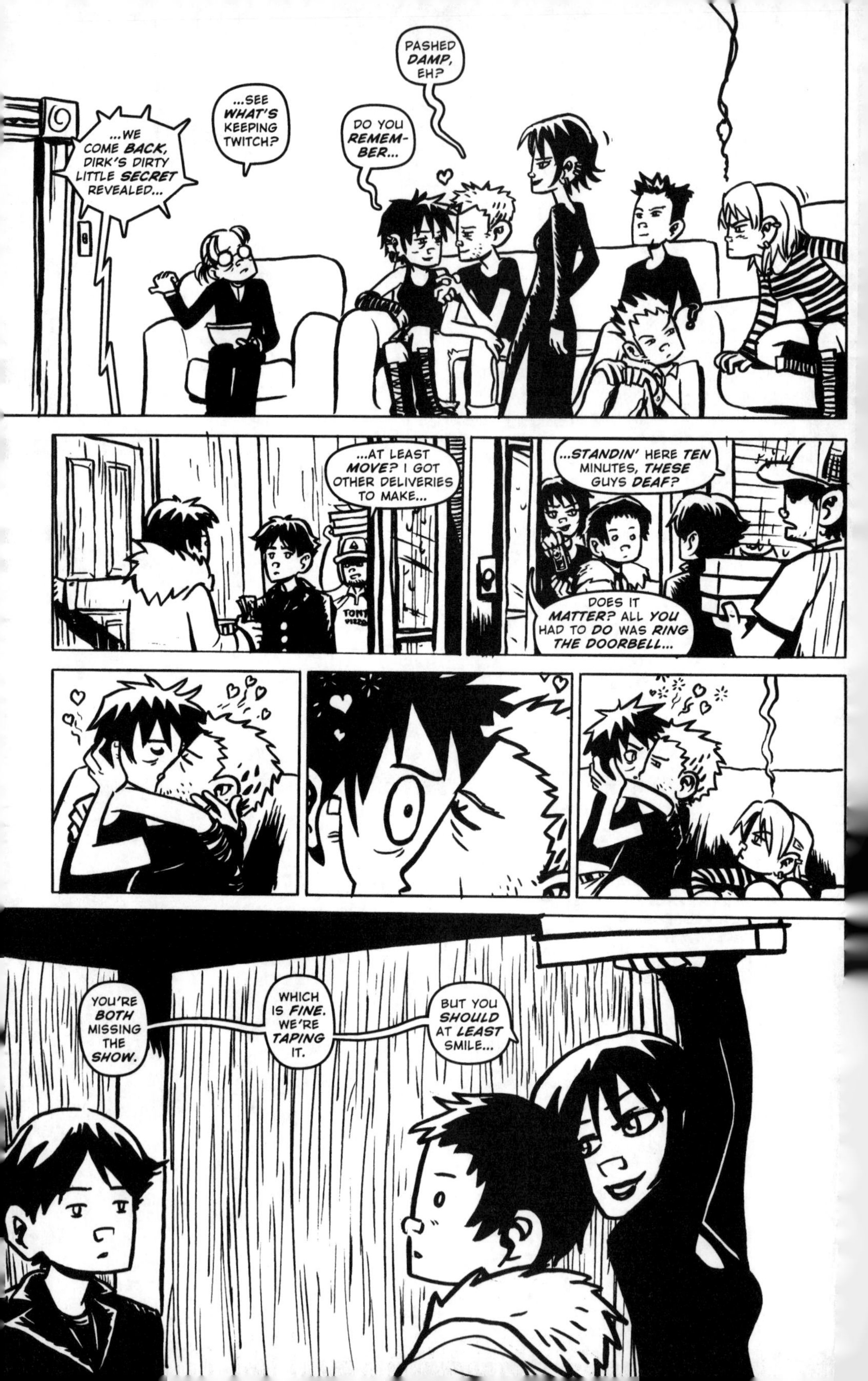
...WE COME BACK, DIRK'S DIRTY LITTLE SECRET REVEALED...
...SEE WHAT'S KEEPING TWITCH?
DO YOU REMEMBER...
PASHED DAMP, EH?
...AT LEAST MOVE? I GOT OTHER DELIVERIES TO MAKE...
TONY PIZZA
...STANDIN' HERE TEN MINUTES, THESE GUYS DEAF?
DOES IT MATTER? ALL YOU HAD TO DO WAS RING THE DOORBELL...
YOU'RE BOTH MISSING THE SHOW.
WHICH IS FINE. WE'RE TAPING IT.
BUT YOU SHOULD AT LEAST SMILE...

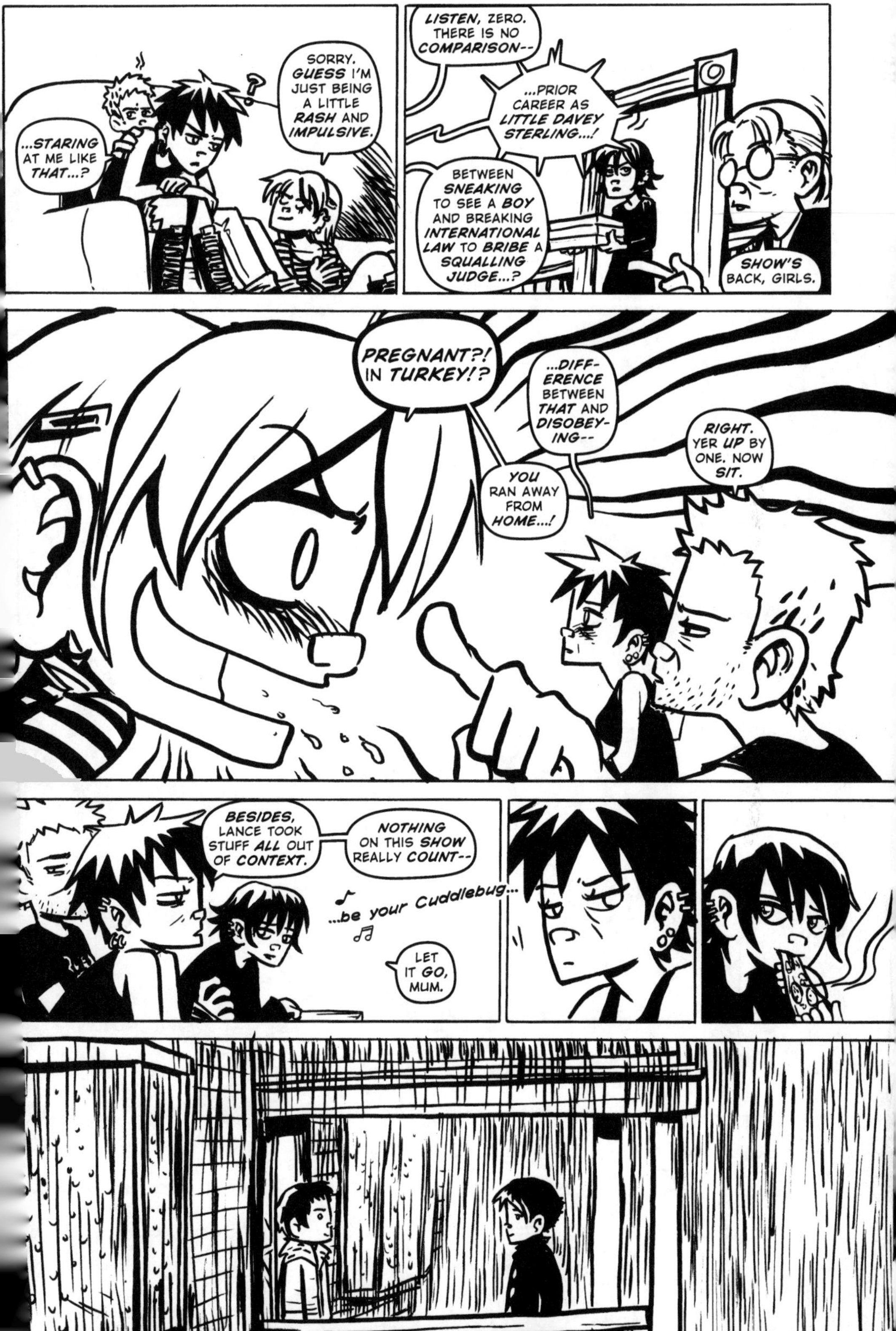

SORRY. GUESS I'M JUST BEING A LITTLE RASH AND IMPULSIVE.
...STARING AT ME LIKE THAT...?
LISTEN, ZERO. THERE IS NO COMPARISON--
...PRIOR CAREER AS LITTLE DAVEY STERLING...!
BETWEEN SNEAKING TO SEE A BOY AND BREAKING INTERNATIONAL LAW TO BRIBE A SQUALLING JUDGE...?
SHOW'S BACK, GIRLS.
PREGNANT?! IN TURKEY!?
YOU RAN AWAY FROM HOME...!
...DIFFERENCE BETWEEN THAT AND DISOBEYING--
RIGHT. YER UP BY ONE. NOW SIT.
BESIDES, LANCE TOOK STUFF ALL OUT OF CONTEXT.
NOTHING ON THIS SHOW REALLY COUNT--
...be your Cuddlebug...
LET IT GO, MUM.

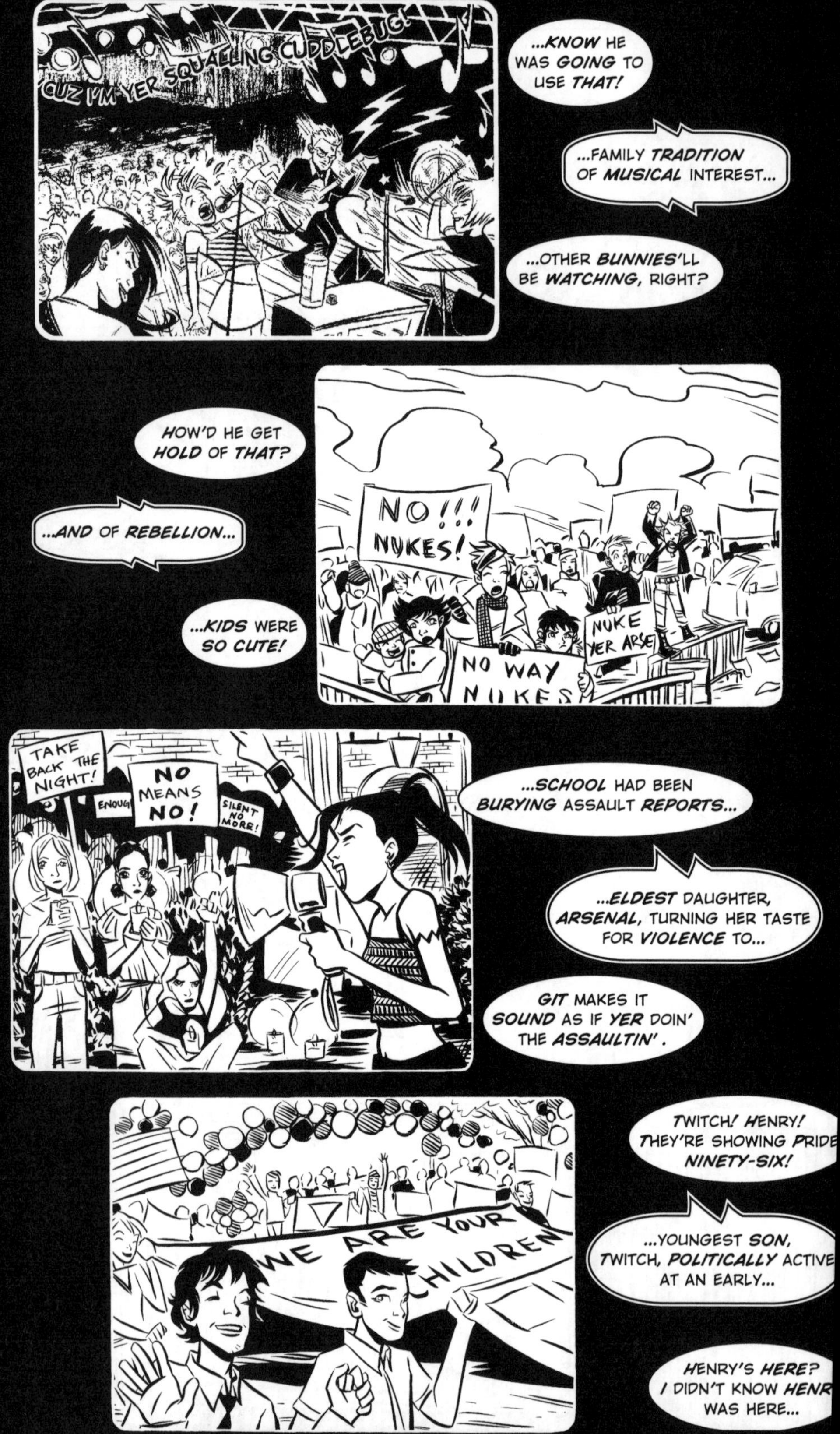
'CUZ I'M YER SQUALLING CUDDLEBUG!
...KNOW HE WAS GOING TO USE THAT!
...FAMILY TRADITION OF MUSICAL INTEREST...
...OTHER BUNNIES'LL BE WATCHING, RIGHT?
HOW'D HE GET HOLD OF THAT?
...AND OF REBELLION...
...KIDS WERE SO CUTE!
NO!!! NUKES!
NUKE YER ARSE
NO WAY NUKES
TAKE BACK THE NIGHT!
ENOUG
NO MEANS NO!
SILENT NO MORE!
...SCHOOL HAD BEEN BURYING ASSAULT REPORTS...
...ELDEST DAUGHTER, ARSENAL, TURNING HER TASTE FOR VIOLENCE TO...
GIT MAKES IT SOUND AS IF YER DOIN' THE ASSAULTIN'.
WE ARE YOUR CHILDREN
TWITCH! HENRY! THEY'RE SHOWING PRIDE NINETY-SIX!
...YOUNGEST SON, TWITCH, POLITICALLY ACTIVE AT AN EARLY...
HENRY'S HERE? I DIDN'T KNOW HENR WAS HERE...

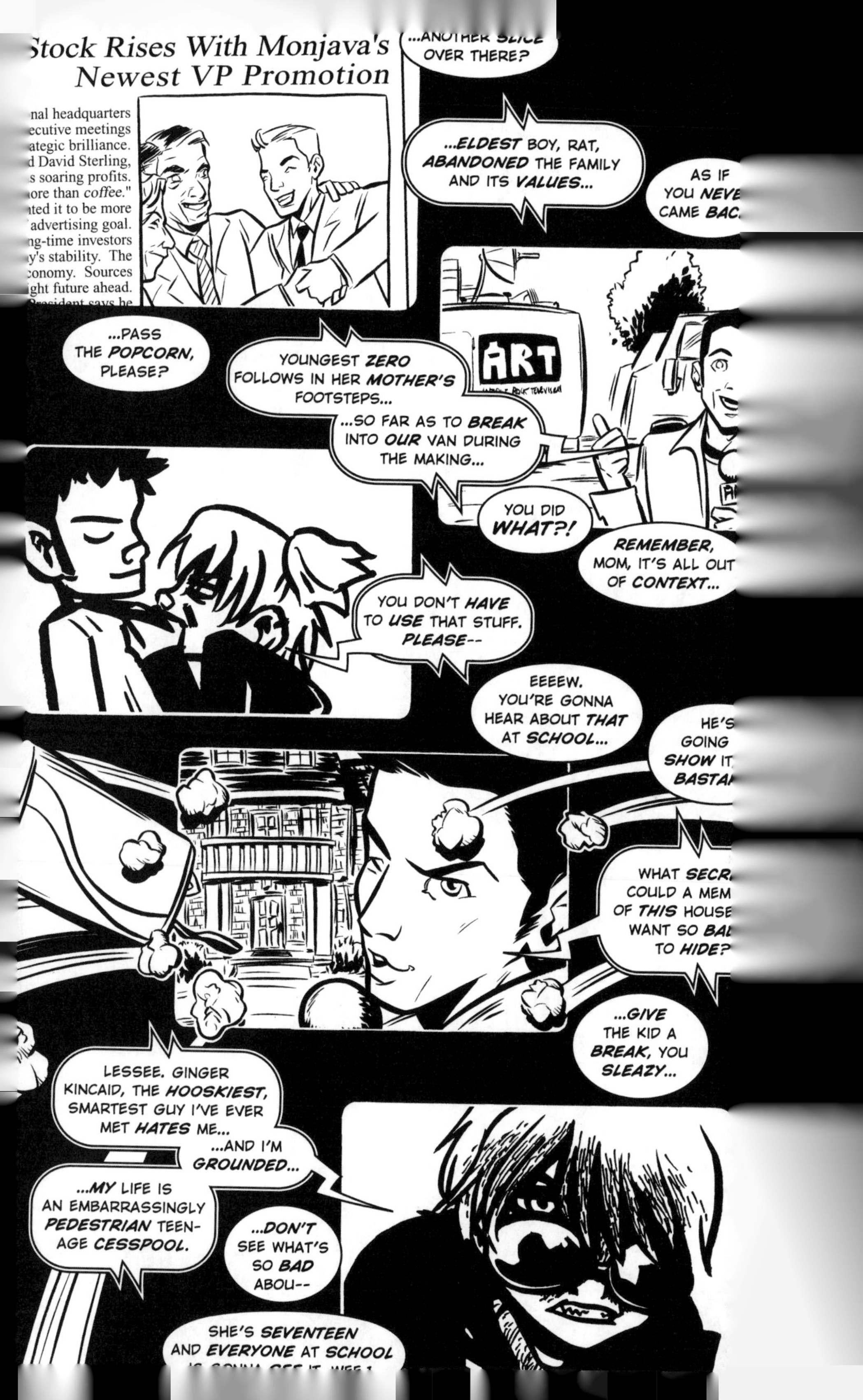
Stock Rises With Monjava's Newest VP Promotion
nal headquarters
ecutive meetings
ategic brilliance.
d David Sterling,
s soaring profits.
ore than coffee."
ted it to be more
advertising goal.
ng-time investors
y's stability. The
conomy. Sources
ight future ahead.
...ANOTHER SLICE OVER THERE?
...ELDEST BOY, RAT, ABANDONED THE FAMILY AND ITS VALUES...
AS IF YOU NEVE CAME BAC
...PASS THE POPCORN, PLEASE?
YOUNGEST ZERO FOLLOWS IN HER MOTHER'S FOOTSTEPS...
...SO FAR AS TO BREAK INTO OUR VAN DURING THE MAKING...
ART
YOU DID WHAT?!
REMEMBER, MOM, IT'S ALL OUT OF CONTEXT...
YOU DON'T HAVE TO USE THAT STUFF. PLEASE--
EEEEW. YOU'RE GONNA HEAR ABOUT THAT AT SCHOOL...
HE'S GOING SHOW IT BASTA
WHAT SECR COULD A MEM OF THIS HOUSE WANT SO BA TO HIDE?
...GIVE THE KID A BREAK, YOU SLEAZY...
LESSEE. GINGER KINCAID, THE HOOSKIEST, SMARTEST GUY I'VE EVER MET HATES ME...
...AND I'M GROUNDED...
...MY LIFE IS AN EMBARRASSINGLY PEDESTRIAN TEEN-AGE CESSPOOL.
...DON'T SEE WHAT'S SO BAD ABOU--
SHE'S SEVENTEEN AND EVERYONE AT SCHOOL

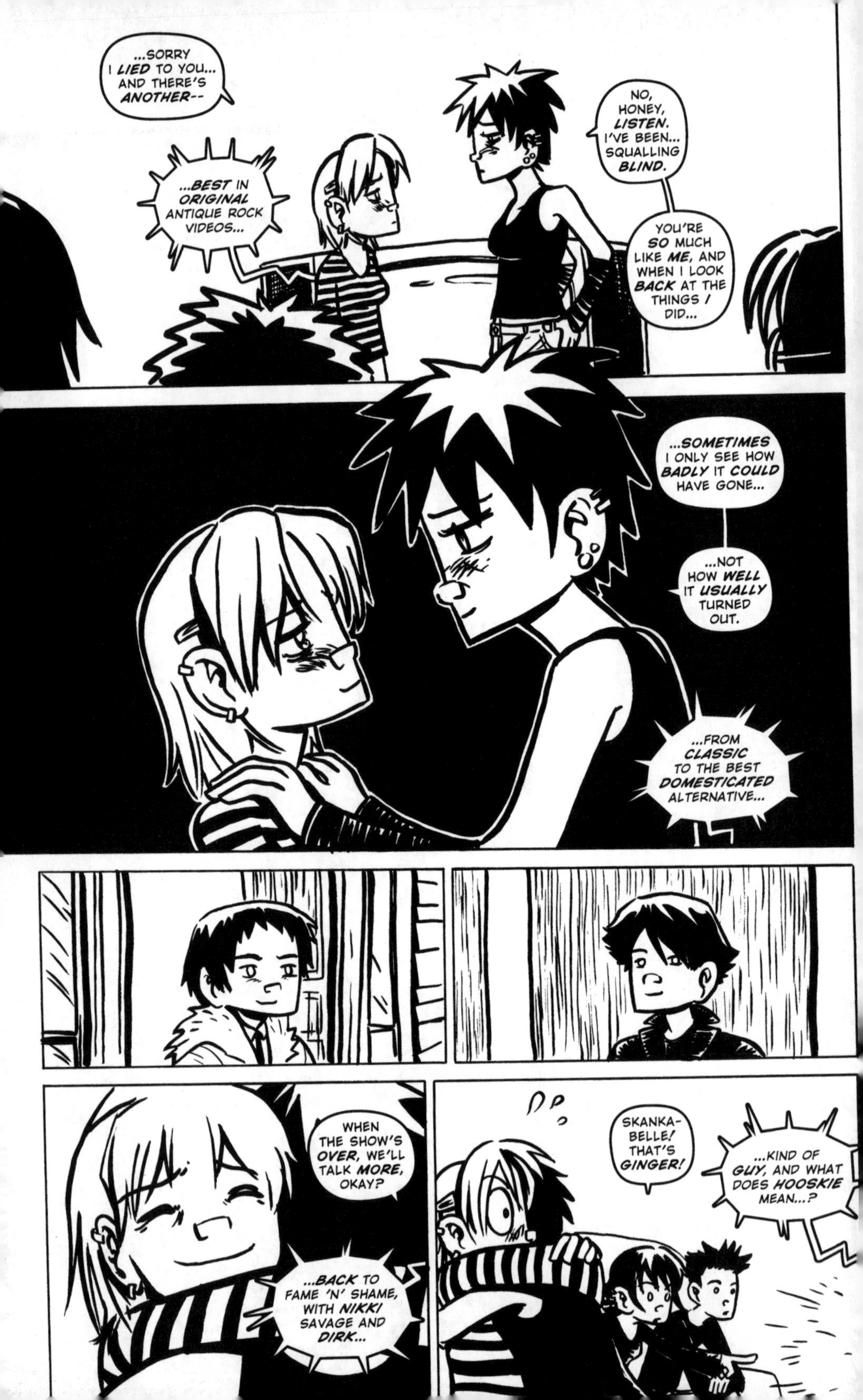
...SORRY I LIED TO YOU... AND THERE'S ANOTHER--
...BEST IN ORIGINAL ANTIQUE ROCK VIDEOS...
NO, HONEY, LISTEN. I'VE BEEN... SQUALLING BLIND.
YOU'RE SO MUCH LIKE ME, AND WHEN I LOOK BACK AT THE THINGS I DID...
...SOMETIMES I ONLY SEE HOW BADLY IT COULD HAVE GONE...
...NOT HOW WELL IT USUALLY TURNED OUT.
...FROM CLASSIC TO THE BEST DOMESTICATED ALTERNATIVE...
WHEN THE SHOW'S OVER, WE'LL TALK MORE, OKAY?
...BACK TO FAME 'N' SHAME, WITH NIKKI SAVAGE AND DIRK...
SKANKA-BELLE! THAT'S GINGER!
...KIND OF GUY, AND WHAT DOES HOOSKIE MEAN...?

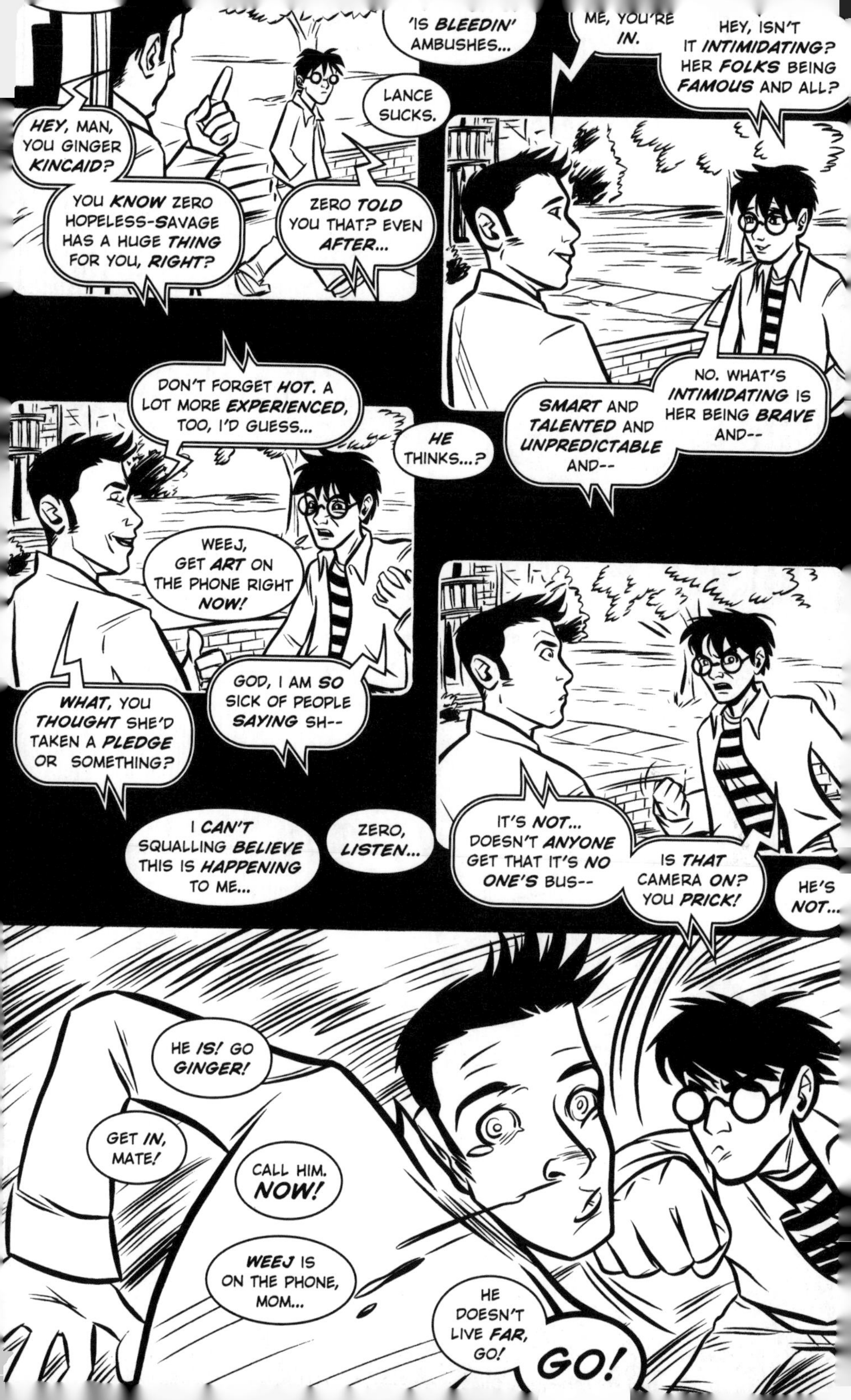
HEY, MAN, YOU GINGER KINCAID?
YOU KNOW ZERO HOPELESS-SAVAGE HAS A HUGE THING FOR YOU, RIGHT?
LANCE SUCKS.
ZERO TOLD YOU THAT? EVEN AFTER...
'IS BLEEDIN' AMBUSHES...
ME, YOU'RE IN.
HEY, ISN'T IT INTIMIDATING? HER FOLKS BEING FAMOUS AND ALL?
NO. WHAT'S INTIMIDATING IS HER BEING BRAVE AND--
SMART AND TALENTED AND UNPREDICTABLE AND--
DON'T FORGET HOT. A LOT MORE EXPERIENCED, TOO, I'D GUESS...
HE THINKS...?
WEEJ, GET ART ON THE PHONE RIGHT NOW!
WHAT, YOU THOUGHT SHE'D TAKEN A PLEDGE OR SOMETHING?
GOD, I AM SO SICK OF PEOPLE SAYING SH--
I CAN'T SQUALLING BELIEVE THIS IS HAPPENING TO ME...
ZERO, LISTEN...
IT'S NOT... DOESN'T ANYONE GET THAT IT'S NO ONE'S BUS--
IS THAT CAMERA ON? YOU PRICK!
HE'S NOT...
HE IS! GO GINGER!
GET IN, MATE!
CALL HIM. NOW!
WEEJ IS ON THE PHONE, MOM...
HE DOESN'T LIVE FAR, GO!
GO!

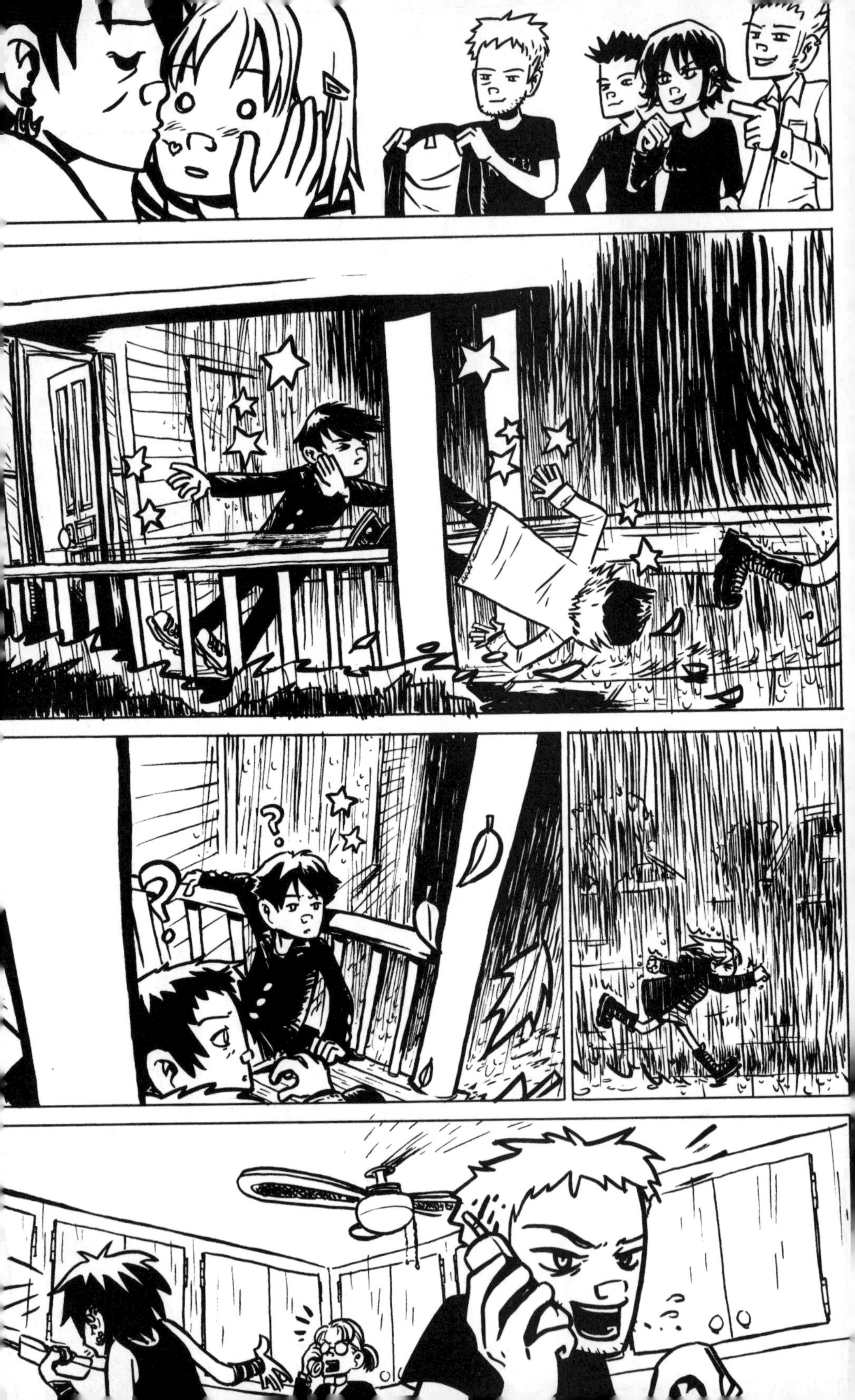

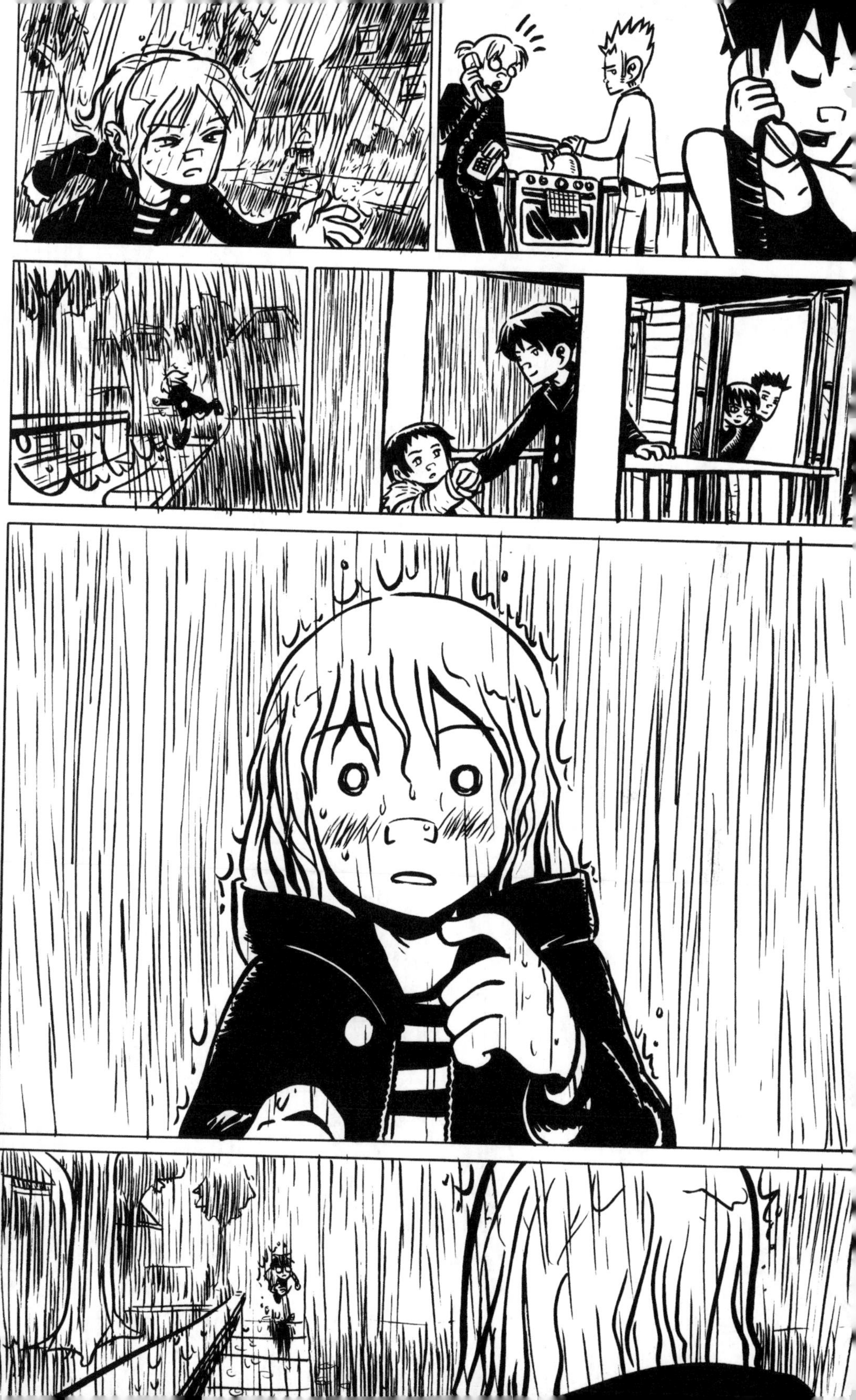

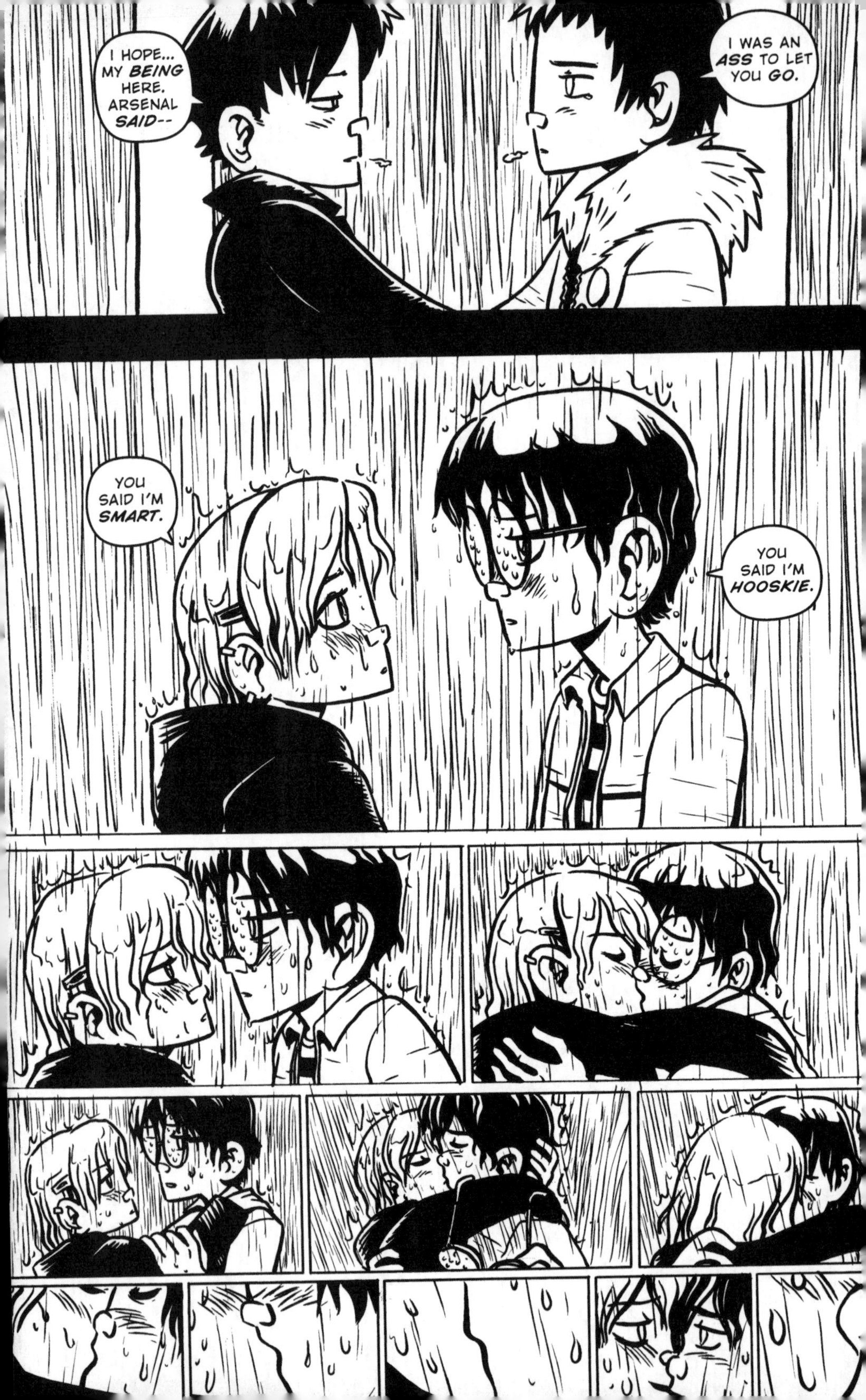
I HOPE... MY BEING HERE. ARSENAL SAID--
I WAS AN ASS TO LET YOU GO.
YOU SAID I'M SMART.
YOU SAID I'M HOOSKIE.

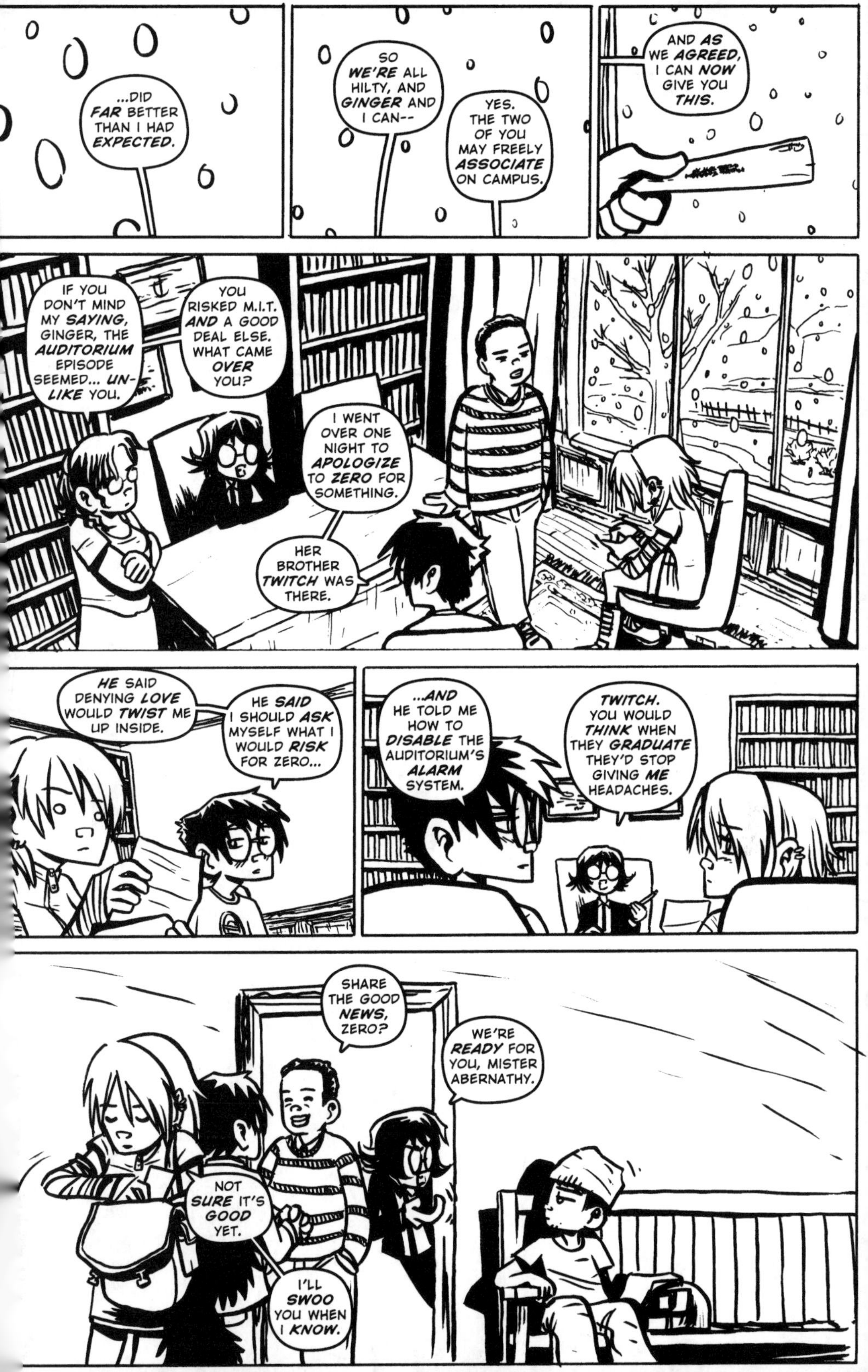
...DID FAR BETTER THAN I HAD EXPECTED.
SO WE'RE ALL HILTY, AND GINGER AND I CAN--
YES. THE TWO OF YOU MAY FREELY ASSOCIATE ON CAMPUS.
AND AS WE AGREED, I CAN NOW GIVE YOU THIS.
IF YOU DON'T MIND MY SAYING, GINGER, THE AUDITORIUM EPISODE SEEMED... UN-LIKE YOU.
YOU RISKED M.I.T. AND A GOOD DEAL ELSE. WHAT CAME OVER YOU?
I WENT OVER ONE NIGHT TO APOLOGIZE TO ZERO FOR SOMETHING.
HER BROTHER TWITCH WAS THERE.
HE SAID DENYING LOVE WOULD TWIST ME UP INSIDE.
HE SAID I SHOULD ASK MYSELF WHAT I WOULD RISK FOR ZERO...
...AND HE TOLD ME HOW TO DISABLE THE AUDITORIUM'S ALARM SYSTEM.
TWITCH. YOU WOULD THINK WHEN THEY GRADUATE THEY'D STOP GIVING ME HEADACHES.
SHARE THE GOOD NEWS, ZERO?
WE'RE READY FOR YOU, MISTER ABERNATHY.
NOT SURE IT'S GOOD YET.
I'LL SWOO YOU WHEN I KNOW.

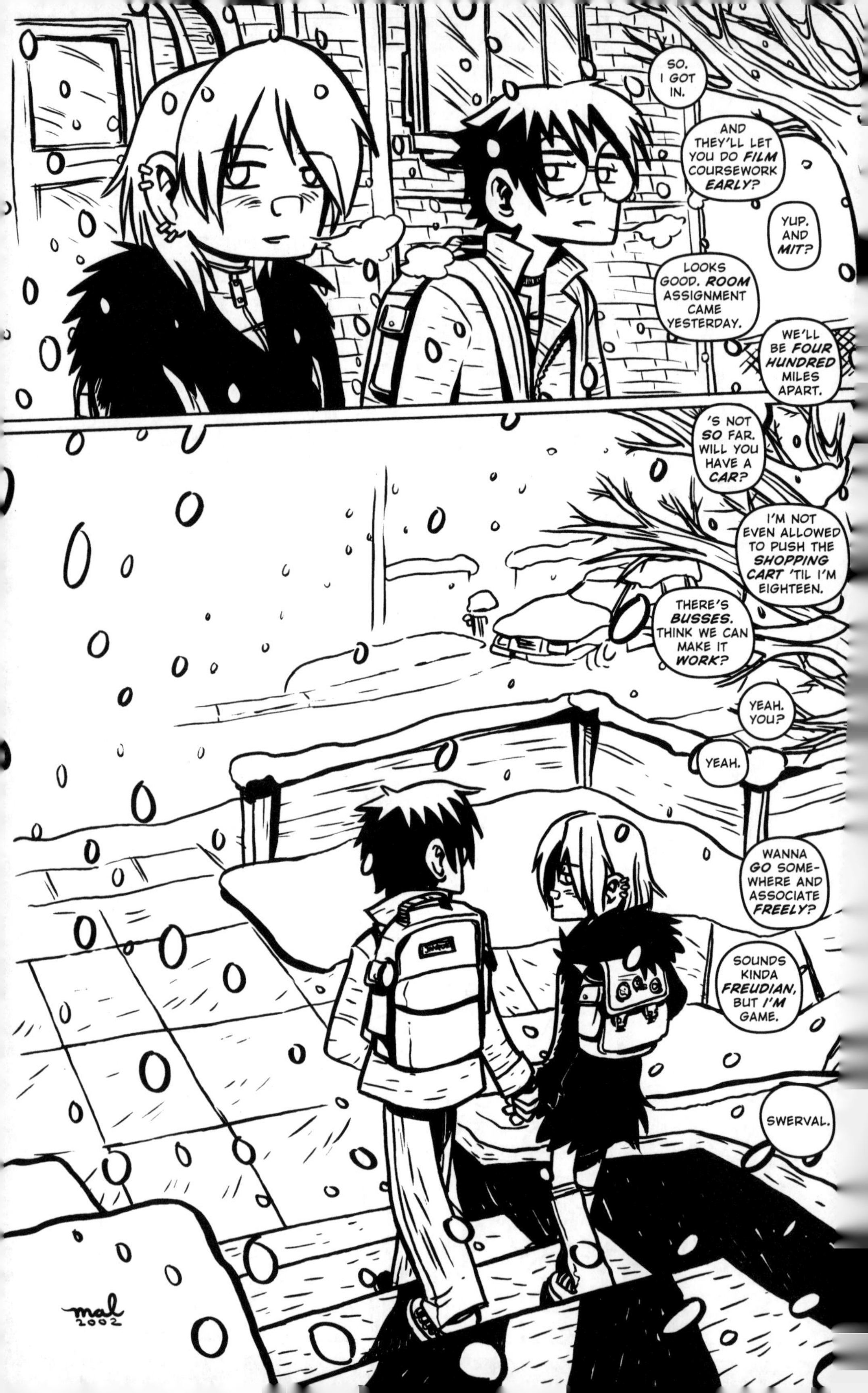
SO. I GOT IN.
AND THEY'LL LET YOU DO FILM COURSEWORK EARLY?
YUP. AND MIT?
LOOKS GOOD. ROOM ASSIGNMENT CAME YESTERDAY.
WE'LL BE FOUR HUNDRED MILES APART.
'S NOT SO FAR. WILL YOU HAVE A CAR?
I'M NOT EVEN ALLOWED TO PUSH THE SHOPPING CART 'TIL I'M EIGHTEEN.
THERE'S BUSSES. THINK WE CAN MAKE IT WORK?
YEAH. YOU?
YEAH.
WANNA GO SOMEWHERE AND ASSOCIATE FREELY?
SOUNDS KINDA FREUDIAN, BUT I'M GAME.
SWERVAL.
mal 2002

HOPELESS SAVAGES

BOOK 3: TOO MUCH HOPELESS SAVAGES

Written by
JEN VAN METER

Chapters 1 & 2 art and chapter 3 finished art by
CHRISTINE NORRIE

Chapter 3 layouts by
CHYNNA CLUGSTON FLORES

Flashback & Chapter 4 finished art by
ROSS CAMPBELL

Lettered by
CHRISTINE NORRIE, ANDY LIS, JAMIE MCKELVIE, TOM ORZECHOWSKI and BRYAN LEE O'MALLEY

Originally edited by
JAMIE S. RICH

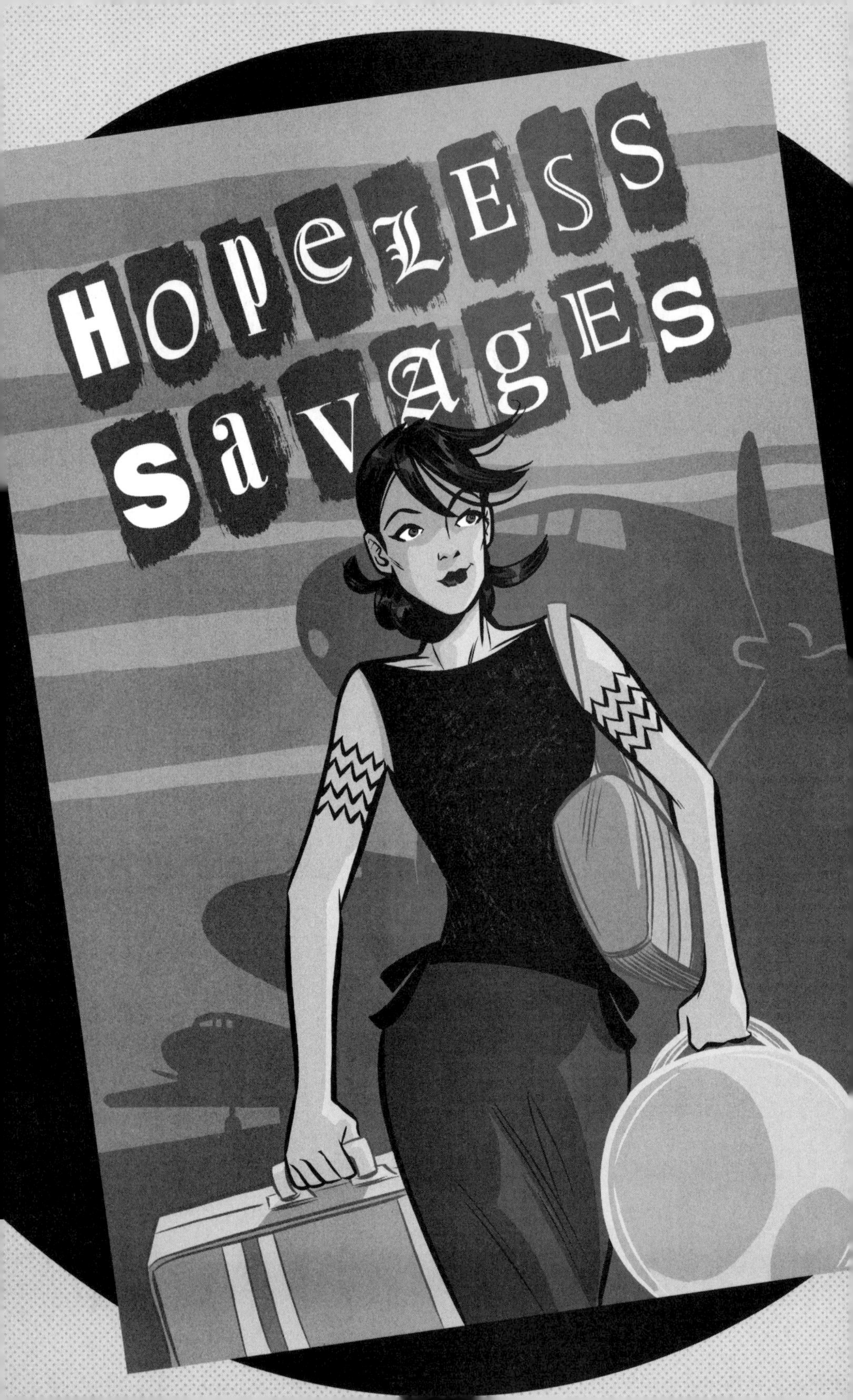
HOPELESS
SAVAGES

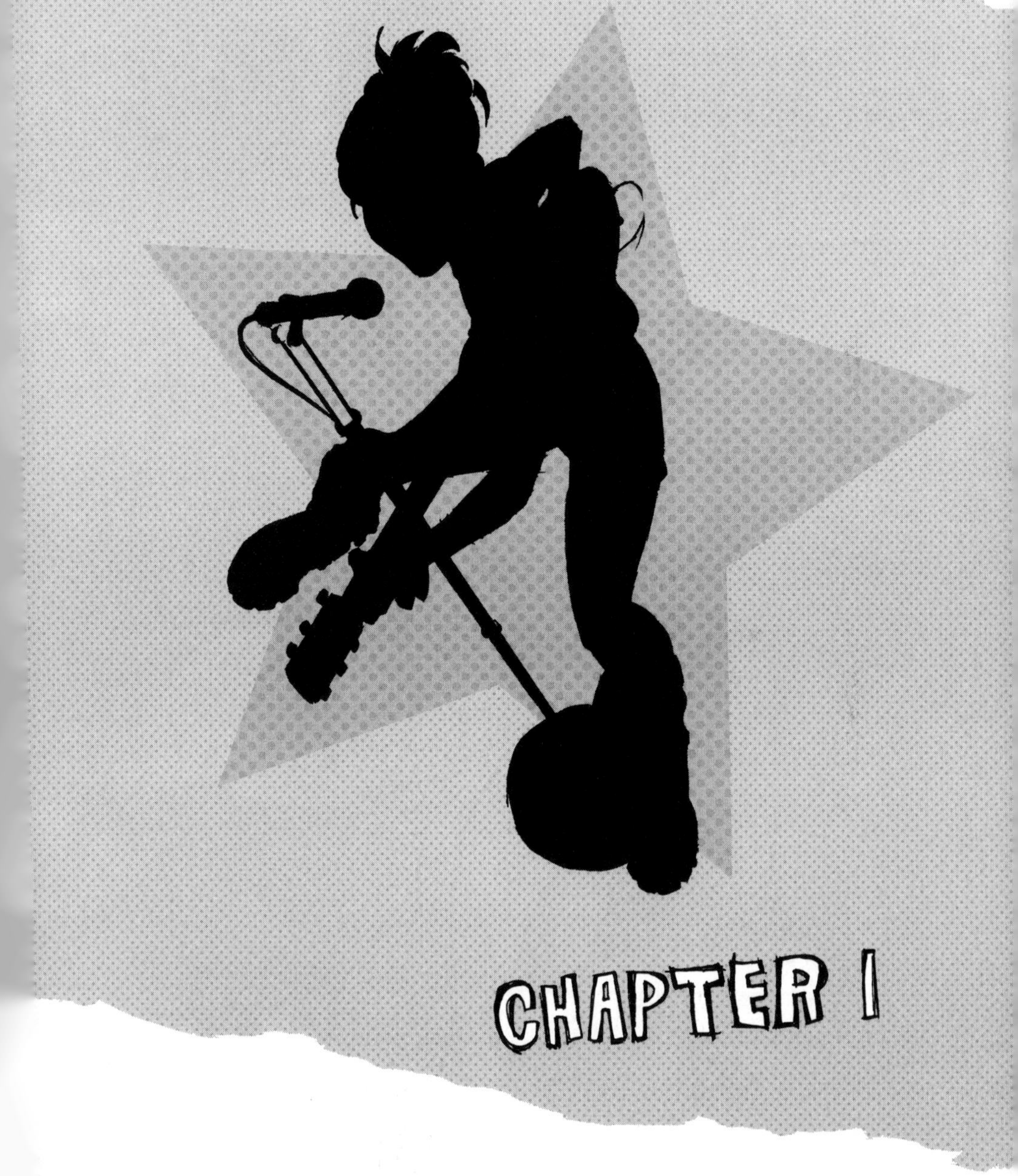

CHAPTER 1

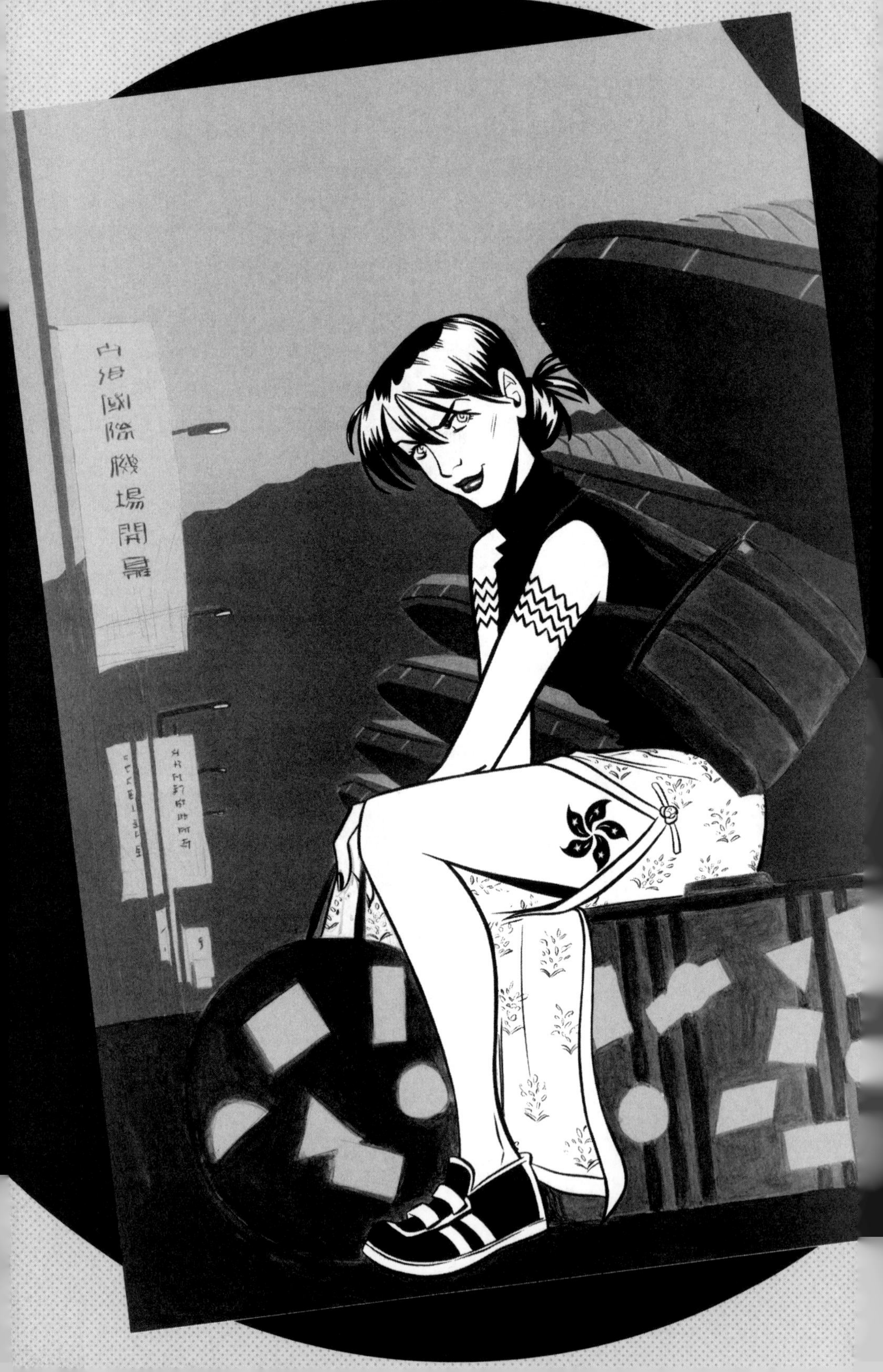

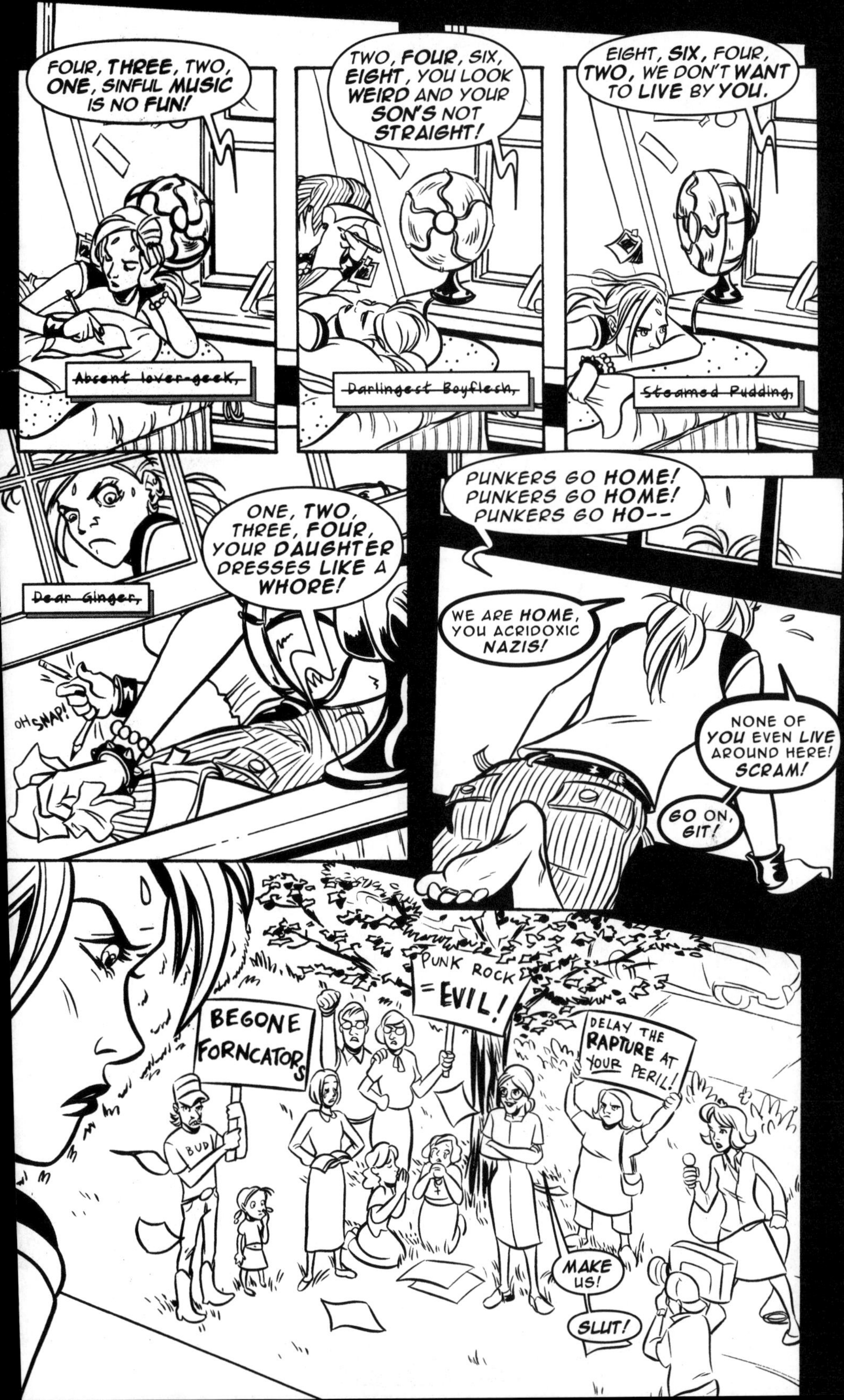
FOUR, THREE, TWO, ONE, SINFUL MUSIC IS NO FUN!
~~Absent lover-geek,~~
TWO, FOUR, SIX, EIGHT, YOU LOOK WEIRD AND YOUR SON'S NOT STRAIGHT!
~~Darlingest Boyflesh,~~
EIGHT, SIX, FOUR, TWO, WE DON'T WANT TO LIVE BY YOU.
~~Steamed Pudding,~~
~~Dear Ginger,~~
ONE, TWO, THREE, FOUR, YOUR DAUGHTER DRESSES LIKE A WHORE!
OH SNAP!
PUNKERS GO HOME! PUNKERS GO HOME! PUNKERS GO HO--
WE ARE HOME, YOU ACRIDOXIC NAZIS!
NONE OF YOU EVEN LIVE AROUND HERE! SCRAM!
GO ON, GIT!
PUNK ROCK = EVIL!
BEGONE FORNCATORS
DELAY THE RAPTURE AT YOUR PERIL!
BUD
MAKE US!
SLUT!

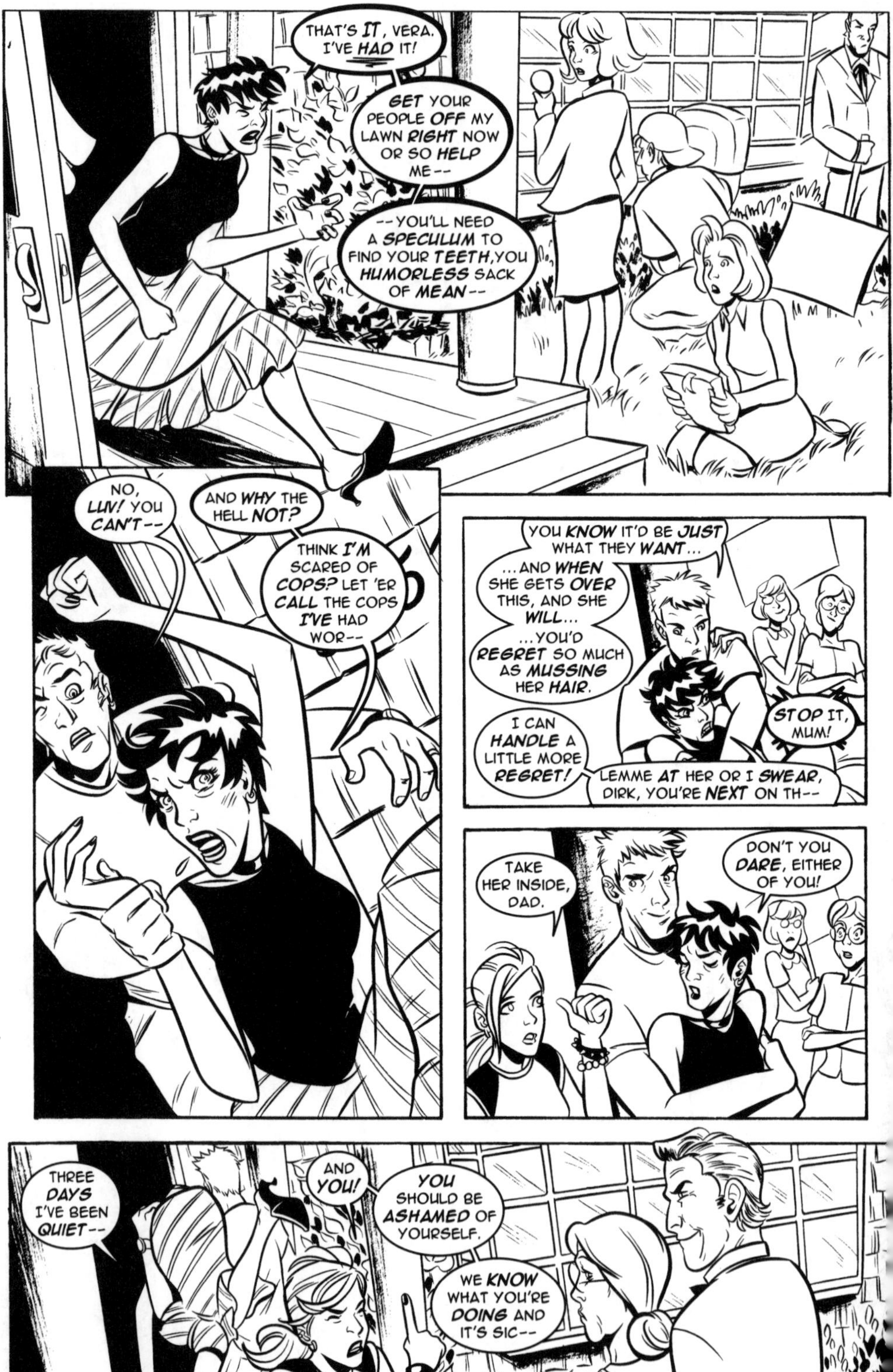
THAT'S IT, VERA. I'VE HAD IT!
GET YOUR PEOPLE OFF MY LAWN RIGHT NOW OR SO HELP ME--
--YOU'LL NEED A SPECULUM TO FIND YOUR TEETH, YOU HUMORLESS SACK OF MEAN--
NO, LUV! YOU CAN'T--
AND WHY THE HELL NOT?
THINK I'M SCARED OF COPS? LET 'ER CALL THE COPS I'VE HAD WOR--
YOU KNOW IT'D BE JUST WHAT THEY WANT...
...AND WHEN SHE GETS OVER THIS, AND SHE WILL...
...YOU'D REGRET SO MUCH AS MUSSING HER HAIR.
I CAN HANDLE A LITTLE MORE REGRET!
LEMME AT HER OR I SWEAR, DIRK, YOU'RE NEXT ON TH--
STOP IT, MUM!
TAKE HER INSIDE, DAD.
DON'T YOU DARE, EITHER OF YOU!
THREE DAYS I'VE BEEN QUIET--
AND YOU!
YOU SHOULD BE ASHAMED OF YOURSELF.
WE KNOW WHAT YOU'RE DOING AND IT'S SIC--

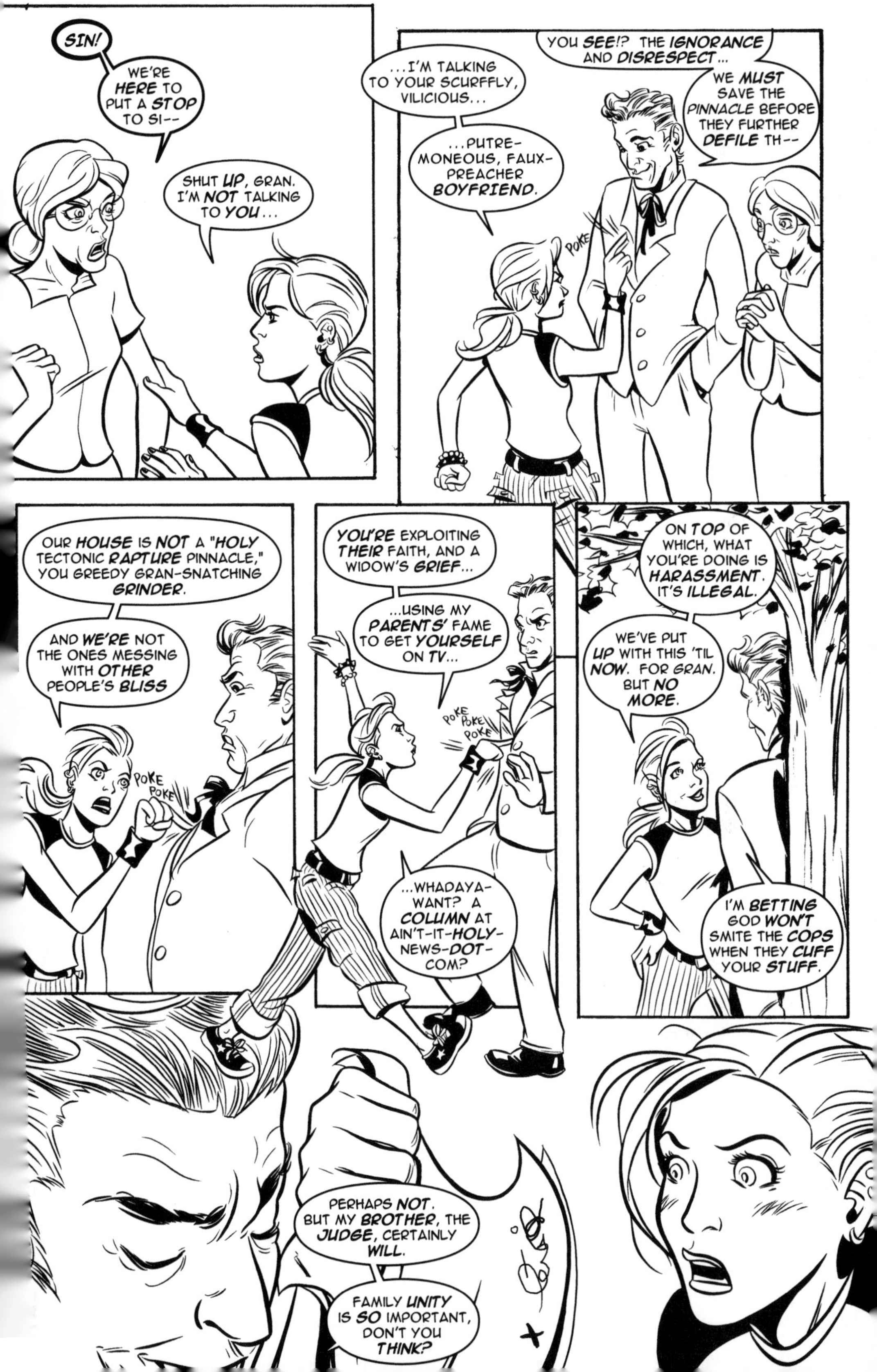
SIN!
WE'RE HERE TO PUT A STOP TO SI--
SHUT UP, GRAN. I'M NOT TALKING TO YOU...
...I'M TALKING TO YOUR SCURFFLY, VILICIOUS...
...PUTRE-MONEOUS, FAUX-PREACHER BOYFRIEND.
POKE
YOU SEE!? THE IGNORANCE AND DISRESPECT...
WE MUST SAVE THE PINNACLE BEFORE THEY FURTHER DEFILE TH--
OUR HOUSE IS NOT A "HOLY TECTONIC RAPTURE PINNACLE," YOU GREEDY GRAN-SNATCHING GRINDER.
AND WE'RE NOT THE ONES MESSING WITH OTHER PEOPLE'S BLISS
POKE POKE
YOU'RE EXPLOITING THEIR FAITH, AND A WIDOW'S GRIEF...
...USING MY PARENTS' FAME TO GET YOURSELF ON TV...
POKE POKE POKE
...WHADAYA-WANT? A COLUMN AT AIN'T-IT-HOLY-NEWS-DOT-COM?
ON TOP OF WHICH, WHAT YOU'RE DOING IS HARASSMENT. IT'S ILLEGAL.
WE'VE PUT UP WITH THIS 'TIL NOW. FOR GRAN. BUT NO MORE.
I'M BETTING GOD WON'T SMITE THE COPS WHEN THEY CUFF YOUR STUFF.
PERHAPS NOT. BUT MY BROTHER, THE JUDGE, CERTAINLY WILL.
FAMILY UNITY IS SO IMPORTANT, DON'T YOU THINK?

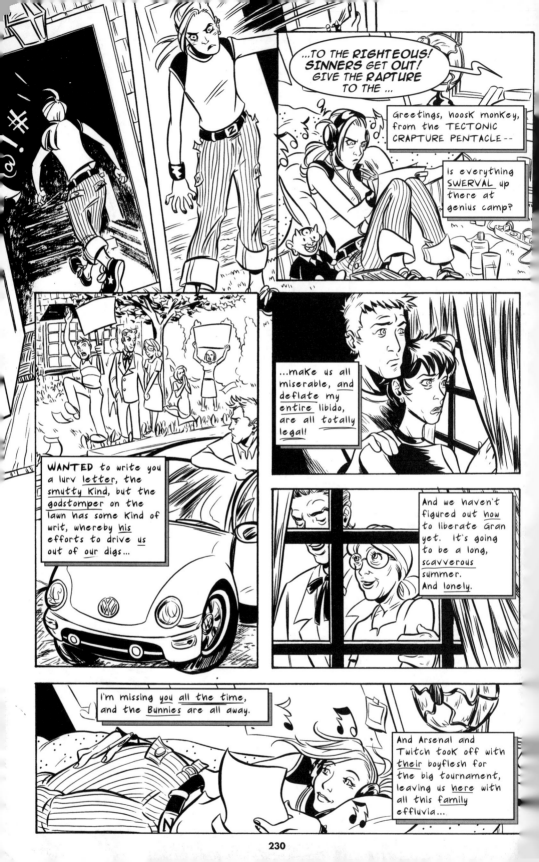

...TO THE **RIGHTEOUS!**
SINNERS GET OUT!
GIVE THE **RAPTURE**
TO THE ...

Greetings, hoosk monkey, from the TECTONIC CRAPTURE PENTACLE--

Is everything SWERVAL up there at genius camp?

...make us all miserable, and deflate my entire libido, are all totally legal!

WANTED to write you a lurv letter, the smutty kind, but the godstomper on the lawn has some kind of writ, whereby his efforts to drive us out of our digs...

And we haven't figured out how to liberate Gran yet. It's going to be a long, scavverous summer.
And lonely.

I'm missing you all the time, and the Bunnies are all away.

And Arsenal and Twitch took off with their boyflesh for the big tournament, leaving us here with all this family effluvia...

230

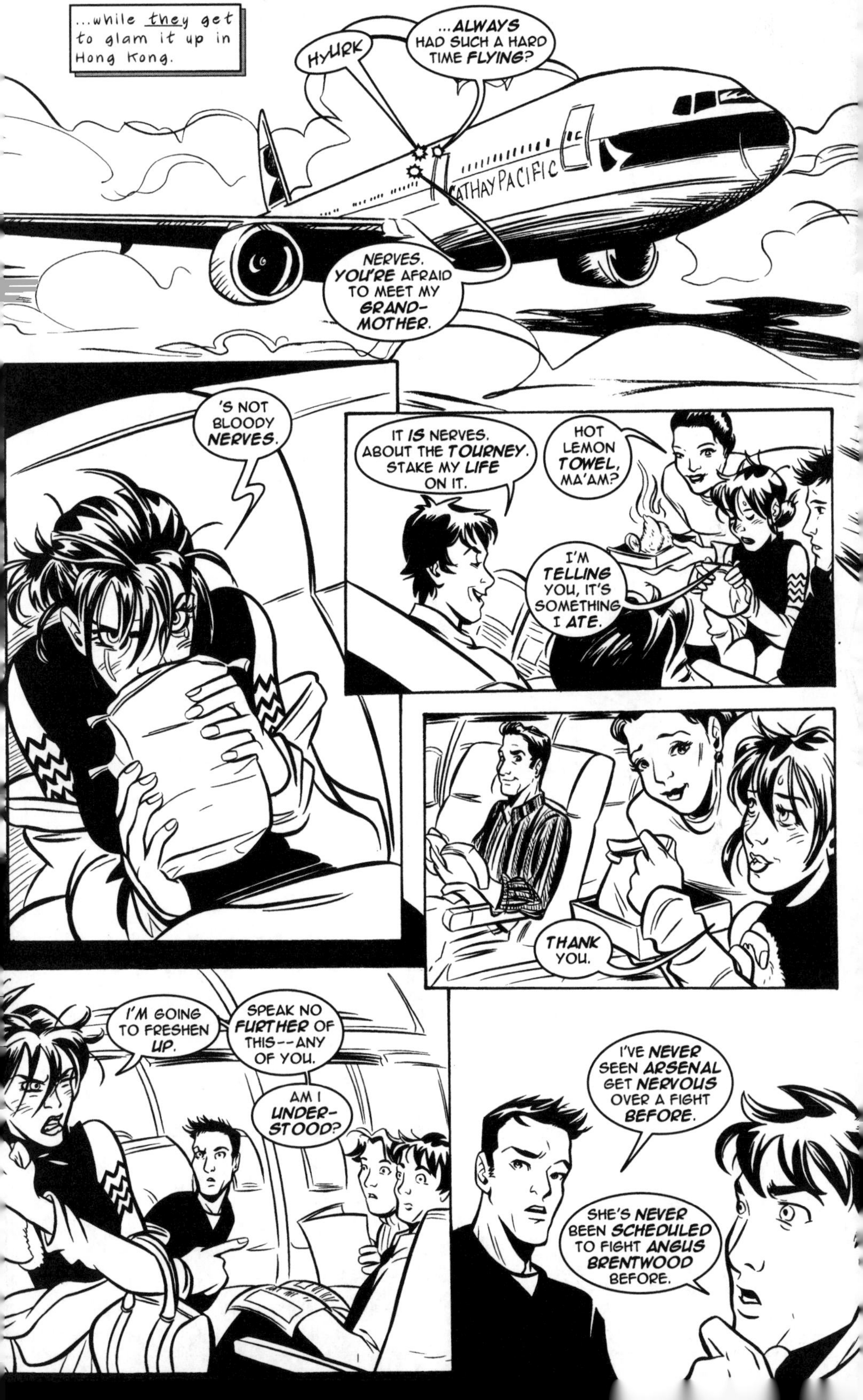

...while they get to glam it up in Hong Kong.
HYURK
...ALWAYS HAD SUCH A HARD TIME FLYING?
NERVES. YOU'RE AFRAID TO MEET MY GRAND-MOTHER.
CATHAY PACIFIC
'S NOT BLOODY NERVES.
IT IS NERVES. ABOUT THE TOURNEY. STAKE MY LIFE ON IT.
HOT LEMON TOWEL, MA'AM?
I'M TELLING YOU, IT'S SOMETHING I ATE.
THANK YOU.
I'M GOING TO FRESHEN UP.
SPEAK NO FURTHER OF THIS--ANY OF YOU.
AM I UNDER-STOOD?
I'VE NEVER SEEN ARSENAL GET NERVOUS OVER A FIGHT BEFORE.
SHE'S NEVER BEEN SCHEDULED TO FIGHT ANGUS BRENTWOOD BEFORE.

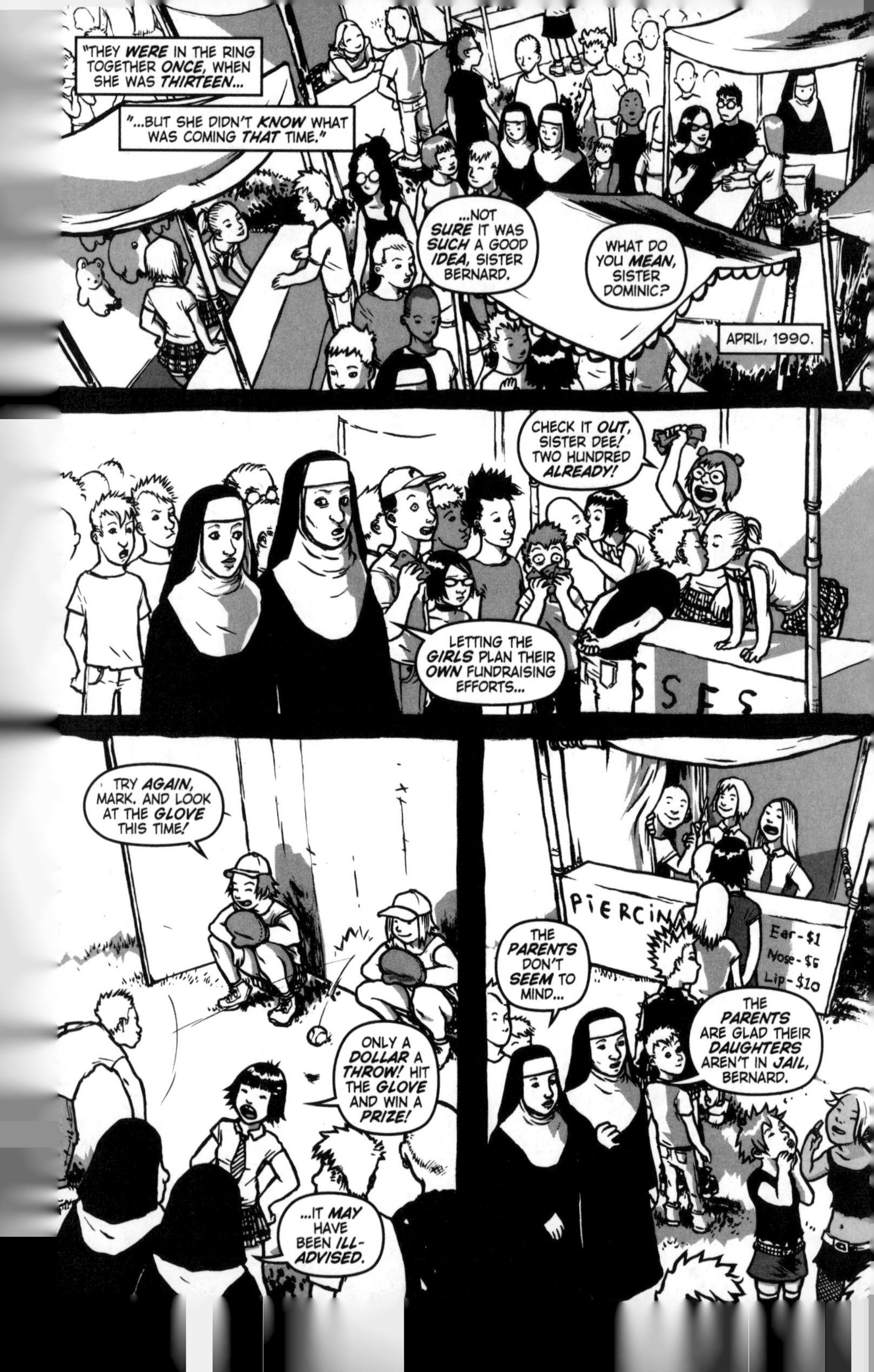

"THEY WERE IN THE RING TOGETHER ONCE, WHEN SHE WAS THIRTEEN...
"...BUT SHE DIDN'T KNOW WHAT WAS COMING THAT TIME."
...NOT SURE IT WAS SUCH A GOOD IDEA, SISTER BERNARD.
WHAT DO YOU MEAN, SISTER DOMINIC?
APRIL, 1990.
CHECK IT OUT, SISTER DEE! TWO HUNDRED ALREADY!
LETTING THE GIRLS PLAN THEIR OWN FUNDRAISING EFFORTS...
SSES
TRY AGAIN, MARK. AND LOOK AT THE GLOVE THIS TIME!
ONLY A DOLLAR A THROW! HIT THE GLOVE AND WIN A PRIZE!
...IT MAY HAVE BEEN ILL-ADVISED.
PIERCIN
Ear-$1
Nose-$5
Lip-$10
THE PARENTS DON'T SEEM TO MIND...
THE PARENTS ARE GLAD THEIR DAUGHTERS AREN'T IN JAIL, BERNARD.

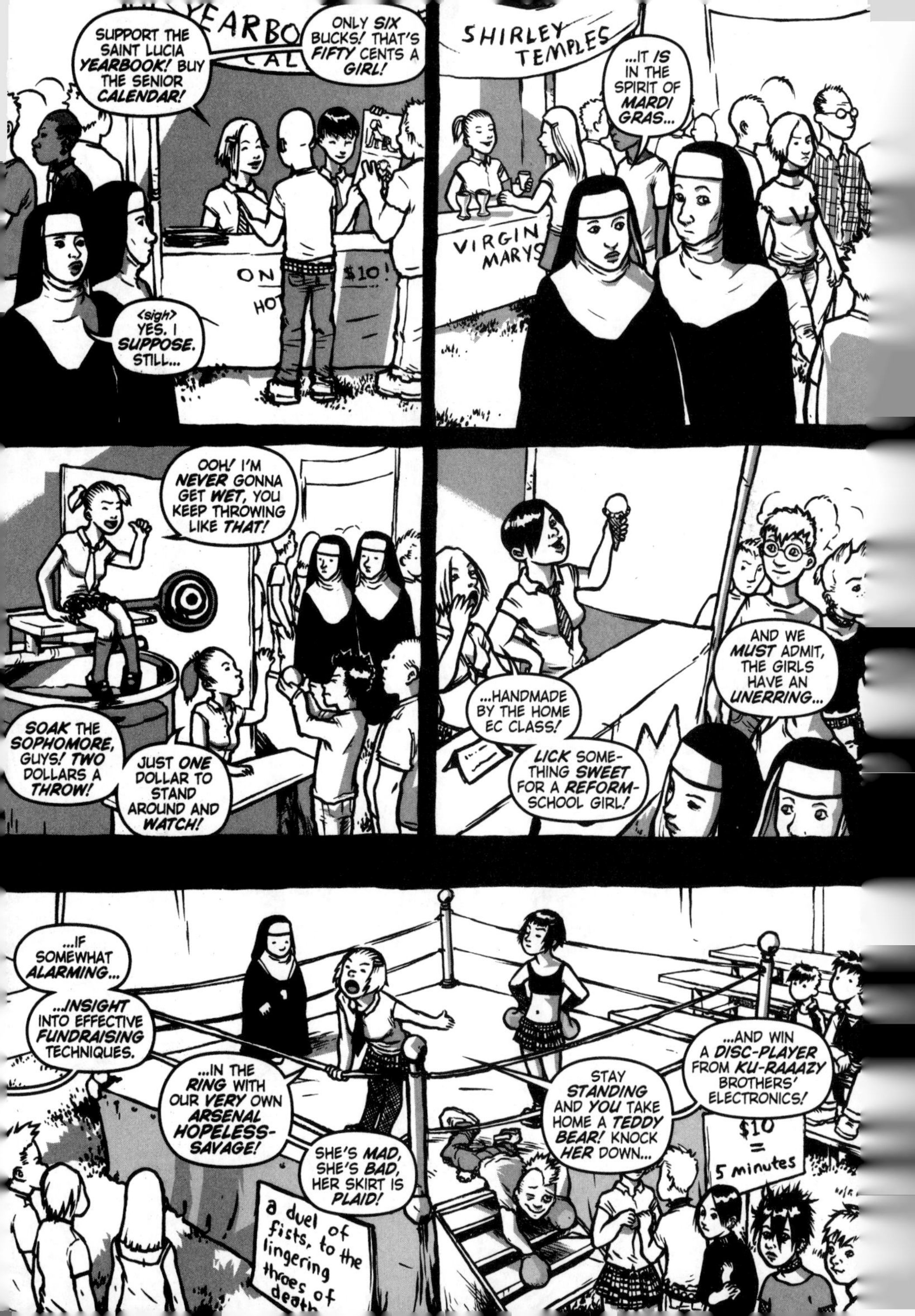
YEARBO
CAL
SUPPORT THE SAINT LUCIA YEARBOOK! BUY THE SENIOR CALENDAR!
ONLY SIX BUCKS! THAT'S FIFTY CENTS A GIRL!
ON $10!
HO
<sigh> YES. I SUPPOSE. STILL...
SHIRLEY TEMPLES
VIRGIN MARYS
...IT IS IN THE SPIRIT OF MARDI GRAS...
OOH! I'M NEVER GONNA GET WET, YOU KEEP THROWING LIKE THAT!
SOAK THE SOPHOMORE, GUYS! TWO DOLLARS A THROW!
JUST ONE DOLLAR TO STAND AROUND AND WATCH!
...HANDMADE BY THE HOME EC CLASS!
LICK SOMETHING SWEET FOR A REFORM-SCHOOL GIRL!
AND WE MUST ADMIT, THE GIRLS HAVE AN UNERRING...
...IF SOMEWHAT ALARMING...
...INSIGHT INTO EFFECTIVE FUNDRAISING TECHNIQUES.
...IN THE RING WITH OUR VERY OWN ARSENAL HOPELESS-SAVAGE!
SHE'S MAD, SHE'S BAD, HER SKIRT IS PLAID!
a duel of fists, to the lingering throes of death
STAY STANDING AND YOU TAKE HOME A TEDDY BEAR! KNOCK HER DOWN...
...AND WIN A DISC-PLAYER FROM KU-RAAAZY BROTHERS' ELECTRONICS!
$10 = 5 minutes

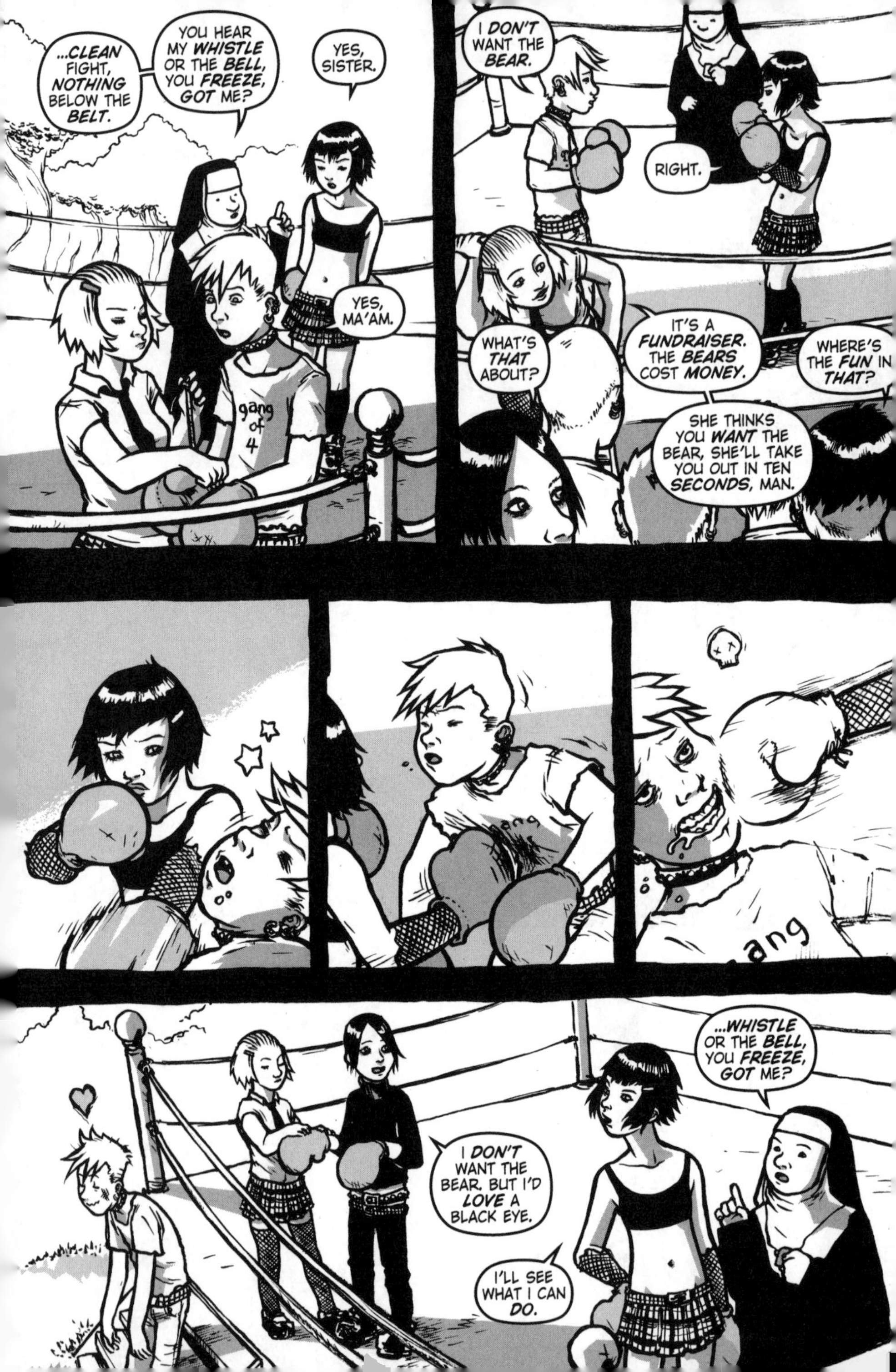
...CLEAN FIGHT, NOTHING BELOW THE BELT.
YOU HEAR MY WHISTLE OR THE BELL, YOU FREEZE, GOT ME?
YES, SISTER.
YES, MA'AM.
gang of 4
I DON'T WANT THE BEAR.
RIGHT.
WHAT'S THAT ABOUT?
IT'S A FUNDRAISER. THE BEARS COST MONEY.
WHERE'S THE FUN IN THAT?
SHE THINKS YOU WANT THE BEAR, SHE'LL TAKE YOU OUT IN TEN SECONDS, MAN.
...WHISTLE OR THE BELL, YOU FREEZE, GOT ME?
I DON'T WANT THE BEAR. BUT I'D LOVE A BLACK EYE.
I'LL SEE WHAT I CAN DO.

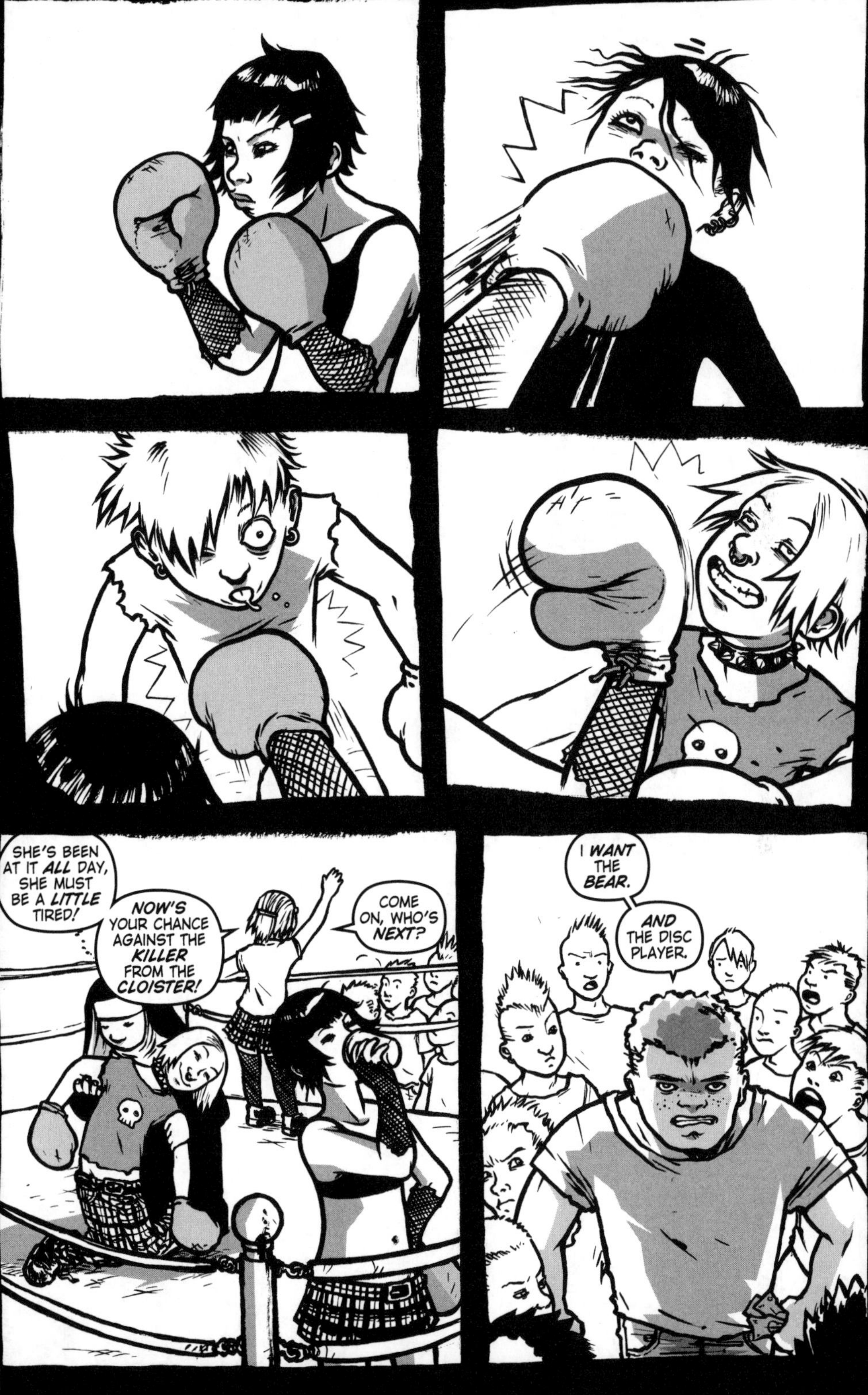
SHE'S BEEN AT IT ALL DAY, SHE MUST BE A LITTLE TIRED!
NOW'S YOUR CHANCE AGAINST THE KILLER FROM THE CLOISTER!
COME ON, WHO'S NEXT?
I WANT THE BEAR.
AND THE DISC PLAYER.

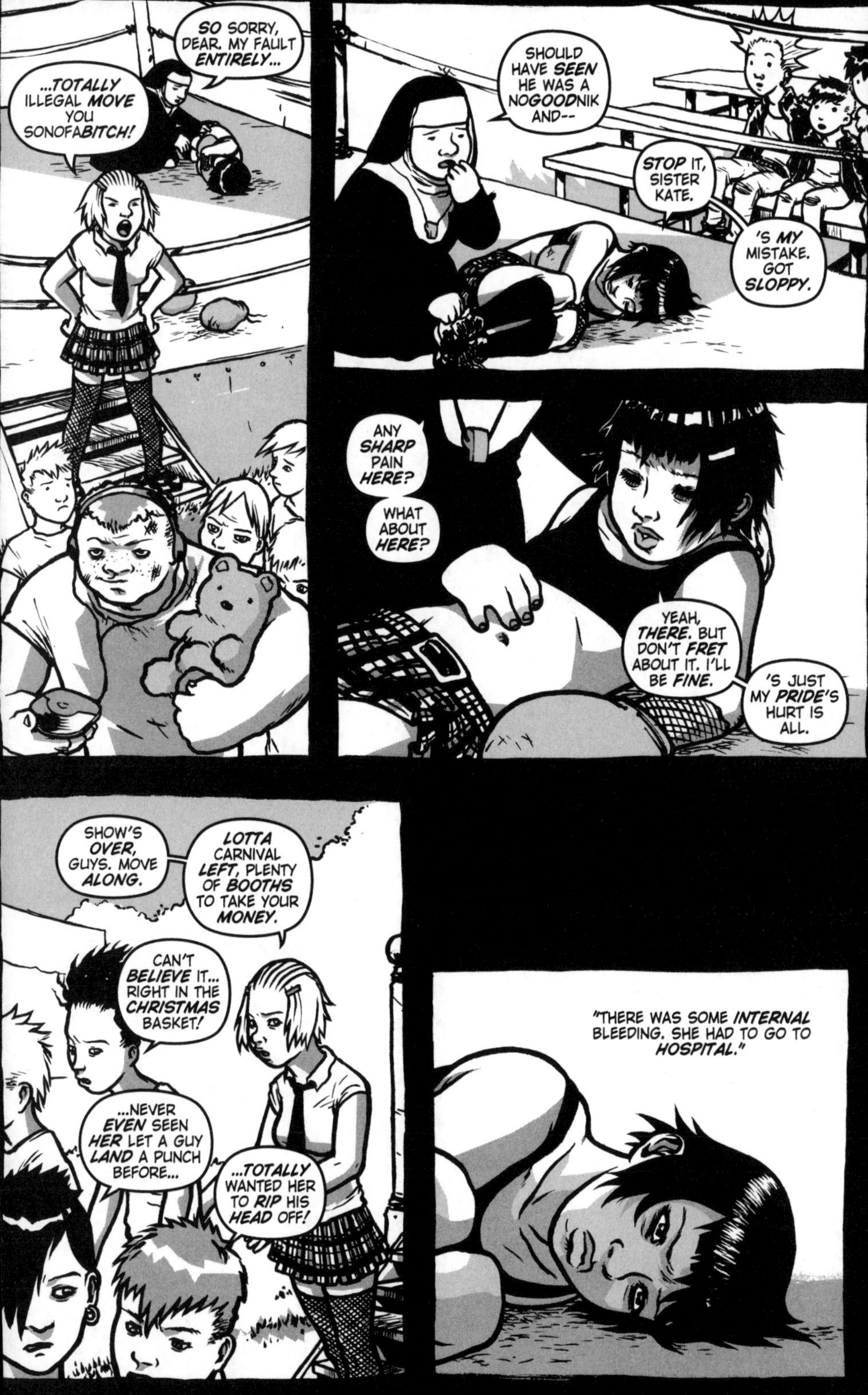

SO SORRY, DEAR. MY FAULT ENTIRELY...
...TOTALLY ILLEGAL MOVE YOU SONOFABITCH!
SHOULD HAVE SEEN HE WAS A NOGOODNIK AND--
STOP IT, SISTER KATE.
'S MY MISTAKE. GOT SLOPPY.
ANY SHARP PAIN HERE?
WHAT ABOUT HERE?
YEAH, THERE. BUT DON'T FRET ABOUT IT. I'LL BE FINE.
'S JUST MY PRIDE'S HURT IS ALL.
SHOW'S OVER, GUYS. MOVE ALONG.
LOTTA CARNIVAL LEFT, PLENTY OF BOOTHS TO TAKE YOUR MONEY.
CAN'T BELIEVE IT... RIGHT IN THE CHRISTMAS BASKET!
...NEVER EVEN SEEN HER LET A GUY LAND A PUNCH BEFORE...
...TOTALLY WANTED HER TO RIP HIS HEAD OFF!
"THERE WAS SOME INTERNAL BLEEDING. SHE HAD TO GO TO HOSPITAL."

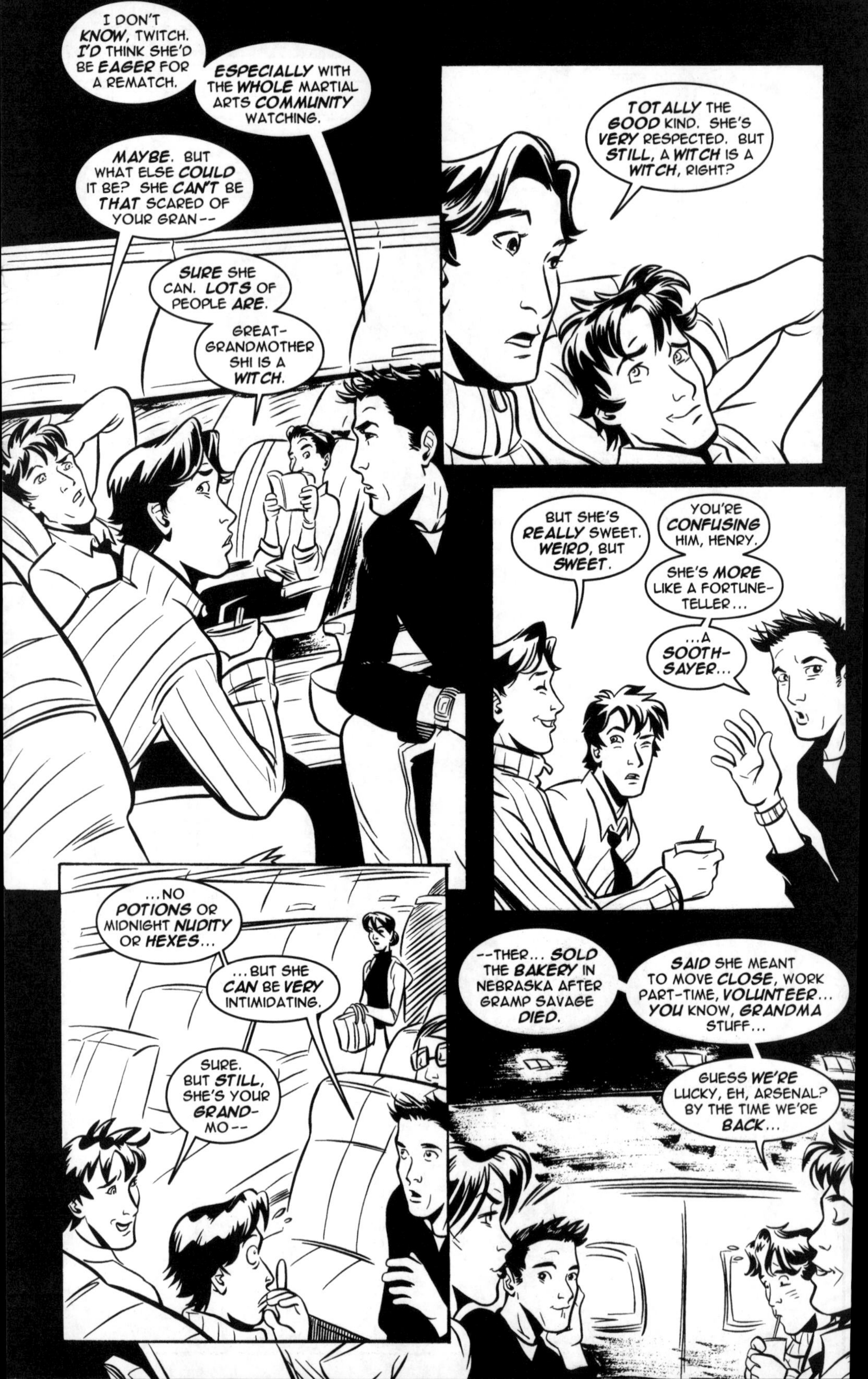
I DON'T KNOW, TWITCH. I'D THINK SHE'D BE EAGER FOR A REMATCH.
ESPECIALLY WITH THE WHOLE MARTIAL ARTS COMMUNITY WATCHING.
MAYBE. BUT WHAT ELSE COULD IT BE? SHE CAN'T BE THAT SCARED OF YOUR GRAN--
SURE SHE CAN. LOTS OF PEOPLE ARE.
GREAT-GRANDMOTHER SHI IS A WITCH.
TOTALLY THE GOOD KIND. SHE'S VERY RESPECTED. BUT STILL, A WITCH IS A WITCH, RIGHT?
BUT SHE'S REALLY SWEET. WEIRD, BUT SWEET.
YOU'RE CONFUSING HIM, HENRY.
SHE'S MORE LIKE A FORTUNE-TELLER...
...A SOOTH-SAYER...
...NO POTIONS OR MIDNIGHT NUDITY OR HEXES...
...BUT SHE CAN BE VERY INTIMIDATING.
SURE. BUT STILL, SHE'S YOUR GRAND-MO--
--THER... SOLD THE BAKERY IN NEBRASKA AFTER GRAMP SAVAGE DIED.
SAID SHE MEANT TO MOVE CLOSE, WORK PART-TIME, VOLUNTEER... YOU KNOW, GRANDMA STUFF...
GUESS WE'RE LUCKY, EH, ARSENAL? BY THE TIME WE'RE BACK...

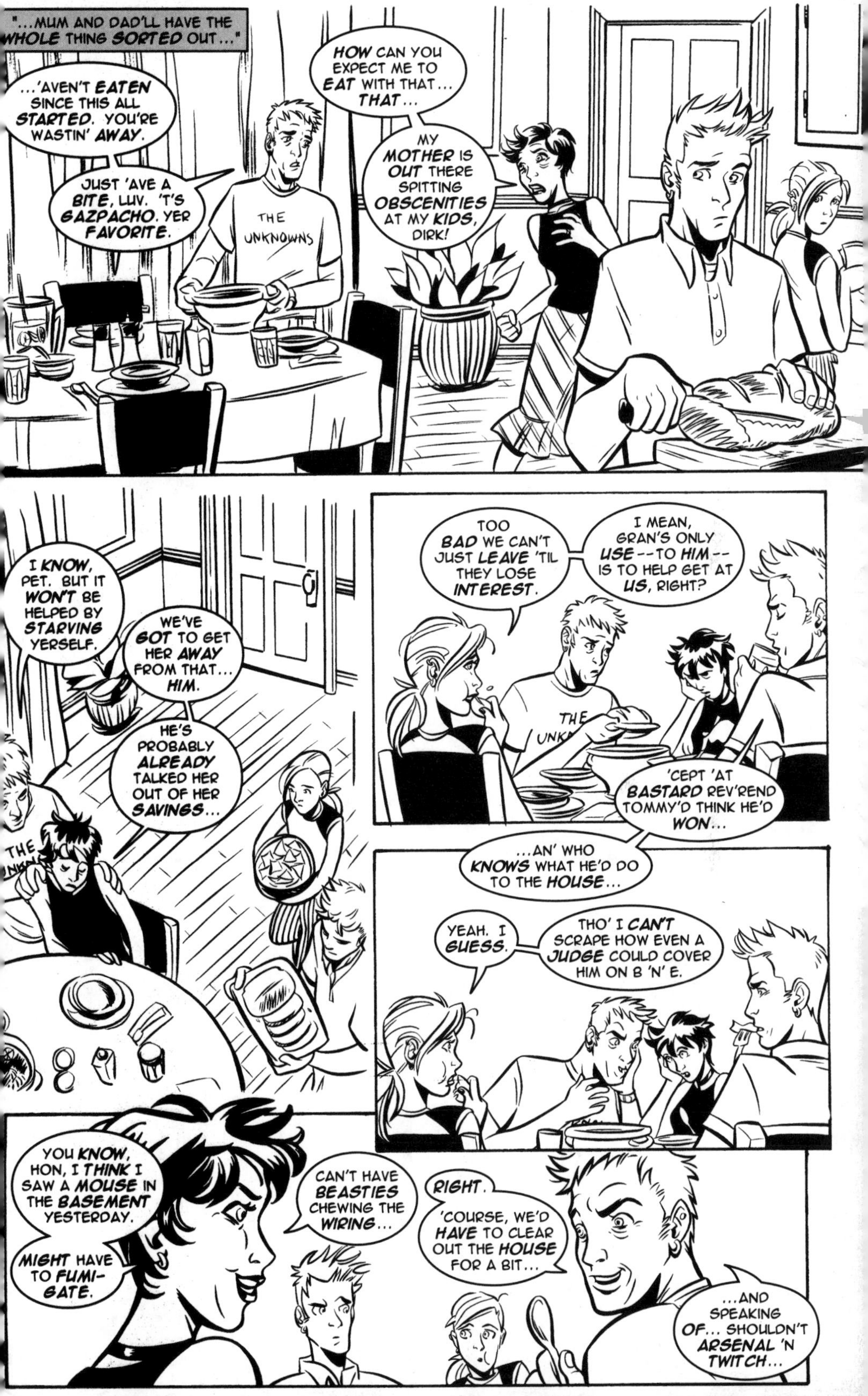
"...MUM AND DAD'LL HAVE THE WHOLE THING SORTED OUT..."
...'AVEN'T EATEN SINCE THIS ALL STARTED. YOU'RE WASTIN' AWAY.
JUST 'AVE A BITE, LUV. 'T'S GAZPACHO. YER FAVORITE.
THE UNKNOWNS
HOW CAN YOU EXPECT ME TO EAT WITH THAT... THAT...
MY MOTHER IS OUT THERE SPITTING OBSCENITIES AT MY KIDS, DIRK!
I KNOW, PET. BUT IT WON'T BE HELPED BY STARVING YERSELF.
WE'VE GOT TO GET HER AWAY FROM THAT... HIM.
HE'S PROBABLY ALREADY TALKED HER OUT OF HER SAVINGS...
TOO BAD WE CAN'T JUST LEAVE 'TIL THEY LOSE INTEREST.
I MEAN, GRAN'S ONLY USE--TO HIM--IS TO HELP GET AT US, RIGHT?
'CEPT 'AT BASTARD REV'REND TOMMY'D THINK HE'D WON...
...AN' WHO KNOWS WHAT HE'D DO TO THE HOUSE...
YEAH. I GUESS.
THO' I CAN'T SCRAPE HOW EVEN A JUDGE COULD COVER HIM ON B 'N' E.
YOU KNOW, HON, I THINK I SAW A MOUSE IN THE BASEMENT YESTERDAY.
MIGHT HAVE TO FUMI-GATE.
CAN'T HAVE BEASTIES CHEWING THE WIRING...
RIGHT.
'COURSE, WE'D HAVE TO CLEAR OUT THE HOUSE FOR A BIT...
...AND SPEAKING OF... SHOULDN'T ARSENAL 'N TWITCH...

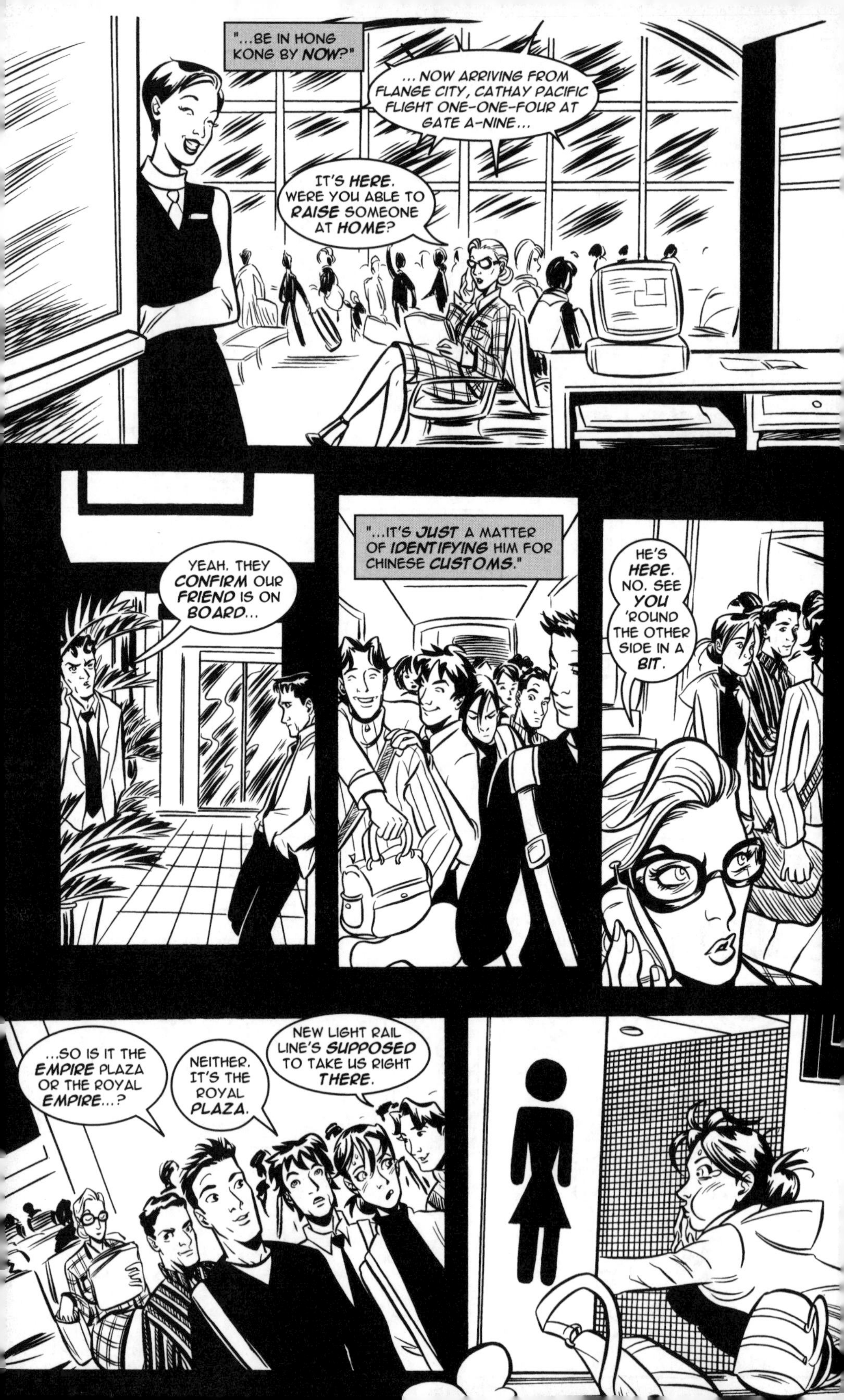
"...BE IN HONG KONG BY NOW?"
... NOW ARRIVING FROM FLANGE CITY, CATHAY PACIFIC FLIGHT ONE-ONE-FOUR AT GATE A-NINE...
IT'S HERE. WERE YOU ABLE TO RAISE SOMEONE AT HOME?
YEAH. THEY CONFIRM OUR FRIEND IS ON BOARD...
"...IT'S JUST A MATTER OF IDENTIFYING HIM FOR CHINESE CUSTOMS."
HE'S HERE. NO. SEE YOU 'ROUND THE OTHER SIDE IN A BIT.
...SO IS IT THE EMPIRE PLAZA OR THE ROYAL EMPIRE...?
NEITHER. IT'S THE ROYAL PLAZA.
NEW LIGHT RAIL LINE'S SUPPOSED TO TAKE US RIGHT THERE.

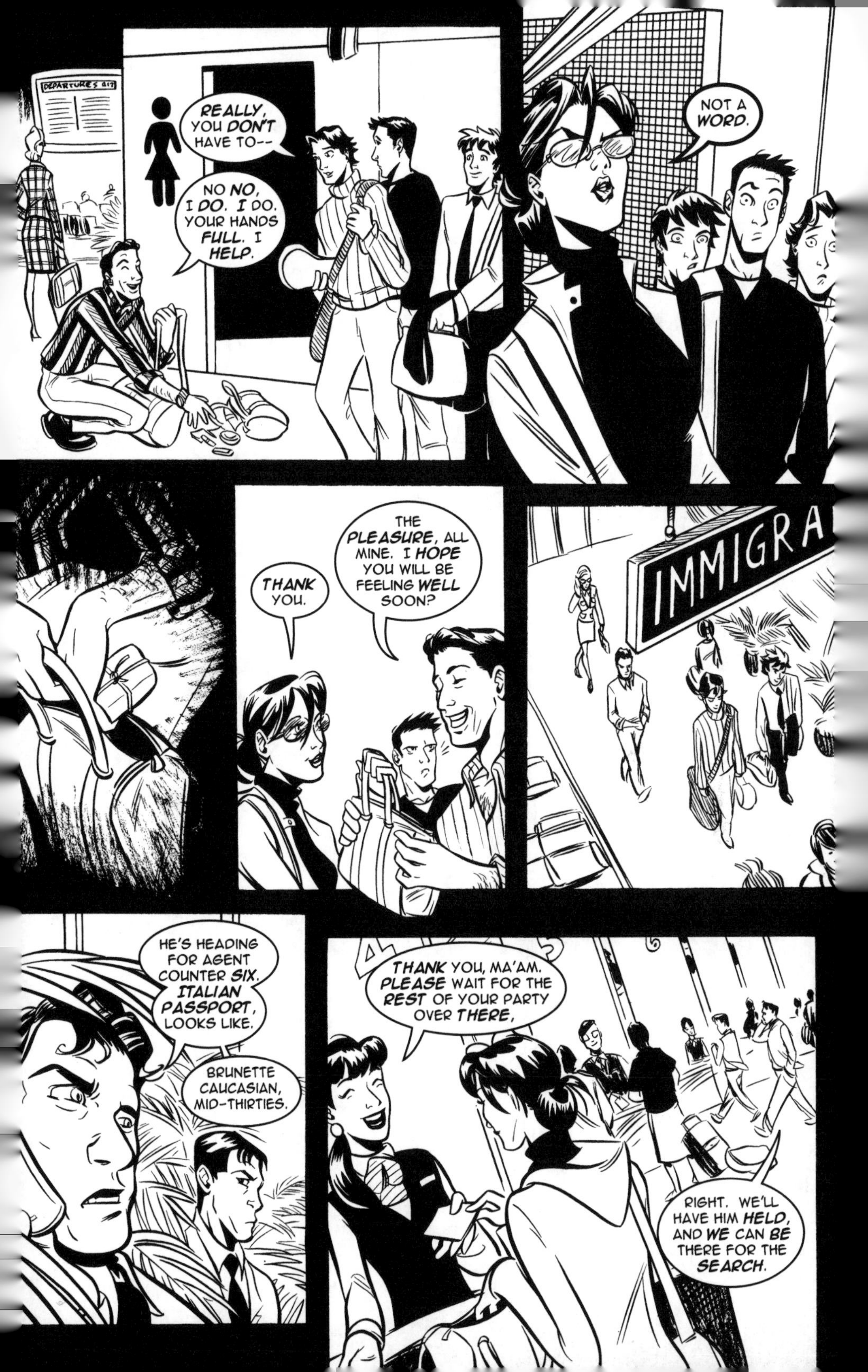
DEPARTURES
REALLY, YOU DON'T HAVE TO--
NO NO, I DO. I DO. YOUR HANDS FULL. I HELP.
NOT A WORD.
THE PLEASURE, ALL MINE. I HOPE YOU WILL BE FEELING WELL SOON?
THANK YOU.
IMMIGRA
HE'S HEADING FOR AGENT COUNTER SIX. ITALIAN PASSPORT, LOOKS LIKE.
BRUNETTE CAUCASIAN, MID-THIRTIES.
THANK YOU, MA'AM. PLEASE WAIT FOR THE REST OF YOUR PARTY OVER THERE,
RIGHT. WE'LL HAVE HIM HELD, AND WE CAN BE THERE FOR THE SEARCH.

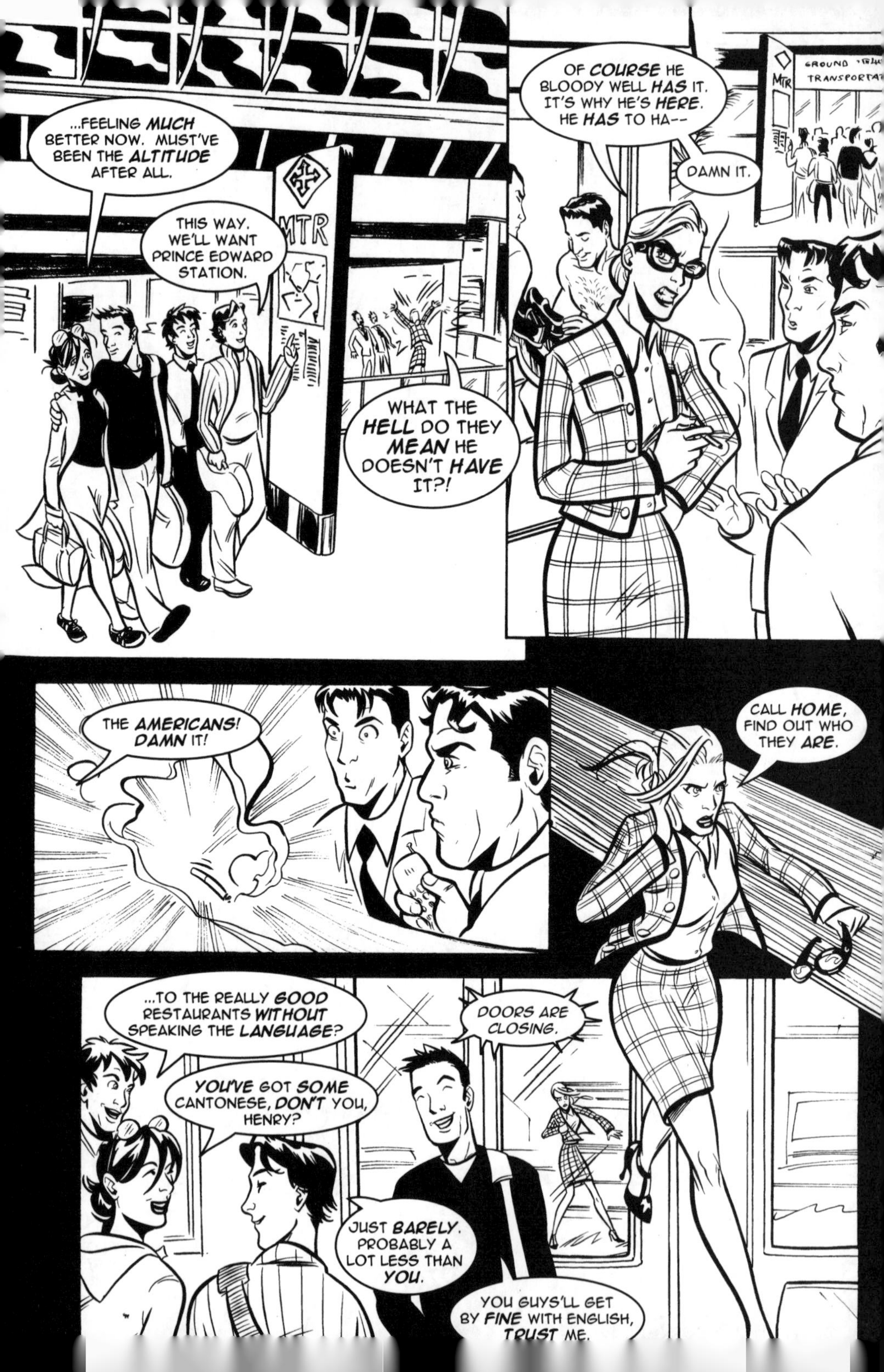

...FEELING MUCH BETTER NOW. MUST'VE BEEN THE ALTITUDE AFTER ALL.
THIS WAY. WE'LL WANT PRINCE EDWARD STATION.
MTR
WHAT THE HELL DO THEY MEAN HE DOESN'T HAVE IT?!
OF COURSE HE BLOODY WELL HAS IT. IT'S WHY HE'S HERE. HE HAS TO HA--
DAMN IT.
MTR
GROUND TRANSPORTAT
THE AMERICANS! DAMN IT!
CALL HOME, FIND OUT WHO THEY ARE.
...TO THE REALLY GOOD RESTAURANTS WITHOUT SPEAKING THE LANGUAGE?
DOORS ARE CLOSING.
YOU'VE GOT SOME CANTONESE, DON'T YOU, HENRY?
JUST BARELY. PROBABLY A LOT LESS THAN YOU.
YOU GUYS'LL GET BY FINE WITH ENGLISH, TRUST ME.

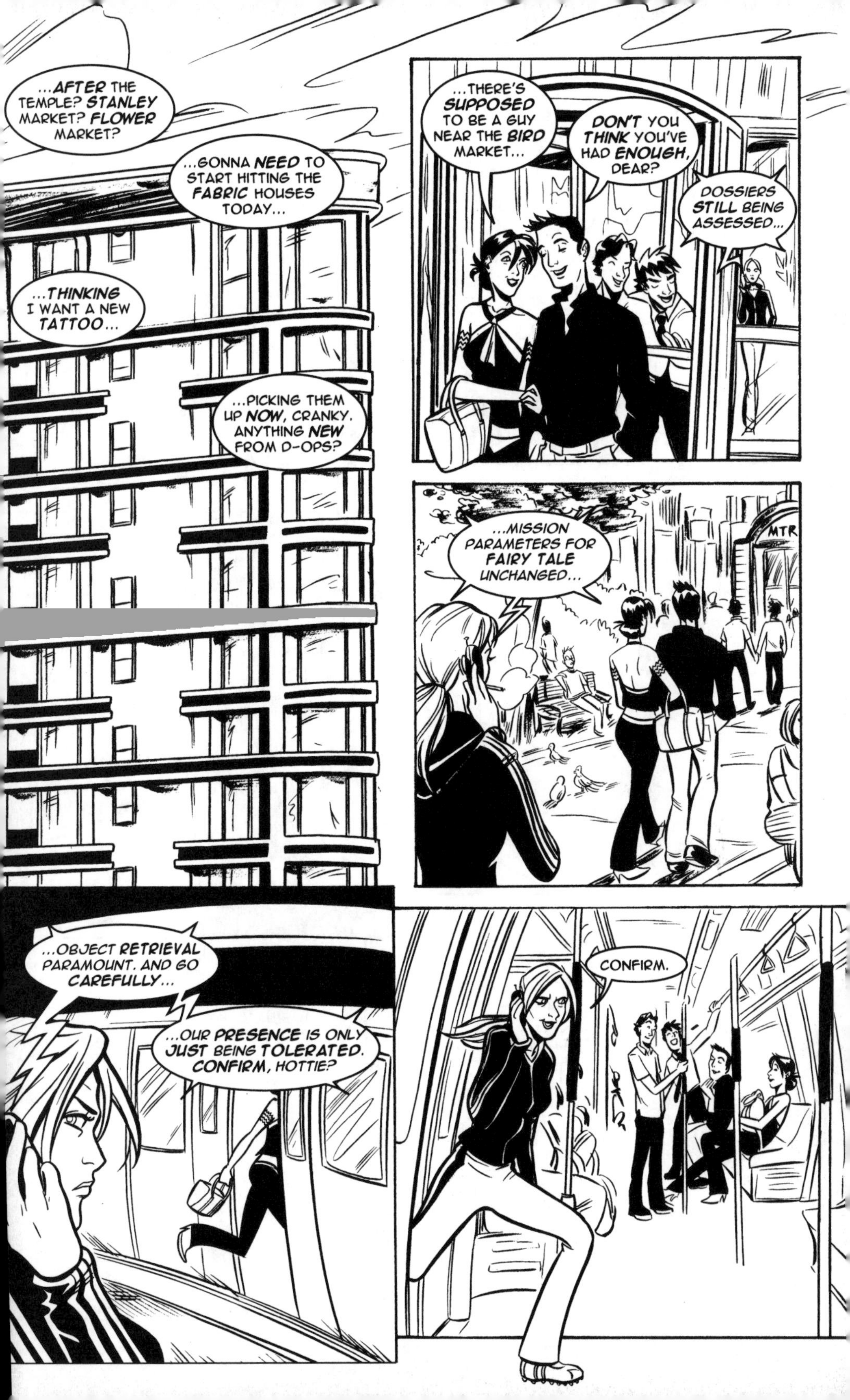
...AFTER THE TEMPLE? STANLEY MARKET? FLOWER MARKET?
...GONNA NEED TO START HITTING THE FABRIC HOUSES TODAY...
...THINKING I WANT A NEW TATTOO...
...PICKING THEM UP NOW, CRANKY. ANYTHING NEW FROM D-OPS?
...THERE'S SUPPOSED TO BE A GUY NEAR THE BIRD MARKET...
DON'T YOU THINK YOU'VE HAD ENOUGH, DEAR?
DOSSIERS STILL BEING ASSESSED...
...MISSION PARAMETERS FOR FAIRY TALE UNCHANGED...
MTR
...OBJECT RETRIEVAL PARAMOUNT. AND GO CAREFULLY...
...OUR PRESENCE IS ONLY JUST BEING TOLERATED. CONFIRM, HOTTIE?
CONFIRM.

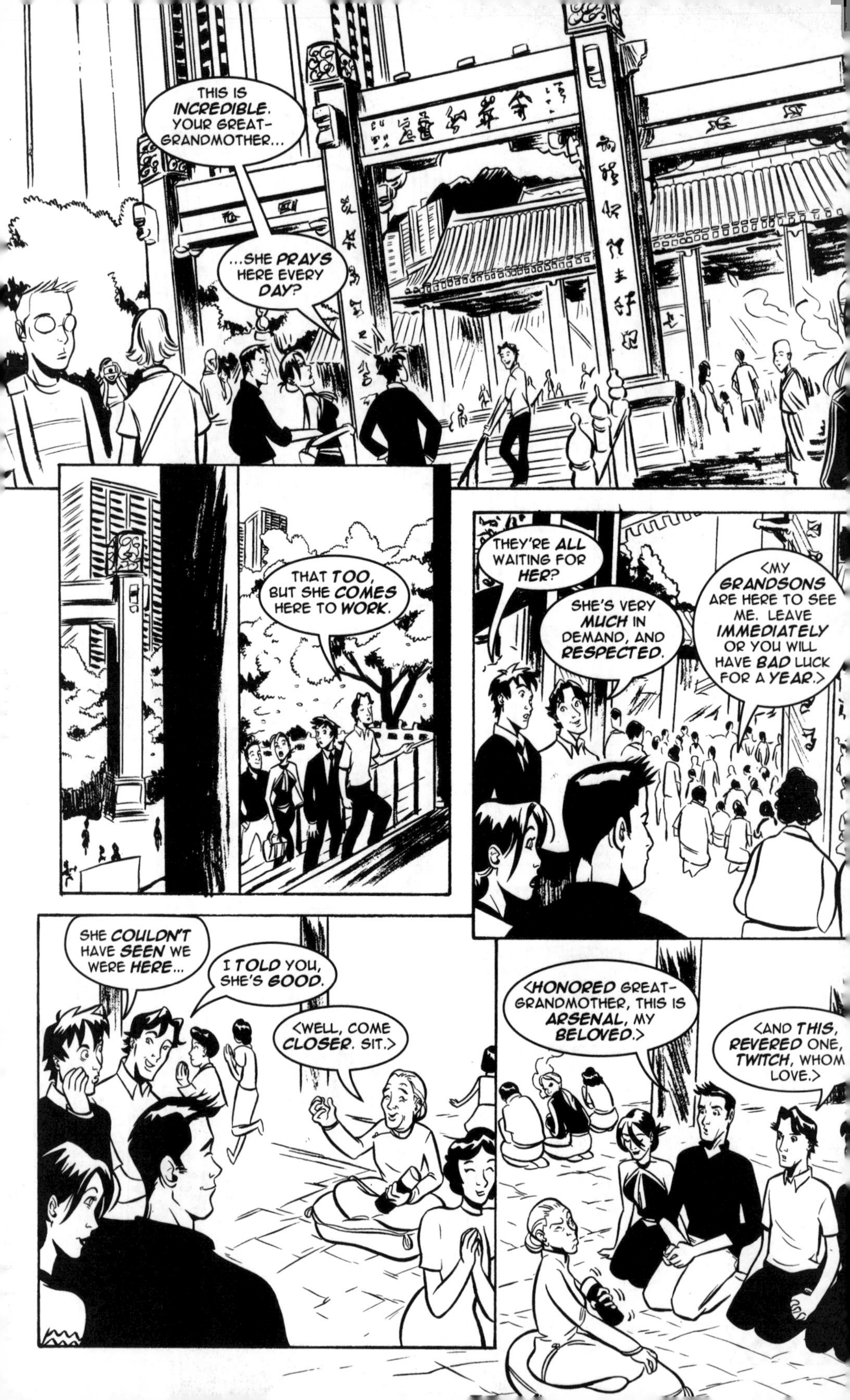
THIS IS INCREDIBLE. YOUR GREAT-GRANDMOTHER...
...SHE PRAYS HERE EVERY DAY?
THAT TOO, BUT SHE COMES HERE TO WORK.
THEY'RE ALL WAITING FOR HER?
SHE'S VERY MUCH IN DEMAND, AND RESPECTED.
<MY GRANDSONS ARE HERE TO SEE ME. LEAVE IMMEDIATELY OR YOU WILL HAVE BAD LUCK FOR A YEAR.>
SHE COULDN'T HAVE SEEN WE WERE HERE...
I TOLD YOU, SHE'S GOOD.
<WELL, COME CLOSER. SIT.>
<HONORED GREAT-GRANDMOTHER, THIS IS ARSENAL, MY BELOVED.>
<AND THIS, REVERED ONE, TWITCH, WHOM I LOVE.>

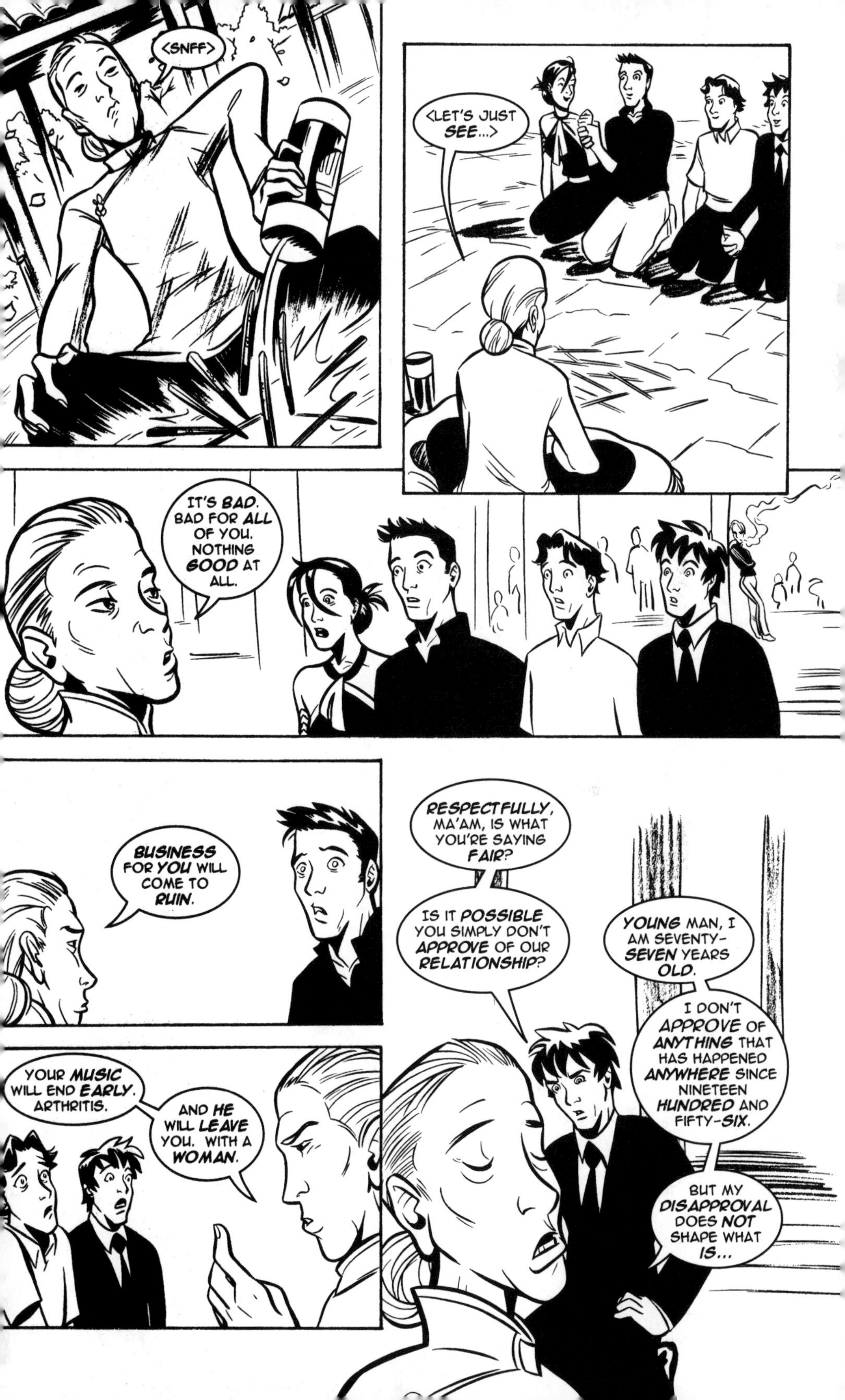
<SNFF>
<LET'S JUST SEE...>
IT'S BAD. BAD FOR ALL OF YOU. NOTHING GOOD AT ALL.
BUSINESS FOR YOU WILL COME TO RUIN.
YOUR MUSIC WILL END EARLY. ARTHRITIS.
AND HE WILL LEAVE YOU. WITH A WOMAN.
RESPECTFULLY, MA'AM, IS WHAT YOU'RE SAYING FAIR?
IS IT POSSIBLE YOU SIMPLY DON'T APPROVE OF OUR RELATIONSHIP?
YOUNG MAN, I AM SEVENTY-SEVEN YEARS OLD.
I DON'T APPROVE OF ANYTHING THAT HAS HAPPENED ANYWHERE SINCE NINETEEN HUNDRED AND FIFTY-SIX.
BUT MY DISAPPROVAL DOES NOT SHAPE WHAT IS...

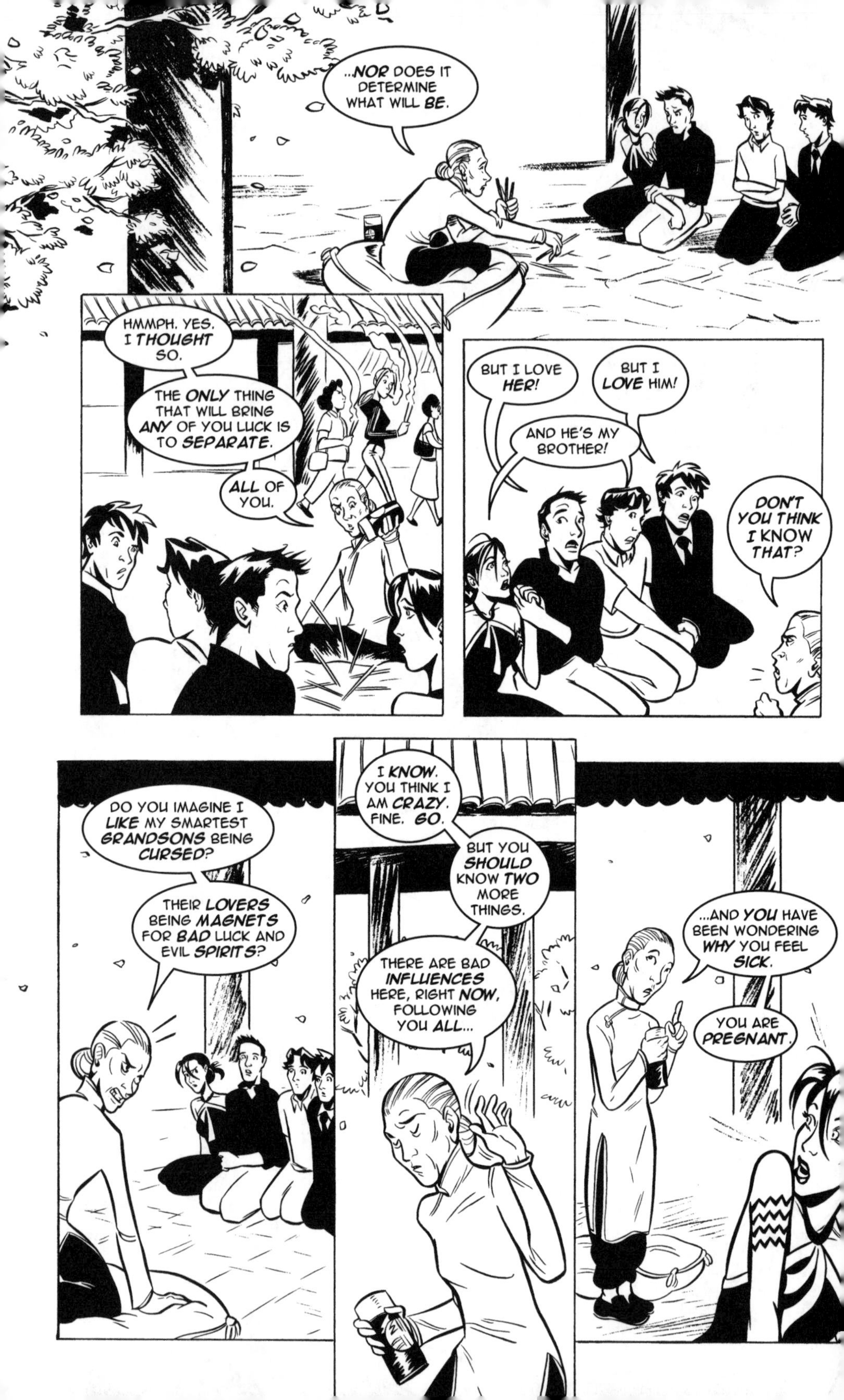
...NOR DOES IT DETERMINE WHAT WILL BE.
HMMPH. YES. I THOUGHT SO.
THE ONLY THING THAT WILL BRING ANY OF YOU LUCK IS TO SEPARATE.
ALL OF YOU.
BUT I LOVE HER!
BUT I LOVE HIM!
AND HE'S MY BROTHER!
DON'T YOU THINK I KNOW THAT?
DO YOU IMAGINE I LIKE MY SMARTEST GRANDSONS BEING CURSED?
THEIR LOVERS BEING MAGNETS FOR BAD LUCK AND EVIL SPIRITS?
I KNOW. YOU THINK I AM CRAZY. FINE. GO.
BUT YOU SHOULD KNOW TWO MORE THINGS.
THERE ARE BAD INFLUENCES HERE, RIGHT NOW, FOLLOWING YOU ALL...
...AND YOU HAVE BEEN WONDERING WHY YOU FEEL SICK.
YOU ARE PREGNANT.

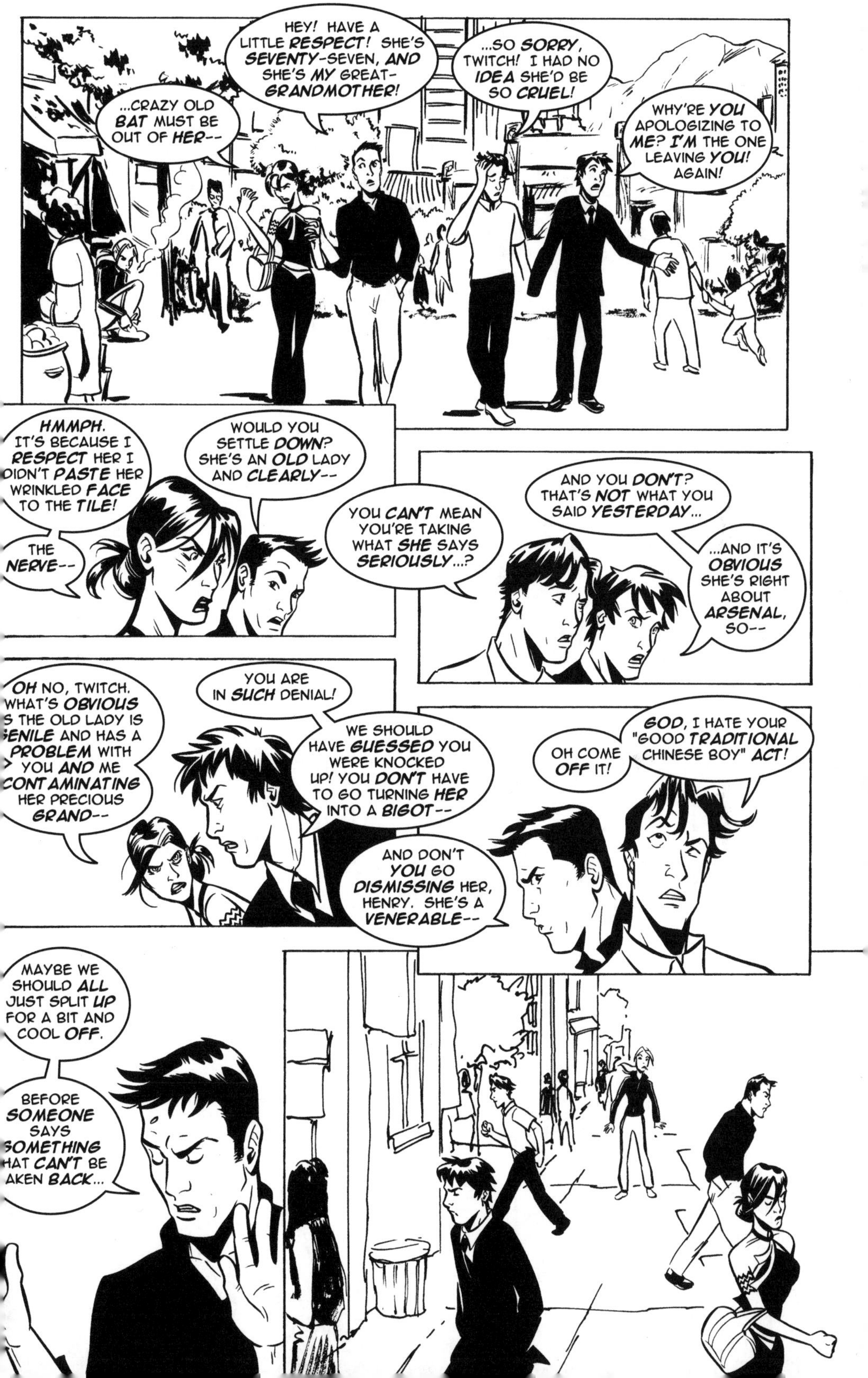

...CRAZY OLD BAT MUST BE OUT OF HER--
HEY! HAVE A LITTLE RESPECT! SHE'S SEVENTY-SEVEN, AND SHE'S MY GREAT-GRANDMOTHER!
...SO SORRY, TWITCH! I HAD NO IDEA SHE'D BE SO CRUEL!
WHY'RE YOU APOLOGIZING TO ME? I'M THE ONE LEAVING YOU! AGAIN!
HMMPH. IT'S BECAUSE I RESPECT HER I DIDN'T PASTE HER WRINKLED FACE TO THE TILE!
THE NERVE--
WOULD YOU SETTLE DOWN? SHE'S AN OLD LADY AND CLEARLY--
YOU CAN'T MEAN YOU'RE TAKING WHAT SHE SAYS SERIOUSLY...?
AND YOU DON'T? THAT'S NOT WHAT YOU SAID YESTERDAY...
...AND IT'S OBVIOUS SHE'S RIGHT ABOUT ARSENAL, SO--
OH NO, TWITCH. WHAT'S OBVIOUS IS THE OLD LADY IS SENILE AND HAS A PROBLEM WITH YOU AND ME CONTAMINATING HER PRECIOUS GRAND--
YOU ARE IN SUCH DENIAL!
WE SHOULD HAVE GUESSED YOU WERE KNOCKED UP! YOU DON'T HAVE TO GO TURNING HER INTO A BIGOT--
OH COME OFF IT!
GOD, I HATE YOUR "GOOD TRADITIONAL CHINESE BOY" ACT!
AND DON'T YOU GO DISMISSING HER, HENRY. SHE'S A VENERABLE--
MAYBE WE SHOULD ALL JUST SPLIT UP FOR A BIT AND COOL OFF.
BEFORE SOMEONE SAYS SOMETHING THAT CAN'T BE TAKEN BACK...

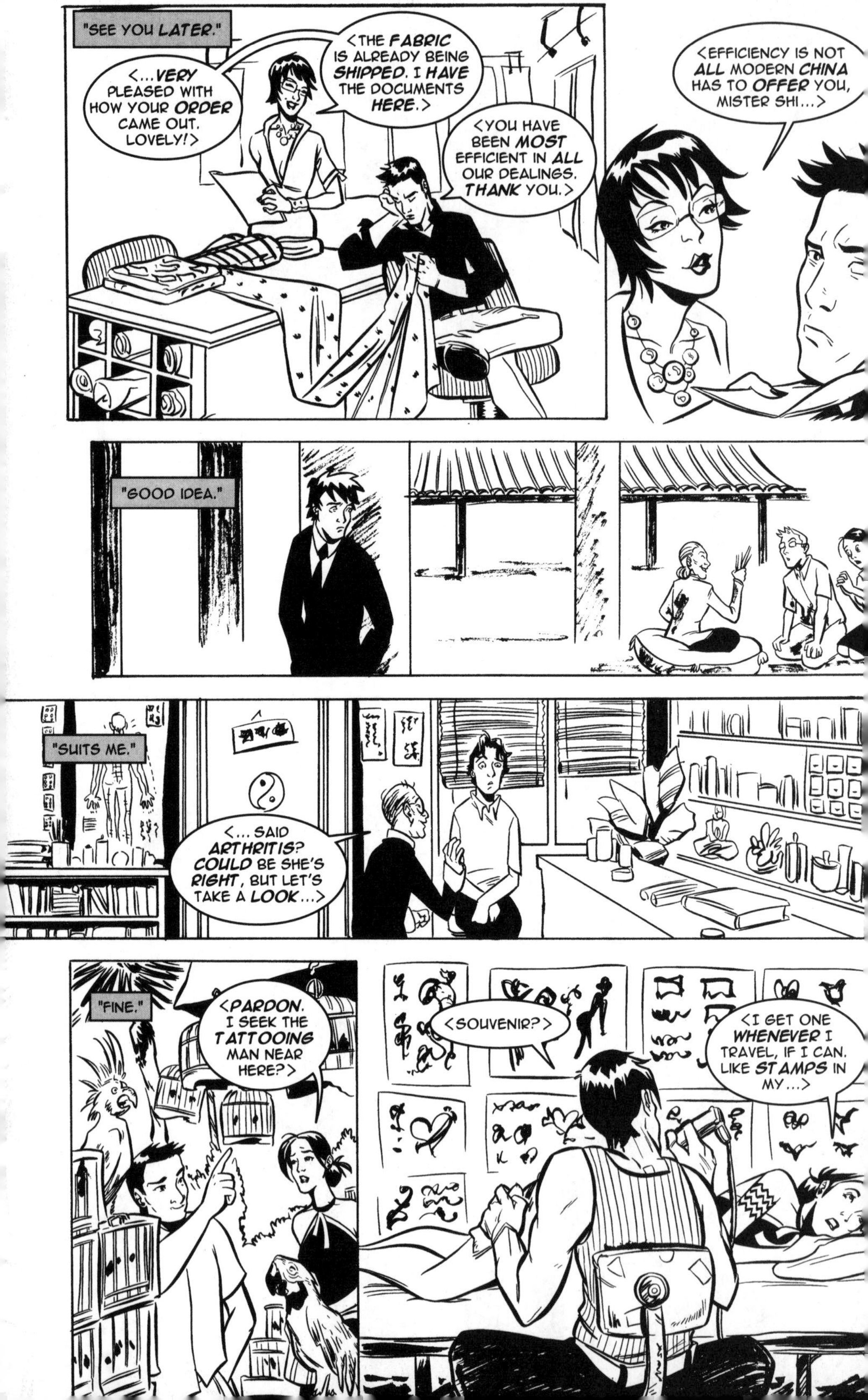
"SEE YOU LATER."
<...VERY PLEASED WITH HOW YOUR ORDER CAME OUT. LOVELY!>
<THE FABRIC IS ALREADY BEING SHIPPED. I HAVE THE DOCUMENTS HERE.>
<YOU HAVE BEEN MOST EFFICIENT IN ALL OUR DEALINGS. THANK YOU.>
<EFFICIENCY IS NOT ALL MODERN CHINA HAS TO OFFER YOU, MISTER SHI...>
"GOOD IDEA."
"SUITS ME."
<... SAID ARTHRITIS? COULD BE SHE'S RIGHT, BUT LET'S TAKE A LOOK...>
"FINE."
<PARDON. I SEEK THE TATTOOING MAN NEAR HERE?>
<SOUVENIR?>
<I GET ONE WHENEVER I TRAVEL, IF I CAN. LIKE STAMPS IN MY...>

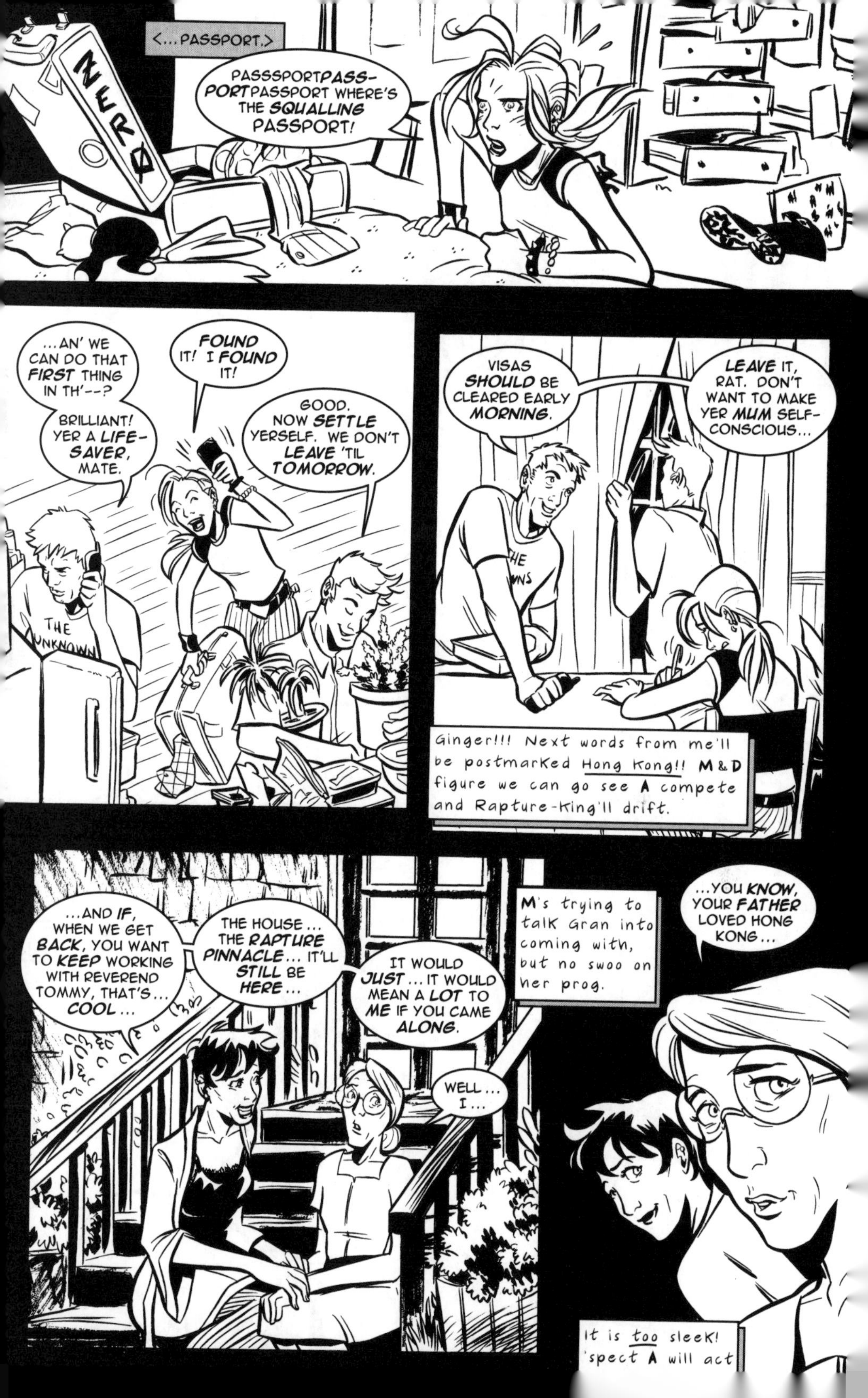
<...PASSPORT.>
PASSSPORTPASS-PORTPASSPORT WHERE'S THE SQUALLING PASSPORT!
...AN' WE CAN DO THAT FIRST THING IN TH'--?
BRILLIANT! YER A LIFE-SAVER, MATE.
FOUND IT! I FOUND IT!
GOOD. NOW SETTLE YOURSELF. WE DON'T LEAVE 'TIL TOMORROW.
THE UNKNOWN
VISAS SHOULD BE CLEARED EARLY MORNING.
LEAVE IT, RAT. DON'T WANT TO MAKE YER MUM SELF-CONSCIOUS...
Ginger!!! Next words from me'll be postmarked Hong Kong!! M & D figure we can go see A compete and Rapture-King'll drift.
...AND IF, WHEN WE GET BACK, YOU WANT TO KEEP WORKING WITH REVEREND TOMMY, THAT'S... COOL...
THE HOUSE... THE RAPTURE PINNACLE... IT'LL STILL BE HERE...
IT WOULD JUST... IT WOULD MEAN A LOT TO ME IF YOU CAME ALONG.
WELL... I...
M's trying to talk Gran into coming with, but no swoo on her prog.
...YOU KNOW, YOUR FATHER LOVED HONG KONG...
It is too sleek! 'spect A will act

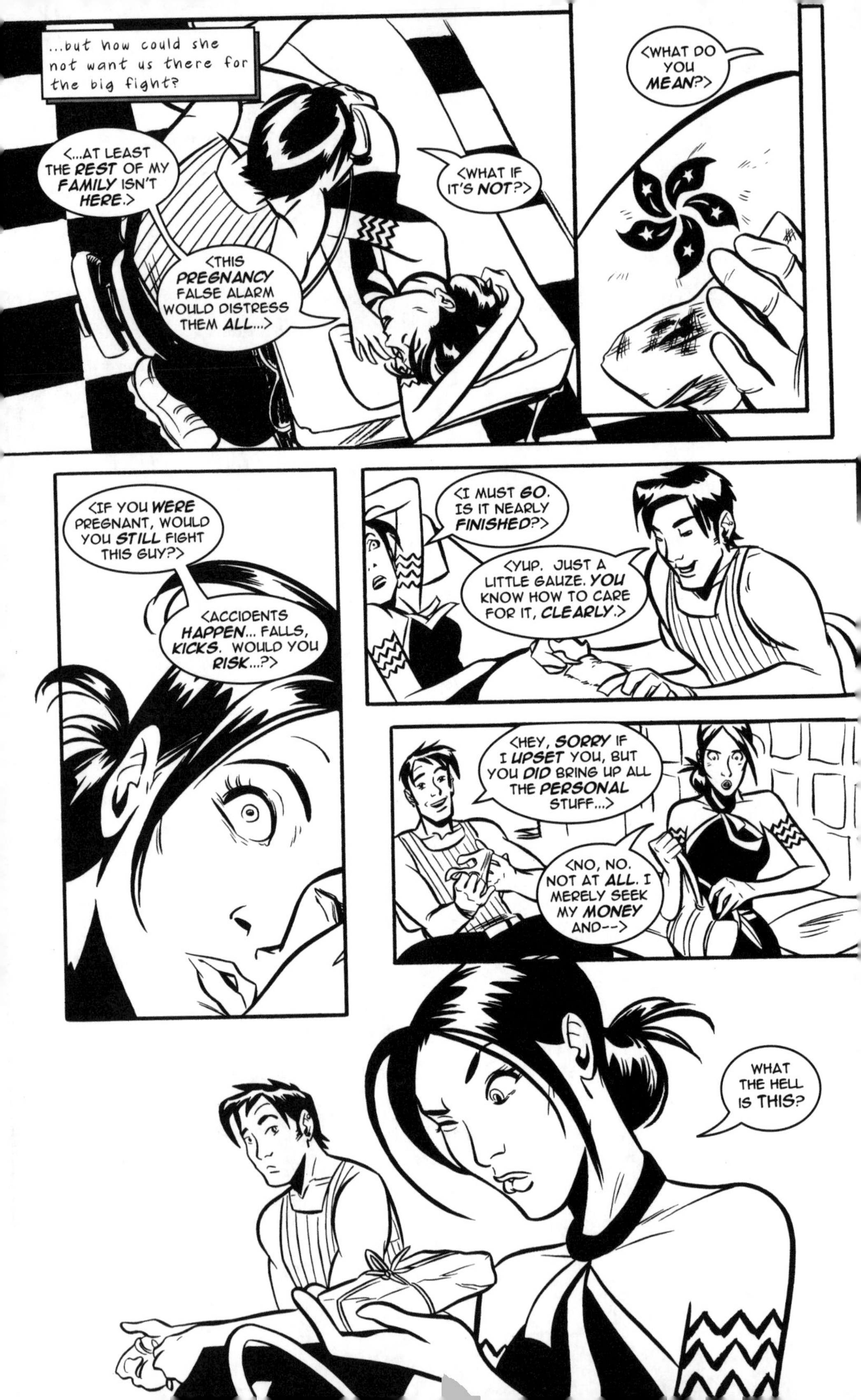
...but how could she not want us there for the big fight?
<...AT LEAST THE REST OF MY FAMILY ISN'T HERE.>
<THIS PREGNANCY FALSE ALARM WOULD DISTRESS THEM ALL...>
<WHAT IF IT'S NOT?>
<WHAT DO YOU MEAN?>
<IF YOU WERE PREGNANT, WOULD YOU STILL FIGHT THIS GUY?>
<ACCIDENTS HAPPEN... FALLS, KICKS. WOULD YOU RISK...?>
<I MUST GO. IS IT NEARLY FINISHED?>
<YUP. JUST A LITTLE GAUZE. YOU KNOW HOW TO CARE FOR IT, CLEARLY.>
<HEY, SORRY IF I UPSET YOU, BUT YOU DID BRING UP ALL THE PERSONAL STUFF...>
<NO, NO. NOT AT ALL. I MERELY SEEK MY MONEY AND-->
WHAT THE HELL IS THIS?

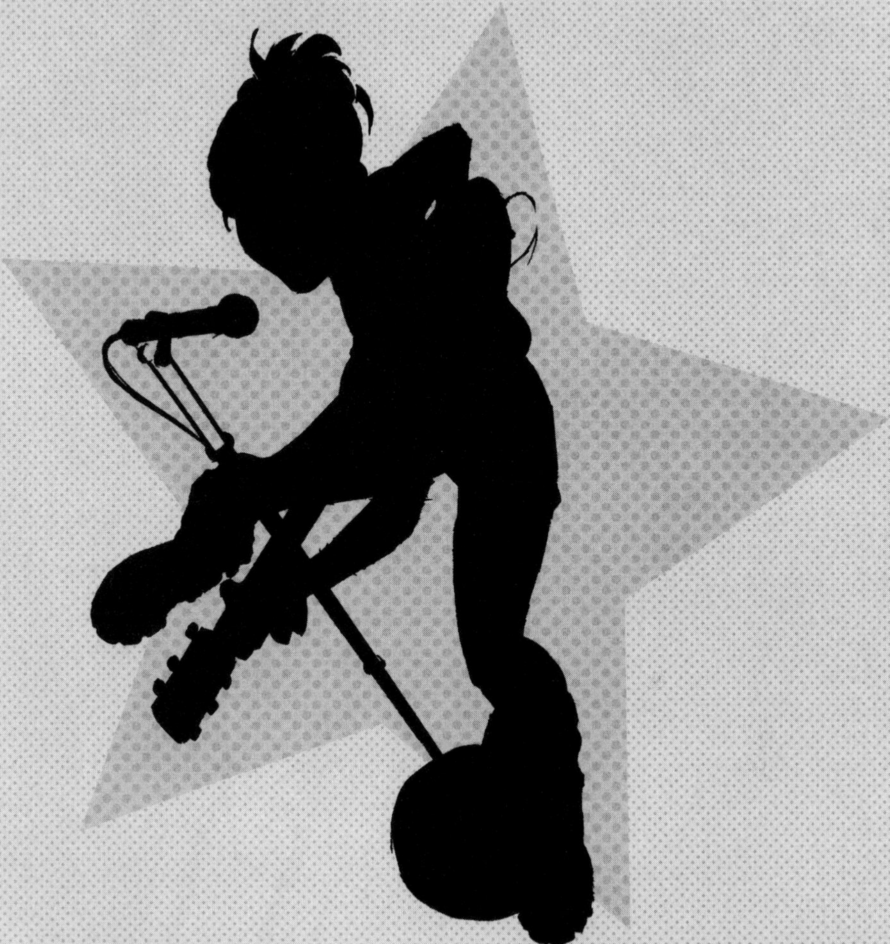

CHAPTER 2

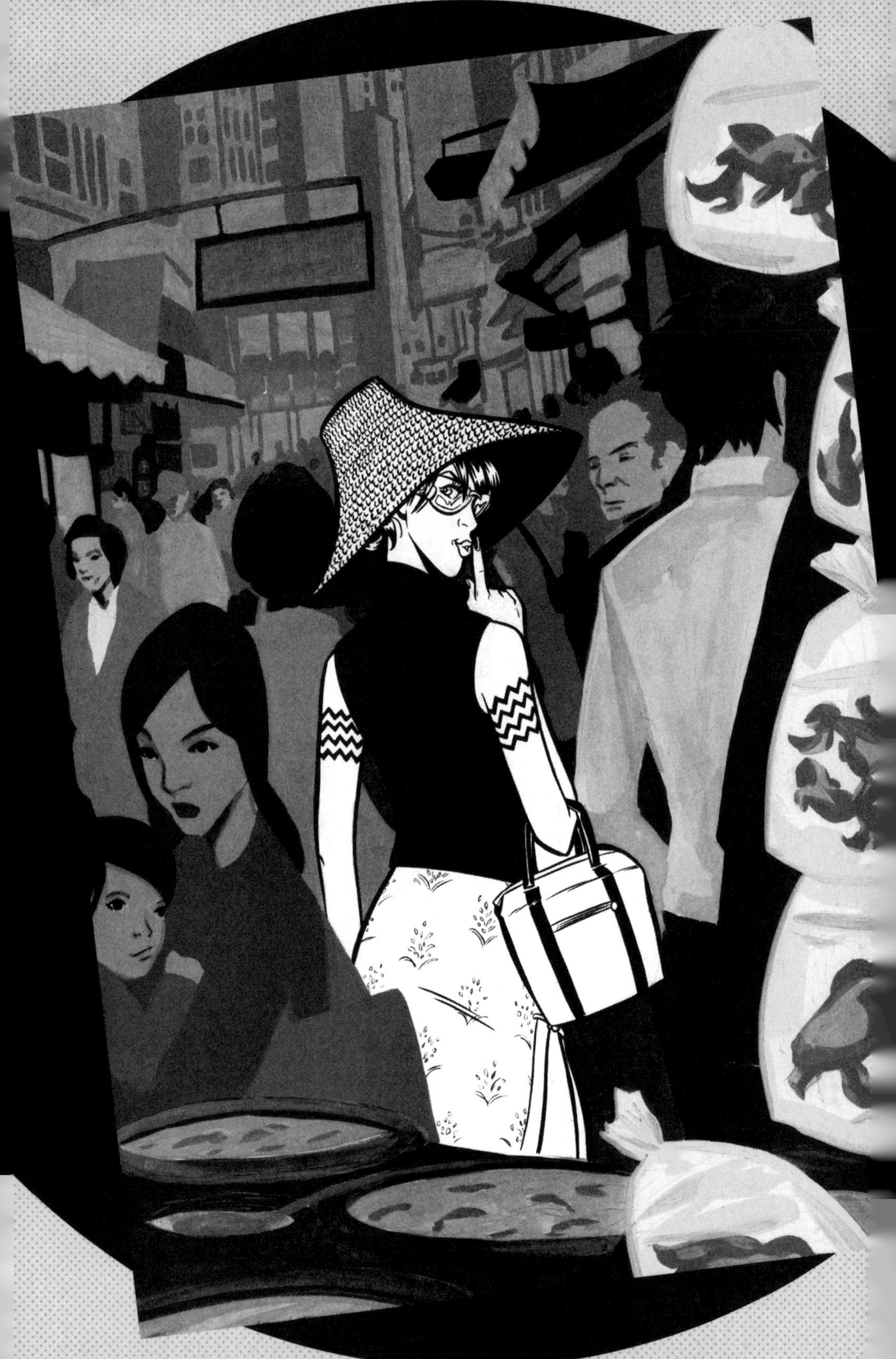

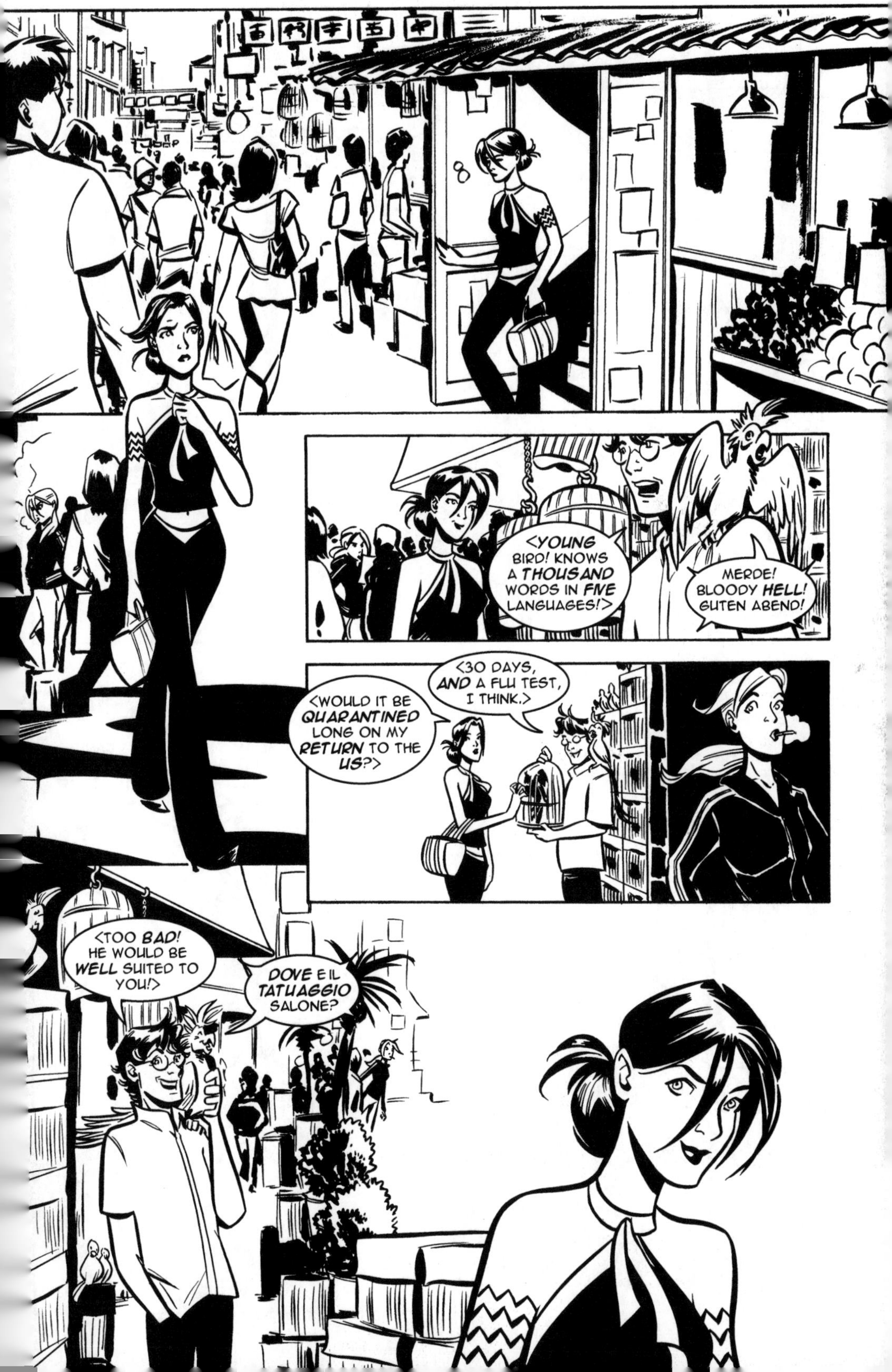
<YOUNG BIRD! KNOWS A THOUSAND WORDS IN FIVE LANGUAGES!>
MERDE! BLOODY HELL! GUTEN ABEND!
<WOULD IT BE QUARANTINED LONG ON MY RETURN TO THE US?>
<30 DAYS, AND A FLU TEST, I THINK.>
<TOO BAD! HE WOULD BE WELL SUITED TO YOU!>
DOVE E IL TATUAGGIO SALONE?

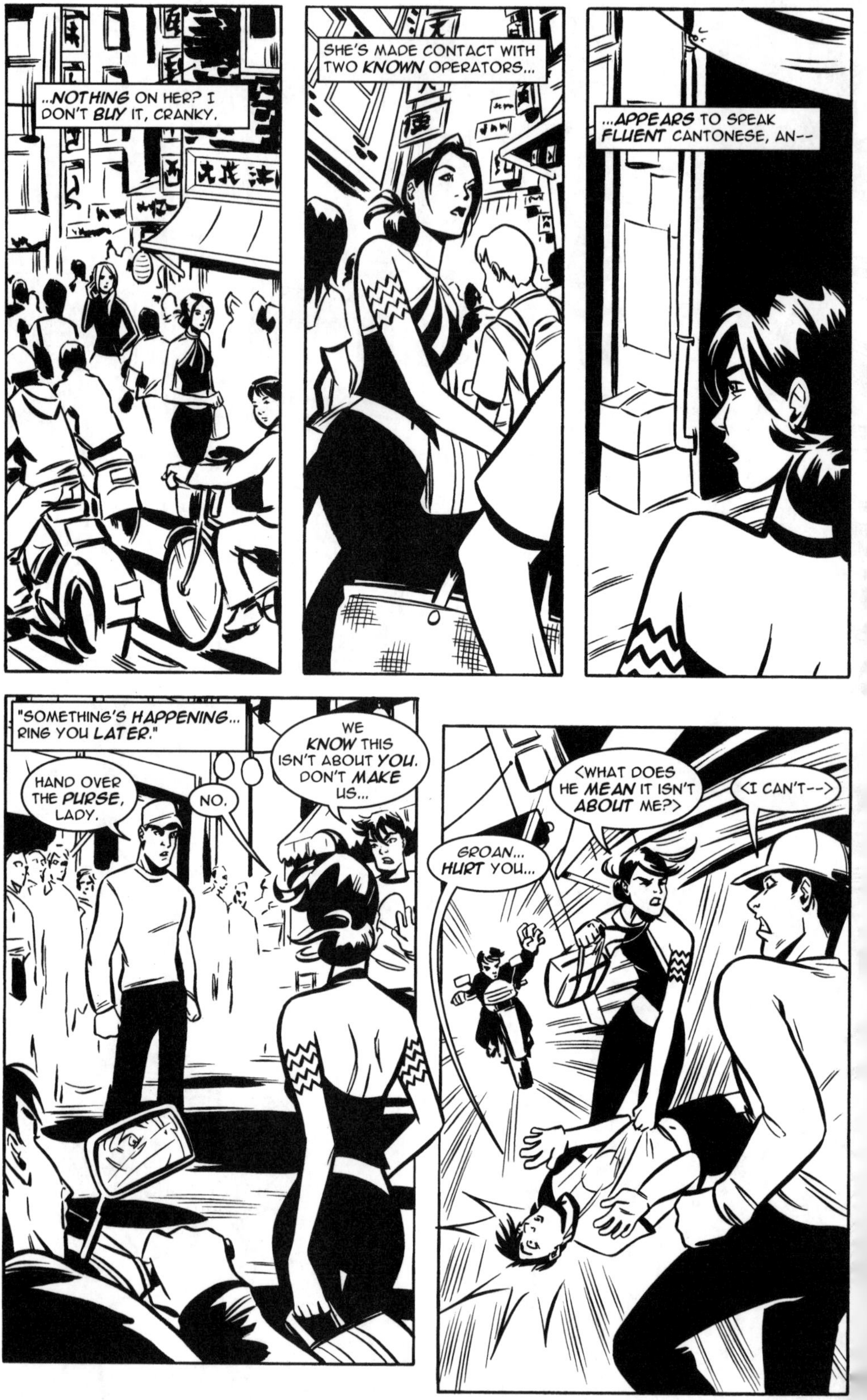
...NOTHING ON HER? I DON'T BUY IT, CRANKY.
SHE'S MADE CONTACT WITH TWO KNOWN OPERATORS...
...APPEARS TO SPEAK FLUENT CANTONESE, AN--
"SOMETHING'S HAPPENING... RING YOU LATER."
HAND OVER THE PURSE, LADY.
NO.
WE KNOW THIS ISN'T ABOUT YOU. DON'T MAKE US...
GROAN... HURT YOU...
<WHAT DOES HE MEAN IT ISN'T ABOUT ME?>
<I CAN'T-->

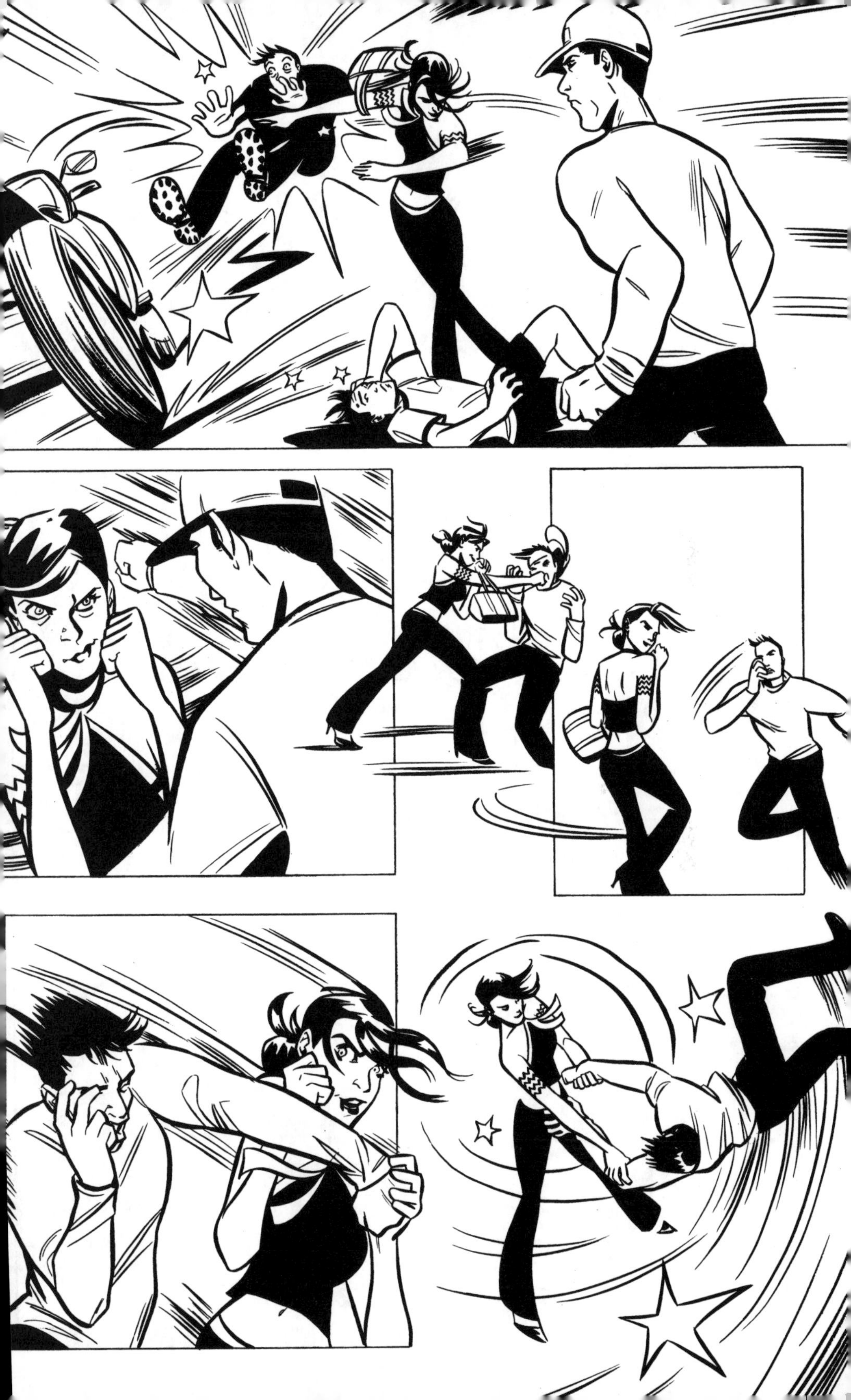

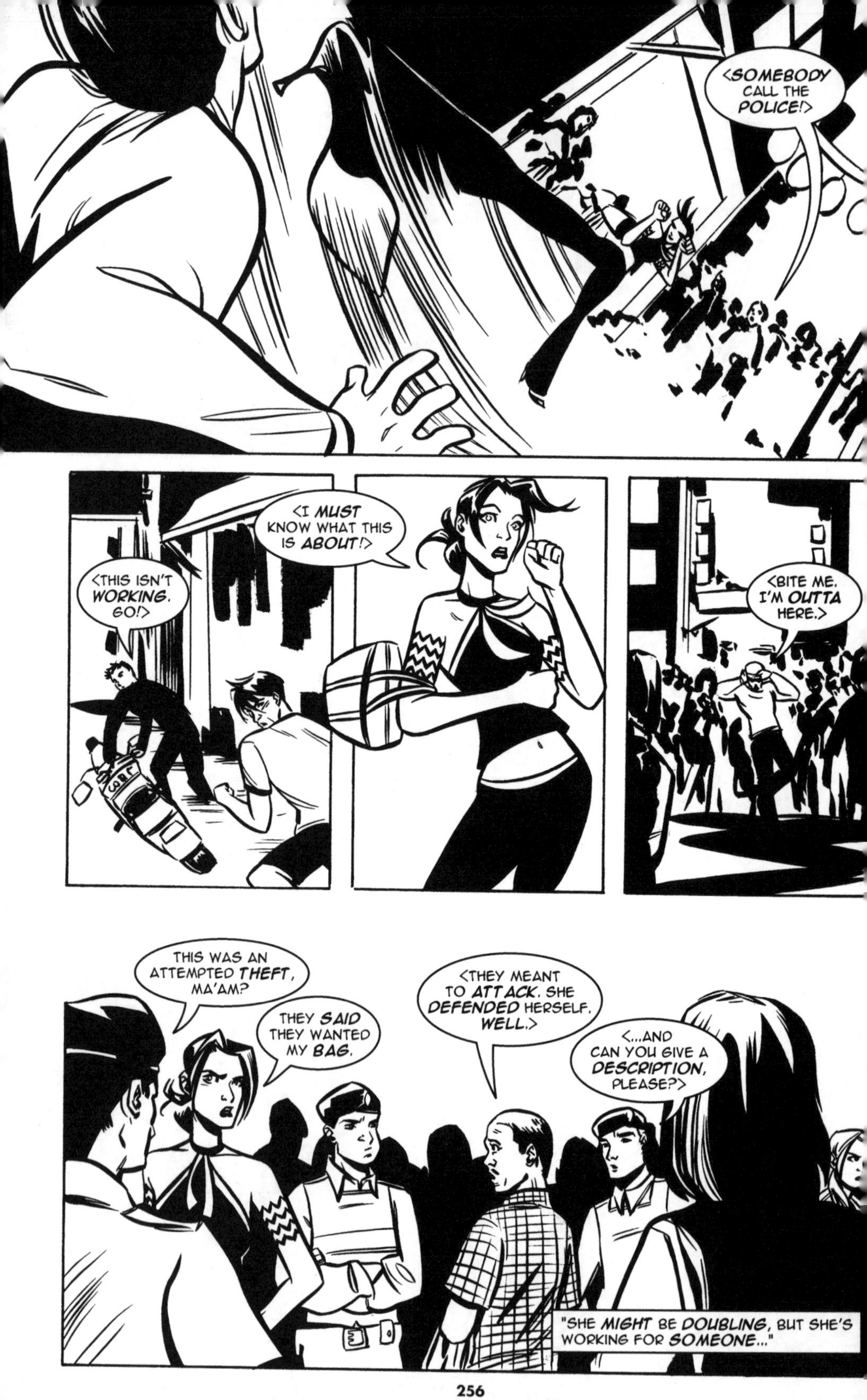
<SOMEBODY CALL THE POLICE!>
<I MUST KNOW WHAT THIS IS ABOUT!>
<THIS ISN'T WORKING. GO!>
<BITE ME. I'M OUTTA HERE.>
THIS WAS AN ATTEMPTED THEFT, MA'AM?
THEY SAID THEY WANTED MY BAG.
<THEY MEANT TO ATTACK. SHE DEFENDED HERSELF. WELL.>
<...AND CAN YOU GIVE A DESCRIPTION, PLEASE?>
"SHE MIGHT BE DOUBLING, BUT SHE'S WORKING FOR SOMEONE..."

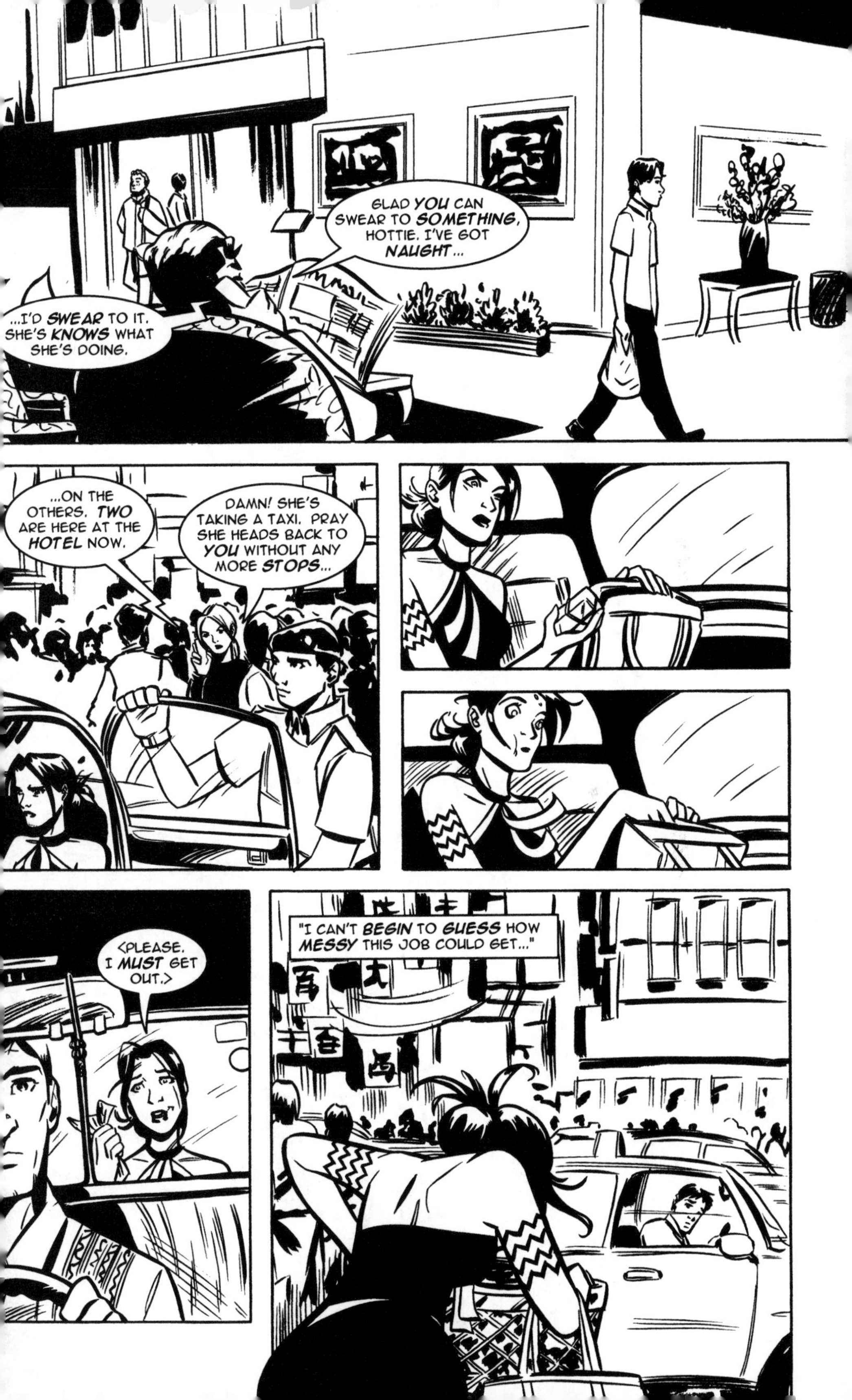
GLAD YOU CAN SWEAR TO SOMETHING, HOTTIE. I'VE GOT NAUGHT...
...I'D SWEAR TO IT. SHE'S KNOWS WHAT SHE'S DOING.
...ON THE OTHERS. TWO ARE HERE AT THE HOTEL NOW.
DAMN! SHE'S TAKING A TAXI. PRAY SHE HEADS BACK TO YOU WITHOUT ANY MORE STOPS...
<PLEASE. I MUST GET OUT.>
"I CAN'T BEGIN TO GUESS HOW MESSY THIS JOB COULD GET..."

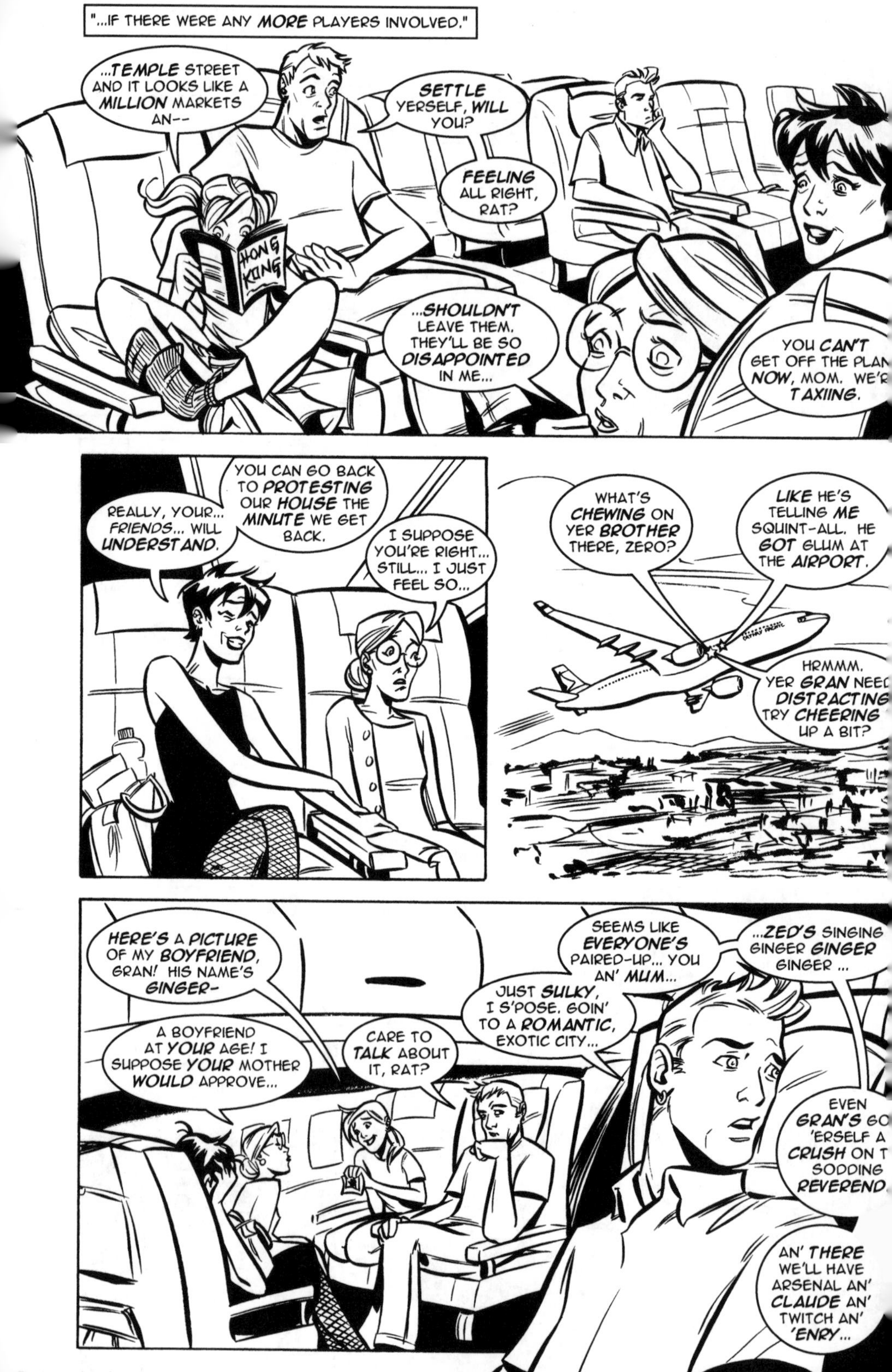
"...IF THERE WERE ANY MORE PLAYERS INVOLVED."
...TEMPLE STREET AND IT LOOKS LIKE A MILLION MARKETS AN--
SETTLE YERSELF, WILL YOU?
FEELING ALL RIGHT, RAT?
...SHOULDN'T LEAVE THEM. THEY'LL BE SO DISAPPOINTED IN ME...
YOU CAN'T GET OFF THE PLAN NOW, MOM. WE'R TAXIING.
HONG KONG
REALLY, YOUR... FRIENDS... WILL UNDERSTAND.
YOU CAN GO BACK TO PROTESTING OUR HOUSE THE MINUTE WE GET BACK.
I SUPPOSE YOU'RE RIGHT... STILL... I JUST FEEL SO...
WHAT'S CHEWING ON YER BROTHER THERE, ZERO?
LIKE HE'S TELLING ME SQUINT-ALL. HE GOT GLUM AT THE AIRPORT.
HRMMM. YER GRAN NEED DISTRACTING TRY CHEERING UP A BIT?
HERE'S A PICTURE OF MY BOYFRIEND, GRAN! HIS NAME'S GINGER-
A BOYFRIEND AT YOUR AGE! I SUPPOSE YOUR MOTHER WOULD APPROVE...
CARE TO TALK ABOUT IT, RAT?
JUST SULKY, I S'POSE. GOIN' TO A ROMANTIC, EXOTIC CITY...
SEEMS LIKE EVERYONE'S PAIRED-UP... YOU AN' MUM...
...ZED'S SINGING GINGER GINGER GINGER ...
EVEN GRAN'S GO 'ERSELF A CRUSH ON T SODDING REVEREND.
AN' THERE WE'LL HAVE ARSENAL AN' CLAUDE AN' TWITCH AN' 'ENRY...

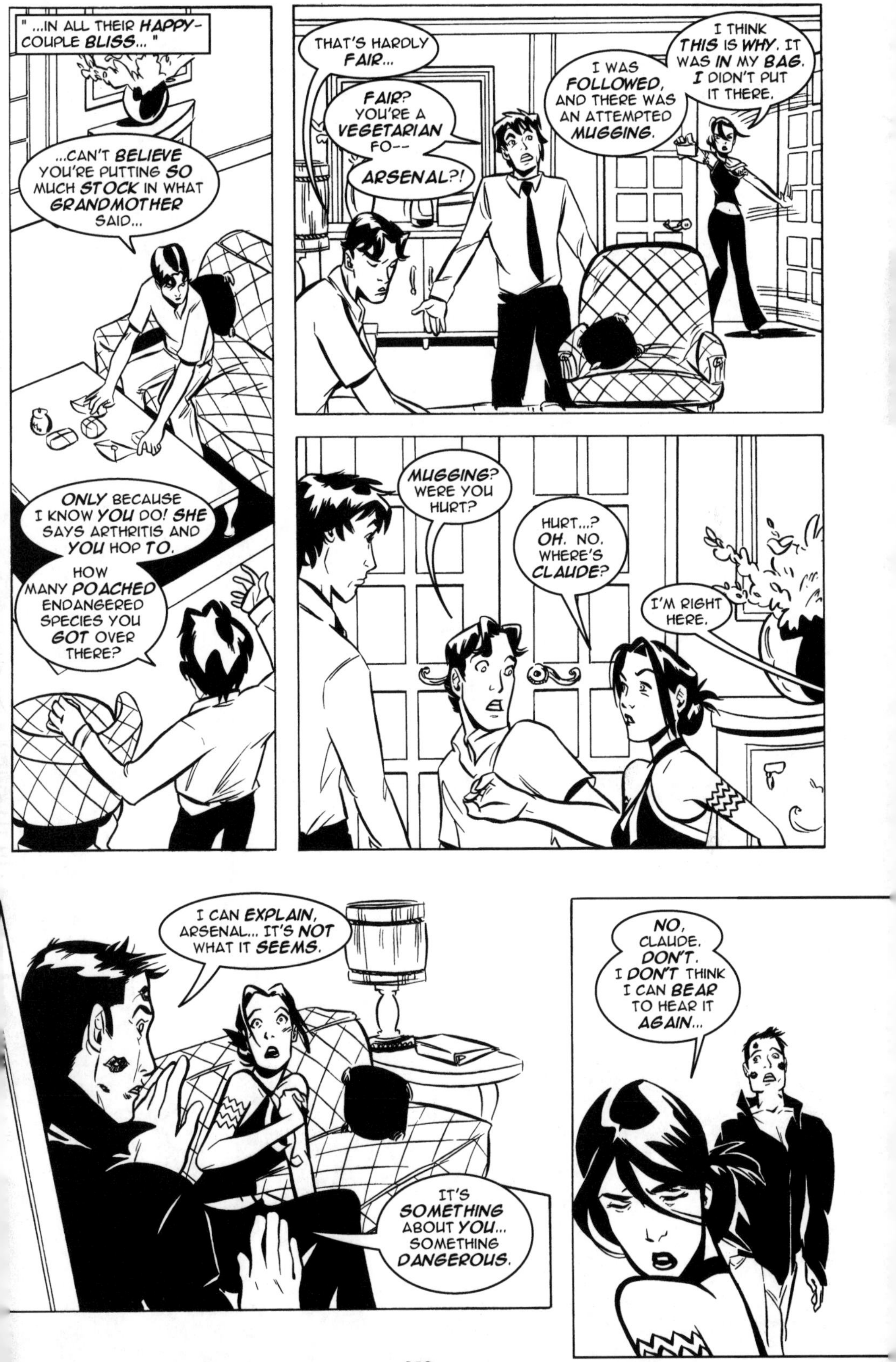
" ...IN ALL THEIR HAPPY-COUPLE BLISS... "
...CAN'T BELIEVE YOU'RE PUTTING SO MUCH STOCK IN WHAT GRANDMOTHER SAID...
ONLY BECAUSE I KNOW YOU DO! SHE SAYS ARTHRITIS AND YOU HOP TO.
HOW MANY POACHED ENDANGERED SPECIES YOU GOT OVER THERE?
THAT'S HARDLY FAIR...
FAIR? YOU'RE A VEGETARIAN FO--
ARSENAL?!
I WAS FOLLOWED, AND THERE WAS AN ATTEMPTED MUGGING.
I THINK THIS IS WHY. IT WAS IN MY BAG. I DIDN'T PUT IT THERE.
MUGGING? WERE YOU HURT?
HURT...? OH. NO. WHERE'S CLAUDE?
I'M RIGHT HERE.
I CAN EXPLAIN, ARSENAL... IT'S NOT WHAT IT SEEMS.
IT'S SOMETHING ABOUT YOU... SOMETHING DANGEROUS.
NO, CLAUDE. DON'T. I DON'T THINK I CAN BEAR TO HEAR IT AGAIN...

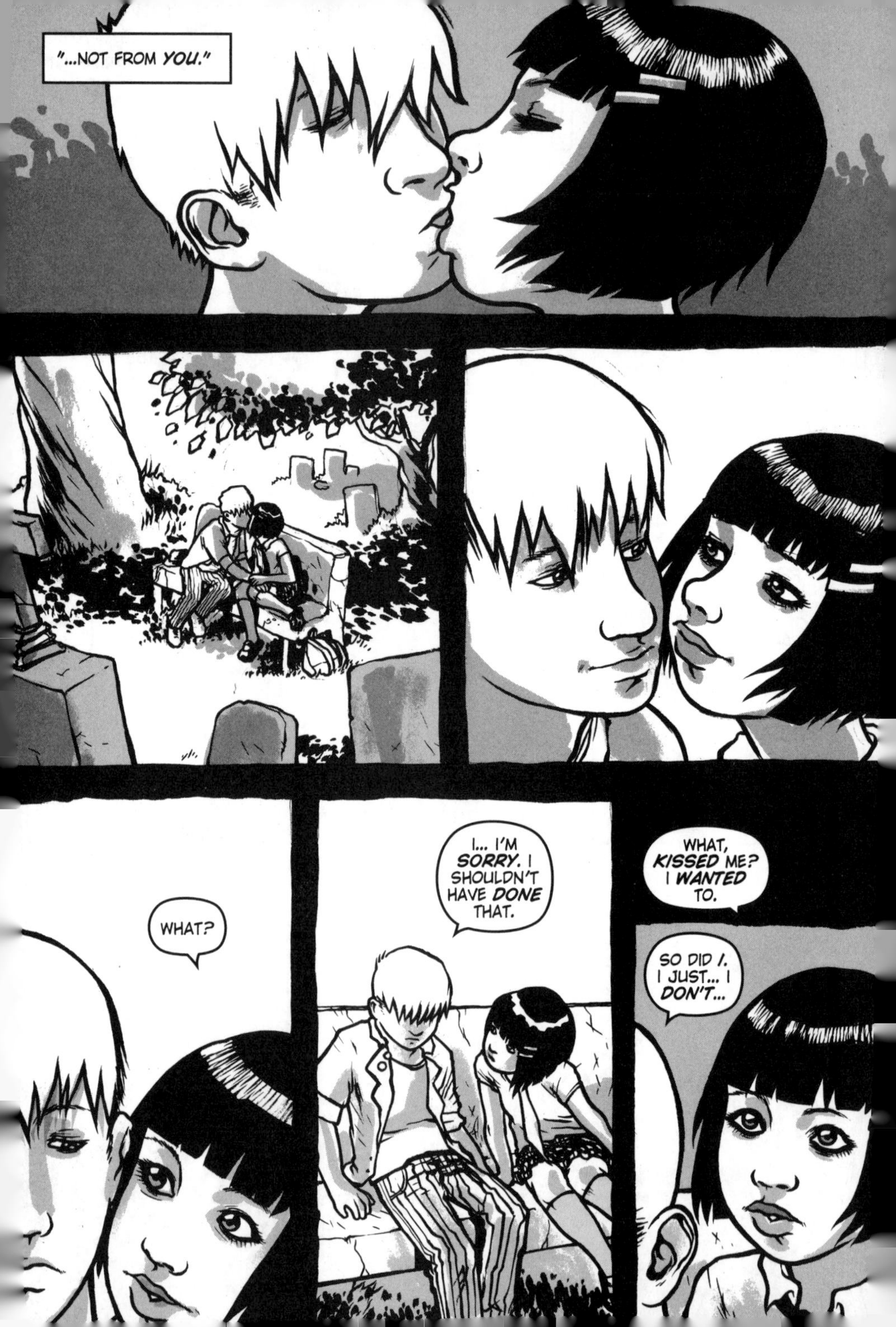
"...NOT FROM *YOU.*"
WHAT?
I... I'M *SORRY*. I SHOULDN'T HAVE *DONE* THAT.
WHAT, *KISSED* ME? I *WANTED* TO.
SO DID *I*. I JUST... I *DON'T*...

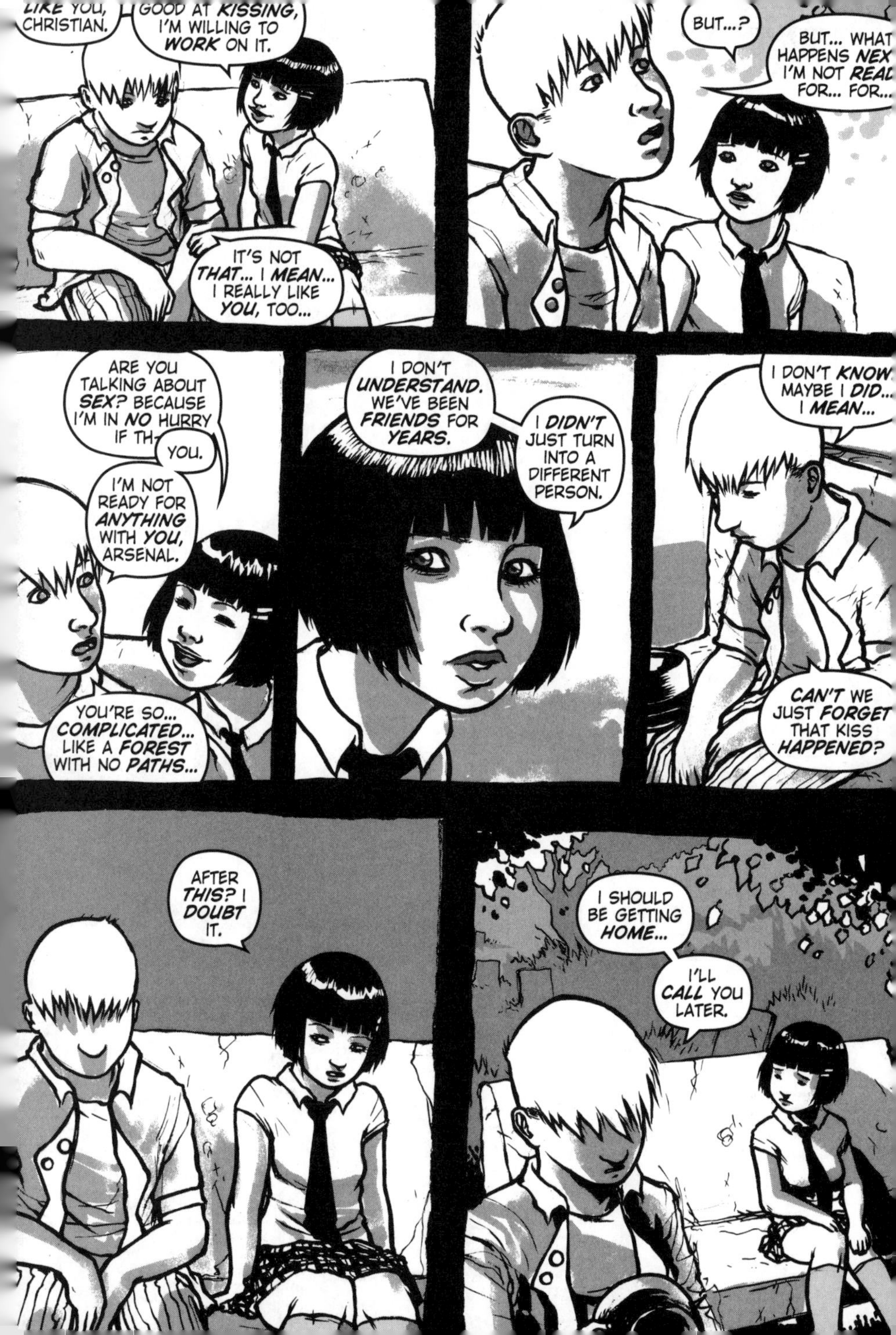
LIKE YOU, CHRISTIAN.
GOOD AT KISSING, I'M WILLING TO WORK ON IT.
IT'S NOT THAT... I MEAN... I REALLY LIKE YOU, TOO...
BUT...?
BUT... WHAT HAPPENS NEX I'M NOT REAL FOR... FOR...
ARE YOU TALKING ABOUT SEX? BECAUSE I'M IN NO HURRY IF TH-
YOU.
I'M NOT READY FOR ANYTHING WITH YOU, ARSENAL.
YOU'RE SO... COMPLICATED... LIKE A FOREST WITH NO PATHS...
I DON'T UNDERSTAND. WE'VE BEEN FRIENDS FOR YEARS.
I DIDN'T JUST TURN INTO A DIFFERENT PERSON.
I DON'T KNOW. MAYBE I DID... I MEAN...
CAN'T WE JUST FORGET THAT KISS HAPPENED?
AFTER THIS? I DOUBT IT.
I SHOULD BE GETTING HOME...
I'LL CALL YOU LATER.

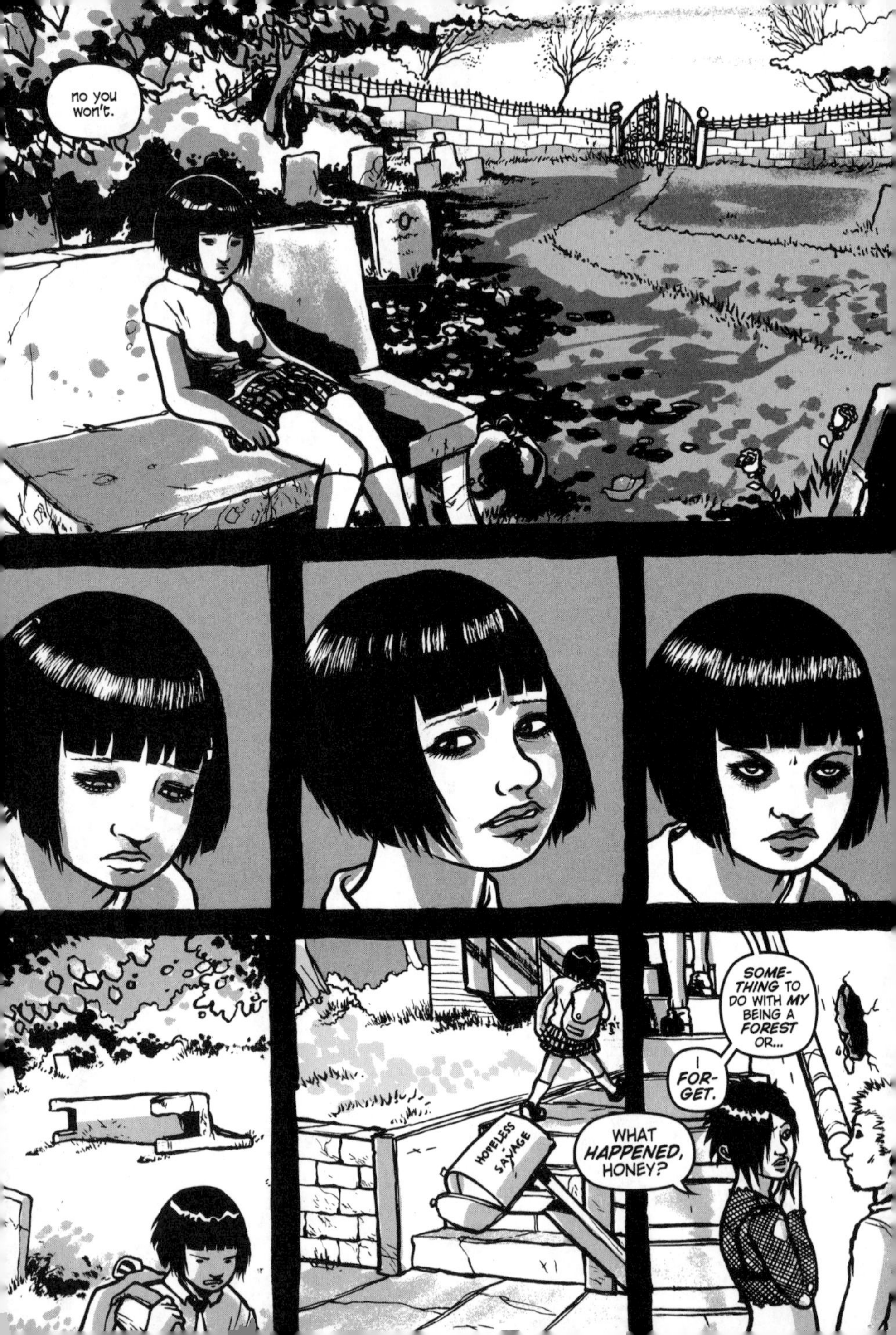
no you won't.
HOPELESS SAVAGE
SOME-THING TO DO WITH MY BEING A FOREST OR...
I FOR-GET.
WHAT HAPPENED, HONEY?

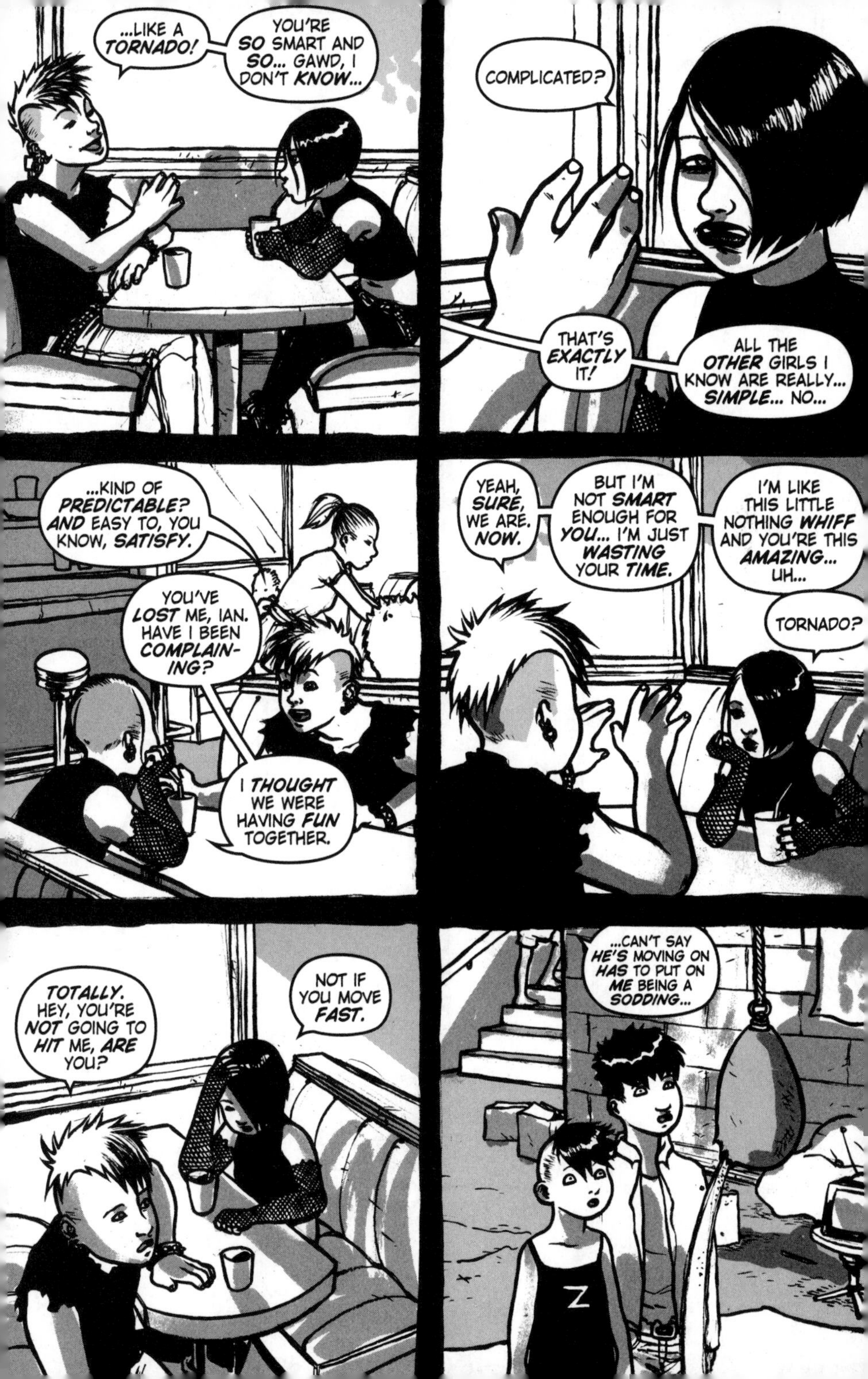
...LIKE A TORNADO!
YOU'RE SO SMART AND SO... GAWD, I DON'T KNOW...
COMPLICATED?
THAT'S EXACTLY IT!
ALL THE OTHER GIRLS I KNOW ARE REALLY... SIMPLE... NO...
...KIND OF PREDICTABLE? AND EASY TO, YOU KNOW, SATISFY.
YOU'VE LOST ME, IAN. HAVE I BEEN COMPLAINING?
I THOUGHT WE WERE HAVING FUN TOGETHER.
YEAH, SURE, WE ARE. NOW.
BUT I'M NOT SMART ENOUGH FOR YOU... I'M JUST WASTING YOUR TIME.
I'M LIKE THIS LITTLE NOTHING WHIFF AND YOU'RE THIS AMAZING... UH...
TORNADO?
TOTALLY. HEY, YOU'RE NOT GOING TO HIT ME, ARE YOU?
NOT IF YOU MOVE FAST.
...CAN'T SAY HE'S MOVING ON HAS TO PUT ON ME BEING A SODDING...

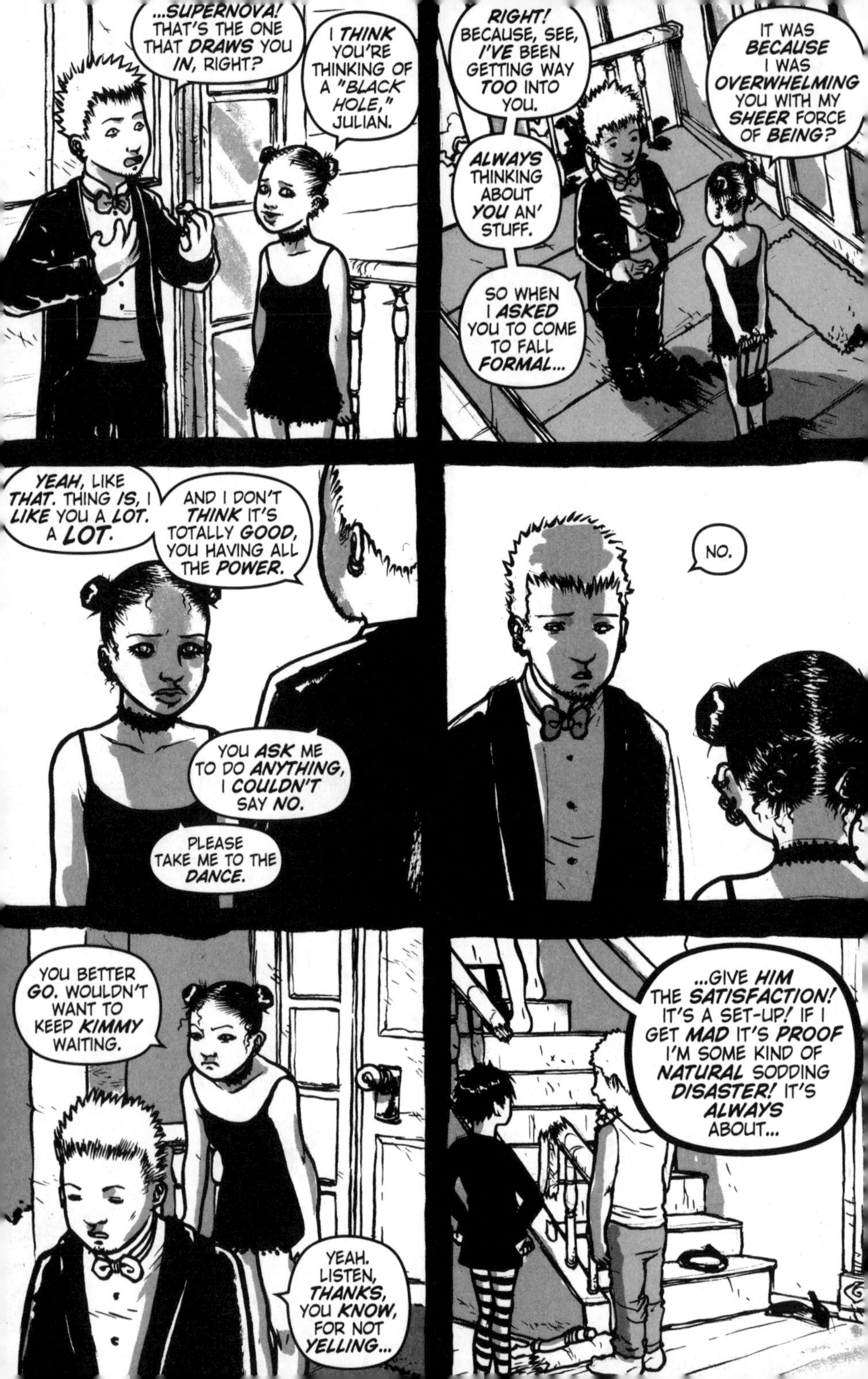

...SUPERNOVA! THAT'S THE ONE THAT DRAWS YOU IN, RIGHT?
I THINK YOU'RE THINKING OF A "BLACK HOLE," JULIAN.
RIGHT! BECAUSE, SEE, I'VE BEEN GETTING WAY TOO INTO YOU.
ALWAYS THINKING ABOUT YOU AN' STUFF.
SO WHEN I ASKED YOU TO COME TO FALL FORMAL...
IT WAS BECAUSE I WAS OVERWHELMING YOU WITH MY SHEER FORCE OF BEING?
YEAH, LIKE THAT. THING IS, I LIKE YOU A LOT. A LOT.
AND I DON'T THINK IT'S TOTALLY GOOD, YOU HAVING ALL THE POWER.
YOU ASK ME TO DO ANYTHING, I COULDN'T SAY NO.
PLEASE TAKE ME TO THE DANCE.
NO.
YOU BETTER GO. WOULDN'T WANT TO KEEP KIMMY WAITING.
YEAH. LISTEN, THANKS, YOU KNOW, FOR NOT YELLING...
...GIVE HIM THE SATISFACTION! IT'S A SET-UP! IF I GET MAD IT'S PROOF I'M SOME KIND OF NATURAL SODDING DISASTER! IT'S ALWAYS ABOUT...

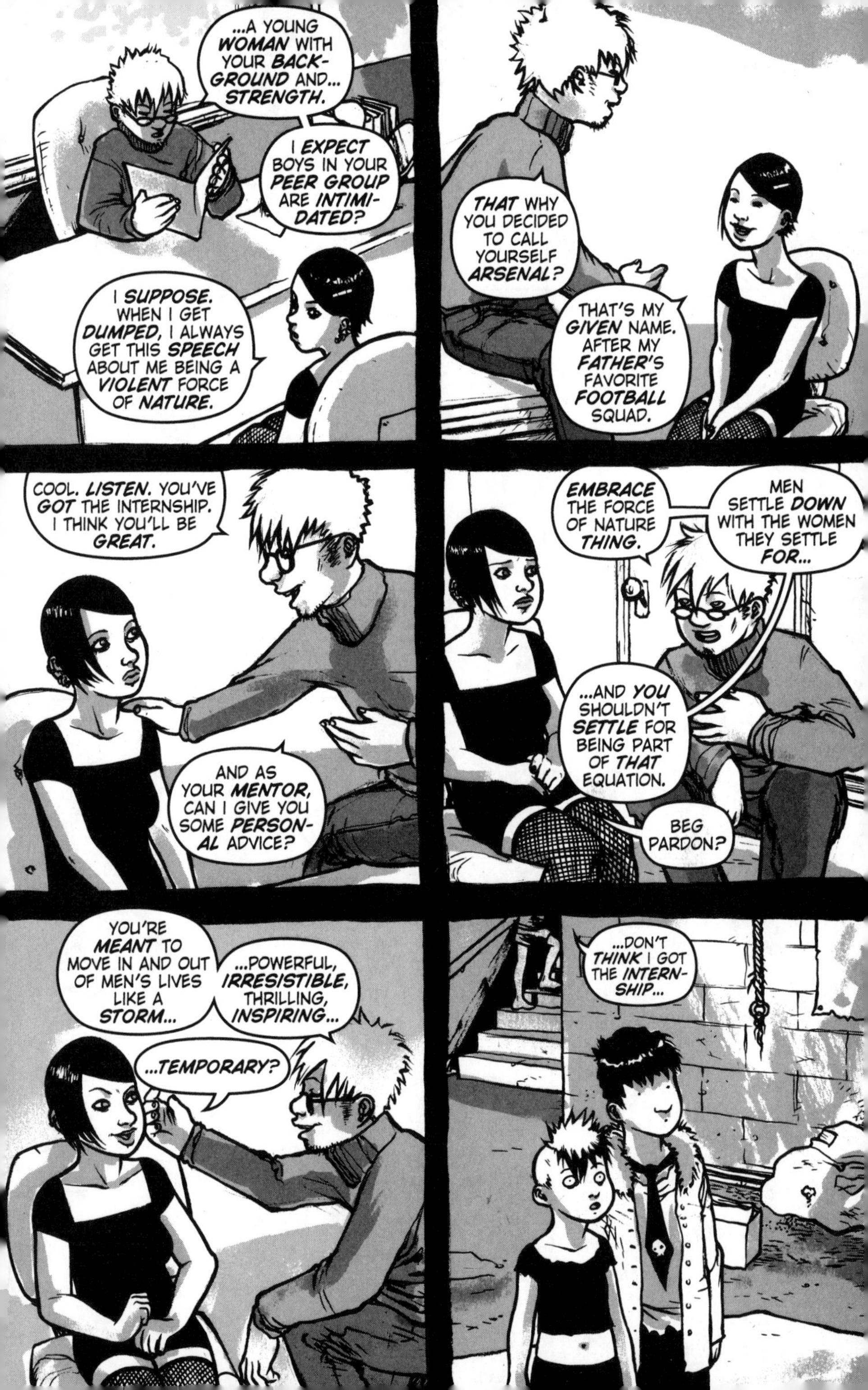
...A YOUNG WOMAN WITH YOUR BACK-GROUND AND... STRENGTH.
I EXPECT BOYS IN YOUR PEER GROUP ARE INTIMI-DATED?
I SUPPOSE. WHEN I GET DUMPED, I ALWAYS GET THIS SPEECH ABOUT ME BEING A VIOLENT FORCE OF NATURE.
THAT WHY YOU DECIDED TO CALL YOURSELF ARSENAL?
THAT'S MY GIVEN NAME. AFTER MY FATHER'S FAVORITE FOOTBALL SQUAD.
COOL. LISTEN. YOU'VE GOT THE INTERNSHIP. I THINK YOU'LL BE GREAT.
AND AS YOUR MENTOR, CAN I GIVE YOU SOME PERSON-AL ADVICE?
EMBRACE THE FORCE OF NATURE THING.
MEN SETTLE DOWN WITH THE WOMEN THEY SETTLE FOR...
...AND YOU SHOULDN'T SETTLE FOR BEING PART OF THAT EQUATION.
BEG PARDON?
YOU'RE MEANT TO MOVE IN AND OUT OF MEN'S LIVES LIKE A STORM...
...POWERFUL, IRRESISTIBLE, THRILLING, INSPIRING...
...TEMPORARY?
...DON'T THINK I GOT THE INTERN-SHIP...

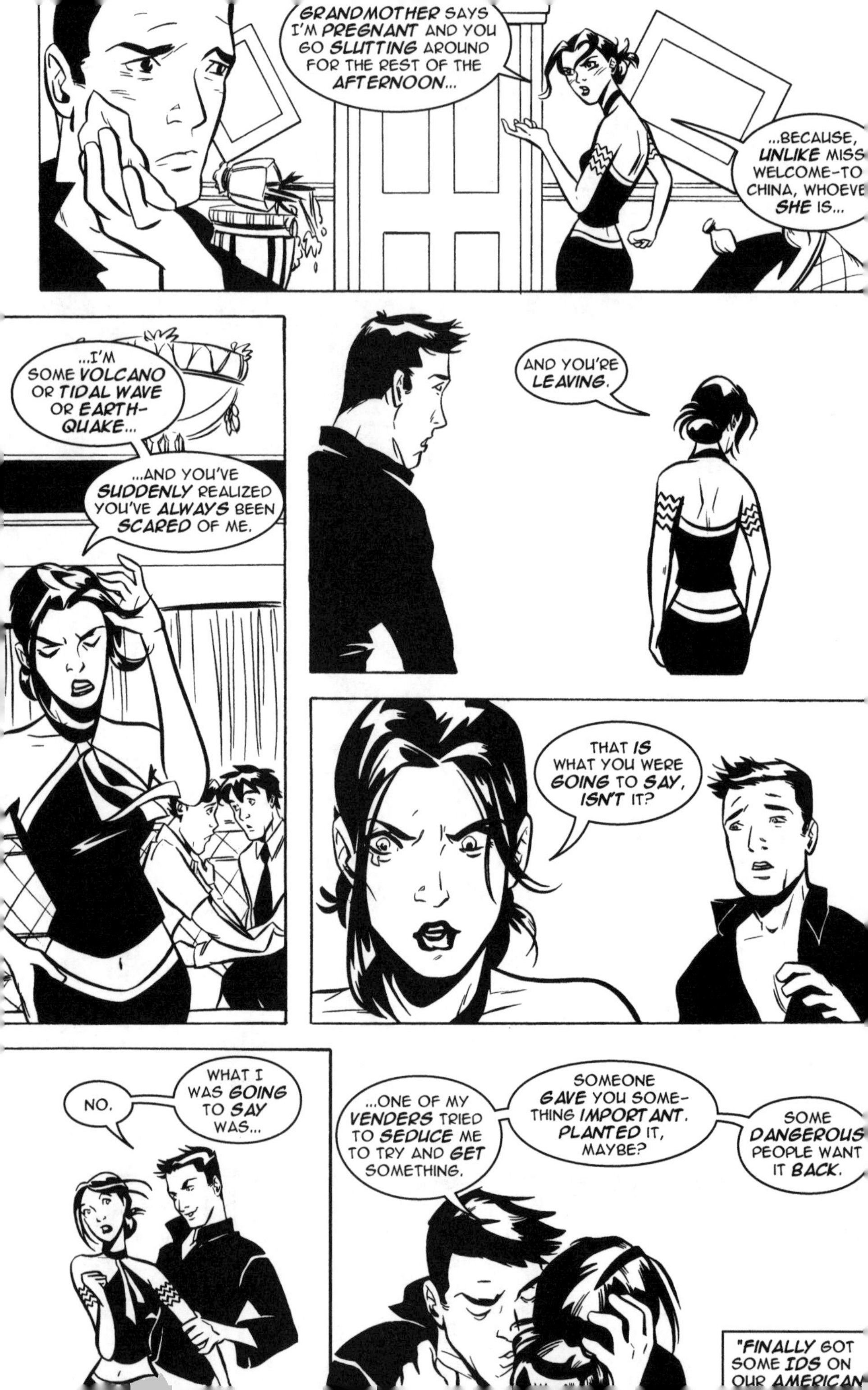
GRANDMOTHER SAYS I'M PREGNANT AND YOU GO SLUTTING AROUND FOR THE REST OF THE AFTERNOON...
...BECAUSE, UNLIKE MISS WELCOME-TO CHINA, WHOEVE SHE IS...
...I'M SOME VOLCANO OR TIDAL WAVE OR EARTH-QUAKE...
...AND YOU'VE SUDDENLY REALIZED YOU'VE ALWAYS BEEN SCARED OF ME.
AND YOU'RE LEAVING.
THAT IS WHAT YOU WERE GOING TO SAY, ISN'T IT?
NO.
WHAT I WAS GOING TO SAY WAS...
...ONE OF MY VENDERS TRIED TO SEDUCE ME TO TRY AND GET SOMETHING.
SOMEONE GAVE YOU SOME-THING IMPORTANT. PLANTED IT, MAYBE?
SOME DANGEROUS PEOPLE WANT IT BACK.
"FINALLY GOT SOME IDS ON OUR AMERICAN

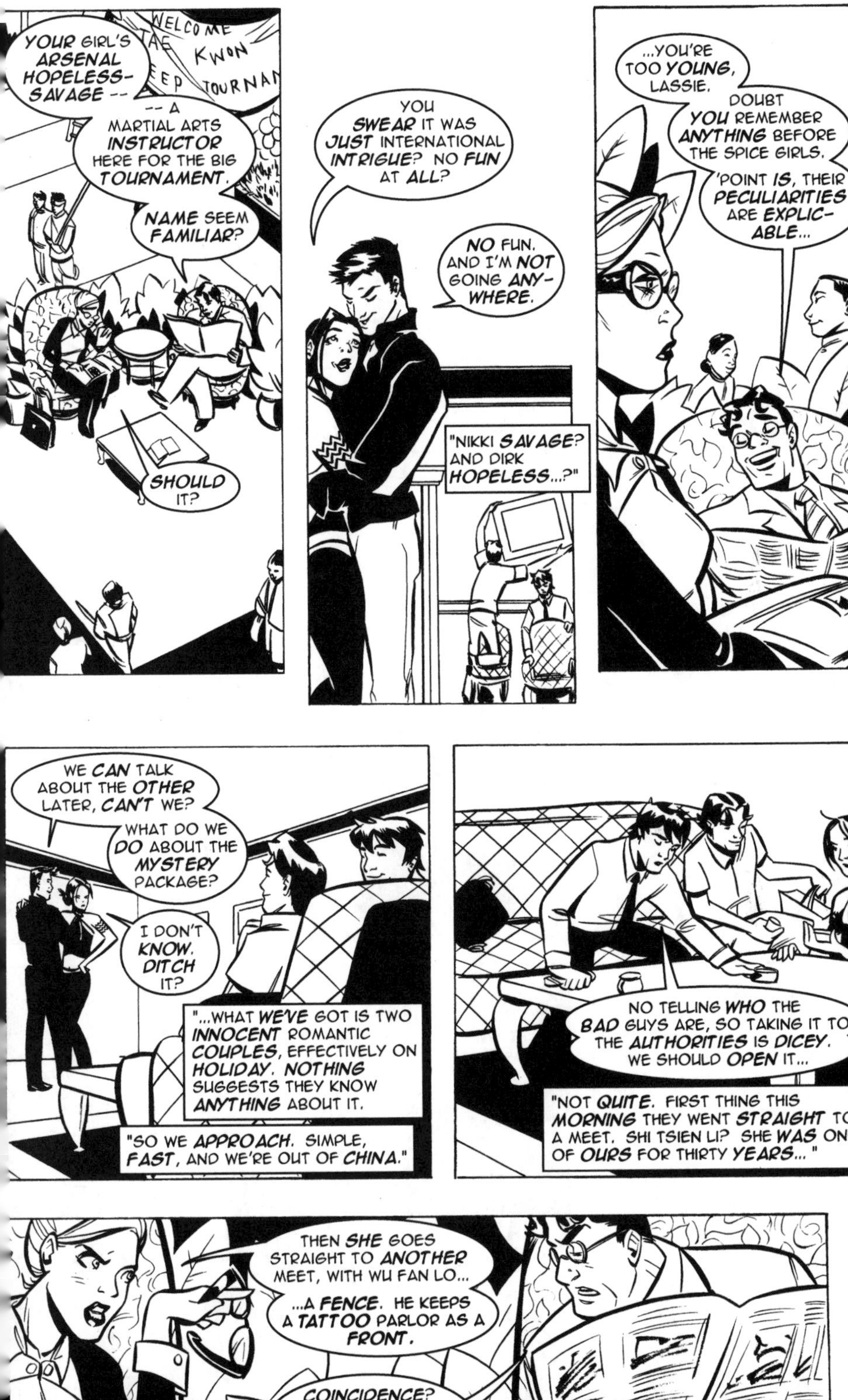

YOUR GIRL'S ARSENAL HOPELESS-SAVAGE --
-- A MARTIAL ARTS INSTRUCTOR HERE FOR THE BIG TOURNAMENT.
NAME SEEM FAMILIAR?
SHOULD IT?
YOU SWEAR IT WAS JUST INTERNATIONAL INTRIGUE? NO FUN AT ALL?
NO FUN. AND I'M NOT GOING ANYWHERE.
"NIKKI SAVAGE? AND DIRK HOPELESS...?"
...YOU'RE TOO YOUNG, LASSIE.
DOUBT YOU REMEMBER ANYTHING BEFORE THE SPICE GIRLS.
'POINT IS, THEIR PECULIARITIES ARE EXPLICABLE...
WE CAN TALK ABOUT THE OTHER LATER, CAN'T WE?
WHAT DO WE DO ABOUT THE MYSTERY PACKAGE?
I DON'T KNOW. DITCH IT?
"...WHAT WE'VE GOT IS TWO INNOCENT ROMANTIC COUPLES, EFFECTIVELY ON HOLIDAY. NOTHING SUGGESTS THEY KNOW ANYTHING ABOUT IT.
"SO WE APPROACH. SIMPLE, FAST, AND WE'RE OUT OF CHINA."
NO TELLING WHO THE BAD GUYS ARE, SO TAKING IT TO THE AUTHORITIES IS DICEY. WE SHOULD OPEN IT...
"NOT QUITE. FIRST THING THIS MORNING THEY WENT STRAIGHT TO A MEET. SHI TSIEN LI? SHE WAS ONE OF OURS FOR THIRTY YEARS..."
THEN SHE GOES STRAIGHT TO ANOTHER MEET, WITH WU FAN LO...
...A FENCE. HE KEEPS A TATTOO PARLOR AS A FRONT.
COINCIDENCE? IT'S POSSIBLE SHE JUST WENT TO GET A TATTOO...

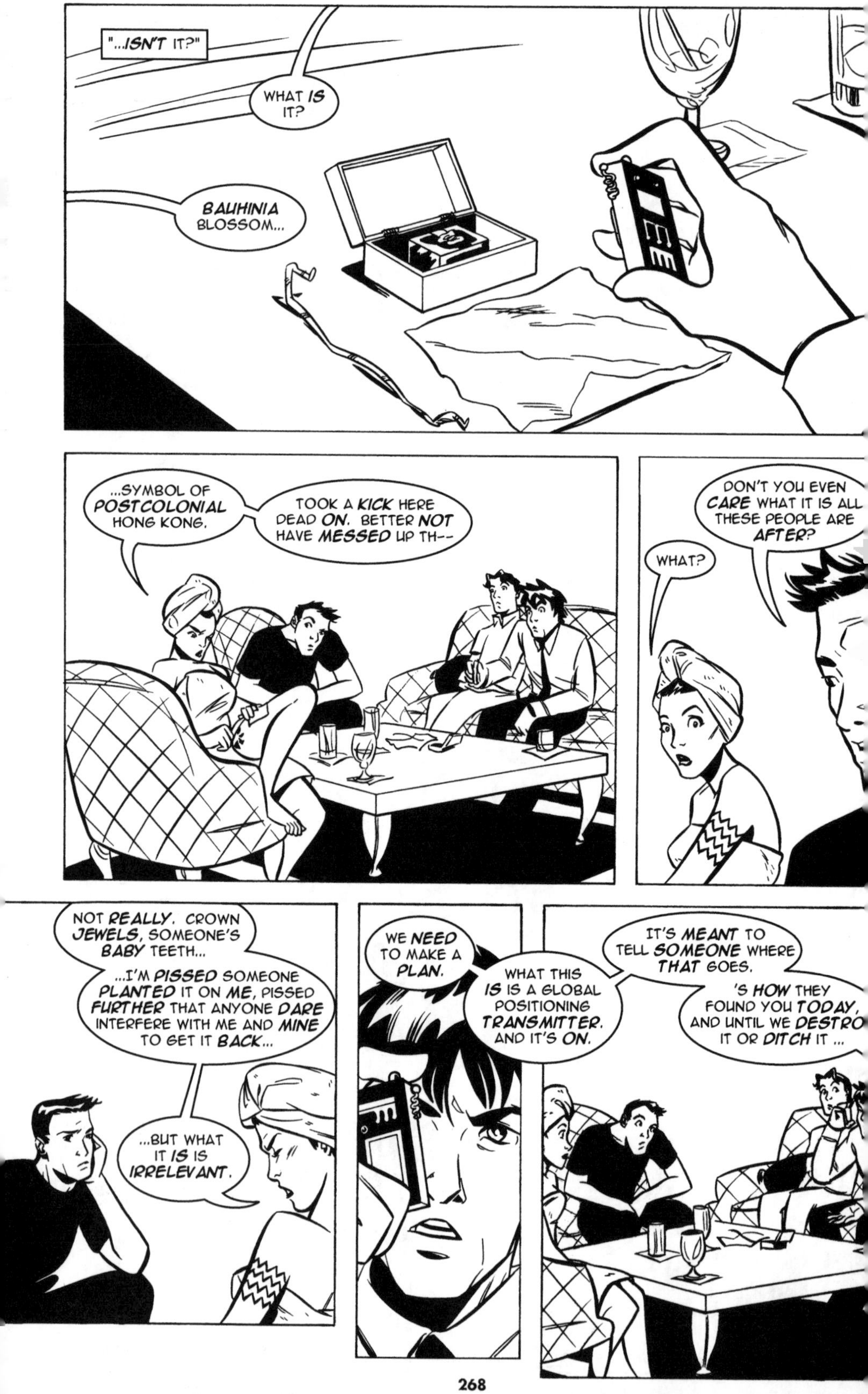
"...ISN'T IT?"
WHAT IS IT?
BAUHINIA BLOSSOM...
...SYMBOL OF POSTCOLONIAL HONG KONG.
TOOK A KICK HERE DEAD ON. BETTER NOT HAVE MESSED UP TH--
DON'T YOU EVEN CARE WHAT IT IS ALL THESE PEOPLE ARE AFTER?
WHAT?
NOT REALLY. CROWN JEWELS, SOMEONE'S BABY TEETH...
...I'M PISSED SOMEONE PLANTED IT ON ME, PISSED FURTHER THAT ANYONE DARE INTERFERE WITH ME AND MINE TO GET IT BACK...
...BUT WHAT IT IS IS IRRELEVANT.
WE NEED TO MAKE A PLAN.
WHAT THIS IS IS A GLOBAL POSITIONING TRANSMITTER. AND IT'S ON.
IT'S MEANT TO TELL SOMEONE WHERE THAT GOES.
'S HOW THEY FOUND YOU TODAY, AND UNTIL WE DESTRO
IT OR DITCH IT ...

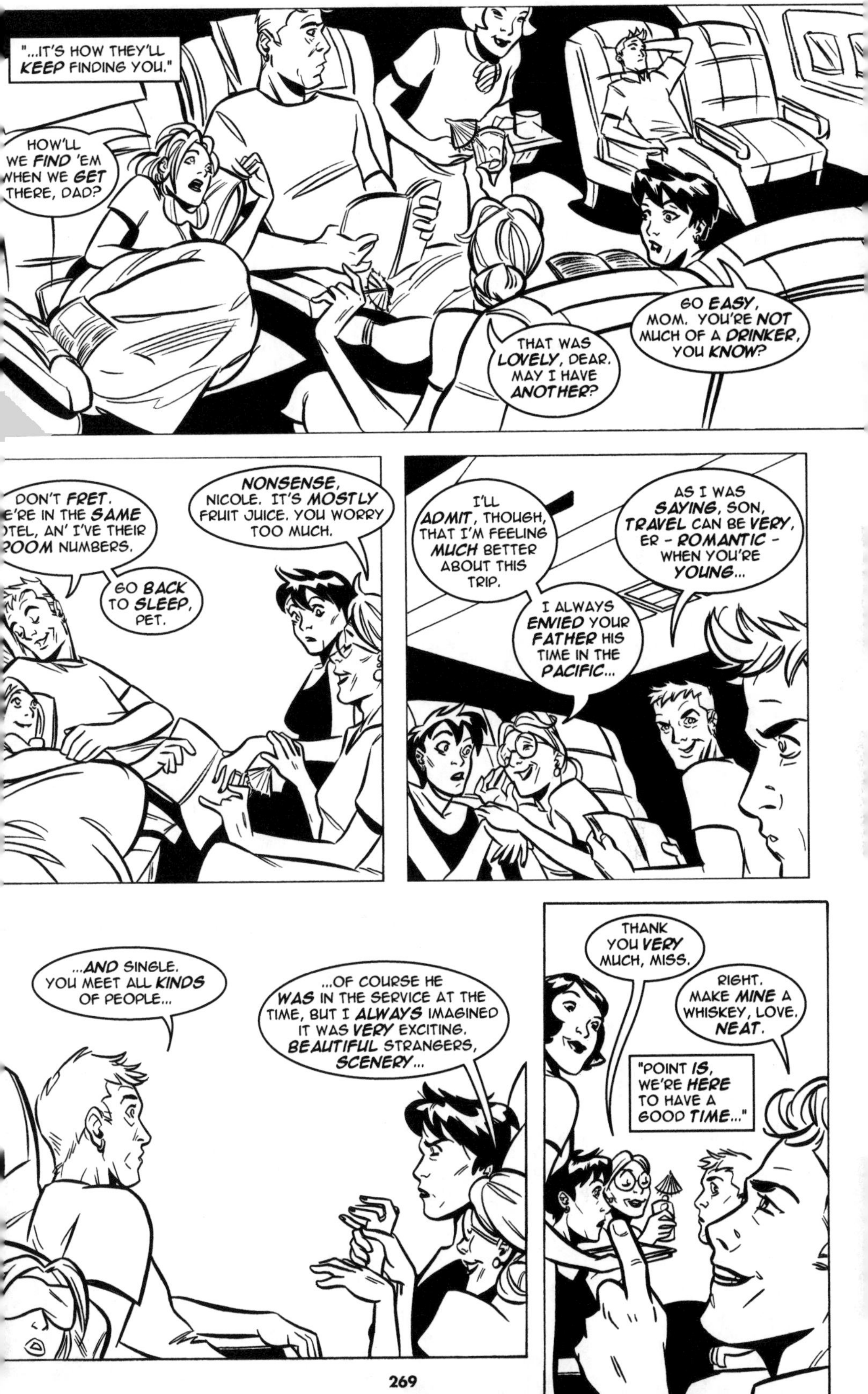
"...IT'S HOW THEY'LL KEEP FINDING YOU."
HOW'LL WE FIND 'EM WHEN WE GET THERE, DAD?
THAT WAS LOVELY, DEAR. MAY I HAVE ANOTHER?
GO EASY, MOM. YOU'RE NOT MUCH OF A DRINKER, YOU KNOW?
DON'T FRET. E'RE IN THE SAME OTEL, AN' I'VE THEIR ROOM NUMBERS.
GO BACK TO SLEEP, PET.
NONSENSE, NICOLE. IT'S MOSTLY FRUIT JUICE. YOU WORRY TOO MUCH.
I'LL ADMIT, THOUGH, THAT I'M FEELING MUCH BETTER ABOUT THIS TRIP.
I ALWAYS ENVIED YOUR FATHER HIS TIME IN THE PACIFIC...
AS I WAS SAYING, SON, TRAVEL CAN BE VERY, ER - ROMANTIC - WHEN YOU'RE YOUNG...
...AND SINGLE. YOU MEET ALL KINDS OF PEOPLE...
...OF COURSE HE WAS IN THE SERVICE AT THE TIME, BUT I ALWAYS IMAGINED IT WAS VERY EXCITING. BEAUTIFUL STRANGERS, SCENERY...
THANK YOU VERY MUCH, MISS.
RIGHT. MAKE MINE A WHISKEY, LOVE. NEAT.
"POINT IS, WE'RE HERE TO HAVE A GOOD TIME..."

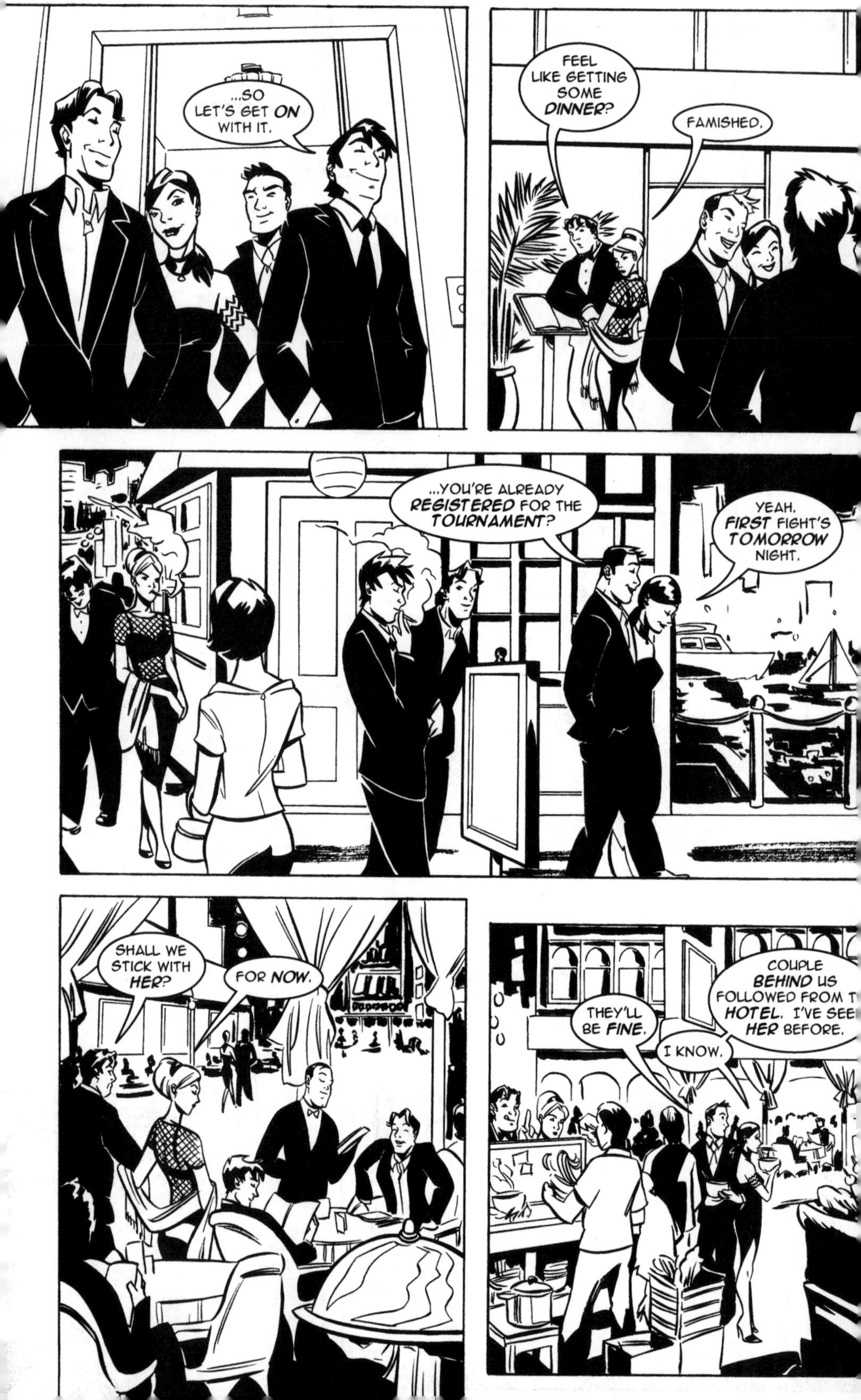
...SO LET'S GET ON WITH IT.
FEEL LIKE GETTING SOME DINNER?
FAMISHED.
...YOU'RE ALREADY REGISTERED FOR THE TOURNAMENT?
YEAH. FIRST FIGHT'S TOMORROW NIGHT.
SHALL WE STICK WITH HER?
FOR NOW.
THEY'LL BE FINE.
I KNOW.

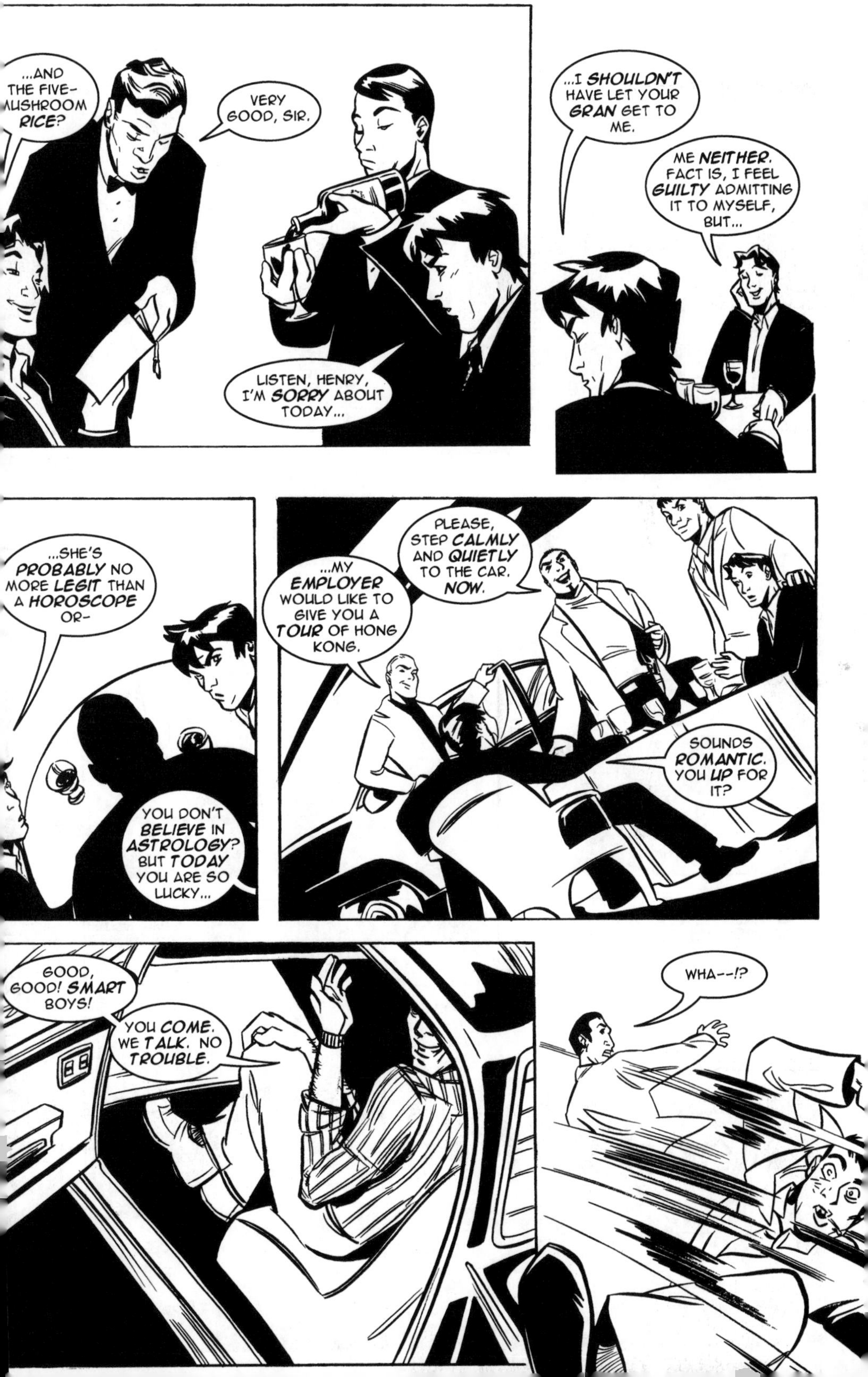
...AND THE FIVE-MUSHROOM RICE?
VERY GOOD, SIR.
LISTEN, HENRY, I'M SORRY ABOUT TODAY...
...I SHOULDN'T HAVE LET YOUR GRAN GET TO ME.
ME NEITHER. FACT IS, I FEEL GUILTY ADMITTING IT TO MYSELF, BUT...
...SHE'S PROBABLY NO MORE LEGIT THAN A HOROSCOPE OR-
YOU DON'T BELIEVE IN ASTROLOGY? BUT TODAY YOU ARE SO LUCKY...
...MY EMPLOYER WOULD LIKE TO GIVE YOU A TOUR OF HONG KONG.
PLEASE, STEP CALMLY AND QUIETLY TO THE CAR. NOW.
SOUNDS ROMANTIC. YOU UP FOR IT?
GOOD, GOOD! SMART BOYS!
YOU COME. WE TALK. NO TROUBLE.
WHA--!?

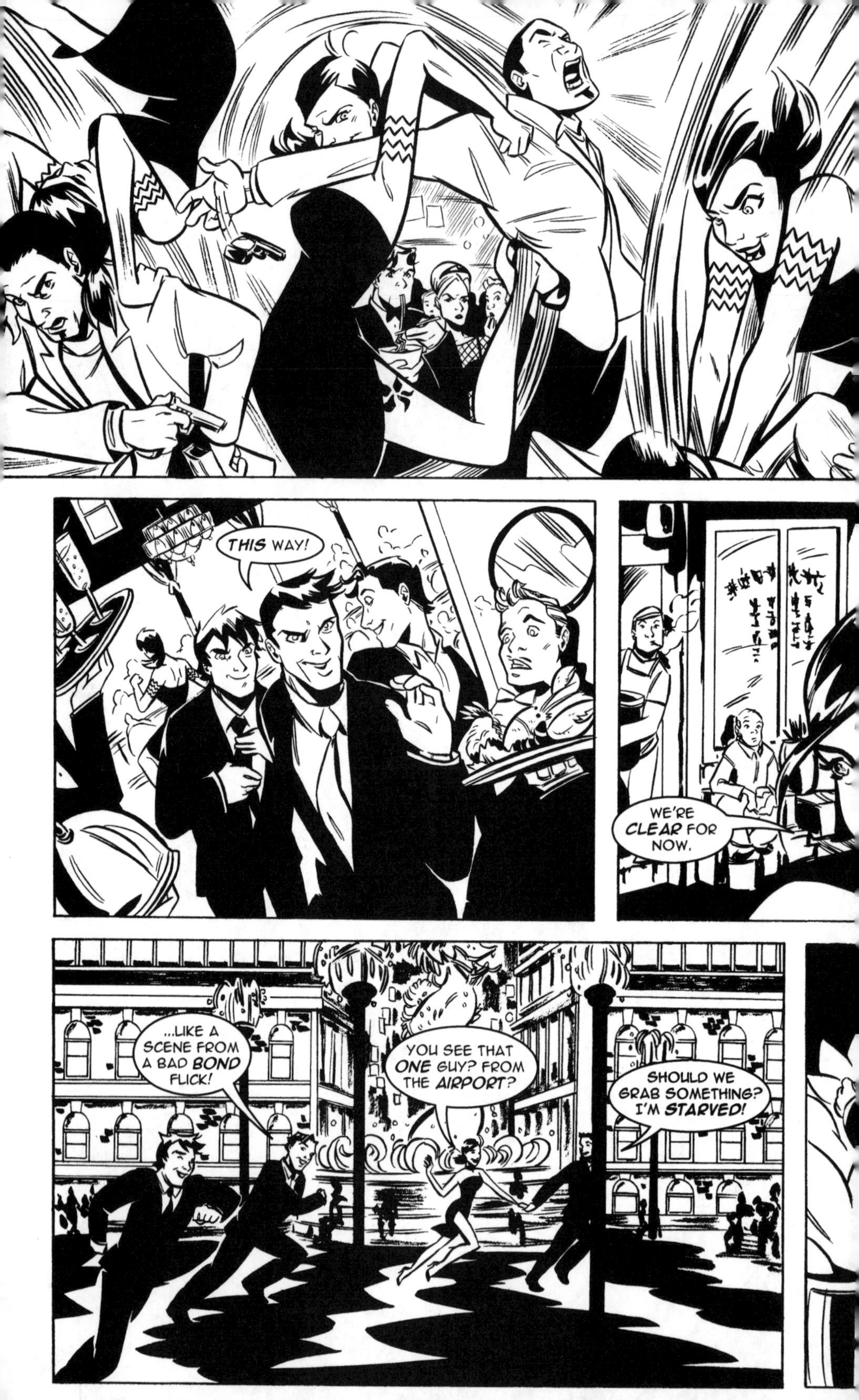
THIS WAY!
WE'RE CLEAR FOR NOW.
...LIKE A SCENE FROM A BAD BOND FLICK!
YOU SEE THAT ONE GUY? FROM THE AIRPORT?
SHOULD WE GRAB SOMETHING? I'M STARVED!

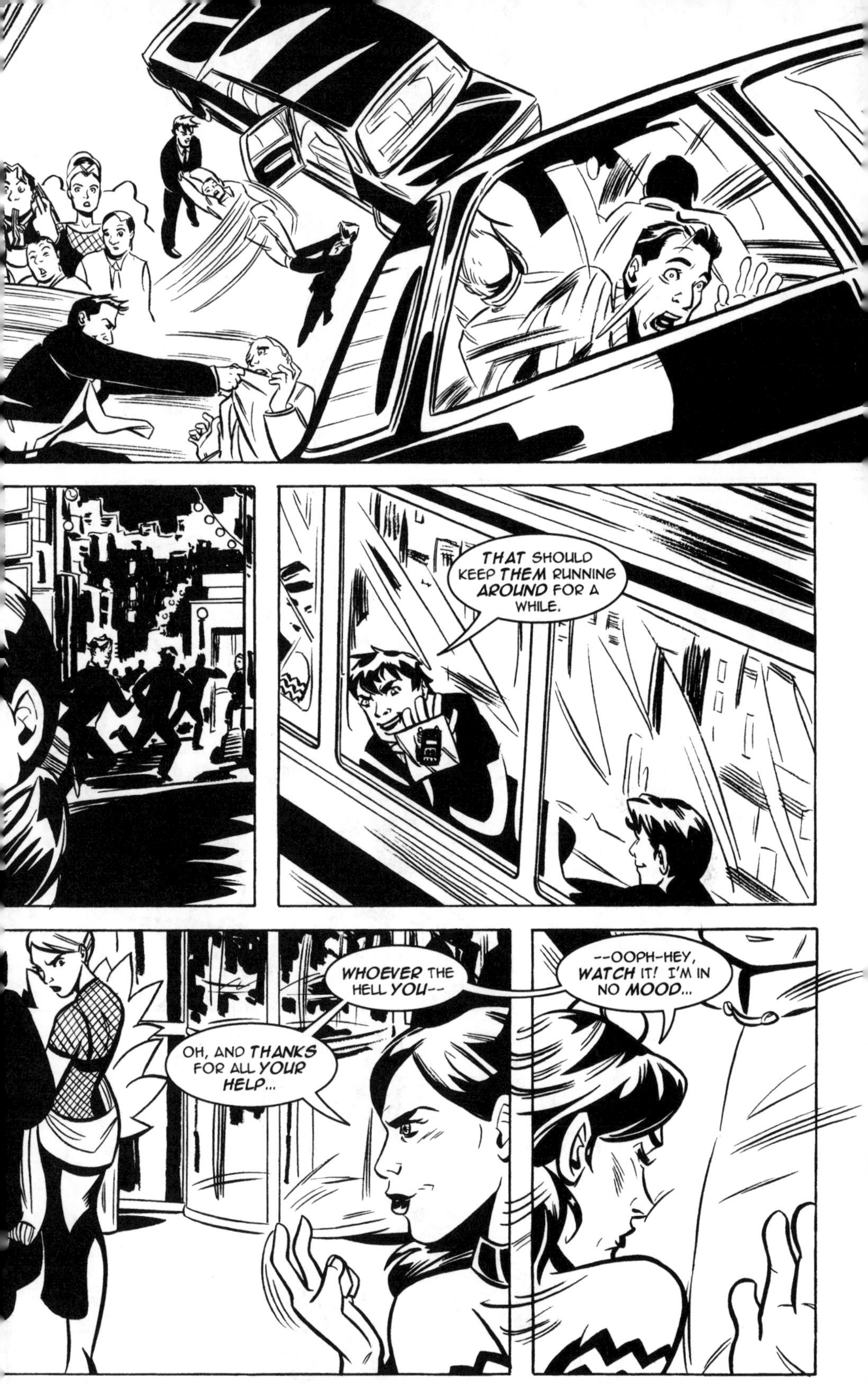
THAT SHOULD KEEP THEM RUNNING AROUND FOR A WHILE.
OH, AND THANKS FOR ALL YOUR HELP...
WHOEVER THE HELL YOU--
--OOPH-HEY, WATCH IT! I'M IN NO MOOD...

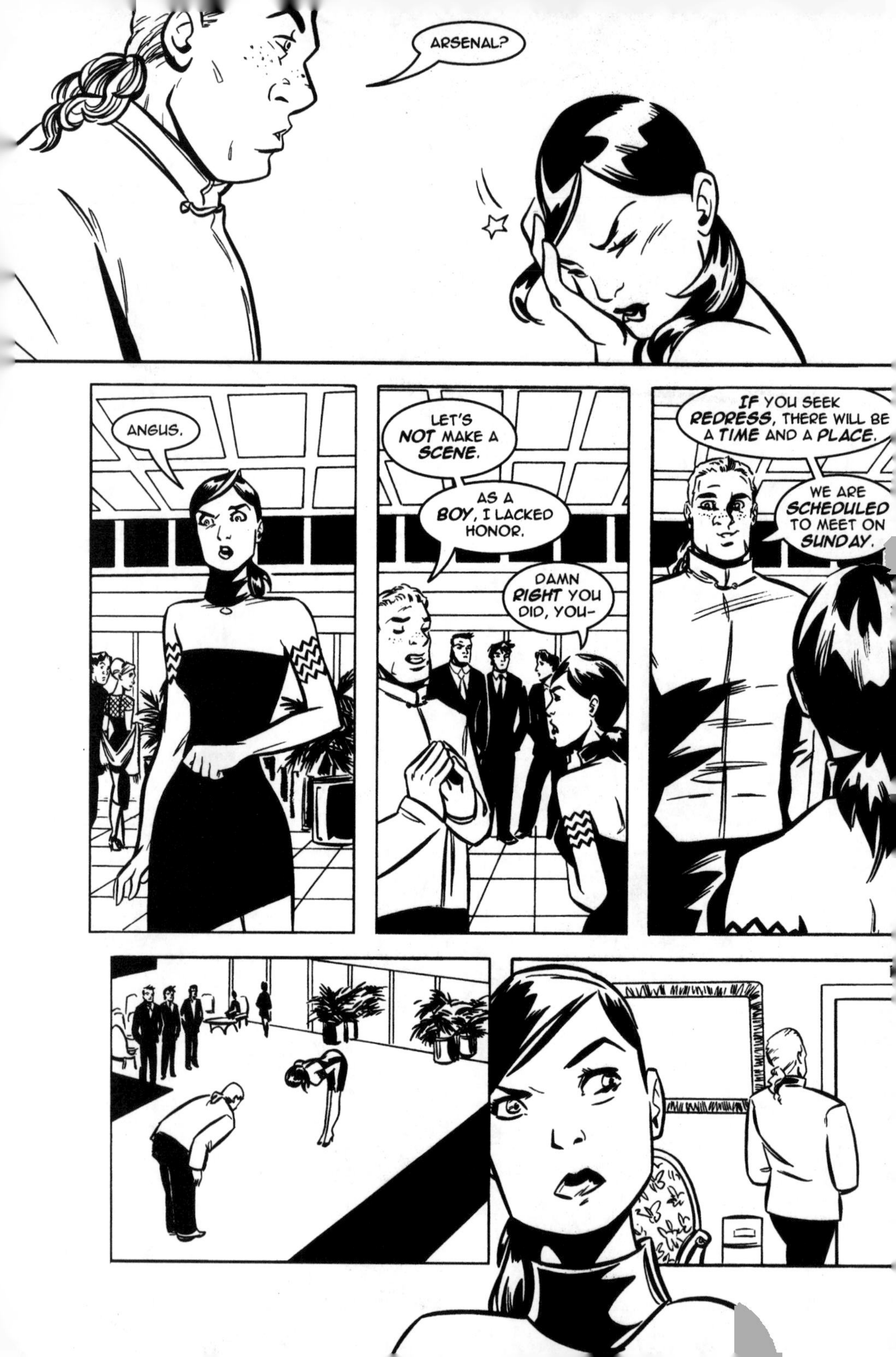
ARSENAL?
ANGUS.
LET'S NOT MAKE A SCENE.
AS A BOY, I LACKED HONOR.
DAMN RIGHT YOU DID, YOU-
IF YOU SEEK REDRESS, THERE WILL BE A TIME AND A PLACE.
WE ARE SCHEDULED TO MEET ON SUNDAY.

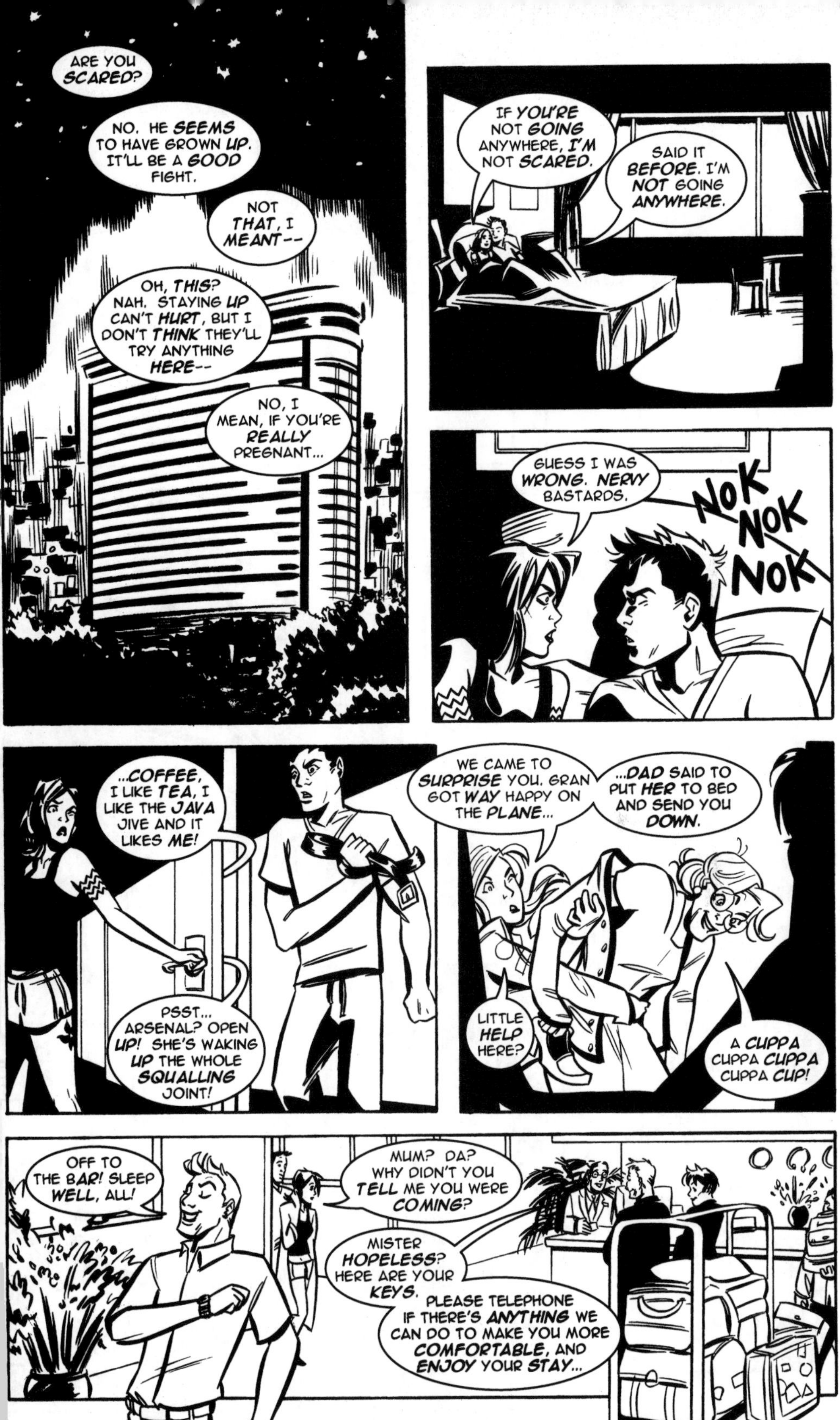
ARE YOU SCARED?
NO. HE SEEMS TO HAVE GROWN UP. IT'LL BE A GOOD FIGHT.
NOT THAT, I MEANT--
OH, THIS? NAH. STAYING UP CAN'T HURT, BUT I DON'T THINK THEY'LL TRY ANYTHING HERE--
NO, I MEAN, IF YOU'RE REALLY PREGNANT...
IF YOU'RE NOT GOING ANYWHERE, I'M NOT SCARED.
SAID IT BEFORE. I'M NOT GOING ANYWHERE.
GUESS I WAS WRONG. NERVY BASTARDS.
NOK NOK NOK
...COFFEE, I LIKE TEA, I LIKE THE JAVA JIVE AND IT LIKES ME!
PSST... ARSENAL? OPEN UP! SHE'S WAKING UP THE WHOLE SQUALLING JOINT!
WE CAME TO SURPRISE YOU. GRAN GOT WAY HAPPY ON THE PLANE...
...DAD SAID TO PUT HER TO BED AND SEND YOU DOWN.
LITTLE HELP HERE?
A CUPPA CUPPA CUPPA CUPPA CUP!
OFF TO THE BAR! SLEEP WELL, ALL!
MUM? DA? WHY DIDN'T YOU TELL ME YOU WERE COMING?
MISTER HOPELESS? HERE ARE YOUR KEYS.
PLEASE TELEPHONE IF THERE'S ANYTHING WE CAN DO TO MAKE YOU MORE COMFORTABLE, AND ENJOY YOUR STAY...

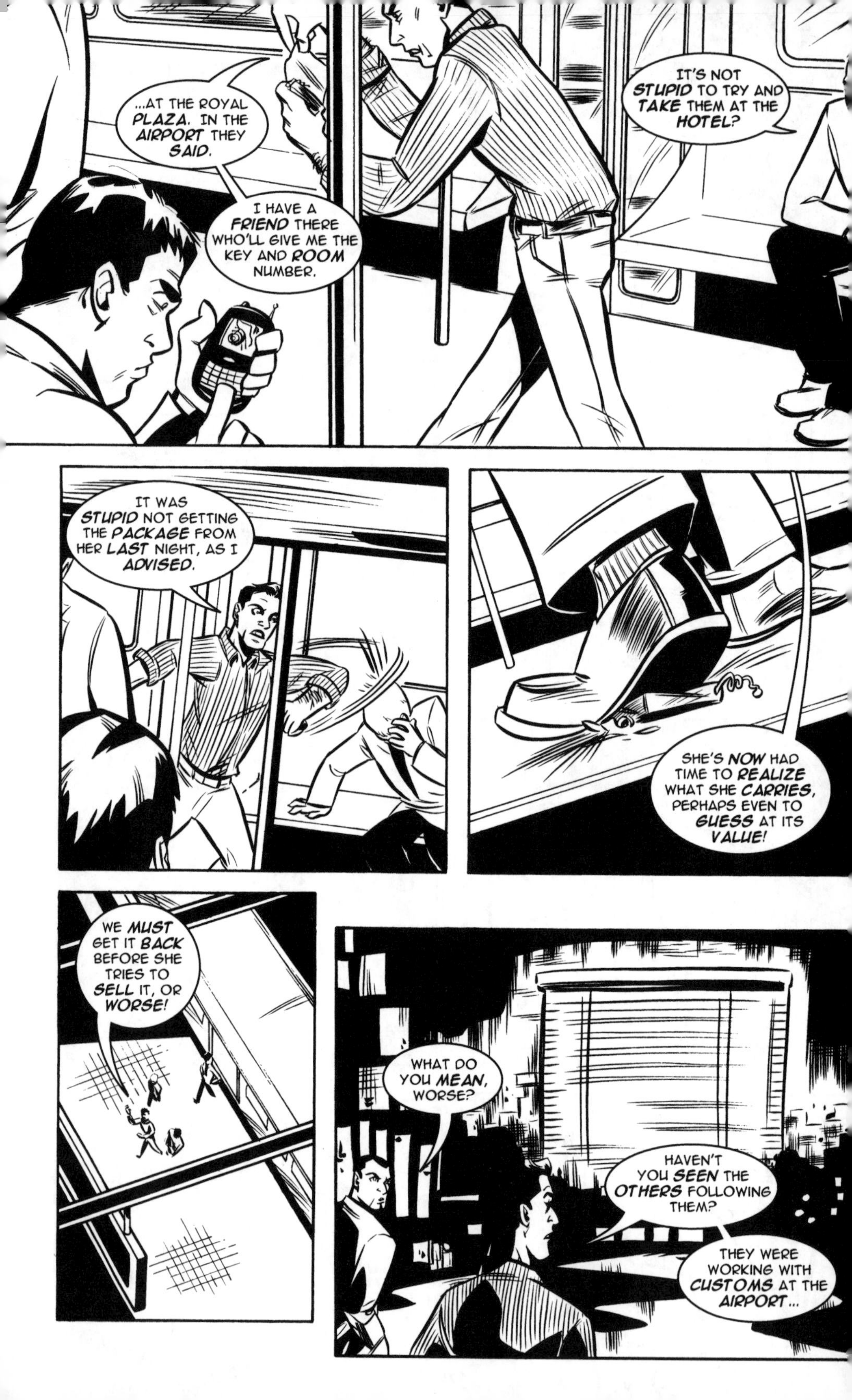
...AT THE ROYAL PLAZA. IN THE AIRPORT THEY SAID.
I HAVE A FRIEND THERE WHO'LL GIVE ME THE KEY AND ROOM NUMBER.
IT'S NOT STUPID TO TRY AND TAKE THEM AT THE HOTEL?
IT WAS STUPID NOT GETTING THE PACKAGE FROM HER LAST NIGHT, AS I ADVISED.
SHE'S NOW HAD TIME TO REALIZE WHAT SHE CARRIES, PERHAPS EVEN TO GUESS AT ITS VALUE!
WE MUST GET IT BACK BEFORE SHE TRIES TO SELL IT, OR WORSE!
WHAT DO YOU MEAN, WORSE?
HAVEN'T YOU SEEN THE OTHERS FOLLOWING THEM?
THEY WERE WORKING WITH CUSTOMS AT THE AIRPORT...

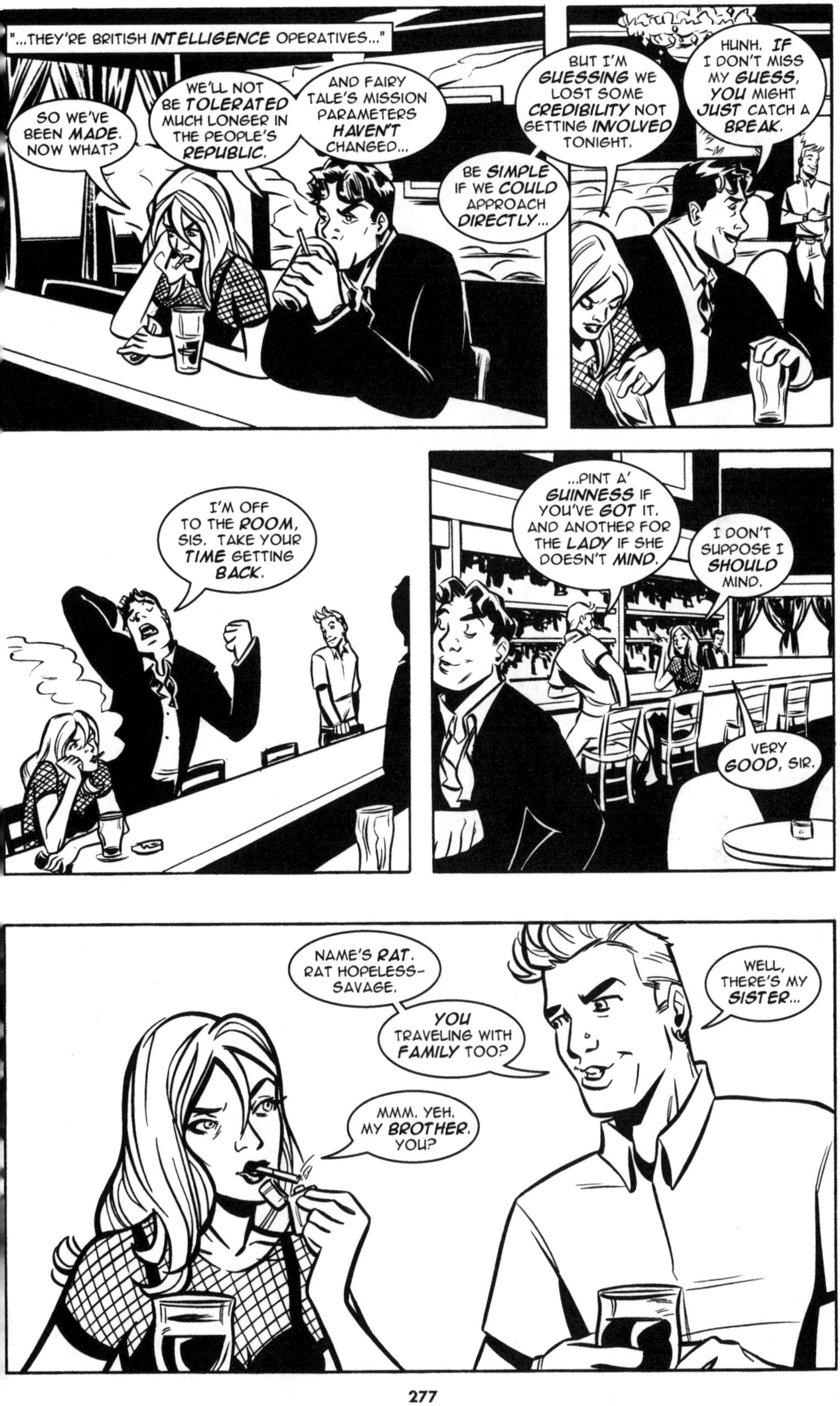
"...THEY'RE BRITISH INTELLIGENCE OPERATIVES..."
SO WE'VE BEEN MADE. NOW WHAT?
WE'LL NOT BE TOLERATED MUCH LONGER IN THE PEOPLE'S REPUBLIC.
AND FAIRY TALE'S MISSION PARAMETERS HAVEN'T CHANGED...
BE SIMPLE IF WE COULD APPROACH DIRECTLY...
BUT I'M GUESSING WE LOST SOME CREDIBILITY NOT GETTING INVOLVED TONIGHT.
HUNH. IF I DON'T MISS MY GUESS, YOU MIGHT JUST CATCH A BREAK.
I'M OFF TO THE ROOM, SIS. TAKE YOUR TIME GETTING BACK.
...PINT A' GUINNESS IF YOU'VE GOT IT. AND ANOTHER FOR THE LADY IF SHE DOESN'T MIND.
I DON'T SUPPOSE I SHOULD MIND.
VERY GOOD, SIR.
NAME'S RAT. RAT HOPELESS-SAVAGE.
YOU TRAVELING WITH FAMILY TOO?
WELL, THERE'S MY SISTER...
MMM. YEH. MY BROTHER. YOU?

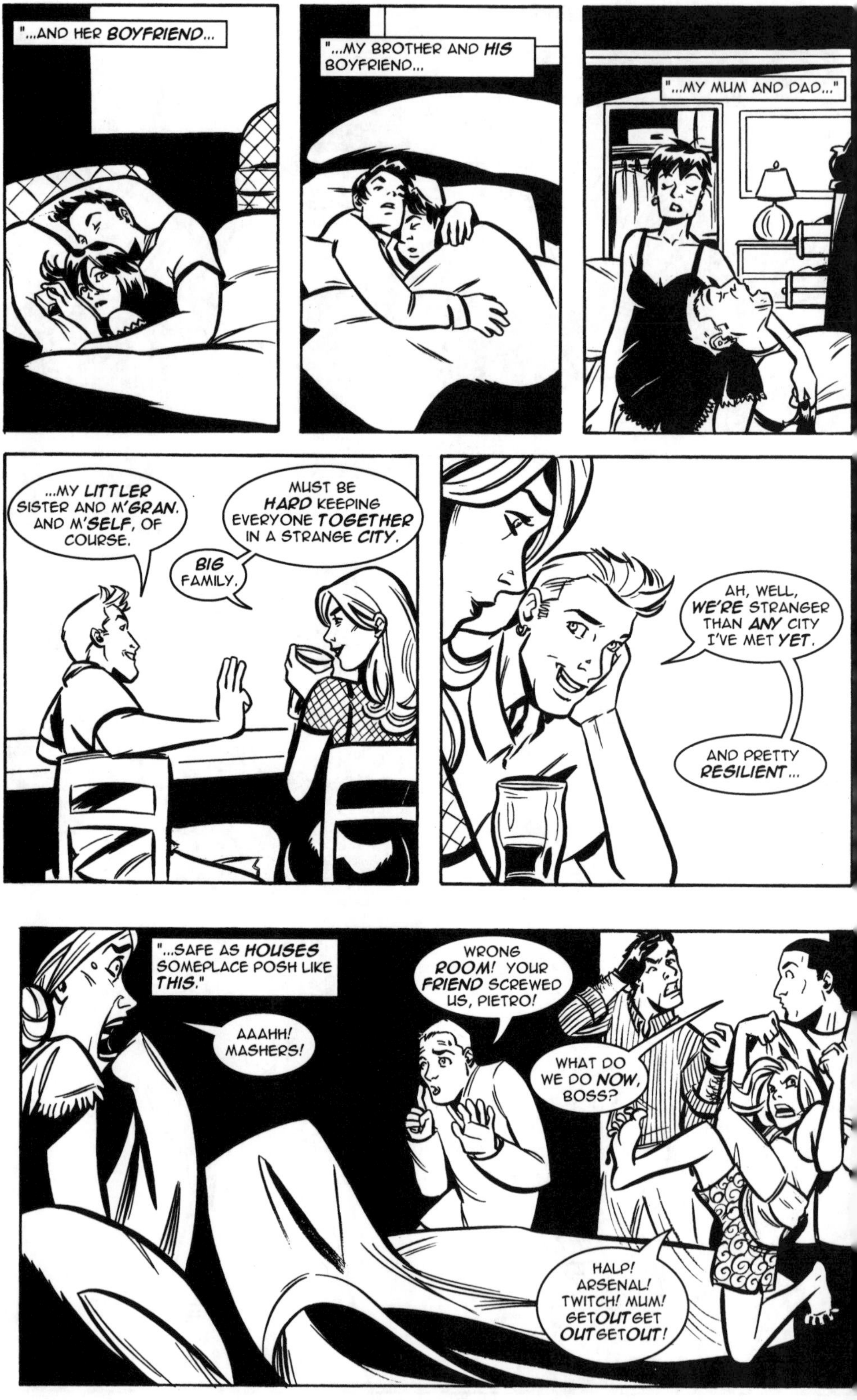
"...AND HER BOYFRIEND...
"...MY BROTHER AND HIS BOYFRIEND...
"...MY MUM AND DAD..."
...MY LITTLER SISTER AND M'GRAN. AND M'SELF, OF COURSE.
BIG FAMILY.
MUST BE HARD KEEPING EVERYONE TOGETHER IN A STRANGE CITY.
AH, WELL, WE'RE STRANGER THAN ANY CITY I'VE MET YET.
AND PRETTY RESILIENT...
"...SAFE AS HOUSES SOMEPLACE POSH LIKE THIS."
AAAHH! MASHERS!
WRONG ROOM! YOUR FRIEND SCREWED US, PIETRO!
WHAT DO WE DO NOW, BOSS?
HALP! ARSENAL! TWITCH! MUM! GETOUTGET OUTGETOUT!

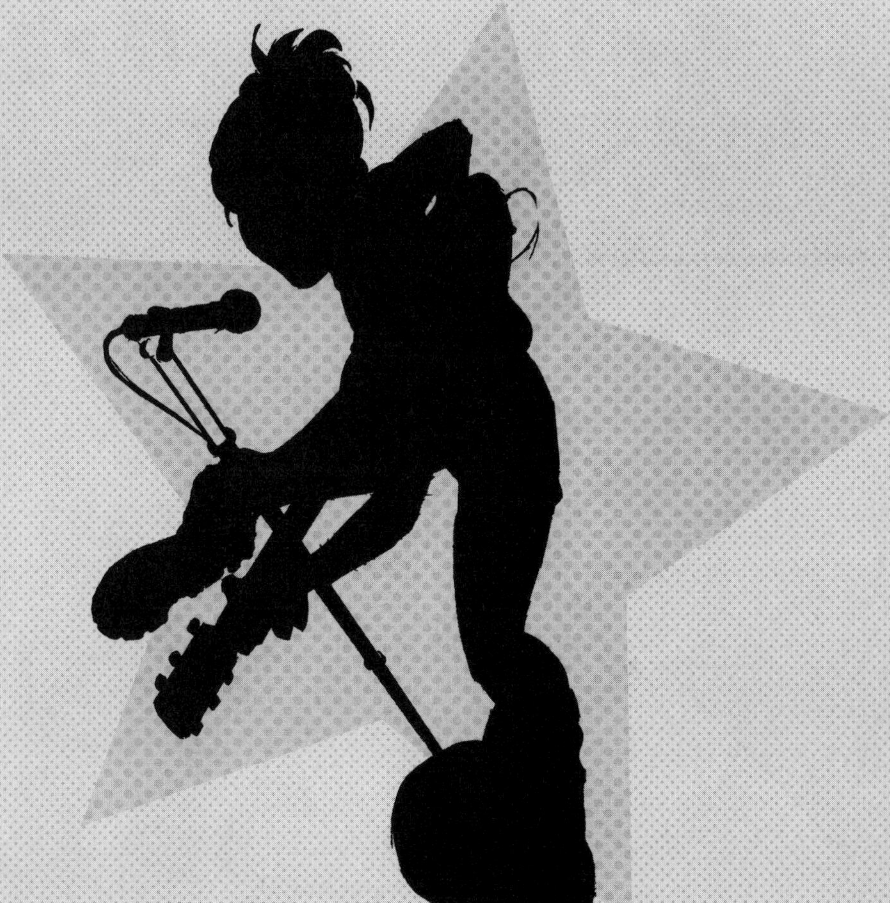

CHAPTER 3

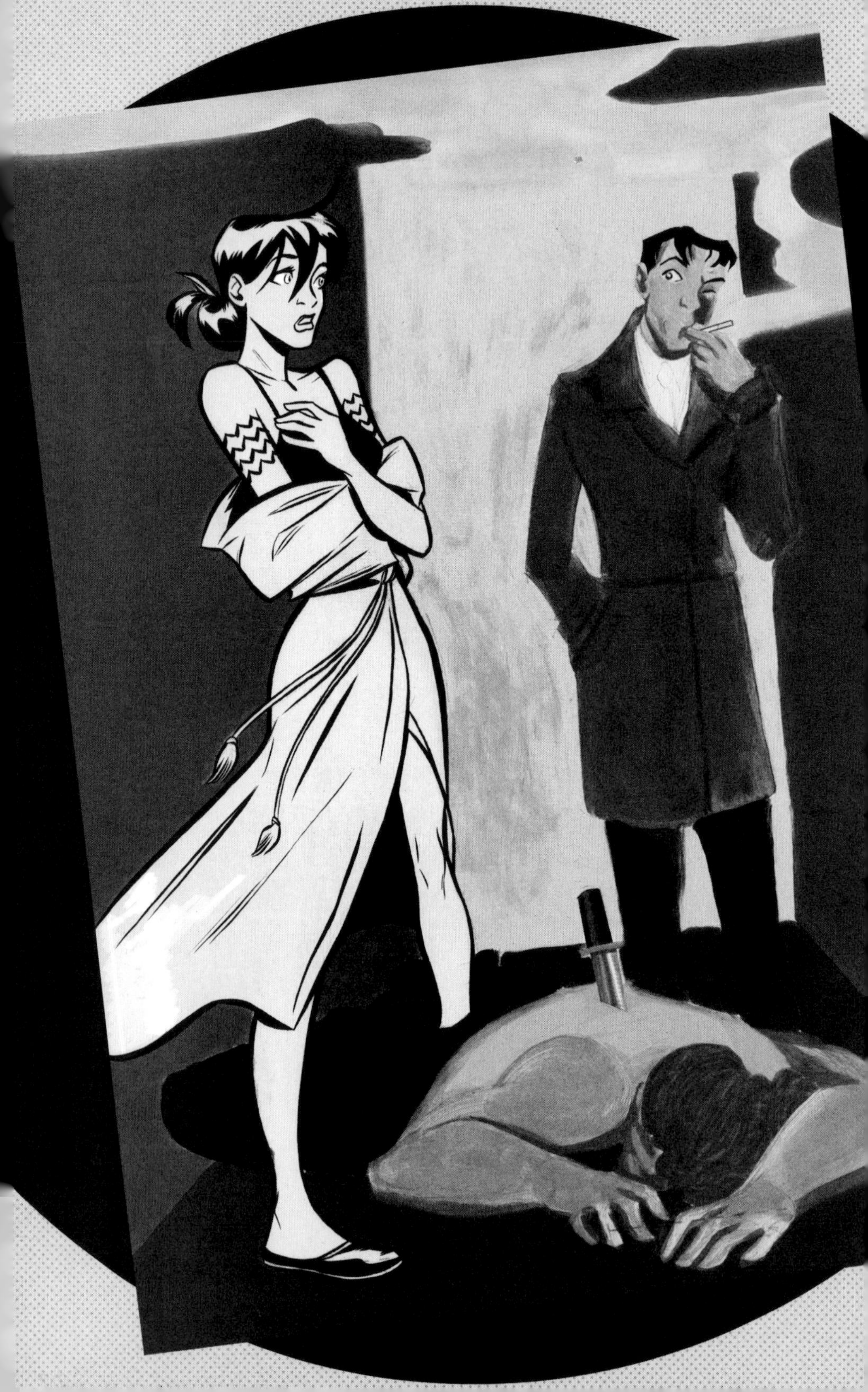

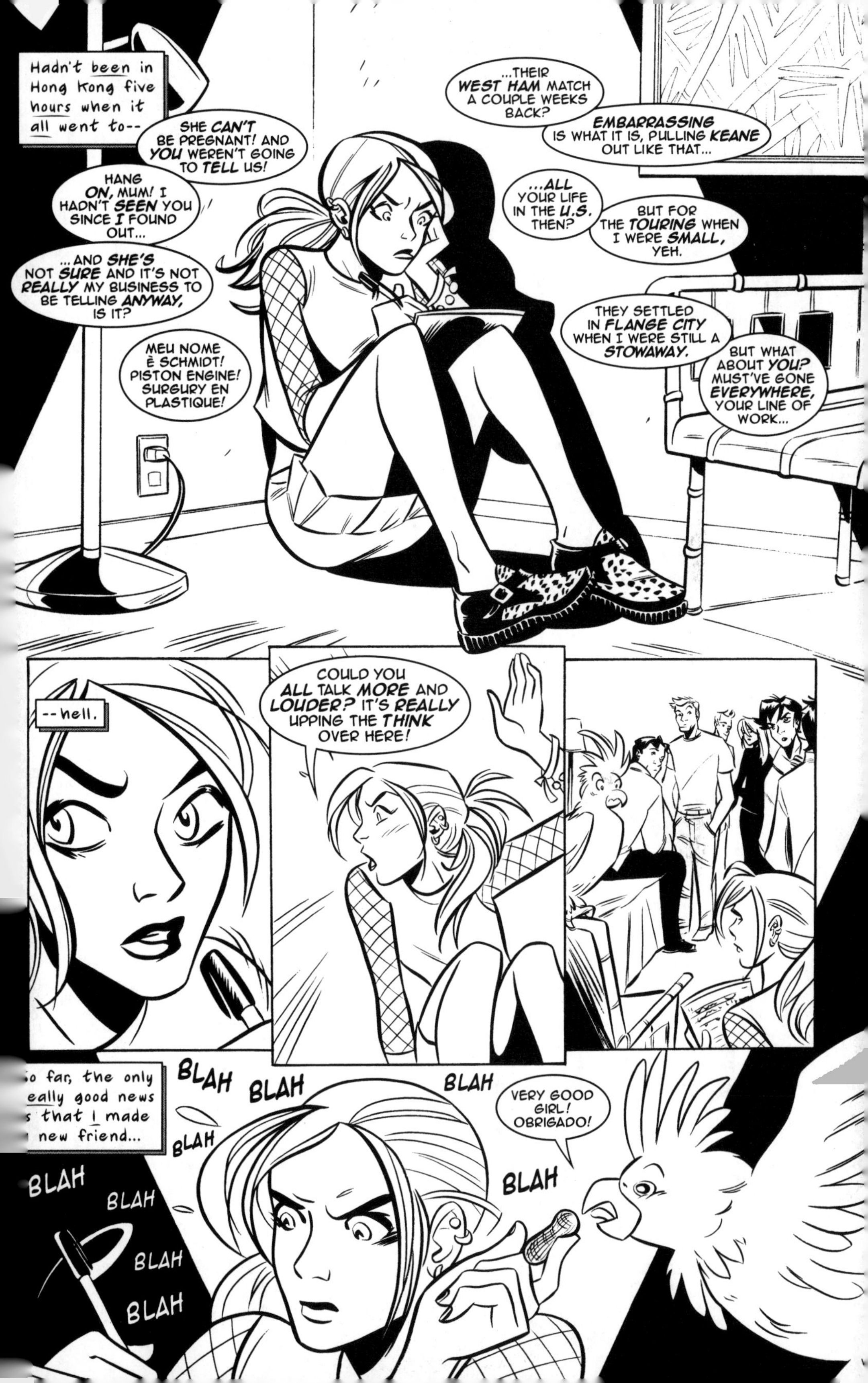

Hadn't been in Hong Kong five hours when it all went to--
SHE CAN'T BE PREGNANT! AND YOU WEREN'T GOING TO TELL US!
HANG ON, MUM! I HADN'T SEEN YOU SINCE I FOUND OUT...
...AND SHE'S NOT SURE AND IT'S NOT REALLY MY BUSINESS TO BE TELLING ANYWAY, IS IT?
MEU NOME È SCHMIDT! PISTON ENGINE! SURGURY EN PLASTIQUE!
...THEIR WEST HAM MATCH A COUPLE WEEKS BACK?
EMBARRASSING IS WHAT IT IS, PULLING KEANE OUT LIKE THAT...
...ALL YOUR LIFE IN THE U.S. THEN?
BUT FOR THE TOURING WHEN I WERE SMALL, YEH.
THEY SETTLED IN FLANGE CITY WHEN I WERE STILL A STOWAWAY.
BUT WHAT ABOUT YOU? MUST'VE GONE EVERYWHERE, YOUR LINE OF WORK...
--hell.
COULD YOU ALL TALK MORE AND LOUDER? IT'S REALLY UPPING THE THINK OVER HERE!
So far, the only really good news is that I made a new friend...
BLAH
BLAH
BLAH
BLAH
VERY GOOD GIRL! OBRIGADO!
BLAH
BLAH
BLAH
BLAH
BLAH

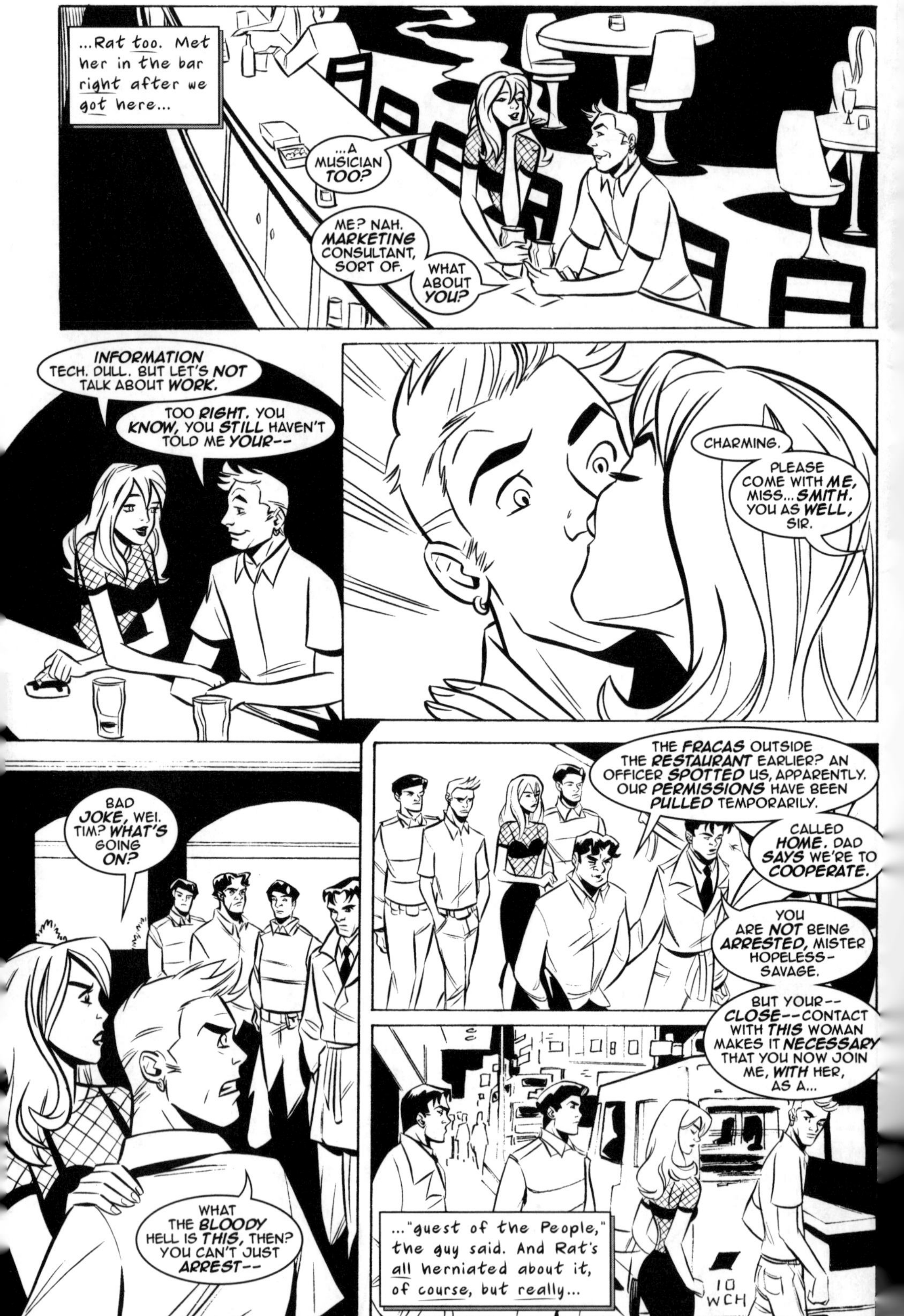
...Rat too. Met her in the bar right after we got here...
...A MUSICIAN TOO?
ME? NAH. MARKETING CONSULTANT, SORT OF.
WHAT ABOUT YOU?
INFORMATION TECH. DULL. BUT LET'S NOT TALK ABOUT WORK.
TOO RIGHT. YOU KNOW, YOU STILL HAVEN'T TOLD ME YOUR--
CHARMING.
PLEASE COME WITH ME, MISS... SMITH. YOU AS WELL, SIR.
BAD JOKE, WEI. TIM? WHAT'S GOING ON?
WHAT THE BLOODY HELL IS THIS, THEN? YOU CAN'T JUST ARREST--
THE FRACAS OUTSIDE THE RESTAURANT EARLIER? AN OFFICER SPOTTED US, APPARENTLY. OUR PERMISSIONS HAVE BEEN PULLED TEMPORARILY.
CALLED HOME. DAD SAYS WE'RE TO COOPERATE.
YOU ARE NOT BEING ARRESTED, MISTER HOPELESS-SAVAGE.
BUT YOUR-- CLOSE--CONTACT WITH THIS WOMAN MAKES IT NECESSARY THAT YOU NOW JOIN ME, WITH HER, AS A...
..."guest of the People," the guy said. And Rat's all herniated about it, of course, but really...
10 WCH

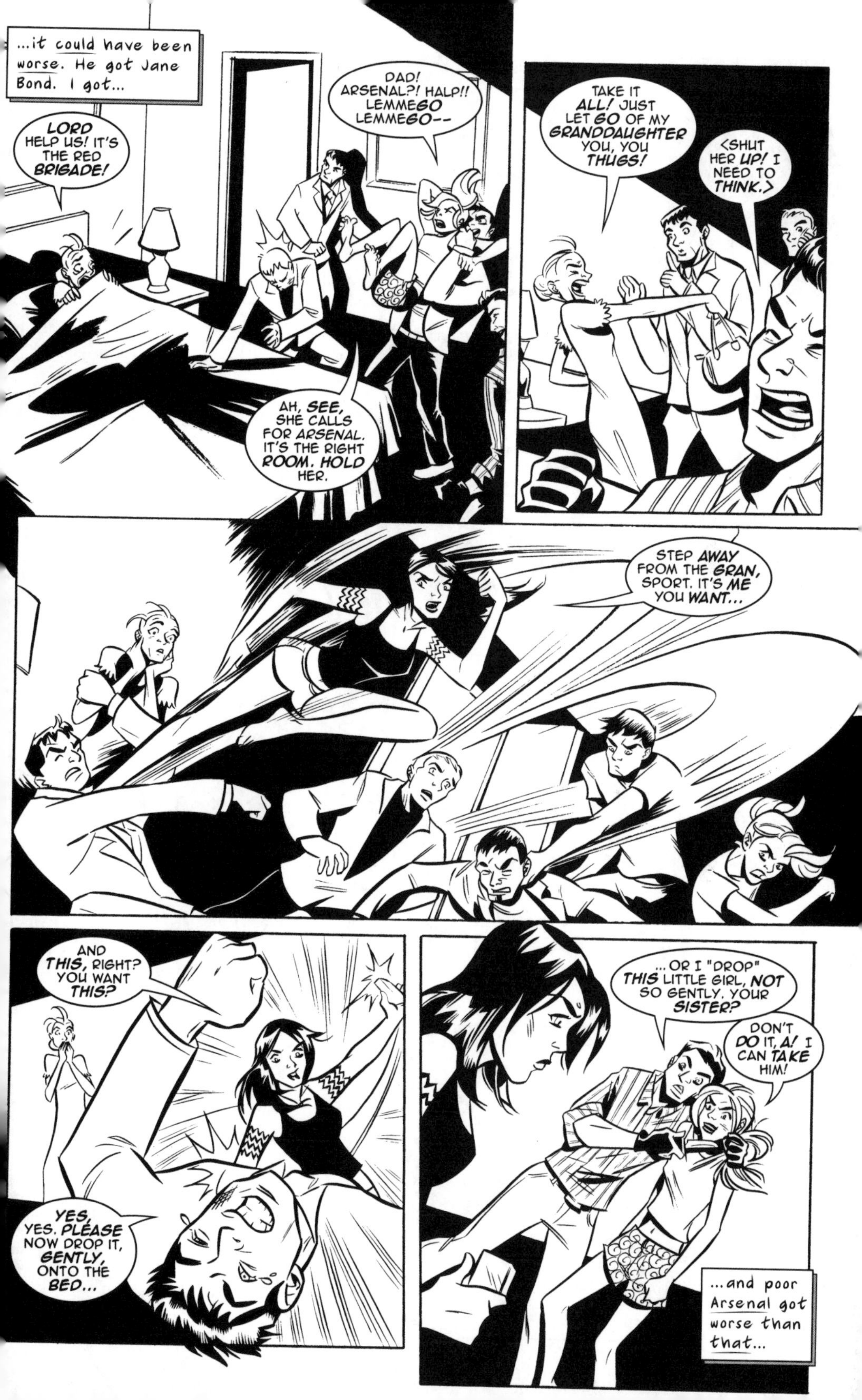
...it could have been worse. He got Jane Bond. I got...
LORD HELP US! IT'S THE RED BRIGADE!
DAD! ARSENAL?! HALP!! LEMMEGO LEMMEGO--
AH, SEE, SHE CALLS FOR ARSENAL. IT'S THE RIGHT ROOM. HOLD HER.
TAKE IT ALL! JUST LET GO OF MY GRANDDAUGHTER YOU, YOU THUGS!
<SHUT HER UP! I NEED TO THINK.>
STEP AWAY FROM THE GRAN, SPORT. IT'S ME YOU WANT...
AND THIS, RIGHT? YOU WANT THIS?
YES, YES. PLEASE NOW DROP IT, GENTLY, ONTO THE BED...
... OR I "DROP" THIS LITTLE GIRL, NOT SO GENTLY. YOUR SISTER?
DON'T DO IT, A! I CAN TAKE HIM!
...and poor Arsenal got worse than that...

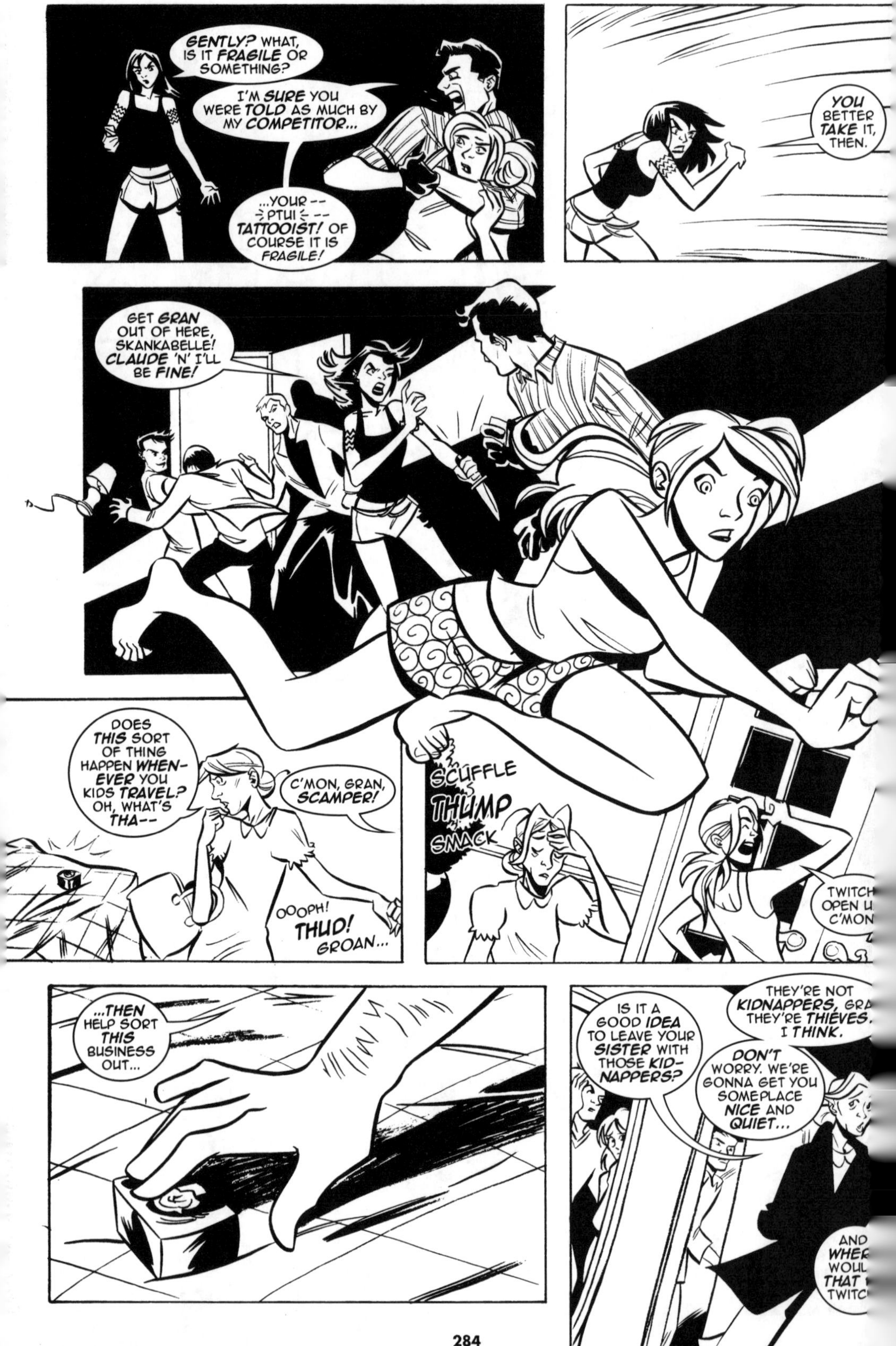
GENTLY? WHAT, IS IT FRAGILE OR SOMETHING?
I'M SURE YOU WERE TOLD AS MUCH BY MY COMPETITOR...
...YOUR -- PTUI -- TATTOOIST! OF COURSE IT IS FRAGILE!
YOU BETTER TAKE IT, THEN.
GET GRAN OUT OF HERE, SKANKABELLE! CLAUDE 'N' I'LL BE FINE!
DOES THIS SORT OF THING HAPPEN WHENEVER YOU KIDS TRAVEL? OH, WHAT'S THA--
C'MON, GRAN, SCAMPER!
OOOPH! THUD! GROAN...
SCUFFLE
THUMP
SMACK
TWITCH OPEN U C'MON
...THEN HELP SORT THIS BUSINESS OUT...
IS IT A GOOD IDEA TO LEAVE YOUR SISTER WITH THOSE KIDNAPPERS?
THEY'RE NOT KIDNAPPERS, GRA THEY'RE THIEVES. I THINK.
DON'T WORRY. WE'RE GONNA GET YOU SOMEPLACE NICE AND QUIET...
AND WHER WOUL THAT TWITC

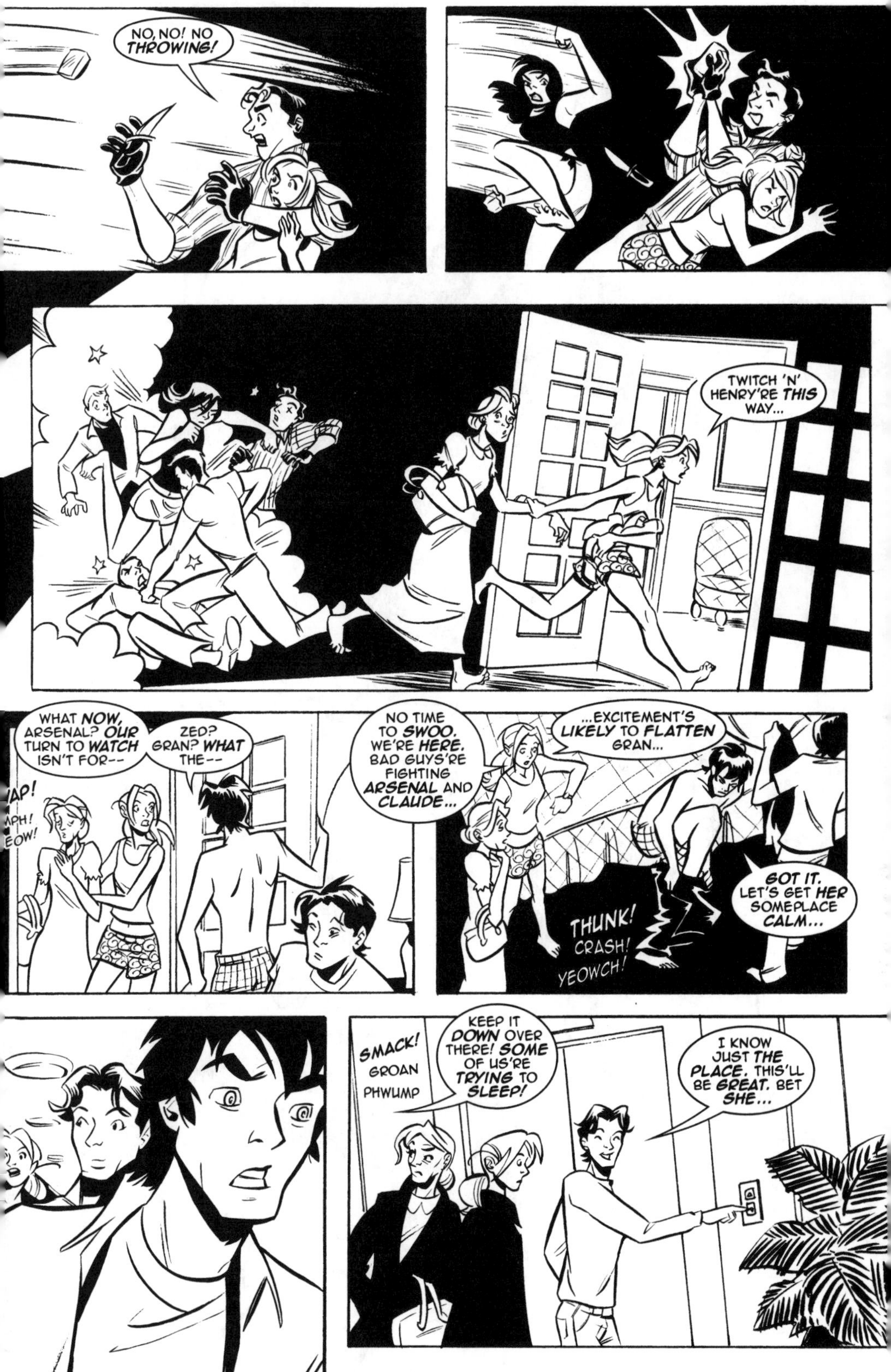
NO, NO! NO THROWING!
TWITCH 'N' HENRY'RE THIS WAY...
WHAT NOW, ARSENAL? OUR TURN TO WATCH ISN'T FOR--
ZED? GRAN? WHAT THE--
NO TIME TO SWOO. WE'RE HERE. BAD GUYS'RE FIGHTING ARSENAL AND CLAUDE...
...EXCITEMENT'S LIKELY TO FLATTEN GRAN...
THUNK! CRASH! YEOWCH!
GOT IT. LET'S GET HER SOMEPLACE CALM...
SMACK! GROAN PHWUMP
KEEP IT DOWN OVER THERE! SOME OF US'RE TRYING TO SLEEP!
I KNOW JUST THE PLACE. THIS'LL BE GREAT. BET SHE...

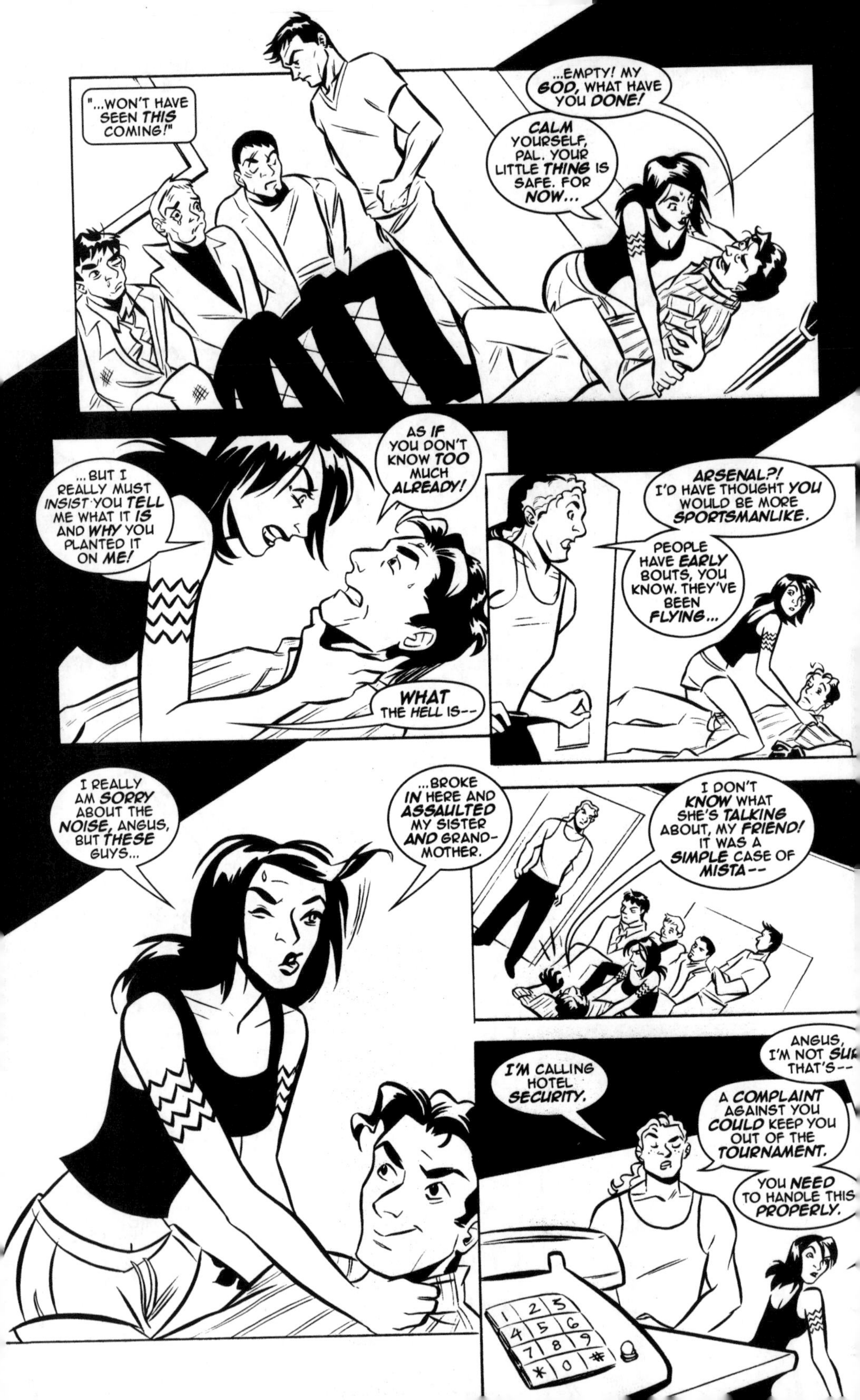

"...WON'T HAVE SEEN THIS COMING!"
...EMPTY! MY GOD, WHAT HAVE YOU DONE!
CALM YOURSELF, PAL. YOUR LITTLE THING IS SAFE. FOR NOW...
...BUT I REALLY MUST INSIST YOU TELL ME WHAT IT IS AND WHY YOU PLANTED IT ON ME!
AS IF YOU DON'T KNOW TOO MUCH ALREADY!
WHAT THE HELL IS--
ARSENAL?! I'D HAVE THOUGHT YOU WOULD BE MORE SPORTSMANLIKE.
PEOPLE HAVE EARLY BOUTS, YOU KNOW. THEY'VE BEEN FLYING...
I REALLY AM SORRY ABOUT THE NOISE, ANGUS, BUT THESE GUYS...
...BROKE IN HERE AND ASSAULTED MY SISTER AND GRAND-MOTHER.
I DON'T KNOW WHAT SHE'S TALKING ABOUT, MY FRIEND! IT WAS A SIMPLE CASE OF MISTA--
I'M CALLING HOTEL SECURITY.
ANGUS, I'M NOT SU THAT'S--
A COMPLAINT AGAINST YOU COULD KEEP YOU OUT OF THE TOURNAMENT.
YOU NEED TO HANDLE THIS PROPERLY.

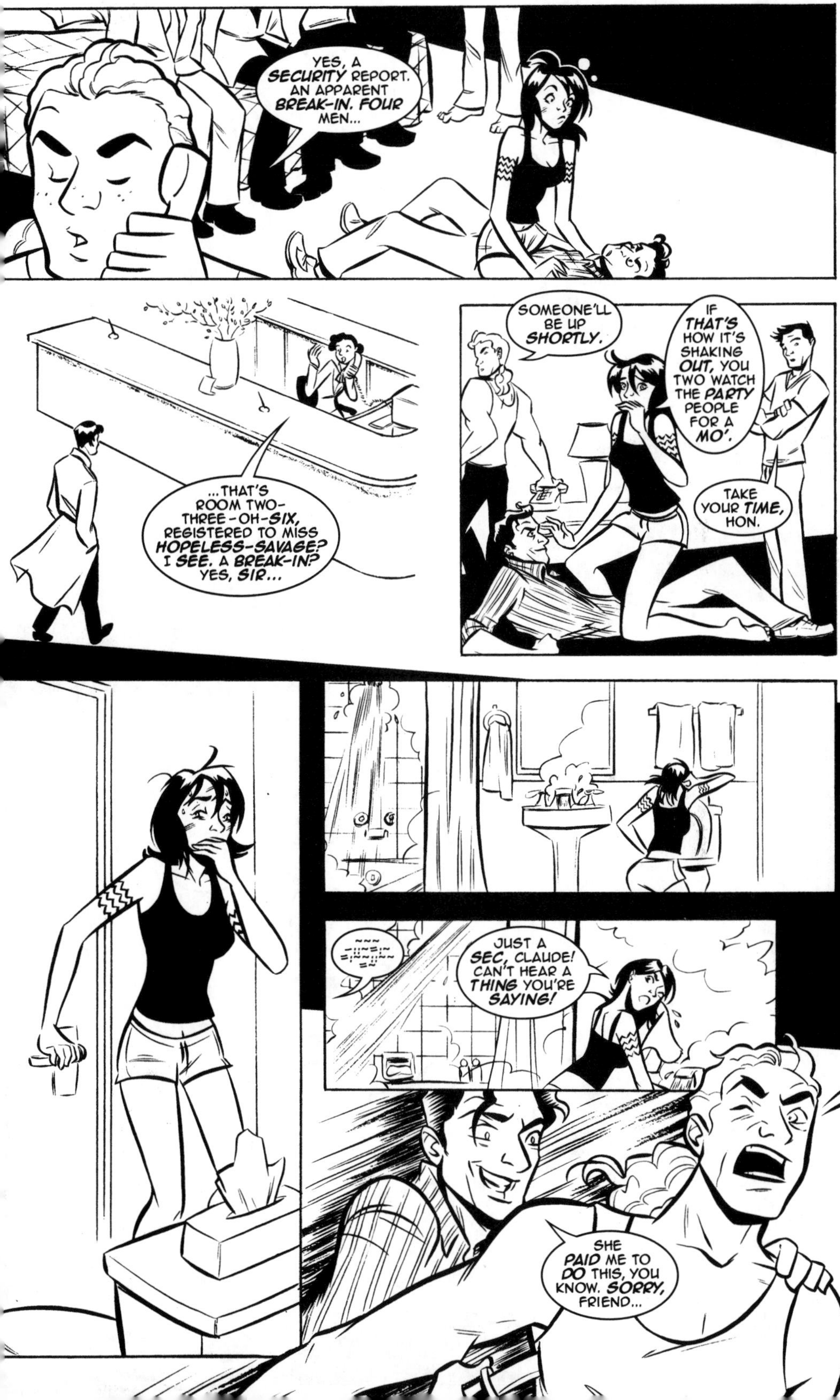

YES, A SECURITY REPORT. AN APPARENT BREAK-IN. FOUR MEN...
...THAT'S ROOM TWO-THREE-OH-SIX, REGISTERED TO MISS HOPELESS-SAVAGE? I SEE. A BREAK-IN? YES, SIR...
SOMEONE'LL BE UP SHORTLY.
IF THAT'S HOW IT'S SHAKING OUT, YOU TWO WATCH THE PARTY PEOPLE FOR A MO'.
TAKE YOUR TIME, HON.
JUST A SEC, CLAUDE! CAN'T HEAR A THING YOU'RE SAYING!
SHE PAID ME TO DO THIS, YOU KNOW. SORRY, FRIEND...

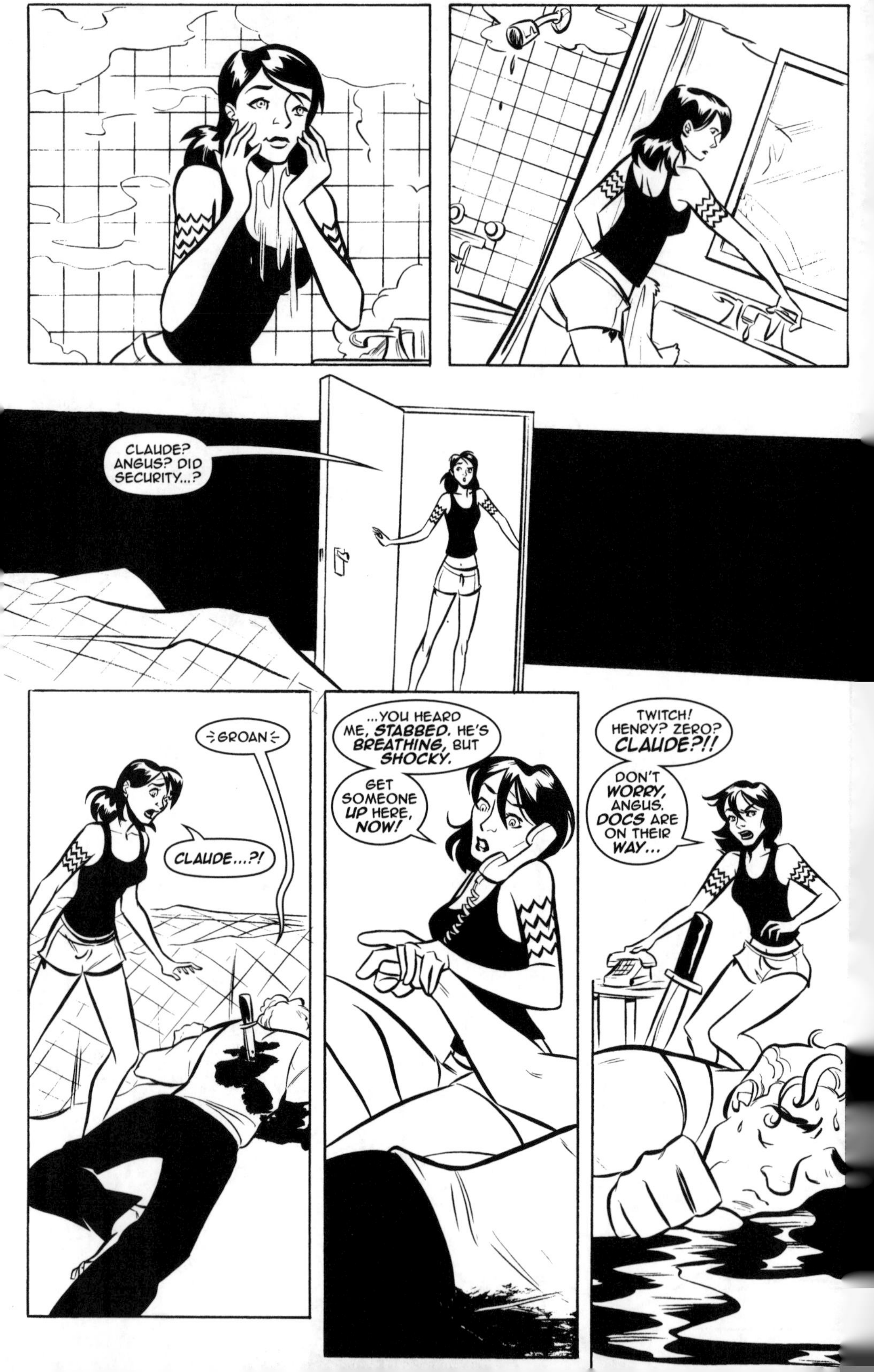
CLAUDE? ANGUS? DID SECURITY...?
GROAN
CLAUDE...?!
...YOU HEARD ME, STABBED. HE'S BREATHING, BUT SHOCKY.
GET SOMEONE UP HERE, NOW!
TWITCH! HENRY? ZERO? CLAUDE?!!
DON'T WORRY, ANGUS. DOCS ARE ON THEIR WAY...

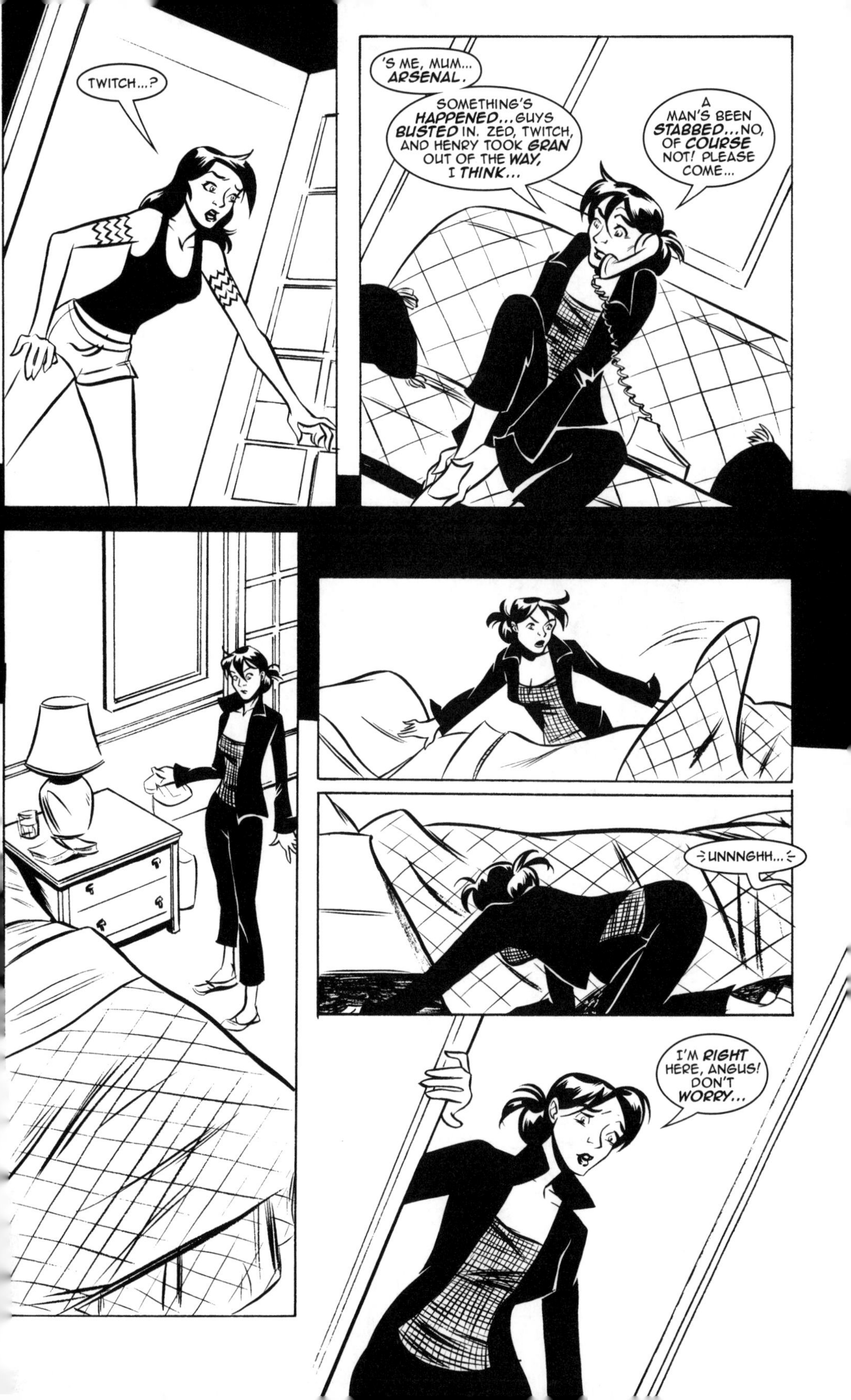
TWITCH...?
'S ME, MUM... ARSENAL.
SOMETHING'S HAPPENED... GUYS BUSTED IN. ZED, TWITCH, AND HENRY TOOK GRAN OUT OF THE WAY, I THINK...
A MAN'S BEEN STABBED... NO, OF COURSE NOT! PLEASE COME...
UNNNGHH...
I'M RIGHT HERE, ANGUS! DON'T WORRY...

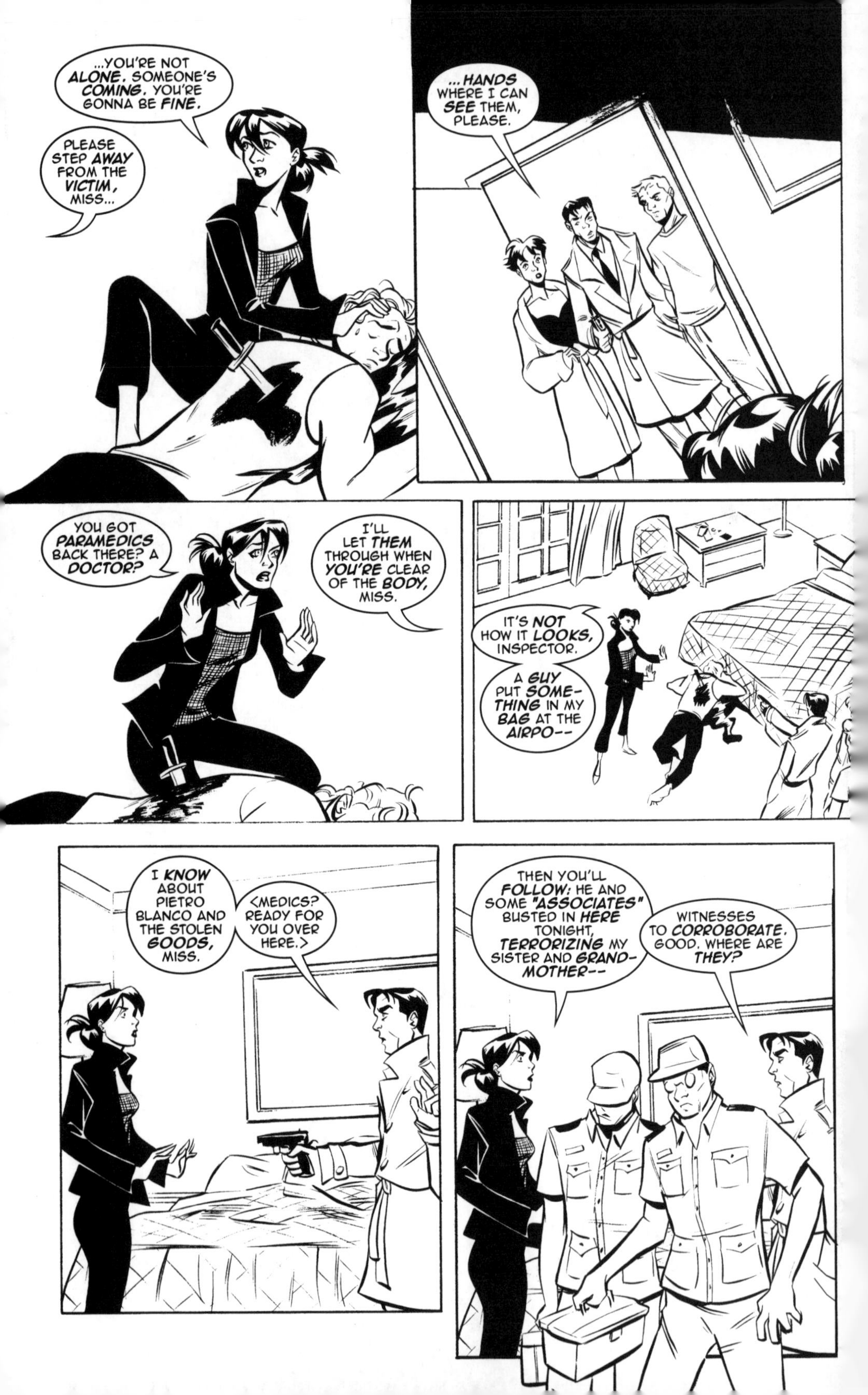
...YOU'RE NOT ALONE. SOMEONE'S COMING. YOU'RE GONNA BE FINE.
PLEASE STEP AWAY FROM THE VICTIM, MISS...
...HANDS WHERE I CAN SEE THEM, PLEASE.
YOU GOT PARAMEDICS BACK THERE? A DOCTOR?
I'LL LET THEM THROUGH WHEN YOU'RE CLEAR OF THE BODY, MISS.
IT'S NOT HOW IT LOOKS, INSPECTOR.
A GUY PUT SOME-THING IN MY BAG AT THE AIRPO--
I KNOW ABOUT PIETRO BLANCO AND THE STOLEN GOODS, MISS.
<MEDICS? READY FOR YOU OVER HERE.>
THEN YOU'LL FOLLOW: HE AND SOME "ASSOCIATES" BUSTED IN HERE TONIGHT, TERRORIZING MY SISTER AND GRAND-MOTHER--
WITNESSES TO CORROBORATE. GOOD. WHERE ARE THEY?

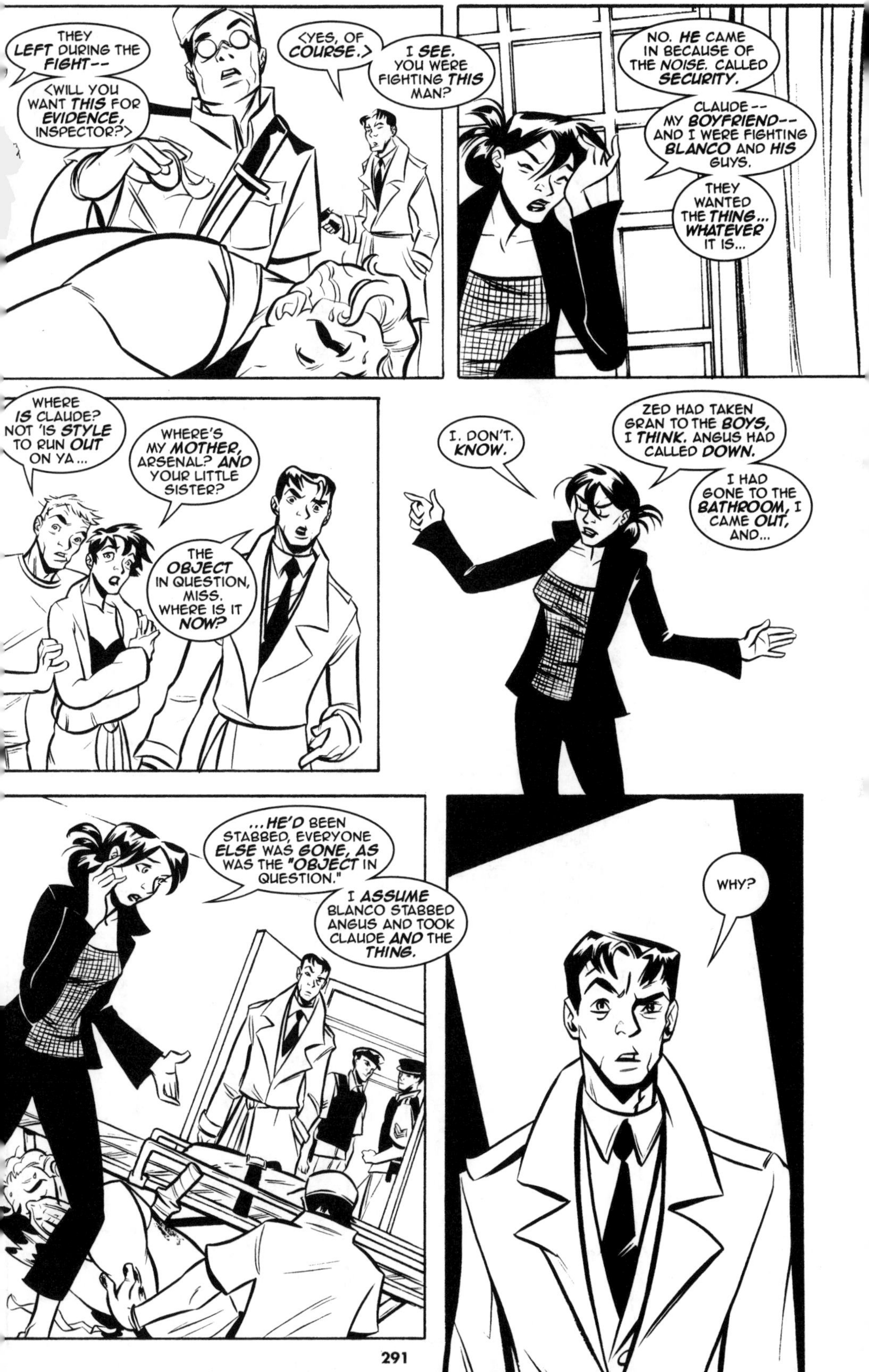
THEY LEFT DURING THE FIGHT--
<WILL YOU WANT THIS FOR EVIDENCE, INSPECTOR?>
<YES, OF COURSE.>
I SEE. YOU WERE FIGHTING THIS MAN?
NO. HE CAME IN BECAUSE OF THE NOISE. CALLED SECURITY.
CLAUDE -- MY BOYFRIEND-- AND I WERE FIGHTING BLANCO AND HIS GUYS.
THEY WANTED THE THING... WHATEVER IT IS...
WHERE IS CLAUDE? NOT 'IS STYLE TO RUN OUT ON YA...
WHERE'S MY MOTHER, ARSENAL? AND YOUR LITTLE SISTER?
THE OBJECT IN QUESTION, MISS. WHERE IS IT NOW?
I. DON'T. KNOW.
ZED HAD TAKEN GRAN TO THE BOYS, I THINK. ANGUS HAD CALLED DOWN.
I HAD GONE TO THE BATHROOM, I CAME OUT, AND...
...HE'D BEEN STABBED, EVERYONE ELSE WAS GONE, AS WAS THE "OBJECT IN QUESTION."
I ASSUME BLANCO STABBED ANGUS AND TOOK CLAUDE AND THE THING.
WHY?

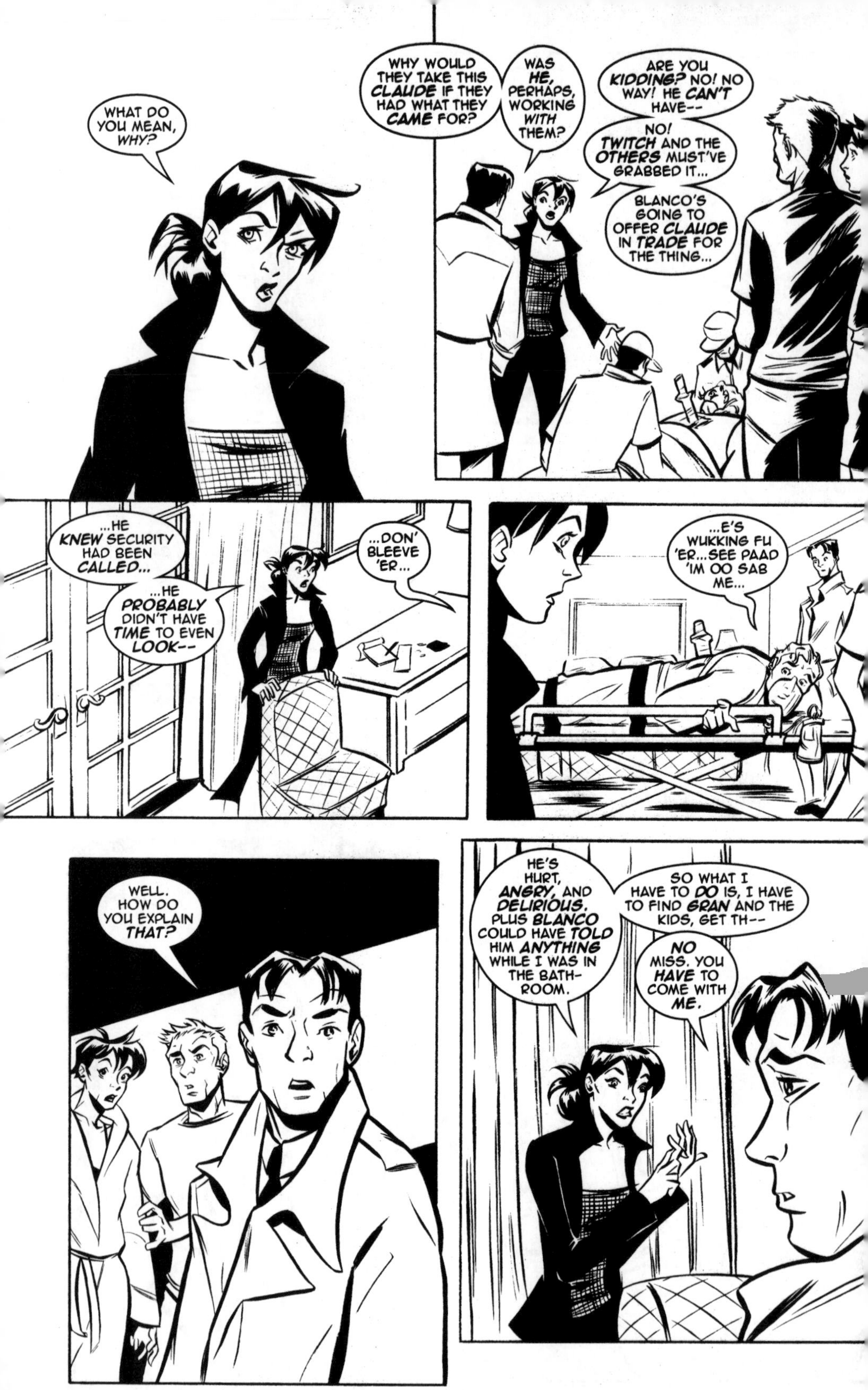
WHAT DO YOU MEAN, WHY?
WHY WOULD THEY TAKE THIS CLAUDE IF THEY HAD WHAT THEY CAME FOR?
WAS HE, PERHAPS, WORKING WITH THEM?
ARE YOU KIDDING? NO! NO WAY! HE CAN'T HAVE--
NO! TWITCH AND THE OTHERS MUST'VE GRABBED IT...
BLANCO'S GOING TO OFFER CLAUDE IN TRADE FOR THE THING...
...HE KNEW SECURITY HAD BEEN CALLED...
...HE PROBABLY DIDN'T HAVE TIME TO EVEN LOOK--
...DON' BLEEVE 'ER...
...E'S WUKKING FU 'ER...SEE PAAD 'IM OO SAB ME...
WELL. HOW DO YOU EXPLAIN THAT?
HE'S HURT, ANGRY, AND DELIRIOUS. PLUS BLANCO COULD HAVE TOLD HIM ANYTHING WHILE I WAS IN THE BATH-ROOM.
SO WHAT I HAVE TO DO IS, I HAVE TO FIND GRAN AND THE KIDS, GET TH--
NO MISS. YOU HAVE TO COME WITH ME.

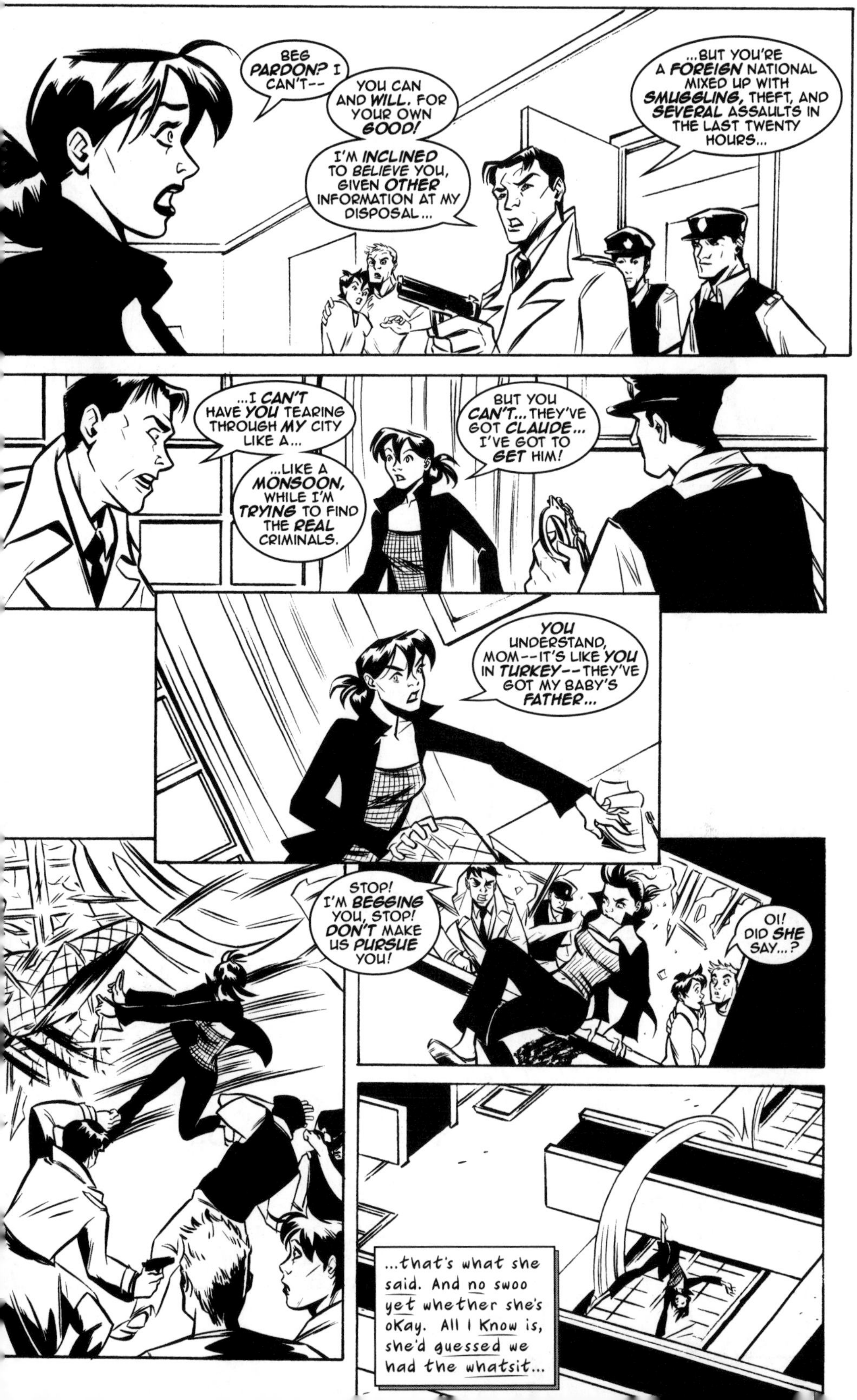
BEG PARDON? I CAN'T--
YOU CAN AND WILL. FOR YOUR OWN GOOD!
I'M INCLINED TO BELIEVE YOU, GIVEN OTHER INFORMATION AT MY DISPOSAL...
...BUT YOU'RE A FOREIGN NATIONAL MIXED UP WITH SMUGGLING, THEFT, AND SEVERAL ASSAULTS IN THE LAST TWENTY HOURS...
...I CAN'T HAVE YOU TEARING THROUGH MY CITY LIKE A...
...LIKE A MONSOON, WHILE I'M TRYING TO FIND THE REAL CRIMINALS.
BUT YOU CAN'T... THEY'VE GOT CLAUDE... I'VE GOT TO GET HIM!
YOU UNDERSTAND, MOM--IT'S LIKE YOU IN TURKEY--THEY'VE GOT MY BABY'S FATHER...
STOP! I'M BEGGING YOU, STOP! DON'T MAKE US PURSUE YOU!
OI! DID SHE SAY...?
...that's what she said. And no swoo yet whether she's okay. All I Know is, she'd guessed we had the whatsit...

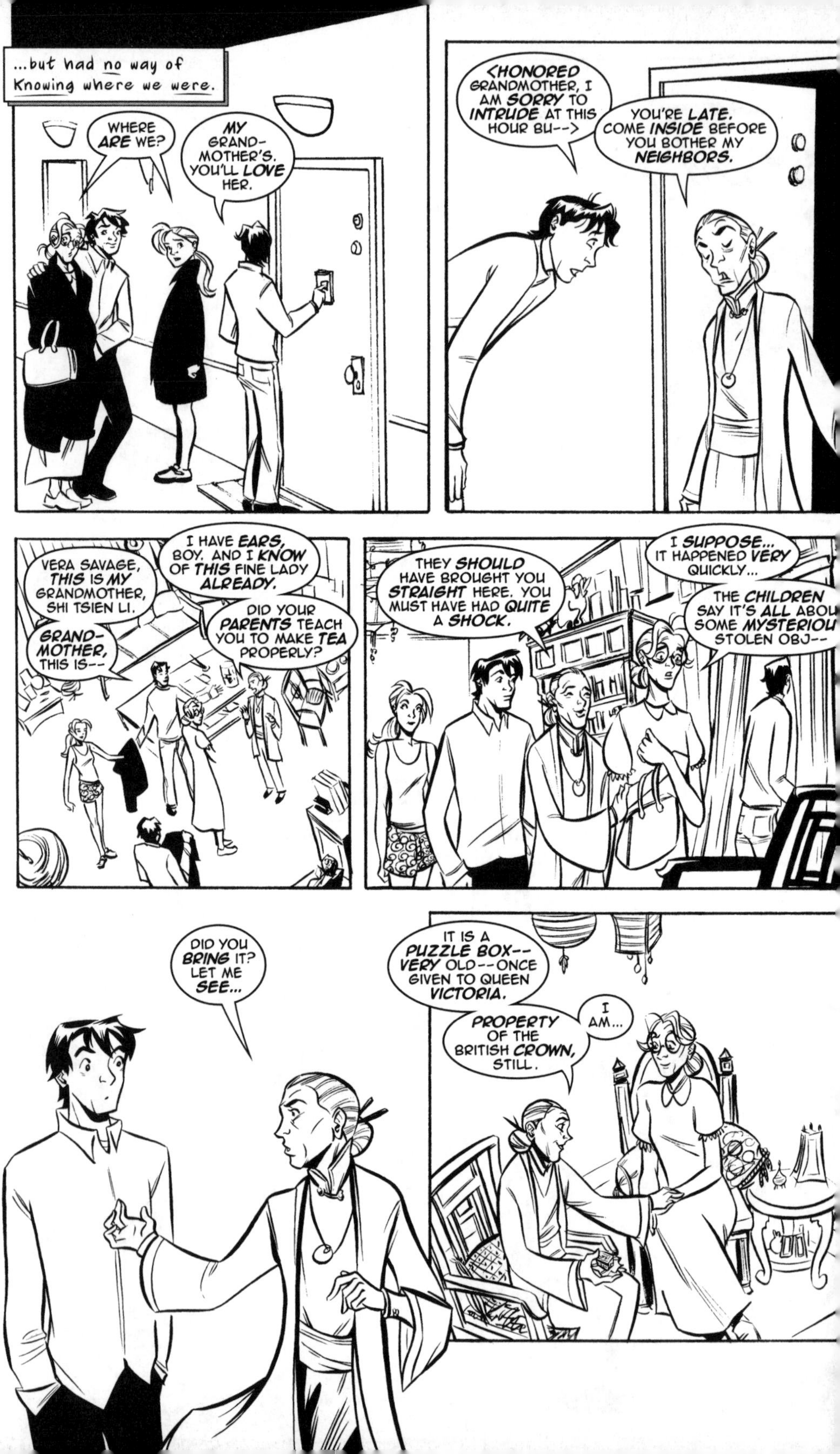
...but had no way of Knowing where we were.
WHERE ARE WE?
MY GRAND-MOTHER'S. YOU'LL LOVE HER.
<HONORED GRANDMOTHER, I AM SORRY TO INTRUDE AT THIS HOUR BU-->
YOU'RE LATE. COME INSIDE BEFORE YOU BOTHER MY NEIGHBORS.
VERA SAVAGE, THIS IS MY GRANDMOTHER, SHI TSIEN LI.
I HAVE EARS, BOY. AND I KNOW OF THIS FINE LADY ALREADY.
GRAND-MOTHER, THIS IS--
DID YOUR PARENTS TEACH YOU TO MAKE TEA PROPERLY?
THEY SHOULD HAVE BROUGHT YOU STRAIGHT HERE. YOU MUST HAVE HAD QUITE A SHOCK.
I SUPPOSE... IT HAPPENED VERY QUICKLY...
THE CHILDREN SAY IT'S ALL ABOU SOME MYSTERIOU STOLEN OBJ--
DID YOU BRING IT? LET ME SEE...
IT IS A PUZZLE BOX-- VERY OLD--ONCE GIVEN TO QUEEN VICTORIA.
PROPERTY OF THE BRITISH CROWN, STILL.
I AM...

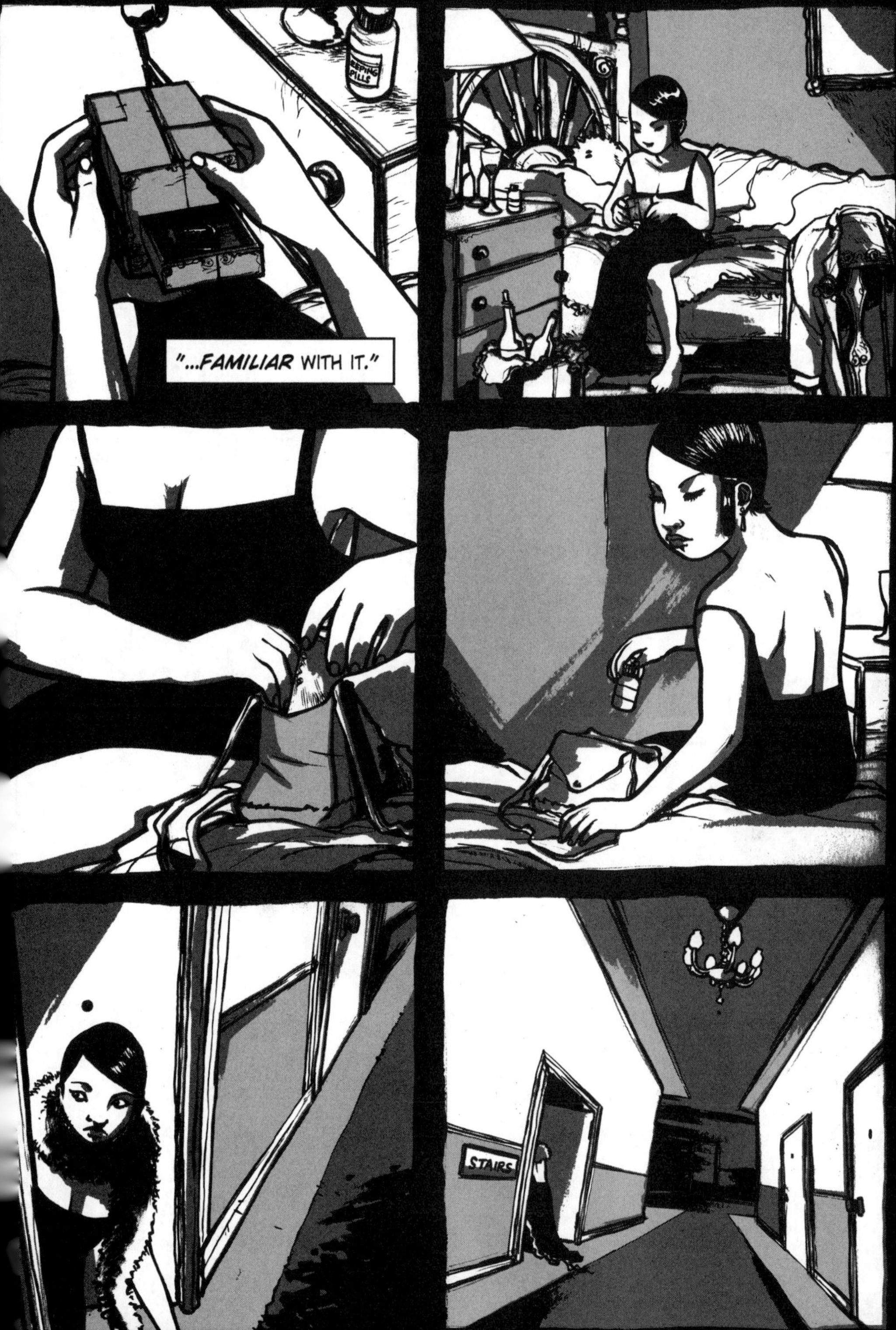
SLEEPING PILLS
"...FAMILIAR WITH IT."
STAIRS

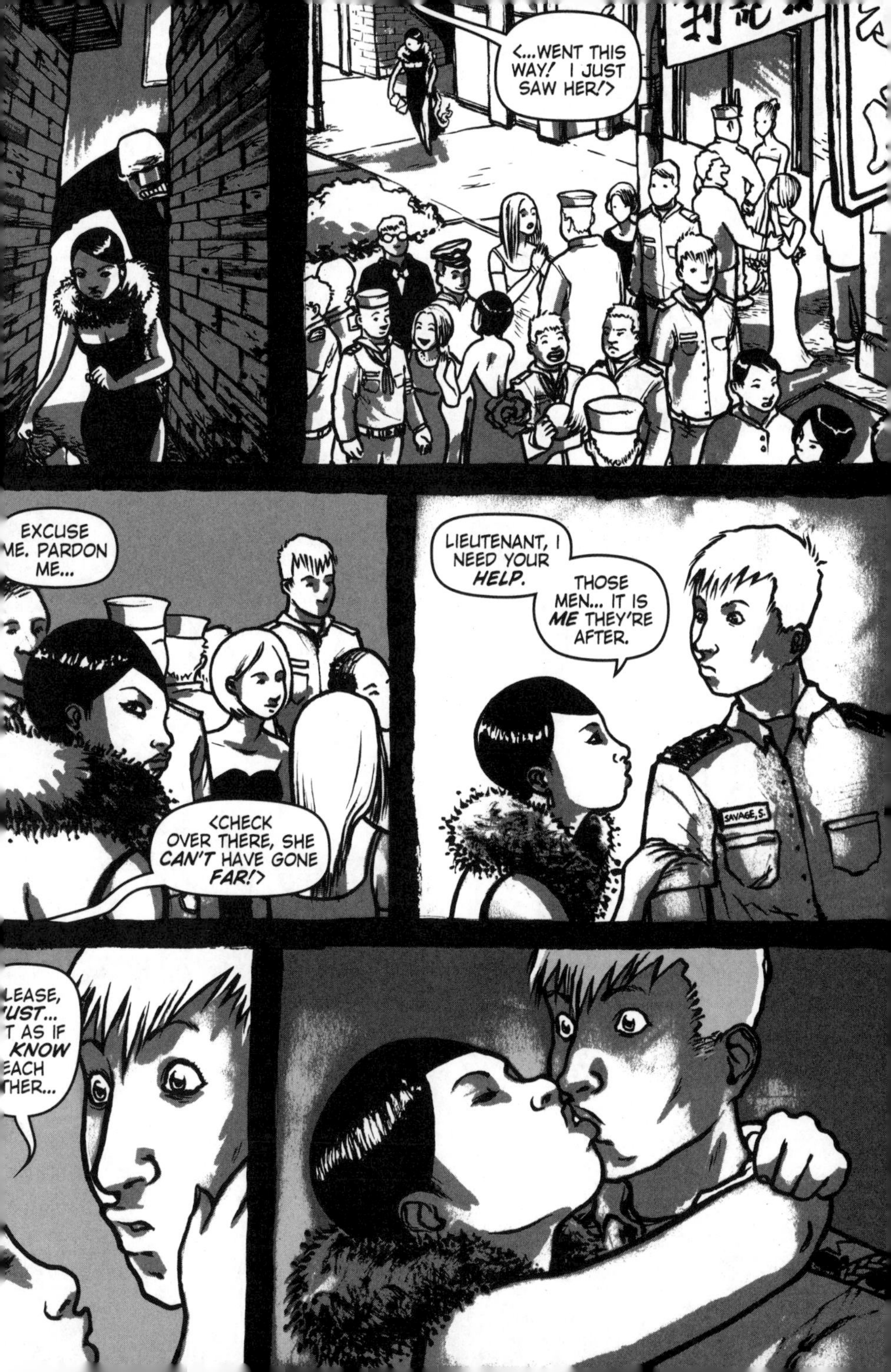
<...WENT THIS WAY! I JUST SAW HER!>
EXCUSE ME. PARDON ME...
<CHECK OVER THERE, SHE CAN'T HAVE GONE FAR!>
LIEUTENANT, I NEED YOUR HELP.
THOSE MEN... IT IS ME THEY'RE AFTER.
SAVAGE, S.
LEASE, UST... T AS IF KNOW EACH THER...

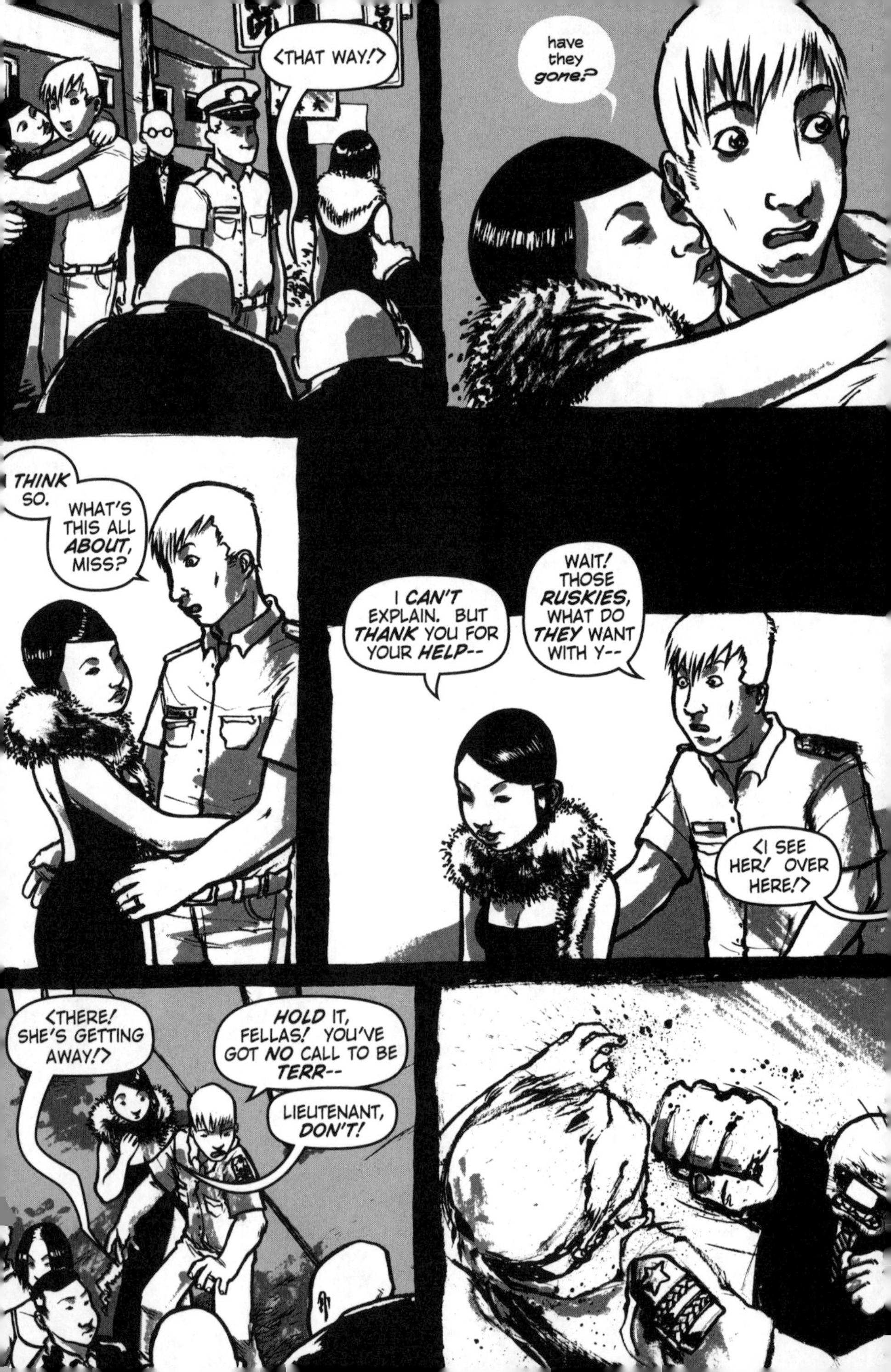
<THAT WAY!>
have they gone?
THINK SO.
WHAT'S THIS ALL ABOUT, MISS?
I CAN'T EXPLAIN. BUT THANK YOU FOR YOUR HELP--
WAIT! THOSE RUSKIES, WHAT DO THEY WANT WITH Y--
<I SEE HER! OVER HERE!>
<THERE! SHE'S GETTING AWAY!>
HOLD IT, FELLAS! YOU'VE GOT NO CALL TO BE TERR--
LIEUTENANT, DON'T!

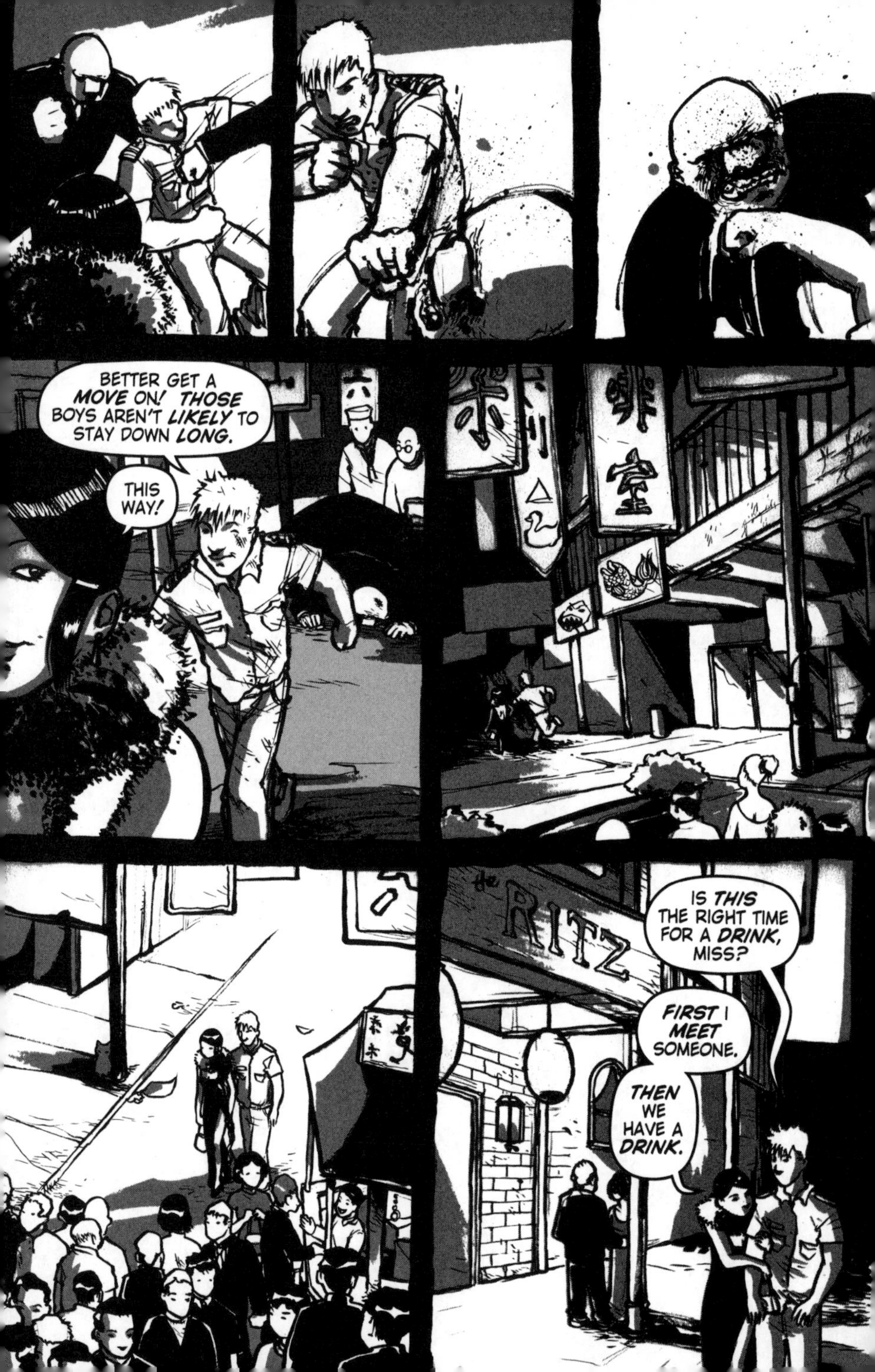
BETTER GET A MOVE ON! THOSE BOYS AREN'T LIKELY TO STAY DOWN LONG.
THIS WAY!
RITZ
IS THIS THE RIGHT TIME FOR A DRINK, MISS?
FIRST I MEET SOMEONE.
THEN WE HAVE A DRINK.

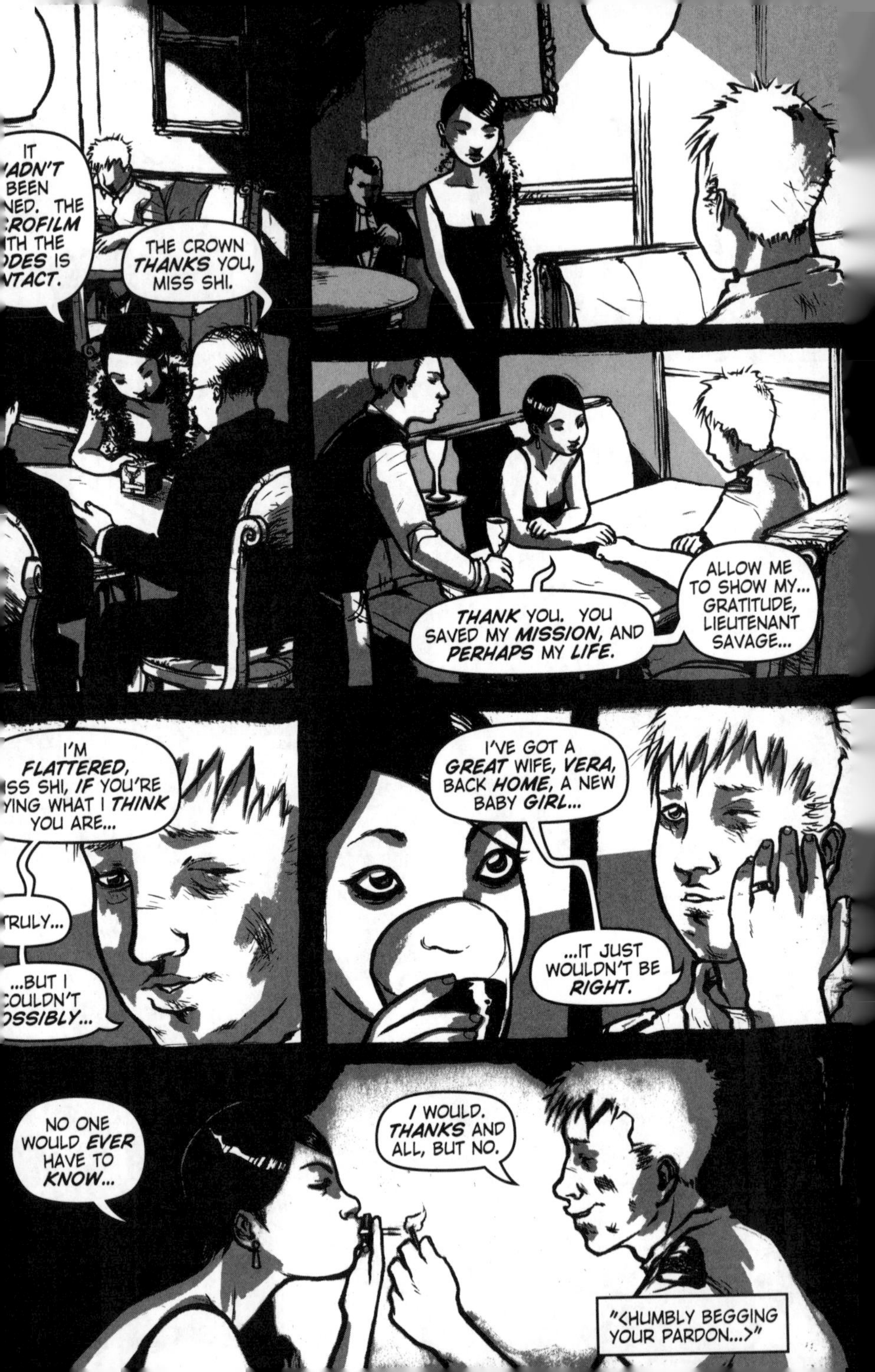
IT ADN'T BEEN NED. THE ROFILM TH THE DES IS NTACT.
THE CROWN THANKS YOU, MISS SHI.
THANK YOU. YOU SAVED MY MISSION, AND PERHAPS MY LIFE.
ALLOW ME TO SHOW MY... GRATITUDE, LIEUTENANT SAVAGE...
I'M FLATTERED, SS SHI, IF YOU'RE YING WHAT I THINK YOU ARE...
TRULY...
...BUT I COULDN'T OSSIBLY...
I'VE GOT A GREAT WIFE, VERA, BACK HOME, A NEW BABY GIRL...
...IT JUST WOULDN'T BE RIGHT.
NO ONE WOULD EVER HAVE TO KNOW...
I WOULD. THANKS AND ALL, BUT NO.
"<HUMBLY BEGGING YOUR PARDON...>"

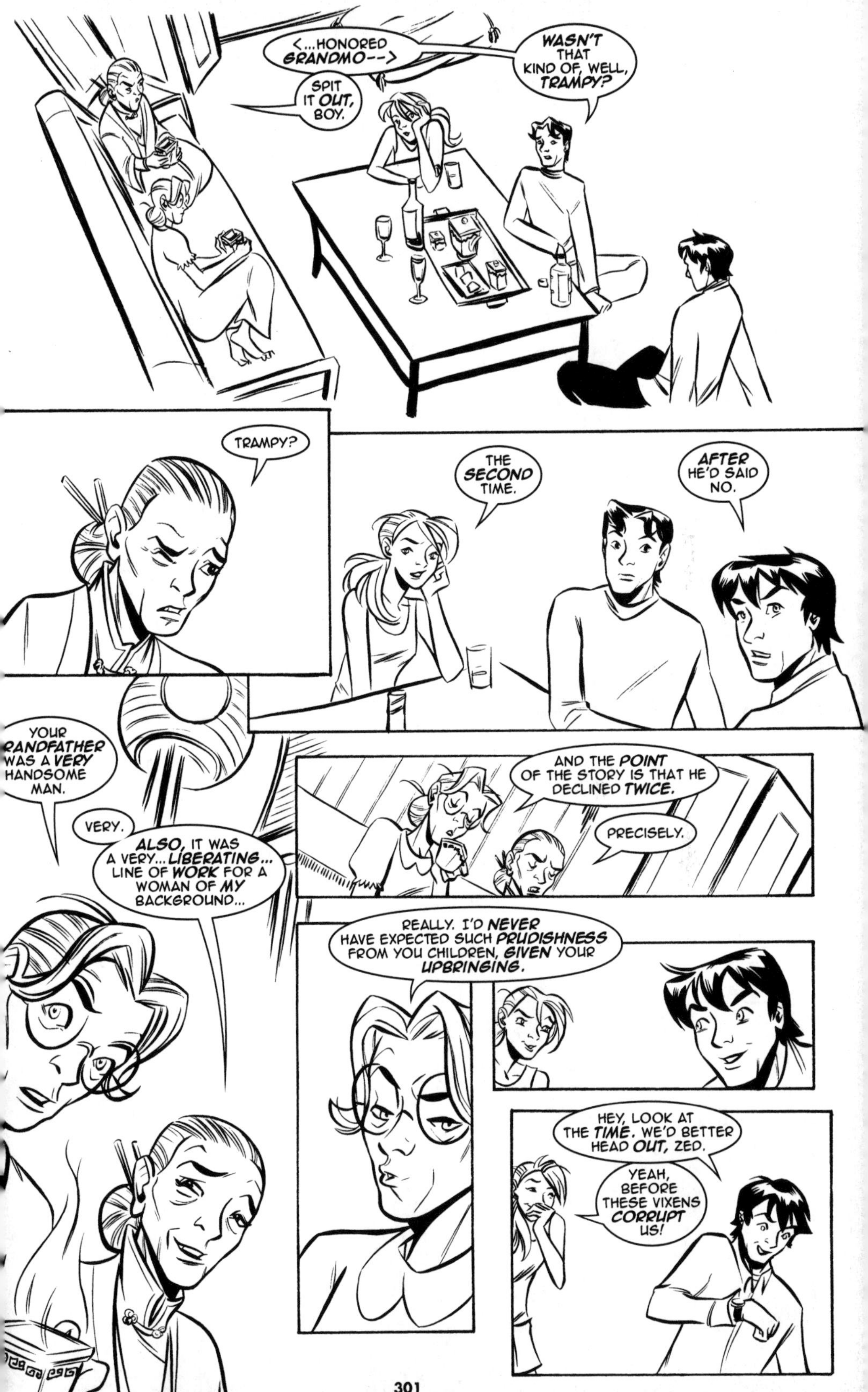
<...HONORED GRANDMO-->
SPIT IT OUT, BOY.
WASN'T THAT KIND OF, WELL, TRAMPY?
TRAMPY?
THE SECOND TIME.
AFTER HE'D SAID NO.
YOUR RANDFATHER WAS A VERY HANDSOME MAN.
VERY.
ALSO, IT WAS A VERY... LIBERATING... LINE OF WORK FOR A WOMAN OF MY BACKGROUND...
AND THE POINT OF THE STORY IS THAT HE DECLINED TWICE.
PRECISELY.
REALLY. I'D NEVER HAVE EXPECTED SUCH PRUDISHNESS FROM YOU CHILDREN, GIVEN YOUR UPBRINGING.
HEY, LOOK AT THE TIME. WE'D BETTER HEAD OUT, ZED.
YEAH, BEFORE THESE VIXENS CORRUPT US!

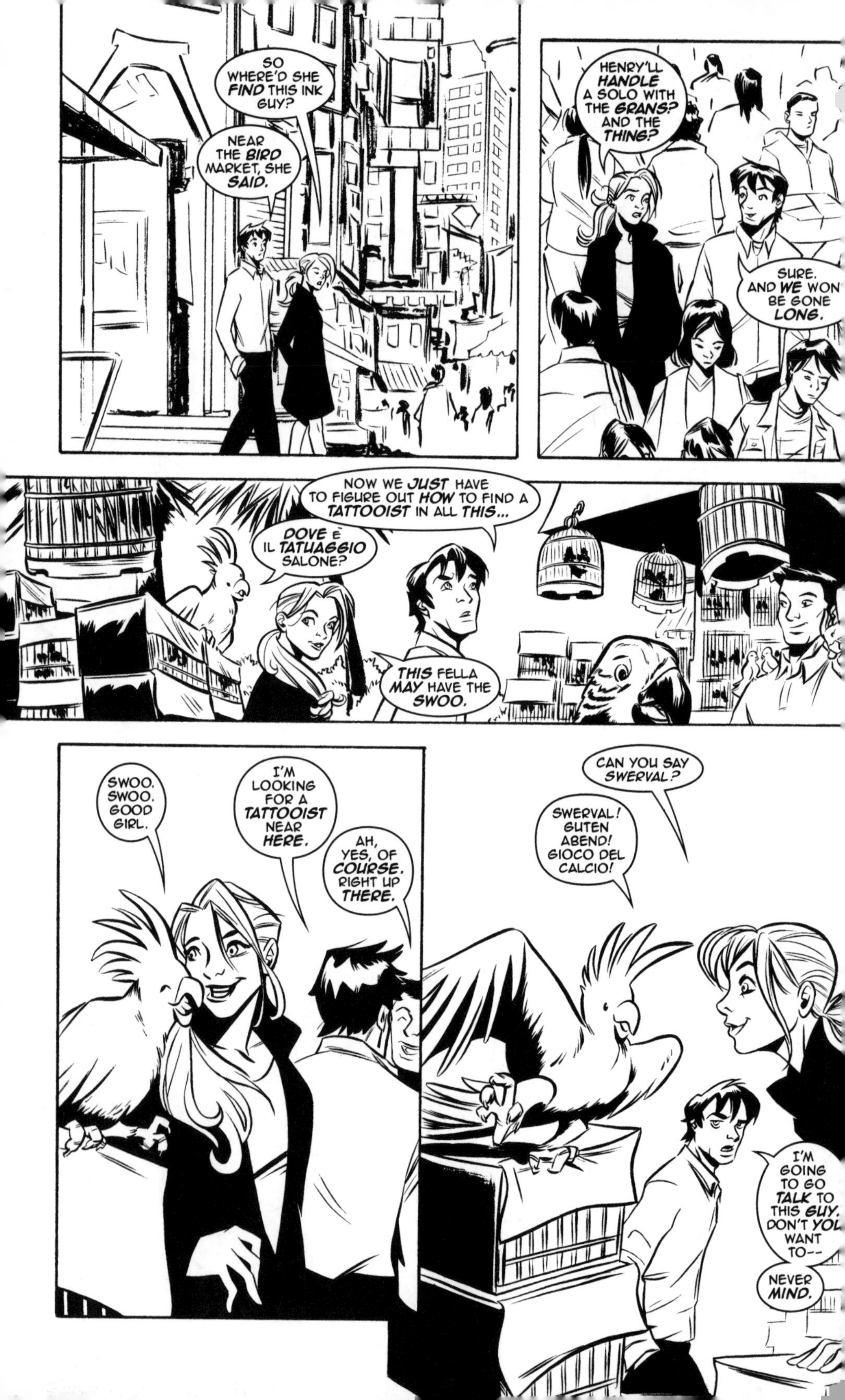
SO WHERE'D SHE FIND THIS INK GUY?
NEAR THE BIRD MARKET, SHE SAID.
HENRY'LL HANDLE A SOLO WITH THE GRANS? AND THE THING?
SURE. AND WE WON' BE GONE LONG.
NOW WE JUST HAVE TO FIGURE OUT HOW TO FIND A TATTOOIST IN ALL THIS...
DOVE È IL TATUAGGIO SALONE?
THIS FELLA MAY HAVE THE SWOO.
SWOO. SWOO. GOOD GIRL.
I'M LOOKING FOR A TATTOOIST NEAR HERE.
AH, YES, OF COURSE. RIGHT UP THERE.
CAN YOU SAY SWERVAL?
SWERVAL! GUTEN ABEND! GIOCO DEL CALCIO!
I'M GOING TO GO TALK TO THIS GUY. DON'T YOU WANT TO--
NEVER MIND.

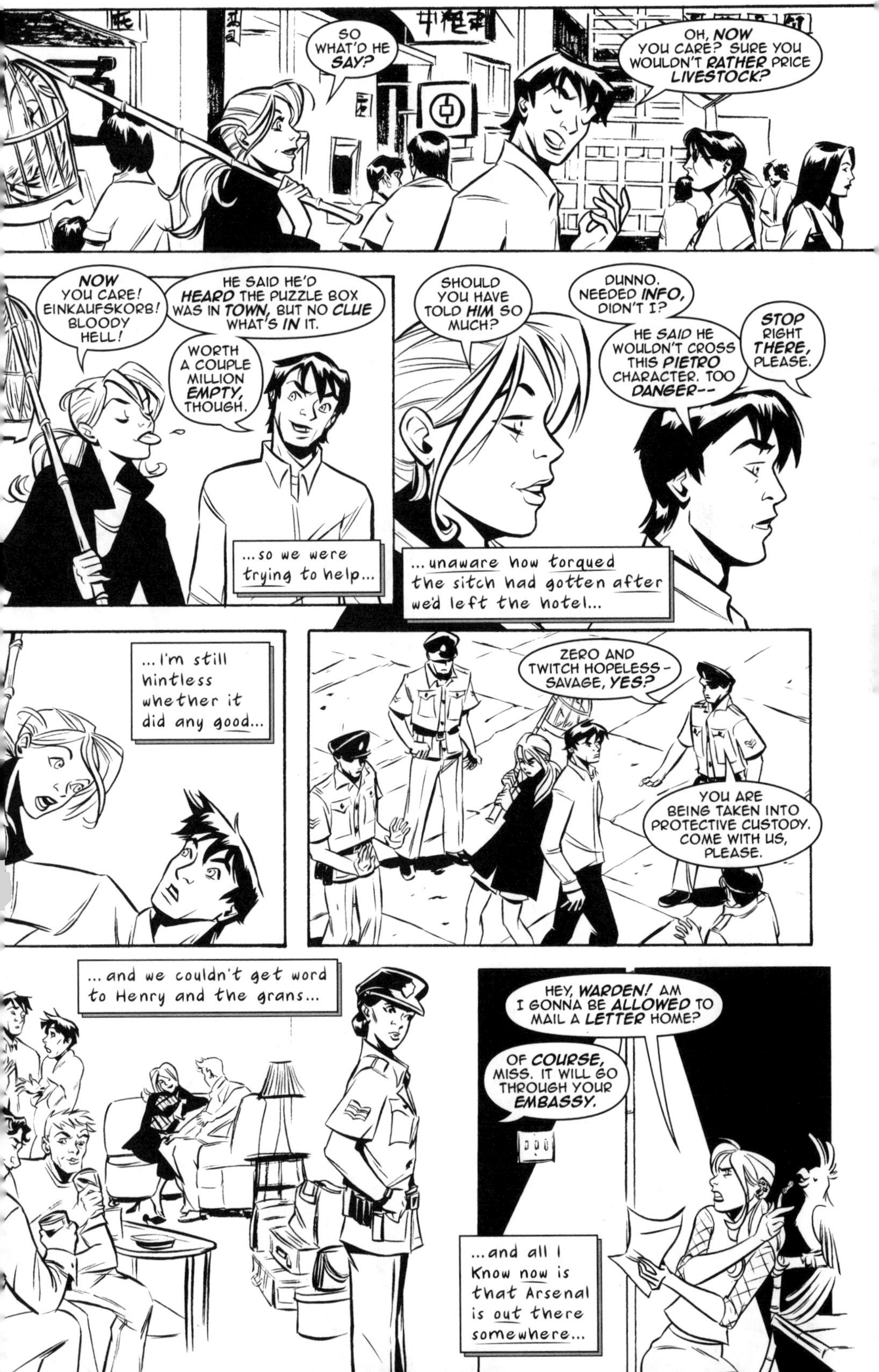
SO WHAT'D HE SAY?
OH, NOW YOU CARE? SURE YOU WOULDN'T RATHER PRICE LIVESTOCK?
NOW YOU CARE! EINKAUFSKORB! BLOODY HELL!
HE SAID HE'D HEARD THE PUZZLE BOX WAS IN TOWN, BUT NO CLUE WHAT'S IN IT.
WORTH A COUPLE MILLION EMPTY, THOUGH.
...so we were trying to help...
SHOULD YOU HAVE TOLD HIM SO MUCH?
DUNNO. NEEDED INFO, DIDN'T I?
HE SAID HE WOULDN'T CROSS THIS PIETRO CHARACTER. TOO DANGER--
STOP RIGHT THERE, PLEASE.
...unaware how torqued the sitch had gotten after we'd left the hotel...
...I'm still hintless whether it did any good...
ZERO AND TWITCH HOPELESS-SAVAGE, YES?
YOU ARE BEING TAKEN INTO PROTECTIVE CUSTODY. COME WITH US, PLEASE.
...and we couldn't get word to Henry and the grans...
HEY, WARDEN! AM I GONNA BE ALLOWED TO MAIL A LETTER HOME?
OF COURSE, MISS. IT WILL GO THROUGH YOUR EMBASSY.
...and all I know now is that Arsenal is out there somewhere...

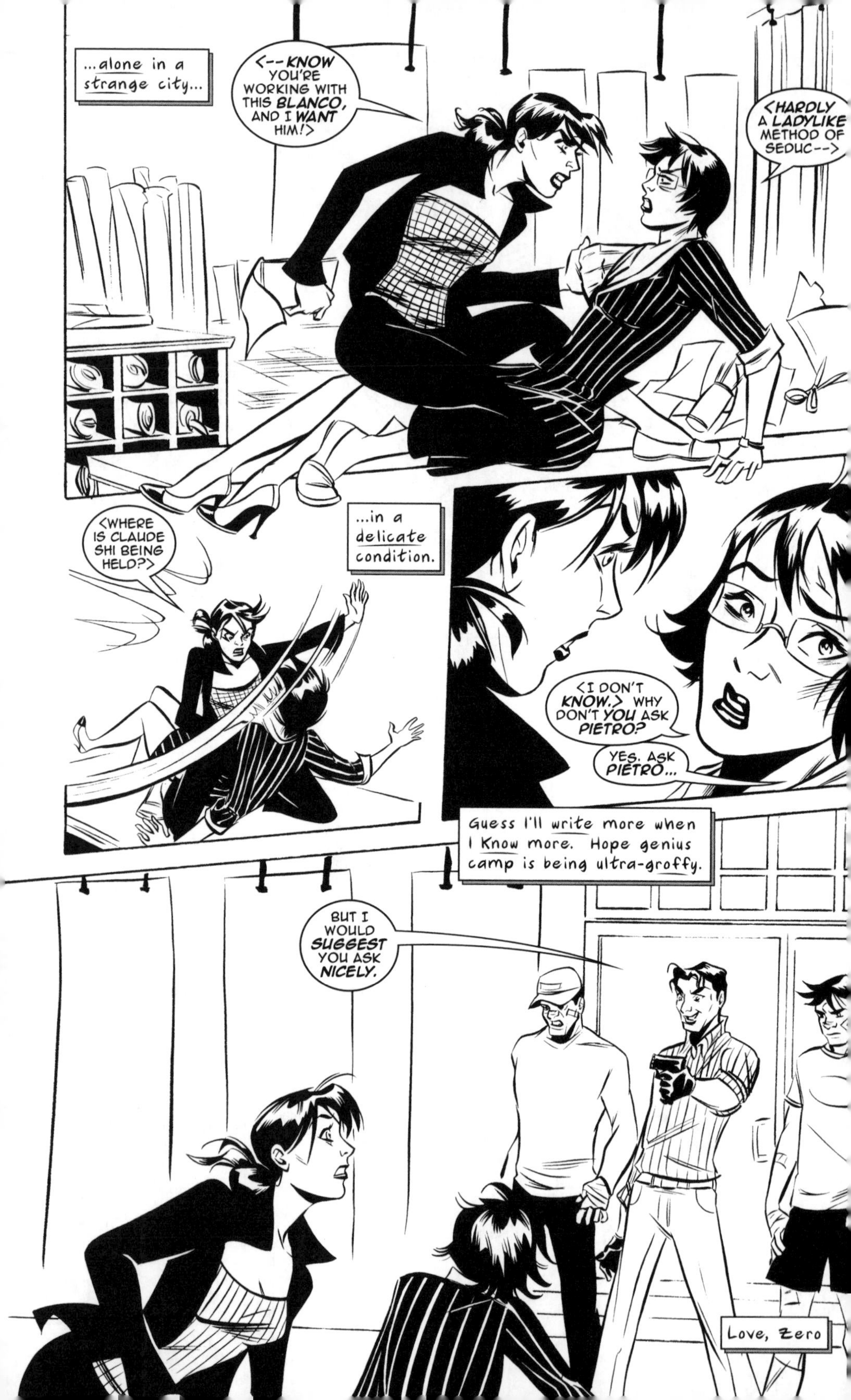
...alone in a strange city...
<--KNOW YOU'RE WORKING WITH THIS BLANCO, AND I WANT HIM!>
<HARDLY A LADYLIKE METHOD OF SEDUC-->
<WHERE IS CLAUDE SHI BEING HELD?>
...in a delicate condition.
<I DON'T KNOW.> WHY DON'T YOU ASK PIETRO?
YES. ASK PIETRO...
Guess I'll write more when I Know more. Hope genius camp is being ultra-groffy.
BUT I WOULD SUGGEST YOU ASK NICELY.
Love, Zero

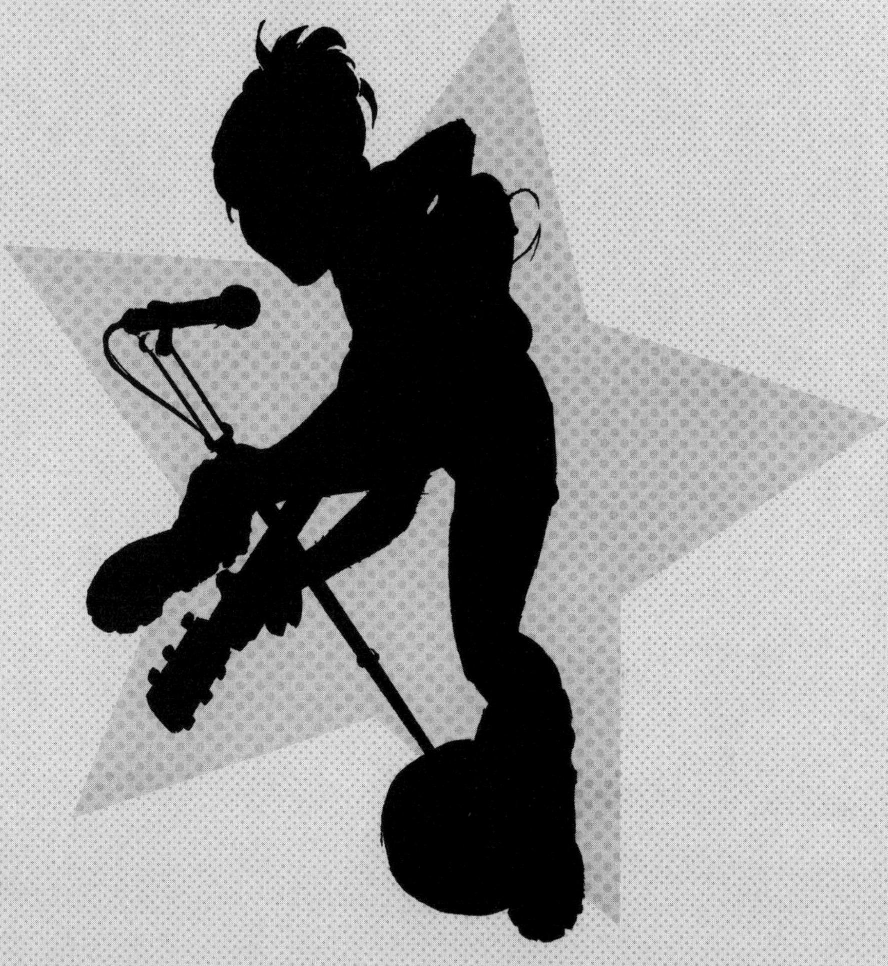

CHAPTER 4

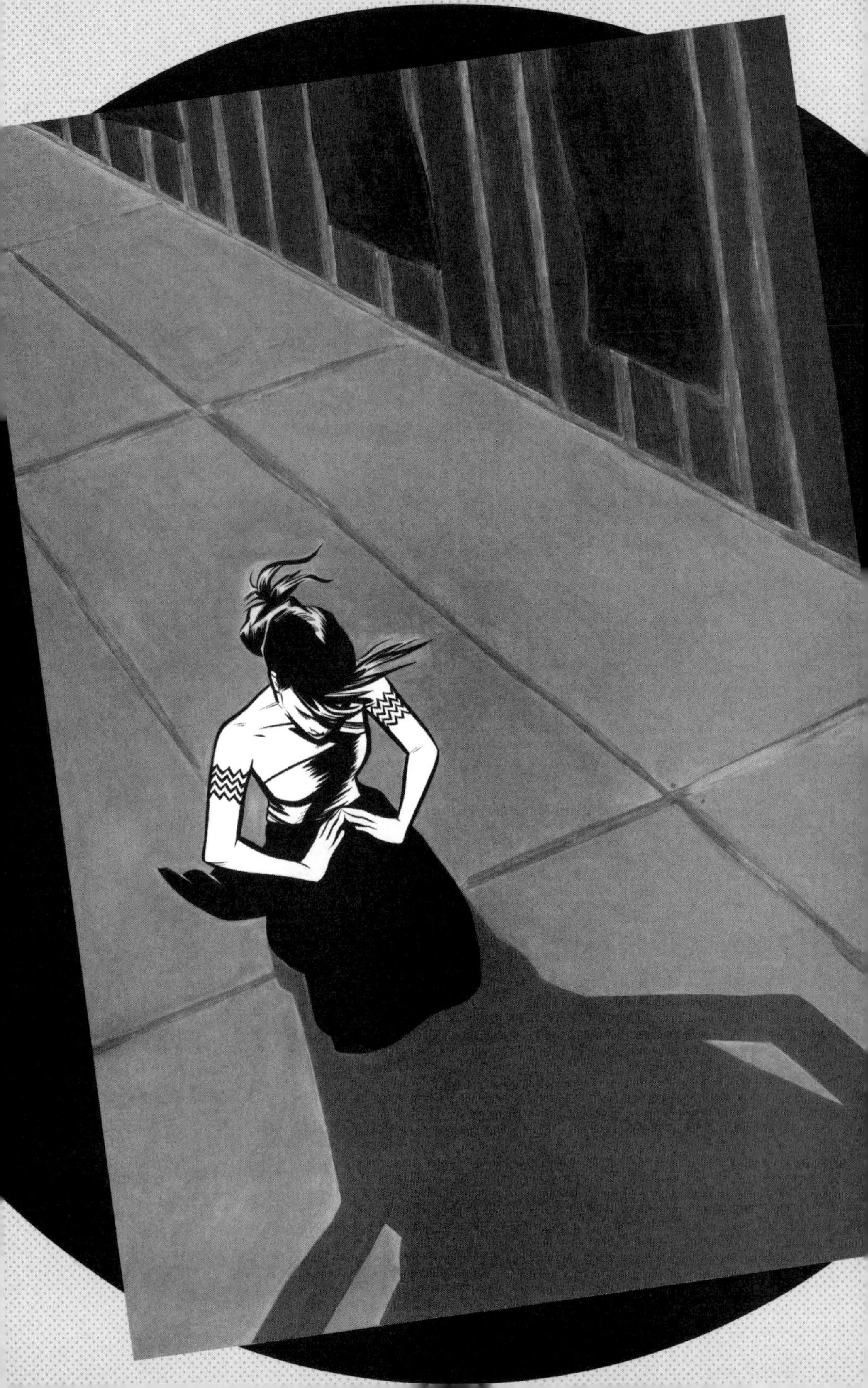

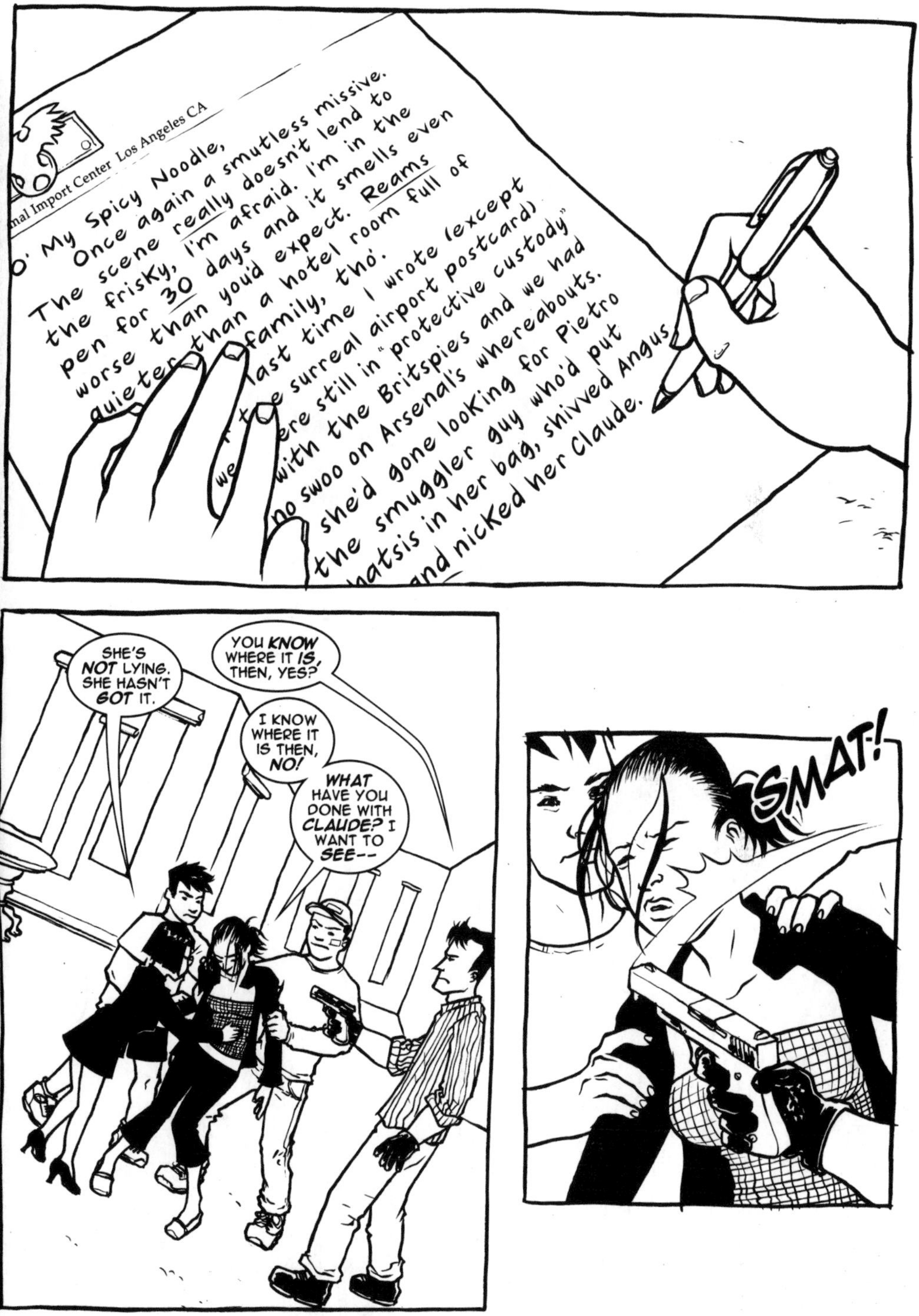

mal Import Center Los Angeles CA
o' My Spicy Noodle,
Once again a smutless missive.
The scene really doesn't lend to
the frisky, I'm afraid. I'm in the
pen for 30 days and it smells even
worse than you'd expect. Reams
quieter than a hotel room full of
family, tho'.
last time I wrote (except
the surreal airport postcard)
we ere still in "protective custody"
with the Britspies and we had
no swoo on Arsenal's whereabouts.
she'd gone looking for Pietro
the smuggler guy who'd put
atsis in her bag, shivved Angus
and nicked her Claude.
SHE'S NOT LYING. SHE HASN'T GOT IT.
YOU KNOW WHERE IT IS, THEN, YES?
I KNOW WHERE IT IS THEN, NO!
WHAT HAVE YOU DONE WITH CLAUDE? I WANT TO SEE--
SMAT!

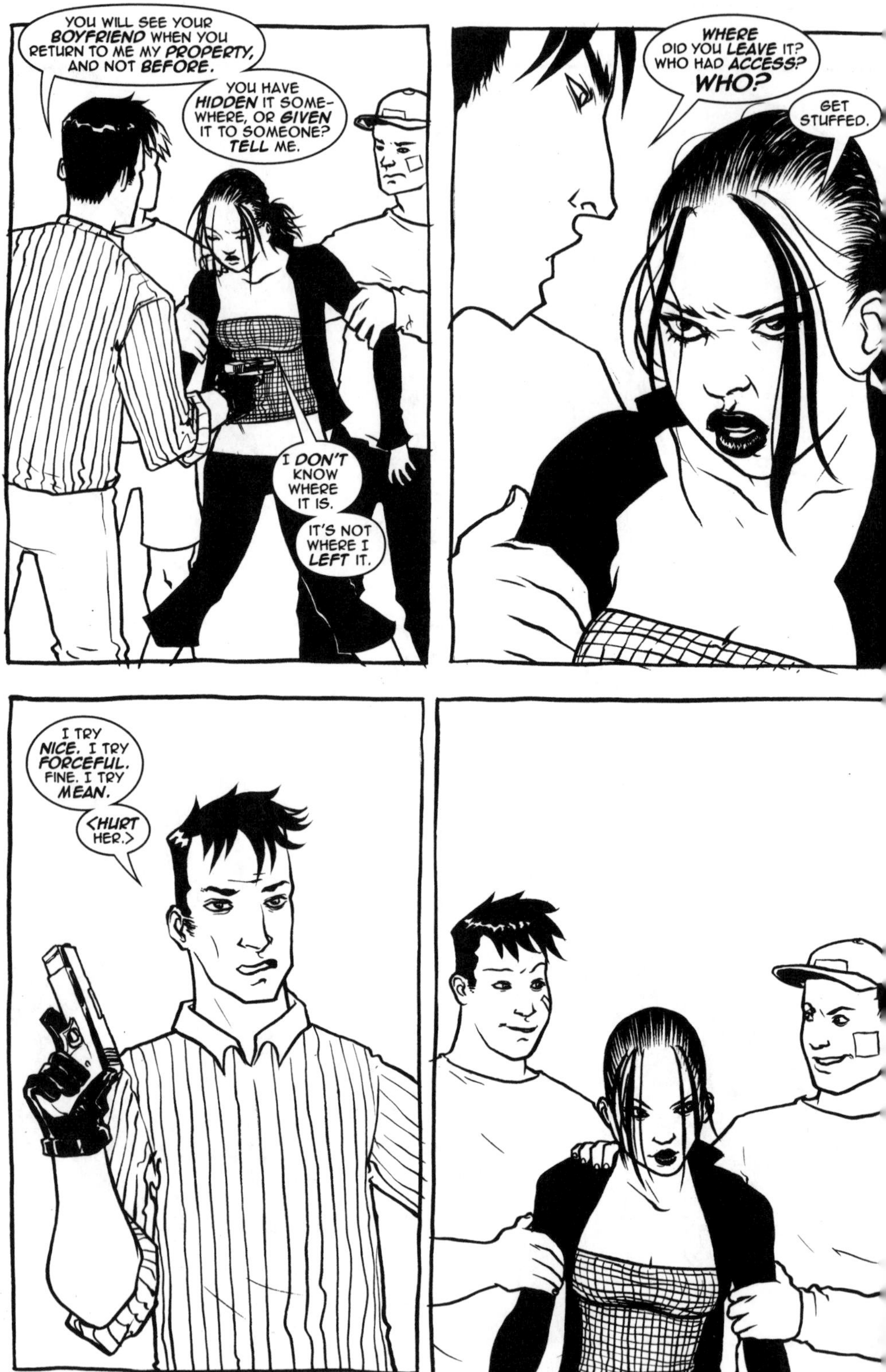
YOU WILL SEE YOUR BOYFRIEND WHEN YOU RETURN TO ME MY PROPERTY, AND NOT BEFORE.
YOU HAVE HIDDEN IT SOME-WHERE, OR GIVEN IT TO SOMEONE? TELL ME.
I DON'T KNOW WHERE IT IS.
IT'S NOT WHERE I LEFT IT.
WHERE DID YOU LEAVE IT? WHO HAD ACCESS? WHO?
GET STUFFED.
I TRY NICE. I TRY FORCEFUL. FINE. I TRY MEAN.
<HURT HER.>

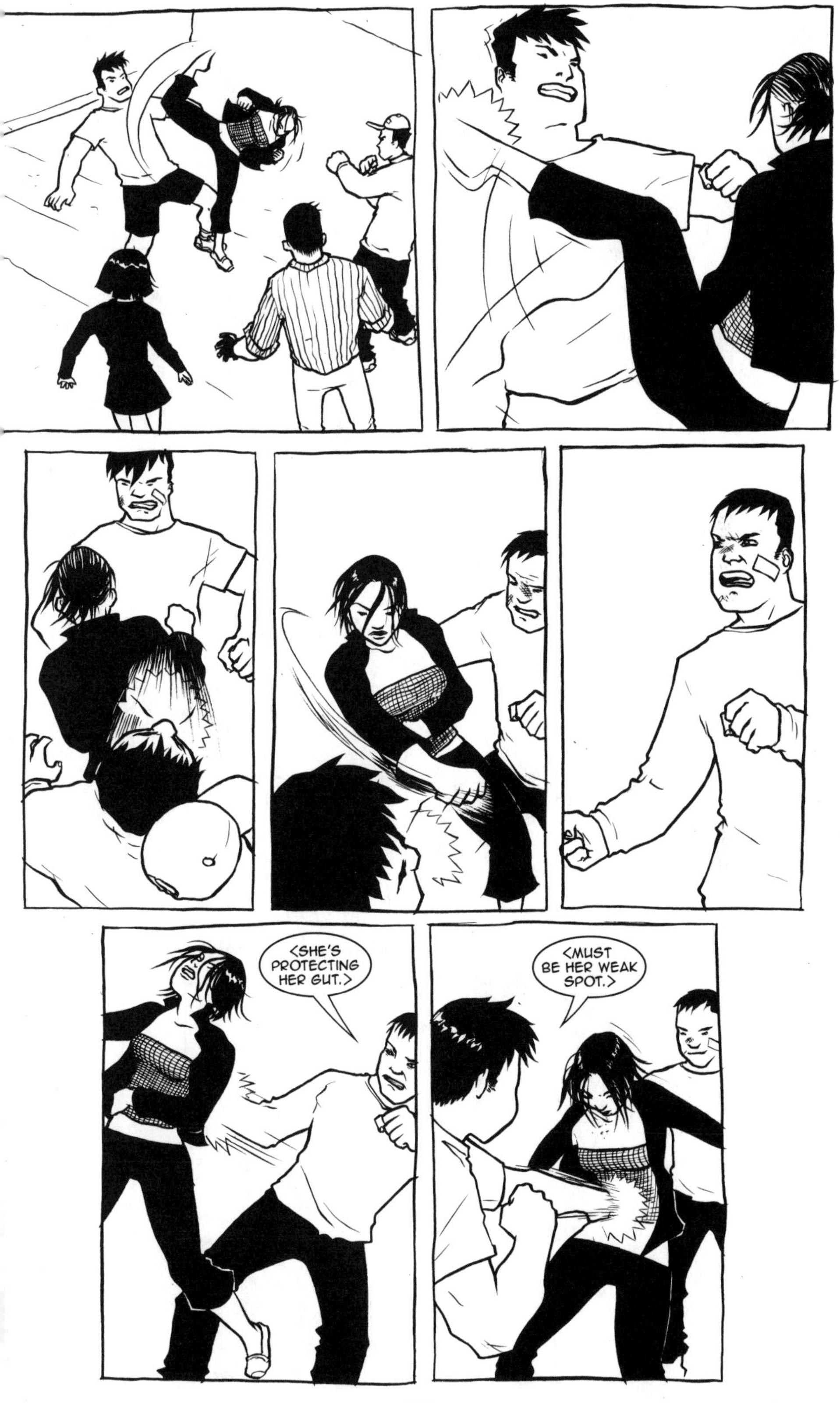
<SHE'S PROTECTING HER GUT.>
<MUST BE HER WEAK SPOT.>

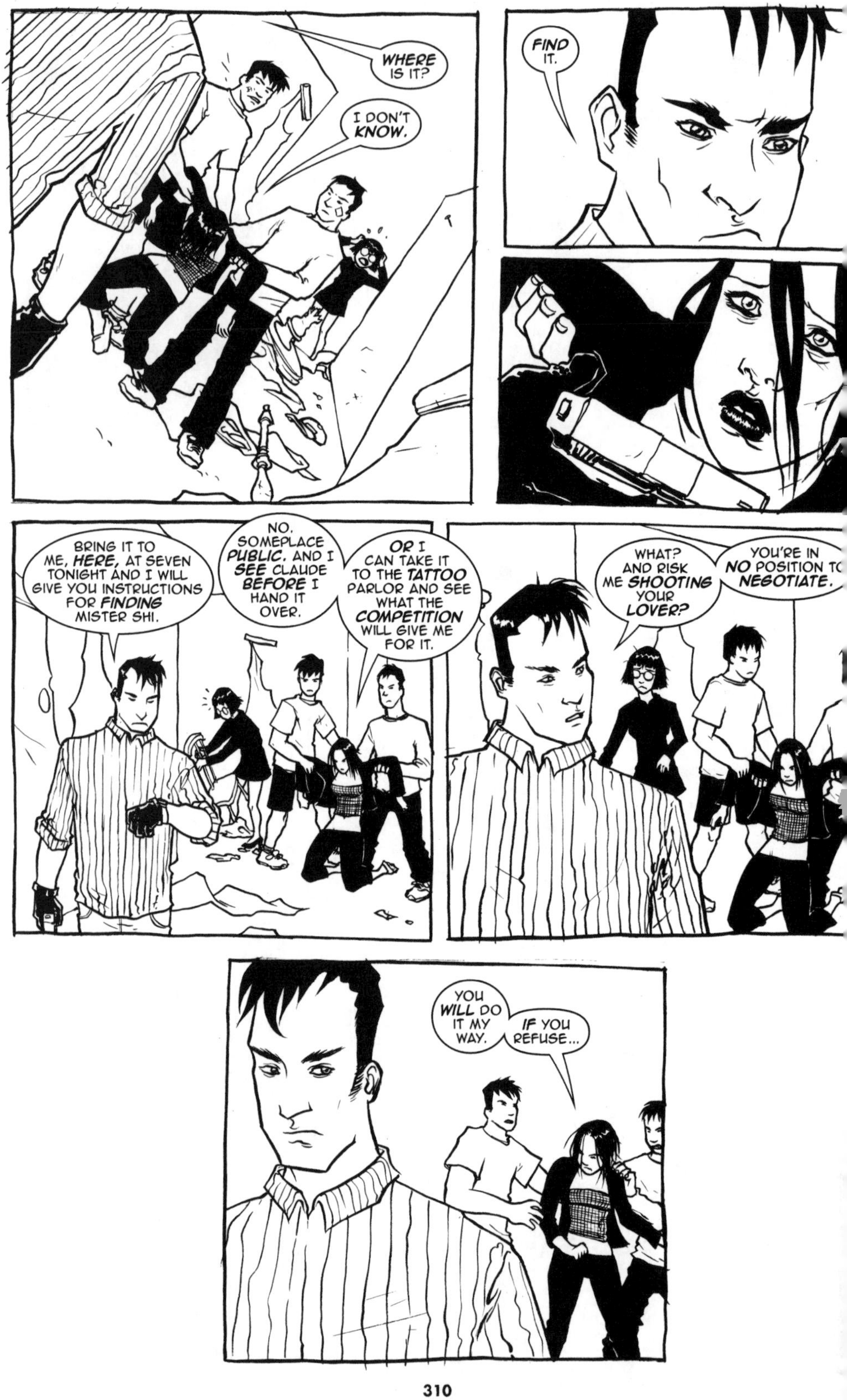
WHERE IS IT?
I DON'T KNOW.
FIND IT.
BRING IT TO ME, HERE, AT SEVEN TONIGHT AND I WILL GIVE YOU INSTRUCTIONS FOR FINDING MISTER SHI.
NO. SOMEPLACE PUBLIC. AND I SEE CLAUDE BEFORE I HAND IT OVER.
OR I CAN TAKE IT TO THE TATTOO PARLOR AND SEE WHAT THE COMPETITION WILL GIVE ME FOR IT.
WHAT? AND RISK ME SHOOTING YOUR LOVER?
YOU'RE IN NO POSITION TO NEGOTIATE.
YOU WILL DO IT MY WAY.
IF YOU REFUSE...

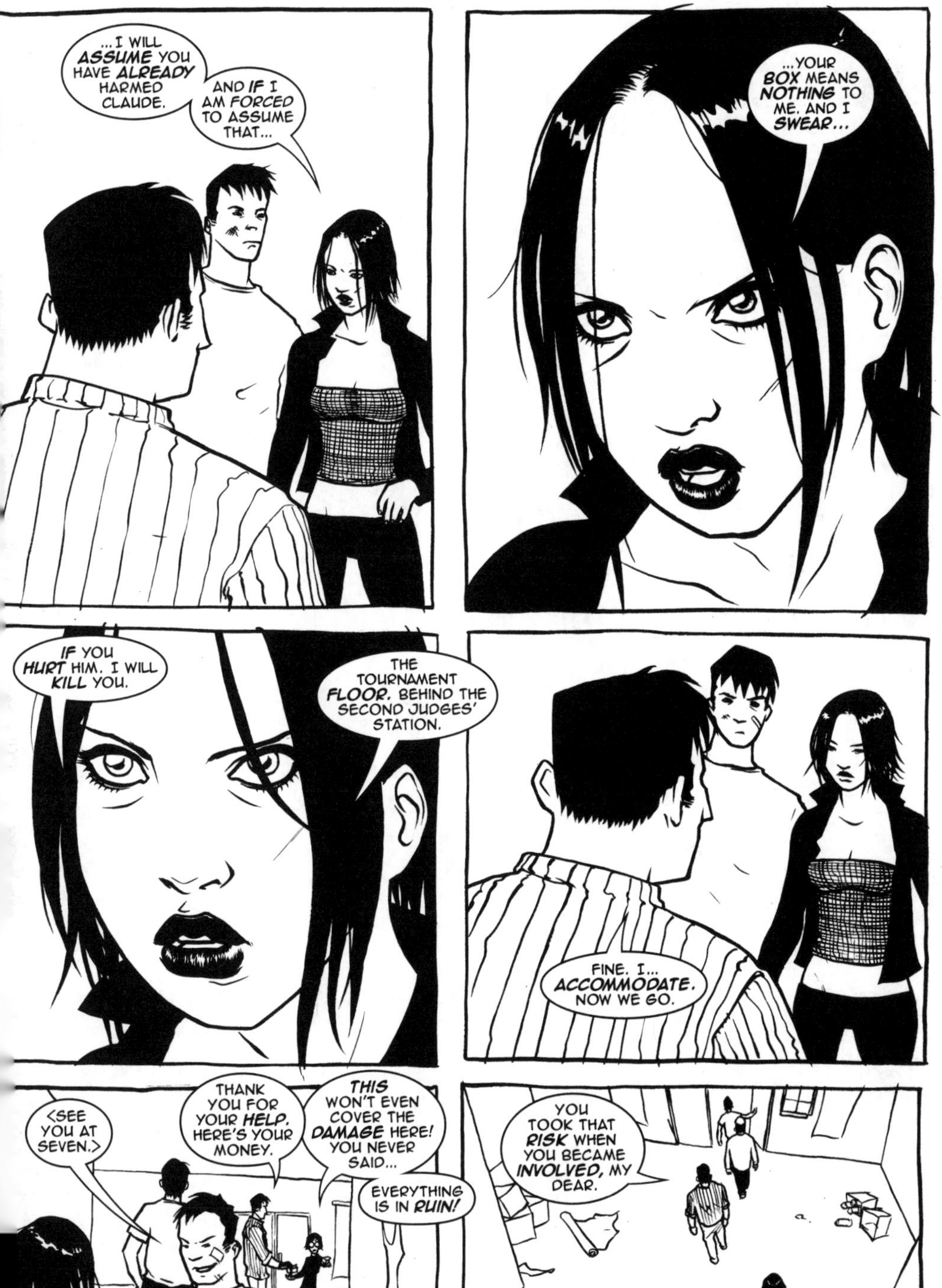
...I WILL ASSUME YOU HAVE ALREADY HARMED CLAUDE.
AND IF I AM FORCED TO ASSUME THAT...
...YOUR BOX MEANS NOTHING TO ME. AND I SWEAR...
IF YOU HURT HIM. I WILL KILL YOU.
THE TOURNAMENT FLOOR. BEHIND THE SECOND JUDGES' STATION.
FINE. I... ACCOMMODATE. NOW WE GO.
<SEE YOU AT SEVEN.>
THANK YOU FOR YOUR HELP. HERE'S YOUR MONEY.
THIS WON'T EVEN COVER THE DAMAGE HERE! YOU NEVER SAID...
EVERYTHING IS IN RUIN!
YOU TOOK THAT RISK WHEN YOU BECAME INVOLVED, MY DEAR.
She's clamming about what happened when she found Blanco...

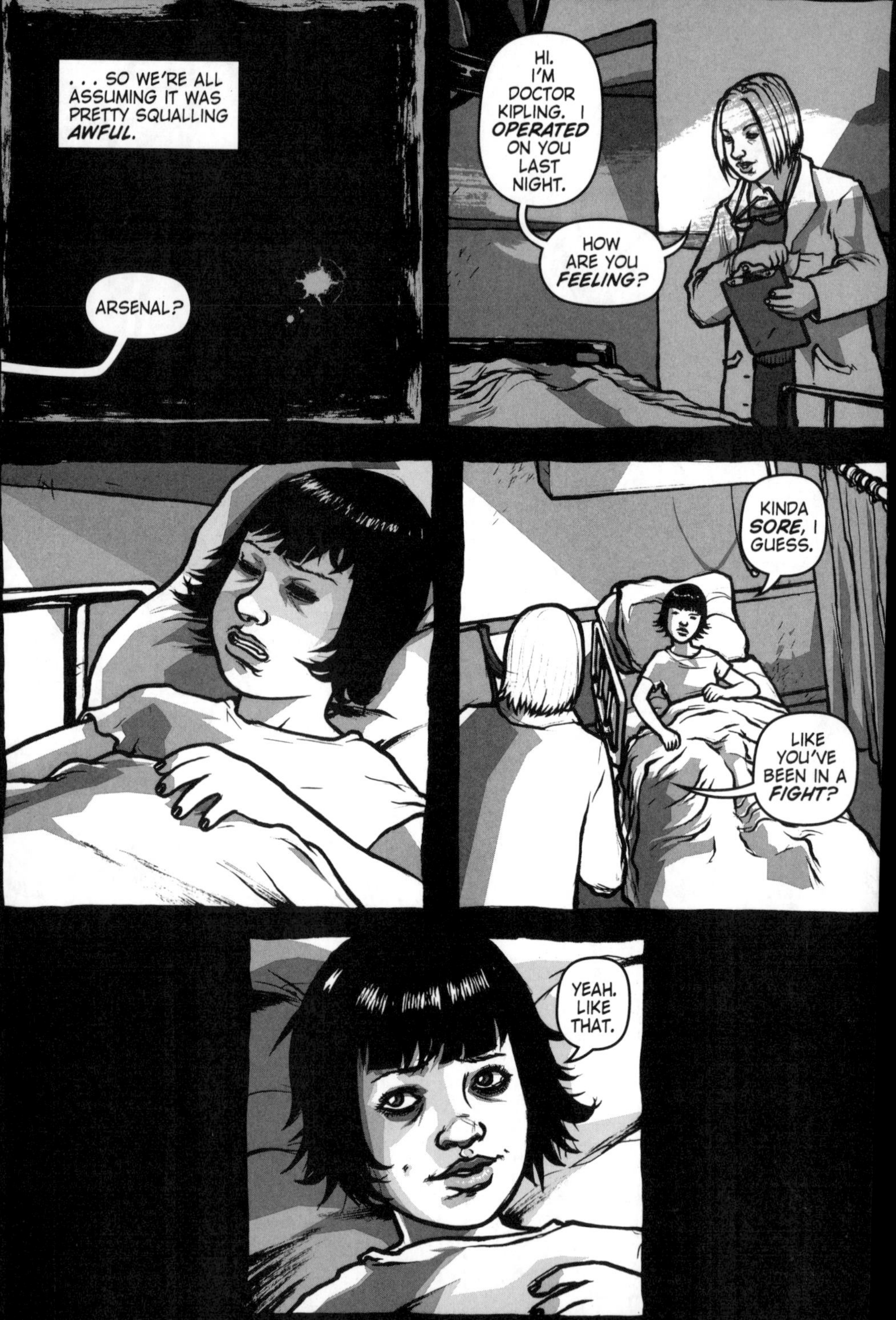
. . . SO WE'RE ALL ASSUMING IT WAS PRETTY SQUALLING **AWFUL.**
ARSENAL?
HI. I'M DOCTOR KIPLING. I **OPERATED** ON YOU LAST NIGHT.
HOW ARE YOU **FEELING?**
KINDA **SORE,** I GUESS.
LIKE YOU'VE BEEN IN A **FIGHT?**
YEAH. LIKE THAT.

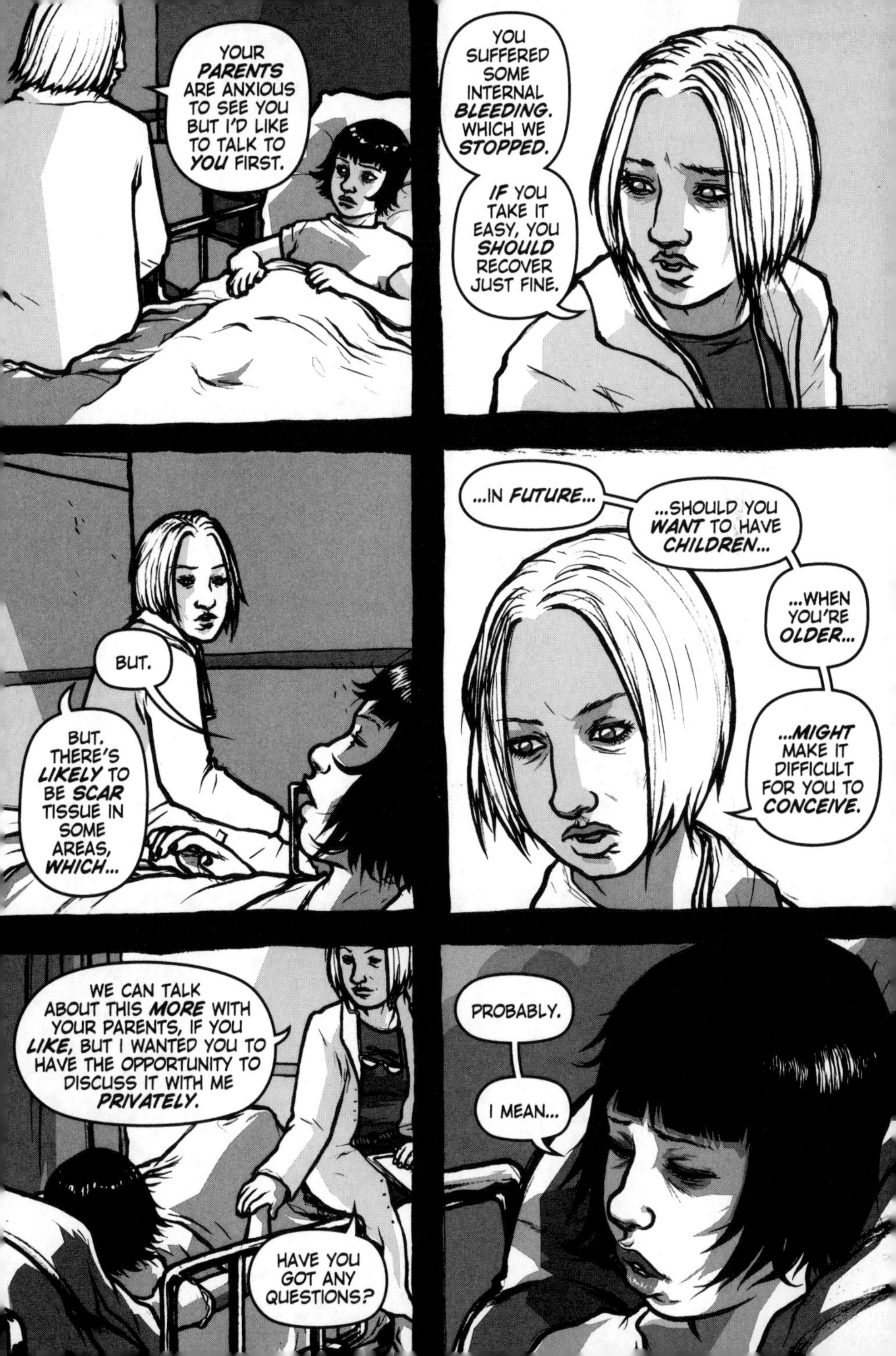
YOUR PARENTS ARE ANXIOUS TO SEE YOU BUT I'D LIKE TO TALK TO YOU FIRST.
YOU SUFFERED SOME INTERNAL BLEEDING. WHICH WE STOPPED.
IF YOU TAKE IT EASY, YOU SHOULD RECOVER JUST FINE.
BUT.
BUT. THERE'S LIKELY TO BE SCAR TISSUE IN SOME AREAS, WHICH...
...IN FUTURE...
...SHOULD YOU WANT TO HAVE CHILDREN...
...WHEN YOU'RE OLDER...
...MIGHT MAKE IT DIFFICULT FOR YOU TO CONCEIVE.
WE CAN TALK ABOUT THIS MORE WITH YOUR PARENTS, IF YOU LIKE, BUT I WANTED YOU TO HAVE THE OPPORTUNITY TO DISCUSS IT WITH ME PRIVATELY.
HAVE YOU GOT ANY QUESTIONS?
PROBABLY.
I MEAN...

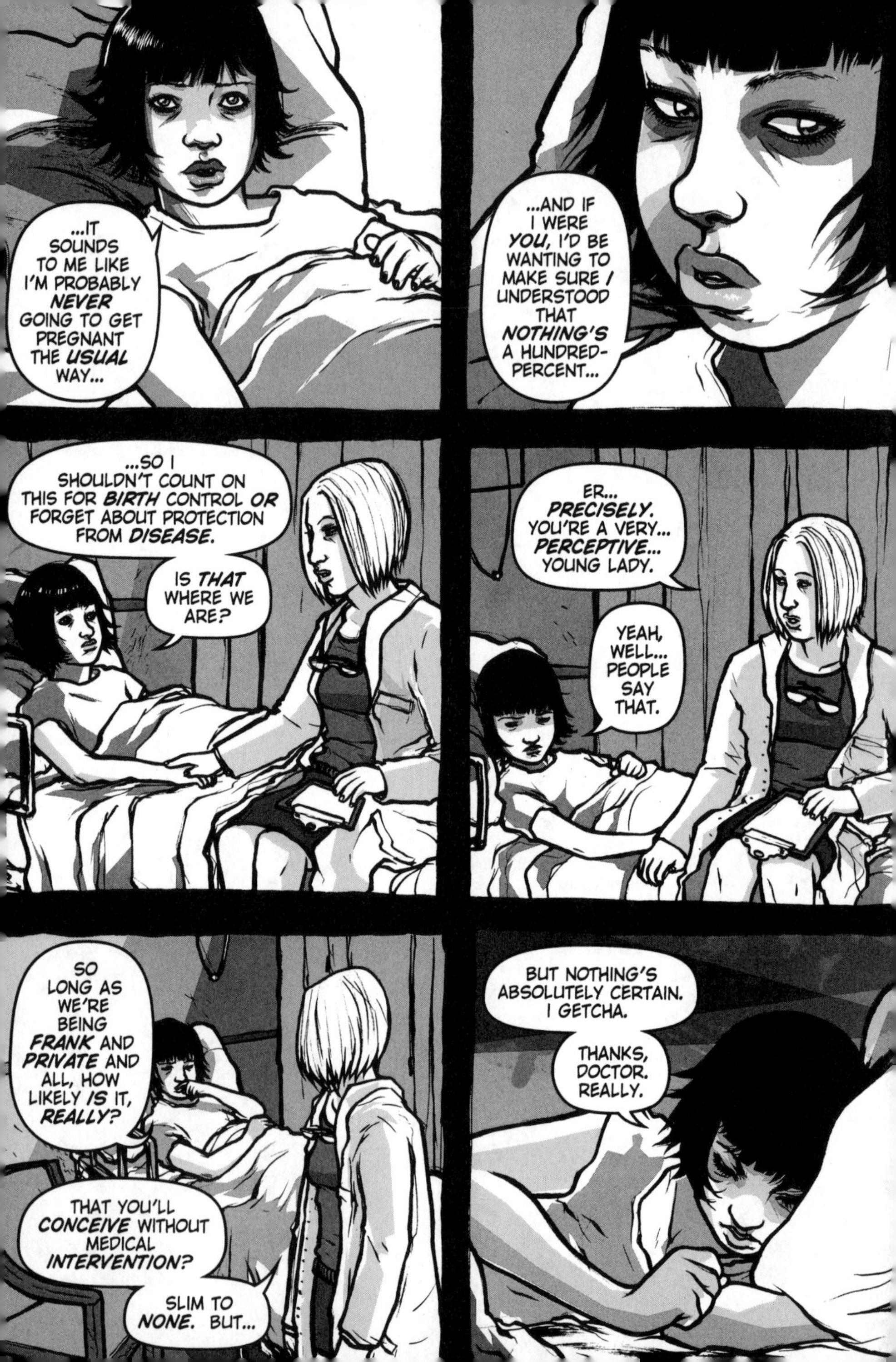
...IT SOUNDS TO ME LIKE I'M PROBABLY *NEVER* GOING TO GET PREGNANT THE *USUAL* WAY...
...AND IF I WERE *YOU*, I'D BE WANTING TO MAKE SURE *I* UNDERSTOOD THAT *NOTHING'S* A HUNDRED-PERCENT...
...SO I SHOULDN'T COUNT ON THIS FOR *BIRTH* CONTROL *OR* FORGET ABOUT PROTECTION FROM *DISEASE*.
IS *THAT* WHERE WE ARE?
ER... *PRECISELY*. YOU'RE A VERY... *PERCEPTIVE*... YOUNG LADY.
YEAH, WELL... PEOPLE SAY THAT.
SO LONG AS WE'RE BEING *FRANK* AND *PRIVATE* AND ALL, HOW LIKELY *IS* IT, *REALLY*?
THAT YOU'LL *CONCEIVE* WITHOUT MEDICAL *INTERVENTION*?
SLIM TO *NONE*. BUT...
BUT NOTHING'S ABSOLUTELY CERTAIN. I GETCHA.
THANKS, DOCTOR. REALLY.

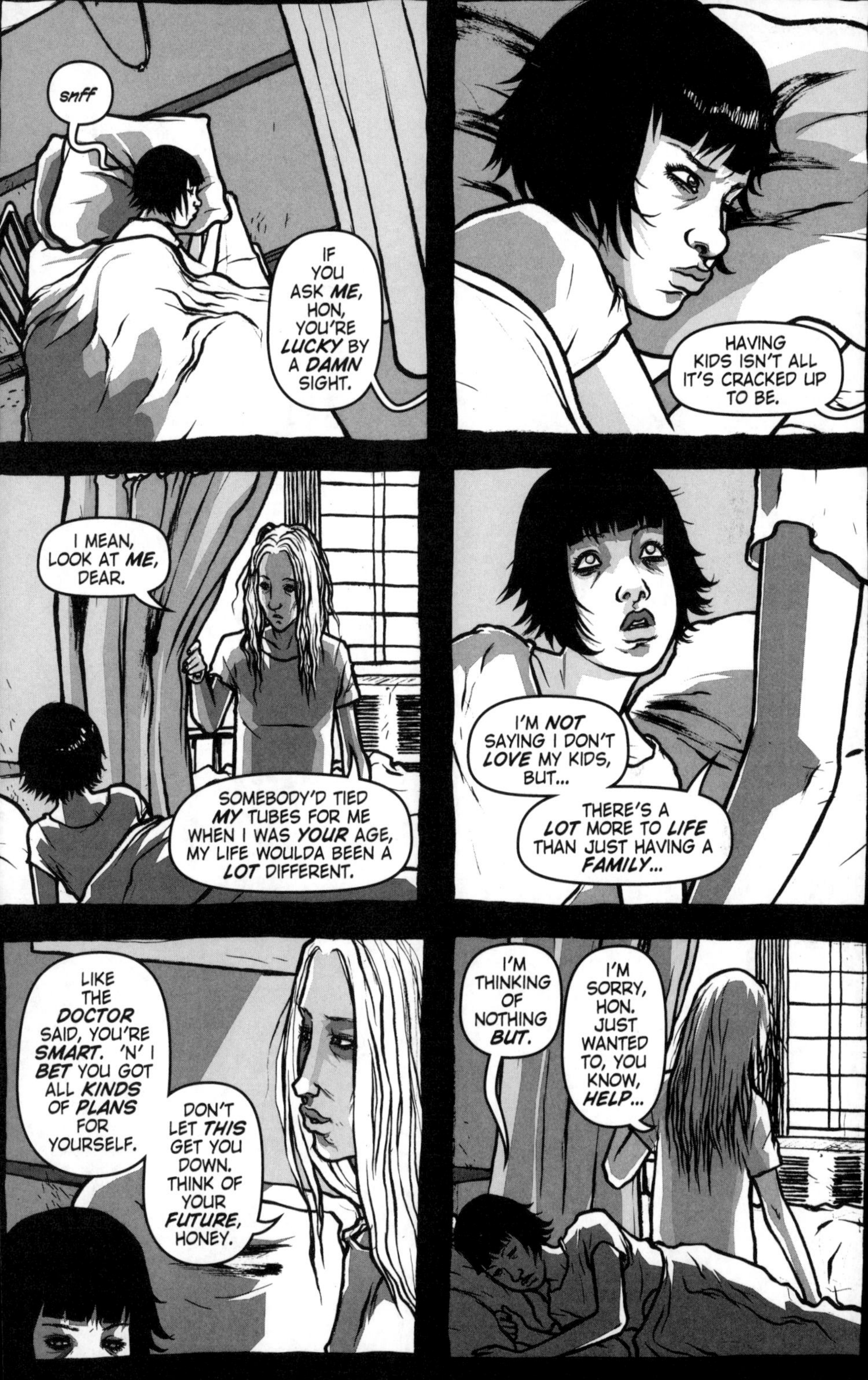
snff
IF YOU ASK ME, HON, YOU'RE LUCKY BY A DAMN SIGHT.
HAVING KIDS ISN'T ALL IT'S CRACKED UP TO BE.
I MEAN, LOOK AT ME, DEAR.
SOMEBODY'D TIED MY TUBES FOR ME WHEN I WAS YOUR AGE, MY LIFE WOULDA BEEN A LOT DIFFERENT.
I'M NOT SAYING I DON'T LOVE MY KIDS, BUT...
THERE'S A LOT MORE TO LIFE THAN JUST HAVING A FAMILY...
LIKE THE DOCTOR SAID, YOU'RE SMART. 'N' I BET YOU GOT ALL KINDS OF PLANS FOR YOURSELF.
DON'T LET THIS GET YOU DOWN. THINK OF YOUR FUTURE, HONEY.
I'M THINKING OF NOTHING BUT.
I'M SORRY, HON. JUST WANTED TO, YOU KNOW, HELP...

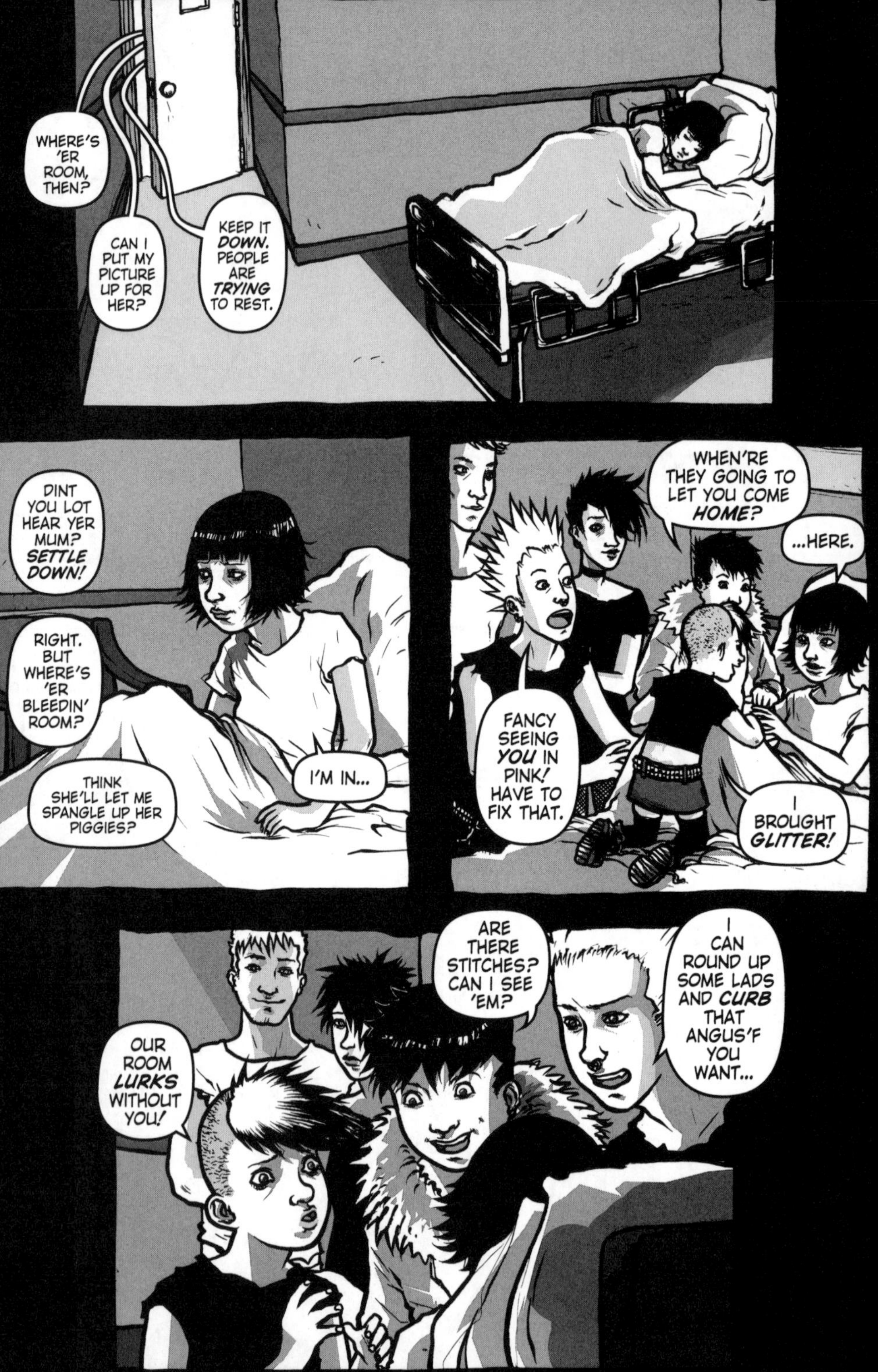
WHERE'S 'ER ROOM, THEN?
CAN I PUT MY PICTURE UP FOR HER?
KEEP IT DOWN. PEOPLE ARE TRYING TO REST.
DINT YOU LOT HEAR YER MUM? SETTLE DOWN!
RIGHT. BUT WHERE'S 'ER BLEEDIN' ROOM?
THINK SHE'LL LET ME SPANGLE UP HER PIGGIES?
I'M IN...
WHEN'RE THEY GOING TO LET YOU COME HOME?
...HERE.
FANCY SEEING YOU IN PINK! HAVE TO FIX THAT.
I BROUGHT GLITTER!
OUR ROOM LURKS WITHOUT YOU!
ARE THERE STITCHES? CAN I SEE 'EM?
I CAN ROUND UP SOME LADS AND CURB THAT ANGUS'F YOU WANT...

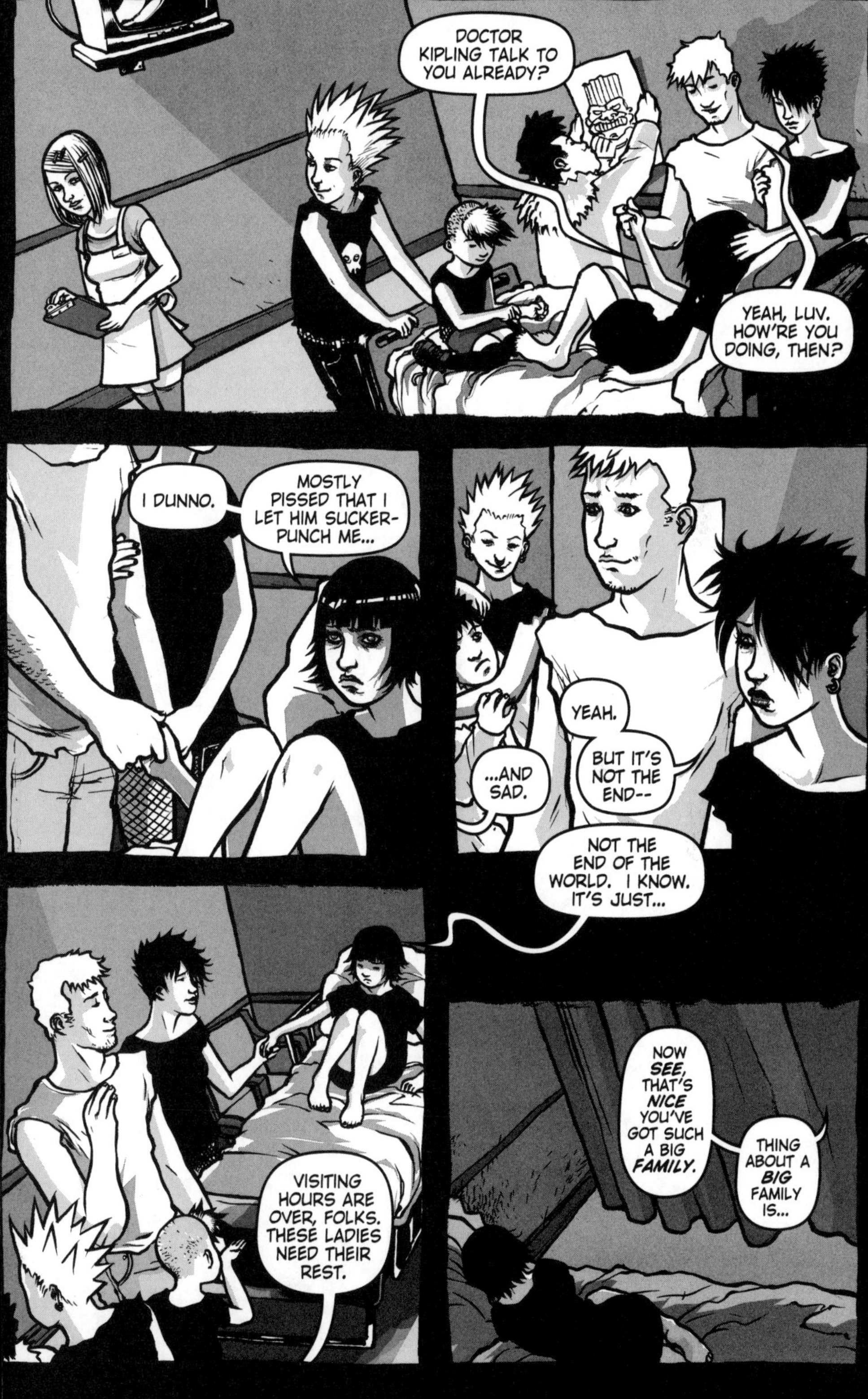
DOCTOR KIPLING TALK TO YOU ALREADY?
YEAH, LUV. HOW'RE YOU DOING, THEN?
I DUNNO.
MOSTLY PISSED THAT I LET HIM SUCKER-PUNCH ME...
YEAH.
BUT IT'S NOT THE END--
...AND SAD.
NOT THE END OF THE WORLD. I KNOW. IT'S JUST...
VISITING HOURS ARE OVER, FOLKS. THESE LADIES NEED THEIR REST.
NOW SEE, THAT'S NICE YOU'VE GOT SUCH A BIG FAMILY.
THING ABOUT A BIG FAMILY IS...

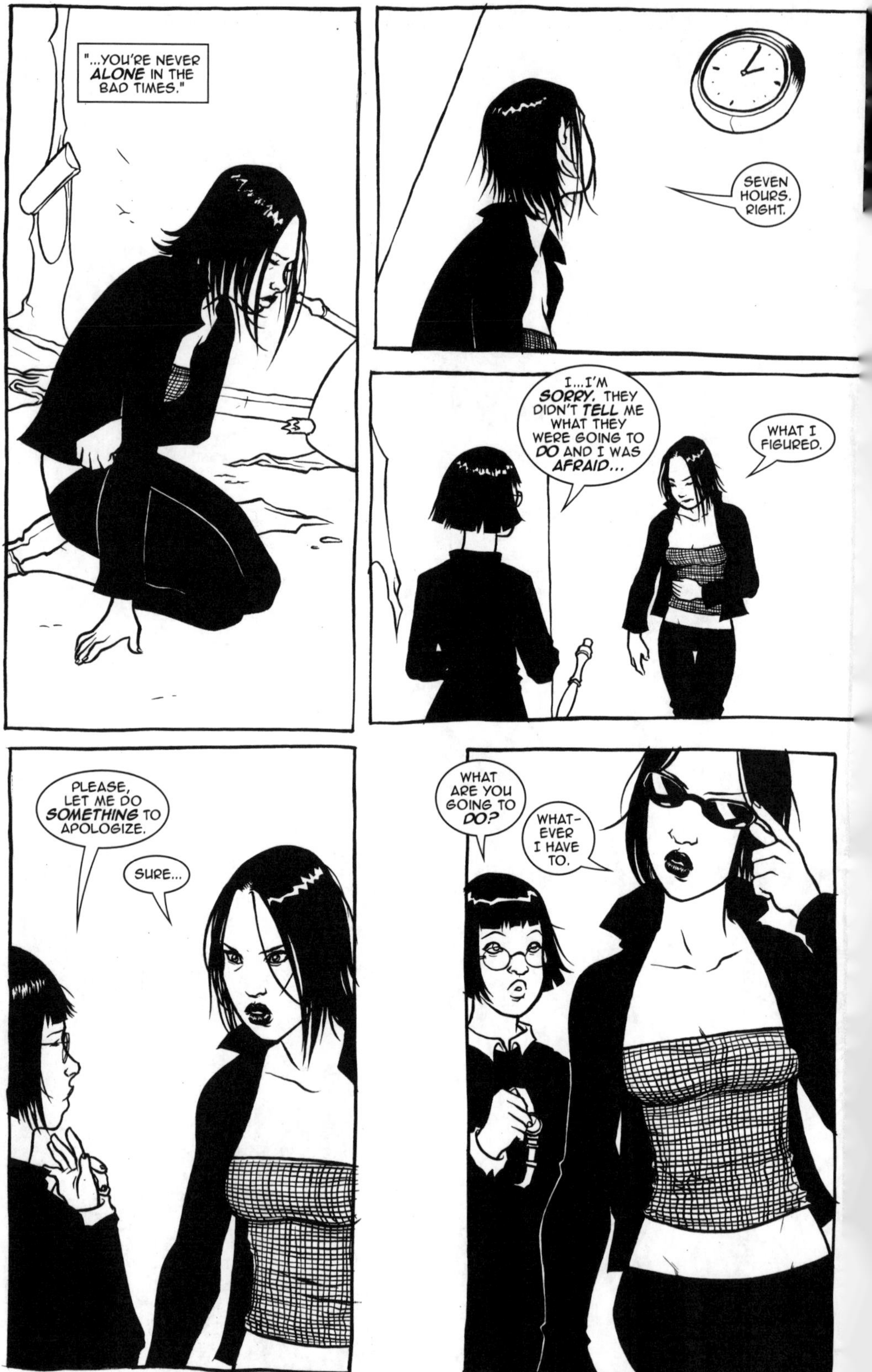
"...YOU'RE NEVER **ALONE** IN THE BAD TIMES."
SEVEN HOURS. RIGHT.
I...I'M **SORRY.** THEY DIDN'T **TELL** ME WHAT THEY WERE GOING TO **DO** AND I WAS **AFRAID...**
WHAT I FIGURED.
PLEASE, LET ME DO **SOMETHING** TO APOLOGIZE.
SURE...
WHAT ARE YOU GOING TO **DO?**
WHAT-EVER I HAVE TO.

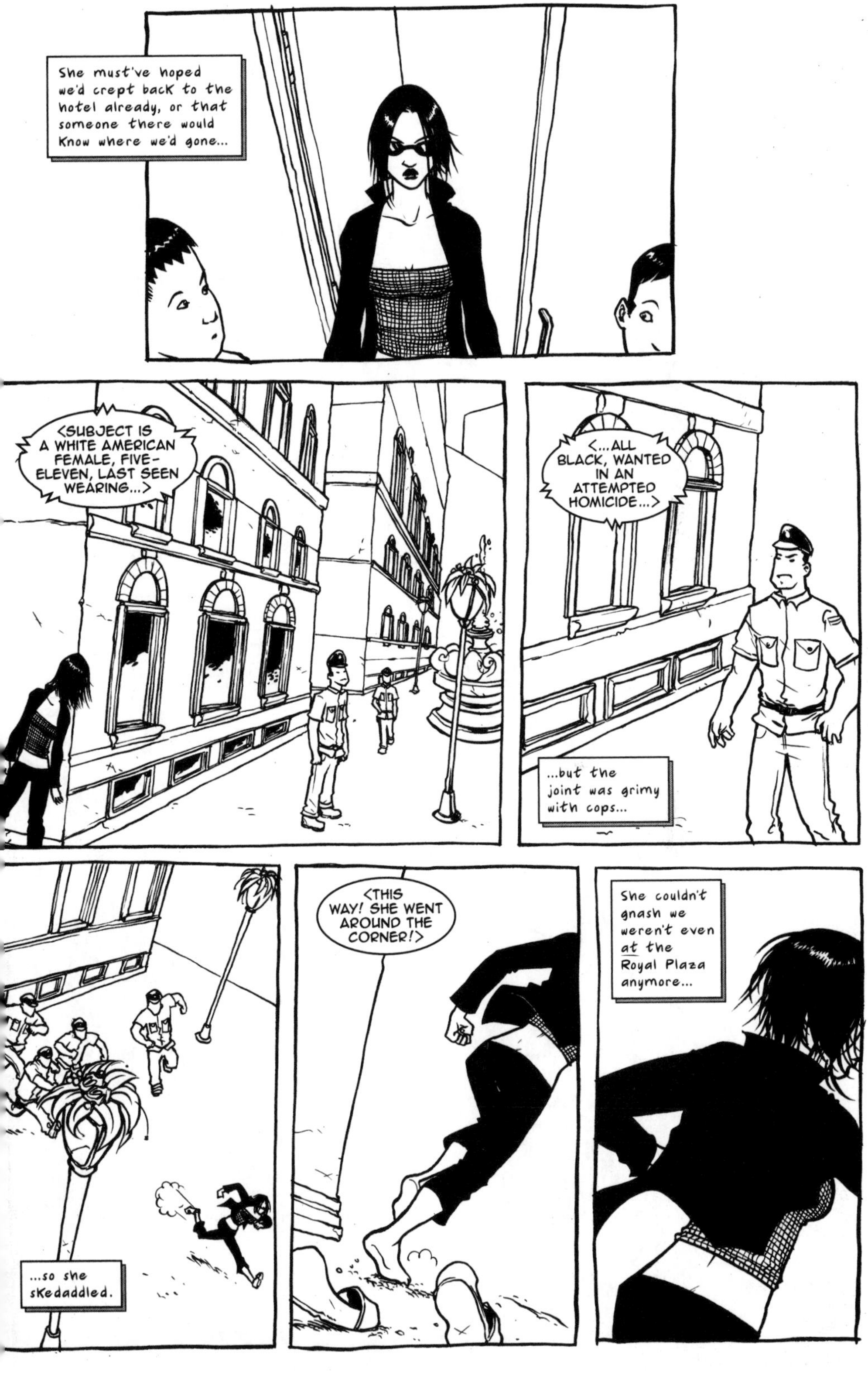
She must've hoped we'd crept back to the hotel already, or that someone there would know where we'd gone...
<SUBJECT IS A WHITE AMERICAN FEMALE, FIVE-ELEVEN, LAST SEEN WEARING...>
<...ALL BLACK, WANTED IN AN ATTEMPTED HOMICIDE...>
...but the joint was grimy with cops...
...so she skedaddled.
<THIS WAY! SHE WENT AROUND THE CORNER!>
She couldn't gnash we weren't even at the Royal Plaza anymore...

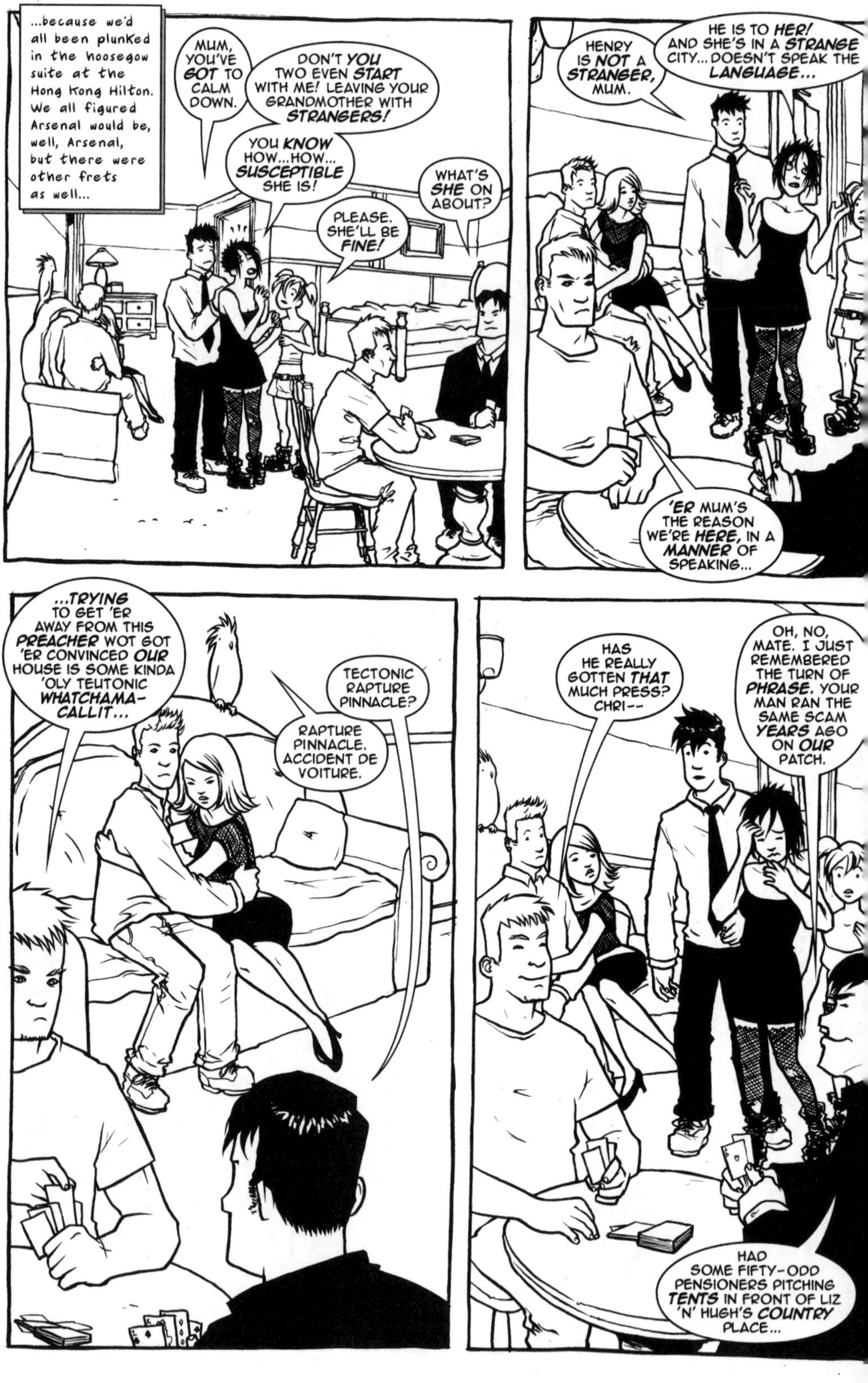
...because we'd all been plunked in the hoosegow suite at the Hong Kong Hilton. We all figured Arsenal would be, well, Arsenal, but there were other frets as well...
MUM, YOU'VE GOT TO CALM DOWN.
DON'T YOU TWO EVEN START WITH ME! LEAVING YOUR GRANDMOTHER WITH STRANGERS!
YOU KNOW HOW...HOW... SUSCEPTIBLE SHE IS!
WHAT'S SHE ON ABOUT?
PLEASE. SHE'LL BE FINE!
HENRY IS NOT A STRANGER, MUM.
HE IS TO HER! AND SHE'S IN A STRANGE CITY... DOESN'T SPEAK THE LANGUAGE...
'ER MUM'S THE REASON WE'RE HERE, IN A MANNER OF SPEAKING...
...TRYING TO GET 'ER AWAY FROM THIS PREACHER WOT GOT 'ER CONVINCED OUR HOUSE IS SOME KINDA 'OLY TEUTONIC WHATCHAMA-CALLIT...
TECTONIC RAPTURE PINNACLE?
RAPTURE PINNACLE. ACCIDENT DE VOITURE.
HAS HE REALLY GOTTEN THAT MUCH PRESS? CHRI--
OH, NO, MATE. I JUST REMEMBERED THE TURN OF PHRASE. YOUR MAN RAN THE SAME SCAM YEARS AGO ON OUR PATCH.
HAD SOME FIFTY-ODD PENSIONERS PITCHING TENTS IN FRONT OF LIZ 'N' HUGH'S COUNTRY PLACE...

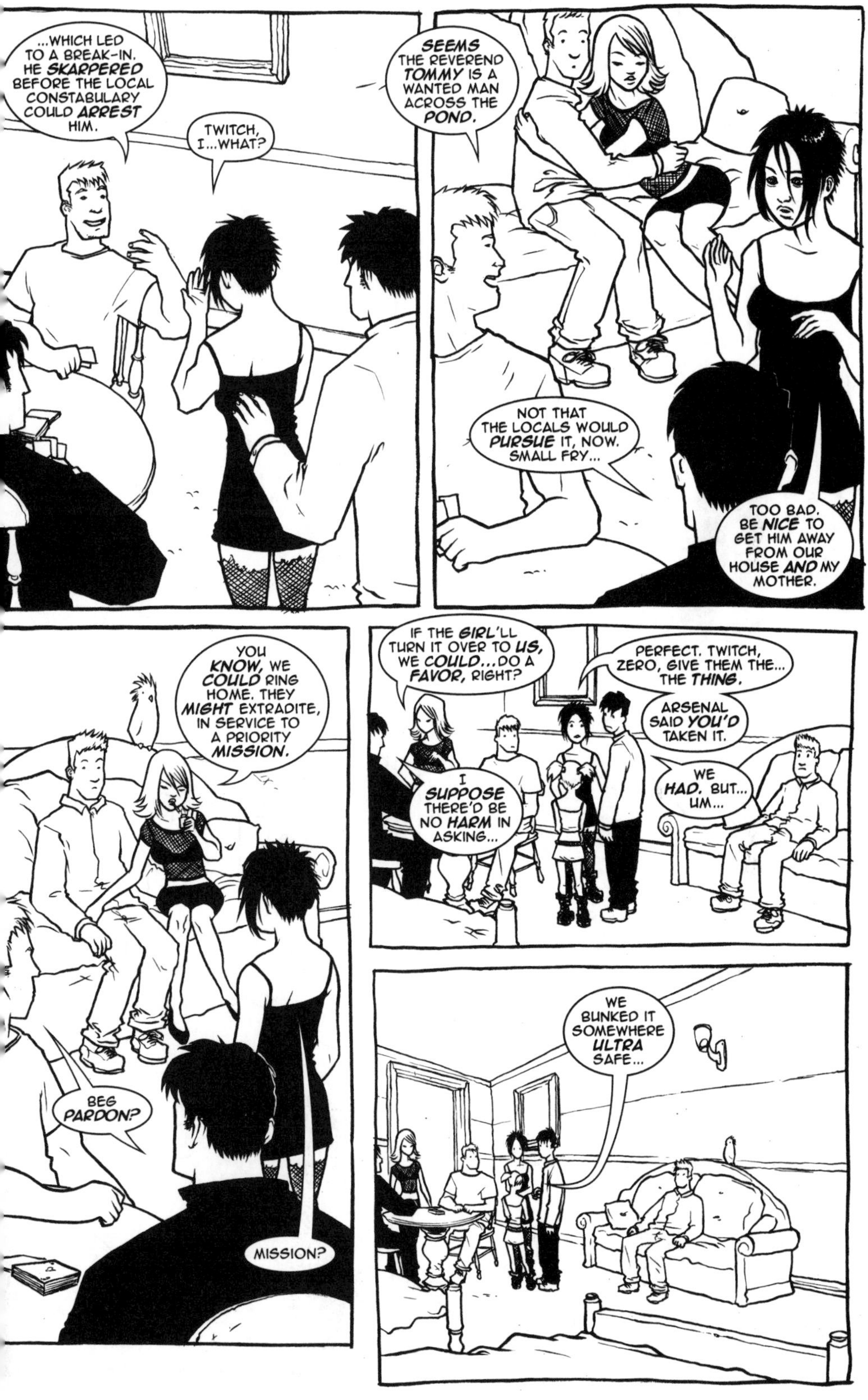
...WHICH LED TO A BREAK-IN. HE SKARPERED BEFORE THE LOCAL CONSTABULARY COULD ARREST HIM.
TWITCH, I...WHAT?
SEEMS THE REVEREND TOMMY IS A WANTED MAN ACROSS THE POND.
NOT THAT THE LOCALS WOULD PURSUE IT, NOW. SMALL FRY...
TOO BAD. BE NICE TO GET HIM AWAY FROM OUR HOUSE AND MY MOTHER.
YOU KNOW, WE COULD RING HOME. THEY MIGHT EXTRADITE, IN SERVICE TO A PRIORITY MISSION.
BEG PARDON?
MISSION?
IF THE GIRL'LL TURN IT OVER TO US, WE COULD... DO A FAVOR, RIGHT?
I SUPPOSE THERE'D BE NO HARM IN ASKING...
PERFECT. TWITCH, ZERO, GIVE THEM THE... THE THING.
ARSENAL SAID YOU'D TAKEN IT.
WE HAD. BUT... UM...
WE BUNKED IT SOMEWHERE ULTRA SAFE...

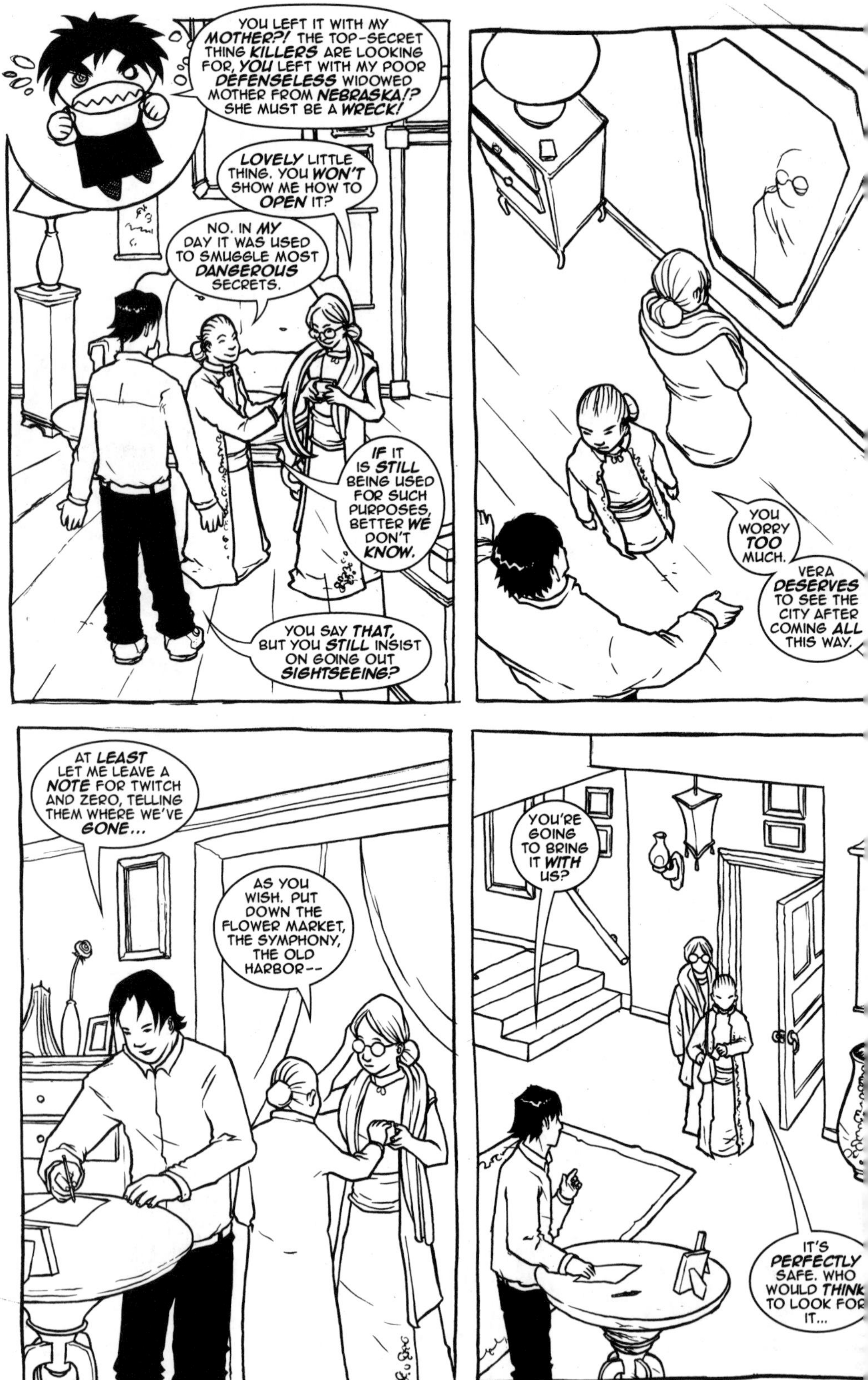
YOU LEFT IT WITH MY MOTHER?! THE TOP-SECRET THING KILLERS ARE LOOKING FOR, YOU LEFT WITH MY POOR DEFENSELESS WIDOWED MOTHER FROM NEBRASKA!? SHE MUST BE A WRECK!
LOVELY LITTLE THING. YOU WON'T SHOW ME HOW TO OPEN IT?
NO. IN MY DAY IT WAS USED TO SMUGGLE MOST DANGEROUS SECRETS.
IF IT IS STILL BEING USED FOR SUCH PURPOSES, BETTER WE DON'T KNOW.
YOU SAY THAT, BUT YOU STILL INSIST ON GOING OUT SIGHTSEEING?
YOU WORRY TOO MUCH.
VERA DESERVES TO SEE THE CITY AFTER COMING ALL THIS WAY.
AT LEAST LET ME LEAVE A NOTE FOR TWITCH AND ZERO, TELLING THEM WHERE WE'VE GONE...
AS YOU WISH. PUT DOWN THE FLOWER MARKET, THE SYMPHONY, THE OLD HARBOR--
YOU'RE GOING TO BRING IT WITH US?
IT'S PERFECTLY SAFE. WHO WOULD THINK TO LOOK FOR IT...

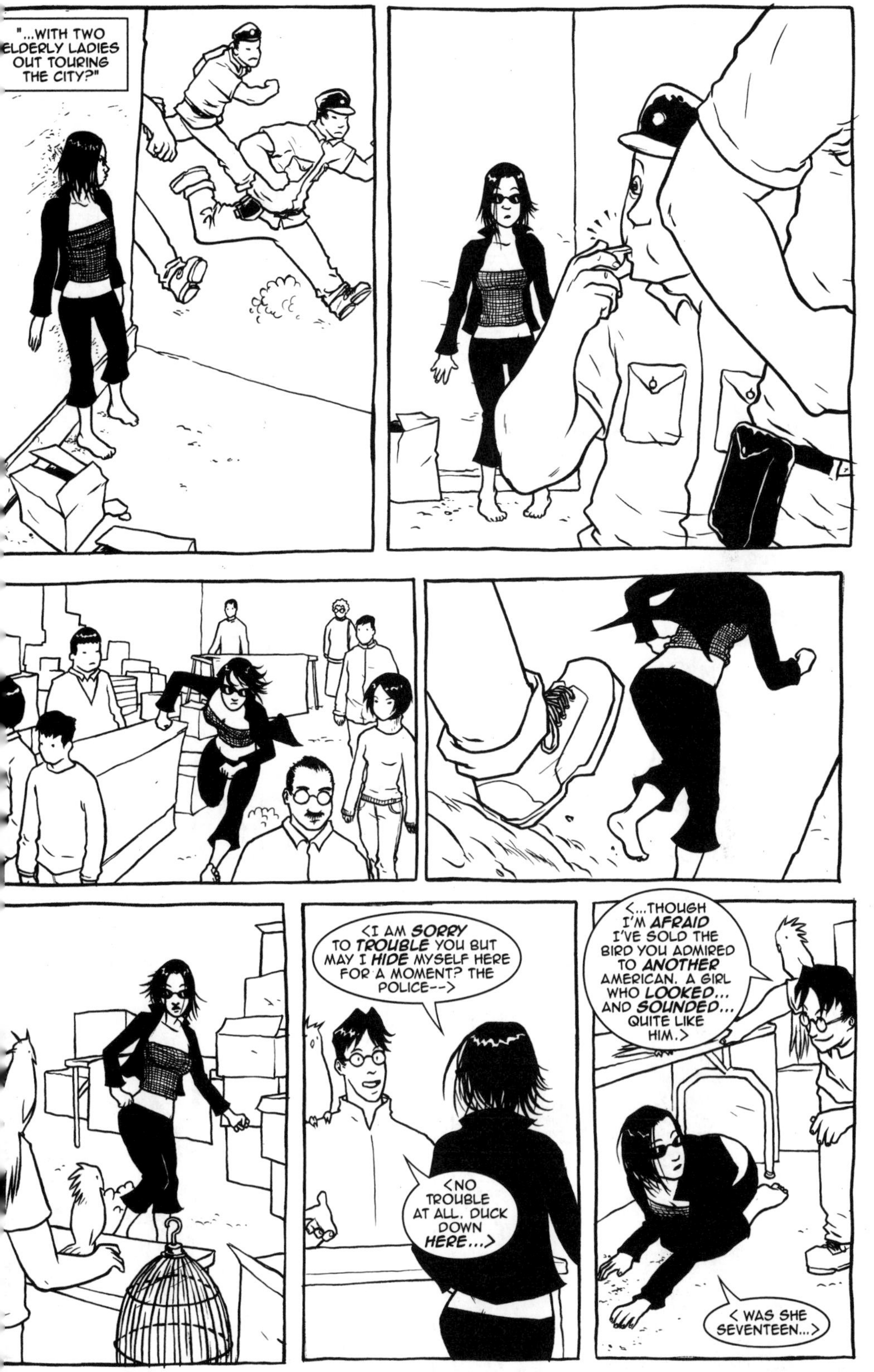
"...WITH TWO ELDERLY LADIES OUT TOURING THE CITY?"
<I AM SORRY TO TROUBLE YOU BUT MAY I HIDE MYSELF HERE FOR A MOMENT? THE POLICE-->
<NO TROUBLE AT ALL. DUCK DOWN HERE...>
<...THOUGH I'M AFRAID I'VE SOLD THE BIRD YOU ADMIRED TO ANOTHER AMERICAN. A GIRL WHO LOOKED... AND SOUNDED... QUITE LIKE HIM.>
< WAS SHE SEVENTEEN...>

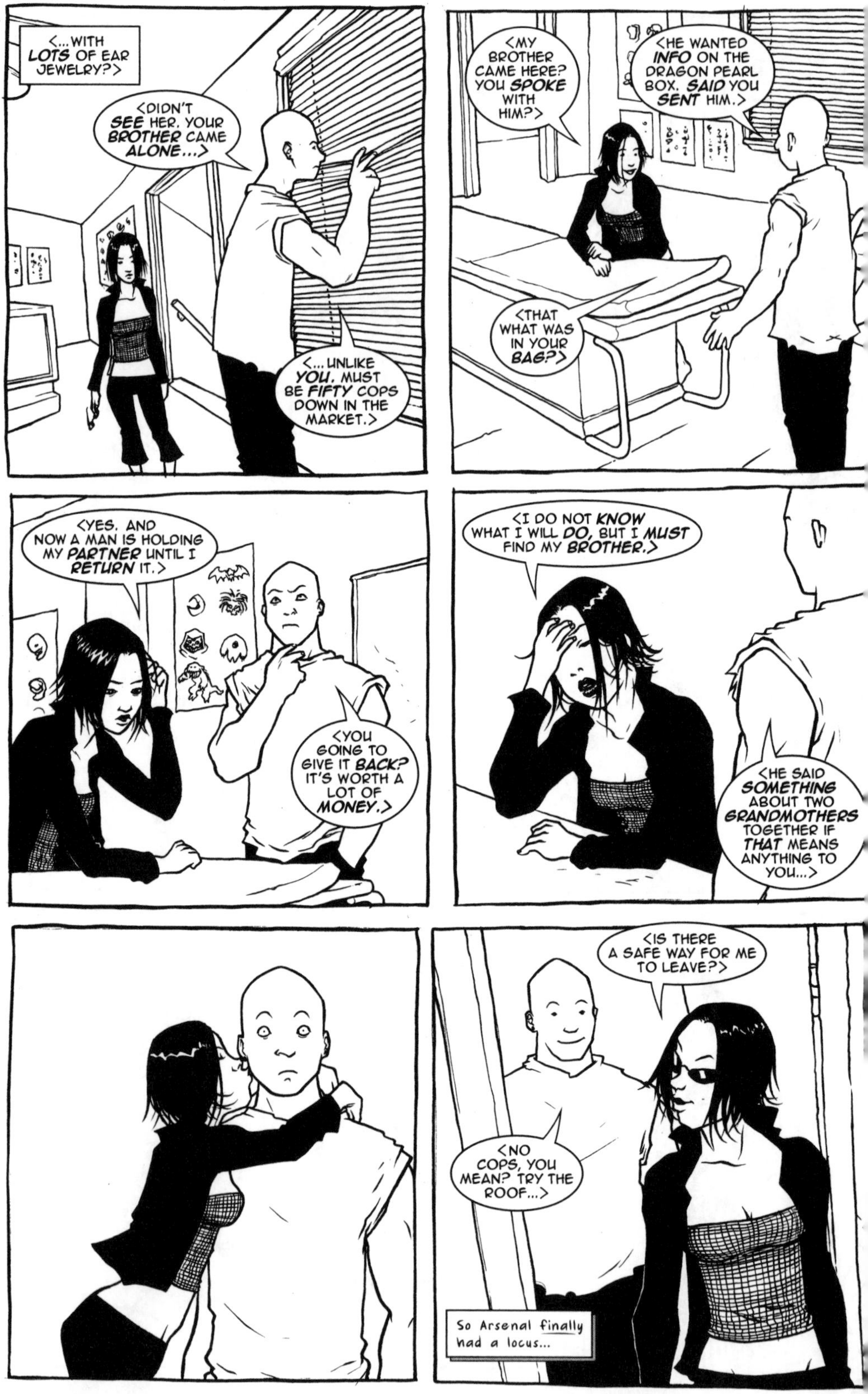

<...WITH LOTS OF EAR JEWELRY?>
<DIDN'T SEE HER. YOUR BROTHER CAME ALONE...>
<...UNLIKE YOU. MUST BE FIFTY COPS DOWN IN THE MARKET.>
<MY BROTHER CAME HERE? YOU SPOKE WITH HIM?>
<HE WANTED INFO ON THE DRAGON PEARL BOX. SAID YOU SENT HIM.>
<THAT WHAT WAS IN YOUR BAG?>
<YES. AND NOW A MAN IS HOLDING MY PARTNER UNTIL I RETURN IT.>
<YOU GOING TO GIVE IT BACK? IT'S WORTH A LOT OF MONEY.>
<I DO NOT KNOW WHAT I WILL DO, BUT I MUST FIND MY BROTHER.>
<HE SAID SOMETHING ABOUT TWO GRANDMOTHERS TOGETHER IF THAT MEANS ANYTHING TO YOU...>
<IS THERE A SAFE WAY FOR ME TO LEAVE?>
<NO COPS, YOU MEAN? TRY THE ROOF...>
So Arsenal finally had a locus...

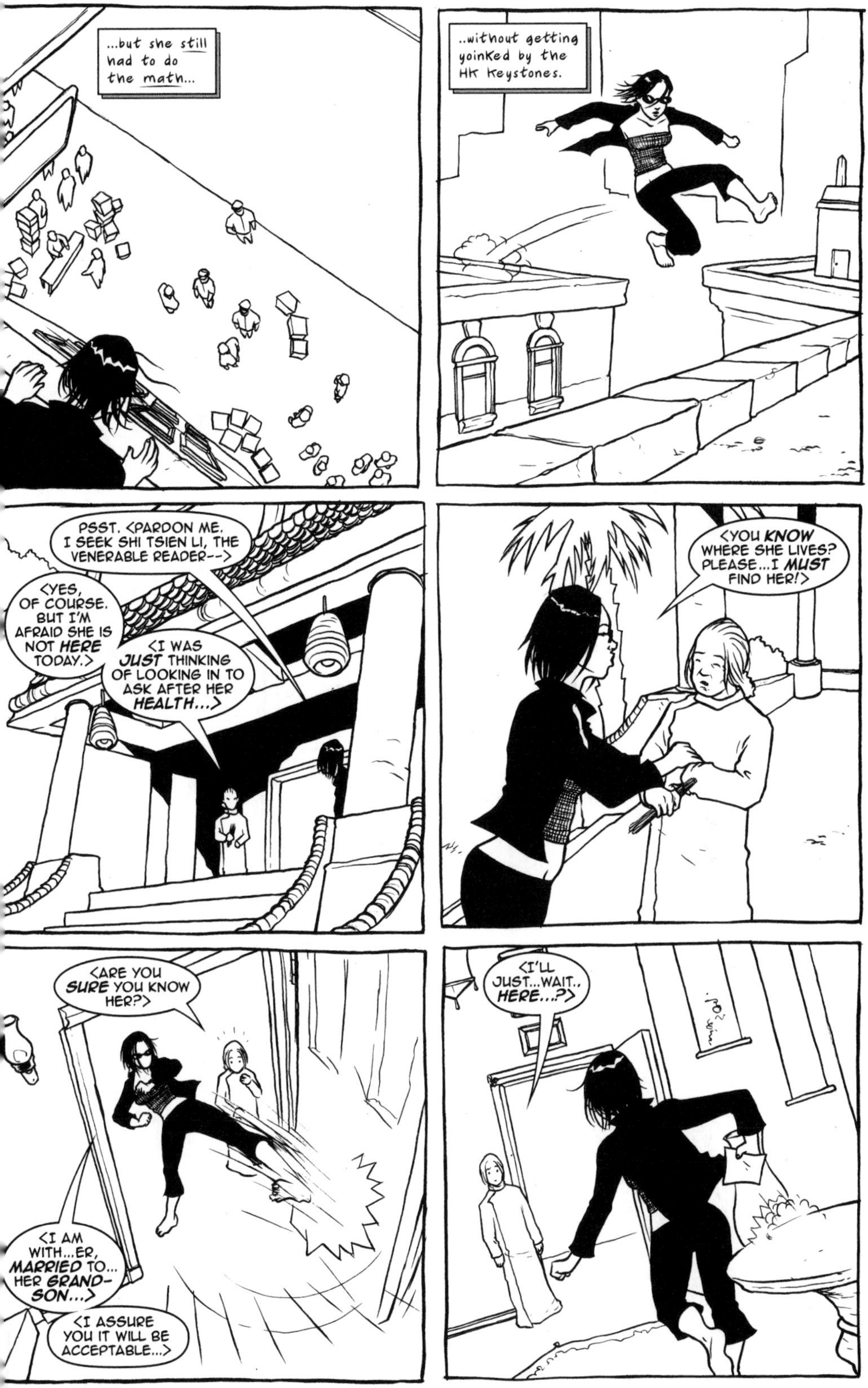
...but she still had to do the math...
..without getting yoinked by the HK Keystones.
PSST. <PARDON ME. I SEEK SHI TSIEN LI, THE VENERABLE READER-->
<YES, OF COURSE. BUT I'M AFRAID SHE IS NOT HERE TODAY.>
<I WAS JUST THINKING OF LOOKING IN TO ASK AFTER HER HEALTH...>
<YOU KNOW WHERE SHE LIVES? PLEASE...I MUST FIND HER!>
<ARE YOU SURE YOU KNOW HER?>
<I AM WITH...ER, MARRIED TO... HER GRAND-SON...>
<I ASSURE YOU IT WILL BE ACCEPTABLE...>
<I'LL JUST...WAIT.. HERE...?>

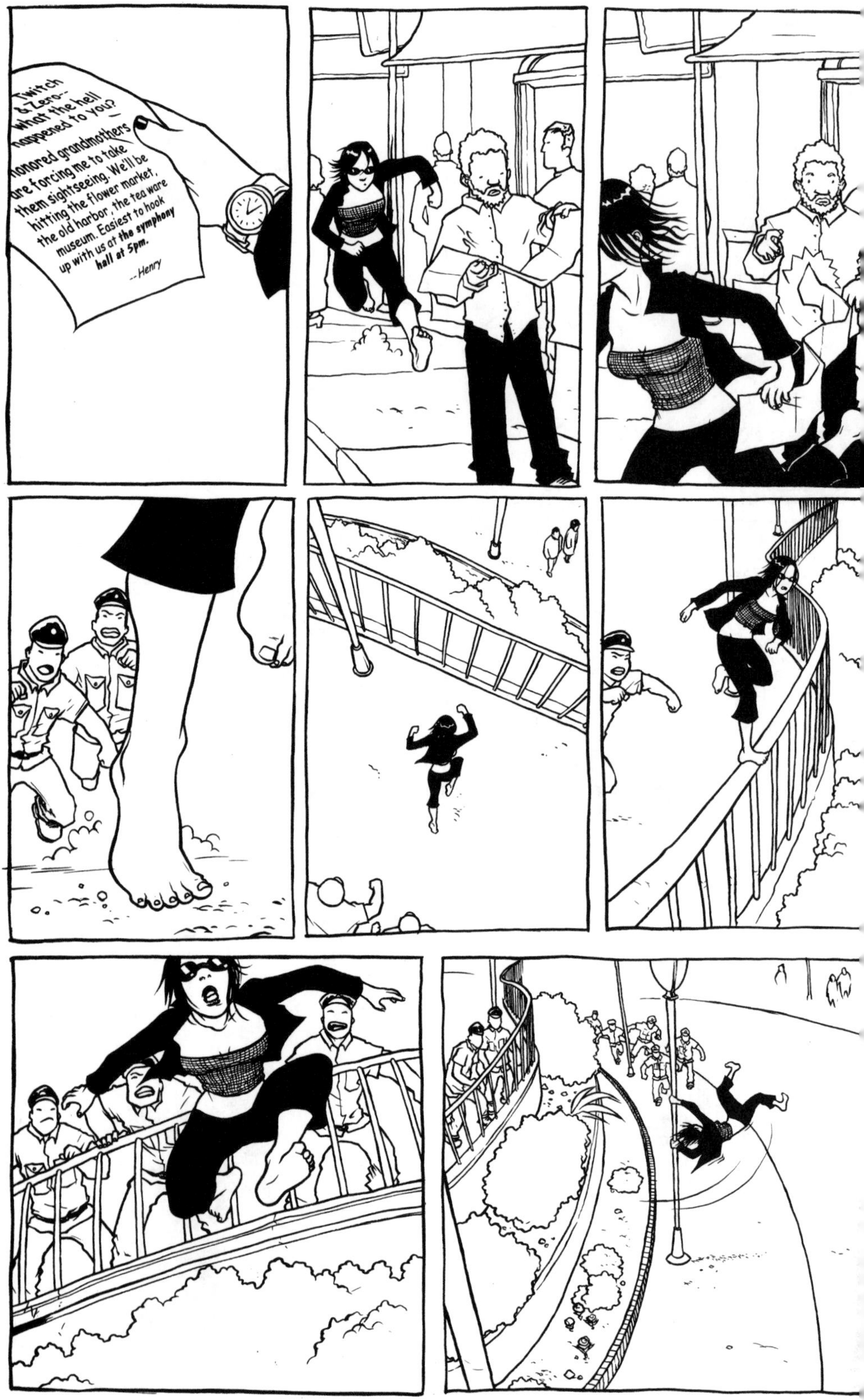
Twitch & Zero--
what the hell happened to you?
Honored grandmothers are forcing me to take them sightseeing. We'll be hitting the flower market, the old harbor, the tea ware museum. Easiest to hook up with us at the symphony hall at 5pm.
--Henry

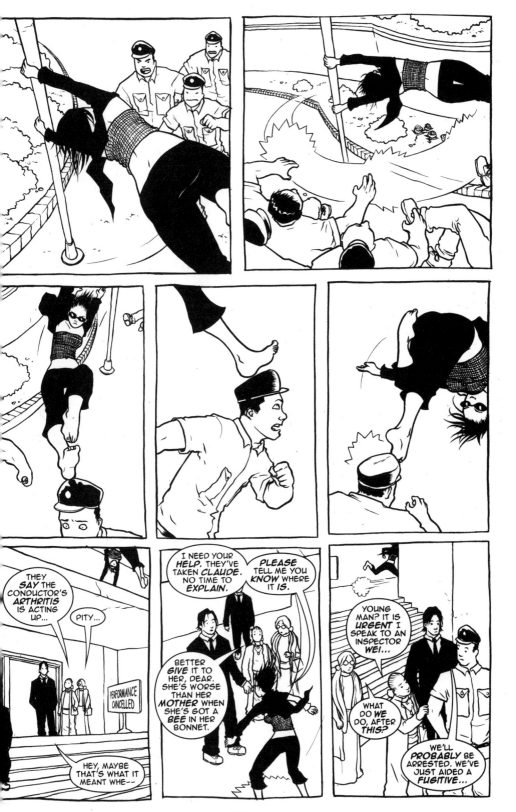

THEY *SAY* THE CONDUCTOR'S *ARTHRITIS* IS ACTING UP...

PITY...

PERFORMANCE CANCELLED

HEY, MAYBE THAT'S WHAT IT MEANT WHE--

I NEED YOUR *HELP.* THEY'VE TAKEN *CLAUDE.* NO TIME TO *EXPLAIN.*

PLEASE TELL ME YOU *KNOW* WHERE IT *IS.*

BETTER *GIVE* IT TO HER, DEAR. SHE'S WORSE THAN HER *MOTHER* WHEN SHE'S GOT A *BEE* IN HER BONNET.

YOUNG MAN? IT IS *URGENT* I SPEAK TO AN INSPECTOR *WEI...*

WHAT DO *WE* DO, AFTER *THIS?*

WE'LL *PROBABLY* BE ARRESTED. WE'VE JUST AIDED A *FUGITIVE...*

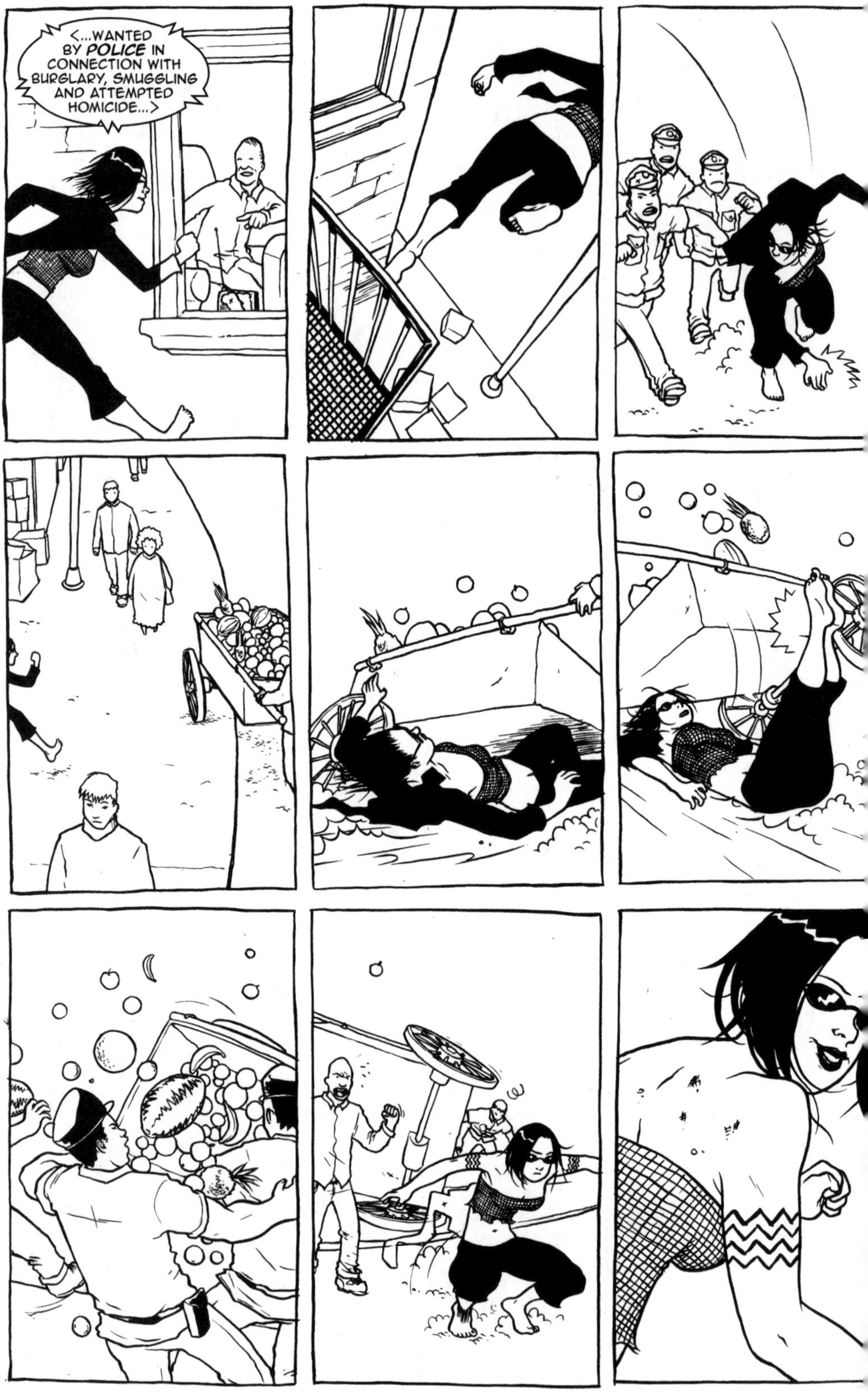

<...WANTED BY POLICE IN CONNECTION WITH BURGLARY, SMUGGLING AND ATTEMPTED HOMICIDE...>

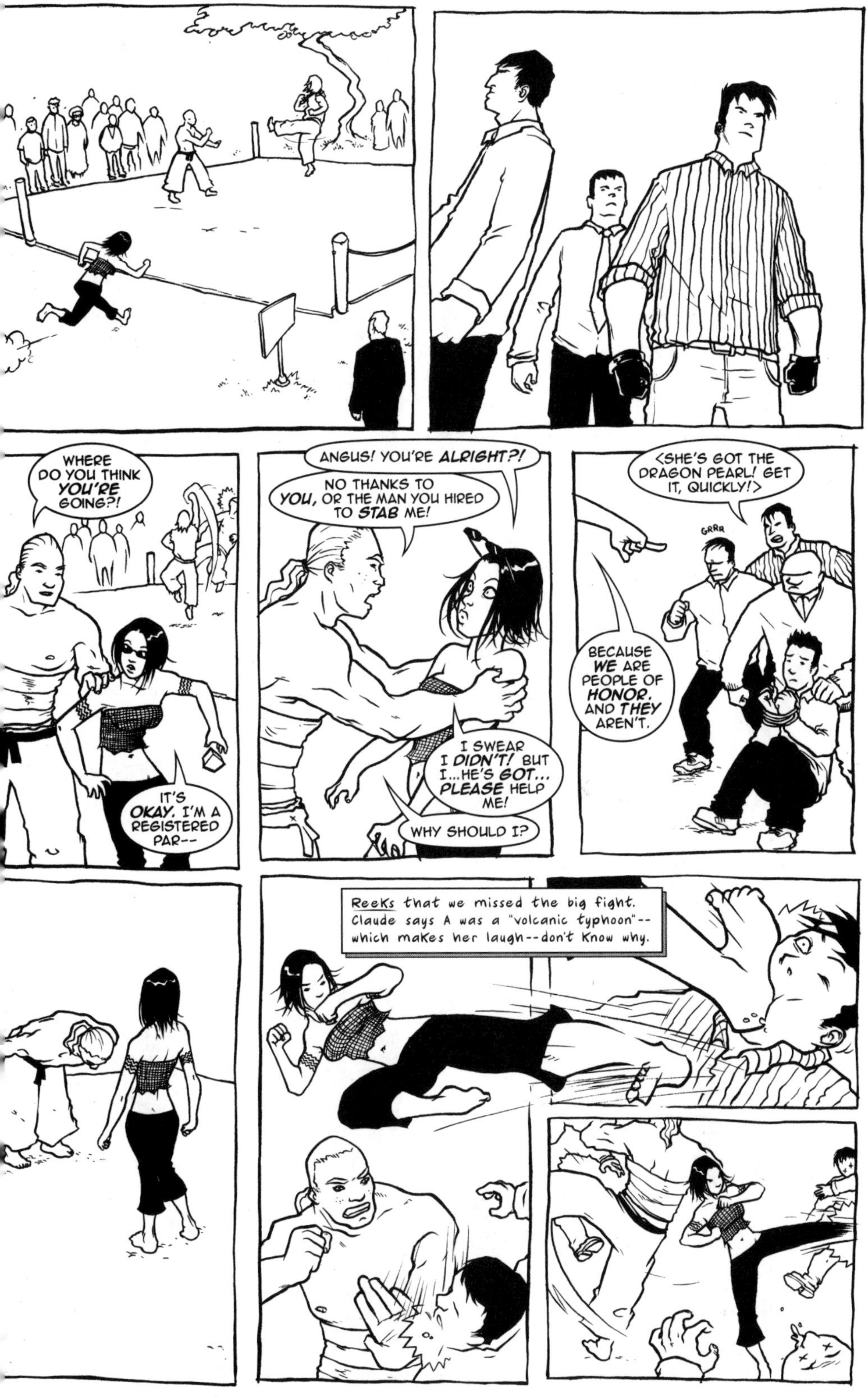
WHERE DO YOU THINK YOU'RE GOING?!
IT'S OKAY. I'M A REGISTERED PAR--
ANGUS! YOU'RE ALRIGHT?!
NO THANKS TO YOU, OR THE MAN YOU HIRED TO STAB ME!
I SWEAR I DIDN'T! BUT I...HE'S GOT... PLEASE HELP ME!
WHY SHOULD I?
<SHE'S GOT THE DRAGON PEARL! GET IT, QUICKLY!>
GRRR
BECAUSE WE ARE PEOPLE OF HONOR. AND THEY AREN'T.
Reeks that we missed the big fight. Claude says A was a "volcanic typhoon"-- which makes her laugh--don't know why.

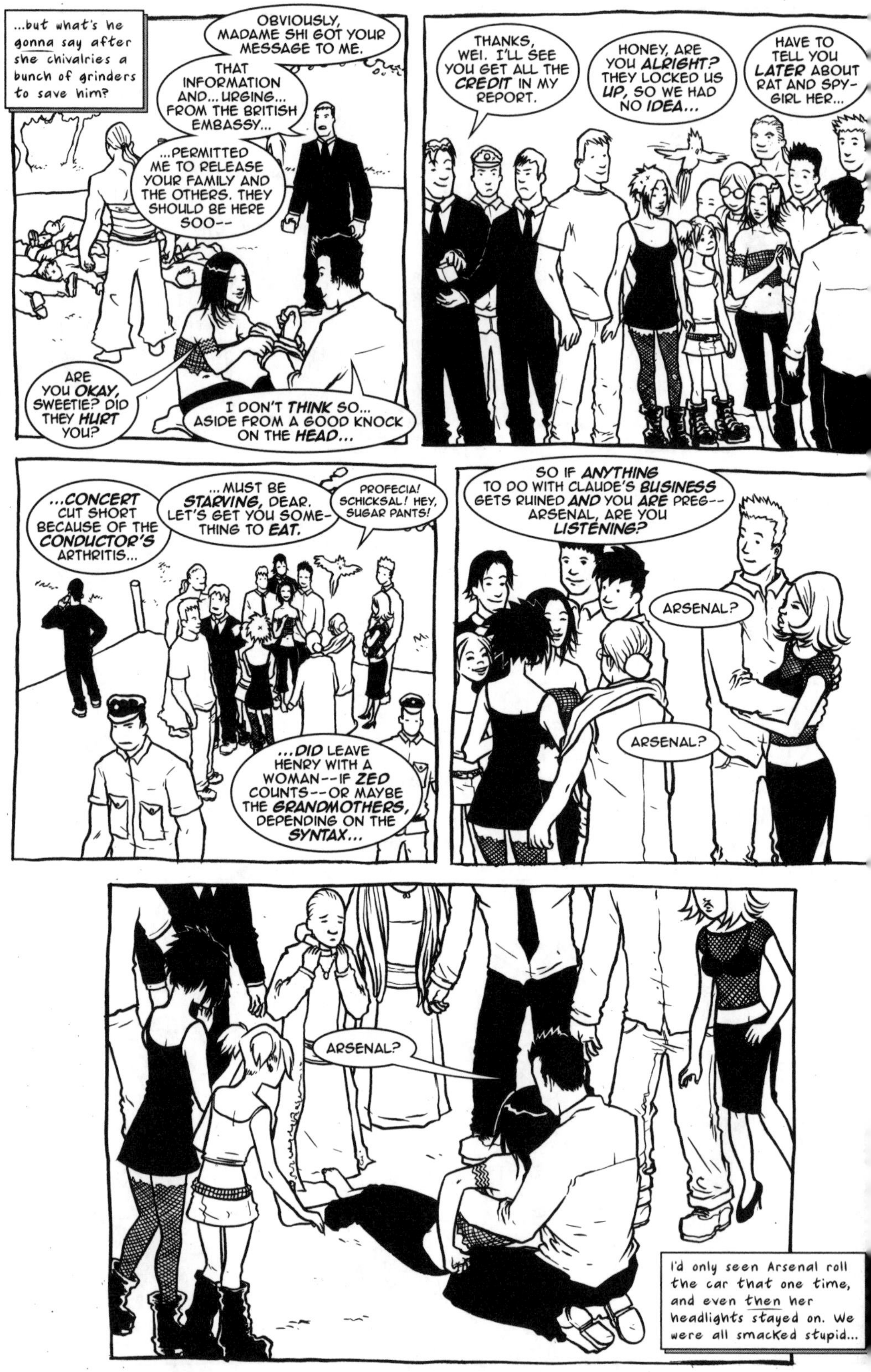
...but what's he gonna say after she chivalries a bunch of grinders to save him?
OBVIOUSLY, MADAME SHI GOT YOUR MESSAGE TO ME.
THAT INFORMATION AND... URGING... FROM THE BRITISH EMBASSY...
...PERMITTED ME TO RELEASE YOUR FAMILY AND THE OTHERS. THEY SHOULD BE HERE SOO--
ARE YOU OKAY, SWEETIE? DID THEY HURT YOU?
I DON'T THINK SO... ASIDE FROM A GOOD KNOCK ON THE HEAD...
THANKS, WEI. I'LL SEE YOU GET ALL THE CREDIT IN MY REPORT.
HONEY, ARE YOU ALRIGHT? THEY LOCKED US UP, SO WE HAD NO IDEA...
HAVE TO TELL YOU LATER ABOUT RAT AND SPY-GIRL HER...
...CONCERT CUT SHORT BECAUSE OF THE CONDUCTOR'S ARTHRITIS...
...MUST BE STARVING, DEAR. LET'S GET YOU SOME-THING TO EAT.
PROFECIA! SCHICKSAL! HEY, SUGAR PANTS!
...DID LEAVE HENRY WITH A WOMAN--IF ZED COUNTS--OR MAYBE THE GRANDMOTHERS, DEPENDING ON THE SYNTAX...
SO IF ANYTHING TO DO WITH CLAUDE'S BUSINESS GETS RUINED AND YOU ARE PREG-- ARSENAL, ARE YOU LISTENING?
ARSENAL?
ARSENAL?
ARSENAL?
I'd only seen Arsenal roll the car that one time, and even then her headlights stayed on. We were all smacked stupid...

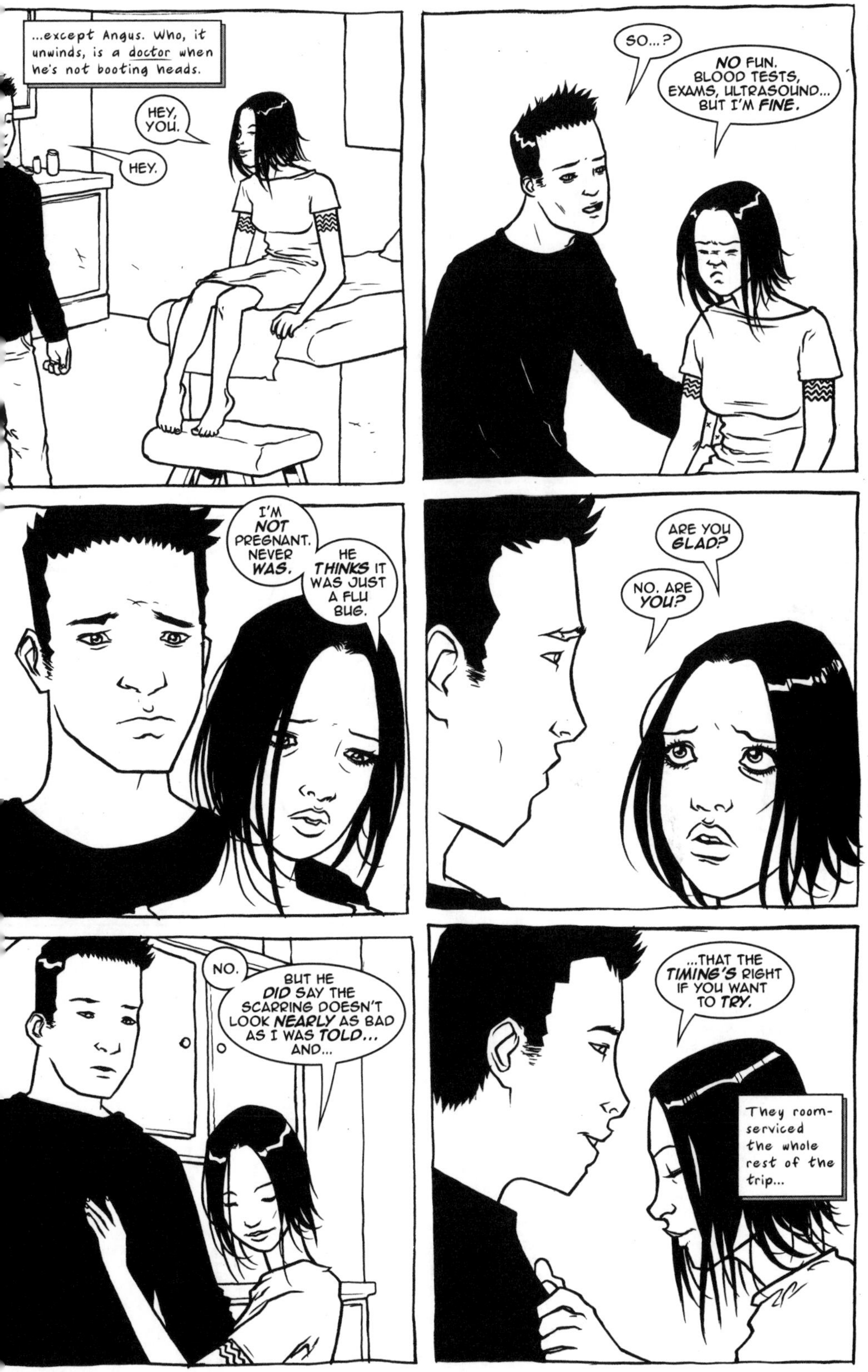
...except Angus. Who, it unwinds, is a doctor when he's not booting heads.
HEY, YOU.
HEY.
SO...?
NO FUN. BLOOD TESTS, EXAMS, ULTRASOUND... BUT I'M FINE.
I'M NOT PREGNANT. NEVER WAS.
HE THINKS IT WAS JUST A FLU BUG.
ARE YOU GLAD?
NO. ARE YOU?
NO.
BUT HE DID SAY THE SCARRING DOESN'T LOOK NEARLY AS BAD AS I WAS TOLD... AND...
...THAT THE TIMING'S RIGHT IF YOU WANT TO TRY.
They room-serviced the whole rest of the trip...

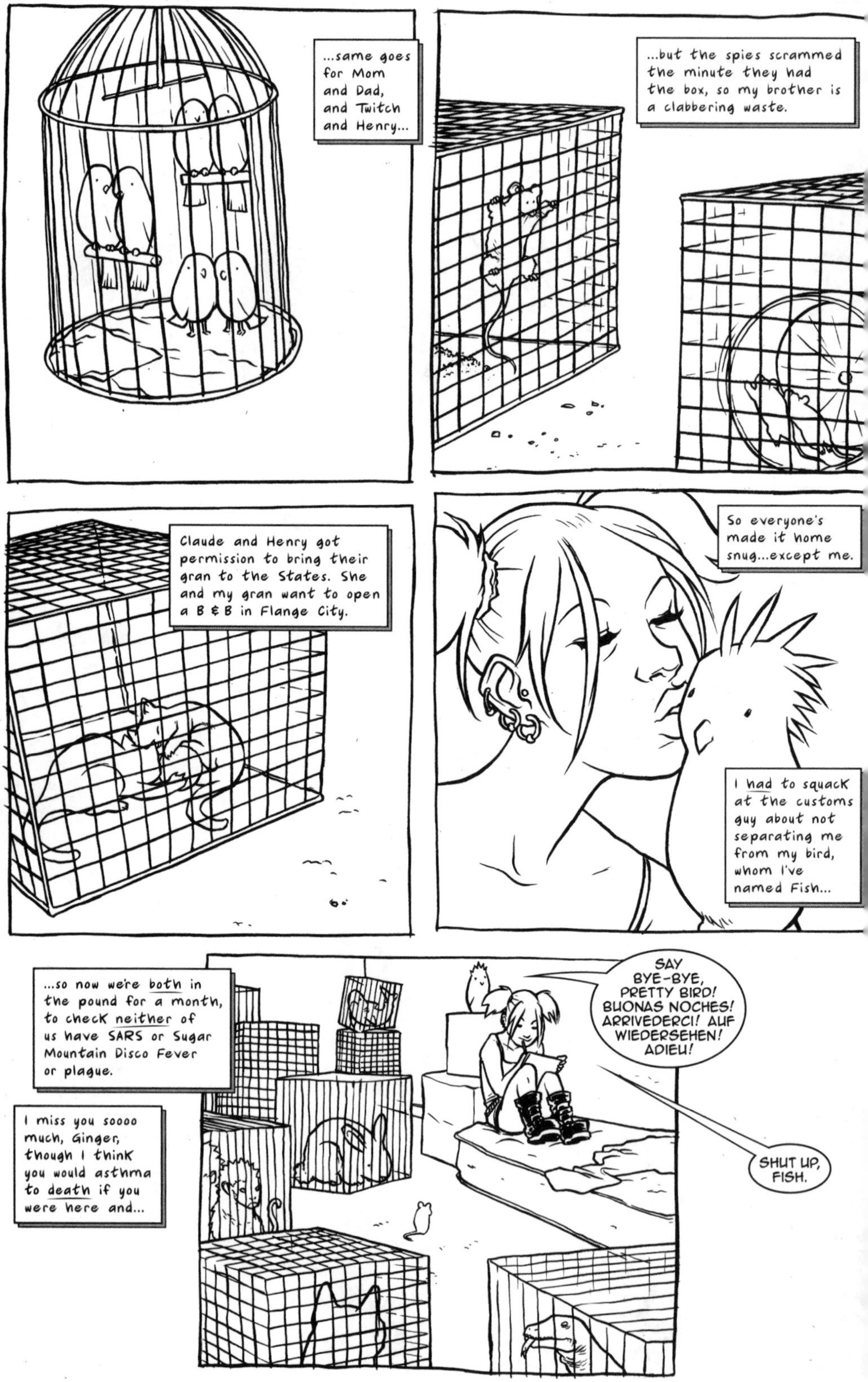
...same goes for Mom and Dad, and Twitch and Henry...
...but the spies scrammed the minute they had the box, so my brother is a clabbering waste.
Claude and Henry got permission to bring their gran to the States. She and my gran want to open a B & B in Flange City.
So everyone's made it home snug...except me.
I had to squack at the customs guy about not separating me from my bird, whom I've named Fish...
...so now we're both in the pound for a month, to check neither of us have SARS or Sugar Mountain Disco Fever or plague.
SAY BYE-BYE, PRETTY BIRD! BUONAS NOCHES! ARRIVEDERCI! AUF WIEDERSEHEN! ADIEU!
I miss you soooo much, Ginger, though I think you would asthma to death if you were here and...
SHUT UP, FISH.

HOPELESS SAVAGES

B-SIDES

Written by
JEN VAN METER

Art by
BECKY CLOONAN, VERA BROSGOL,
and **MIKE NORTON**

Lettering by
HOPE LARSON and
BRYAN LEE O'MALLEY

Chapter break art by
BRYAN LEE O'MALLEY and
CHRISTINE NORRIE

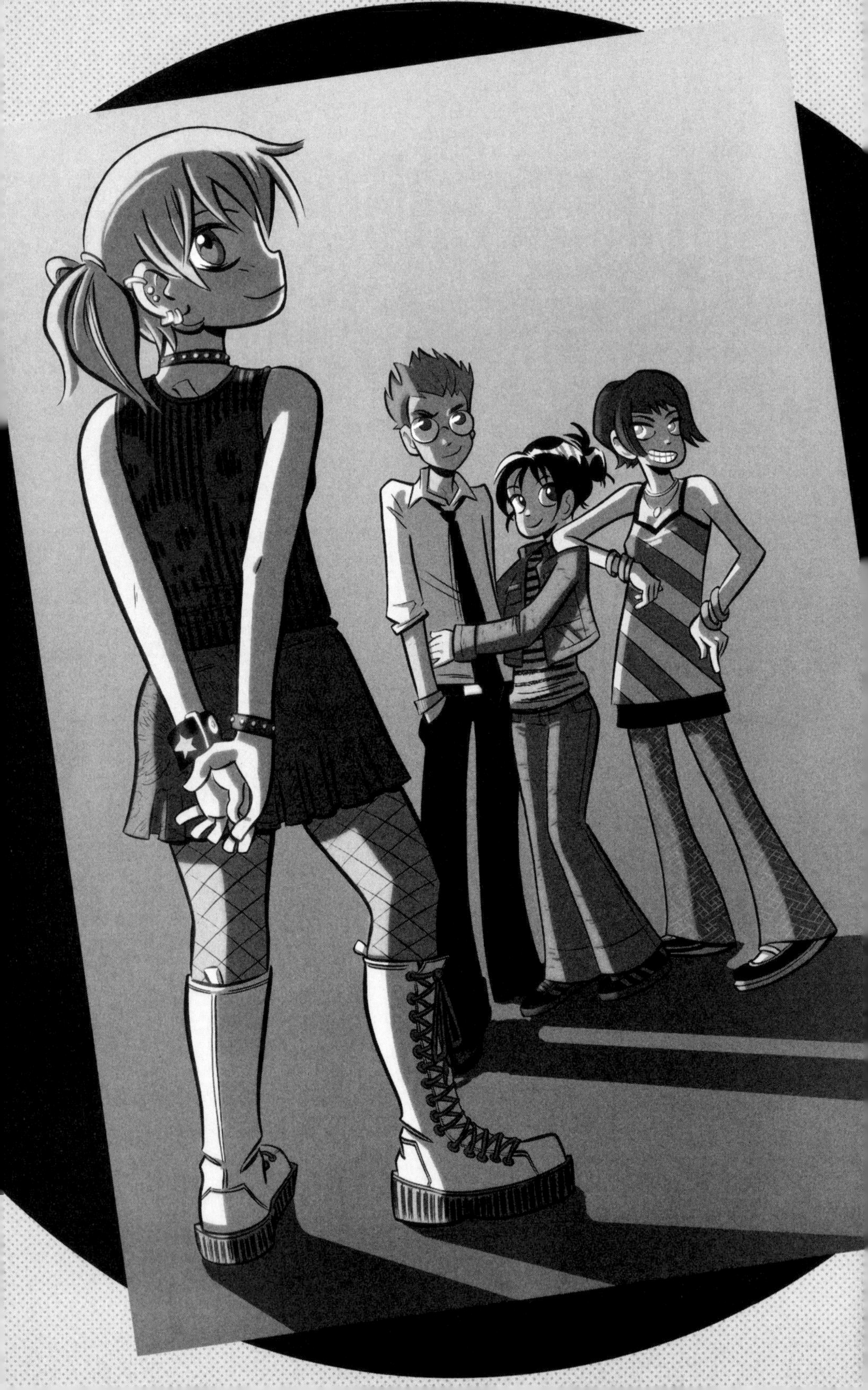

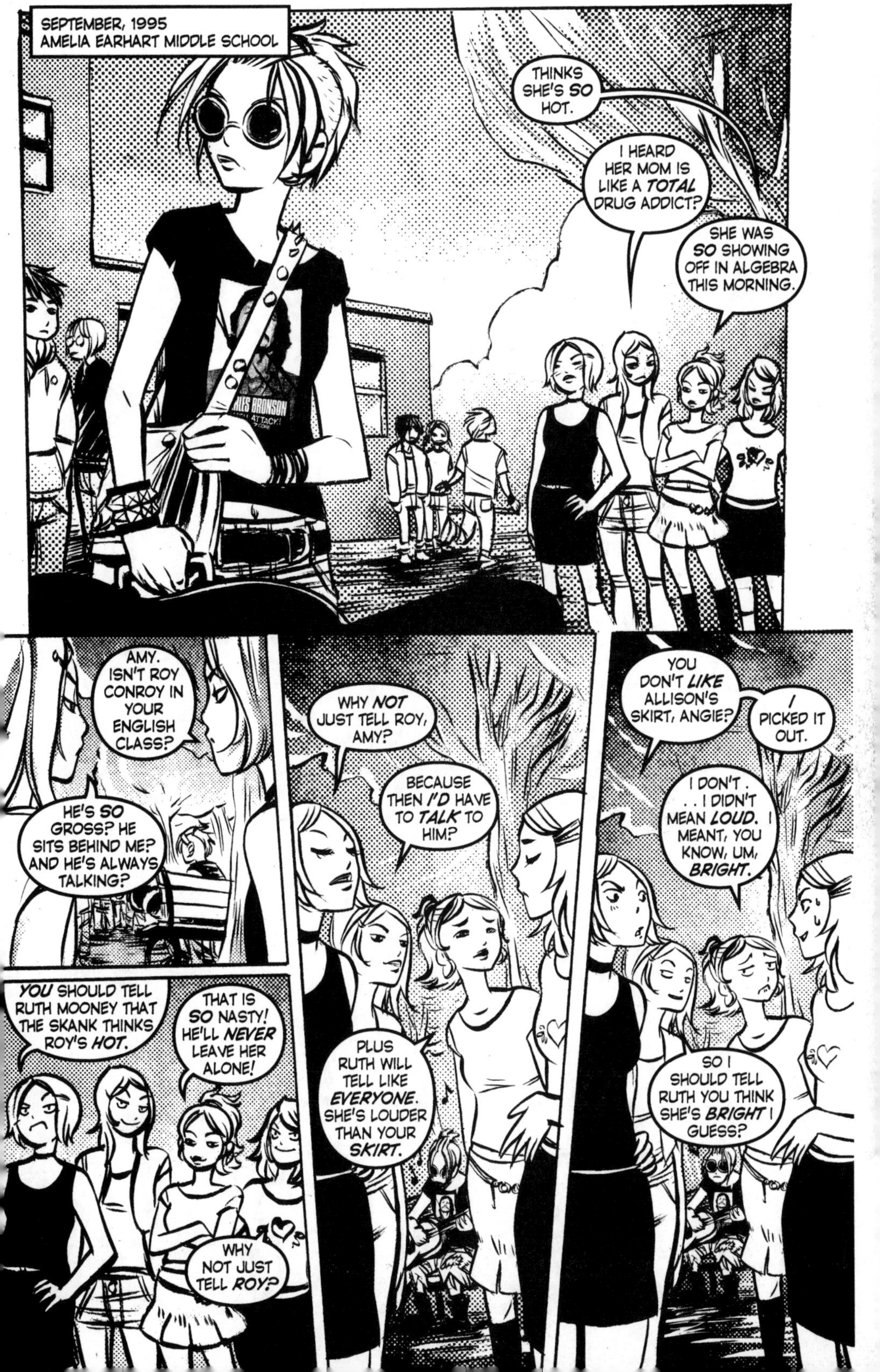
SEPTEMBER, 1995
AMELIA EARHART MIDDLE SCHOOL
THINKS SHE'S SO HOT.
I HEARD HER MOM IS LIKE A TOTAL DRUG ADDICT?
SHE WAS SO SHOWING OFF IN ALGEBRA THIS MORNING.
AMY. ISN'T ROY CONROY IN YOUR ENGLISH CLASS?
HE'S SO GROSS? HE SITS BEHIND ME? AND HE'S ALWAYS TALKING?
YOU SHOULD TELL RUTH MOONEY THAT THE SKANK THINKS ROY'S HOT.
THAT IS SO NASTY! HE'LL NEVER LEAVE HER ALONE!
WHY NOT JUST TELL ROY?
WHY NOT JUST TELL ROY, AMY?
BECAUSE THEN I'D HAVE TO TALK TO HIM?
PLUS RUTH WILL TELL LIKE EVERYONE. SHE'S LOUDER THAN YOUR SKIRT.
YOU DON'T LIKE ALLISON'S SKIRT, ANGIE?
I PICKED IT OUT.
I DON'T . . . I DIDN'T MEAN LOUD. I MEANT, YOU KNOW, UM, BRIGHT.
SO I SHOULD TELL RUTH YOU THINK SHE'S BRIGHT I GUESS?

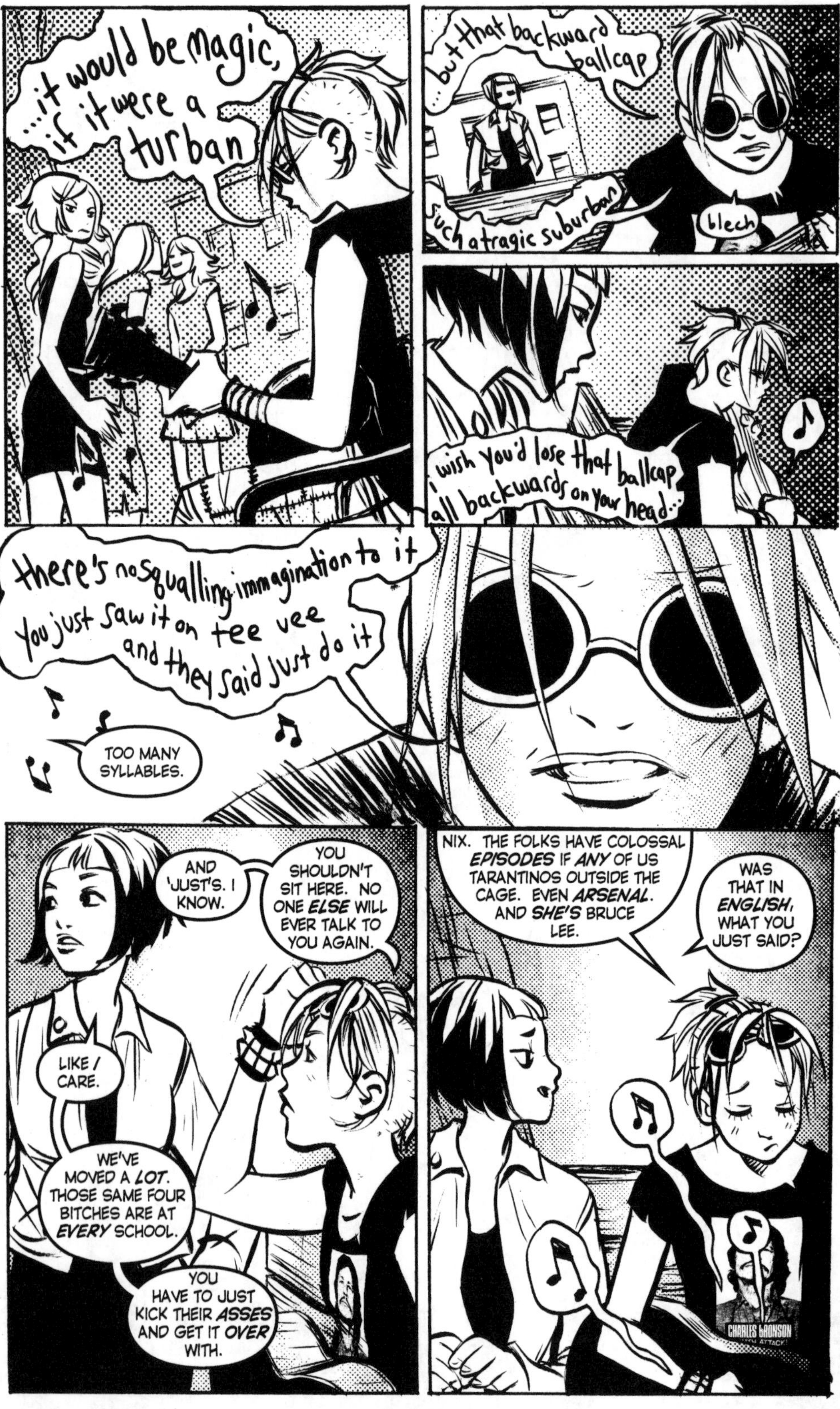

...it would be magic, if it were a turban
...but that backward ballcap
such a tragic suburban
blech
i wish you'd lose that ballcap all backwards on your head...
there's no squalling immagination to it
you just saw it on tee vee
and they said just do it
TOO MANY SYLLABLES.
AND 'JUST'S. I KNOW.
YOU SHOULDN'T SIT HERE. NO ONE ELSE WILL EVER TALK TO YOU AGAIN.
LIKE I CARE.
WE'VE MOVED A LOT. THOSE SAME FOUR BITCHES ARE AT EVERY SCHOOL.
YOU HAVE TO JUST KICK THEIR ASSES AND GET IT OVER WITH.
NIX. THE FOLKS HAVE COLOSSAL EPISODES IF ANY OF US TARANTINOS OUTSIDE THE CAGE. EVEN ARSENAL. AND SHE'S BRUCE LEE.
WAS THAT IN ENGLISH, WHAT YOU JUST SAID?
CHARLES BRONSON

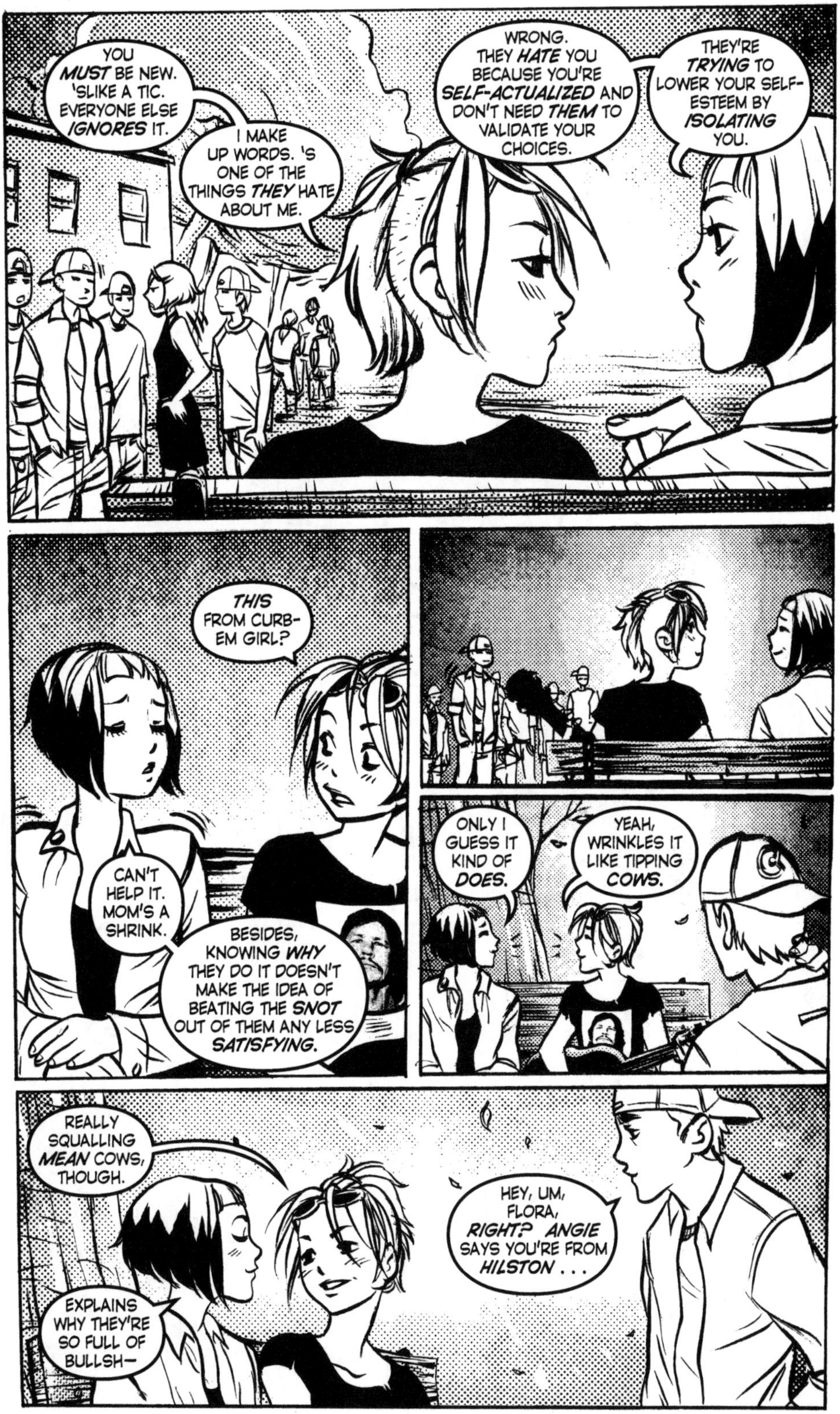
YOU MUST BE NEW. 'SLIKE A TIC. EVERYONE ELSE IGNORES IT.
I MAKE UP WORDS. 'S ONE OF THE THINGS THEY HATE ABOUT ME.
WRONG. THEY HATE YOU BECAUSE YOU'RE SELF-ACTUALIZED AND DON'T NEED THEM TO VALIDATE YOUR CHOICES.
THEY'RE TRYING TO LOWER YOUR SELF-ESTEEM BY ISOLATING YOU.
THIS FROM CURB-EM GIRL?
CAN'T HELP IT. MOM'S A SHRINK.
BESIDES, KNOWING WHY THEY DO IT DOESN'T MAKE THE IDEA OF BEATING THE SNOT OUT OF THEM ANY LESS SATISFYING.
ONLY I GUESS IT KIND OF DOES.
YEAH, WRINKLES IT LIKE TIPPING COWS.
REALLY SQUALLING MEAN COWS, THOUGH.
EXPLAINS WHY THEY'RE SO FULL OF BULLSH—
HEY, UM, FLORA, RIGHT? ANGIE SAYS YOU'RE FROM HILSTON . . .

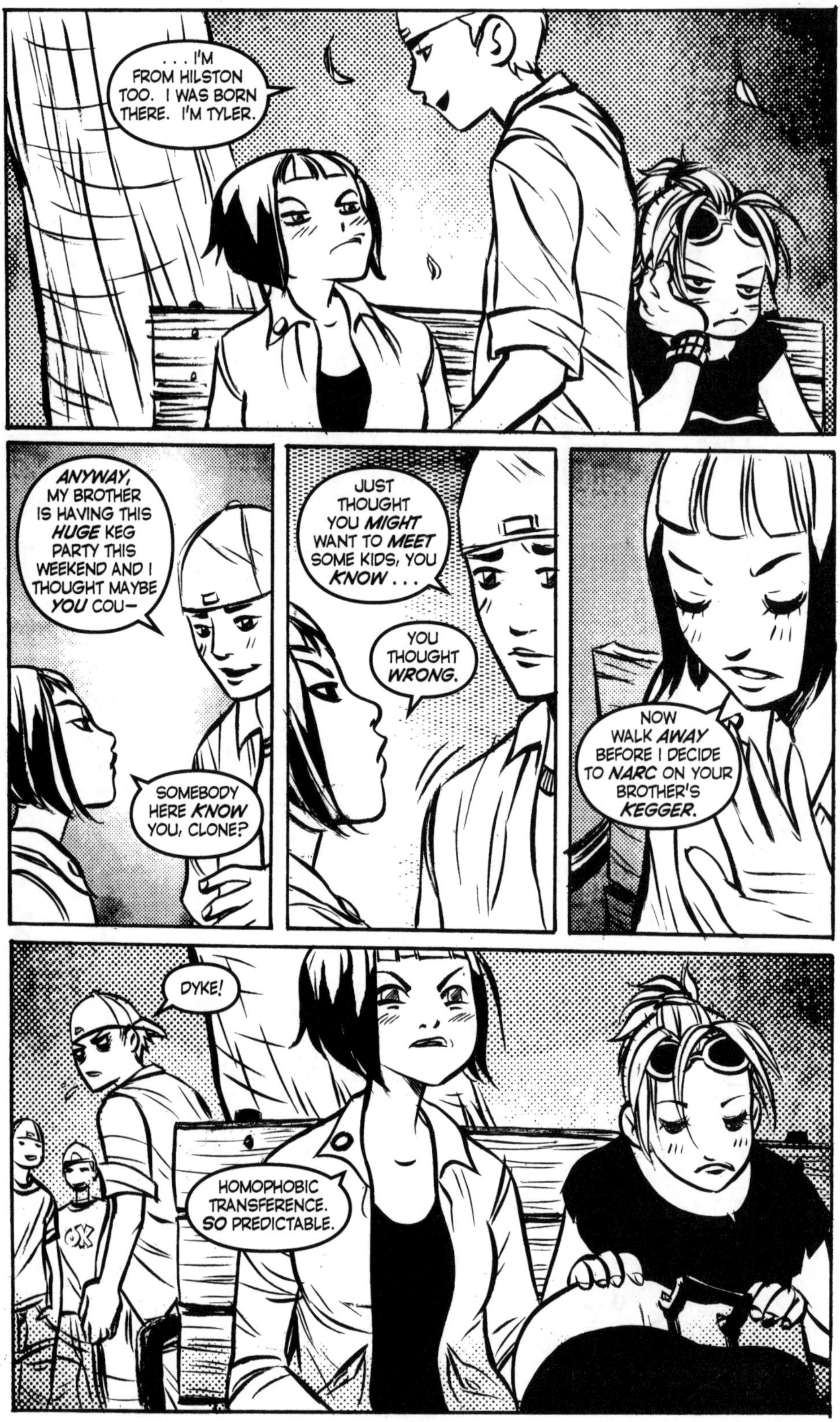
. . . I'M FROM HILSTON TOO. I WAS BORN THERE. I'M TYLER.
ANYWAY, MY BROTHER IS HAVING THIS HUGE KEG PARTY THIS WEEKEND AND I THOUGHT MAYBE YOU COU–
SOMEBODY HERE KNOW YOU, CLONE?
JUST THOUGHT YOU MIGHT WANT TO MEET SOME KIDS, YOU KNOW . . .
YOU THOUGHT WRONG.
NOW WALK AWAY BEFORE I DECIDE TO NARC ON YOUR BROTHER'S KEGGER.
DYKE!
HOMOPHOBIC TRANSFERENCE. SO PREDICTABLE.

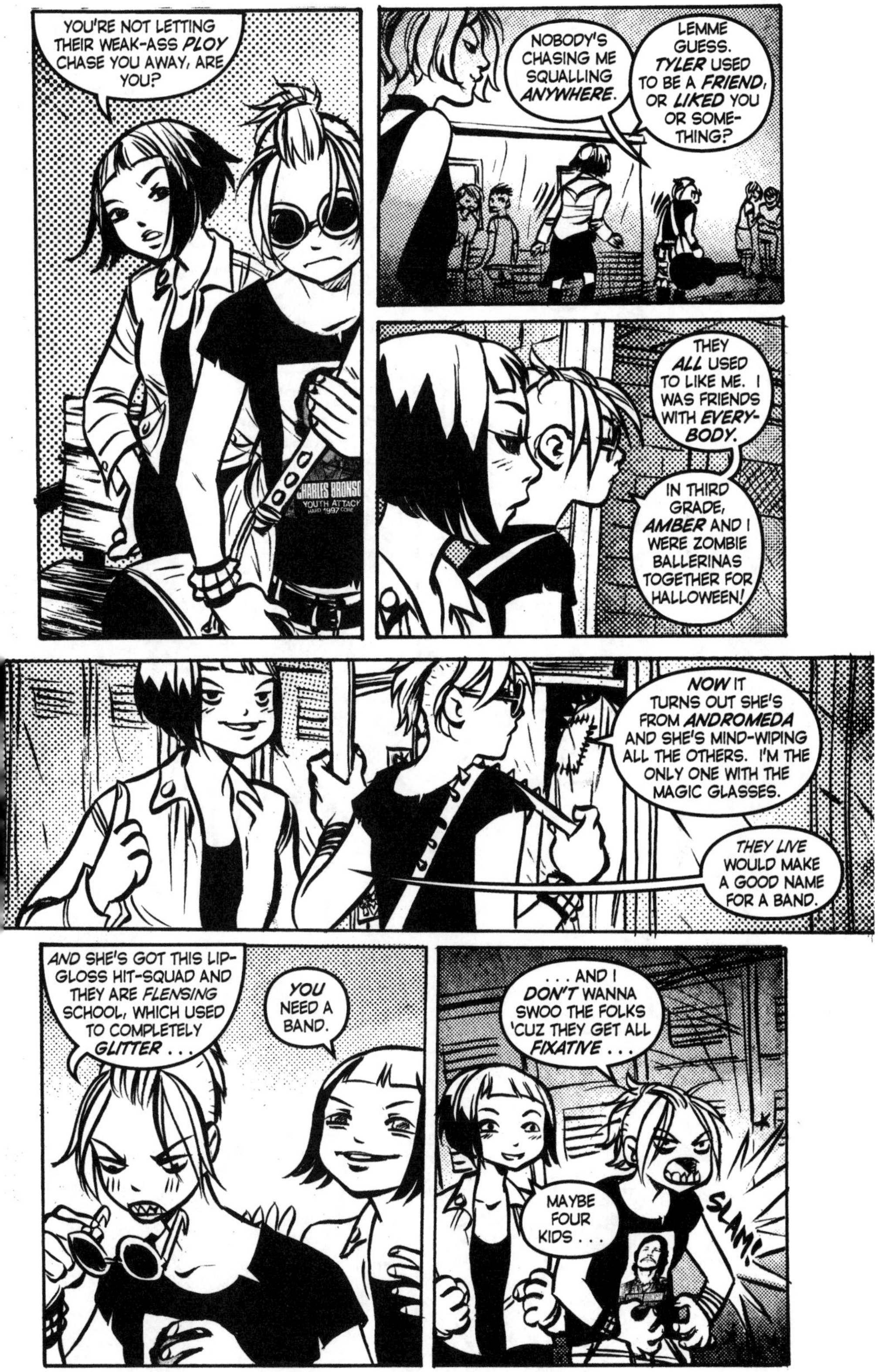
YOU'RE NOT LETTING THEIR WEAK-ASS PLOY CHASE YOU AWAY, ARE YOU?
NOBODY'S CHASING ME SQUALLING ANYWHERE.
LEMME GUESS. TYLER USED TO BE A FRIEND, OR LIKED YOU OR SOME-THING?
CHARLES BRONSO
YOUTH ATTACK
HARD 1997 CORE
THEY ALL USED TO LIKE ME. I WAS FRIENDS WITH EVERY-BODY.
IN THIRD GRADE, AMBER AND I WERE ZOMBIE BALLERINAS TOGETHER FOR HALLOWEEN!
NOW IT TURNS OUT SHE'S FROM ANDROMEDA AND SHE'S MIND-WIPING ALL THE OTHERS. I'M THE ONLY ONE WITH THE MAGIC GLASSES.
THEY LIVE WOULD MAKE A GOOD NAME FOR A BAND.
AND SHE'S GOT THIS LIP-GLOSS HIT-SQUAD AND THEY ARE FLENSING SCHOOL, WHICH USED TO COMPLETELY GLITTER . . .
YOU NEED A BAND.
. . . AND I DON'T WANNA SWOO THE FOLKS 'CUZ THEY GET ALL FIXATIVE . . .
MAYBE FOUR KIDS . . .
SLAM!

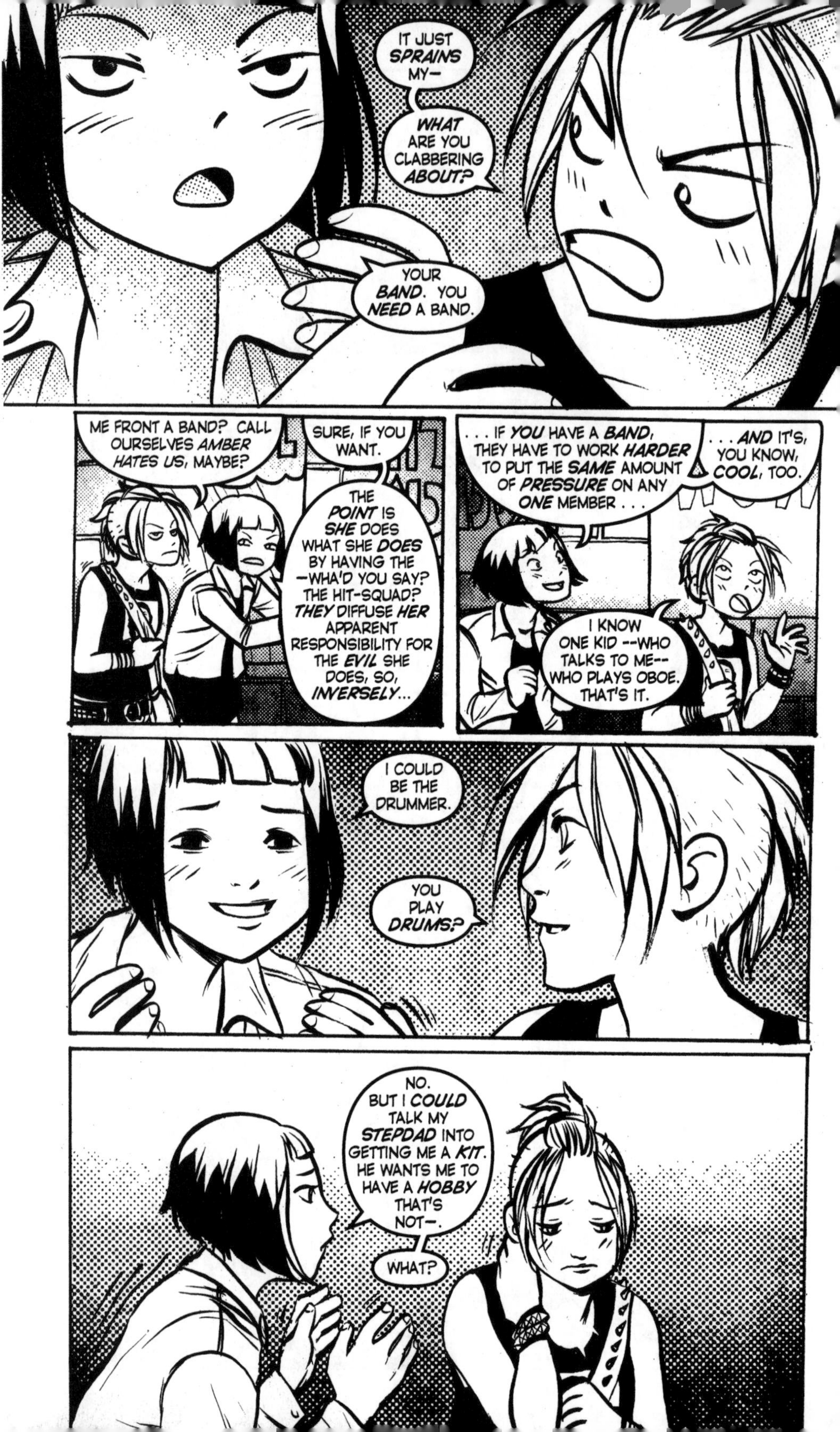

IT JUST SPRAINS MY—
WHAT ARE YOU CLABBERING ABOUT?
YOUR BAND. YOU NEED A BAND.
ME FRONT A BAND? CALL OURSELVES AMBER HATES US, MAYBE?
SURE, IF YOU WANT.
THE POINT IS SHE DOES WHAT SHE DOES BY HAVING THE —WHA'D YOU SAY? THE HIT-SQUAD? THEY DIFFUSE HER APPARENT RESPONSIBILITY FOR THE EVIL SHE DOES, SO, INVERSELY...
. . . IF YOU HAVE A BAND, THEY HAVE TO WORK HARDER TO PUT THE SAME AMOUNT OF PRESSURE ON ANY ONE MEMBER . . .
. . . AND IT'S, YOU KNOW, COOL, TOO.
I KNOW ONE KID --WHO TALKS TO ME-- WHO PLAYS OBOE. THAT'S IT.
I COULD BE THE DRUMMER.
YOU PLAY DRUMS?
NO. BUT I COULD TALK MY STEPDAD INTO GETTING ME A KIT. HE WANTS ME TO HAVE A HOBBY THAT'S NOT—.
WHAT?

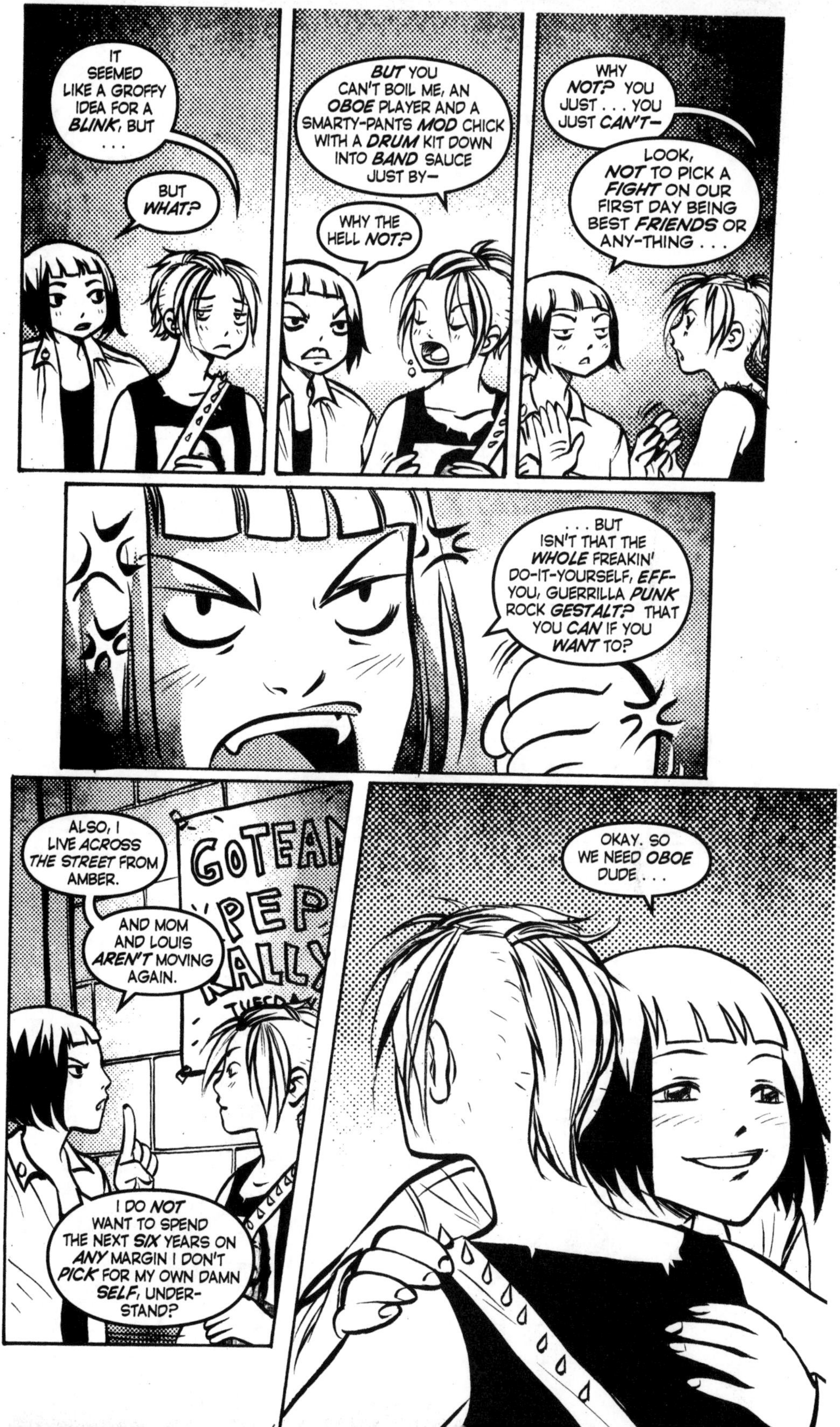

IT SEEMED LIKE A GROFFY IDEA FOR A BLINK, BUT . . .
BUT WHAT?
BUT YOU CAN'T BOIL ME, AN OBOE PLAYER AND A SMARTY-PANTS MOD CHICK WITH A DRUM KIT DOWN INTO BAND SAUCE JUST BY—
WHY THE HELL NOT?
WHY NOT? YOU JUST . . . YOU JUST CAN'T—
LOOK, NOT TO PICK A FIGHT ON OUR FIRST DAY BEING BEST FRIENDS OR ANY-THING . . .
. . . BUT ISN'T THAT THE WHOLE FREAKIN' DO-IT-YOURSELF, EFF-YOU, GUERRILLA PUNK ROCK GESTALT? THAT YOU CAN IF YOU WANT TO?
ALSO, I LIVE ACROSS THE STREET FROM AMBER.
AND MOM AND LOUIS AREN'T MOVING AGAIN.
I DO NOT WANT TO SPEND THE NEXT SIX YEARS ON ANY MARGIN I DON'T PICK FOR MY OWN DAMN SELF, UNDER-STAND?
OKAY. SO WE NEED OBOE DUDE . . .

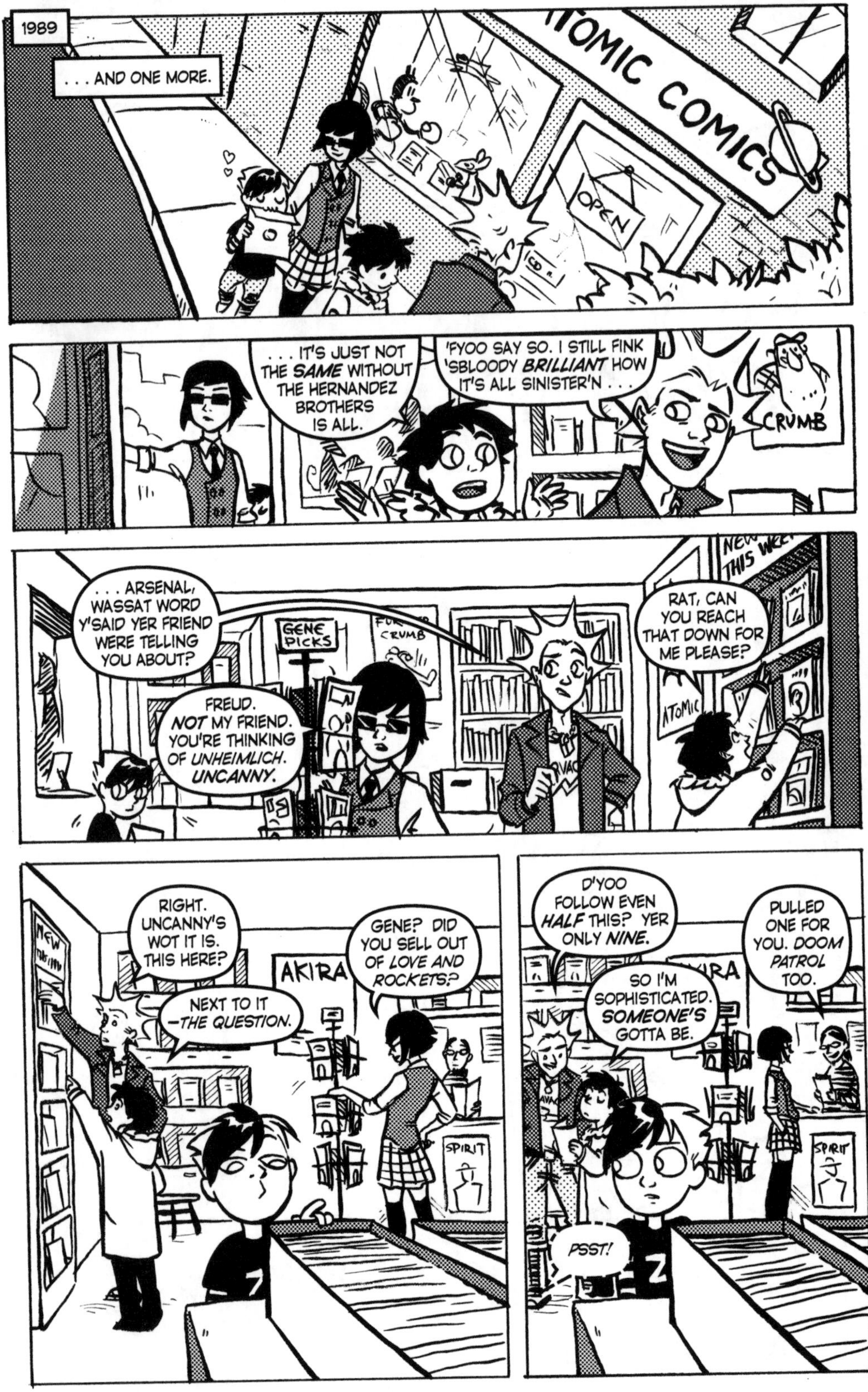

1989
. . . AND ONE MORE.
ATOMIC COMICS
OPEN
. . . IT'S JUST NOT THE SAME WITHOUT THE HERNANDEZ BROTHERS IS ALL.
'FYOO SAY SO. I STILL FINK 'SBLOODY BRILLIANT HOW IT'S ALL SINISTER'N . . .
CRUMB
. . . ARSENAL, WASSAT WORD Y'SAID YER FRIEND WERE TELLING YOU ABOUT?
GENE PICKS
RAT, CAN YOU REACH THAT DOWN FOR ME PLEASE?
FREUD. NOT MY FRIEND. YOU'RE THINKING OF UNHEIMLICH. UNCANNY.
ATOMIC
RIGHT. UNCANNY'S WOT IT IS. THIS HERE?
NEXT TO IT —THE QUESTION.
AKIRA
GENE? DID YOU SELL OUT OF LOVE AND ROCKETS?
SPIRIT
D'YOO FOLLOW EVEN HALF THIS? YER ONLY NINE.
PULLED ONE FOR YOU. DOOM PATROL TOO.
SO I'M SOPHISTICATED. SOMEONE'S GOTTA BE.
PSST!
SPIRIT

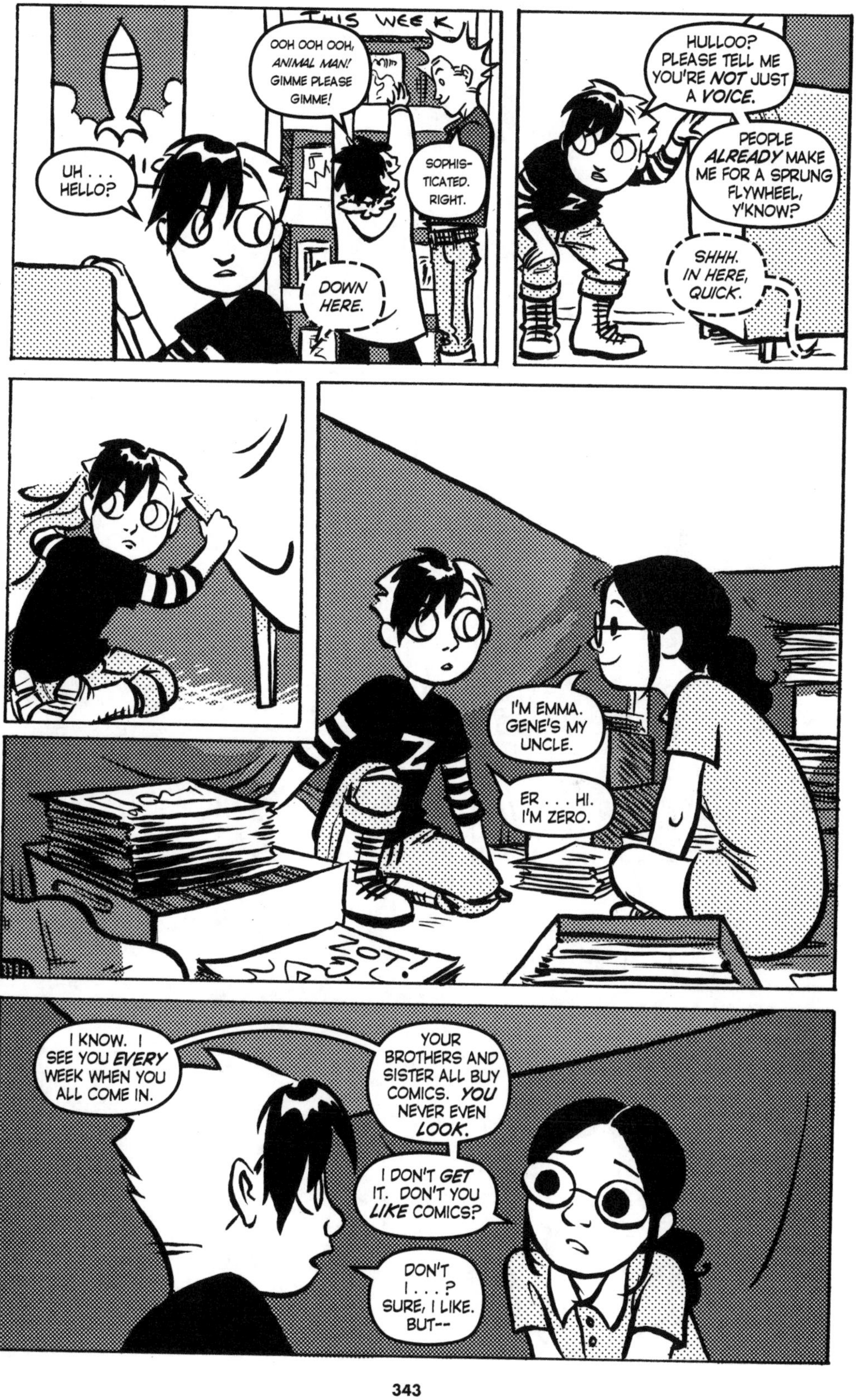
THIS WEEK
UH . . . HELLO?
OOH OOH OOH, ANIMAL MAN! GIMME PLEASE GIMME!
SOPHISTICATED. RIGHT.
DOWN HERE.
HULLOO? PLEASE TELL ME YOU'RE NOT JUST A VOICE.
PEOPLE ALREADY MAKE ME FOR A SPRUNG FLYWHEEL, Y'KNOW?
SHHH. IN HERE, QUICK.
I'M EMMA. GENE'S MY UNCLE.
ER . . . HI. I'M ZERO.
ZOT!
I KNOW. I SEE YOU EVERY WEEK WHEN YOU ALL COME IN.
YOUR BROTHERS AND SISTER ALL BUY COMICS. YOU NEVER EVEN LOOK.
I DON'T GET IT. DON'T YOU LIKE COMICS?
DON'T I . . . ? SURE, I LIKE. BUT--

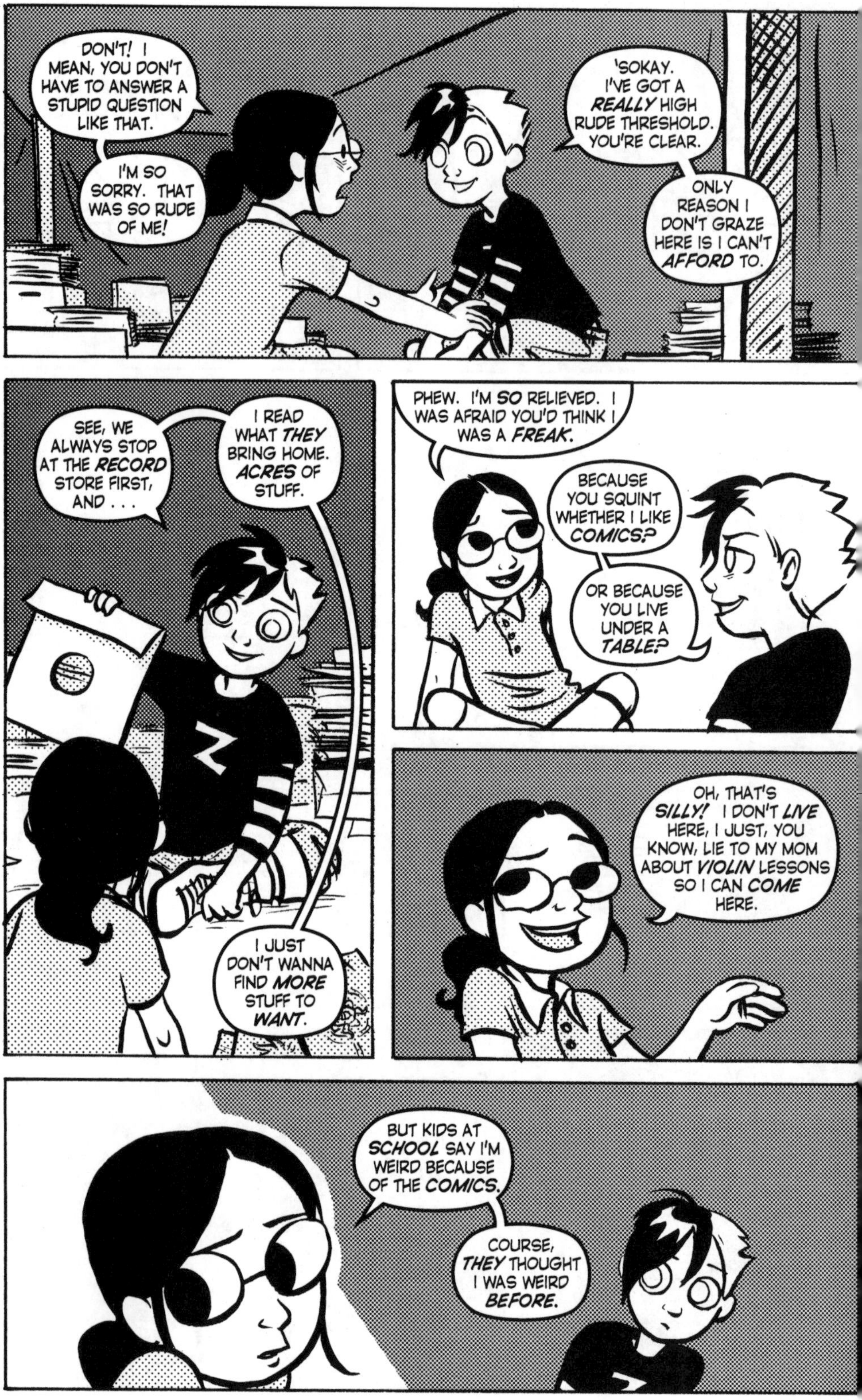
DON'T! I MEAN, YOU DON'T HAVE TO ANSWER A STUPID QUESTION LIKE THAT.
I'M SO SORRY. THAT WAS SO RUDE OF ME!
'SOKAY. I'VE GOT A REALLY HIGH RUDE THRESHOLD. YOU'RE CLEAR.
ONLY REASON I DON'T GRAZE HERE IS I CAN'T AFFORD TO.
SEE, WE ALWAYS STOP AT THE RECORD STORE FIRST, AND . . .
I READ WHAT THEY BRING HOME. ACRES OF STUFF.
I JUST DON'T WANNA FIND MORE STUFF TO WANT.
PHEW. I'M SO RELIEVED. I WAS AFRAID YOU'D THINK I WAS A FREAK.
BECAUSE YOU SQUINT WHETHER I LIKE COMICS?
OR BECAUSE YOU LIVE UNDER A TABLE?
OH, THAT'S SILLY! I DON'T LIVE HERE, I JUST, YOU KNOW, LIE TO MY MOM ABOUT VIOLIN LESSONS SO I CAN COME HERE.
BUT KIDS AT SCHOOL SAY I'M WEIRD BECAUSE OF THE COMICS.
COURSE, THEY THOUGHT I WAS WEIRD BEFORE.

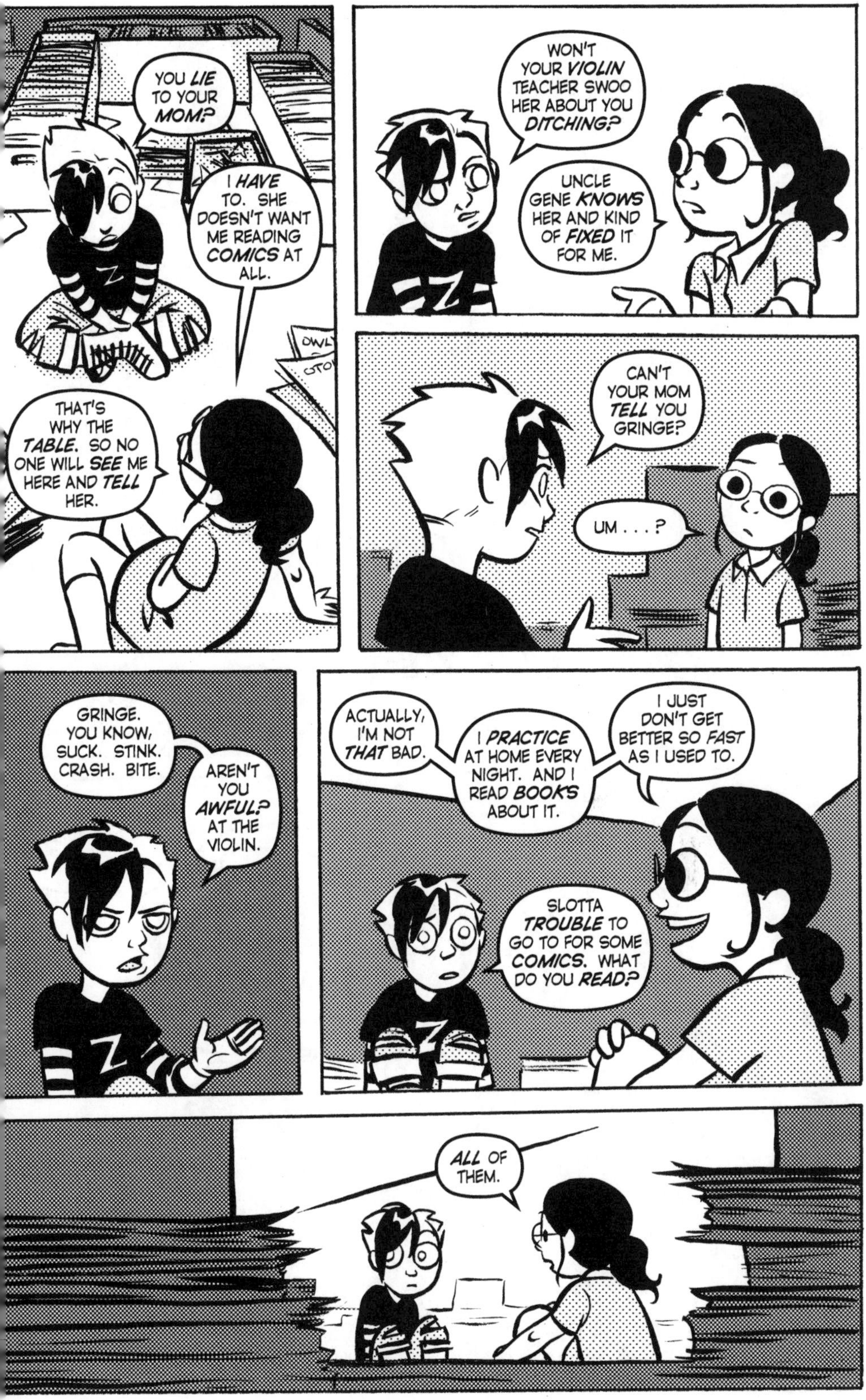
YOU LIE TO YOUR MOM?
I HAVE TO. SHE DOESN'T WANT ME READING COMICS AT ALL.
THAT'S WHY THE TABLE. SO NO ONE WILL SEE ME HERE AND TELL HER.
WON'T YOUR VIOLIN TEACHER SWOO HER ABOUT YOU DITCHING?
UNCLE GENE KNOWS HER AND KIND OF FIXED IT FOR ME.
CAN'T YOUR MOM TELL YOU GRINGE?
UM . . . ?
GRINGE. YOU KNOW, SUCK. STINK. CRASH. BITE.
AREN'T YOU AWFUL? AT THE VIOLIN.
ACTUALLY, I'M NOT THAT BAD.
I PRACTICE AT HOME EVERY NIGHT. AND I READ BOOKS ABOUT IT.
I JUST DON'T GET BETTER SO FAST AS I USED TO.
SLOTTA TROUBLE TO GO TO FOR SOME COMICS. WHAT DO YOU READ?
ALL OF THEM.

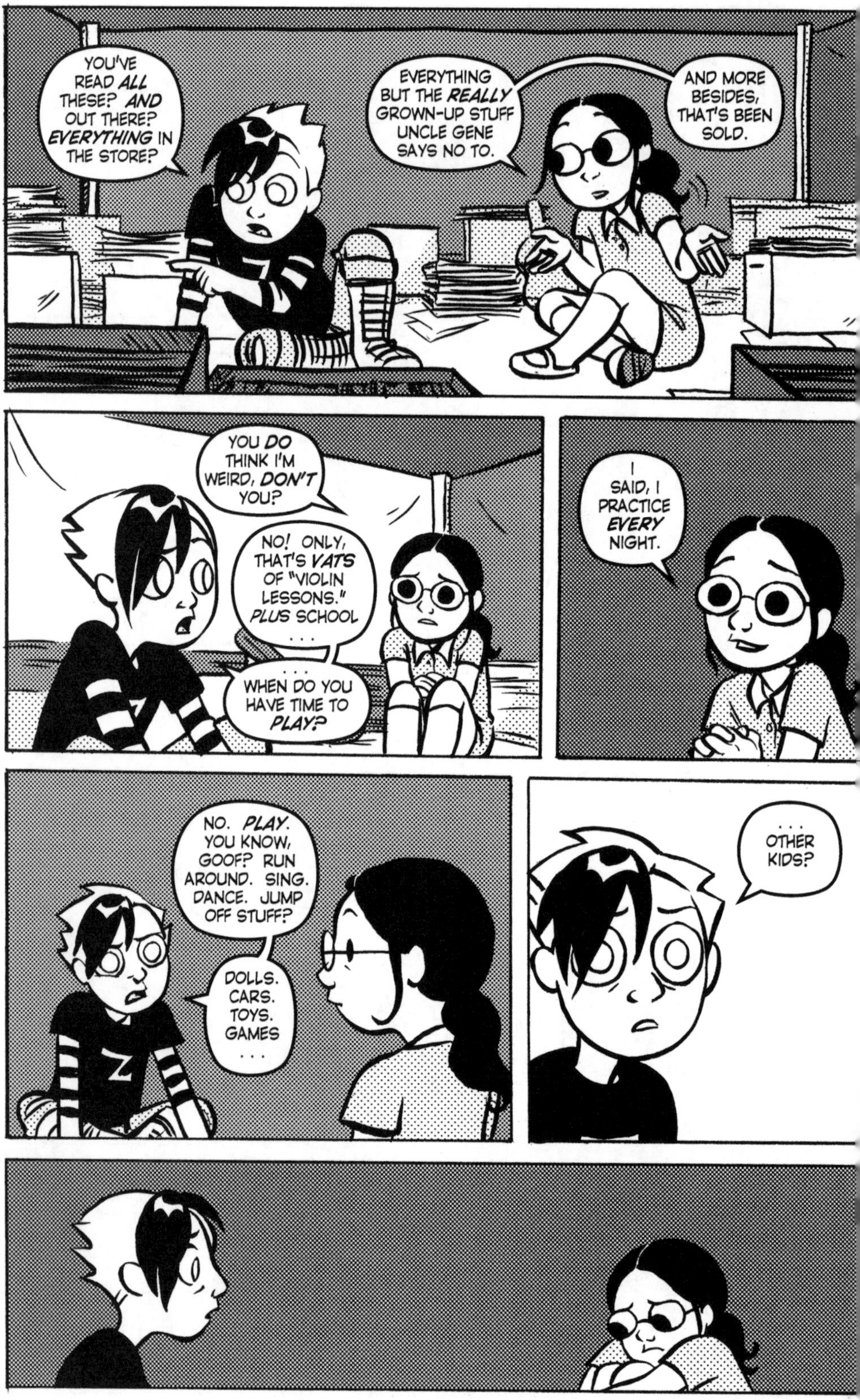
YOU'VE READ ALL THESE? AND OUT THERE? EVERYTHING IN THE STORE?
EVERYTHING BUT THE REALLY GROWN-UP STUFF UNCLE GENE SAYS NO TO.
AND MORE BESIDES, THAT'S BEEN SOLD.
YOU DO THINK I'M WEIRD, DON'T YOU?
NO! ONLY, THAT'S VATS OF "VIOLIN LESSONS." PLUS SCHOOL . . .
. . . WHEN DO YOU HAVE TIME TO PLAY?
I SAID, I PRACTICE EVERY NIGHT.
NO. PLAY. YOU KNOW, GOOF? RUN AROUND. SING. DANCE. JUMP OFF STUFF?
DOLLS. CARS. TOYS. GAMES . . .
. . . OTHER KIDS?

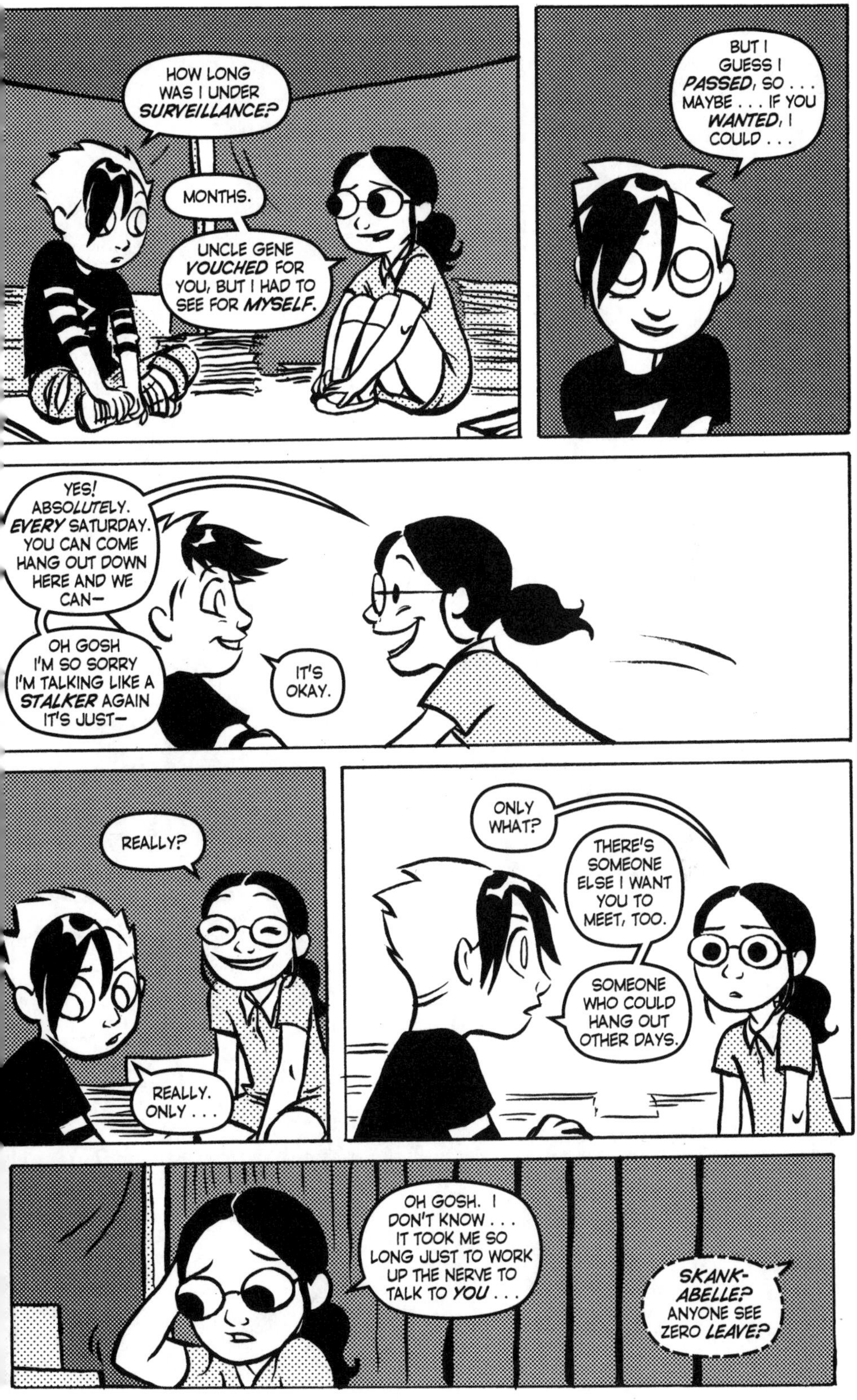
HOW LONG WAS I UNDER SURVEILLANCE?
MONTHS.
UNCLE GENE VOUCHED FOR YOU, BUT I HAD TO SEE FOR MYSELF.
BUT I GUESS I PASSED, SO . . . MAYBE . . . IF YOU WANTED, I COULD . . .
YES! ABSOLUTELY. EVERY SATURDAY. YOU CAN COME HANG OUT DOWN HERE AND WE CAN—
OH GOSH I'M SO SORRY I'M TALKING LIKE A STALKER AGAIN IT'S JUST—
IT'S OKAY.
REALLY?
REALLY. ONLY . . .
ONLY WHAT?
THERE'S SOMEONE ELSE I WANT YOU TO MEET, TOO.
SOMEONE WHO COULD HANG OUT OTHER DAYS.
OH GOSH. I DON'T KNOW . . . IT TOOK ME SO LONG JUST TO WORK UP THE NERVE TO TALK TO YOU . . .
SKANK-ABELLE? ANYONE SEE ZERO LEAVE?

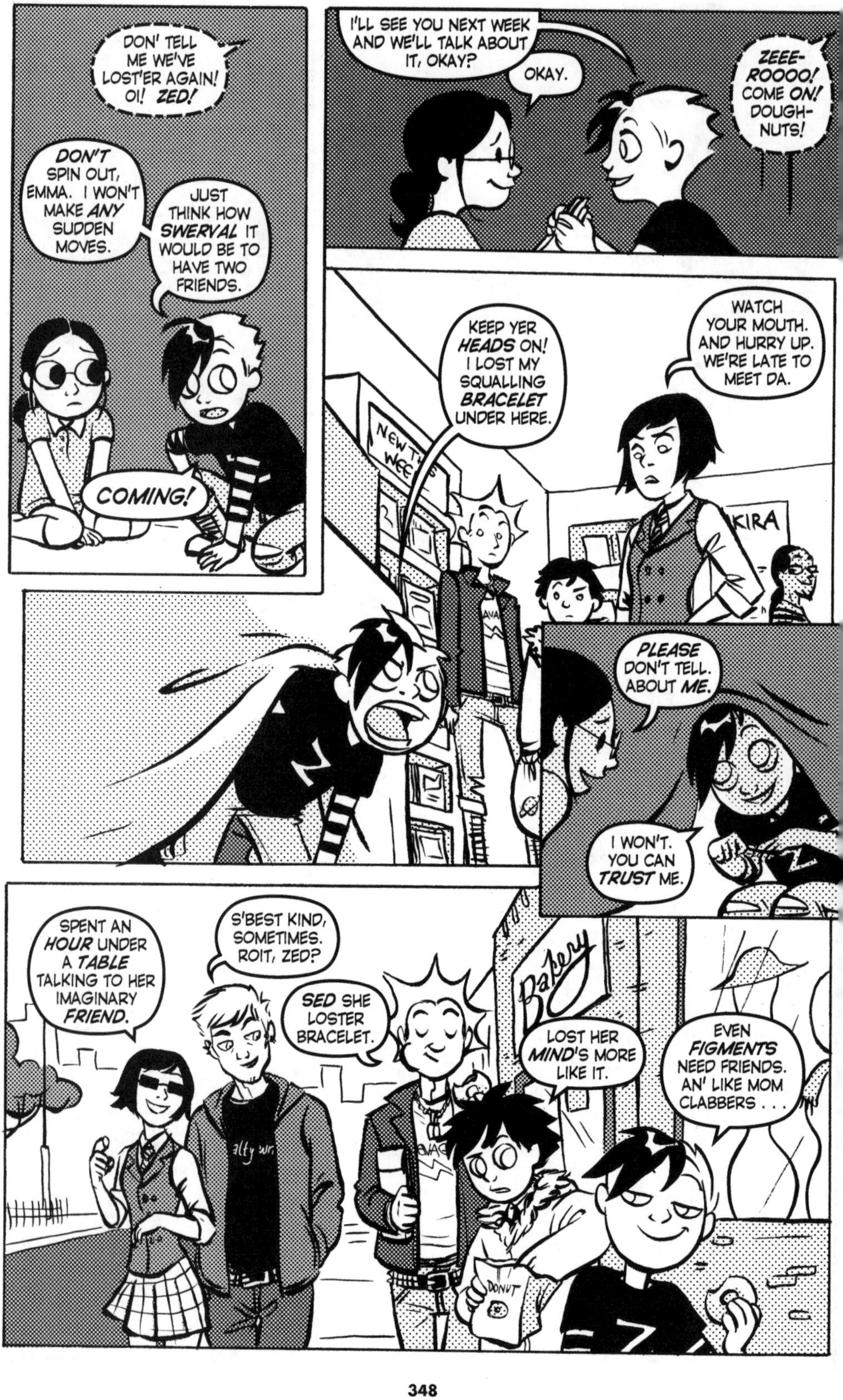
DON' TELL ME WE'VE LOST'ER AGAIN! OI! ZED!
DON'T SPIN OUT, EMMA. I WON'T MAKE ANY SUDDEN MOVES.
JUST THINK HOW SWERVAL IT WOULD BE TO HAVE TWO FRIENDS.
COMING!
I'LL SEE YOU NEXT WEEK AND WE'LL TALK ABOUT IT, OKAY?
OKAY.
ZEEE-ROOOO! COME ON! DOUGH-NUTS!
KEEP YER HEADS ON! I LOST MY SQUALLING BRACELET UNDER HERE.
WATCH YOUR MOUTH. AND HURRY UP. WE'RE LATE TO MEET DA.
KIRA
PLEASE DON'T TELL. ABOUT ME.
I WON'T. YOU CAN TRUST ME.
SPENT AN HOUR UNDER A TABLE TALKING TO HER IMAGINARY FRIEND.
S'BEST KIND, SOMETIMES. ROIT, ZED?
SED SHE LOSTER BRACELET.
Bakery
LOST HER MIND'S MORE LIKE IT.
EVEN FIGMENTS NEED FRIENDS. AN' LIKE MOM CLABBERS . . .
DONUT

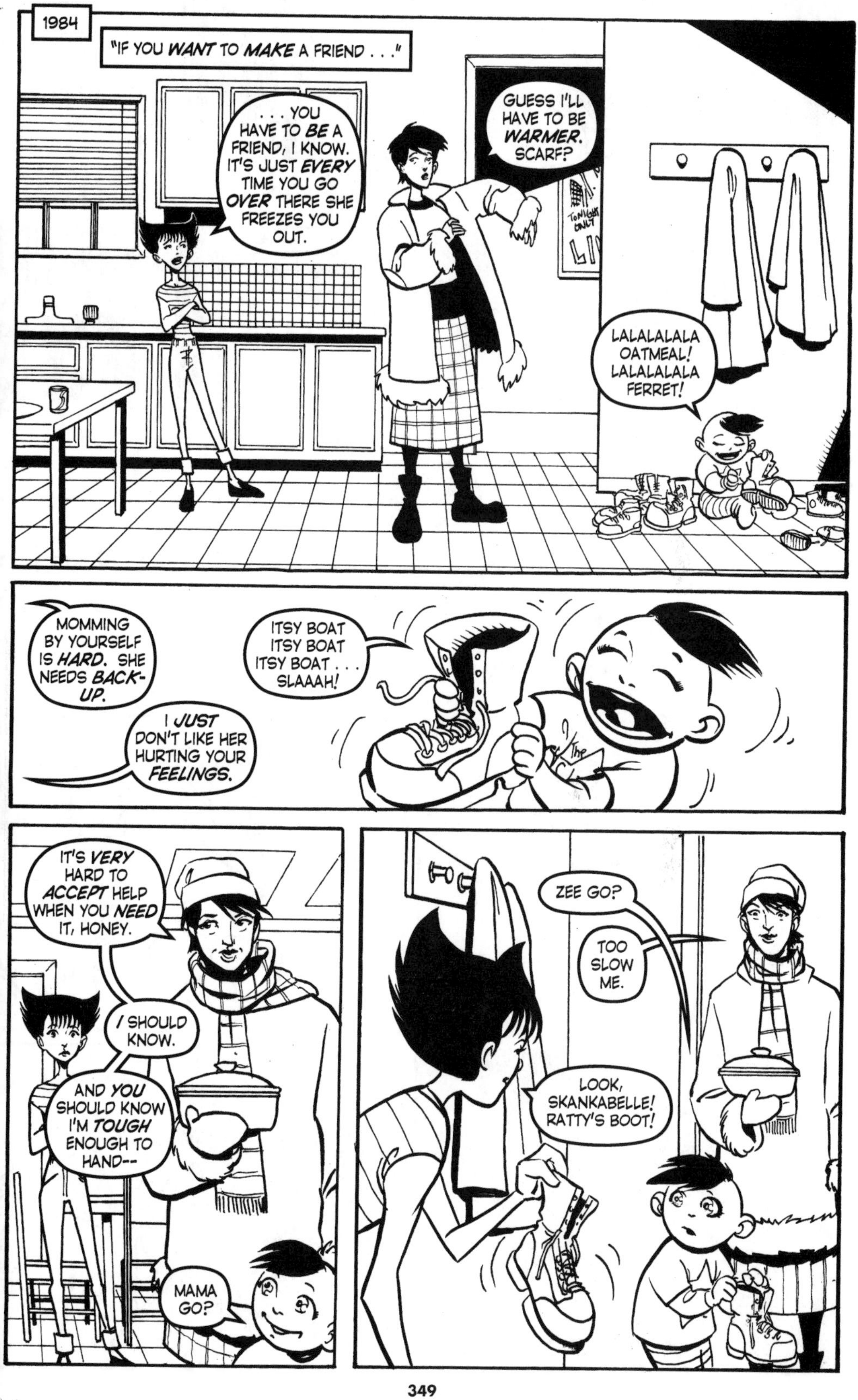
1984
"IF YOU WANT TO MAKE A FRIEND . . ."
. . . YOU HAVE TO BE A FRIEND, I KNOW. IT'S JUST EVERY TIME YOU GO OVER THERE SHE FREEZES YOU OUT.
GUESS I'LL HAVE TO BE WARMER. SCARF?
LALALALALA OATMEAL! LALALALALA FERRET!
MOMMING BY YOURSELF IS HARD. SHE NEEDS BACK-UP.
I JUST DON'T LIKE HER HURTING YOUR FEELINGS.
ITSY BOAT ITSY BOAT ITSY BOAT . . . SLAAAH!
IT'S VERY HARD TO ACCEPT HELP WHEN YOU NEED IT, HONEY.
I SHOULD KNOW.
AND YOU SHOULD KNOW I'M TOUGH ENOUGH TO HAND--
MAMA GO?
ZEE GO?
TOO SLOW ME.
LOOK, SKANKABELLE! RATTY'S BOOT!

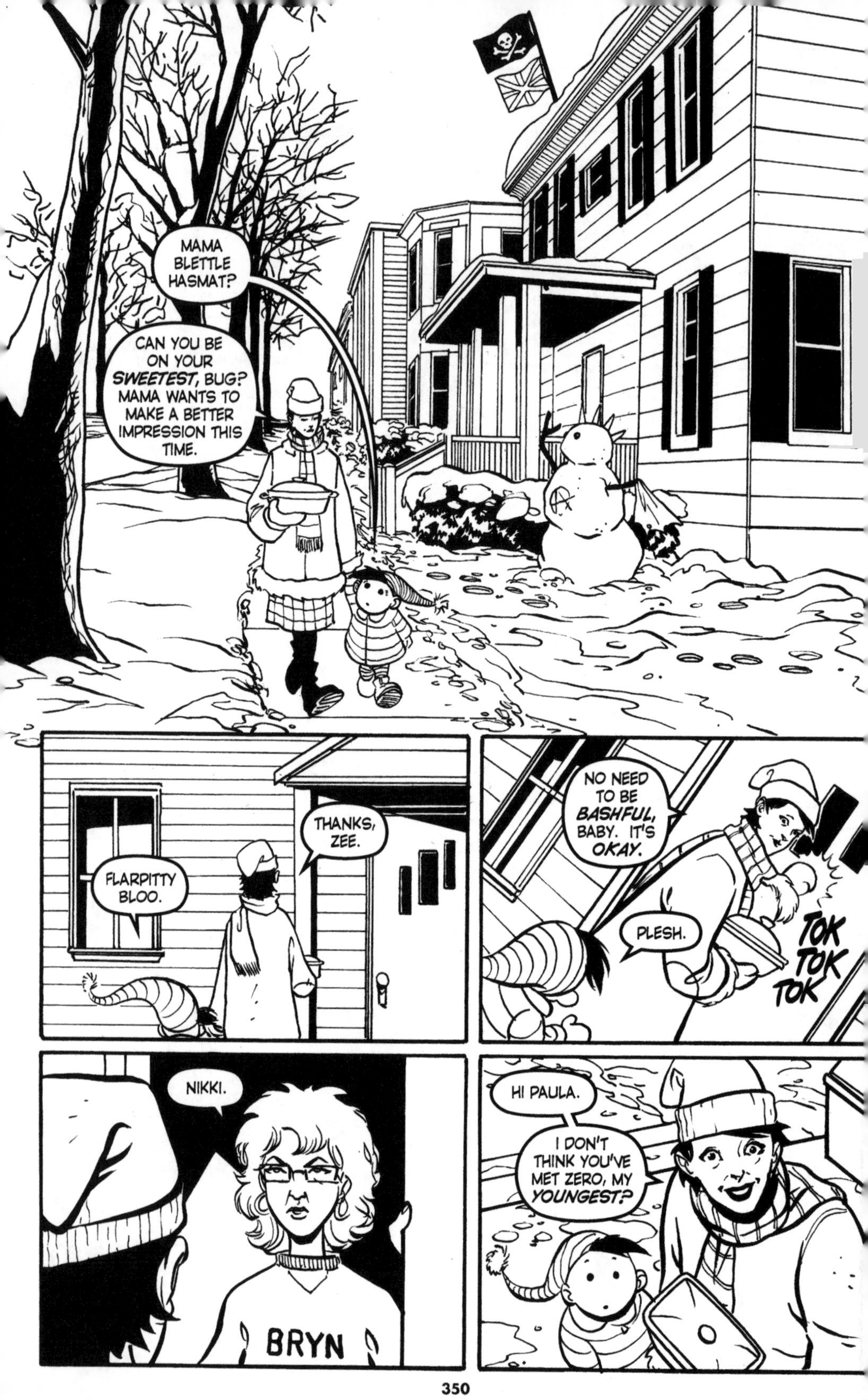
MAMA BLETTLE HASMAT?
CAN YOU BE ON YOUR SWEETEST, BUG? MAMA WANTS TO MAKE A BETTER IMPRESSION THIS TIME.
FLARPITTY BLOO.
THANKS, ZEE.
NO NEED TO BE BASHFUL, BABY. IT'S OKAY.
PLESH.
TOK TOK TOK
NIKKI.
BRYN
HI PAULA.
I DON'T THINK YOU'VE MET ZERO, MY YOUNGEST?

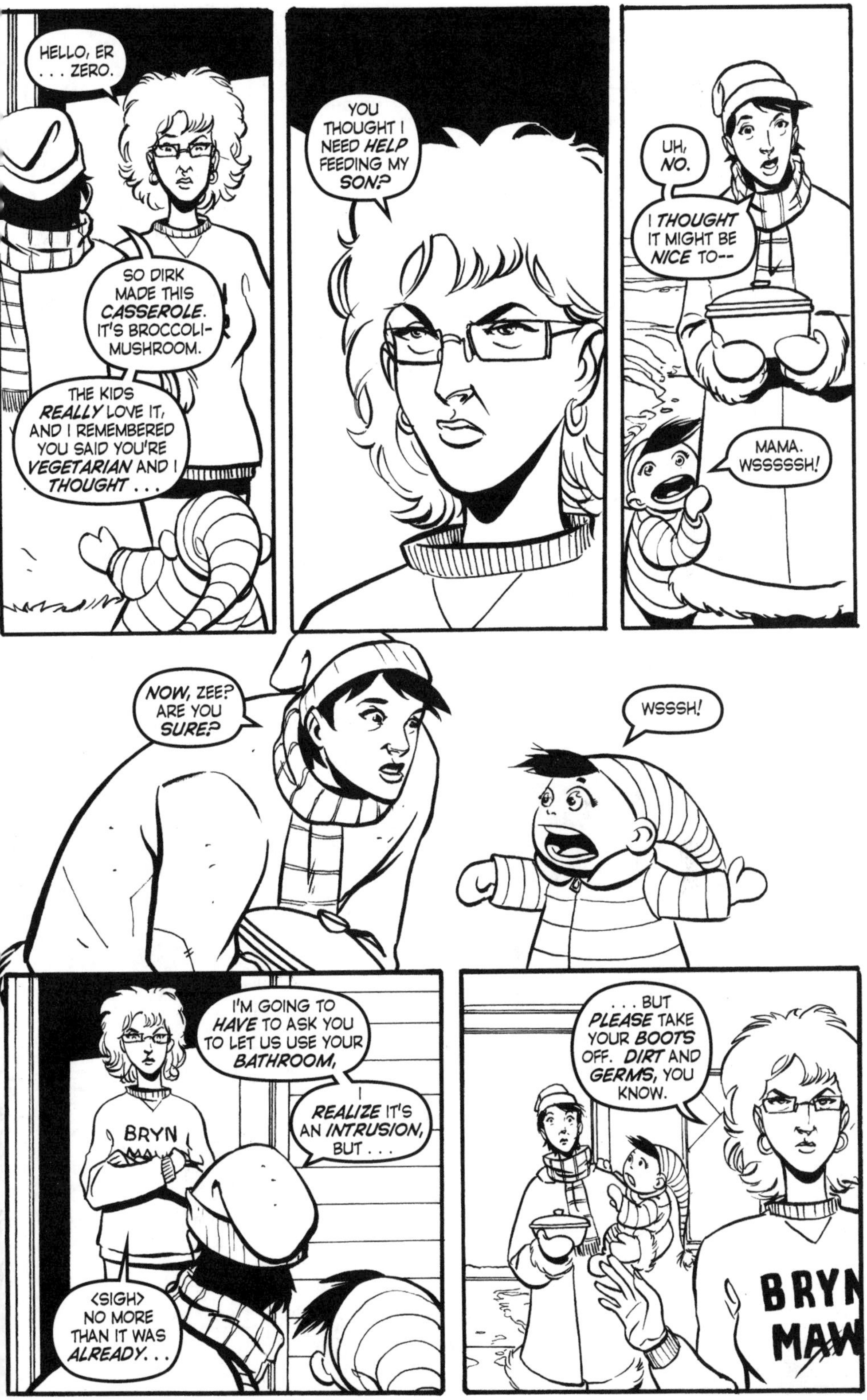
HELLO, ER . . . ZERO.
SO DIRK MADE THIS CASSEROLE. IT'S BROCCOLI-MUSHROOM.
THE KIDS REALLY LOVE IT, AND I REMEMBERED YOU SAID YOU'RE VEGETARIAN AND I THOUGHT . . .
YOU THOUGHT I NEED HELP FEEDING MY SON?
UH, NO.
I THOUGHT IT MIGHT BE NICE TO--
MAMA. WSSSSSH!
NOW, ZEE? ARE YOU SURE?
WSSSH!
I'M GOING TO HAVE TO ASK YOU TO LET US USE YOUR BATHROOM,
I REALIZE IT'S AN INTRUSION, BUT . . .
BRYN MAW
<SIGH> NO MORE THAN IT WAS ALREADY. . .
. . . BUT PLEASE TAKE YOUR BOOTS OFF. DIRT AND GERMS, YOU KNOW.
BRYN MAW

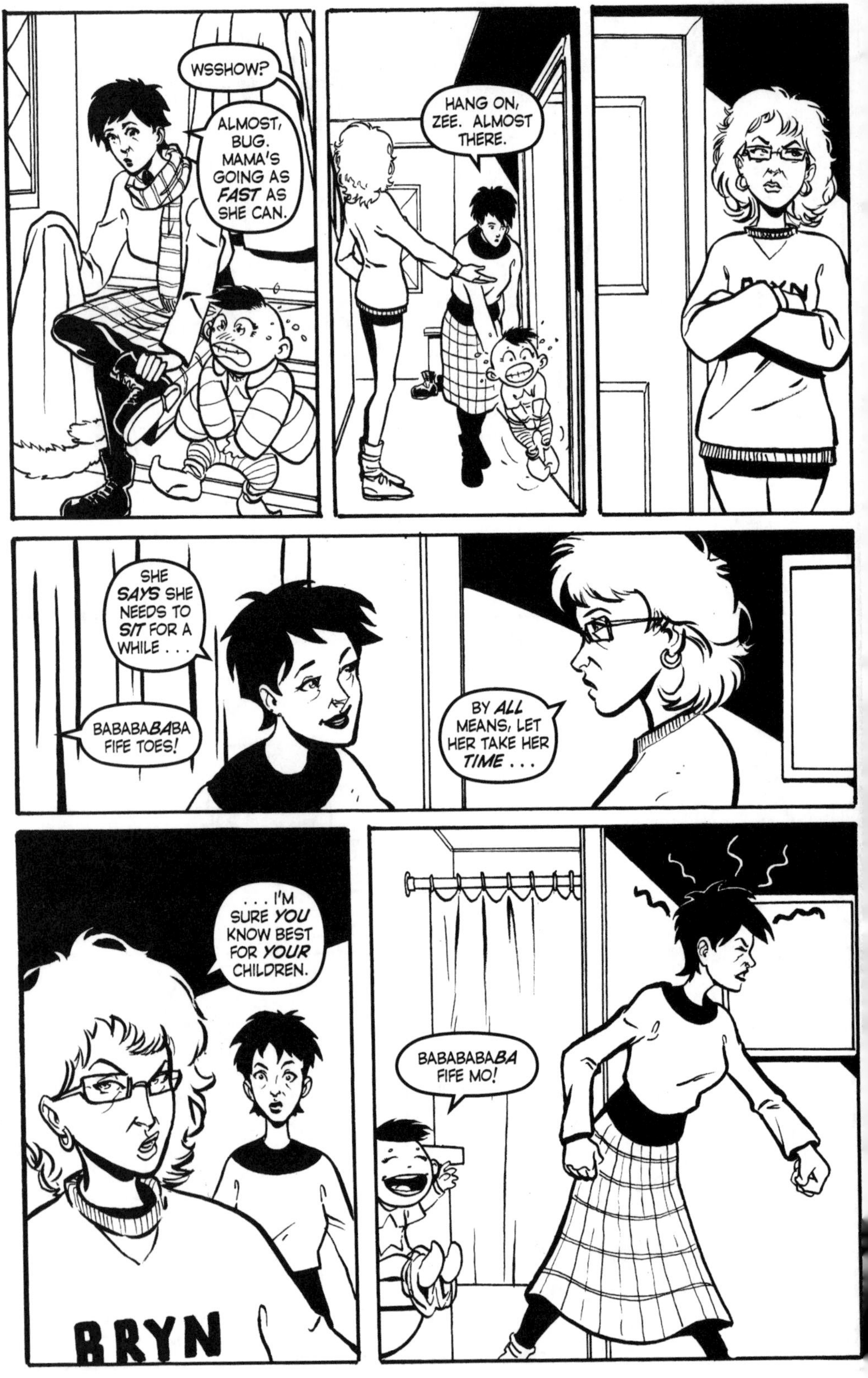
WSSHOW?
ALMOST, BUG. MAMA'S GOING AS FAST AS SHE CAN.
HANG ON, ZEE. ALMOST THERE.
BRYN
SHE SAYS SHE NEEDS TO SIT FOR A WHILE . . .
BABABABABA FIFE TOES!
BY ALL MEANS, LET HER TAKE HER TIME . . .
. . . I'M SURE YOU KNOW BEST FOR YOUR CHILDREN.
BRYN
BABABABABA FIFE MO!

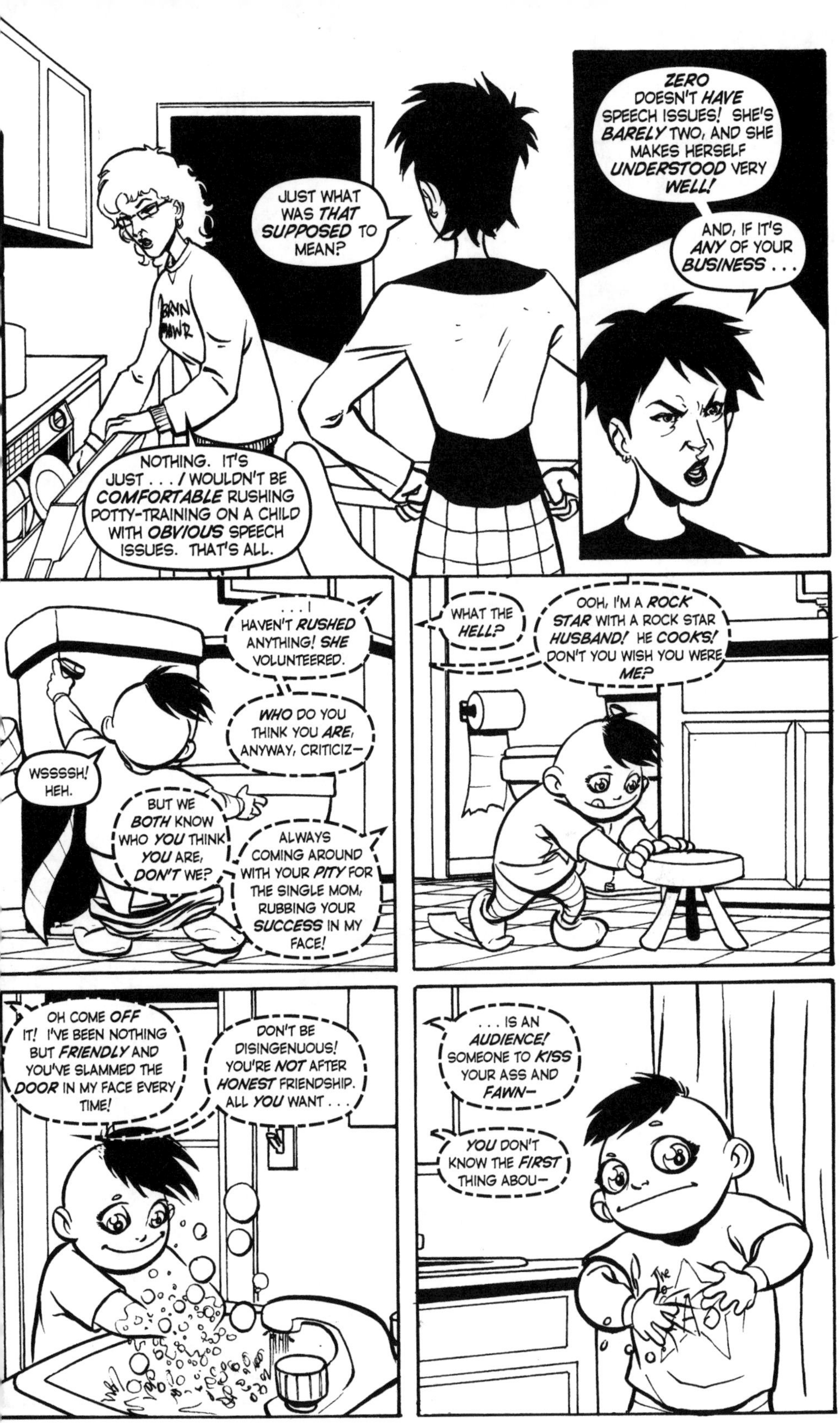
JUST WHAT WAS THAT SUPPOSED TO MEAN?
NOTHING. IT'S JUST . . . I WOULDN'T BE COMFORTABLE RUSHING POTTY-TRAINING ON A CHILD WITH OBVIOUS SPEECH ISSUES. THAT'S ALL.
ZERO DOESN'T HAVE SPEECH ISSUES! SHE'S BARELY TWO, AND SHE MAKES HERSELF UNDERSTOOD VERY WELL!
AND, IF IT'S ANY OF YOUR BUSINESS . . .
. . . I HAVEN'T RUSHED ANYTHING! SHE VOLUNTEERED.
WHO DO YOU THINK YOU ARE, ANYWAY, CRITICIZ—
WSSSSH! HEH.
BUT WE BOTH KNOW WHO YOU THINK YOU ARE, DON'T WE?
ALWAYS COMING AROUND WITH YOUR PITY FOR THE SINGLE MOM, RUBBING YOUR SUCCESS IN MY FACE!
WHAT THE HELL?
OOH, I'M A ROCK STAR WITH A ROCK STAR HUSBAND! HE COOKS! DON'T YOU WISH YOU WERE ME?
OH COME OFF IT! I'VE BEEN NOTHING BUT FRIENDLY AND YOU'VE SLAMMED THE DOOR IN MY FACE EVERY TIME!
DON'T BE DISINGENUOUS! YOU'RE NOT AFTER HONEST FRIENDSHIP. ALL YOU WANT . . .
. . . IS AN AUDIENCE! SOMEONE TO KISS YOUR ASS AND FAWN—
YOU DON'T KNOW THE FIRST THING ABOU—

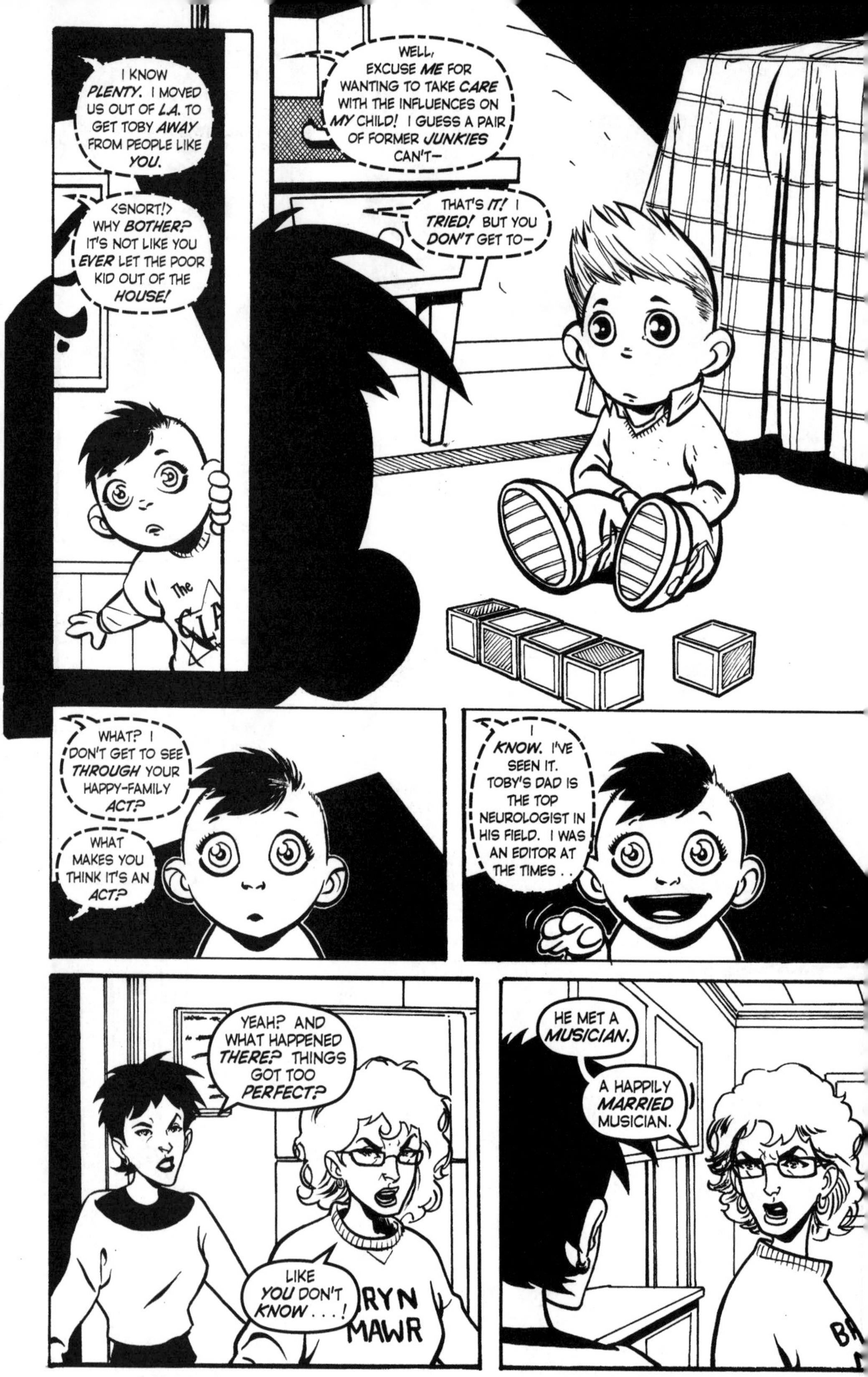
I KNOW PLENTY. I MOVED US OUT OF L.A. TO GET TOBY AWAY FROM PEOPLE LIKE YOU.
WELL, EXCUSE ME FOR WANTING TO TAKE CARE WITH THE INFLUENCES ON MY CHILD! I GUESS A PAIR OF FORMER JUNKIES CAN'T—
<SNORT!> WHY BOTHER? IT'S NOT LIKE YOU EVER LET THE POOR KID OUT OF THE HOUSE!
THAT'S IT! I TRIED! BUT YOU DON'T GET TO—
WHAT? I DON'T GET TO SEE THROUGH YOUR HAPPY-FAMILY ACT?
WHAT MAKES YOU THINK IT'S AN ACT?
I KNOW. I'VE SEEN IT. TOBY'S DAD IS THE TOP NEUROLOGIST IN HIS FIELD. I WAS AN EDITOR AT THE TIMES . .
YEAH? AND WHAT HAPPENED THERE? THINGS GOT TOO PERFECT?
LIKE YOU DON'T KNOW . . . !
RYN MAWR
HE MET A MUSICIAN.
A HAPPILY MARRIED MUSICIAN.

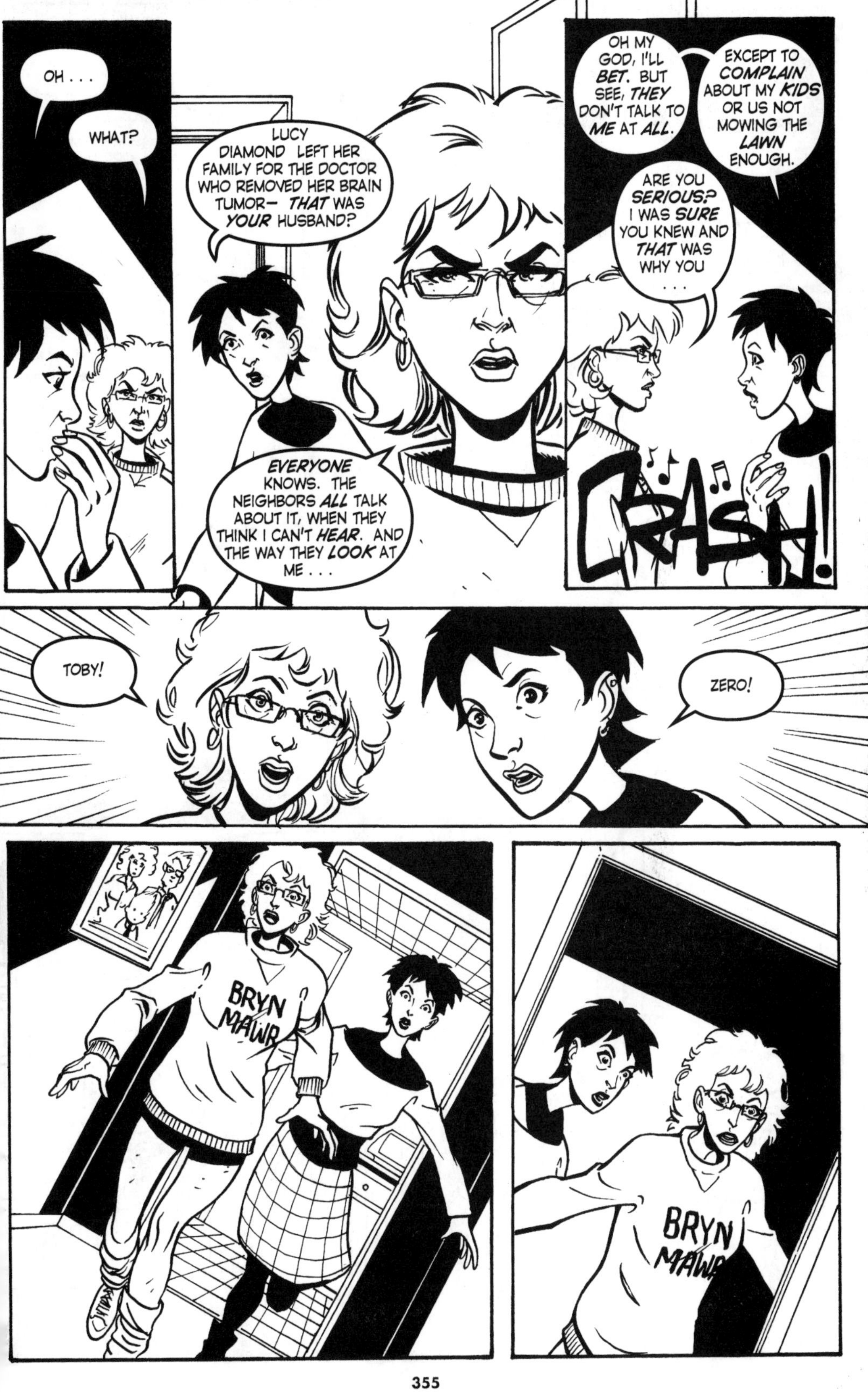

OH . . .
WHAT?
LUCY DIAMOND LEFT HER FAMILY FOR THE DOCTOR WHO REMOVED HER BRAIN TUMOR— THAT WAS YOUR HUSBAND?
EVERYONE KNOWS. THE NEIGHBORS ALL TALK ABOUT IT, WHEN THEY THINK I CAN'T HEAR. AND THE WAY THEY LOOK AT ME . . .
OH MY GOD, I'LL BET. BUT SEE, THEY DON'T TALK TO ME AT ALL.
EXCEPT TO COMPLAIN ABOUT MY KIDS OR US NOT MOWING THE LAWN ENOUGH.
ARE YOU SERIOUS? I WAS SURE YOU KNEW AND THAT WAS WHY YOU . . .
CRASH!
TOBY!
ZERO!
BRYN MAWR
BRYN MAWR

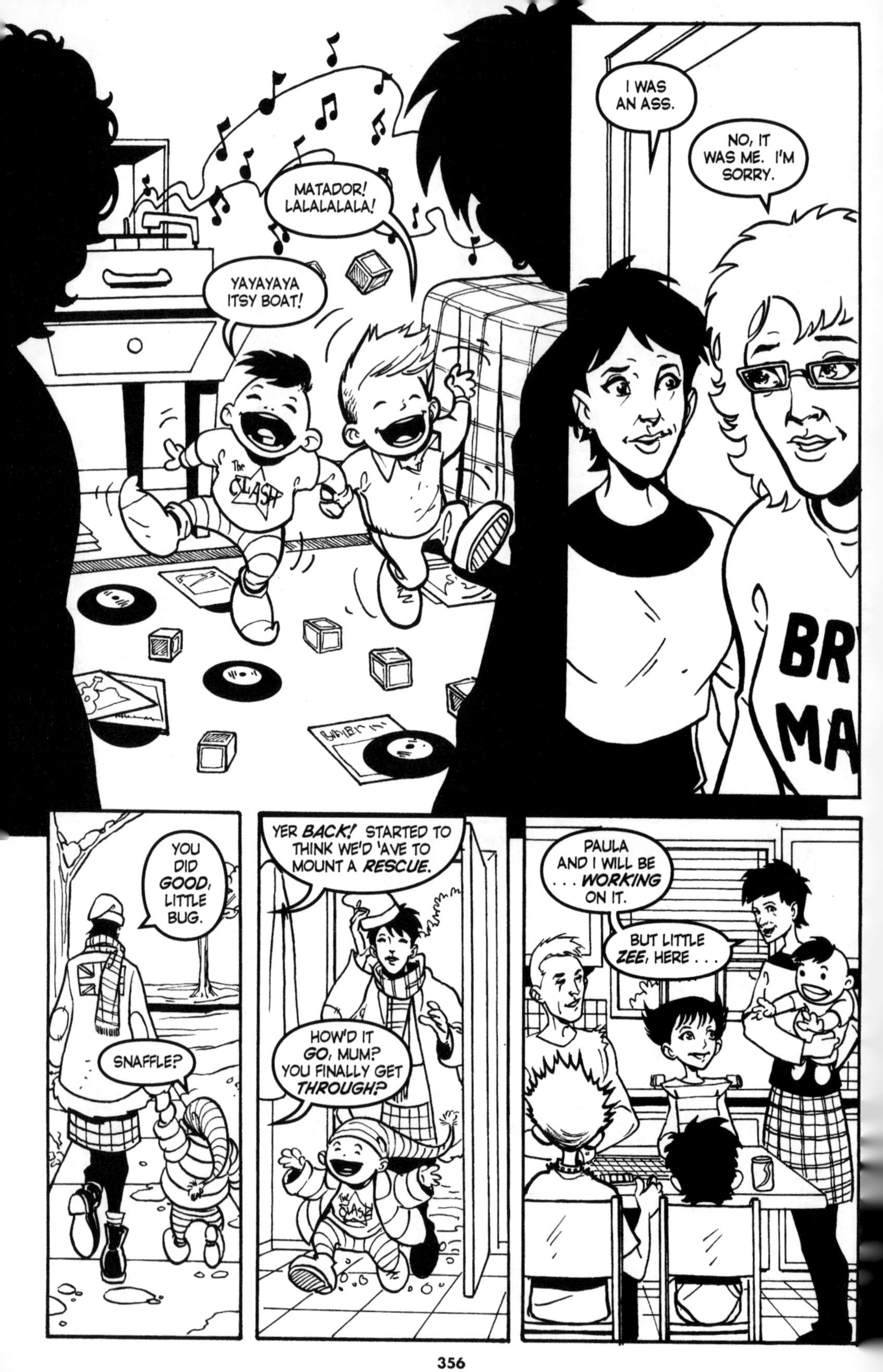
MATADOR! LALALALALA!
YAYAYAYA ITSY BOAT!
I WAS AN ASS.
NO, IT WAS ME. I'M SORRY.
YOU DID GOOD, LITTLE BUG.
SNAFFLE?
YER BACK! STARTED TO THINK WE'D 'AVE TO MOUNT A RESCUE.
HOW'D IT GO, MUM? YOU FINALLY GET THROUGH?
PAULA AND I WILL BE . . . WORKING ON IT.
BUT LITTLE ZEE, HERE . . .

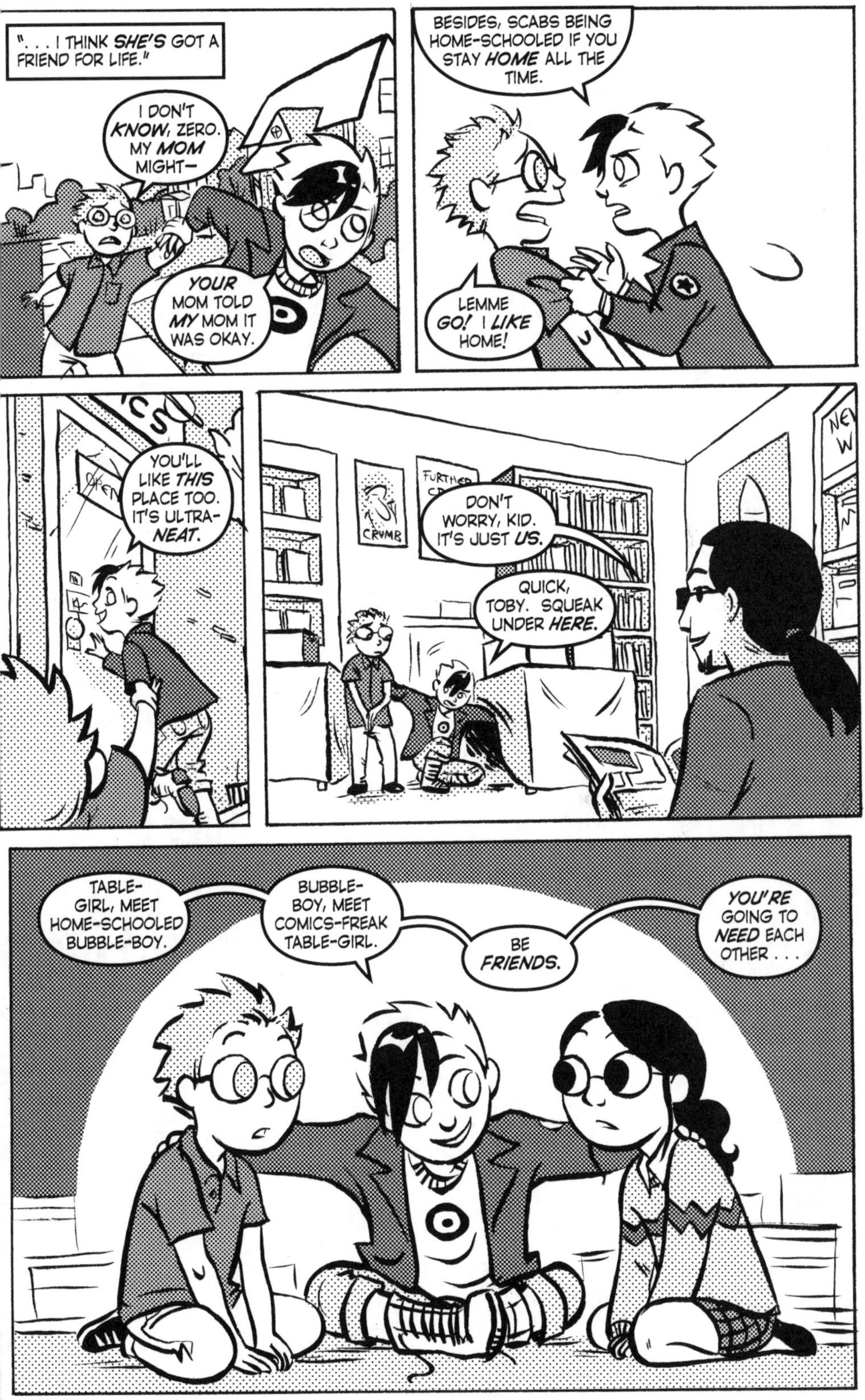
". . . I THINK SHE'S GOT A FRIEND FOR LIFE."
I DON'T KNOW, ZERO. MY MOM MIGHT—
YOUR MOM TOLD MY MOM IT WAS OKAY.
BESIDES, SCABS BEING HOME-SCHOOLED IF YOU STAY HOME ALL THE TIME.
LEMME GO! I LIKE HOME!
YOU'LL LIKE THIS PLACE TOO. IT'S ULTRA-NEAT.
CRUMB
DON'T WORRY, KID. IT'S JUST US.
QUICK, TOBY. SQUEAK UNDER HERE.
TABLE-GIRL, MEET HOME-SCHOOLED BUBBLE-BOY.
BUBBLE-BOY, MEET COMICS-FREAK TABLE-GIRL.
BE FRIENDS.
YOU'RE GOING TO NEED EACH OTHER . . .

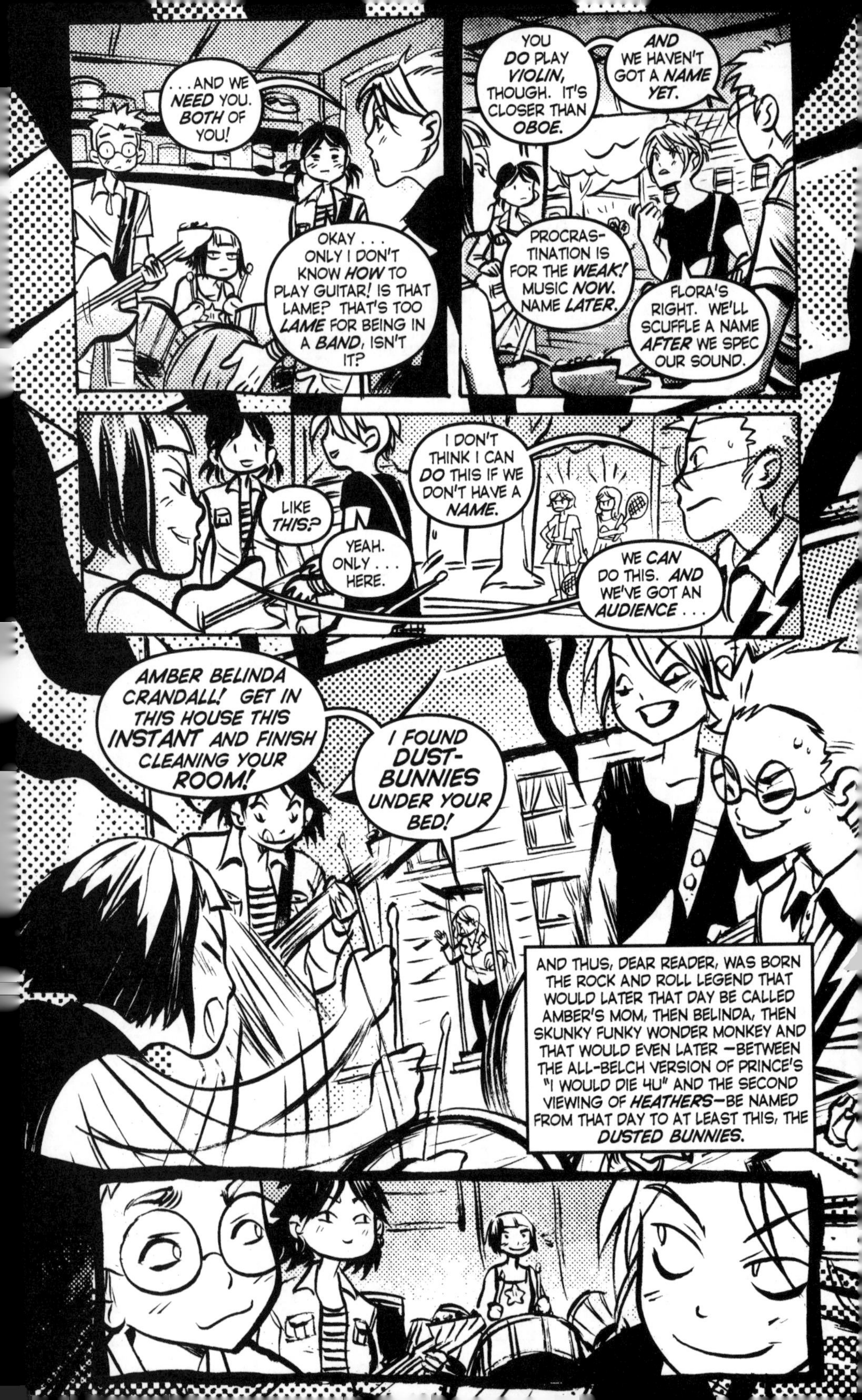

. . . AND WE NEED YOU. BOTH OF YOU!
OKAY . . . ONLY I DON'T KNOW HOW TO PLAY GUITAR! IS THAT LAME? THAT'S TOO LAME FOR BEING IN A BAND, ISN'T IT?
YOU DO PLAY VIOLIN, THOUGH. IT'S CLOSER THAN OBOE.
AND WE HAVEN'T GOT A NAME YET.
PROCRASTINATION IS FOR THE WEAK! MUSIC NOW. NAME LATER.
FLORA'S RIGHT. WE'LL SCUFFLE A NAME AFTER WE SPEC OUR SOUND.
LIKE THIS?
YEAH. ONLY . . . HERE.
I DON'T THINK I CAN DO THIS IF WE DON'T HAVE A NAME.
WE CAN DO THIS. AND WE'VE GOT AN AUDIENCE . . .
AMBER BELINDA CRANDALL! GET IN THIS HOUSE THIS INSTANT AND FINISH CLEANING YOUR ROOM!
I FOUND DUST-BUNNIES UNDER YOUR BED!
AND THUS, DEAR READER, WAS BORN THE ROCK AND ROLL LEGEND THAT WOULD LATER THAT DAY BE CALLED AMBER'S MOM, THEN BELINDA, THEN SKUNKY FUNKY WONDER MONKEY AND THAT WOULD EVEN LATER —BETWEEN THE ALL-BELCH VERSION OF PRINCE'S "I WOULD DIE 4U" AND THE SECOND VIEWING OF HEATHERS—BE NAMED FROM THAT DAY TO AT LEAST THIS, THE DUSTED BUNNIES.

BONUS TRACKS

WRITTEN BY
JEN VAN METER

"OPEN HOUSE"
ART BY CHRISTINE NORRIE
LETTERING BY DOUGLAS E. SHERWOOD

"SOME OF MY BEST WORDS ARE FRIENDS"
ART BY MEREDITH A. MCCLAREN
LETTERING BY DOUGLAS E. SHERWOOD

"ROMANCE #1"
ART BY CHRISTINE NORRIE
COLORS BY ANDI WATSON   LETTERING BY ANDY LIS

"STICKS AND STONES"
ART BY CHYNNA CLUGSTON FLORES
COLORS BY GUY MAJOR   LETTERING BY AMIE GRENIER

"MUSIC BOXES"
ART BY TIM FISH

"GOOD FENCES"
ART & LETTERING BY CHRISTINE NORRIE

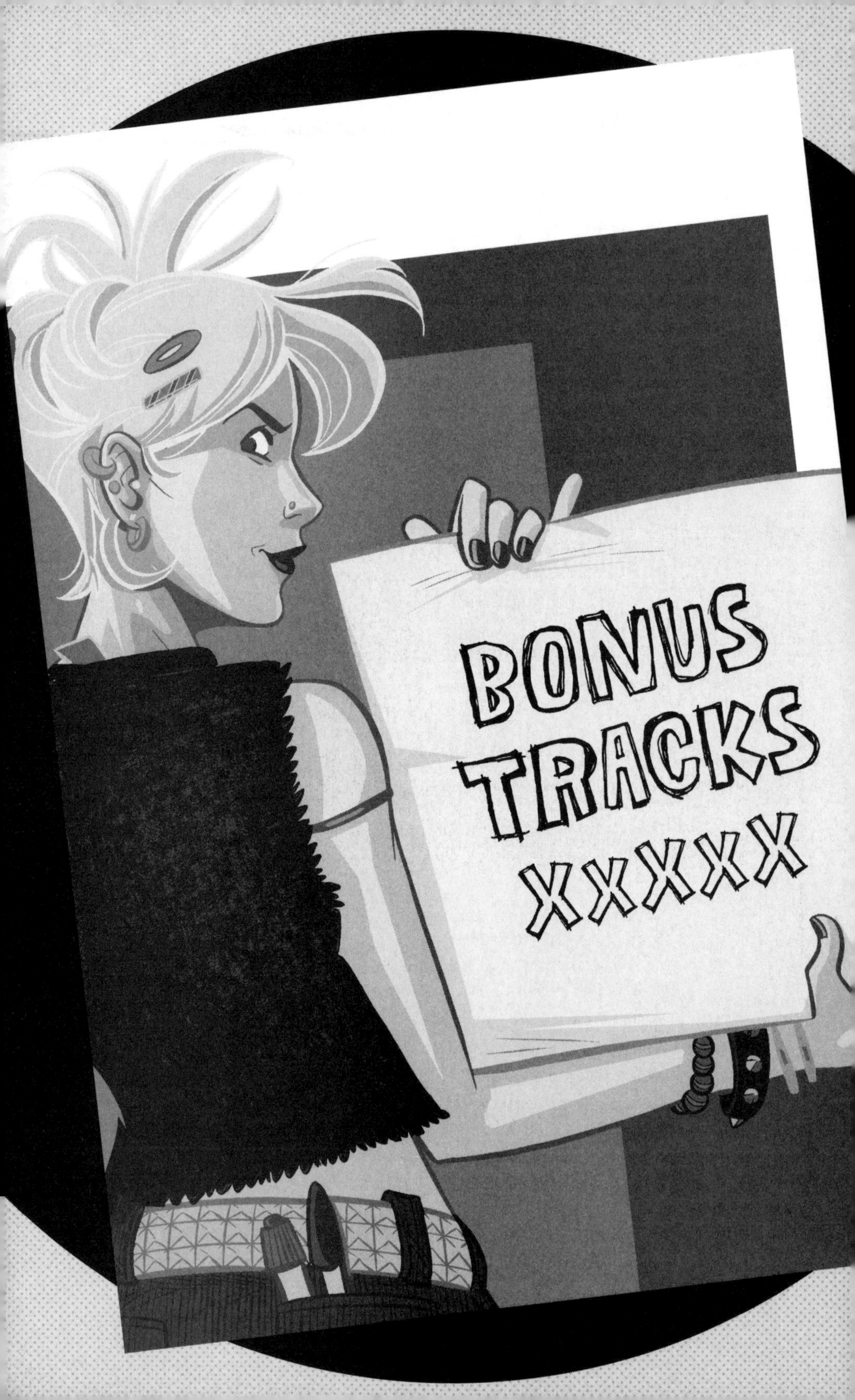
BONUS
TRACKS
XXXXX

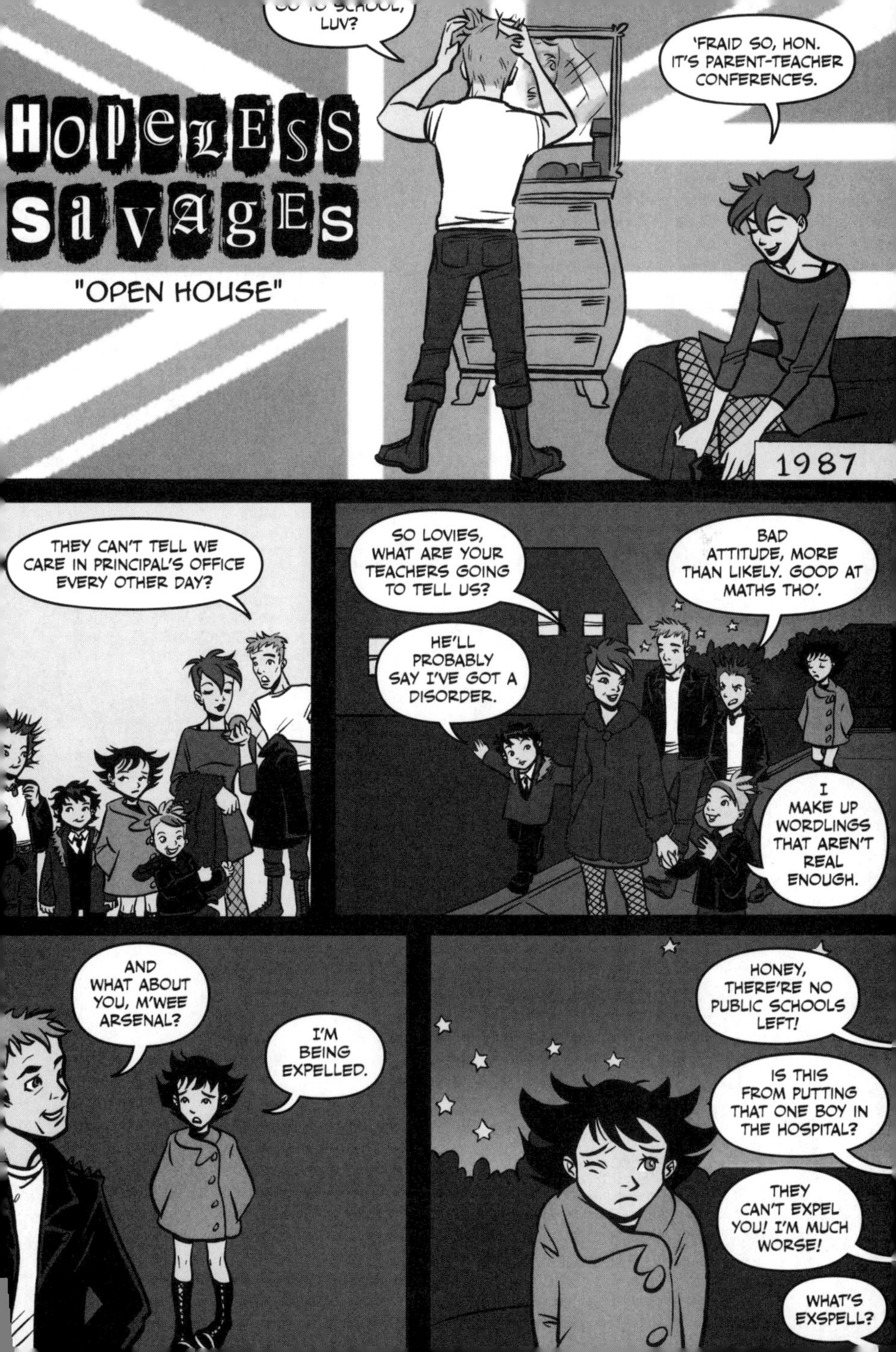

HOPELESS SAVAGES
"OPEN HOUSE"
LUV?
'FRAID SO, HON. IT'S PARENT-TEACHER CONFERENCES.
1987
THEY CAN'T TELL WE CARE IN PRINCIPAL'S OFFICE EVERY OTHER DAY?
SO LOVIES, WHAT ARE YOUR TEACHERS GOING TO TELL US?
BAD ATTITUDE, MORE THAN LIKELY. GOOD AT MATHS THO'.
HE'LL PROBABLY SAY I'VE GOT A DISORDER.
I MAKE UP WORDLINGS THAT AREN'T REAL ENOUGH.
AND WHAT ABOUT YOU, M'WEE ARSENAL?
I'M BEING EXPELLED.
HONEY, THERE'RE NO PUBLIC SCHOOLS LEFT!
IS THIS FROM PUTTING THAT ONE BOY IN THE HOSPITAL?
THEY CAN'T EXPEL YOU! I'M MUCH WORSE!
WHAT'S EXSPELL?

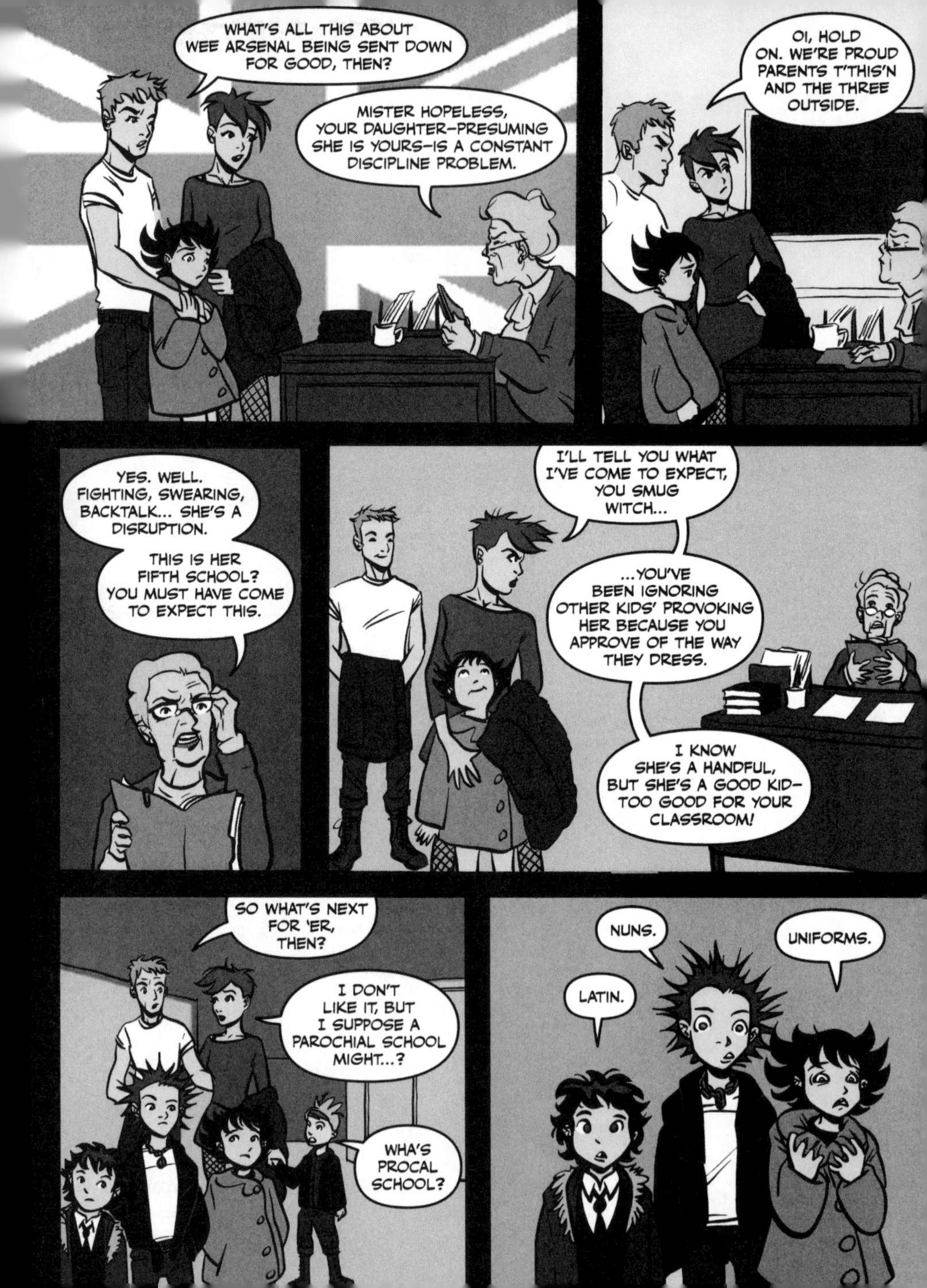
WHAT'S ALL THIS ABOUT WEE ARSENAL BEING SENT DOWN FOR GOOD, THEN?
MISTER HOPELESS, YOUR DAUGHTER–PRESUMING SHE IS YOURS–IS A CONSTANT DISCIPLINE PROBLEM.
OI, HOLD ON. WE'RE PROUD PARENTS T'THIS'N AND THE THREE OUTSIDE.
YES. WELL. FIGHTING, SWEARING, BACKTALK... SHE'S A DISRUPTION.
THIS IS HER FIFTH SCHOOL? YOU MUST HAVE COME TO EXPECT THIS.
I'LL TELL YOU WHAT I'VE COME TO EXPECT, YOU SMUG WITCH...
...YOU'VE BEEN IGNORING OTHER KIDS' PROVOKING HER BECAUSE YOU APPROVE OF THE WAY THEY DRESS.
I KNOW SHE'S A HANDFUL, BUT SHE'S A GOOD KID– TOO GOOD FOR YOUR CLASSROOM!
SO WHAT'S NEXT FOR 'ER, THEN?
I DON'T LIKE IT, BUT I SUPPOSE A PAROCHIAL SCHOOL MIGHT...?
WHA'S PROCAL SCHOOL?
NUNS.
LATIN.
UNIFORMS.

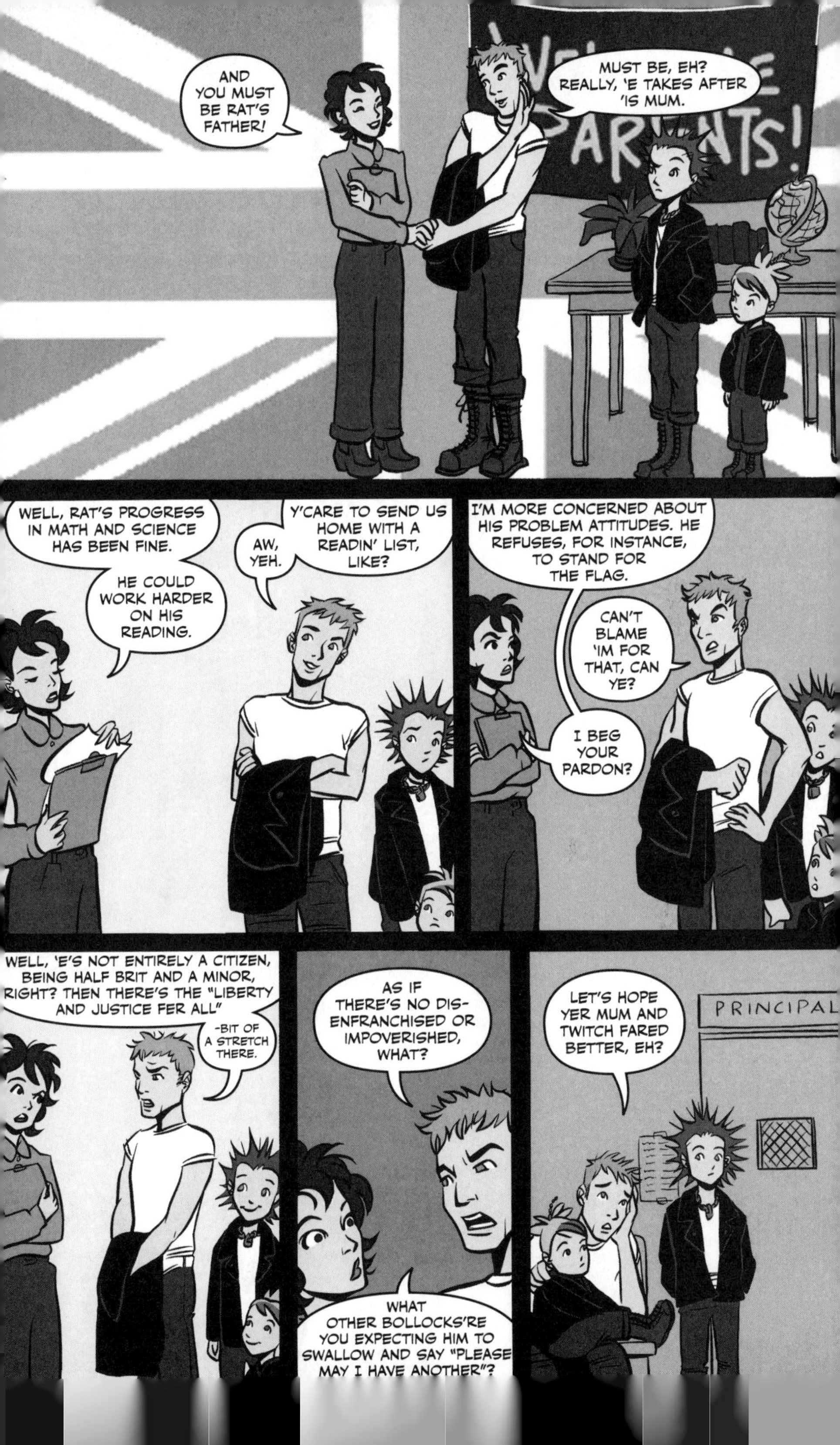
AND YOU MUST BE RAT'S FATHER!
MUST BE, EH? REALLY, 'E TAKES AFTER 'IS MUM.
WELL, RAT'S PROGRESS IN MATH AND SCIENCE HAS BEEN FINE.
HE COULD WORK HARDER ON HIS READING.
AW, YEH.
Y'CARE TO SEND US HOME WITH A READIN' LIST, LIKE?
I'M MORE CONCERNED ABOUT HIS PROBLEM ATTITUDES. HE REFUSES, FOR INSTANCE, TO STAND FOR THE FLAG.
CAN'T BLAME 'IM FOR THAT, CAN YE?
I BEG YOUR PARDON?
WELL, 'E'S NOT ENTIRELY A CITIZEN, BEING HALF BRIT AND A MINOR, RIGHT? THEN THERE'S THE "LIBERTY AND JUSTICE FER ALL"
-BIT OF A STRETCH THERE.
AS IF THERE'S NO DIS-ENFRANCHISED OR IMPOVERISHED, WHAT?
WHAT OTHER BOLLOCKS'RE YOU EXPECTING HIM TO SWALLOW AND SAY "PLEASE MAY I HAVE ANOTHER"?
LET'S HOPE YER MUM AND TWITCH FARED BETTER, EH?
PRINCIPAL

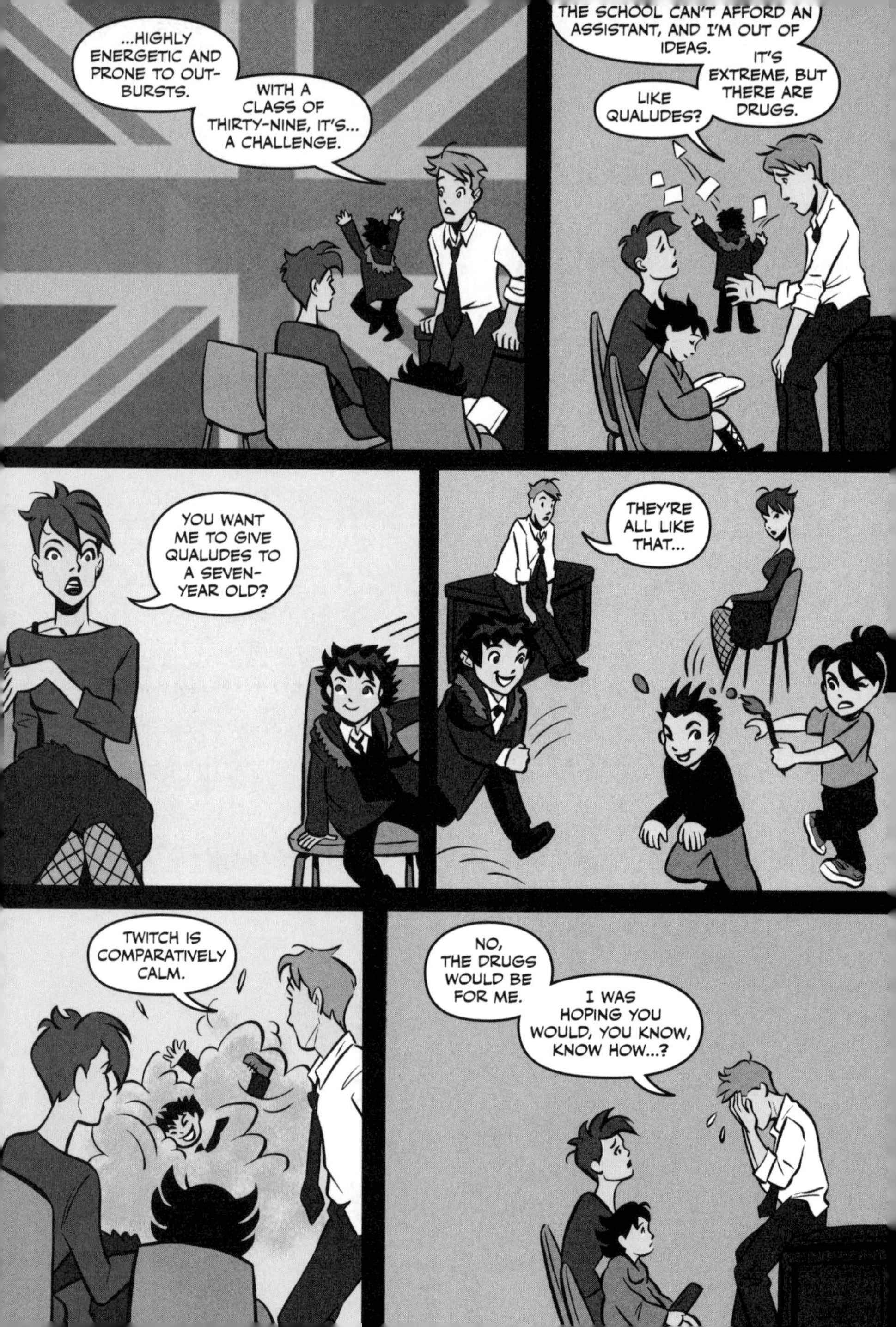
...HIGHLY ENERGETIC AND PRONE TO OUT-BURSTS.
WITH A CLASS OF THIRTY-NINE, IT'S... A CHALLENGE.
THE SCHOOL CAN'T AFFORD AN ASSISTANT, AND I'M OUT OF IDEAS.
IT'S EXTREME, BUT THERE ARE DRUGS.
LIKE QUALUDES?
YOU WANT ME TO GIVE QUALUDES TO A SEVEN-YEAR OLD?
THEY'RE ALL LIKE THAT...
TWITCH IS COMPARATIVELY CALM.
NO, THE DRUGS WOULD BE FOR ME.
I WAS HOPING YOU WOULD, YOU KNOW, KNOW HOW...?

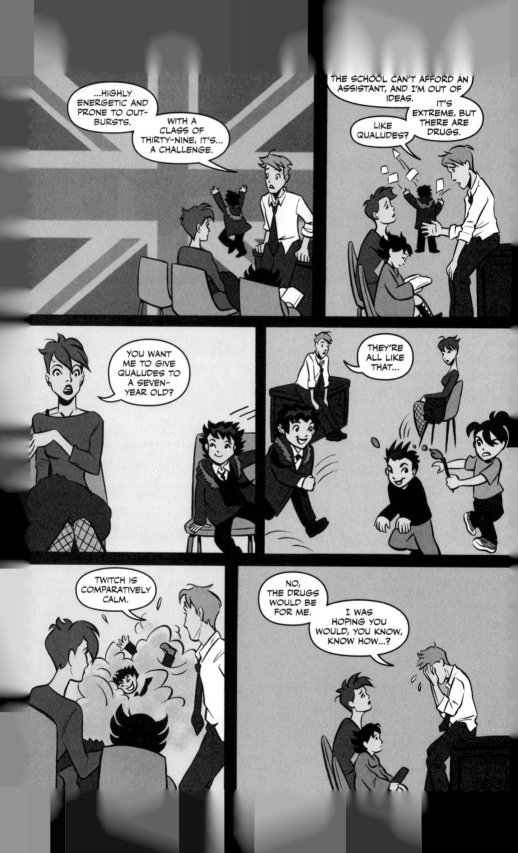

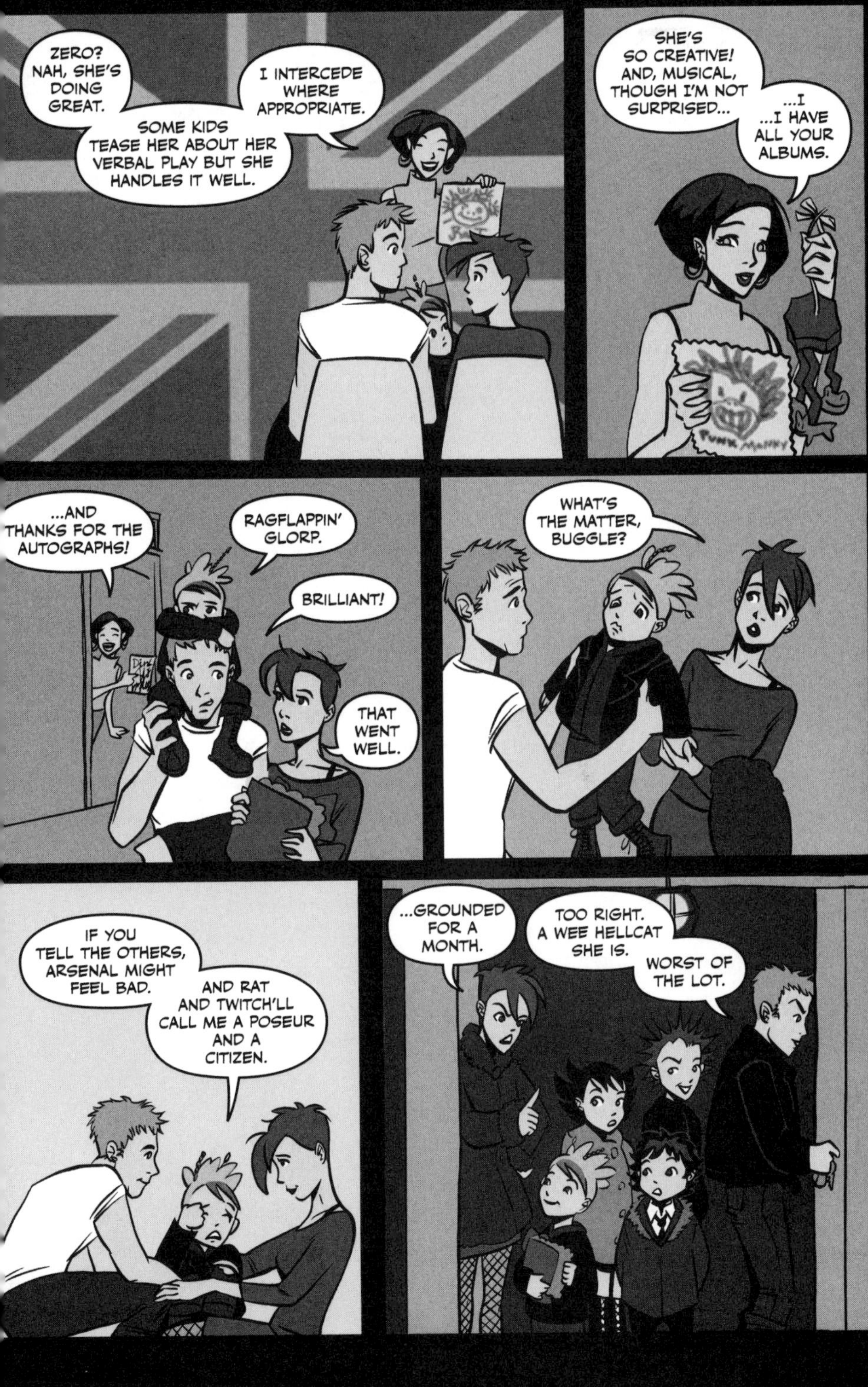
ZERO? NAH, SHE'S DOING GREAT.
SOME KIDS TEASE HER ABOUT HER VERBAL PLAY BUT SHE HANDLES IT WELL.
I INTERCEDE WHERE APPROPRIATE.
SHE'S SO CREATIVE! AND, MUSICAL, THOUGH I'M NOT SURPRISED...
...I ...I HAVE ALL YOUR ALBUMS.
...AND THANKS FOR THE AUTOGRAPHS!
RAGFLAPPIN' GLORP.
BRILLIANT!
THAT WENT WELL.
WHAT'S THE MATTER, BUGGLE?
IF YOU TELL THE OTHERS, ARSENAL MIGHT FEEL BAD.
AND RAT AND TWITCH'LL CALL ME A POSEUR AND A CITIZEN.
...GROUNDED FOR A MONTH.
TOO RIGHT. A WEE HELLCAT SHE IS.
WORST OF THE LOT.

SOME OF MY BEST WORDS ARE FRIENDS

BY SKANK ZERO HOPELESS-SAVAGE

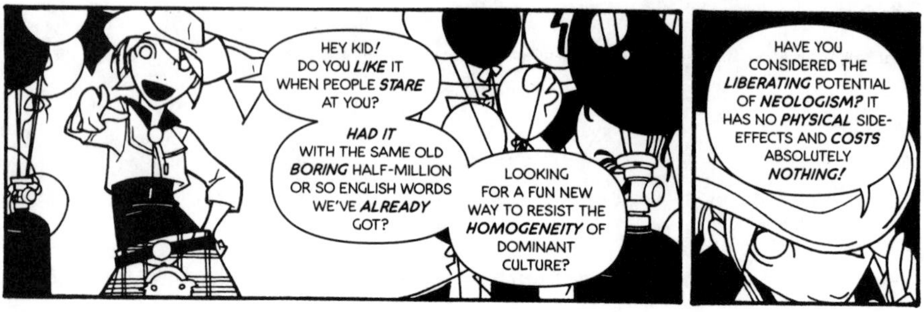
HEY KID! DO YOU *LIKE* IT WHEN PEOPLE *STARE* AT YOU?
HAD IT WITH THE SAME OLD *BORING* HALF-MILLION OR SO ENGLISH WORDS WE'VE *ALREADY* GOT?
LOOKING FOR A FUN NEW WAY TO RESIST THE *HOMOGENEITY* OF DOMINANT CULTURE?
HAVE YOU CONSIDERED THE *LIBERATING* POTENTIAL OF *NEOLOGISM?* IT HAS NO *PHYSICAL* SIDE-EFFECTS AND *COSTS* ABSOLUTELY *NOTHING!*

acridoxy (n) oppressive conservativism; portmanteau of *acrid* + *orthodox* —**acridoxic** (adj) as above, + toxic

bagboiling (adj) having a stressful influence; because some stuff makes you feel kinship with those boil-in-bag frozen vegetables

blark (vti) vocalize without meaningful content, either reflexively or as an expression of overwhelming emotion; portmanteau: bleat + bark —**blarking** (adj) angry or upset beyond coherence

blister (n) an unpleasant, parasitic or shallow person

blurrish (adj) 1. foggy, overcast 2. confused, muddled

brablister (n) deliberately insulting term for a woman whose attractiveness to men is a high personal priority

catblender (n) an unnecessary person or object; cats do not need blenders

clabber (vti) speak, say, prattle

crotchwash (n) nonsense, rubbish —**crotchwashing** (adj)—wasteful, imprudent; derives from non-potable condition of water used to wash your stuff

crudcranking (adj) noxious, repugnant

custard (n) a self-serving or emotionally careless person; acts sweet, but pretty bad for you

dragging (adj) painful, depressing

fixative (adj) intrusively helpful; adhering to you with annoying good intentions. Like a cuddly barnacle.

flabber-jammer (n) unspecified or speculative object; as widget or whatsit.

flan (n) a harmlessly flirtatious or uninhibited person; a lower-calorie, more benign custard (see above)

flap (vti) shout, throw a tantrum, rant

flink (vt) 1. know 2. guess accurately; if you do it, you don't *flunk*

foam over (vi) to make a display of one's delight or excitement

glob (vti) 1. speak 2. blurt abruptly or inappropriately

glorp (n) a number of useless, unappealling or outmoded objects: *We have a glorp of old floppy drives in the garage or, My boss has a glorp of awkward generational bigotries*

gnash (vti) understand, comprehend

gratter (vi) snarl, growl —**grattered** (adj) angered

graze (vi) shop for non-essential items

grinder (n) an infuriating individual; some folks grind away every last shred of your civilized instincts until you want to kill them with your teeth.

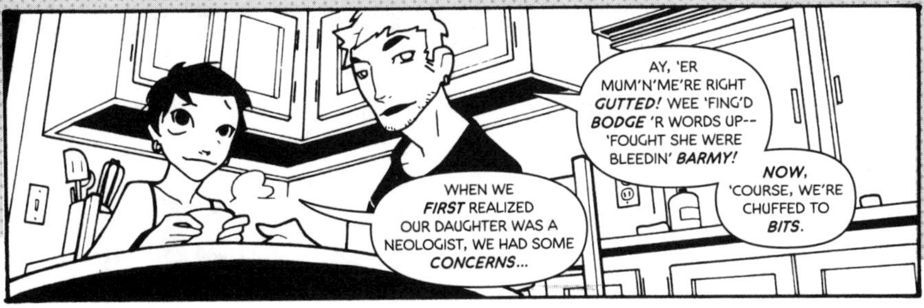
WHEN WE FIRST REALIZED OUR DAUGHTER WAS A NEOLOGIST, WE HAD SOME CONCERNS...
AY, 'ER MUM'N'ME'RE RIGHT GUTTED! WEE 'FING'D BODGE 'R WORDS UP-- 'FOUGHT SHE WERE BLEEDIN' BARMY!
NOW, 'COURSE, WE'RE CHUFFED TO BITS.

gringe (vi) perform badly; as the slang: *suck, stink, crash, bite*

groff (vti) know, understand —**groffy** (adj) well-suited to one's temperament

grotty (adj) filthy, corroded; unpleasant quality of a music venue can often be determined by how ________ the potty is. See, you get it.

grutt (vi) 1. to make an unpleasant display or presumption of masculine dominance 2. to act or speak in haste without basis or preamble; portmanteau of *grunt + rutt*—**grutting** (adj) intensive, usually implying speed and distaste: *If I have to go to the mall, I do it grutting early.*

gumsnapping (adj) obnoxious, impolite

hargully (adv) intensifier; *as really, very, indeed, wicked* or *hella*

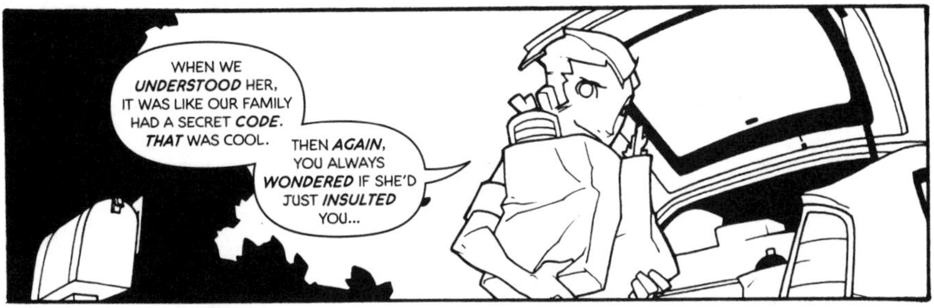
WHEN WE UNDERSTOOD HER, IT WAS LIKE OUR FAMILY HAD A SECRET CODE. THAT WAS COOL.
THEN AGAIN, YOU ALWAYS WONDERED IF SHE'D JUST INSULTED YOU...

hilty (adj) effortless, untroubled, smooth

hooskie (adj) compelling, intriguing; applies to humans only —**hoosk** (n) attractive intensity of character or manner

hounder (n) 1. a worrisome or upsetting thing 2. a belligerent or cruel person

hubsmashing (adj) pointlessly destructive; as a baseball bat to a hubcap

hunkering (adj) terrifyingly enormous, awesome; inspires retreat, submission, groveling

implant (n) an unwelcome or uninvited guest; one who does not fit in

infuscate (v) clarify, illuminate

mugsmack (v) brag, boast

mumgrinding (adj) cruel, sadistic

murkish (adj) sullen, embittered

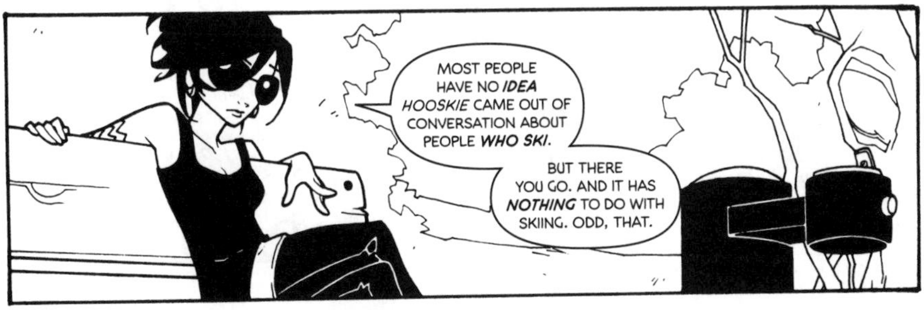
MOST PEOPLE HAVE NO IDEA HOOSKIE CAME OUT OF CONVERSATION ABOUT PEOPLE WHO SKI.
BUT THERE YOU GO. AND IT HAS NOTHING TO DO WITH SKIING. ODD, THAT.

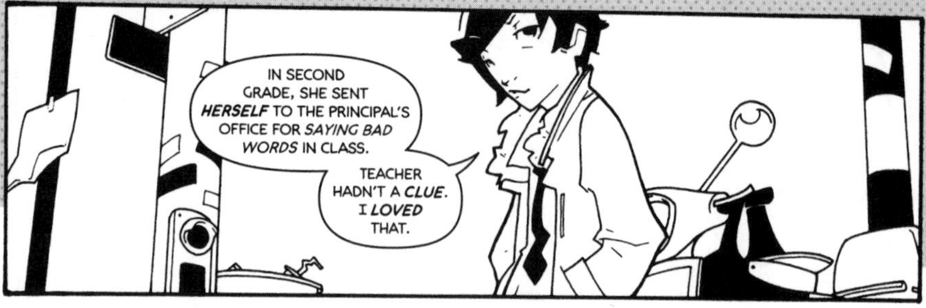
IN SECOND GRADE, SHE SENT ***HERSELF*** TO THE PRINCIPAL'S OFFICE FOR *SAYING BAD WORDS* IN CLASS.
TEACHER HADN'T A ***CLUE***. I ***LOVED*** THAT.

plunk (vt) want, be inclined toward: *I could plunk a soda if you're buying; often used with like: You plunk like a movie?*

putremony (n) cruelty or destruction masked as piety

raffish (adj) strange, unsettling

ragflapping (adj) ridiculous, stupid

ratchet (vti) to break or disable an object

scab (vt) 1. irritate 2. cause worry, concern 3. spoil, render imperfect

scavverous (adj) infested yet barren; as a field stripped by locusts, or a bed empty but for the bedbugs

scrape (vti) comprehend

scruffling (adj) misleading, spurious

seatlifter (n) a human male; derogatory

sherp (vt) carry, transport

skurffly (adj) untrustworthy, suspicious, up to no good

slagamuffin (n) A woman who uses flirtation for business or social advantage, or who derives satisfaction from vying with other women for romantic attention; derogatory

smatchet (vi) 1. converse with another person 2. speak for one's own amusement 3. flirt

spec (v) examine closely, as with special spectacles

squall (vi) to cause turmoil or mayhem (vti) complain, over-dramatize (n) 1. a dramatic or tense situation 2. used as an intensive: *What the squall happened here?* 3. (interj) used to express extreme displeasure —**squalling** (adj) intensive: *I've got a squalling rock in my squalling shoe!*

squint (vti) to concern oneself with something, usually a small or insignificant object (pron) an unknown or unspecified tiny object

stalinate (vt) impose or dictate one's will, usually without discussion

swerval (adj) very good, pleasing; applies to something good enough you would swerve to get to it

yoink (vt) withdraw or retrieve an object suddenly; end abruptly

swoo (n) information (v) tell, inform (adj) smooth, uninterrupted, clear

tarantino (vi) use violence on another person

vilicious (adj) compelling or attractive despite or because of underlying wickedness

waggling (adj) delightful, silly.

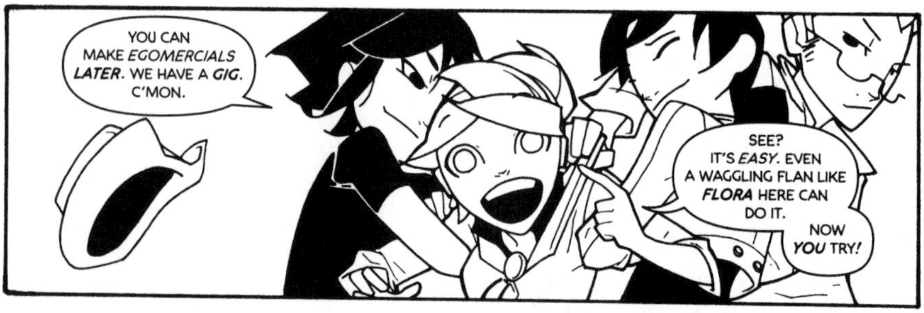
YOU CAN MAKE *EGOMERCIALS* ***LATER***. WE HAVE A ***GIG***. C'MON.
SEE? IT'S *EASY*. EVEN A WAGGLING FLAN LIKE ***FLORA*** HERE CAN DO IT.
NOW ***YOU*** TRY!

words – Jen Van Meter / pictures – Meredith McClaren

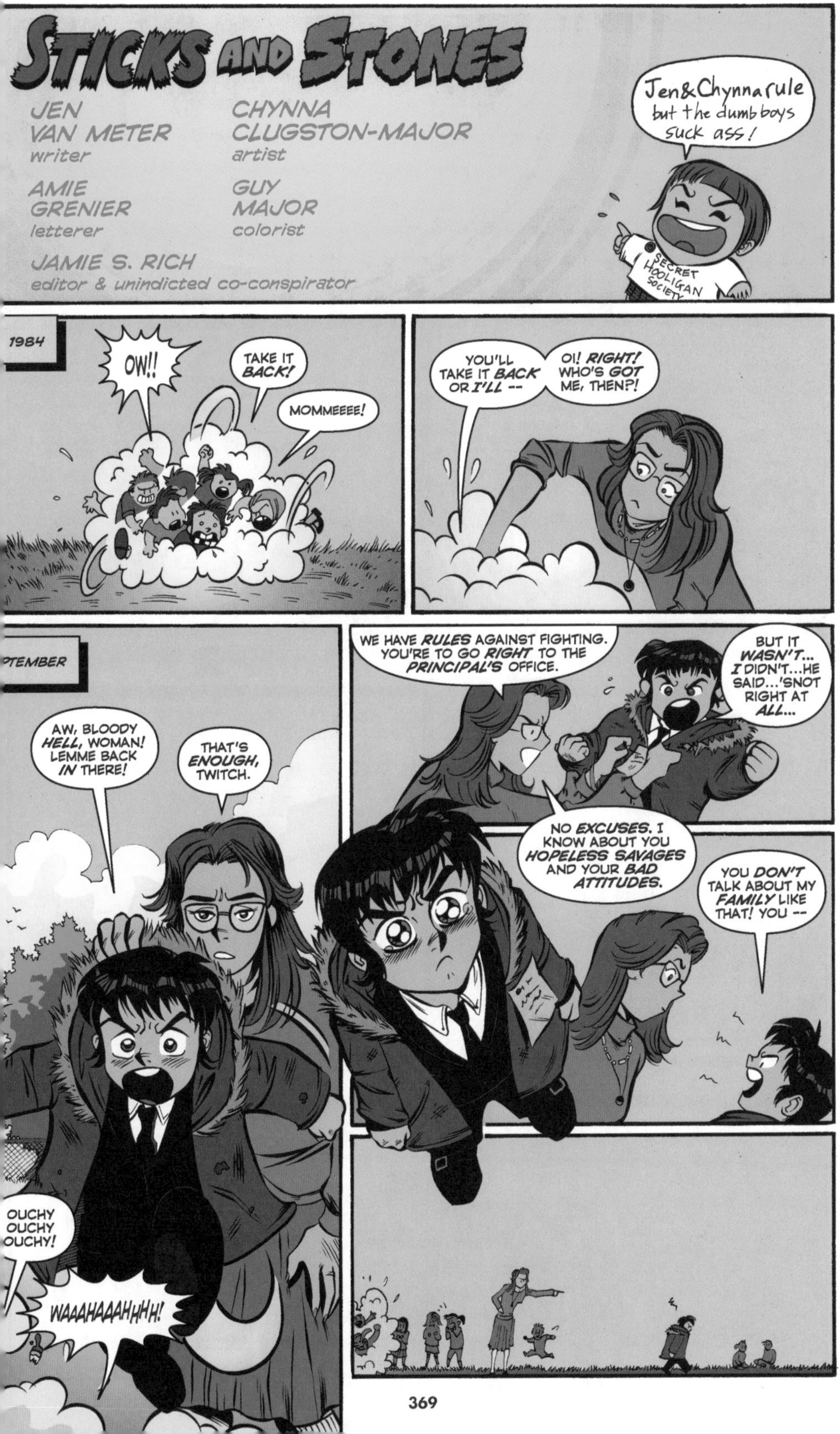
STICKS AND STONES
JEN VAN METER
writer
CHYNNA CLUGSTON-MAJOR
artist
AMIE GRENIER
letterer
GUY MAJOR
colorist
JAMIE S. RICH
editor & unindicted co-conspirator
Jen&Chynna rule but the dumb boys suck ass!
SECRET HOOLIGAN SOCIETY
1984
OW!!
TAKE IT BACK!
MOMMEEEE!
YOU'LL TAKE IT BACK OR I'LL --
OI! RIGHT! WHO'S GOT ME, THEN?!
PTEMBER
AW, BLOODY HELL, WOMAN! LEMME BACK IN THERE!
THAT'S ENOUGH, TWITCH.
OUCHY OUCHY OUCHY!
WAAAHAAAHHHH!
WE HAVE RULES AGAINST FIGHTING. YOU'RE TO GO RIGHT TO THE PRINCIPAL'S OFFICE.
BUT IT WASN'T... I DIDN'T...HE SAID...'SNOT RIGHT AT ALL...
NO EXCUSES. I KNOW ABOUT YOU HOPELESS SAVAGES AND YOUR BAD ATTITUDES.
YOU DON'T TALK ABOUT MY FAMILY LIKE THAT! YOU --

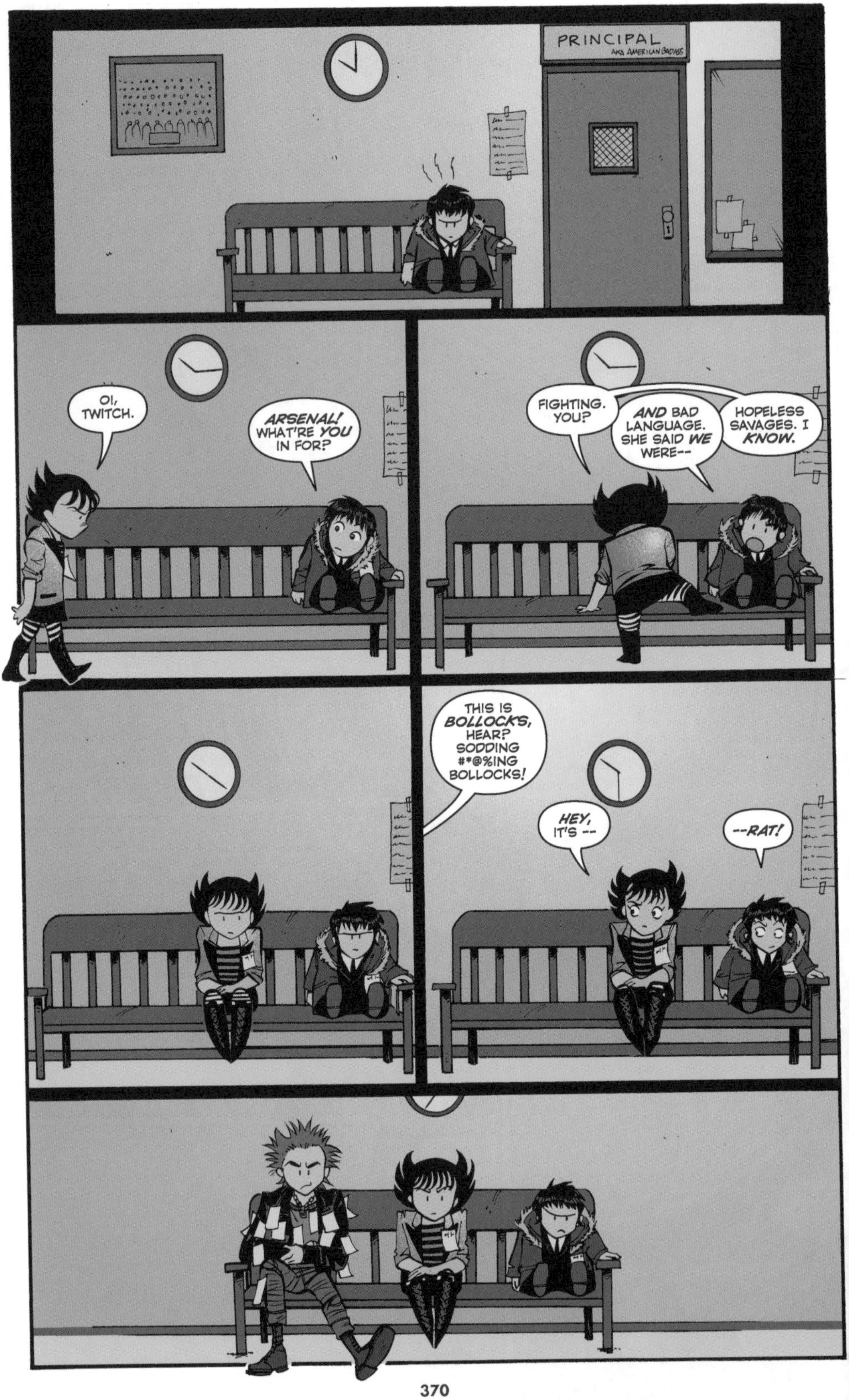

PRINCIPAL
AKA AMERICAN BADASS
OI, TWITCH.
ARSENAL! WHAT'RE YOU IN FOR?
FIGHTING. YOU?
AND BAD LANGUAGE. SHE SAID WE WERE--
HOPELESS SAVAGES. I KNOW.
THIS IS BOLLOCKS, HEAR? SODDING #*@%ING BOLLOCKS!
HEY, IT'S --
--RAT!

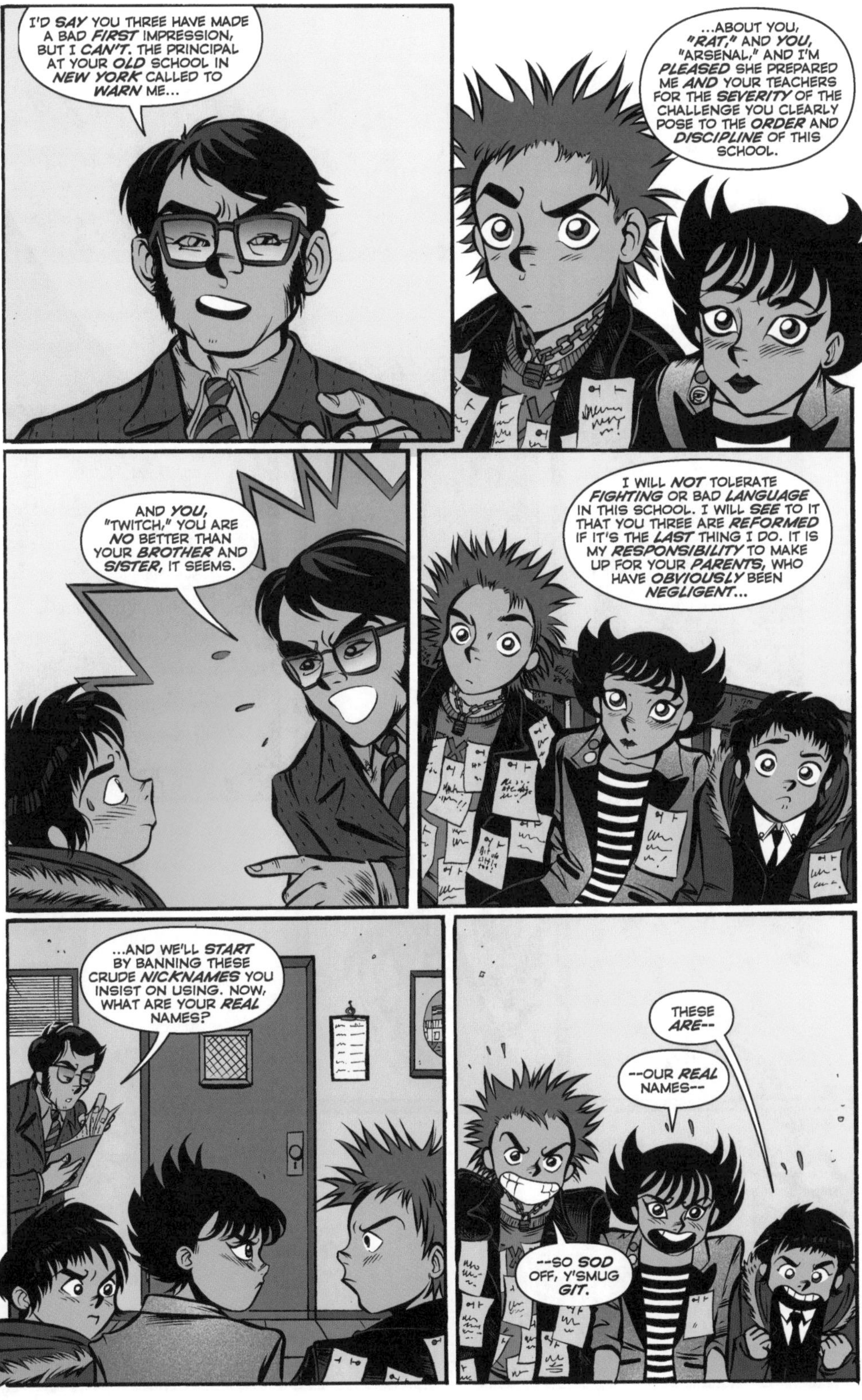
I'D SAY YOU THREE HAVE MADE A BAD FIRST IMPRESSION, BUT I CAN'T. THE PRINCIPAL AT YOUR OLD SCHOOL IN NEW YORK CALLED TO WARN ME...
...ABOUT YOU, "RAT," AND YOU, "ARSENAL," AND I'M PLEASED SHE PREPARED ME AND YOUR TEACHERS FOR THE SEVERITY OF THE CHALLENGE YOU CLEARLY POSE TO THE ORDER AND DISCIPLINE OF THIS SCHOOL.
AND YOU, "TWITCH," YOU ARE NO BETTER THAN YOUR BROTHER AND SISTER, IT SEEMS.
I WILL NOT TOLERATE FIGHTING OR BAD LANGUAGE IN THIS SCHOOL. I WILL SEE TO IT THAT YOU THREE ARE REFORMED IF IT'S THE LAST THING I DO. IT IS MY RESPONSIBILITY TO MAKE UP FOR YOUR PARENTS, WHO HAVE OBVIOUSLY BEEN NEGLIGENT...
...AND WE'LL START BY BANNING THESE CRUDE NICKNAMES YOU INSIST ON USING. NOW, WHAT ARE YOUR REAL NAMES?
THESE ARE--
--OUR REAL NAMES--
--SO SOD OFF, Y'SMUG GIT.

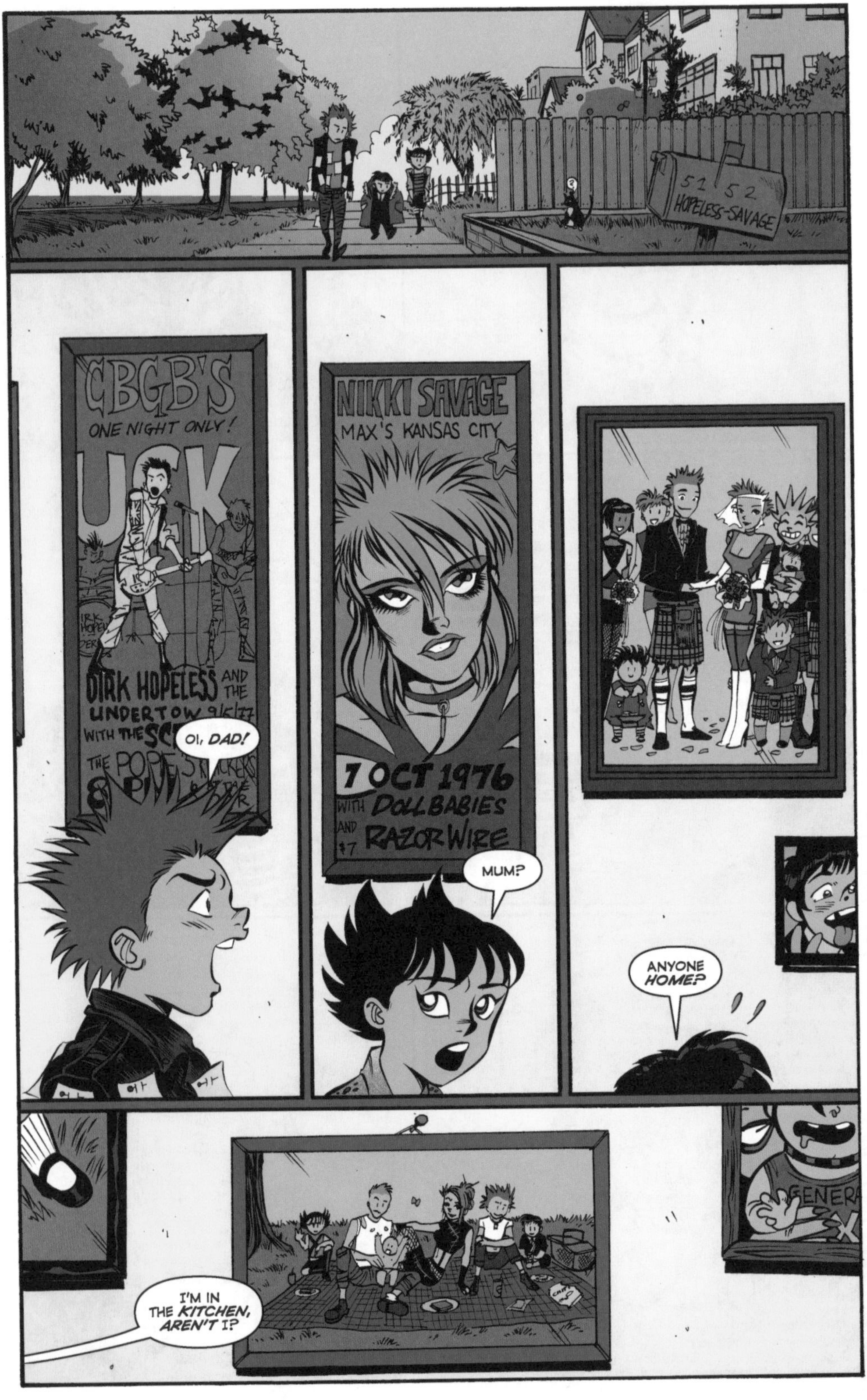
51 52
HOPELESS-SAVAGE
CBGB'S
ONE NIGHT ONLY!
DIRK HOPELESS AND THE UNDERTOW 9/5/77
NIKKI SAVAGE
MAX'S KANSAS CITY
7 OCT 1976
WITH DOLLBABIES AND RAZOR WIRE
$7
OI, DAD!
MUM?
ANYONE HOME?
I'M IN THE KITCHEN, AREN'T I?

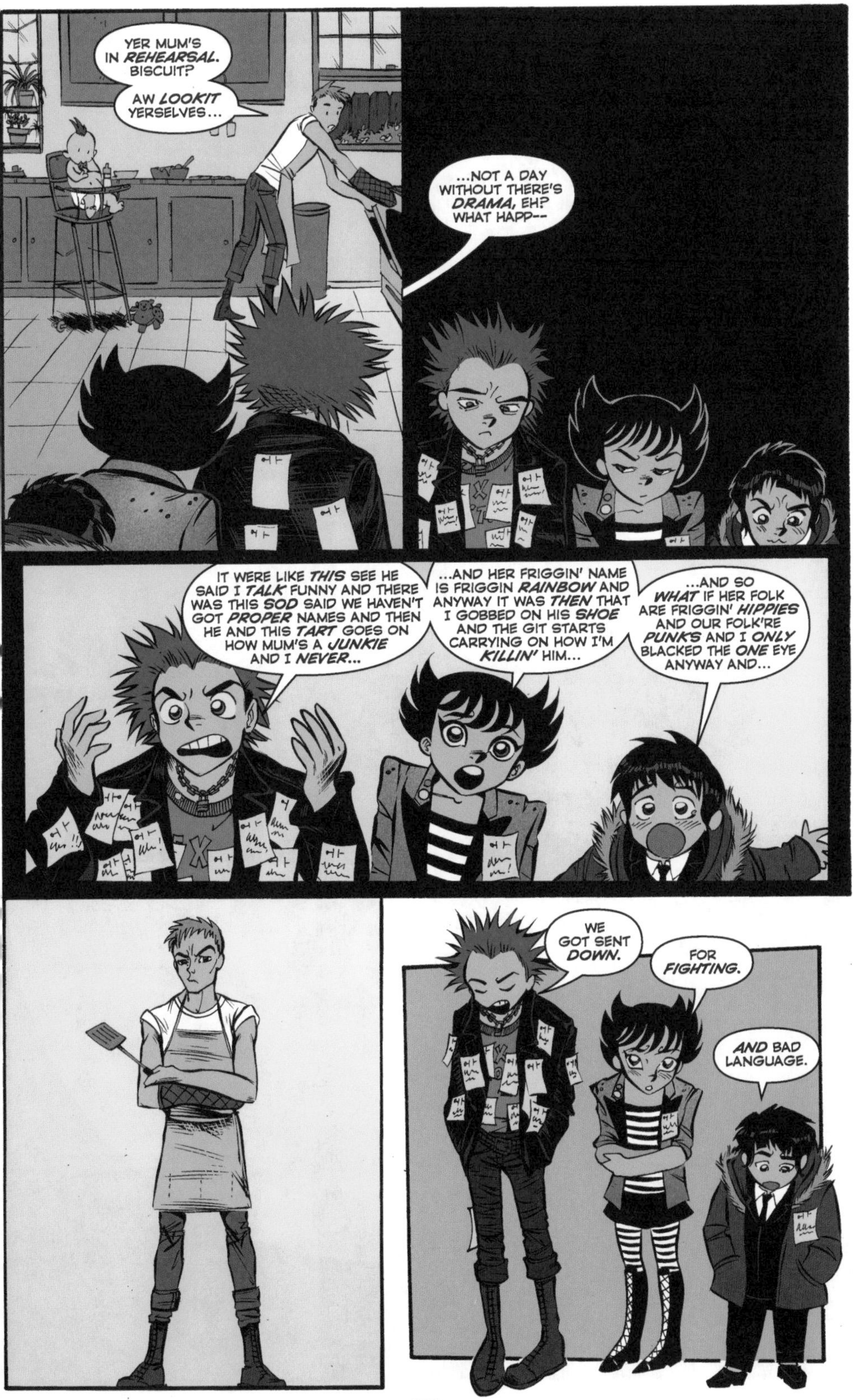
YER MUM'S IN REHEARSAL. BISCUIT?
AW LOOKIT YERSELVES...
...NOT A DAY WITHOUT THERE'S DRAMA, EH? WHAT HAPP--
IT WERE LIKE THIS SEE HE SAID I TALK FUNNY AND THERE WAS THIS SOD SAID WE HAVEN'T GOT PROPER NAMES AND THEN HE AND THIS TART GOES ON HOW MUM'S A JUNKIE AND I NEVER...
...AND HER FRIGGIN' NAME IS FRIGGIN RAINBOW AND ANYWAY IT WAS THEN THAT I GOBBED ON HIS SHOE AND THE GIT STARTS CARRYING ON HOW I'M KILLIN' HIM...
...AND SO WHAT IF HER FOLK ARE FRIGGIN' HIPPIES AND OUR FOLK'RE PUNKS AND I ONLY BLACKED THE ONE EYE ANYWAY AND...
WE GOT SENT DOWN.
FOR FIGHTING.
AND BAD LANGUAGE.

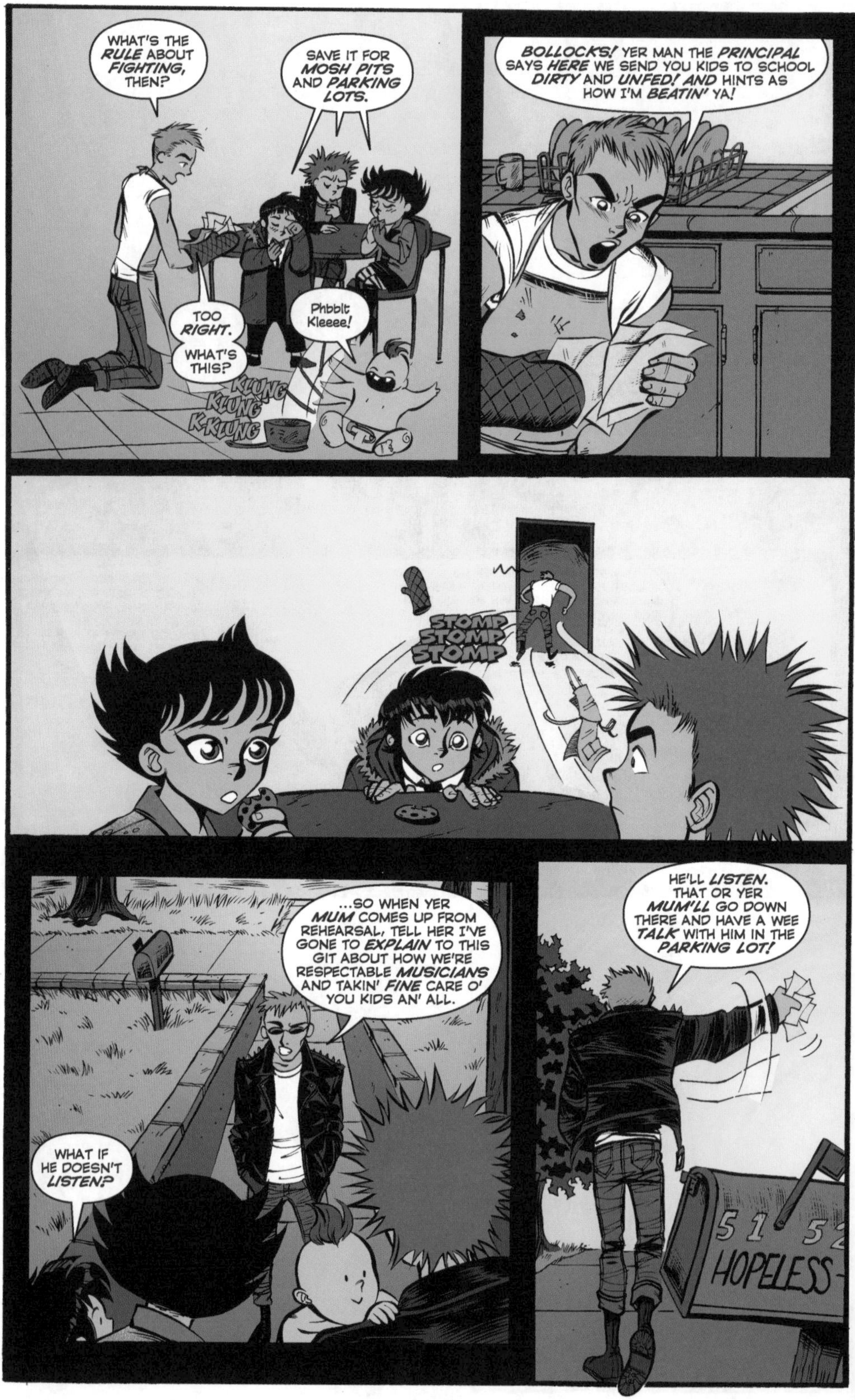
WHAT'S THE RULE ABOUT FIGHTING, THEN?
SAVE IT FOR MOSH PITS AND PARKING LOTS.
TOO RIGHT.
WHAT'S THIS?
Phbblt Kleeee!
KLUNG KLUNG K-KLUNG
BOLLOCKS! YER MAN THE PRINCIPAL SAYS HERE WE SEND YOU KIDS TO SCHOOL DIRTY AND UNFED! AND HINTS AS HOW I'M BEATIN' YA!
STOMP STOMP STOMP
...SO WHEN YER MUM COMES UP FROM REHEARSAL, TELL HER I'VE GONE TO EXPLAIN TO THIS GIT ABOUT HOW WE'RE RESPECTABLE MUSICIANS AND TAKIN' FINE CARE O' YOU KIDS AN' ALL.
WHAT IF HE DOESN'T LISTEN?
HE'LL LISTEN. THAT OR YER MUM'LL GO DOWN THERE AND HAVE A WEE TALK WITH HIM IN THE PARKING LOT!
51 52
HOPELESS

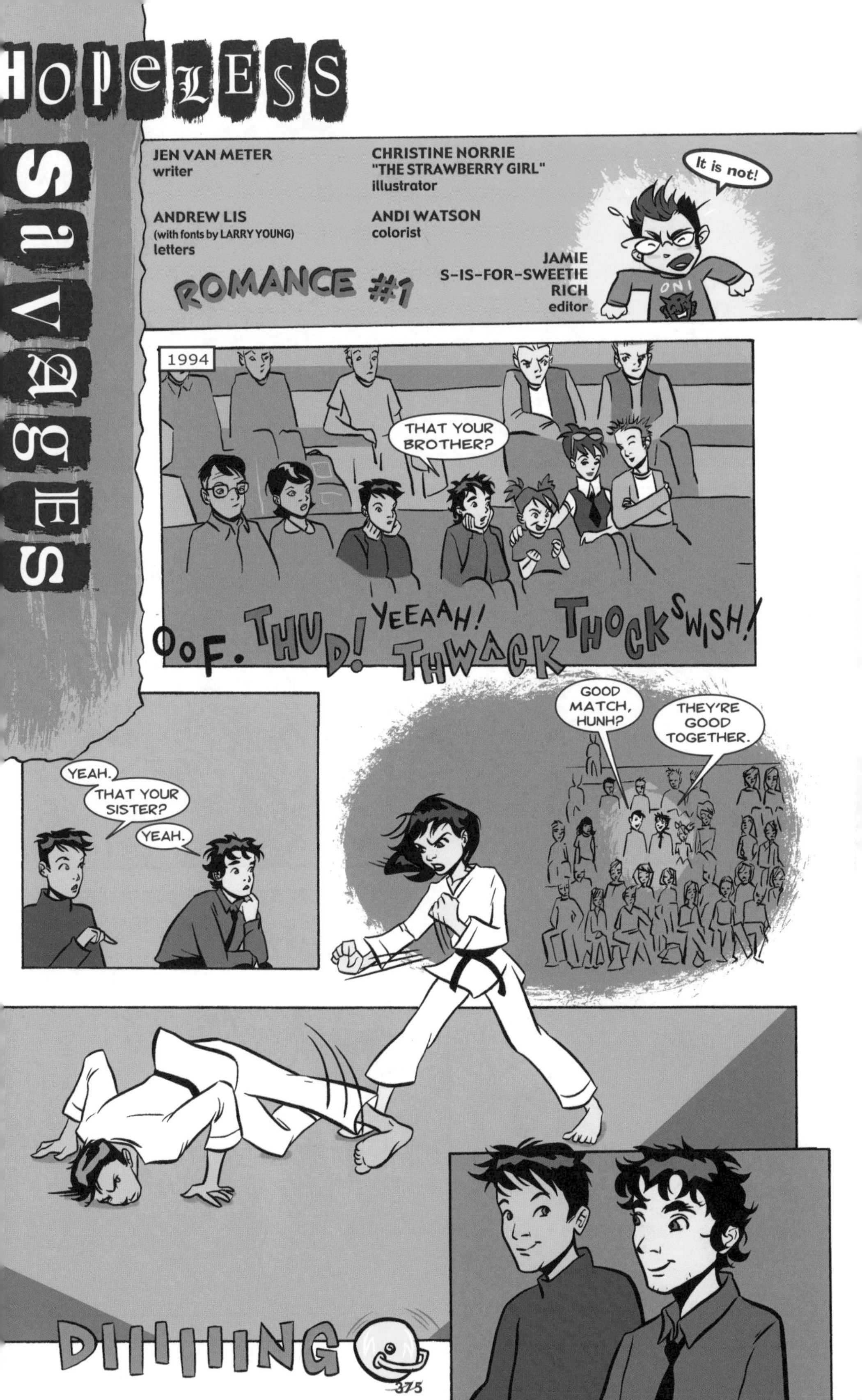
HOPELESS SAVAGES
JEN VAN METER
writer
CHRISTINE NORRIE
"THE STRAWBERRY GIRL"
illustrator
ANDREW LIS
(with fonts by LARRY YOUNG)
letters
ANDI WATSON
colorist
JAMIE
S-IS-FOR-SWEETIE
RICH
editor
It is not!
ROMANCE #1
1994
THAT YOUR BROTHER?
OOF. THUD! YEEAAH! THWACK THOCK SWISH!
YEAH.
THAT YOUR SISTER?
YEAH.
GOOD MATCH, HUNH?
THEY'RE GOOD TOGETHER.
DIIIIING

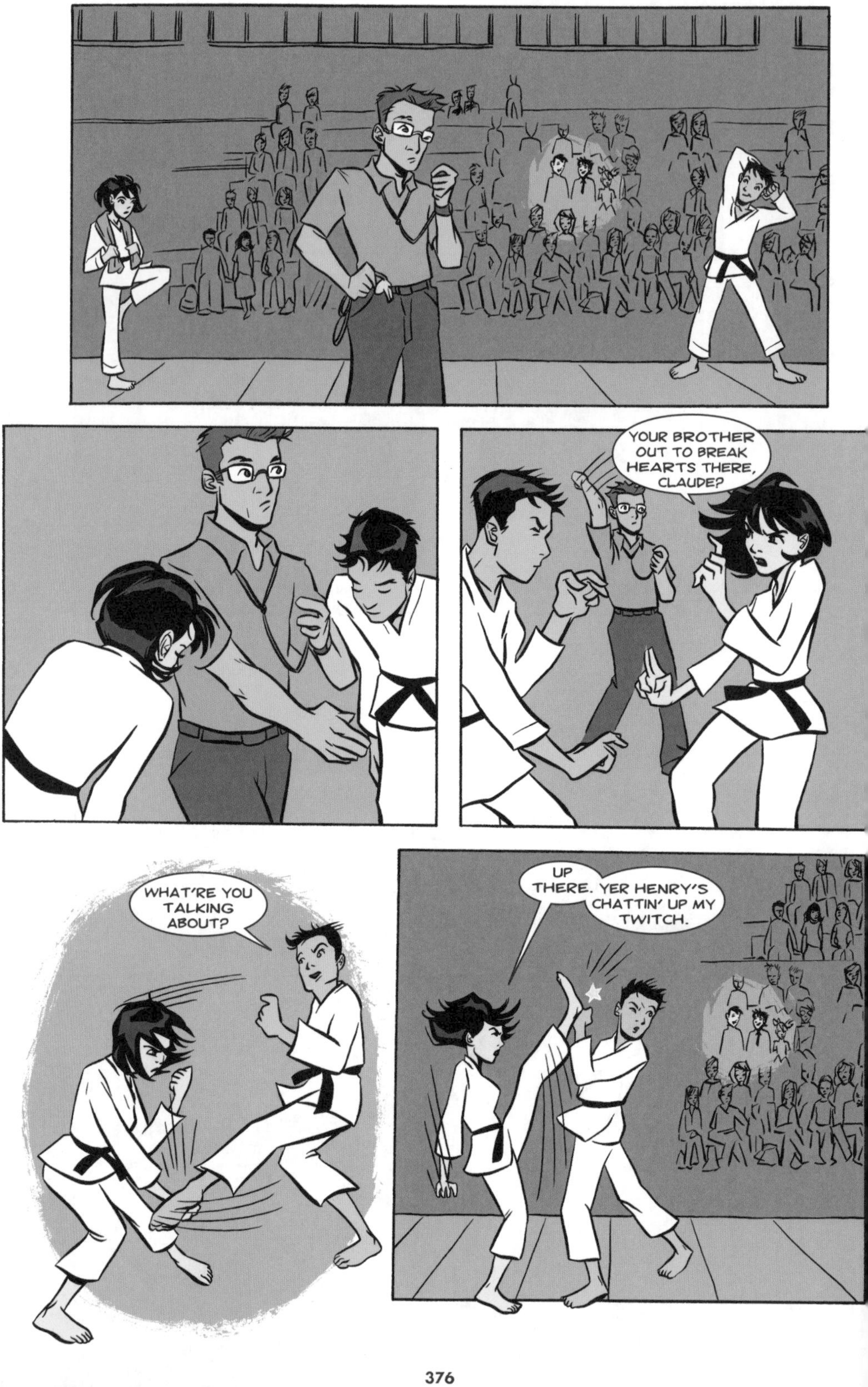
YOUR BROTHER OUT TO BREAK HEARTS THERE, CLAUDE?
WHAT'RE YOU TALKING ABOUT?
UP THERE. YER HENRY'S CHATTIN' UP MY TWITCH.

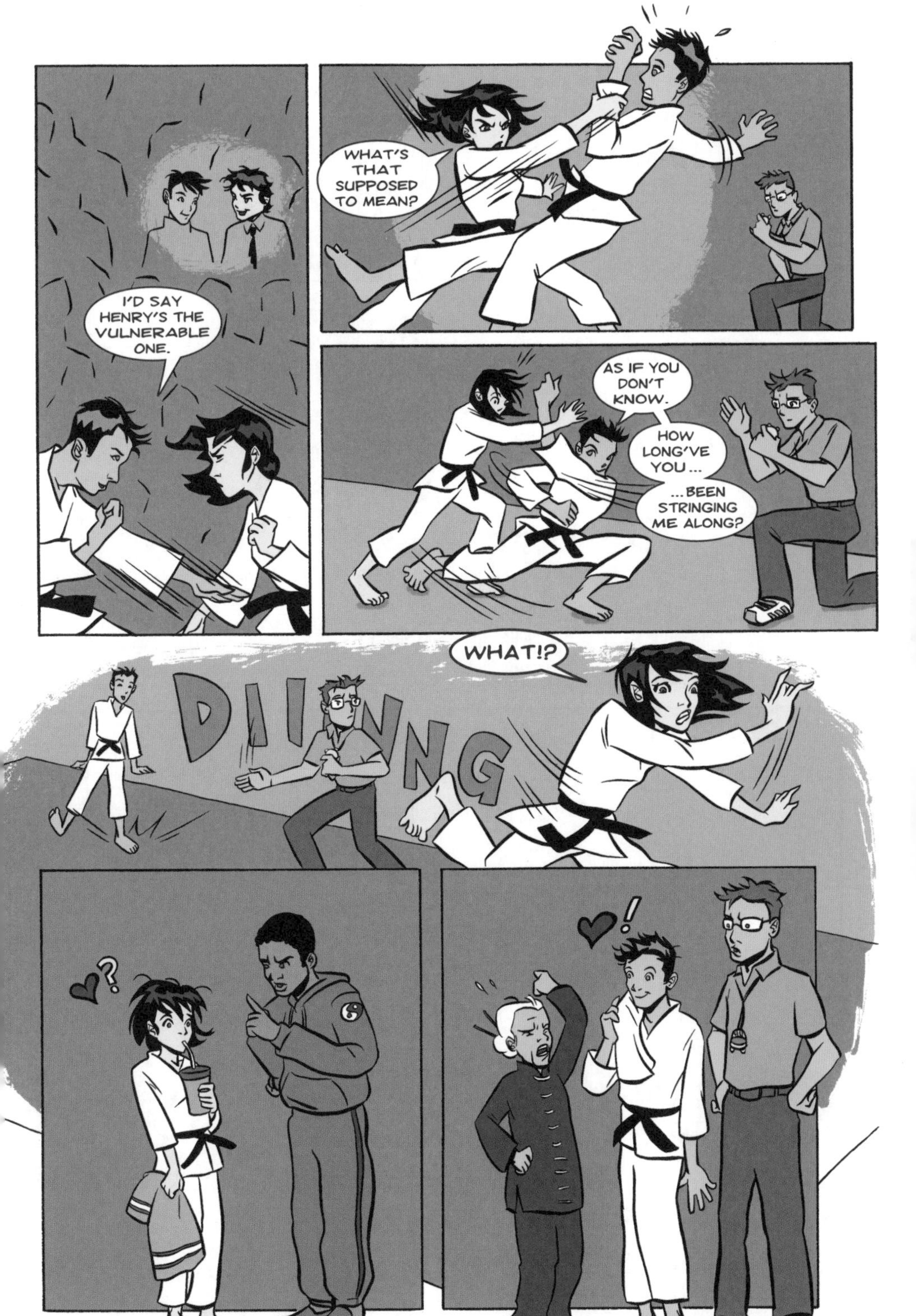
I'D SAY HENRY'S THE VULNERABLE ONE.
WHAT'S THAT SUPPOSED TO MEAN?
AS IF YOU DON'T KNOW.
HOW LONG'VE YOU...
...BEEN STRINGING ME ALONG?
WHAT!?
DIINNG

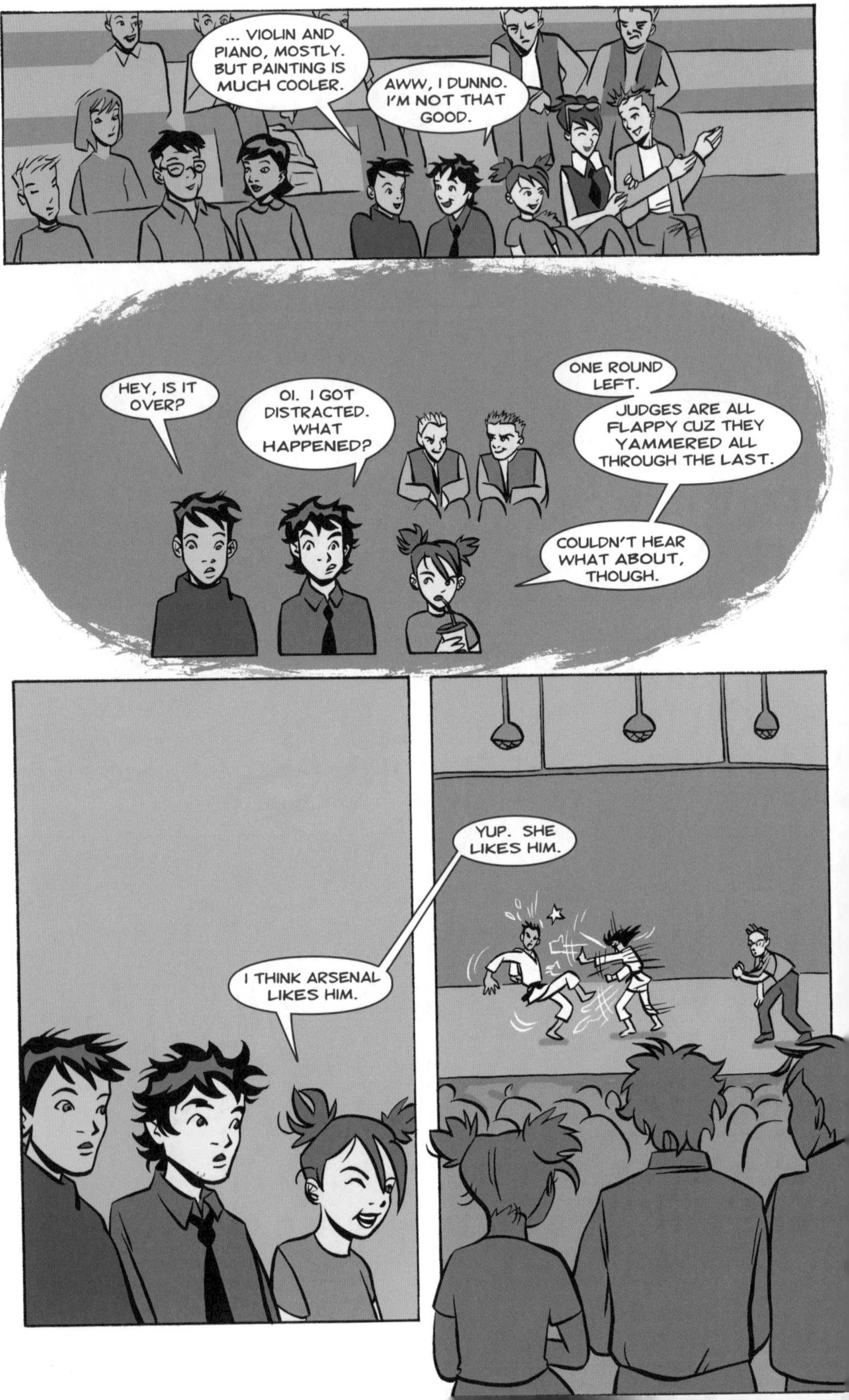
... VIOLIN AND PIANO, MOSTLY. BUT PAINTING IS MUCH COOLER.
AWW, I DUNNO. I'M NOT THAT GOOD.
HEY, IS IT OVER?
OI. I GOT DISTRACTED. WHAT HAPPENED?
ONE ROUND LEFT.
JUDGES ARE ALL FLAPPY CUZ THEY YAMMERED ALL THROUGH THE LAST.
COULDN'T HEAR WHAT ABOUT, THOUGH.
I THINK ARSENAL LIKES HIM.
YUP. SHE LIKES HIM.

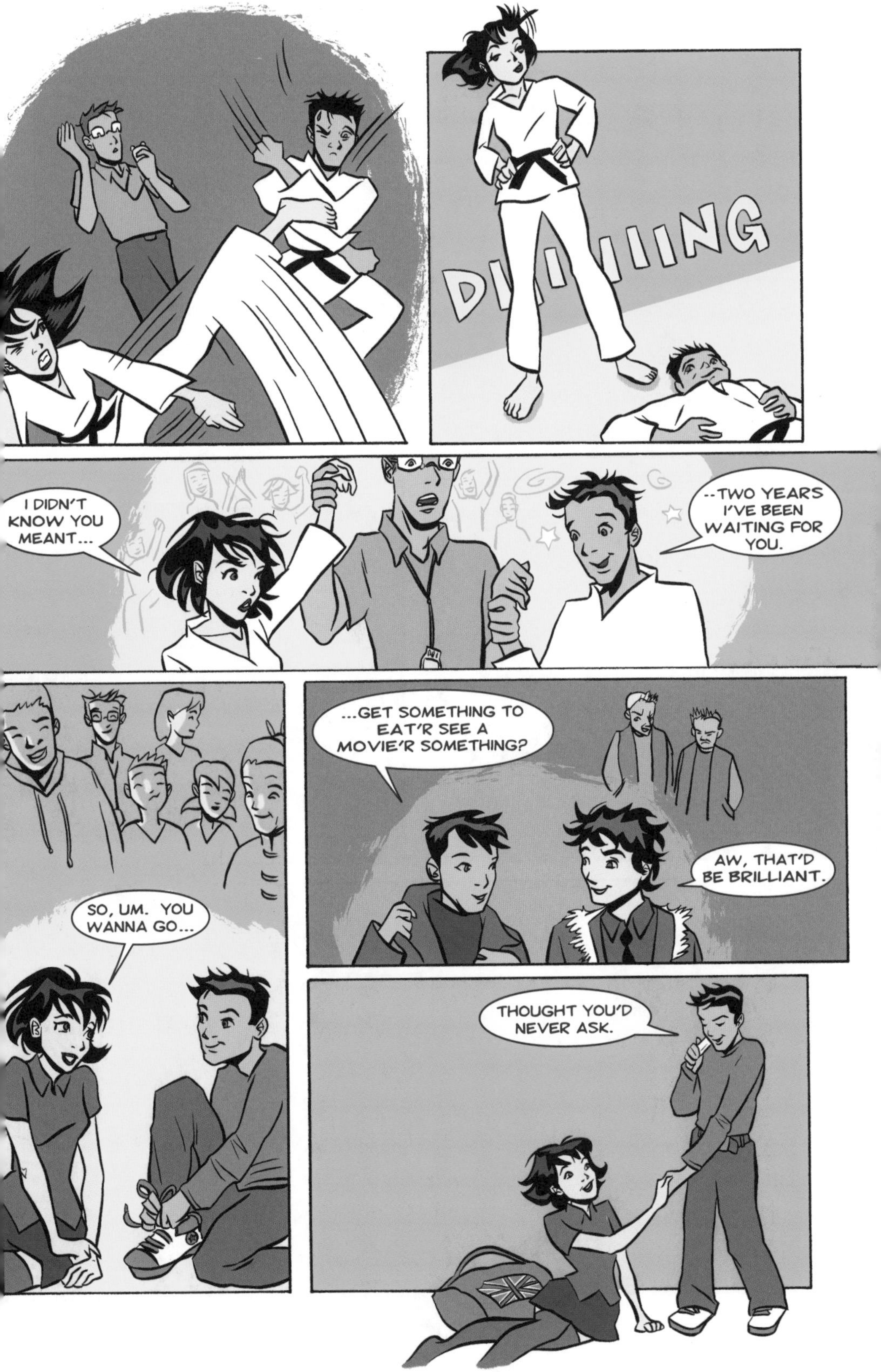
DIIIIIIING
I DIDN'T KNOW YOU MEANT...
--TWO YEARS I'VE BEEN WAITING FOR YOU.
...GET SOMETHING TO EAT'R SEE A MOVIE'R SOMETHING?
AW, THAT'D BE BRILLIANT.
SO, UM. YOU WANNA GO...
THOUGHT YOU'D NEVER ASK.

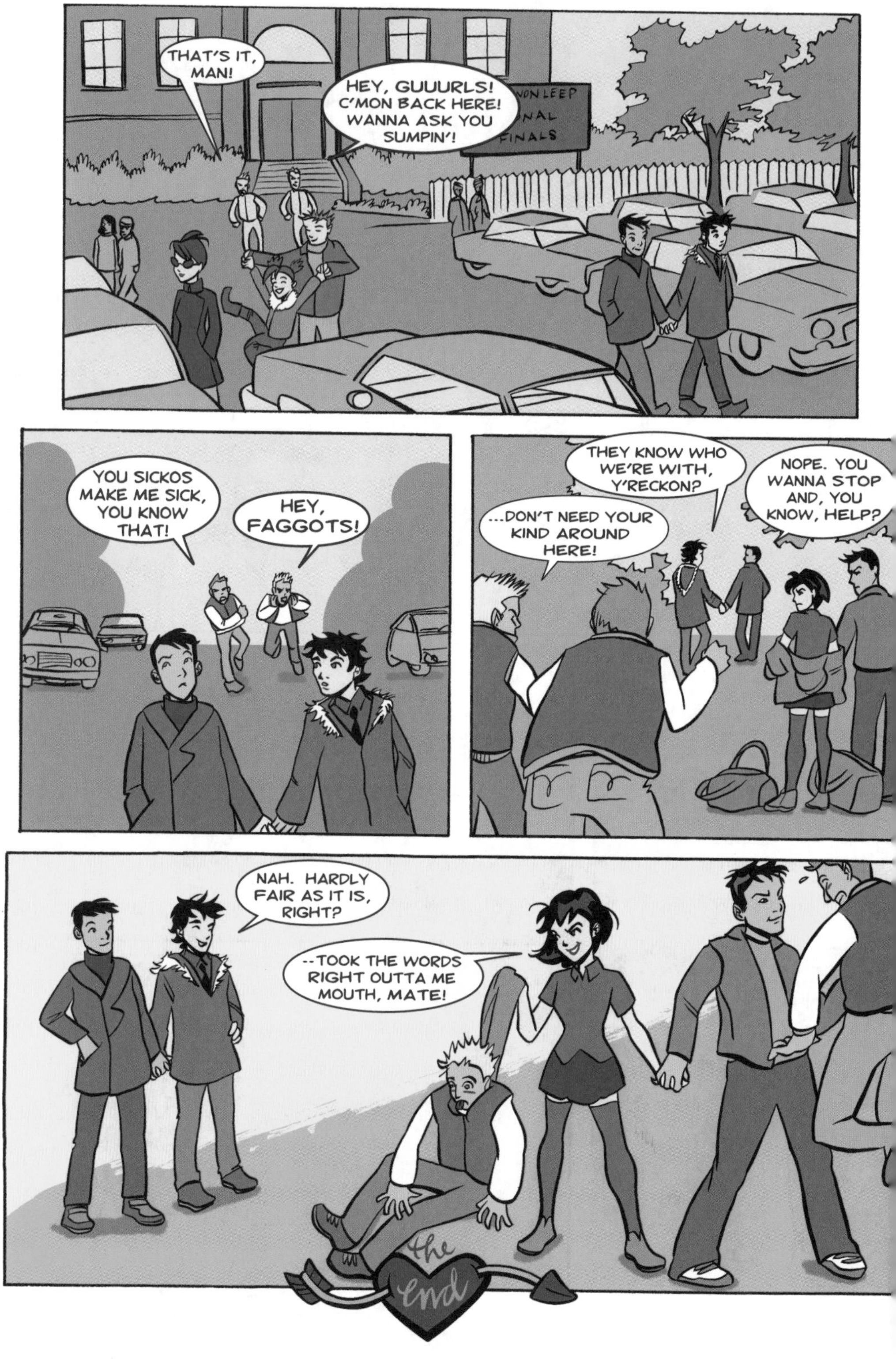

THAT'S IT, MAN!
HEY, GUUURLS! C'MON BACK HERE! WANNA ASK YOU SUMPIN'!
YOU SICKOS MAKE ME SICK, YOU KNOW THAT!
HEY, FAGGOTS!
THEY KNOW WHO WE'RE WITH, Y'RECKON?
...DON'T NEED YOUR KIND AROUND HERE!
NOPE. YOU WANNA STOP AND, YOU KNOW, HELP?
NAH. HARDLY FAIR AS IT IS, RIGHT?
--TOOK THE WORDS RIGHT OUTTA ME MOUTH, MATE!
the end

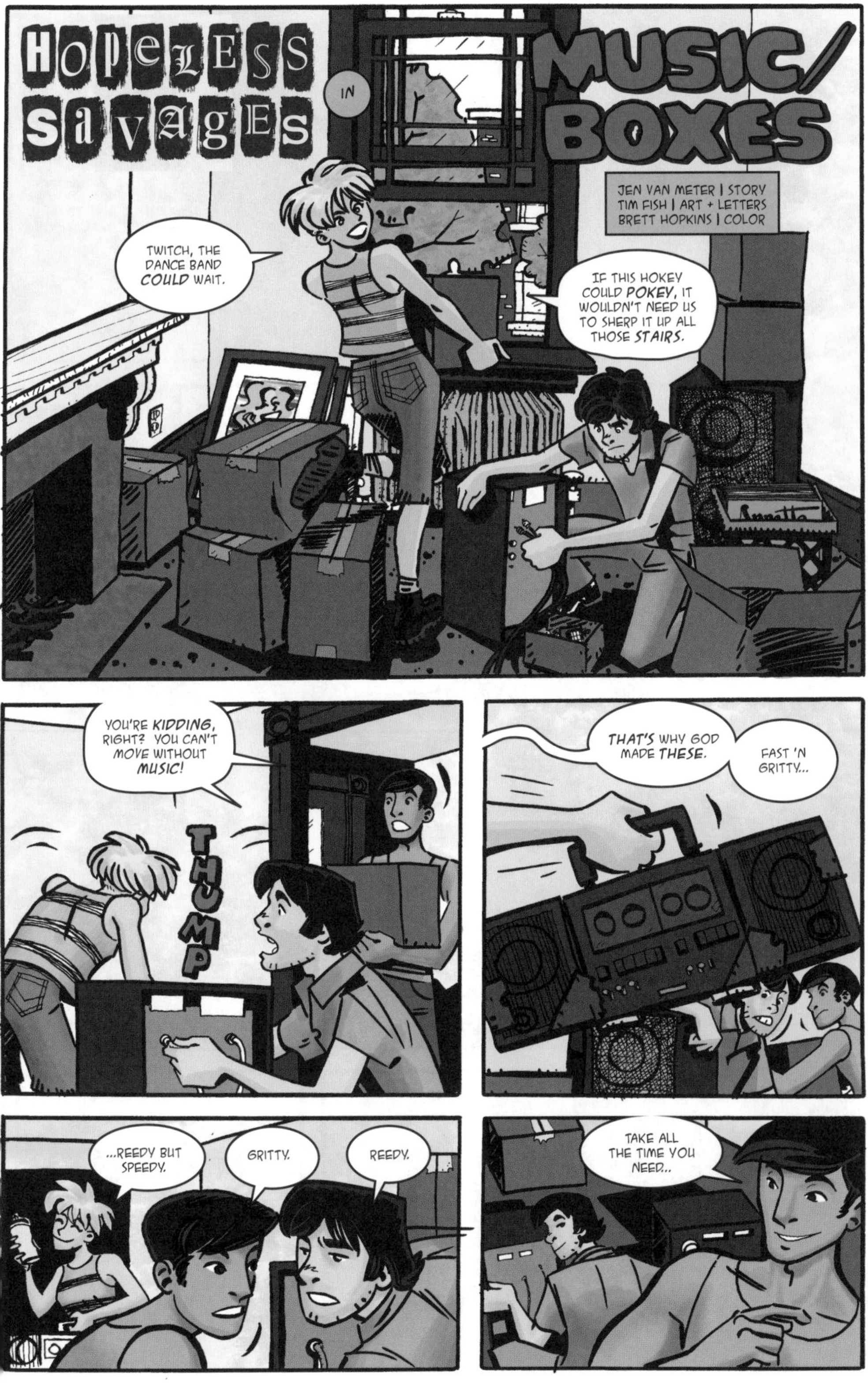
HOPELESS SAVAGES
IN
MUSIC/BOXES
JEN VAN METER | STORY
TIM FISH | ART + LETTERS
BRETT HOPKINS | COLOR
TWITCH, THE DANCE BAND COULD WAIT.
IF THIS HOKEY COULD POKEY, IT WOULDN'T NEED US TO SHERP IT UP ALL THOSE STAIRS.
YOU'RE KIDDING, RIGHT? YOU CAN'T MOVE WITHOUT MUSIC!
THUMP
THAT'S WHY GOD MADE THESE.
FAST 'N GRITTY...
...REEDY BUT SPEEDY.
GRITTY.
REEDY.
TAKE ALL THE TIME YOU NEED...

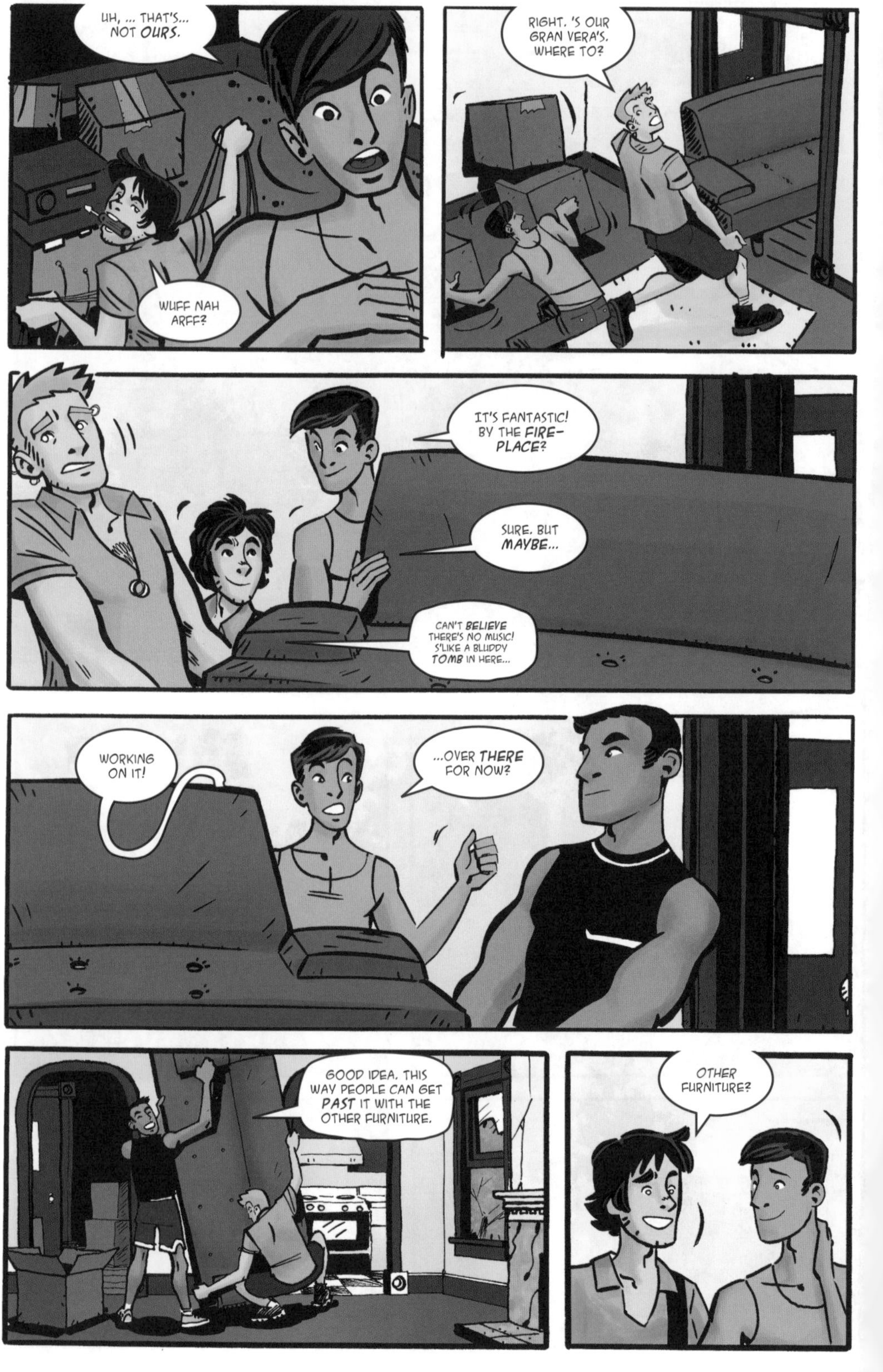
UH, ... THAT'S... NOT OURS.
WUFF NAH ARFF?
RIGHT. 'S OUR GRAN VERA'S. WHERE TO?
IT'S FANTASTIC! BY THE FIRE-PLACE?
SURE. BUT MAYBE...
CAN'T BELIEVE THERE'S NO MUSIC! S'LIKE A BLUDDY TOMB IN HERE...
WORKING ON IT!
...OVER THERE FOR NOW?
GOOD IDEA. THIS WAY PEOPLE CAN GET PAST IT WITH THE OTHER FURNITURE.
OTHER FURNITURE?

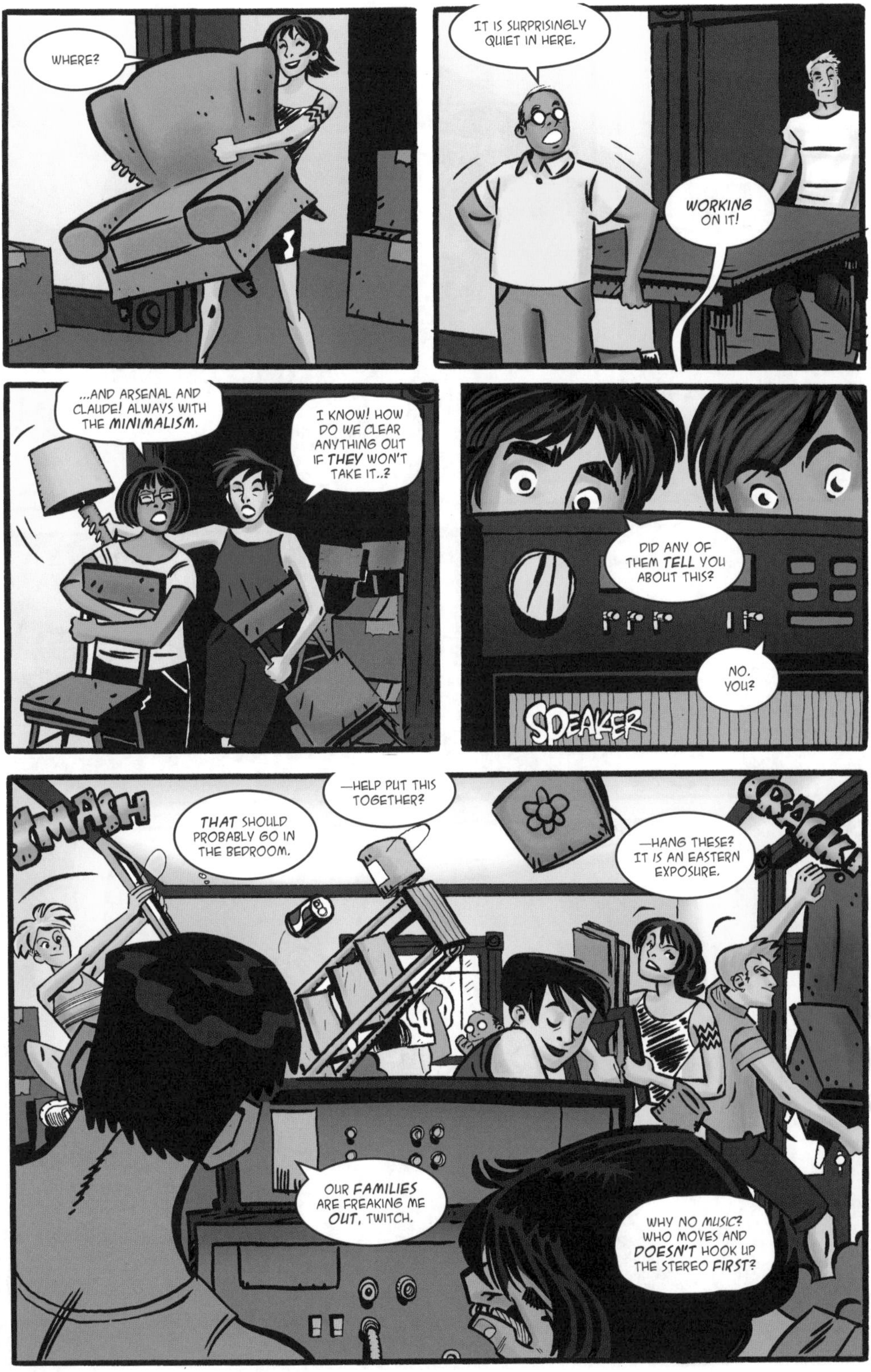
WHERE?
IT IS SURPRISINGLY QUIET IN HERE.
WORKING ON IT!
...AND ARSENAL AND CLAUDE! ALWAYS WITH THE MINIMALISM.
I KNOW! HOW DO WE CLEAR ANYTHING OUT IF THEY WON'T TAKE IT..?
DID ANY OF THEM TELL YOU ABOUT THIS?
NO. YOU?
SPEAKER
MASH
THAT SHOULD PROBABLY GO IN THE BEDROOM.
—HELP PUT THIS TOGETHER?
—HANG THESE? IT IS AN EASTERN EXPOSURE.
CRACK!
OUR FAMILIES ARE FREAKING ME OUT, TWITCH.
WHY NO MUSIC? WHO MOVES AND DOESN'T HOOK UP THE STEREO FIRST?

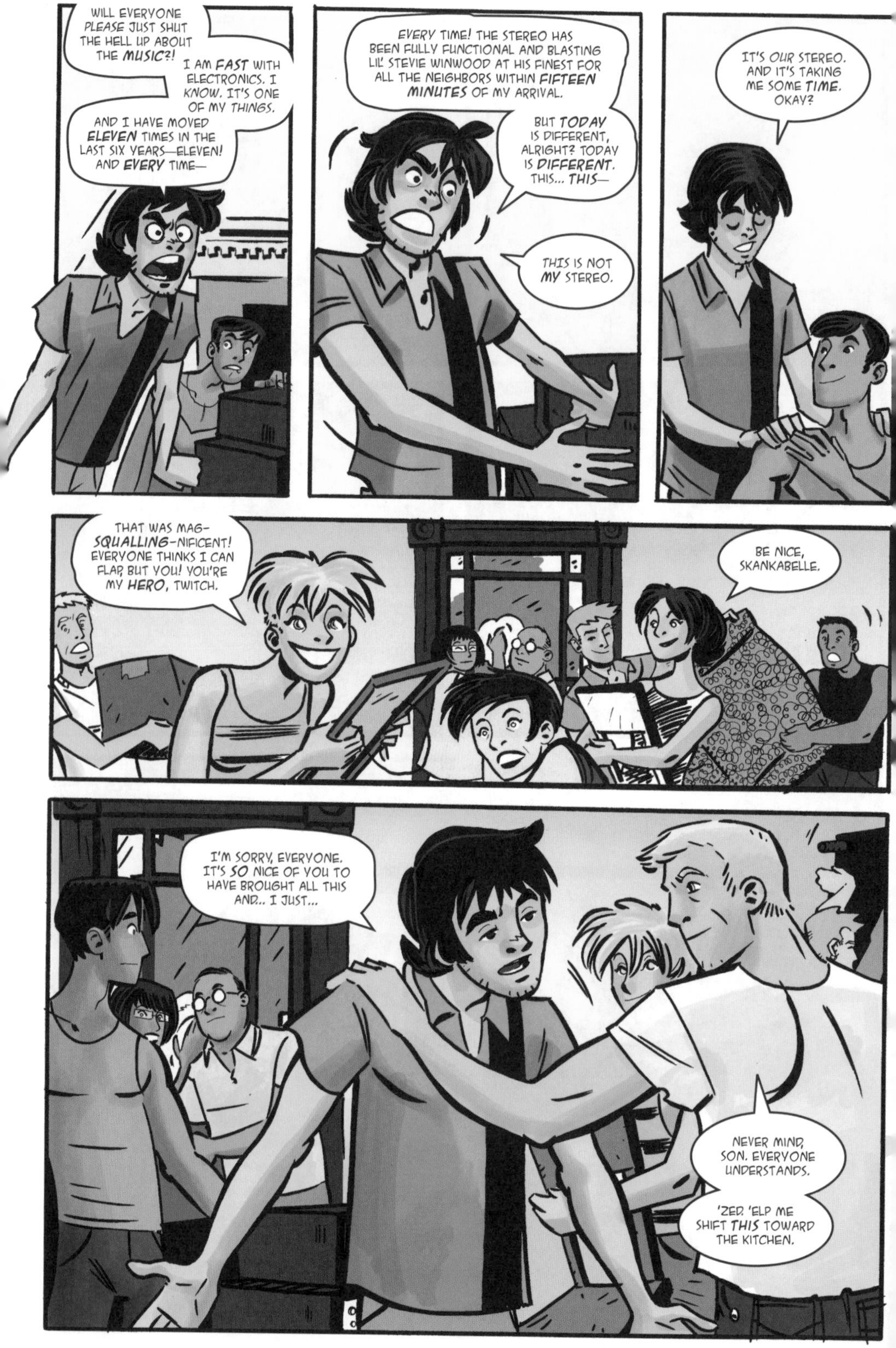
WILL EVERYONE PLEASE JUST SHUT THE HELL UP ABOUT THE MUSIC?!
I AM FAST WITH ELECTRONICS. I KNOW. IT'S ONE OF MY THINGS.
AND I HAVE MOVED ELEVEN TIMES IN THE LAST SIX YEARS—ELEVEN! AND EVERY TIME—
EVERY TIME! THE STEREO HAS BEEN FULLY FUNCTIONAL AND BLASTING LIL' STEVIE WINWOOD AT HIS FINEST FOR ALL THE NEIGHBORS WITHIN FIFTEEN MINUTES OF MY ARRIVAL.
BUT TODAY IS DIFFERENT, ALRIGHT? TODAY IS DIFFERENT. THIS... THIS—
THIS IS NOT MY STEREO.
IT'S OUR STEREO. AND IT'S TAKING ME SOME TIME. OKAY?
THAT WAS MAG-SQUALLING-NIFICENT! EVERYONE THINKS I CAN FLAP, BUT YOU! YOU'RE MY HERO, TWITCH.
BE NICE, SKANKABELLE.
I'M SORRY, EVERYONE. IT'S SO NICE OF YOU TO HAVE BROUGHT ALL THIS AND... I JUST...
NEVER MIND, SON. EVERYONE UNDERSTANDS.
'ZED, 'ELP ME SHIFT THIS TOWARD THE KITCHEN.

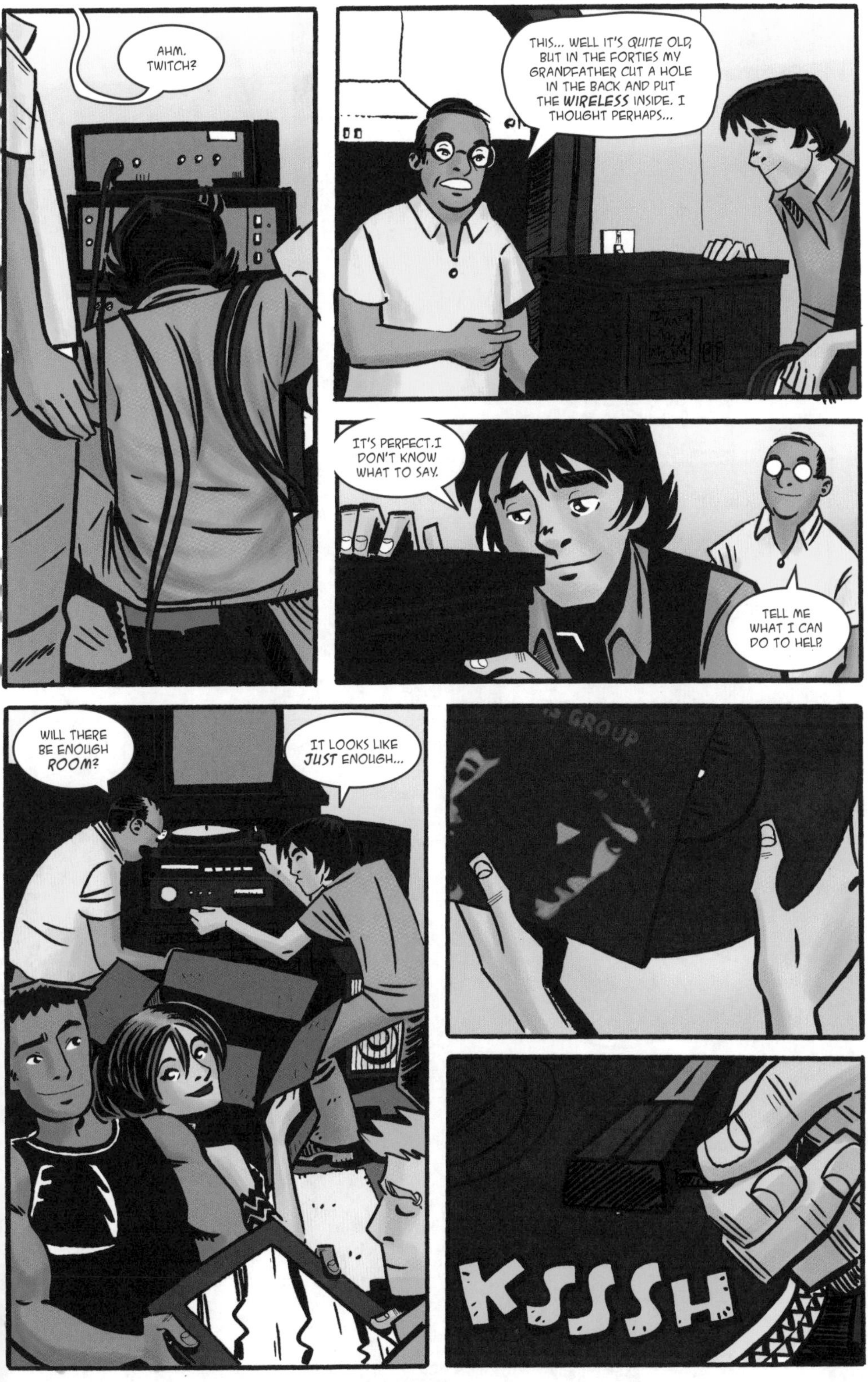
AHM. TWITCH?
THIS... WELL IT'S QUITE OLD, BUT IN THE FORTIES MY GRANDFATHER CUT A HOLE IN THE BACK AND PUT THE WIRELESS INSIDE. I THOUGHT PERHAPS...
IT'S PERFECT. I DON'T KNOW WHAT TO SAY.
TELL ME WHAT I CAN DO TO HELP?
WILL THERE BE ENOUGH ROOM?
IT LOOKS LIKE JUST ENOUGH...
KSSSH

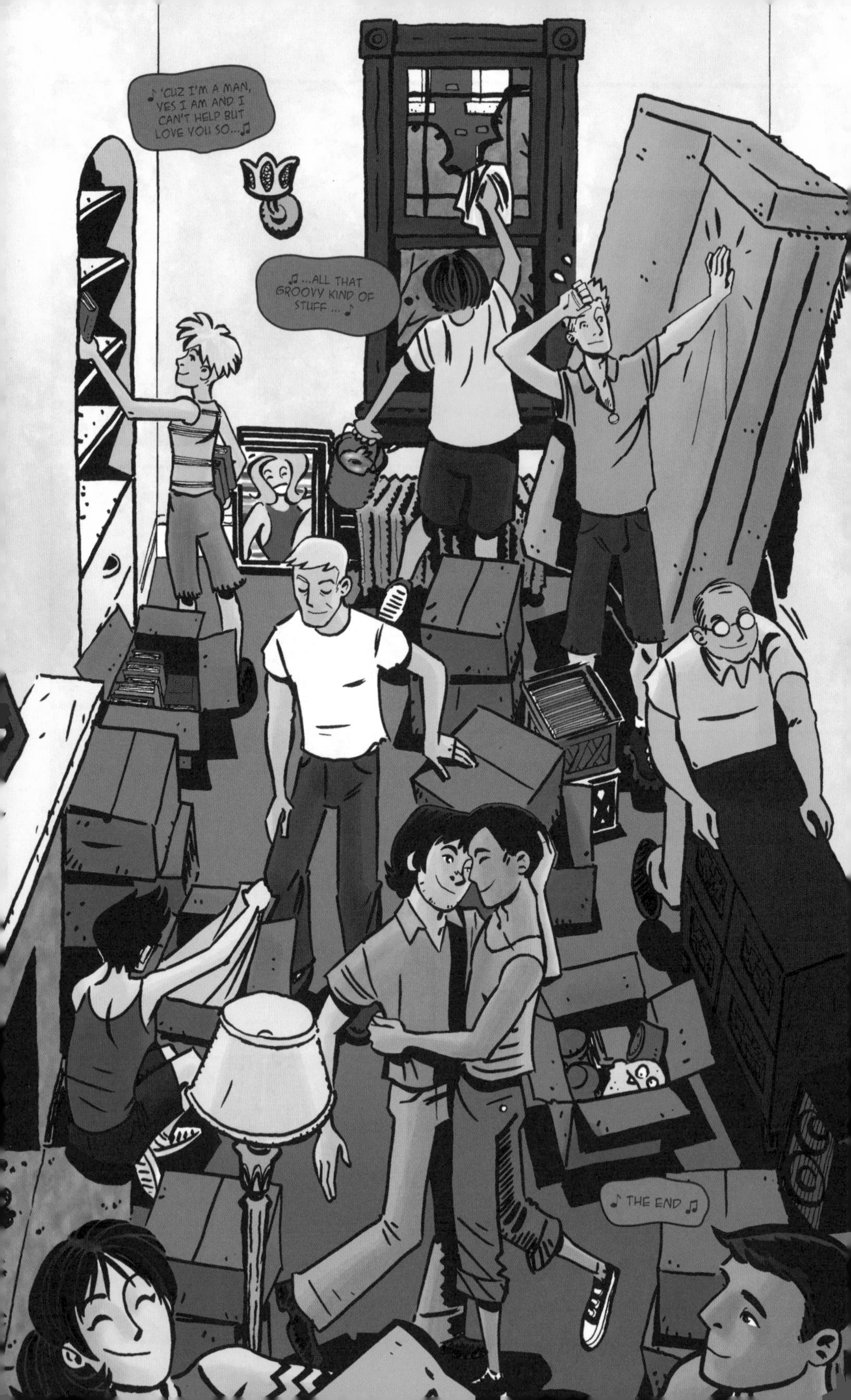
♪ 'CUZ I'M A MAN, YES I AM AND I CAN'T HELP BUT LOVE YOU SO... ♫
♫ ...ALL THAT GROOVY KIND OF STUFF... ♪
♪ THE END ♫

"Good Fences"

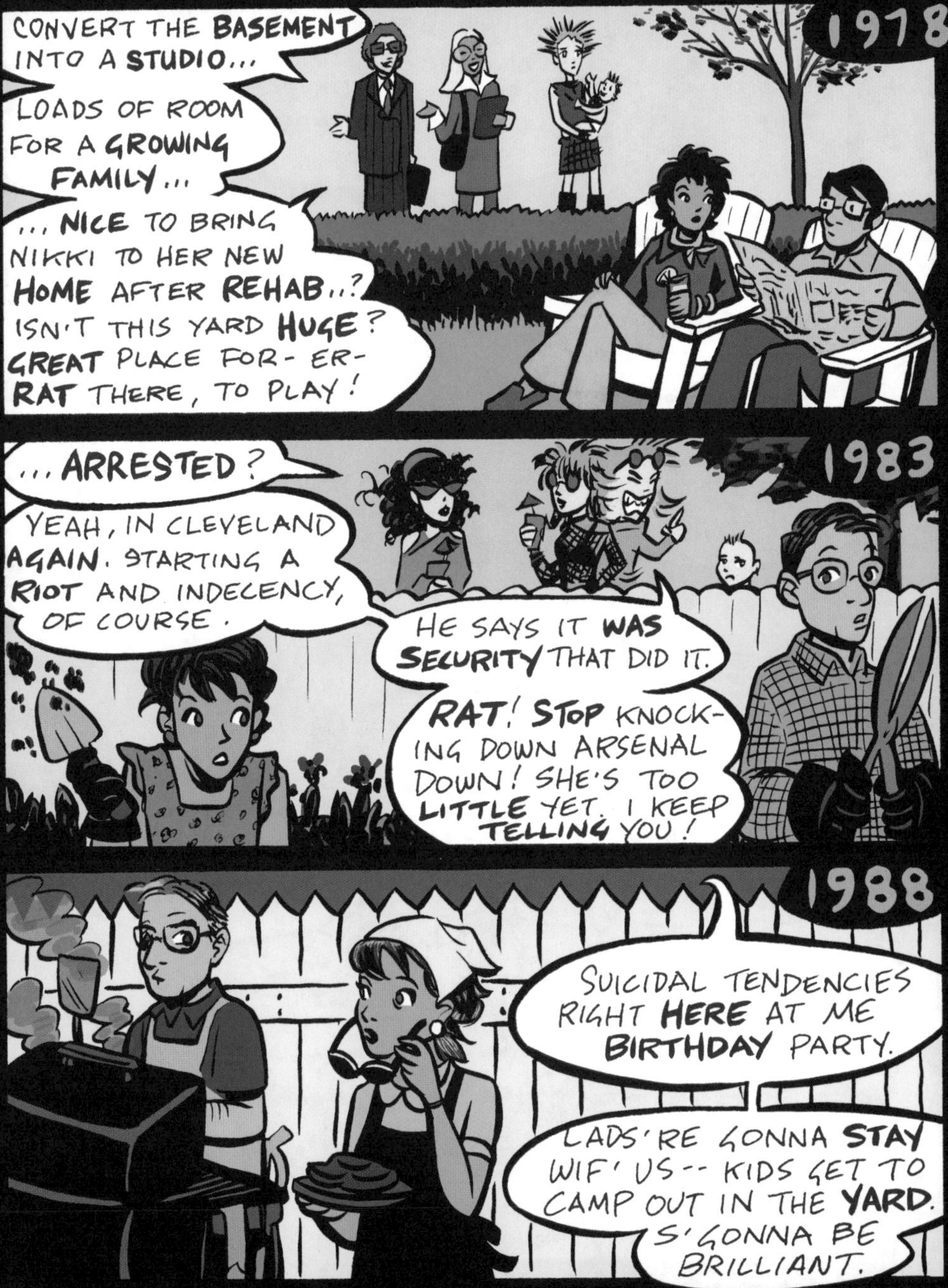
1978
CONVERT THE BASEMENT INTO A STUDIO...
LOADS OF ROOM FOR A GROWING FAMILY...
...NICE TO BRING NIKKI TO HER NEW HOME AFTER REHAB..? ISN'T THIS YARD HUGE? GREAT PLACE FOR- ER- RAT THERE, TO PLAY!
1983
...ARRESTED?
YEAH, IN CLEVELAND AGAIN. STARTING A RIOT AND INDECENCY, OF COURSE.
HE SAYS IT WAS SECURITY THAT DID IT.
RAT! STOP KNOCKING DOWN ARSENAL DOWN! SHE'S TOO LITTLE YET. I KEEP TELLING YOU!
1988
SUICIDAL TENDENCIES RIGHT HERE AT ME BIRTHDAY PARTY.
LADS'RE GONNA STAY WIF' US -- KIDS GET TO CAMP OUT IN THE YARD.
S'GONNA BE BRILLIANT.

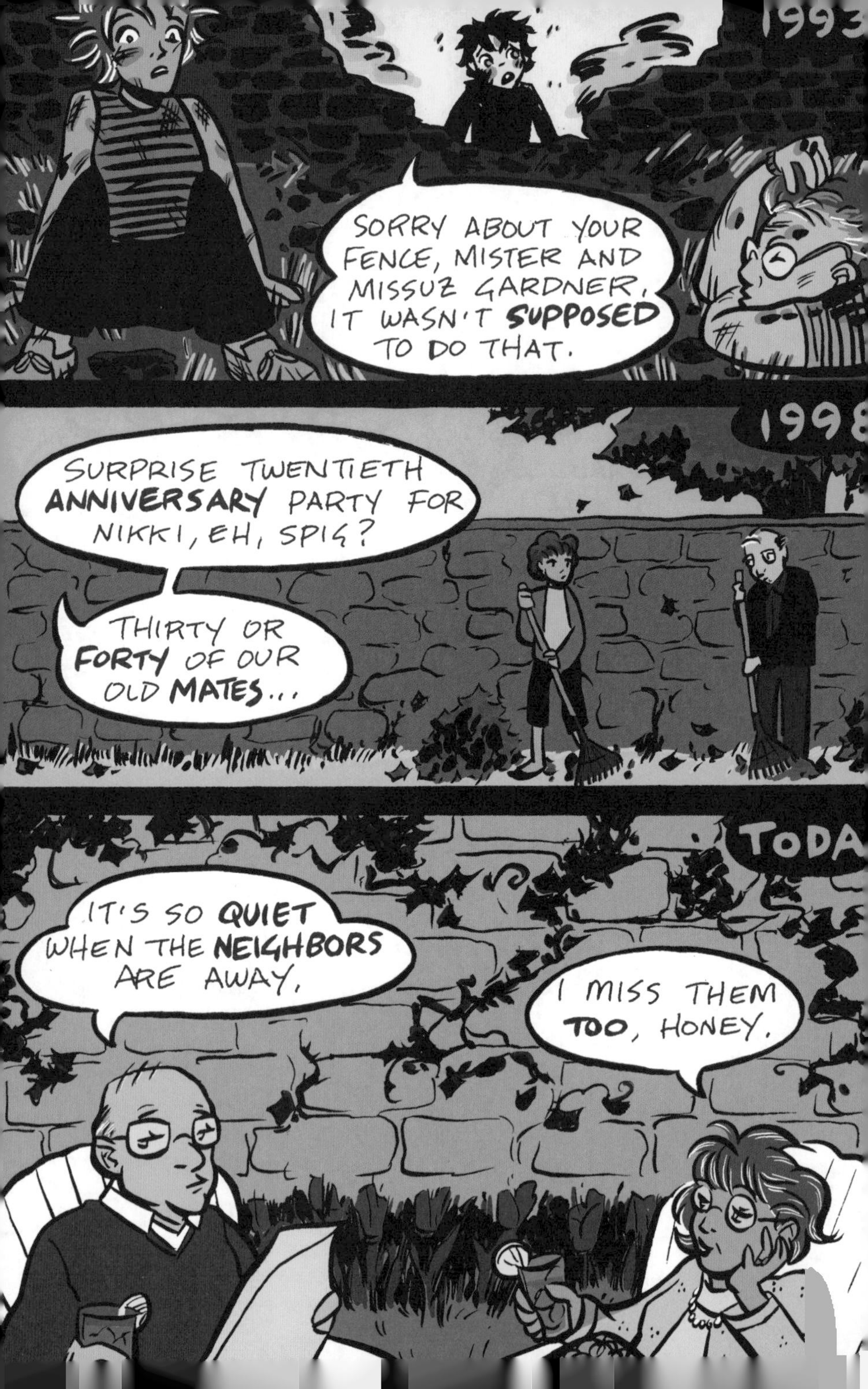
1993
SORRY ABOUT YOUR FENCE, MISTER AND MISSUZ GARDNER, IT WASN'T SUPPOSED TO DO THAT.
1998
SURPRISE TWENTIETH ANNIVERSARY PARTY FOR NIKKI, EH, SPIG?
THIRTY OR FORTY OF OUR OLD MATES...
TODA
IT'S SO QUIET WHEN THE NEIGHBORS ARE AWAY.
I MISS THEM TOO, HONEY.